FLOWERS
IN THE
BLOOD

❧ ❧ ❧

FLOWERS
IN THE
BLOOD

❦ ❦ ❦

GAY COURTER

AN AUTHORS GUILD BACKINPRINT.COM EDITION

Flowers in the Blood

AN AUTHORS GUILD BACKINPRINT.COM EDITION

Published by iUniverse, Inc.

For information address:
iUniverse, Inc.
5220 S. 16th St., Suite 200
Lincoln, NE 68512
www.iuniverse.com

Originally published by Dutton

ISBN: 0-595-24249-9

Printed in the United States of America

In loving memory of
Aunt Edith and Aunt Mary

Contents

PART I

❦ ❦ ❦

Poppy Fields

In India . . . Everything that has happened,
is happening or will happen to the human race
is there and visible to the naked eye.

—ANDRÉ MALRAUX

A. Sassoon Salem
11 Alwyne Place
London N 1
11 July 1960

Clara Luna Weiss
605 Park Avenue
New York, New York

Dear Clara,

We are still sorting out the details of Mother's estate, and nothing much has changed since we spoke in London after the memorial service. However, amongst the possessions left to you is that ghastly desk that Mother referred to as "Clive's Bureau." She must have remembered your admiring comments on it, although I am not certain if they were in praise or in jest.

In any case, her papers directed Mr. Jhirad to remove a package which he found in one of the drawers and to forward it to you. As per Mother's instructions, it has been left intact in its wrapping. We're all panting to know if it is a packet of love letters, or, as Uncle Asher has suggested, a stack of worthless rupee notes saved "for emergencies." Zachariah says if it contains unpaid bills to burn them. Knowing Mother's sentimental side, I'll go on record as guessing the parcel contains school reports, childish scrawls, pictures, and the like. The reason she sent them to you is that you inherited her tendency never to toss anything out.

If you wish, I will ship out the desk "under separate cover" or dispose of it as per your instructions. Your more substantial share of the loot will be forthcoming once the tax men on both sides of the Atlantic pick over the bones.

Do let us know about the mystery bundle.

Love from Nancy and the children,

Aaron

1

Calcutta, 1878

Ever since that dreadful day, I have been unable to tolerate one sound: the slapping of a shutter. Almost twenty years would pass before I could order someone to remove the wooden abominations from that room and replace them with the hush of draperies. And even today, three-quarters of a century later, I recall with loathing the peculiar clatter that woke me the morning my mother was murdered.

Yet here I am in the room where it took place, writing as much as I can recall after so much time. Parts of my past are public knowledge, the stuff of criminal records and newspaper headlines. The rest has been kept within the tight circle of the Sassoons of Calcutta. Because I am departing India, the letters, clippings, photographs, ledgers, and official documents are stacked in the corridors. Perusing them for the last time, I recognize that what seemed a senseless ending is in fact the beginning of my story.

I also now see this tale has elements of revenge, both sweet and bitter, calculated and accidental. Although for most of its telling my narrative will refer to this brooding river, this vindictive undercurrent, I managed to ignore the silent swells for many a year. And yet, as a tap with an intermittent drip eventually fills the bucket, this wall of water, though inevitable if one recalled the source, came as a surprise when it finally rushed its bank. Like the victim of a catastrophe, I would face the moment when I would be swept into the sea to flounder or to prevail. However, that time of reckoning was many years off from the discovery of my mother's mutilated body.

Today, this house looks little different from the way it did in 1878. The clatter of cars and lorries has replaced the clomping of horses pulling carriages, but the traffic still mostly consists of sweating rickshaw-*wallahs* and other forms of human powered vehicles. Of the mansions lining both sides of the street, Number Four Theatre Road continues to be the most prestigious address, at least for the present. What will happen once the Chatterjees take over is anyone's guess.

The room where I am writing is the largest corner suite. Once it was my father's bedroom. The family slept on the second story because the high ceilings and large windows helped cajole the most elusive breezes to pass over us at night. My mother's room adjoined my father's, but since he was away most of the year trading opium to China, she usually slept in his bed, which was raised on a platform to the level of the three walls of windows. "He likes to know I am waiting for him here," she once said to me. At the time the words were a comfort, for my father was a shadowy figure. Whenever I wanted something special or had a difficult question, I was told to wait for his return. The date was never set—it could be weeks or months—yet my mother's presence in my father's bed promised he indeed would come home.

My bedroom was next to my mother's dressing room. I occupied the one bed, and Yali, my *ayah*, slept on a mat on the floor. Next to me was a large nursery washroom with doors leading to my room and the infants' area, where my brothers were in the care of Selima, the *dai*, or wet nurse. Asher, who was less than a year, slept in a swing cradle; Jonah, who at two was four years younger than I, in a railed bed. The other members of the household staff, including the cook, his assistant, the coachman, the bearer, and the *durwan*, or gatekeeper, lived in the *godowns*, which were outbuildings behind the kitchen.

That calamitous night, the first of October, Jonah had a heat rash, so my mother asked the ayahs to take shifts in fanning the babies. The clapping sound woke me before dawn. At first I thought it was Yali, who sometimes snored. I looked down, saw her mat rolled like a snail, and remembered her duties had been shifted. Sitting up, I focused on the noise. Perhaps it was the slap of the *punkah*, the long, flat fan. One of the ayahs would sit in a rocking chair and pull the rope that led to the stiff curtain in a long, slow rhythm. She could close her eyes and doze for five or ten minutes before the movement of the chair in concert with the fan would terminate, and the rope tied to her wrist would tighten enough to nudge her awake. Stirred by a sense that something was not as it should be, I peeked into the babies' room. The punkah was still. Selima lay on her mat, her stout arms and legs looking like stuffed sausages. Skinny Yali was stretched like a child's stick figure on the floor beside her. My brothers slept peacefully. I returned to my bed.

Just as I lay down, a louder bang startled me. It came from the far end of the hall, where my mother slept. Her shutter must have come loose. I decided to fix it, then lie down on the chaise in the corner of the room—where I was permitted to rest if I had a bad dream or a fever—until she awakened. I passed through her dressing room because the corridor door was always fastened from the inside.

At once I saw the difficulty. One of the double corner shutters, which were hinged in the center, had been opened intentionally, but had not been hooked into place. Moonlight, mixed with the amber rays that herald the tropical sun, spilled into the room. The luminescence slashed across the bed where my mother was sleeping. The pearly skin of her face glowed in contrast to the satin cape that draped from her shoulders onto the bed. I had never seen this covering before. It was red, glistening. It matched her nightdress fold for fold.

As I latched the shutter securely, I noticed an odd aroma in the room. Usually the odor of jasmine bushes alongside that end of the house dominated at night, but as I moved toward Mother I was assaulted by a peculiar pungent smell that caused my eyes to water and my throat to burn.

"Mama," I choked.

I climbed to the rim of the platform and touched the satin cloak at her shoulder. It slid away from me, the shiny surface adhering to my fingertips, warm and sticky. I brought my hand to my face and sniffed the rusty residue.

"Mama . . ." The cloying odor made me gag.

Holding my breath, I touched her forehead. It was cool as stone. Something splashed my bare toes. In the darkness I could not see what was seeping down the front of my legs, and for one horrifying moment I thought I was urinating. I tried to hold myself, only to discover the wetness poured from the bedclothes. With both hands I clasped my mother's arm and pulled it toward me. It flopped limply beside the bed, its crimson cover slithering along with it. As I lifted her wrist upward, a warm fluid sprayed my face.

"Mama! Mama! Mama!"

My shrieks brought the ayahs running. They found me in the middle of the bed, bending over my prostrate mother. I thrust my bloodied hands forward in supplication. My nightgown—acting like a wick—was hemmed with scarlet streaks.

Yali touched my mother's mouth and lips, then reached for me. "At least she lives!" Yali said as Selima handed me to her.

"Mama!" I cried, but the ayahs seemed unconcerned with her. They rushed me to the kitchen courtyard and laid me down on the cold stones. I struggled to be free, but they held me fast. The cook cut away my gown with a curved knife. His assistant poured tepid water over me. What sort of a bath was this? The cook ran his fingers across my scalp, checked my ears, my nose. Yali, who was strong and wiry enough to hold me down, bathed my flailing limbs, then pressed a cloth between my legs and wiped me like a baby. When that too came out clean, she fell upon Selima with joyful sobs.

A few days later I came to understand what they had been doing: searching my bloodied body for wounds. However, at that moment I could not fathom how they could be so happy when their mistress had been attacked. I jumped up and beat Yali with my fists. She took the blows without resistance. When I tired, she carried me, pink and naked, into the drawing room, where stout Selima was waiting with a fresh gown. Jonah and Asher lay nearby on blankets set like islands on the Kashmir carpet. The doors to the rest of the house were shut. I crawled into Selima's generous lap. In Hindustani she suggested that Yali might want to attend to herself. I looked up. Yali's sari was streaked with vermilion patches. I clutched Selima. Holding me like an infant, the wet nurse stroked my cheek. My tears flowed freely. I had moistened her blouse, so she lifted it away, and my cheek rested against her brown breast. The buttery cleft smelled of cardamon. Even though I had not nursed for several years, I took her firm teat in my mouth. Sucking, I fell asleep.

❦   ❦   ❦

Later in the day, after the police had taken control of the house, Grandmother Flora Raymond came to fetch us. I called her Nani, the Hindustani name for one's maternal grandmother. She barely moved her mouth as she asked me to come outside with her. The cook's assistant brought a glass of water. Grandmother sprinkled in some salt and made me take a few sips.

"Ugh!" I pushed it away.

"For the fright," she said, forcing me to take another swallow. She then went to the kitchen, which was in an outbuilding, took a long iron spoon, placed a rough hunk of lead in the hollow, and held it over the fire. When the spoon glowed, the cook was told to hold a large *dekchi*, or pot, over my head, and into this she doused the molten lead. The sizzling made me jump. Next, she reached in to examine the shape into which the ball of lead had formed. Displeased, she repeated the procedure two more times. Satisifed at last, she wrapped the lead in paper and placed this under my foot.

"Stamp on it, Dinah."

"Why?"

Her response was a stern, not-to-be-disobeyed expression.

"*Ayn-faksit-ayn-ilraa,*" she chanted in Arabic, the original language of the Calcutta Jews. "May the evil eye be destroyed." This was the first time I had heard a *tarkah*, a superstitious Baghdadi charm, used as an antidote to fright.

Nani decided to take us back to her house in Lower Chitpur Road in the older Jewish district near the earliest synagogues. A few clothes were fetched from my room, and I was asked what else I might want.

"The white robe with the blue border."

Yali looked perplexed. "You have nothing like that."

"I want it."

"Some books perhaps, your dolls?" Nani suggested sweetly.

"The robe. Mama's robe."

"Why would she want such a thing?" Yali asked.

With an impatient gesture Nani indicated the nurse was to fetch it. Moments later, though, Yali returned crying. The police would not allow her to enter the room where the crime had occurred.

"I'll see to it," Nani announced.

That night, when she settled me in the garden room at her house, she placed the robe at the foot of my bed. "There it is, dearest Dinah. Your mother loved you very much."

"No, she didn't. If she loved me, she would be here."

As my grandmother stood up, I saw only her back, curved with defeat. She replied in a garbled voice, "I will send Yali in now. She will sleep at your bedside. If you awake, she will fetch me."

Before I closed my eyes, I pulled the dressing gown across myself. Running my fingers down the plump edge, I was able to blot out the image of my mother under the red cloak by replacing it with the white moiré robe. I envisioned Mama reading a book—one of her favorites was *Lorna Doone*—the lamplight playing on the silk swirls like oil skimming water. Sometimes I would sit beside her and she would read to me. She was so slender, it was a simple matter for us to share the narrow chaise longue. Mama would begin from wherever she was in her own story. Not that it mattered to me. Though I had a passing interest in the tale, I mostly wanted to hear her voice: lyrical, whispery, with the faintest of lisps. After I had fallen asleep or slipped away, she would continue silently. Usually she wore this white gown, banded with a two-inch border of blue silk. Over and over I would run my hands along the smooth seam, from the hem to the shawl collar, idly trying to fathom where it began, where it ended. I would press my cheek against her breast. She smelled mostly of roses. Sometimes Mama would clasp my other hand to her lips and kiss each finger, one by one. That's my most vivid memory: kisses, her thin, tentative voice, her languid sprawl on the chaise, the same volumes read again and again.

In a week or two, the robe's silk began to lose the scent, and long before my father returned, the last essence of rose had vanished.

❦ ❦ ❦

The day after I discovered my mother, I awoke to find Yali and Nani staring down at me, muttering. After I bathed, Yali dressed me in a white pinafore embroidered with butterflies. Nani unbound my light brown hair and signaled Yali to brush it out. When it was obvious they would not braid it again, I was about to comment. Then I noticed my grandmother looked peculiar. Her own hair was also unbound and fell in gray clumps about her face.

"Why is your hair out, Nani?"

"A mark of respect." She nodded to Yali that she was satisfied with my appearance. "Now you must eat something."

"I'm not hungry."

A servant brought a tray with tea and fruit and placed it on the bedside table.

"Take some tea." Yali held the cup while I sipped. "Good. Doesn't that feel better?"

"I suppose so."

"Now some slices of banana." Grandmother kissed my cheek. "Many people are coming to see us today."

"Why?"

She took my hand. "Today we say good-bye to your mother."

"Where will she go?"

"To the cemetery."

"And then?"

"Into the ground."

"Why?"

"Because that is what we do."

I stamped my foot and cried out, "No! Not *my* mother!"

Grandmother reached out to steady herself on my washstand, her eyes brimming. "You must not say that, Dinah." Her mouth set into a firm line with little vertical creases above and below. She squeezed my hand and led me out to see the others.

During the morning, there was a constant stream of visitors. I wandered among them, permitting them to touch me and fuss. I felt as though I was acting a part in an elaborate fairy tale. As long as I was passive, brave, and quiet, nobody banished me from the places where the activities were taking place. The scene became even more interesting when the Sassoon contingent arrived.

The members of my father's family were almost strangers. Both his parents were dead and the others came around only when he was home from his travels. They filled the entire parlor, relegating the Raymonds and Cohens to other wings of the house. Anyone could tell the difference between the two sides of the family by their dress alone. Grandfather Ephraim Raymond wore the attire of his Arabic origins, including a turban, a long gown, called a *dagla*, and a loose outer coat, known as a *jubba*. Nani was dressed in a *dariyee kassa*, the traditional open-fronted dress with an embroidered chemise. Other relations on the maternal side wore variations on this Baghdadi style of garment, with both men and women covering their heads with a *fez*—the women's decorated with gold thread and pearls.

The Sassoons had begun to adopt European dress. All four of my father's brothers wore tailored suits. My father's one sister, Bellore, held court in the fashion of the day known as a *wrapper*, a loose garment that reached to her ankles, with a frilly collar, sleeves, and hem. The children in the family were outfitted like our British counterparts.

Reuben, the second Sassoon brother, called me over and offered me some *jelebis*, the syrupy candy I liked best. I took two, but did not taste them.

"Don't you like sweets?"

"Sometimes."

He rattled the tin. "Plenty more here. Go ahead, after yesterday—"

I jutted out my chin and handed them back with a regal gesture that caught him off-guard.

"You are upset, of course you are." He lowered his head until his thick beard grazed my cheek. When I pulled back, he firmly drew me toward him. "You can tell your uncle about it. What did you see?"

Aunt Bellore swooped forward and I squirmed as she locked her stout arms around me. Her massive breasts jiggled in my face. Even though she was supposedly in mourning, a heavy layer of powder covered her pasty skin and perfect rouged circles had been smudged under her padded cheekbones. "Hush! How could you?" she chastised her brother. Clasping me to her bosom, she led me away.

Later that afternoon, when the cart carrying Mother arrived, the wailing of the women rose to such a pitch that the china, the glassware, even my bones began to vibrate. Following the others outside, I saw the body lying in an *aron*, a long lidless bier with wicker sides. She was completely wrapped in a white shroud.

"That's not Mama."

"It most certainly is," Aunt Bellore declared firmly.

"Take it off," I screamed. "I want to see Mama!" I pushed forward, but the sickly-sweet smell of rosewater emanating from the aron sent me running to Yali.

"They wouldn't let me see her. Why?"

"You're a child," my ayah replied softly.

"But I saw her in the bed," I sobbed.

I did not return to the family until the men gathered in preparation for the funeral ceremony. From a far doorway I watched as poles were attached to the aron; then it was covered by a sheet. Six torches were carried on either side of the bier. The procession, with the corpse held aloft on the shoulders of my father's brothers, organized itself outside the house. Then began the slow four-mile journey to the cemetery. Prayers were read as the party walked. My grandfather, whom I called Nana, and his assistant, Dr. Hyam, followed behind in the carriage. In the failing light the ribbon of men, their white garments reflecting dusky roses and purples, swayed before me like a sari in a breeze.

"No! Don't take her!" I ran after them, but two of the mourners grabbed me and carried me home.

While they were away, the women tried to divert my grandmother. Nobody seemed concerned with me. Even Yali was occupied with the younger children.

Confusion accompanied my grandfather's return. Dr. Hyam helped him into his rolling chair. I followed as he was wheeled to his room and lifted into bed.

"What's wrong?" Aunt Bellore asked.

"He broke down at the grave," Dr. Hyam replied. "When he saw where it was placed, he could not bring himself to do his part."

"I thought she'd be with her husband's family—"

"No, the site for Luna's burial was on the south side of the cemetery and separated from the regular plots by a low wall," the doctor whispered.

"My God, not beside the suicides!"

"No, but nearby. The place where the other—" He caught himself. "Where some disreputables are buried."

"No," my aunt groaned, but I could see her expression was an odd mixture of consternation and pleasure. "What did Ephraim do?"

"He raised his fist toward the Sassoons. I had to help lower him into the grave."

"He did it, then?"

"Yes, he finally did his duty as her nearest male relative."

"And?" she prodded.

"He uncovered Luna's eyes and sprinkled a handful of earth into each of them. Afterward, it took three men to hoist Ephraim level with the grass."

For two days I had managed without losing my equilibrium, but this vivid detail unhinged me. I remembered my mother's almond-shaped eyes—the same amber color as mine—and her long, curling lashes. I thought about my grandfather forcing the lids up and soiling the delicate white orbs with grit.

"Mama, I want my mama!" Fighting back, I pounded the wall with my foot.

Dr. Hyam had not noticed my presence in the shadows, and he started. "What is she doing up?"

"Mama! Mama!" Aunt Bellore pinned me under her arm. I kicked her legs. "Let me go to Mama!"

"Dinah," she hissed. "Control yourself. You cannot go to your mother. Your mother is never coming back."

"Yes she is!" Furiously struggling, I sank my teeth into the tender flesh inside her elbow. She bellowed in anger, released me for a second, then caught me with the other arm. Defeated by her superior strength, I slumped in the hallway. She kept one hand on me so I could not flee.

Nani came running. "What are you doing to her? Let the child go!"

"She's gone crazy. This is what comes from letting her run wild. We should have sent her away today. But no, you wouldn't listen to me."

As Nani possessively yanked me to her, the jolting motion caused my gut to twist and I vomited on my pinafore.

"Look what you've done now," Aunt Bellore accused as she backed away shaking her head. "I don't know why nobody ever listens to me."

❈   ❈   ❈

On the conclusion of the prayers on the seventh day, the tea table was laden with delicious foods, including my favorite sweets: *sumboosaks*, cakes filled with cheese or almonds; *dol-dol*, made from molasses and coconut milk; *babas*, pastries filled with mashed dates. There was far more than any family—or even the guests who flocked to the house—could eat in a month.

Nani said, "Take whatever you like. The rest will be given to the poor."

I filled my plate. "Why not save it?"

"Someone should benefit from our grief."

"Good to see her appetite returning," my grandfather replied in a shaky voice. "Benu will be pleased she looks so well." A few weeks later I would overhear Dr. Hyam tell my grandmother that Nana's palsy of the past few years had taken a sharp turn for the worse after the funeral.

"How long until word reaches Benu?" Nani muttered.

"A ship leaves for China and the Pearl River delta this week. No telling where he might be or how long a message might take to reach him. A month at the least."

Nani replaced her silver water goblet. "When was he due back?"

I strained to understand what they were saying about my father.

"Saul did not expect him until February. If he hears the news sooner, he will certainly come before then. If not—"

"Will I have to go back to Theatre Road?" I asked.

Nana's trembling increased and the fork fell from his fingers. "That's your home," he said gently.

"I do not want to live there ever again."

The adults' eyes shifted from one to the other. Dr. Mordecai Hyam, my grandfather's assistant, filled in. "Dinah, nobody knows what will happen in the future. We shall have to wait and see."

In the next few weeks, the atmosphere in my grandparents' house changed palpably, partly due to the weather. Well into October the air had been drier than usual. The monsoon had withdrawn early. Breathing seemed easier, as though the weight of humidity and melancholy were lifting in tandem. During that time, the question of where we would live was discussed repeatedly. Concerns revolved around my grandfather's failing health and occupation more than the needs of the three motherless children. Although Nana was only nominally working, he did continue to see patients and advise young Dr. Hyam on their treatments. Transferring his consulting room to Theatre Road was impractical. My grandmother's moving without him was impossible. On the other hand, the Raymonds' home in the old Jewish district was not large enough to accommodate three children, two ayahs, and a nursery cook on a permanent basis in anything but cramped conditions. Dr. Hyam had been given a bed with neighbors, so he could be available for either my grandfather or patients, but this was supposed to be a temporary arrangement. The nursery cook was offered time off to visit his family, with Nani supervising our meals herself. I was content, and balked anytime a change was mentioned. I promised myself they could never force me to leave. I would scream, I would shout, I would do anything to prevent them from transporting me to that dreadful house, with that bloody bed, those creaking shutters.

*   *   *

Grandfather Raymond had a following in an unusual quarter: the lepers of Calcutta. On Wednesdays those experiencing problems with their rotting limbs would make their way to the consulting room. Laden with garlands of flowers, fruits, or whatever meager offerings they had managed to assemble, they waited for medical attention. They were devoted to my grandfather because he had been one of the first physicians of his day to offer pain relief to his patients—whether nobleman or pauper—in the form of chloroform and opium drops.

One particular Wednesday, almost two months after my mother's funeral, I came upon three lepers waiting at the back door of his clinic. The only woman beckoned me closer. After a few hesitant steps I could see she was waving with a discolored stump of an arm. I fled back to the courtyard. In less than an hour I heard a door slam and I peeked around the side wall. The lepers were being helped into the back of a cart. The woman's chest and shoulder were wrapped in a bandage. As the cart carrying her turned down the street, Aunt Bellore and her husband, Samuel Lanyado, drove up in their *gharry*.

"Hello, Dinah," Uncle Samuel called out brightly when he saw me.

"Where's your grandfather?" Aunt Bellore asked brusquely.

"In the consulting room."

She pushed by me and made for the door, Uncle Samuel puffing behind. I ran after her and blocked the path. "He's been—"

"Dinah, let us pass," my aunt barked sternly.

Nobody had spoken to me in anything but a solicitous tone since the day of my mother's murder. Stung into silence, I fell behind as Aunt Bellore blustered her way forward. The door between the anteroom and the procedure room was slightly ajar. She pushed it open with her foot. Grandfather's sweeper, a white-bearded Hindu, was scrubbing the floor. Neatly laid out on a cloth on the table was the day's gruesome harvest: one leg, one hand, one arm. Aunt Bellore's screams brought Dr. Hyam running from the office.

I hid behind the door and listened until the commotion passed, then made my way as close as I dared, to listen.

". . . so he's been arrested . . . they're still looking for the other . . . I thought you would want to know . . . the evidence in his rooms . . . the rubber shoe . . . chloroform vials . . ." were some of the phrases I caught before scurrying back to the courtyard.

Yali gave me my supper with the boys, saying the adults could not be disturbed. Nani did not come in to see me until I was in bed. Her face, which had softened somewhat since the ordeal of the funeral, was again a map streaked by long lines leading in every direction. Her hug was short, tense, and she almost flew from the room.

Disturbed, I could not sleep and begged Yali to tell me what was wrong.

"Are they going to send me away?"

"No, no."

"Are we going back to Theatre Road?"

"No, no."

"What is happening, then?"

Yali twisted the hem of her sari and looked away as she whispered, "Do you remember a friend of your mother's, the sahib Mr. Sadka?"

"Uncle Nissim?"

She grimaced. "He's not your true uncle."

"Are you certain?"

"He was merely a friend of your mother's."

"And mine. He brought me sweets and toys."

"No."

"But he did!"

"He was not a real friend."

"Mama liked him. She was always happy to see him."

"She was mistaken. He is a wicked man."

"Why do you say that?"

Yali sat on my bed and attempted to drape my mother's robe over my shoulders. I brushed it away. "No! I don't want it."

Yali refolded it and sat down on her mat. "You sleep now, Dinah."

"No!"

"Shall I stay?"

"Yes!"

I clenched my teeth and stared at the poles from which the mosquito-netting tent hung over my bed. Something inside me twisted and crushed me painfully. I must have cried out, for Yali appeared beside me, stroking my shoulders. Barely noticing her, I lay still as images of Mama and Uncle Nissim flashed before me: quick glances, a light touch on the hand, lying together side by side on the veranda cushions passing the mouthpiece of a gurgling water pipe, called a *hookah*, between them, Uncle Nissim's long, drooping lashes, his protuberant lower lip mimicking a bulbul, Mother dancing in front of him in a diaphanous gown, him clapping in response. I remembered joining in, linking hands in a circle, and recalled how out of place I had felt because they were in step with each other, but out of step with me. That memory was jolted by others: a grim expression in Uncle Nissim's black velvet eyes, a slammed door, loud voices, a broken glass. They had argued. Most people did. Even so, how could a man who had been so gentle, so funny, have harmed my mother? No, Uncle Nissim could never have done that! It was someone else. Someone had made a mistake. There had to be another answer.

From that moment I developed a precocious curiosity about the crime.

2

‖ ‖ ‖

A daughter learns her mother in sequence as the years pass. At each stage there are revelations, mysteries revealed. But what of the child who loses her mother before the age of reason? That child learns as I did—from others. I had few memories of our early years together, but these I began to gather and store as if in preparation for the long winter of life without a maternal guardian.

Luna's mother, Flora, was a direct descendant of Shalom Aaron Cohen, who came from Aleppo, Syria, arriving in Calcutta in 1798. He is considered the founder of the city's Jewish community. Soon thereafter Jewish settlers began to flood into Calcutta, the majority emigrating from Baghdad in order to flee the harsh rule of Daud Pasha in the early 1800's. India, a land of many religions, welcomed the Jews. Here they could live in perfect freedom; here their traditions could be preserved. Flora had been promised to Ephraim Rahamin (who later anglicized his last name to Raymond) through intermediary contracts in Baghdad. Her father, Obadiah Cohen, had been a gem dealer to the *nawabs* of Oudh, as had been his father, Shalom. Obadiah was said to have been a charming man who loved to weave stories and entertain—a skill that made him popular with the princes of northern India. Once he received a gift of priceless pearls, and the most valuable were set into a pearl ring, which my grandmother gave, along with many matching pieces, to Luna on her wedding day.

Obadiah was one of the first Jews to build a mansion in the elegant Park Street district—as fine as any in this "City of Palaces." To maintain his family's scholarly tradition, Obadiah insisted tutors from Baghdad educate his children. Determined to raise the Jewish community to new standards, he wanted to establish a Jewish clinic. His daughter's dowry was astounding, as was Obadiah's offer to construct not only a home for the couple but also whatever medical facility the young man

17

desired. Thus he was able to entice a medical student from Baghdad to come out to India.

My grandfather, Ephraim, was the first Jewish physician in Calcutta. He won the confidence of maharajahs, British generals, the kings of commerce, and others who traveled far to entrust themselves to his care. Not only those with the rupees to pay his fees were healed by him. Paupers, who had been refused admittance to the city hospital, would find their way to his clinic and plead for a cure. Throughout my life I have met people who felt they owed me a service to pay back a debt of gratitude to my grandfather.

If another woman complained about her match, Flora, who was delighted by Ephraim, would claim, "If you accept a marriage joyfully, everything will be right." She had no patience for women who believed a natural incompatibility could exist. "With acceptance, the bonds will tighten. Pull together, not apart."

In spite of their happiness with each other, good fortune did not visit my grandparents during the early years of their union. The Raymonds' first child, a son, died two weeks after birth. The following year Flora had a stillbirth. Ten months later, Luna was born. There were other pregnancies—nobody knows how many—but no further issue.

Luna was an enchanting newborn. "Your mother was tiny and frail," Nani boasted. "She had the most extraordinary wide-set eyes, a perfectly shaped bow of a mouth, and skin the color of fresh cream."

"Did I look like her?"

"Only the eyes. Your skin was darker, your mouth thinner. And of course you weighed almost twice as much."

At first I was disheartened to learn of the charms she possessed and I lacked. Eventually I was to be grateful I was so little like my mother.

Luna continued to be delicate of frame and constitution. Artists captured the child's fragile beauty in a series of portraits that hung in the Raymonds' parlor. One by one they depicted dark hair framing milk-white skin and enormous oval eyes fringed with long, feline lashes. Her nose and chin were like finely chiseled ivory. Always tiny for her age, she was dressed in clothes to match her mother's, taking on the aura of a miniature adult.

Since both parents had the benefit of education, they began Luna's studies in Hebrew at the age of five. Luna learned her alphabet, mastered simple sums, and made progress for several years. After becoming literate in English around the age of ten, though, her interest waned.

When my grandmother realized I was almost seven, and other than having learned the rudiments of reading by listening to my mother's stories, I had never been given any proper schooling, she took on the task of educating me, as she had her daughter. After a discussion with Grandfather, she decided I should not begin my studies in Arabic or Hebrew—as they had—but would learn English first. I studied harder than she expected, and learned rapidly.

"You are a much better scholar than your mother ever was," Nani said to encourage me.

As Luna approached puberty, both parents worried that the custom of marrying a daughter while she was in her early teens might cause Luna difficulties, since her skeleton was narrow. When she was fifteen—two years past the age when most girls were betrothed—inquiries for a husband were made through their Baghdadi connections. Ephraim was keen on having another physician as a son-in-law. Luna's dowry would surpass even Flora's, so there were many candidates from whom to choose.

Their daughter had other ideas. She had several friends with whom she met at the synagogue for supervised social activities, and the girl she most admired was Bellore Sassoon. Bellore was a year older, a head taller, a third heavier, and more outspoken and daring than the diffident Luna. The youngest of a family of six, Bellore was the only daughter. Fascinated by this gregarious, hardy family, Luna spent many a day with Bellore at the Sassoon mansion on Kyd Street.

Bellore's great-grandfather, Sheikh Sason ben Saleh, gave her a superior lineage to Luna's descent from Shalom Cohen. For centuries the Sassoons had prospered in Baghdad. The clan's chieftain had worn gold raiments for appearances at the pasha's palace. As he made his way through the streets for a royal audience, peasants would bow to him and his retinue. However, the status, security, and glamour of that family's station vanished under the rule of the cruel Daud Pasha.

Sheikh Sason was born in 1750. Following his forefathers, he became the pasha's civil head of the Jewish community, or *nasi*, in 1778. For thirty-eight years he collected taxes from his community, while guarding both their secular and spiritual welfare. He married and bore seven sons. The oldest died in a plague. His second son, David, was expected to become nasi when his father retired. Learning that Daud Pasha did not want another Jewish nasi, David Sassoon respectfully declined the hereditary appointment, then was arrested along with his wife's brother, who was strangled. Sheikh Sason rushed to the palace to plead for his son's life. The pasha agreed that if the sheikh would pay a huge ransom, David would be freed—as long as he agreed to leave Baghdad for Basra. Thus began David's wanderings that led him to Bombay, where he opened a countinghouse in 1832.

He arrived in India at the dawn of a boom. He and his family prospered. Moses, his youngest son, moved to Calcutta—fast becoming the commercial hub of the Indian subcontinent—and set up a branch of the business in that port city. There he discovered the most profitable commodity in which to trade: opium.

Arab merchants had introduced opium to the Chinese as a remedy for everything from stomach troubles to leprosy. Later, Portuguese sailors cultivated a taste for what they called *yang yien*, or foreign smoke, among the mandarins. When the British East India Company exported far more silk and tea—which had to be paid for in silver— with less than equal value in Indian cotton or British woolens to sell back to the Chinese, the trade imbalance became problematic. The solution—selling opium to the Chinese—leveled this deficit, eventually tilting the equation in the company's favor.

Compact compared with most crops, opium was almost as dear as precious metals in price per weight. Packed in tidy chests, it shipped easily. Once processed, it was not perishable. Its customers were loyal and constant. Best of all, the demand for opium escalated year after year. The ownership of the opium lands was deeded to the British government of India, who leased the cultivation rights to local farmers. The harvested crop was then auctioned by the government to the merchants, who speculated on the price and accepted the hazards of shipping and trading a substance the Chinese people craved, but their lords did not wish them to consume, even though trading in opium was entirely lawful as far as the British were concerned.

One of the first Jews to become active in what he came to call "the flower trade," Moses Sassoon established the practice of boycotting auctions when the prices were too steep, thus depressing the market. When the value had fallen to his satisfaction, he would turn around and buy up the harvest. His sons followed him into the business and made solid marriages with girls from the Baghdadi community. For his youngest, Benjamin, he was looking for an alliance with one of the Jewish families who had settled in Hong Kong in the 1840's, right after the Treaty of Nanking created the British colony, so he could better control that end of the transactions.

Neither Moses Sassoon nor Ephraim Raymond expected either of their children would have romantic ambitions of their own.

"Luna startled us when she announced she wanted to marry Benu Sassoon," Nani told me, enjoying the excuse to talk about my mother.

"What would have happened if you had refused her?" I recall asking.

"There would have been some wailing, but Luna would have accepted the decision of her elders, as your grandfather and I had done. Either father—Luna's or Benu's—would have been well within his rights to dismiss the matter and order obedience."

Fortunately for my parents, Moses Sassoon saw advantages to an alliance with Luna Raymond.

"Let me tell you something about Moses Sassoon." Nani strained to keep a neutral tone. "He was the poor relation of that family. In Bombay he would have been at the bottom of the ladder. Only by making his way in Calcutta could he distinguish himself. With such a large family and that daughter to marry off in style, there was not much left for his youngest son. With the Raymond dowry as a base, however, Benu could have a palace to match the richest of the Bombay Sassoons."

"Was Mama truly in love with Papa?" I ventured the question as though I were testing the temperature of bathwater.

"She was in love with the idea of your father. The one she adored was Bellore, who represented everything she wanted to be: taller, healthier, stronger, older, wiser, and the sister of five handsome boys."

I mulled this over. "So a marriage with Bellore's brother was a way of showing her love for Bellore."

"Yes, that's partially it. Also, Luna did not show an interest in any of the Sassoon men until after the announcement of Bellore's engagement. When she heard the news, Luna cried for days."

"Why? Was she jealous?"

"She thought she was losing the attention of her dearest friend. That's when she told me she wanted to get married too. I tried to explain that Bellore was sixteen—a very grown-up sixteen—and was more than ready for marriage, whereas she was physically a child."

"Why did she pick Benu?"

"He was a striking young man. And he had been kind to her."

"She fell in love with him, didn't she?" I asked, searching for confirmation that my parents' union had been tinged with the glow of true love.

"Yes, Dinah, I believe she felt a deep attraction for him."

"Did my father feel as strongly about her?"

"Your mother was an appealing young woman."

A complicated process of negotiations was set in motion when Luna and Benu made their wishes known. First, the alliance with the Baghdadi medical student had to be severed. Next, an agreement had to be negotiated. Grandfather Raymond had not the business acumen of a Sassoon, who knew this father would pay any price to indulge his daughter.

"Your Nana made only one condition: the marriage would not take place until after Luna's seventeeth birthday. We agreed that immature children must not marry. Boys must be ready for responsibility; girls must be strong enough to carry and tend babies."

"Cousin Sarah was married last month, and she's only thirteen," I said, referring to Reuben Sassoon's oldest daughter.

"A practice born of ignorance—and fear."

"What are they afraid of?"

Nani sucked in her lower lip, a sign that she was weighing her words. I knew she would speak the truth, but perhaps not all of it. "They are afraid the best matches will be gone if they wait too long."

I returned to the subject of my mother. "So Grandfather Moses agreed to what my mother and father wanted."

"We were presented with no arguments, only a list of demands that included building the house in Theatre Road to the Sassoons' specifications."

During the long engagement, both fathers agreed that Benu might undertake the first of his journeys to escort the opium to China. There he hoped to establish the trust of the Chinese middlemen who controlled the retail market. Also, with the young lovers separated by half a continent, they could not be the subjects of the gossip that would surely ensue by permitting children to have a say in their marriage.

The wedding took place the day after Luna's seventeenth birthday.

"Were they happy together?" I asked Nani.

Her answer was guarded. "No more, no less than any newlyweds until Benu's father sent him back to China."

"Didn't Mama mind?"

"She wept, she carried on, but what could she do? By then, of course, she was expecting you."

Contrary to her parents' fearful expectations, Luna maintained robust health during her pregnancy, but my birth was a long, protracted nightmare. Nobody told me about it directly, but over the years I overheard murmurings about how she had suffered. "Such an enormous baby for such a slender woman! At least my babies were small and I had the hips to carry them easily," I heard Aunt Bellore brag.

I learned how my grandfather had agonized over how to help his daughter. Unable to withstand her screams and prayers to die rather than go on, he had dosed her with opium drops. Even afterward, during her long period of recuperation, he had continued to medicate her so she could sleep while her lacerations healed.

"Did she return to Theatre Road?"

"Of course. The Sassoons said a child should be raised in the home of the father and a wife must follow her husband's family's wishes. A Baghdadi girl does not run to her parents when she is unhappy."

"I thought Dadi Sassoon died before I was born and Dada Sassoon followed when I was a baby. Couldn't she have returned to you then?"

"She did not enjoy living alone or managing a large home, but we told her she had her duties." Nani sighed. "That was our mistake. There is a fine line between doing what is right and doing what looks right. If your grandfather or I had known the consequences . . ."

"Was it a mistake to let Mama and Papa have their way?" I asked.

"Who can know? We even might have made that same match for her if Ephraim hadn't wanted to bring another doctor to Calcutta. But my belief that arranged marriages are, if not superior, then at least as workable, was strengthened by Luna's experiences. What did she understand? How could she choose? She loved Bellore, she was impressed with the Sassoon name, she wanted to be married because Bellore was. At least her father and I might have selected someone who better understood her nature."

❦ ❦ ❦

The arrest of Nissim Sadka for my mother's murder gave a provocative focus to every conversation. Even if I were nearby, voices would merely lower, not cease. Alternating between fear and a hunger to know more, I pieced together snippets from various sources and in the process learned that in order to cajole an adult into telling a child about a forbidden subject, the child must follow this rule: never ask a direct question.

I began my probe with my grandmother. Sitting at the parlor table doing my schoolwork, I had completed a page of difficult sums when I mustered the courage to mention the unmentionable. "I don't think Uncle Nissim is a bad man." His name rolled off my tongue like a bitter root.

Nani, who had been embroidering a cushion, put down her needle. "The authorities think he is."

"Mama liked him."

"He may have pretended to be kind, but some believe he hurt your mother."

"No, he did not."

Nani paled. "Why do you say that?"

"He liked Mama. And he liked me too."

"Sometimes friends become angry with each other."

"Uncle Nissim once shouted at Mama, but that doesn't mean that—"

"No, of course not, but sometimes if a man drinks too much or overindulges with . . . well, never mind. When did they argue?"

"I don't remember."

"He came to visit often, didn't he?"

"Yes, every few days."

"Did he have supper in your mother's room?"

"Sometimes."

"Is that where they argued?"

"Yes."

"Do you know what they talked about?"

"No. I only heard loud voices."

"Did he strike your mother?"

"No!"

"He stayed until after you had gone to bed, didn't he?"

"Sometimes."

"Did he visit with friends, other men or women, or alone?"

"Mostly alone."

At so young an age I would not have questioned my mother's propriety. When her husband was away, the downstairs rooms were rarely used and she often entertained instead in the dark coolness of my father's bedroom. I had sensed a logic to this. When my father was home, we were a more social family. The public rooms were suffused with light, music, conversation. The Sassoon relatives came and went freely. Mama wore elegant gowns, organized feasts. When my father was away, she withdrew upstairs and her friends visited her there. Besides, how could anything have been amiss when the servants were about? Except during the coolest weather, the blind punkah-wallah fanned her while she had guests, while she ate, even while she slept.

Frequent visitors included her best friend, Aunt Bellore, her three daughters, and members of their social set and their children. In the hot weather, mattresses covered with thick layers of carpets would be laid out on the upstairs veranda. During the day Jonah and I might frolic there. After sunset Mama would sit outside alone or with her companions laughing and trading short breaths from the hookah.

Nani's dark opinion of Mama's favorite companion altered my perception of Mama's activities. Indeed, I would soon learn Nissim Sadka was a rather unsavory character with questionable associates. Sadka, whose father had once been in service to the King of Oudh, was the lifelong friend of another Jew, Moosa Chachuk, who was rumored to have provided services as an assassin against the enemies of the King of Oudh. Chachuk had degenerated into a pitied alcoholic who lived near the Radha Bazaar in rooms for brethren down on their luck. Moosa, and several other men in similarly reduced circumstances, worked for Nissim as carpenters. A few days after Sadka's arrest, Chachuk was also incarcerated, as he was thought to be either an accessory or the one who committed the crime.

Only a month before the murder, Sadka had made a visit to Grandfather's clinic. Dr. Hyam repeated the story many times in the following weeks, then again in the courtroom. I recall him relating it to Aunt Bellore's husband in the Raymonds' garden a few days after the first arrest.

"This man Sadka asked for me before consulting-room hours. Apparently one of his Hindu workmen had sustained a nasty wound to his hand the week before, and Sadka said the poor man was terrified that he might lose several fingers. I told Sadka to bring the fellow around immediately, for the whole arm could be lost to gangrene if he delayed. Nobody ever appeared."

"So what is the connection?" Uncle Samuel asked.

"I don't believe there ever was a man with an injured hand. Sadka's chief concern was the anesthesia. He persisted in asking how it was done, what the name of the chemical was, and even how much was required to deliver 'a small man unconscious.' When I said 'chloroform' to him, he asked me to write the word so he would not forget it."

"Have you told this to the inspector?"

"Certainly."

This unusual word, "chloroform," which sounded to me like the name for a pretty English girl, was heard again in the next few days. Inquisitive about this new person, I asked Yali. "Who is Miss Form?"

"Who?"

"Chloro Form."

"I have no idea," she said, dismissing me.

I thought better of questioning my grandparents. When I pumped Dr. Hyam, he laughed with his head thrown back. "She's not a person, she's—I mean, it's—a medicine. We use it to help people sleep when they need to have cuts sewn. Why?"

"I heard it mentioned," I said, smarting from my stupidity. After that I was alert anytime the word was used. This is how I learned Sadka had acquired a considerable quantity of the drug. The chemists Messrs. Smith and Stanistreet in Dalhousie Square reported they had sold a one-ounce vial of chloroform to Moosa Chachuk on the fifteenth of September, two weeks before the murder. The next day, another firm in Lal Bazaar was asked for the same amount by Nissim Sadka. Because he was unknown to the proprietor, he refused to sell it to him. Nevertheless, the firm of Scott Thompson and Company in Old Court House Street complied. Armed with this information, police inspectors questioned Sadka's employees.

Terrified of being implicated, his manservant, Arup, supplied the evidence that led to his master's arrest.

Dr. Hyam reported this confession. "Arup says that Sadka and Chachuk took breakfast together the day before the tragedy. Sadka ordered Arup to accompany Chachuk to the market and make whatever transactions his friend desired because 'Jews could not handle money that day since it was Succoth, the Feast of the Tabernacles.' At Moulali, in Lower Circular Road, Arup used his master's money to buy a twelve-foot bamboo ladder for five *annas*. After selecting a box of matches at Tiretta Bazaar, Chachuk told Arup to have a coolie deliver the ladder to his house by evening, since it was needed at a carpentry job the next day. Arup identified this as the same ladder found in the garden at Theatre Road."

The final piece of evidence, an empty chloroform vial with a wrapper from Smith and Stanistreet, also discovered in the garden, led to the arrest of Moosa Chachuk, who protested he had been at home with three men—including Nissim Sadka—on the night of the first of October. Unfortunately for Chachuk, the third man's name could not be recalled and he could not be located.

Other proof emerged. One rubber shoe, spotted with blood only on the outside, had been discovered under my father's bed. The inside was clean, an indication the shoe must have been on the murderer's foot. Arup confirmed the shoe matched a pair that had belonged to his master.

Once this much was known, once the men were jailed, the gloom in my grandparents' house dissipated markedly. Yali asked me if I still wished her to sleep in my room. I did. Grandmother asked me if I was ready to increase my lessons. I was. Aunt Bellore came to tea and asked if I wouldn't feel more at home in Theatre Road.

"No! No shutters!"

"What is this business about shutters?" she asked in a disgruntled tone.

"The bad man came in through the window."

Aunt Bellore looked meaningfully at my grandfather. She knew he did not like having me drawn into the matter.

"No, he didn't," my grandfather said soothingly.

"Yes, he did."

"Then how do you explain the shutters being latched from the inside?" Aunt Bellore asked in an exasperated voice.

"I closed them," I responded, startling them both.

"Don't tell tales," she chastised angrily.

"But I did!" I shouted. Why wouldn't anyone believe me when I was the one who was there?

"When did you do this?" Nana asked.

"I heard them banging. That was what woke me. So I went in to latch them. After that—"

Aunt Bellore placed her hand on my shoulder. "When you looked outside, did you see anyone moving about?"

"No."

"Did you hear other noises?"

"No. It was quiet in the house."

"Nothing outside?"

"No."

"Has anyone else asked you about this?"

"No." I sniffed. "So that's why I want to stay here."

Nana gave Bellore Lanyado a warning glance. "And so you shall, until it is entirely safe to return home" was his final word on the matter.

* * *

I was soon to learn that "safety" was a relative word. Another disaster would send us back to Theatre Road sooner than my grandfather could have anticipated, but this time its origin was natural, rather than man-made.

Calcutta is situated south of the Tropic of Cancer on the left bank of the Hooghly River, sixty miles from the sea. Constructed on the eastern side of the Indo-Gangetic plain, the city lies only twenty feet above sea level and is prone to flooding whenever it rains heavily. The region has three predominant seasons: hot, wet, and cool. The hot weather arrives at the beginning of March, bringing scorching temperatures that often exceed one hundred and ten degrees. During this period, heat prostration, breathing difficulties due to the swirling dust, dehydration, and stomach ailments tortured Grandfather's patients. By the time the monsoon sweeps through the region in June, it is a great relief, even though the daily downpours flood the streets with more than ten inches of rain each month. The high humidity combined with temperatures hovering in the nineties makes it impossible to exert oneself even slightly without becoming bathed in perspiration. In that season my grandfather would treat collapses, fungal and skin eruptions, pestilence from sewage leaking into water supplies, and diseases borne by the increased population of insects. Just after the cyclone season, typically taking place in September, the air becomes drier. If no tropical storms develop, this is a most agreeable, trouble-free time of year. The "cold weather," lasting from the beginning of December to mid-February, brings a welcome respite, with pleasant days and nights rarely lower than fifty degrees.

By the first of November everyone had concluded that it was too late in the year to be concerned about a cyclone. As if in perverse response, barometers around Calcutta began to drop. Aunt Bellore began insisting, because of a twinge in her shoulder, that a huge storm was on the way.

In a few days her predictions seemed on target. Even Nani complained of strange chest-crushing sensations. The next morning Yali woke me and asked me to stand in the courtyard and raise my hands.

"Can you grasp it?"

"What?"

"The thick air."

"No, you're silly."

"Remember the feeling, then. It's like a panting beast. You will know its breath when it comes again."

I pondered this during the morning while devilish squalls blew sheets of rain across the Hooghly River. Sudden gusts tore shutters from houses and crushed rickshaws against buildings like flimsy toys. Between the slashing torrents were periods of relief when no rain would fall and the air would ripple with an eerie crackling sound. Nani put me to bed during one of these lulls.

Yali woke me in the middle of the night. Her soft voice made a queer echoing sound in my room. As I swung my feet around, thinking she wanted to take me to the toilet, she pushed me back. "I must carry you."

Thundering volleys cracked in the hellish sky. Dr. Hyam arrived with a bullock-cart that could carry only our family. The durwan helped the ayahs and other servants climb onto the flat roof above the kitchen and wrapped blankets about them. In the splintering light of the storm I rolled away, waving and calling to Yali.

Eventually we arrived at the house where my father had been born— now the Lanyados' residence—which was built on higher ground. In the rain, which poured off the roof in liquid sheets, Grandmother carried Asher. I took Jonah's hand. Dr. Hyam lifted Grandfather inside. We were not the only refugees from the storm. The entire Sassoon clan had united there.

The next morning, I surveyed the filthy ribbons of water that snaked through the district. A sea interspersed with queer concrete islands sprawled from the Hooghly. The city seemed an aquatic burial ground. The Maidan, Calcutta's vast park, rippled with swirling eddies. I thought about transformations, how quickly everything that has been an accepted part of one's life can be altered by a single event. A mother's death leaves a child awash. A cyclone does the same to a city. Children splashed in the turgid water. Stranded families huddled on the few raised porches.

Oblivious of the turmoil, the sun shone. I could not find my clothes, so I went in search of Yali. Aunt Bellore stopped me before I could reach the kitchens.

"Where's Yali?"

Aunt Bellore gave a massive groan. "Look around you! Confusion. Upset. So many to feed, to care for. I can't keep track of everyone's servants, can I?"

"I need a dress."

"You can borrow something of Sultana's." Aunt Bellore had three girls. Sultana, her oldest, was nearly my age, but much smaller.

In the nursery Aunt Bellore had me try on several dresses. "I can't believe how much bigger you are than Sultana. You certainly won't be turning out like your moth—" She caught herself. Piqued, she gave me a robe. "Try this. Just tie it loosely at the waist."

"No. Yali will do it. Where is Yali?"

"She has gone to find her own family."

"Liar!"

"Dinah!" Aunt Bellore slapped my cheek. "Mind your words."

"Liar!" Blinded by tears, I ran to find Nani.

Yali did not return to the Lanyados' house. After the flood dissipated, the Raymonds' house was declared uninhabitable, but my father's residence in Theatre Road was undamaged.

My grandfather took me on his lap in his rolling chair. "Dinah, would you rather stay with your Aunt Bellore or with us in Theatre Road?"

I touched the cheek that my aunt had slapped and replied without hesitation, "Theatre Road, Nana."

❧ ❧ ❧

The prisoners were to stand trial at the next criminal sessions, in December. As the day approached, everyone kept asking whether my father would arrive before the trial.

"Better that he stays away" was Nani's attitude.

Nana disagreed. "He should see justice done, or else he will question forever the way the matter was handled."

With no knowledge of my father's whereabouts, the trial began on Monday, the second of December, 1878. Moosa Chachuk was charged with the willful murder of Luna Sassoon, and Nissim Sadka was arraigned as his accomplice. The suspects were tried before Chief Justice Sir John Neville and Sir Peter Grant, the second justice. Mr. Gardner, the advocate-general, conducted the case for the crown. Mr. Hicks defended Sadka, while Mr. O'Reilly defended Chachuk. My grandfather was well enough to attend the sessions, fully expecting that by the end of that week the men who had taken his daughter's life would be pronounced guilty and would face their just punishment. In the beginning, my grandmother could not bring herself to visit the courtroom.

After the first day of the trial, Uncle Saul, my father's eldest brother, and Aunt Bellore and her husband, Samuel Lanyado, escorted Grandfather back to Theatre Road. Uncle Saul took my father's place in the drawing room—in our family it was called the "hall." Grandmother poured tea. Asher and Jonah were brought in for a few minutes. I was permitted to remain for some chutney sandwiches.

Aunt Bellore clucked her tongue when she saw the short hem on my dress. "We'll have to see you have some new ones ordered. After this is over, I'll have the dressmaker in for the girls."

Uncle Saul tapped his foot.

"Dinah, why don't you go upstairs with the boys now?" Aunt Bellore asked in a honey-smooth voice.

I looked to Grandmother for confirmation that I might stay.

"Yes, Dinah," Nani said, meaning I had to do as I had been told.

I walked over to my grandfather and held his hand. He patted mine. I took this to mean he had championed my cause.

Uncle Saul was glaring.

Nana gave me a squeeze. "G-go now . . . later . . ."

I turned away as slowly as I could. Out in the corridor I made a loud clomping sound, then removed my shoes and slipped into the serving pantry, where a door had been left slightly ajar. I pressed my back to the wall and breathed silently.

"The adovcate-general's implications about the fact that the participants are Jewish are bothering me," Uncle Saul bellowed.

"What would that have to do with the case?" Grandmother asked.

Nana answered in short, stuttering phrases: "The advocate-general was t-trying to justify . . . that Ch-Chachuk would not act alone . . . t-to help prove that . . . S-Sadka had the m-m—"

Uncle Saul filled in for him. "A motive. Or vice versa. We do not yet know which one committed the violent act. The problem seems to be that if Nissim acted in a frenzy of passion—a crime that might receive a lesser sentence than premeditated murder—then he would not have organized the murder and brought in a second to assist. The sum of the early evidence—why, the chloroform alone—leads us to think it was planned in advance."

Nani spoke slowly. "What does being Jewish have to do with it?"

Uncle Saul tried again. "I believe the advocate-general reasoned that if Sadka selected someone to assist him in a premeditated crime, the accomplice would—as he put it—'be of the same creed, inferior in position, but strong and accustomed to violence, and desperate—for either money or acceptance.' "

"An excellent description of Chachuk—after the fact," Uncle Samuel remarked. "I wonder if he would have come up with that argument if Chachuk had not been implicated."

"My thoughts exactly," Aunt Bellore agreed.

Through the cracked door, I could see Uncle Saul pacing. "All that aside, I thought the advocate-general's arguments were laid out with excellent logic," he continued. "He mentioned the need to silence the victim and the knowledge that the men had acquired chloroform recently. He introduced the purchase of the ladder and matches, both needed to scale a wall at night." He paused. "As the evidence is developed, each point should be proved beyond a doubt."

"What about Dinah?" my aunt mumbled.

My heart pounded as I strained to hear the whispers that followed. Maybe they would listen to me at last.

". . . testify . . . not a child . . ."

". . . but the shutters . . ."

". . . shouldn't be necessary." Uncle Saul's statement ended on a peremptory tone, and I could hear the scrape of chairs against the hard floor. They were probably getting ready to leave.

"At least this should be over in short order," I heard Aunt Bellore say as I tiptoed away in case anyone came looking for me.

The second day of the trial, the family was less ebullient. They were also more careful about closing doors and excluding me. Later I would learn the accuseds' lawyers had begun to discuss the circumstantial nature of the evidence, the lack of eyewitnesses, and the fact that Chachuk and Sadka claimed they had people who would substantiate testimony of their whereabouts that evening.

Concerned that the men might possibly be acquitted, Nani steeled herself and accompanied her husband on the third day. When they returned, she went directly to her room, and I was permitted to greet her for only a few moments.

"Nani!" I cried when I saw her flushed and trembling. "Are you ill?"

"No, dearest Dinah, just tired."

"Where are Uncle Saul and Aunt Bellore?"

"I asked them not to come today because I will be retiring early. Why don't you go in to see your grandfather for a few minutes before you have your supper?" She gave me a limp hug. My mother's former servant, a plump Bengali woman who rarely spoke, brought her some fizzy tablets and pushed me out the door.

When I went to Grandfather's room, which previously had been a day nursery on the ground floor, I found him trembling in his chair. His eyes were weeping continuously. Whatever had happened in the courts that day had sucked dry his reservoir of strength. Dr. Hyam was giving him an injection in his thigh.

"What's that?" I asked as I watched with more curiosity than horror.

"Something to make him more comfortable," the doctor said softly.

When the hypodermic was withdrawn, I threw my arms around Nana. "Is that better?" Nana made a feeble attempt to reach over and pat me. His palsied fingers ruffled my hair and glanced off my cheek.

Short, heavyset Dr. Hyam sat with a sigh and waited until the medicine began to work. Grandfather's head lolled to the side and his limbs twitched intermittently.

I touched his cheek, his lips, his pulse, in a pantomime of Dr. Hyam's usual actions. "He will rest now," I pronounced.

Dr. Hyam stood up and left the room. "Come with me, Dinah," he said as I lingered behind.

I rose to my feet, but on my way out the door I fingered the vial of medicine that had calmed my grandfather. "Laudanum" it said, but I misread the label as "Loudanum" and wondered how something with "loud" in it had quieted him so quickly. Next to it was another with a milky liquid. I touched it, and its label rolled into view. Chloroform! I lifted it and twisted the cap. An acrid fume stung my eyes. That had been the aroma about my mother's face that terrible morning.

❦   ❦   ❦

The next day Grandfather Ephraim was confined at home, and my grandmother went to court in his stead. After that, the Sassoons visited no longer. When Nani returned, she would tell her husband what had happened. Huddled in the alcove outside their door, I listened to her explanations, trembling first at the idea of being caught, second at the revelations about my mother.

"They know, everyone knows," Nani said, sobbing. "They even brought in the hookah and witnesses swore they had seen her smoke from it."

I did not understand my grandmother's horrified expression. My mother's routine was hardly a secret. The silver-inlaid hookah was always in place by her chaise. Her partaking had seemed as natural as sipping water or wine.

"Who spoke against Luna?" Nana choked.

"Several friends of the family and Bellore Sassoon were sworn in."

"Hypocrites. All those d-damned Sassoons!" he sputtered. "You would think that a family who has built their fortune on the buying and selling of opium would not condemn one of their own for using their product. A cigar, a brandy, a pipe of opium. What's the difference to them?"

"Don't you see? In order to wipe themselves clean of any blame, they are attacking us," my grandmother said slowly.

"Us!" Nana exploded. "Who was the cause of her loneliness? Not us. What about Benu? How did he think a woman as lovely as his wife would occupy herself for most of the year without a husband? If he had been by her side—"

"They referred to your medical practice," my grandmother replied evenly. "Several men testified you prescribed opiates freely. Bellore Sassoon swore you gave morphine to Luna during and after the births of her children."

There was a long silence.

"If it had been up to me, I could have regulated her better," Nana sighed. "Benu gave her access to any quantity she desired. He thought it would keep her content. And in a way it did. It also attracted the wrong sort of friends to Theatre Road . . ."

Their voices trailed away. I sat in my niche thinking it over. Opium . . . Mama . . . the wrong sort of friends. The story was a tangled skein that could never be unraveled and yet the silver hookah with its sweet, fruity smoke had somehow been the root of this misery. A door creaked. It was too late to get out of the way. My grandmother left the room dabbing her eyes with a handkerchief. Fortunately, she was far too disturbed to have noticed me trembling in her wake.

The next evening, I took my hiding place with less concern. The adults were far too preoccupied to care for my whereabouts.

"Preliminary arguments have been completed," Nani reported. "The worst is over. At least they seem to be focusing on the love affair more than the opium."

"Luna wasn't the criminal!"

"I know. If Benu was here, he would defend her," my grandmother said, but without conviction, I thought.

"What happened?" my grandfather ordered. "Tell me exactly what was said."

"At the end of his arguments, the advocate-general suggested the motive for the murder."

"Yes, what then?" Nana demanded.

"He said, 'As the French say, "A woman may be satisfied with only one husband, but never with one lover." ' I don't recall his exact words after that, but he suggested that Sadka's awareness that he might not have been the only man Luna invited to her bed had driven him to desperation."

"Do you think that is true?"

"Yes, I do," Nani muttered. "They brought enough witnesses to support the theory. Benu's servants, most especially the blind punkah-wallah, recalled several angry conversations between the lovers."

"What would the Bengali servants know? Luna and Sadka would have spoken in Arabic."

"They understand more than you think. Besides, from the tone, the servant had the impression Luna was telling her visitor that she never wanted to see him again."

"When was that?"

"He claims it was a week before her death, and the counsel for the defendants did not refute this. The man stood up and said, 'Yes, Nissim and Luna may have disagreed—all men and women do. What else is new in the world?' Instead they developed long lists of the men who may have visited Luna while Benu was absent. Every servant was interviewed about her guests. Even the *mehtar* was interrogated."

"The mehtar!" Nana raged.

I understood his fury. How could anyone take the word of one of the lowest classes of Hindu, a man who cleaned the toilets and performed the most menial tasks, on so important a matter?

"And the durwan," Grandmother added with more respect. The durwan was the gatekeeper, whose job it was to monitor comings and goings in the house. Ours was a heavy, dark Hindu man with a frightening face and a gentle disposition whom we trusted with our lives. He insisted that Sadka was the most frequent male visitor and that he had been there many times that week. Under cross-examination he described how he had let Sadka into our home at eight on the evening of her death and how he had seen them out on the upstairs veranda, where memsahib smoked her hookah while the punkah-wallah fanned her. Of course, the prosecutor asked how he knew they were on the veranda when a durwan is normally down by the gate."

"Exactly." Nana coughed. "What did he reply?"

"He said the voices were so loud, he came around the side of the house to see if something was the matter."

"What did he say he overheard?" Nana asked impatiently.

"He could not be exact, just loud words."

"That proves nothing."

"I suppose you are right." Nani sniffed and blew her nose. "The testimony of the blind punkah-wallah was more damaging. I don't know how she could have been so indiscreet! Did she think the man was also deaf and dumb?"

"Well, *abdalak*"—Grandfather used a soothing endearment—"it doesn't matter what they say about Luna. The guilt of the men has been proved by many facts and much evidence. They bought the chloroform with no reasonable explanation why they should require the substance. They purchased the ladder and matches. The ladder was abandoned in the garden, and marks made by the same ladder were found on the garden wall. One of Sadka's shoes was discovered beneath Luna's bed with traces of her blood on it. Chachuk's servant admitted washing his master's shirt and fez because of bloodstains. Scratches on Sadka's knees and Chachuk's wrists correspond to either a struggle or scaling a wall."

"What about Sadka's story that another man committed the murder?"

"They have established nothing on that point."

"I suppose you're right," Nani said, though her groaning belied the words.

By then I thought it prudent to disappear, and missed whatever might have been said afterward.

♔ ♔ ♔

The Sunday before the summing up, no visitors came to the house. The weather was cool and bright. I wandered through the somnambulant corridors until I found my grandmother in my mother's old bedroom. She wiped her eyes as I came toward her. "May we go to Aunt Bellore's house today?"

"That is not possible," my grandmother said in a thick voice.

"Why?" I persisted.

"It wouldn't be proper," was her curt reply.

I went to my grandfather's room. He was snoring in his chair. Upstairs, Jonah and Asher were taking a long nap. In the outer building the *borchi*, or cook, had undertaken to clean the *choola*, a large rectangular brick structure set against one of the walls. Coals were being raked into a basket, and ashes flew everywhere. A few large flakes landed on my dress. When I brushed them away, an oily smudge remained. The borchi apologized profusely and tried to clean it up, but the stain soaked in.

In my room I changed into a fresh dress, lay down on my bed, and stared at the ceiling. I had not been able to sleep in the afternoons since the funeral. I wandered down the hall and into my mother's dressing room. Mama's clothes had been packed away in metal trunks. The dressing table remained with a silver brush-and-comb set laid out as usual. Also intact were her two shelves of books. The spines were organized by color. In the green section I recognized *Lorna Doone*. I opened the book and stared at the illustration opposite the title page. A woman's arms were reaching out through a barred but open window, clasping the hands of a man. His walking stick rested against the rude stone wall of the house; his straw hat lay upside down on the ground. The words underneath read, "So I got the other hand." Ever since I had lived with my grandparents, my studies had progressed. By the end of that year I could read anything, even newspapers. Curious about the picture, I opened *Lorna Doone*. The print was tiny; the words were too difficult. I pulled down a volume of poetry from the blue section. With the white spaces of the margins and between the stanzas, the lines appeared simpler. I carried the book to the end of the hall. The door to my father's bedroom was ajar. The shutters were hooked open. Wide slashes of sunlight streaked across the room, marking the pattern of the panes on the polished floor. The platform bed had been dismantled. The mattress was standing against the wall. The personal effects of both my parents had been removed. No longer was this the darkened den where my mother spent her lonesome days. Nor was it the gloomy hell of the last evening of her life. For some reason there was a bouquet of roses in a cut-glass vase on the marble table beside the chaise.

I dared myself to step inside. My footsteps echoed as I made a tour of the margins of the barren room. Tentatively I touched the velvety petal of one red rose and stared out the window on the north side. The *mali* clipped untidy stalks of grass one by one. Pleased by the gardener's attempt at orderliness, I sat down on the edge of the chaise longue. I leaned back. Lifting my legs, I stretched out full. The cushion was wider than I remembered. My elbows could not reach the armrests. I opened the book and turned to a poem. William Wordsworth. The title was simple: *Lucy.* I could read every single word of the first two stanzas.

She dwelt among the untrodden ways
   Beside the springs of Dove;
A maid whom there were none to praise,
   And very few to love.

A violet by a mossy stone
   Half hidden from the eye!
Fair as a star, when only one
   Is shining in the sky.

Keeping my finger at the place, I glanced at the bunch of roses. Who had placed them there? A servant? My grandmother? I recalled the scent embedded in Mama's satin robe: mostly roses. Had she always kept bouquets on the table? I closed my eyes, trying to remember if she had. Then, irritated that I could not picture roses or my mother, I forced myself to focus on the printed page.

She lived unknown, and few could know
   When Lucy ceased to be;
But she is in her grave, and O,
   The difference to me!

"The difference to me . . ." I whispered in awe, and, shivering, pulled my knees up to my chest. The simple words had magnified my longing. Swept up by the conflicting sensations that eddied about me, I did not hear the first footsteps coming down the corridor. Nor did it occur to me that whoever it was—probably Yali—might be disturbed to find me there. So when I looked up and the form in the doorway adjusted itself through the mist of tears that had caused me to stop reading, the shock numbed me.

My father had returned.

Slowly he walked toward the chaise. Even then I knew he must have been thinking about my mother and not me. In the distance I could see Yali backing away. Sunlight from the window streaked his face so half was darkness, half squinted in brightness. He shielded his eyes and awkwardly sank to his knees.

"Dinah." His voice was huskier than I recalled.

I had done something wrong. I should not have been in my mother's place. I should not have been reading her book. To make amends, I flung my arms about his neck. He lifted me up. Nuzzling my cheek, he swung me around. My feet swirled out and knocked over the vase of roses.

The clatter of glass caused me to cry out.

I slipped from his arms and ran from the room. Halfway to the hall I turned back for a split second. My father was bending down, gingerly picking up the thorny stems of the fallen roses.

3

🌱 🌱 🌱

The last day of the trial I awoke to the gurgling and hissing of water pipes. Because pressure in Calcutta was so low that water could not rise above the ground floor, we had on our roof a cube-shaped reservoir that was pumped full every morning. When I opened my eyes, though, the world was still dark. Why would the tank be draining so early?

Yali stroked my shoulder and told me I was to have a bath.

"But I had one last night," I said groggily.

"Yes, Dinah-*baba*, but the *sahib* says—"

The sahib . . . ?

My father! I sat upright. I had not seen him since I had run from his bedroom the night before. He had dined with his brothers, and I had been put to bed before his return.

Yali undressed me and carried me to the nursery bath. She lowered me into the copper tub. "No!" I leapt out. On summer days the water from the tank ran unbearably hot, but this time of the year the temperature was so chilly I felt as if I had been pierced with needles.

"Dinah-baba . . ." Yali coaxed in her singsong voice.

I shivered. "Too cold."

"You must. I will wash you quickly."

"No!"

Yali picked me up and dunked me, soaking even the crown of my head. I came up sputtering and would have cried out another protest if the shouting hadn't stilled me.

"You cannot do this!" echoed down the corridor. I could not determine who was speaking.

"I most certainly can." The reply was the gruff voice of my father.

"Benu, I implore you, how can I make you see?" Nani was less strident, more recognizable in this plea.

"Don't you think I know what is best for my own daughter?"

38

"No, you don't. You have been away most of her life. You were not here when this happened. She has just begun to recover from the shock. Who can tell what this might do to her?"

"This is precisely what she needs. Once she sees the resolution with her own eyes, she can put the unpleasantness behind her."

"Please, Benu, won't you at least wait until Mordecai gets here? She trusts him. Perhaps if he explains it to her—"

"I can explain it better than the good doctor, thank you."

"You haven't been there. Every day curious crowds pack the room. And those two men in the box are so close you could touch them. A courtroom is no place for a child."

"I have made up my mind." A door slammed.

Not a ripple disturbed my tub. The only sounds were the pings of water droplets dripping from my hair onto the metallic rim. Yali waited a few beats before scrubbing me roughly with a cloth. Selima brought me a banana and a cup of warm milk.

"Drink before you are dressed," Yali said.

I did as I was told. Selima shook out my white starchy petticoats and knickers. After I had eaten, she affixed the straps at my shoulders and waist. Normally fidgety at times like this, I remained immobile. My white dress was lowered over my head. Yali tied my sash.

Selima redid it to her satisfaction. "Now she is ready."

Yali took my hand. "Where am I going?"

"The sahib wishes you to join him for his *chota hazri*."

"Where am I going after that?" I asked curtly.

"With your father."

"Yali!" I complained, but she would tell me nothing more.

My father was taking his "little breakfast" on a small table set up by the windows in the hall. "Dinah!" He stood up as I appeared in the door, as though I were an important lady entering the room. I didn't move. "Come, I will pour you some tea."

"I had milk upstairs, Papa."

"Then come and sit with me."

Yali pushed me at the base of my spine, and I edged forward involuntarily. Papa pulled out a chair for me. Still reluctantly, I fussed with my petticoats as I positioned myself on the chair.

He in turn sat down and beamed at me. "What a pretty girl you have become."

I looked away, out the windows at the silver cast in the dawning sky.

"You will spend today with me."

I did not respond.

He waited for a beat. "Won't you like that?"

"I think so, Papa."

Hearing a scraping sound, I looked across the table. My father had lathered a slice of toast with more butter than Yali would ever have permitted. He passed it across to me. "Thank you, Papa."

We both munched quietly for a long while. From time to time I glanced up at the stranger who was my father. He was a tall man, the largest of the Sassoon brothers. His head was unusually elongated, or perhaps it only seemed so because there was a great deal of flesh showing from his high polished forehead to the V of his pointed beard. His eyes were small dark beads set under drooping lids. Without asking again, my father prepared a cup of tea for me with three sugars and a third of a cup of milk. I took a few sips to help me swallow the bread, leaning across my saucer so as not to soil anything. My father's gaze continued to unsettle me. I thought his limbs were bonier than I recalled. When he had been talking, the gauntness was not as noticeable, but when he stared at me, his demeanor took on the same threatening aspect that had sent me running when we were reunited the day before.

He replaced his empty cup with a clatter. "Dinah, you do know what is happening today, don't you?"

"Well . . ."

"There is a trial—"

"Yes," I cut him off. "Dr. Hyam told me about it."

"I see. Then you know that today will be the last of it." As he stood up, Abdul, his bearer, who had been waiting in the shadows, rushed to brush the crumbs from his waistcoat. "We will leave in half an hour. You may go to say good morning to your grandparents for a few minutes, but you mustn't stay long. They are quite . . . ah, tired. Taking care of everything while I was away has been too much of a strain on them. Now that I am home, they can return to Lower Chitpur Street."

"I don't want them to go, Papa."

"And why is that?"

"I shall be lonely without them."

"We must think of their feelings now."

"I want them to stay with us."

"That won't be possible, Dinah."

"But, Papa—"

He came around to my side of the table, took my hand, and pulled me to my feet. "Now that I am home, I will care for my own children." Realizing that he was speaking too stridently, he lowered his voice. "Now, do as I say." He looked away from me to the view across the garden. The sky was a muted pink and orange with a golden band at the bottom, like the border of a Brahmin's sari. "Today will be one of the most important days of your life. Today you will see evil punished and goodness restored."

❦ ❦ ❦

Riding for the first time in my father's office *jaun*, I arrived at the High Court, an impressive Gothic building modeled on the town hall of Ypres, Belgium. My first surprise was the crowd of people waiting to enter, a throng that filled the square out to the statue of Lord Bentinck. The second was that, unlike at synagogue, I did not have to sit in a gallery with the women, but was permitted to remain at my father's side.

Inside, the courtroom was almost filled. I recognized many faces from Sabbath services. There were a few gasps as I passed, then a buzz of words I could not quite make out as we made our way down the aisle. Instead I gripped my father's hand, wishing we could hurry to our places faster. Friends who had not seen him for more than six months greeted him cordially. He acknowledged them with a curt lowering of his chin. Most of my Sassoon aunts and uncles were already seated on the back benches on the right, with the eldest, Uncle Saul, on an aisle. My father sat directly in front of him. As I sat beside my father, I noticed that Aunt Bellore was behind me. Three seats to my right were empty until the proceedings were about to begin. My grandparents slipped in last. We had come in separate carriages.

Since it was December, and by Calcutta standards relatively cool, only one punkah-wallah pulled the rope on his fan, which was directly over the officials and not the audience.

There was a pounding sound. "Be upstanding!" a clerk cried. Everyone stood at attention. A small door behind a raised platform opened. Two men in black robes entered the room.

"Who are they?" I asked Papa.

"The justices."

"What is a justice?"

"Hush, I'll explain later."

The two justices, one considerably older than the other, took their places against the wall. They were followed by two Indian guards resplendent in crimson uniforms and white turbans, each carrying an enormous black staff topped with a club-shaped silver ornament.

I lifted my hand and pointed. "What's that? And who are they?"

My father caught my fingers and placed them in my lap. "A mace. And they are *chobdars*—guards for the justices."

"What do they use those poles for? To hit someone?"

"No, they are symbols of authority."

"Oh," I replied, not really comprehending. I contemplated the unfamiliar array of people before me. Below the justices' table was another surrounded by men making notes. In the center of the area, at an even longer table, were more men. Some were wearing white collars, bands, and robes like the justices.

My father seemed distracted by something, so I asked my grand-mother, this time discreetly pointing from my lap. "Who are they, Nani?"

"They are called barristers, Dinah. Those are the men who will try to make us believe that Mr. Sadka and Mr. Chachuk are innocent."

"But they are not."

"No, they are not, but it remains for the jury to decide that."

"What is the jury?"

Nani tilted her head to an area enclosed by a balustrade. "Do you see the twelve men sitting there?"

"Yes."

"Those men will listen carefully to what is said, then decide who is telling the truth."

"But . . ." My question faded as I recognized Uncle Nissim and another man being escorted into the room. They were led into an enclosed box opposite the jury box.

A man in a robe rose and began to speak. This time Nani did not wait for my questions, but bent over and whispered, "He's the advocate-general. He presents the case for the crown. That means he wishes to prosecute the men who hurt your mother."

The man spoke for almost an hour, using the bulk of the time trying to dismiss the circumstantial nature of the evidence and the lack of witnesses. He concluded, "Let us assume the crime was both deliber-ate and planned. Would not the planning include elaborate measures to ensure that no eyewitness should be available to give evidence? Would not any criminal do his utmost to prevent anyone from know-ing beforehand? Does this not suggest a devious mind? If, according to the defense, no punishment can be given if there is no positive evi-dence, that would therefore confer immunity on the worst transgres-sors." His voice rose to the pitch of a fervent plea. "What a travesty it would be if the only criminals who could be punished were the less artful culprits whose offenses were unpremeditated, or committed un-der the duress of so great a passion as to be unaware of the presence of a witness!"

I turned to where Nissim Sadka was standing. His accomplice, Chachuk, was looking off into the distance, but Uncle Nissim's squinty, narrow black eyes were focused directly at me. His thick hair had been greased back so purposely that the comb lines formed tracks on his scalp. Even though I looked at him squarely, his face appeared crooked, probably because his long nose had a twist to one side. Could there really be a connection between this man and my lifeless, rigid mother covered in sticky crimson?

"Dinah!" Aunt Bellore whispered at the back of my neck.

Transfixed by Sadka's stare, I did not turn around.

She reached over and shoved my chin toward my grandmother, breaking the link. Nani clasped both my hands in hers and stroked them rhythmically, as if to the beat of a soldier's march. I leaned on my father's shoulder and was soon dozing as the proceedings droned on.

I was awakened for a break in the trial. A luncheon was held in Kyd Street. Before Aunt Bellore had inherited the house as part of her dowry, it had been home to all her brothers. After her marriage she had lived in one wing, taking it over entirely on the death of her father. I ate in the nursery with Sultana, Abigail, and Lulu and would have been quite content to spend the rest of the afternoon there. Sultana ventured downstairs at one point and came back to report there was much shouting and unpleasantness in the dining room. I felt certain the animosity had to do with me.

The Lanyados' ayah washed my hands and face, fluffed up my dress, and retied my sash. Even before the nurse was satisfied, my father appeared and said it was time to go.

At the door, Aunt Bellore sided with the Raymonds. "Are you certain, Benu? Dinah may spend the day here. She would rather be with Sultana and the others." My aunt patted my head. "Wouldn't you, Dinah?"

I looked from brother to sister. "No." I reached for my father's hand. "I'd rather be with Papa."

He did not reply, but I sensed his pleasure. He marched past his sister and my grandparents and lifted me into the office jaun, pulled by a large white horse. On the way, he explained what would happen next. "One of the two judges will now retell both sides of the story to the jurors. They may be confused by conflicting statements that have been said by the men who claim Chachuk and Sadka are innocent and the men who claim they are guilty. The chief justice will tell the jury they must decide."

"Will it be today?"

"I do not think there is much doubt in the matter, so it should be over rather quickly."

"That's good," I said, since I dreaded too many more hours of sitting quietly.

"Very good," he replied, though his meaning was far different from mine.

As we approached the municipal buildings, I dared ask the question that most weighed on my mind. "Papa, what will they do to them?"

"In the Bible it says, 'Eye for an eye, tooth for tooth, hand for hand, foot for foot.' "

A horrid image of extractions of teeth and eyes, of amputations—like the ones my grandfather performed for the lepers—nauseated me. "Will they cut off their hands and pull out their teeth?"

My father smiled crookedly, but spoke in a dignified voice. "No, they will lose the privilege of their lives."

"The men in the robes, the judges, will one of them kill them?"

"No, another official will do it."

"Oh!" I thought I had it now. The men with the heavy maces would beat the criminals. One or two blows should do it. Wanting confirmation, I asked, "How?"

He hugged me close.

"With the mace?"

My father's grin widened. "No, the gallows. They shall hang by their necks until they are dead."

॥⁄ ॥⁄ ॥⁄

Even without the transcript of the chief justice's summation, I can recall portions of his lengthy speech—it lasted almost four hours—because he enunciated so slowly, so carefully for the jurors, even I could follow what he was saying.

He spoke of the necessity not to rush to simple conclusions in so complex a case. "I urge the jury to exercise caution in accepting the story created by the advocate-general, who has neatly developed a line of thinking that leads to the conclusion that these men collaborated to murder Luna Sassoon. Whilst this may be the very case, not all evidence follows in agreement. There are many controversial items to consider."

He went on to list the areas he felt the prosecution had introduced weakly: ". . . Mr. Sadka was at the Sassoon house that evening, but there is no certainty that it was he who returned to that place or he who made a final departure in the early-morning hours. . . . There is no proof to support that the dagger introduced as evidence was ever in the possession of the accused. Even the servant claims there was no one present when he found it and cleaned it."

A flurry of gasps rolled across the audience, visibly annoying the older judge. On my left, my father's spine stiffened; on my right, Nani's arm began to vibrate. My grandfather's lips twitched.

"With regard to the chloroform . . ." My attention was riveted when I again heard that familiar word. ". . . Even if you were to consider there is some evidence the prisoners were anxious to acquire it, there is no positive connection with the murder, since there is no proof the chloroform vial, which was not found near the body, was used on Luna Sassoon."

"But—" I started to say. Aunt Bellore reached forward and put her finger over my mouth. Still determined to speak up, I rose to my feet. My grandfather pushed me down. Stunned into obedience, I muttered, "But the smell on my mother matched the doctor's vial. I'm sure of it. Why doesn't anyone care about what I have to say?"

Angrily I sat back and listened as the younger judge spoke about a mysterious third man who had been identified by witnesses to have been with Sadka that evening and was definitely not Chachuk. At last the chief justice concluded his remarks. "Gentlemen of the jury, I must caution you in accepting the evidence of native witnesses. Most of the witnesses for the prosecution have been of the servant class, whose ignorance and loose ideas as to time—as well as the necessity for adhering to facts and circumstances as they actually occur—invest their testimony with a tenuous character. Further, one of these witnesses, the punkah-wallah, is blind, and we have no diagnosis as to which other faculties may be impaired."

When the summation concluded, the men of the jury left the room. As Papa turned around to confer with his brothers, their voices were muted, but their tone was outraged. Why had the younger judge twisted the facts in favor of the criminals? Why had he discredited the testimony of his trusted servants? How could he discount the bloody dagger, the ladder, the chloroform?

"Could someone have paid him off?" Uncle Saul whispered hoarsely.

Aunt Bellore's husband was aghast. "Bribe a judge?"

"The decision hasn't been made," Uncle Reuben reminded in a conciliatory tone.

Since almost everyone else had dispersed outside, I walked around the perimeter of the courtroom. I was thirsty and wondered how much longer this would continue.

In less than half an hour the jury members walked back into the room. The tableau of men, guards, and prisoners rearranged themselves rapidly.

"See!" Aunt Bellore announced as the family took their seats. "Their guilt was irrefutable."

As I fastened my gaze on the prisoners' box, I felt a peculiar shudder in my chest. "Eye for eye . . ." The men would be dead soon. Under the earth with dirt in their eyes. Like Mama. Sadka and Chachuk stared straight ahead.

"Not guilty," said a soft voice.

"Not guilty!" reverberated in the audience.

"They won't die?" I asked. No one responded.

My grandmother swooned, but I barely noticed it as my grandfather shot up from his seat. Straight and tall, without a tremble in his hand or a warble in his voice, he shouted, "Impossible! How could this be so?"

Dr. Hyam raised his arms to restrain his mentor, but Grandfather Ephraim pushed him away with such force that Dr. Hyam twisted his foot and fell beside his seat. Grandfather Ephraim stepped over him and made his way to the platform, where a policeman halted him. I could not believe how sturdy, how healthy Grandfather—in the potency of his fury—appeared. He marched to the table where the stunned advocate-general stood and pounded his fist.

"An outrage! How could this be? Where is justice?"

Dr. Hyam finally caught up to him, and the prosecutor and the doctor assisted Grandfather out of the court.

I turned to the men in the box. Moosa Chachuk had fallen and was being braced by a guard. Nissim Sadka was shaking so violently he had to clutch the rails for support. I thought an odd transference had just taken place: the weak had been given the strength of the murderer; the murderer had been blighted with the disease of his victim's parent.

"Now they won't die, will they?" I asked my aunt.

"Of course they will die, everyone does."

"Not for this, for what they did—"

"No," she gagged.

"But Papa said they would hang."

"Well, they won't!" Noticing her face had turned purple, I tugged on her arm and her breath returned. She composed herself and pulled me along with her.

"They will suffer," I said as cruelly as I could. In the aisle of the noisy chamber, she could not hear me. She led me outside. This was a mistake, because Moosa Chachuk already was at the curb, getting into his barrister's closed landau. "Where is he going?" I shouted above the throng.

"Wherever he wishes, Dinah. He is a free man."

"Not fair!" I screamed.

"You should never have been brought here!" she seethed, and spun around to see who was watching this spectacle.

I twisted away from her and began to run toward the street. She caught me and yanked me back so roughly my arm burned. My eyes burst with tears of pain and confusion.

"There's nothing you or anyone else can do about it. At least it is finally over," she pronounced in a tone that was too accepting for my taste.

"It is not fair—to Mama," I sputtered.

"Your mother was a part of this, I'm sorry to say."

"Then it's your fault too."

"What?" Aunt Bellore stared at me as though I were crazed.

"If it weren't for you, my mother would have married the Baghdadi doctor and had a different life."

As her grimace furrowed her firm high brow, she looked repulsive. "Dinah, we must get you home." She tightened her grip on my shoulder while furiously searching for her family.

"Stop him!" I screamed toward Chachuk's carriage, now stalled by the mob. "Make him come back!"

"Hush. Don't shout. There is nothing we can—"

"I can! I can do it." I pulled away and went rushing to where the second carriage, with Sadka inside, was driving off. The startled driver jerked on the reins as I flew in front of the horse. A bystander tugged me to safety. Struggling, I looked up. Sadka's simian face leered from the window. "Make him stop," I sobbed to the stranger.

"Where is your father?" she asked.

I looked around. The crowd of onlookers was multiplying, and nobody familiar could be recognized in the crush. Everyone's eyes focused on me.

"At least she doesn't have her mother's face," I heard someone say.

"Have you looked closely at the eyes?" commented another.

"In any case, she's not a beauty, but even if she was, who would have her now?"

"Poor child, poor little girl."

"What will become of her?"

"The family is ruined."

Aunt Bellore whisked me to her. "Don't mind what people are saying, Dinah."

For the first time I felt soiled, dirty. I wanted to hide myself away.

"Bellore! Here!" a voice called from a carriage as it drew closer.

My aunt lifted me into the open gharry, where Dr. Hyam was riding with my grandparents. She rushed for the next, which held her husband and my father. We drove off as rapidly as possible through the crowd that had spilled onto the streets.

I turned back and looked at the High Court Building. In the rising dust, the spire seemed to vibrate like strings on a harp.

The core of my resentment burst like a rotten mango. "Not fair . . . not fair . . . not fair . . ." I muttered in rhythm with the beat of the horses' hooves. If only they had listened to me! I knew more than they did about the shutters, the chloroform. Everyone in that courtroom had made an error in not paying attention to me. Somehow I would get back at all of them—especially Nissim Sadka—I vowed.

No doubt most people in the crowd that day felt justice had not been served. Nevertheless, few concerned themselves with the matter for more than several minutes. If they remembered anything, they may have heard my protests ringing in the air. Others who have been wronged must have felt as passionately as I did that day. Many a child must have had romantic hopes of being able to right the injustices of the adult world. However, few would have the opportunity to carry out the retribution that I would be offered many years later.

4

Whereas I directed the barbs of my hate toward Sadka and Chachuk, my father's revulsion took a different turn. The next afternoon I awoke from a nap with a start to sounds of bumping, scraping, banging. The shutters!

"Yali! Yali!" I screamed in terror.

I could hear the slap of her sandals in the corridor. As she rushed into the room, her violet sari flew out behind her like dragonfly wings. She took me in her arms and stroked my hair. "Hush, Dinah-baba. You will see them soon."

She must have thought I was upset because my grandparents had packed and left the house that morning.

"You will come to us as often as you like," Nani had said as she kissed me on the doorstep.

"In fact, you shall see us the day after tomorrow at services and then return home to spend the Sabbath with us," Grandfather said with hardly a stutter. He had declined since his impressive recovery the day before, yet he seemed far better than he had in more than a year.

The memory of their departure faded, replaced by the feel of Yali wiping my tears with the edge of her sari. She kept her cool hand on my brow until I calmed. Then Jonah poked his head in the door, dragging his favorite toy—an elephant on wooden wheels—behind him. Was that the sound I had heard?

Yali shooed him away and washed my hands and face. Selima brought in tea and set it out on the table in my room. I could hear the creaking wheels of Jonah's toy as he ran down the halls and called, "Jonah, come have tea with me."

Grinning broadly, he pushed the elephant in front of him with his foot until the toy grazed my leg. "Akbar wants a biscuit."

"Very well, Akbar, you may have mine." I broke off a piece, pretended to feed the elephant, then popped it into Jonah's nearby mouth.

48

He took the seat beside mine and fingered the border on the cloth. The design was of elephants linked trunk to tail. Jonah named them. "Akbar, Zakbar, Flakbar, Nackbar, Hackbar . . ." He giggled.

I was about to join his game when I heard the bumping noise again, I rushed to the door in time to see the durwan and the mali carrying Mama's chaise down the staircase. I followed them to the downstairs terrace, watching as they crossed the garden to a pile beside the far wall. Logs had been stacked in a neat pyre, like the *ghats* on the riverbank where the Hindus cremated their dead. On top was mounded the entire contents of my father's bedroom: the platform bed, the mattresses and coverings, the poles that supported the mosquito netting, the marble table that had held flowers and books. I watched, horrified, as the chaise was positioned precariously on top. No!

I ran upstairs and threw open the bedroom door. Discovering only a few pieces of paper and cloth scattered about in the empty room, I looked back in the hallway. Outside my mother's dressing-room door, clothing and books were accumulating. Where was Papa? His dressing-room door was closed. I tried the handle, but it was locked. I banged on it. "Papa! Papa!" There was no response. Jonah came up behind me and joined in the noisemaking. "Papa, Papa, Papa!" he called cheerily.

The door opened. "Hello, children," Papa said in a smooth voice. He was dressed as he had been for the courtroom the day before. In fact, his clothing was so rumpled, he must not have changed. He stumbled backward and caught himself on the wall. His face was blotched with ruddy patches, his nose swollen and red, his lips oddly blanched.

"Do you know what they are doing?" I asked, knowing full well the servants must have acted under his orders.

"Yes, Dinah, it is for the best—a fresh start . . ." he mumbled.

"No!" I sobbed as I tried to think of some way to deter him. I pictured *Lorna Doone* in flames. "Not her books—" I choked.

His jaw clenched. His high Sassoon forehead rippled. For a moment his oblong face looked like a skull. "Books?" he said as though he was coming out of a daze. "Yes, you like books, don't you? Is that what this is about? You would like to have the books."

I had not thought this through, but it seemed wise to salvage whatever I might. I glanced into my mother's disheveled dressing room next door. "Please, Papa." My mind raced. What else? "And the dressing-table set and—"

He cut me off. "Take whatever you like, as long as it stays out of my sight." He shooed invisible flies from his face. "I never wish to see anything that once belonged to . . ." He could not say the name. Then he spied my mother's inlaid hookah. Picking it up, he muttered fiercely, "Except this."

I did not use the door between the dressing rooms, but went out into the corridor and began to carry books to my room. The dur-wan followed and helped me layer them under my bed, ten high, five deep. When that area was filled, I had rescued most of them. Mama's clothing already had been removed from the shelves. I grabbed an empty hat box and swept her silver dresser set into it, hurrying in case my father changed his mind. Yali came in and saw what I was doing. From the drawers I salvaged two ivory combs, a leather pocket toilet case, an ebony traveling set, her collection of atomizers, three beaded chatelaine purses, embroidered silk handker-chiefs, pompadour combs, silk and ivory fans, neck ruffs, spools of fancy ribbon, hairpins, a box of buttons, two pairs of evening gloves. All were treasures to me.

While I was busy, I noticed Yali removing several long flat jewelry boxes. "What are you doing?"

"Taking these for safekeeping."

"Not to burn?"

"No, no. Never!"

I returned to my task. After stowing as much as I could, I went out on the upstairs veranda in time to see Mama's dressing-room furniture—her daybed, her wooden bookcases with the glass windows, her tufted parlor chair, even her dressing table with its dainty French legs, draw-ers with brass handles, and oval mirror that tilted—being added to the pyre. This last, unruly item caused the tower to shift. The dressing table slipped to the ground, shattering the glass. The mali replaced it at a lower level, then with the coarse broom he used on the paths swept the shards under the firewood.

The servants milled around, waiting. The durwan watched the house expectantly. I sank to the floor of the porch so they would not see me as I peered through the railing. Father's bearer arrived and said a few words to the mali. He nodded and poured an oily substance made from clarified butter, called *ghee*, over everything. The servants looked up at the house again, waiting. At a signal, the mali lit the mound of Mama's earthly possessions. An enormous flame arched skyward. Soon the dusking sky was riddled with billowing smoke.

A moment later the durwan rushed forward and threw an object into the inferno. Its distinctive curve caught my attention. The hookah! I fixed my eyes on the sparks as they flew upward around the glowing torso-shaped metal. If only the monsoon rains would come and drench everything! But that could not happen, not in December. Sparks fly upward; rains fall downward. The contrasting images—and the finality of each—preoccupied me as I watched.

"What shall we do, Dinah?"

I jumped up from my hiding position. The whole while, Papa had been nearby on the other side of the veranda. He must have been the one who signaled for the conflagration to commence. I turned away from him.

"Dinah!" He opened his arms to me.

There was a loud whooshing sound. A long tongue of fire shot up to the sky, crackled like lightning, and was followed by a crunch and a tumble as some of the furniture shifted as it was engulfed. For a few seconds the hot light formed an outline around the delicate curved legs of Mama's dressing table. Some combination of smoke and firelight gave the spectral illusion of a human form staring into the broken glass. My stomach contracted as the vision was sucked away by a burst of wind. The fire, devouring its delicacies, burned on hotter, redder, almost bloody.

Hearing my father muttering, I thought at first he was saying "Dinah" —but no, it was "Luna . . . Luna . . ."

Unanswered questions flickered like sparks in the firelight, glowing momentarily, then turning to crumbling ash. Why had Papa left us alone for so long, causing Mama to invite the wrong sort of friend into our house? Why had the men who had murdered her been set free? Why was Mama now being blamed for everything? Why had Papa stopped loving her because she was gone, and why had he punished me by sending my grandparents away?

Feeling his hand on my shoulder, I pushed him away and backed into a cobweb in the corner. As I madly brushed the sticky fibers from my arms, my bitterness burned white as the coals forming on the firebed. He leaned against the rail, his chin sagging, his mouth agape. The spots on his face had enlarged into blistering blotches. His upper lip twitched. "What shall become of us?" he asked, his voice trembling.

Ever since the murder, I had held the elusive hope that when my father came home, he would somehow stitch the seams of our life back together and make our family whole again. This husk of a man was not about to perform any such miracle.

"Now who shall take care of us?" he asked, looking up to the acrid cloud that hovered over our garden.

I thought: From now on I shall have to take care of myself. Then I turned from the silhouette almost obliterated by smoke and abandoned him.

❦ ❦ ❦

The next day, I remained in my room. Papa did not interfere, for which I was both grateful and resentful. The day after that, I ventured as far as the nursery sitting room to play with my brothers, but I would not go downstairs for meals, even when told I was invited to dine with my father. On the third day, he came to my room. When I did not respond to his knock, he let himself in.

"Dinah, will you come for a walk with me?"

I kept reading the first of Mama's books that seemed meant for a child—*Alice in Wonderland.*

"Is that a good book?" He came closer and looked over my shoulder at the illustration. "What a funny rabbit!" he said in a forced voice. "Dinah!" He stroked the top of my head. I shot up and away from him. Holding the book in front of me like a shield, I backed against the far wall. He rubbed the bump on the side of his nose and waited. I felt powerful, as if invisible claws extended from me into his heart. His chest convulsed, and he left. Good! I thought, vowing never to talk to him again. Why, then, did I feel more bereft than victorious?

He did not approach me for the rest of the week, not even to take me to the synagogue on Saturday morning. The following Monday, renovations began on the upper story of the house. The veranda was to be extended, his dressing-room partitions taken down to make a new bedroom for himself, and a larger room carved for me from my mother's old bedroom. The corner room was shuttered, bolted, locked.

I found the bustling activity a diversion in my self-imposed exile. Workmen scurried around, not caring if I crouched to watch.

Papa came into the nursery and announced, "I have decided that Selima and the boys should stay at Aunt Bellore's until the work is completed."

"Am I going too?" I had spoken against my will. He had tricked me!

"No." His jaw clenched, frightening me.

Was this a punishment for my muteness? I must have looked as crestfallen as I felt.

"You don't wish to stay here with me?"

"I would like to go with Jonah and Asher."

"That will not be possible."

"Couldn't I go to my grandparents' house for a visit?"

He crossed the room and sat on my bed. "No, Dinah. You mustn't bother them."

"They *want* me." I stared at him accusingly—an expression I had perfected. Unexpectedly his face softened. This was more like the kind father of my memories, the father whose lips seemed to smile in repose.

"I have a better plan." He waited a few beats. "I need to do some traveling. Would you like to come with me upriver to Patna?"

"No, thank you," I said politely to ward off the scary face.

"Why ever not?"

How could I trust this man who had been absent so much of my life? The moment he had returned, everything had gone wrong at the trial, with my grandparents, and then the final insult, the destruction of my mother's possessions. What might he do if I displeased him someday?

He gave me a fair chance to respond, then looked at me with a sleepy half-lidded expression. "Perhaps you will change your mind."

I forced my lips to remain immobile.

"All right, Dinah, I will leave now, but if you decide you might like to come with me—"

"I won't change my mind!"

"If that is so, you will be the first woman on earth to be so steadfast." His head tipped back, then flung forward like a rag doll's, and the noise was meant as a laugh, but it sounded more like a wooden wheel arguing with the road.

The next week dragged by unmercifully, until a Sabbath visit with my grandparents. My grandfather did not leave his bed and his power of speech was diminished to a few grunts. My grandmother, on the other hand, was attentive to me. When I told her about my father's offer, I expected she would side with me.

Instead she said, "You must do as he says. He means well."

"I don't want to go."

Nani was thoughtful. Then she spoke with deliberate pauses. "Benu has always tried to do . . . what is . . . correct. He is . . . confused, as you are . . . and your grandfather and I are." Pain lashed her brow. She must have known that he had burned her daughter's possessions and had been attempting to wipe away his association with her family. She must have known how the Raymonds were perceived by the Sassoons and the rest of the Jewish community. Even so, she struggled to leave me with healing words. "Try to be . . . kind to him."

I was furious. "But, Nani—"

She cut me off. "He is your father and he . . . cares for you."

Before I left, she gave me a few lessons, but these I completed in less than a week, and soon was left with time on my hands. There was little to do, no babies to amuse. The workmen's progress was of interest for but a few moments a day. Otherwise I stayed at the far end of the house attempting to read my mother's books. Laboriously I copied from the first chapter of *Lorna Doone*:

Here by the time I was twelve years old, I had risen into the upper school, and could make bold with Eutropius and Caesar—by aid of an English version—and as much as six lines of Ovid. Some even said that I might before manhood, rise almost to the third form, being of a persevering nature; albeit, by full consent of all (except my mother), thick-headed.

As I replaced my pen, wondering what it might be like to attend a real school, my father walked into the room and studied my penmanship from behind my chair.

"Why are you doing this?"

I did not look up. "I am going to school."

"Who gave you this to write?"

"My teacher."

"Your Nani?"

"No, my teacher."

Despite his attempt to speak genially, his tone became exasperated. "I do not recall hiring a teacher."

"I teach myself." I tried to concentrate on the next line: "But that would have been, as I now perceive, an ambition beyond—"

He lifted the pen from my grasp. "When we return, I will find you a proper school. Would you like that?"

I still had not looked at him. "After we return?"

"From our journey on the Ganga."

My head spun around. His lips were pressed tightly; his eyes were clear, purposeful. Where would an argument get me? Besides, I was more than ready to be released from the boredom of the house.

"May I bring some books?"

"A few."

"And my paints?"

"If you wish. Now, go upstairs to Yali. She is preparing your clothing. After you tell her what else to pack, we are going to your grandparents' for a final visit." He grimaced as he saw the effect of his news. Large droplets skimmed my round cheeks, bounced off my chin, and puddled on my blouse.

"Dinah, please . . ." He scrambled for his handkerchief and tried to dab at the flow, not daring to hold me.

The crying brought relief. Suddenly my hostility toward him dissolved even though my bitterness did not disappear. It was as if it had been distilled into a fine elixir which I had bottled, corked, and left to be retasted at a later date.

My father's voice was muffled, but I think he said, "What have we done to you?"

5

✴ ✴ ✴

The day after my seventh birthday, a new phase of my life began. As my father and I wheeled toward the wharf south of the Howrah Bridge, we left the confines of my little world behind and I saw—as if for the first time—the city of Calcutta. At that time it was the second-largest city in the British Empire— "What Calcutta thinks today, the rest of the world thinks tomorrow" was its prideful boast—and in those days, before the capital moved to New Delhi, it was the most European of Indian cities. I was to discover far more than this, though. I was on my way to the vast countryside that is the true heart of India.

A pang stabbed my chest as we passed the immense park called the Maidan—which means a flat, open space. I recalled Mama taking me to hear a band playing in the Eden Gardens section. She had danced me around in a circle, her body moving so sinuously that not only was I enthralled, but two British officers stood by utterly captivated. I saw them before she did, reached for her hand, and tried to follow her steps. She laughed at my clumsiness and turned around. The taller man caught her eye. She did not speak to him, but the intensity of their eye contact frightened me.

"Mama, don't," I begged.

She turned back to the man, smiling conspiratorially at him. "Must do as she says." Reluctantly she allowed me to pull her away from the imaginary harm.

I glanced at my father, who was smiling blithely next to me as we turned in the direction of Clive Street so that he could pick up some documents at his office. Soon we headed toward the waterfront.

At the wharf the British India Steam Navigation Company's steamer *Lord Bentinck* was waiting for us with a crew of beturbaned sailors standing by smartly. The craft was built like a wedding cake, with five decks, each smaller than the last, until the most diminutive, framed by intricate Indian latticework, crowned the top. Along the sides were two large paddle wheels painted yellow. My father had arranged for three cabins, one for himself, one for Yali and me, and a private sitting room where we could also take our meals.

"Where will your bearer stay?" I asked after seeing the accommodations.

"Abdul will sleep on deck outside your door."

This made sense to me, since a male servant had protected me every night since the murder.

With a child's eagerness, I surveyed the harbor scene. There were barges as broad as they were long, with bamboo cottages mounted on top. Flat boats with cargoes mounded high with hay drifted by. Slim craft with pointed prows leaned precariously in the direction the wind directed their colored lateens to fly. A file of boats kept to the center of the river, including Chinese junks with high curved poop decks and a huge triangular rudder thrust into the muddy current. Ships even larger than ours were berthed three and four deep along the shore, including many full-rigged, four-masted barks.

My father stood at the railing outside our cabin in quiet contemplation. Then he spoke in a voice of renewed confidence, perhaps because the matter was in the dispassionate realm of facts. "There are three Calcuttas," he began. "The first is the winter capital of India, the second is the metropolis of the largest white population in Asia, and the third is the tightest-packed sardine tin outside of China."

"Why do so many English people live here?"

"The city was founded by an Englishman when this"—his hand gestured to include the bustling panorama before us—"was but a stinking marsh."

"When was that?"

"Almost two hundred years ago."

"Who was he? Mr. Calcutta?"

My father roared. "His name was Job Charnock."

"What does 'Calcutta' mean?" I asked cautiously, in case my father was tiring of questions.

"You know who the Indian goddess Kali is, don't you?"

I nodded. Yali had told me many Hindu myths, and no child could but be intrigued with Kali, the wife of Shiva. She appeared in her beneficent form as Parvati or in her terrifying form as Kali, the black one. I had often shivered at descriptions of her brandishing weapons, her long menacing tongue, her necklace of human skulls.

"And you know what a *ghat* is, don't you?"

"The steps along a riverbank."

"So 'Kali-ghat'—or the stairway for the goddess Kali—is what this village on the Hooghly was called."

"Oh!" The simplicity of the explanation delighted me. "Why ever did Mr. Charnock come here?"

"Well, Charnock came out as an agent of the East Indian Company. He found the site to be excellent because it was near the sea and on a mighty river that could handle large ships."

"Like that one?" I pointed at the *Somali* from Liverpool.

"Yes, exactly."

"It's the biggest in the harbor, isn't it?"

"Not only this harbor, it is the greatest British sailing ship." He pointed in the opposite direction. "Over there is the broadest-beamed boat in the world. Twice she tore her own masts out because of the weight of her cargo." As he went on telling me what he knew about the visiting craft, I became transfixed by their enormous gossamer webs of spars and tackles.

"See those coolies?"

I followed his nod to a procession of glistening laborers carrying coal baskets on their heads up the gangway of a freighter. "In India men are cheaper than using a mechanical lift."

"Not in other places?"

"No, Dinah, at least not in England."

"That must be why the boats come here," I said, surprising my father. He started to touch me in praise, but fearing my recoil, caught himself and slipped his hand in his pocket.

"Where are the ships going?"

"I believe that one is being readied for Sumatra, the one across the way for Mombasa."

"Sumatra . . . Mombasa . . ." As I began to wonder about the places I never knew existed, a whistle blew. Sailors clad only in *dhotis*—loincloths draped to form trousers—scurried along the wharf and up onto the decks to untie, throw, and coil ropes. There was much shouting and complaining. The ship groaned as it slipped away from its bollards. Then there was a bump and a crash as it unexpectedly slammed back against the wharf. Two sailors ran across the decks screaming curses at the deckhands below, who kicked their legs overboard and held the ship off so it would not bounce a second time, then swung themselves back on board as the gap widened beneath them. I clapped my hands at the successful acrobatics, not noticing that my father's arms had surrounded me.

⚜ ⚜ ⚜

Anticipation of the unknown muted the pain of departure.

"It is always easier to leave than to be left," Papa said, expressing the thought for me.

"Is that why you go away so often?" I asked, but received no reply. At least his pink lips did not blanch in disapproval.

We were headed north along the Hooghly River, one of the dozens of branches of the most sacred of Indian rivers: the Ganga, or, as the English called it, the Ganges. On the outskirts of Calcutta many riparian settlements were clustered along the banks, but soon the villages came at wider intervals, and their inhabitants seemed more lethargic the farther upstream we chugged. Bathing and laundry ghats lined the river's edge. Temples with spires that looked like obelisks enchanted me. We glided past an industrial area that processed jute, then dignified houses in faded blues, pinks, grays, and yellows. At Chandernagore I waved to children running in front of a pink church with green shutters. At Chinsura we passed an octagonal Dutch church surrounded by sleeping sacred cows.

Abdul and Yali served our luncheon in our sitting room; then I was expected to nap, if only to give my father a respite from my incessant questions. When I joined him on the deck in time to witness the sunset, he greeted me with enthusiasm.

"You have brought pens and papers with you, haven't you, Dinah?" he asked, with what I took to be a hint of harshness in his voice.

"Oh, shouldn't I have?"

"Yes, yes." He seemed distracted. "Since you seem to like schooling so much, I thought we could make this trip more educational."

"I do like to study . . ." I ventured warily.

"Good. Then tomorrow you shall begin a list. You shall try to discover the one hundred and eight names for the river we will soon join up with."

"The Ganges . . . the Ganga."

"Right, those are two." He waited. I loved the way his mouth turned up at the edges, almost in a smile, when he was not preoccupied with his own thoughts.

"Are there truly a hundred and eight?"

"Yes."

"How shall I ever find them out?"

"Ask. Ask everyone you meet."

"Do you know them?"

"Not all, but a few."

"Tell me another."

"*Sindu-gamini*, or flowing into the ocean."

"*Sindu-gamini*." I rolled the words on my tongue. "That's lovely. And another?"

"*Sighra-ga*, swift-flowing."

"Another!"

"If I tell you all of them, you will not have to find them for yourself."

"One more," I begged.

"All right. *Bhiti-hrt*." He did not translate.

"What does it mean?"

He started to speak, but his voice cracked. The sun slipped behind a shining black herd of water buffalo on the western shore. Once again he tried. "It means . . ." I followed his eyes to the current that turned milky under the churning paddle wheel. "The Hindus say it means carrying away fear."

On a lower deck a plump musician in a shabby turban was strumming a tinny Bengali melody on a sitar—an Indian instrument with a bulbous body and spidery strings. The stars began to dot the purple canopy of sky. We stayed at the rail long after most of the other passengers had taken shelter inside, waiting, waiting, for the river to stand by its name.

❦ ❦ ❦

Accompanying us along the route were Englishmen and -women who had embarked at the capital to head up to their posts, to join family members, to visit friends. Native Indians also sailed with us, but on different decks. We were not supposed to mingle. In order to have the run of the ship, I told everyone I needed to accumulate more names of the Ganges for my list.

"*Puta*, pure," offered the pilot of the steamer.

"*Siddha*, holy," stated a Brahmin pilgrim who embarked in Monghyr.

"*Punya*, auspicious," suggested a merchant from Ghoga.

The hours on the river flowed with a rhythm quite unlike any I had known on land. There were no set times for arrivals or departures from the riverbank ports. Tides and winds, the ritual bathing of the Hindu passengers and crew, the fancy of the captain, the exigency of a notable on board—any of these events could alter the plan—so it was wisest to have no expectations, to take each hour as it came.

Over the next ten days my list of names grew to include *Nandini*, for happiness, *Satya-sandha-priya*, meaning dear to the faithful, and *Ananta*, or eternal, and then we arrived at our destination.

Patna—at least along the ghat—seemed somnolent compared with Calcutta, even though for centuries it had been one of the chief cities of an Indian empire. Sprawling along the southern bank of the Ganges, it was the loading point for the profitable plantation crops grown in the alluvial soil of the Ganges Plain.

My father sent Yali and his bearer to prepare the rooms the Sassoons kept in a large house off the maidan while he took me to visit the sights. To my surprise, I was lifted upon an elephant. My father scrambled up clumsily beside me in the *howdah*. We poked along through crowds of natives to a ninety-foot-tall beehive of a building.

"What temple is this?" I wondered.

"The *gola*—the storehouse that was built after a famine a hundred years ago. Mr. Hastings, who became the governor-general before

India had viceroys, decided that if during the good years they stored the harvest in large granaries, there would be a surplus for the bad years, so he hired a man named Captain Garstin to build one."

I peered inside an open door. "Why is it empty?"

"It has never been used."

"Why not?"

"Can you figure it out?"

I strolled around the structure, musing at this monstrous brick egg. "How does it get filled?"

My father pointed up. "Through that hole at the top."

I scampered up one of the two sets of staircases that spiraled to the peak. In the distance the river looked like a ribbon wrapping the banks of the city in a bow-shaped curve. I ran down to my father. "I know! Nobody wanted to make the effort to climb all that distance carrying sacks of grain."

"That is partially correct."

I tiptoed inside. The muskiness tickled my nose and I began to sneeze. A millisecond after I stopped, the sound came back to me in a crashing echo. I clapped my hands: this was better still. Papa had entered the door on the opposite side and whispered, "Dinah, can you hear me?"

I started. "Papa!" I shouted, hearing several reverberations before he spoke again.

"Quietly, in your lowest voice."

"Like this?"

"Yes. Have you figured out the rest of the secret?"

"The echoes frightened them."

His laugh rang out like bells of a cathedral.

I looked up and tried to imagine the grain raining down among the shafts of light and filling the upside-down cone. Then I walked out, blinked from the harsh light, and tripped over a mound of earth. I leaned against the door to regain my balance. "The doors!" I shouted. "They open to the inside. If the gola was even partway filled, the bottom would be so packed, the doors could not open. How could anyone make such a gigantic mistake?"

"Everybody makes mistakes. Many vast plans have gone awry during their execution, especially if ignorant men blindly follow their leaders."

"Why didn't anyone question the plan?"

"I do not know, Dinah. There is something to remember here. Obedience to duty has value, but mindless heeding may be foolhardy. Besides, even if some of the laborers doubted the captain, he probably would not have listened. The British rarely believe anything an Indian tells them."

I wondered if he also was remembering the judge who warned the jury not to trust the words of our servants.

Atop the elephant, I laid my head in Papa's lap. He stroked my hair, murmuring, "How very clever you are."

The next morning, I awoke much earlier than usual, due in part to the strangeness of the bed, which did not sway like the one on the ship. Because there was no chamber pot in my room, I went to look for the washing area I had sleepily used the night before. I opened the door where I thought it was, but discovered my father's room. A head lifted from the pillow. I saw only a long braid and large almond eyes before I ran back to my room.

In a few minutes I heard the slap of bare feet on the wooden floors and a door closing smoothly. Only then did I dare get up and try again to find the pot. After I had used it, I saw that my father's door was open. There was no evidence of a visitor. Standing in my nightgown, I shivered in the cool river breeze. I climbed on his bed as unobtrusively as possible.

"Did you have a bad dream?" my father asked when he found me in his bed.

"Sort of."

He did not seem angry. His face was softer, more filled out, and he smiled more warmly than he had in Calcutta. "Let's get up, then," he said with more manly vigor than I had heard in a long time.

After drinking a third cup of tea, he opened the window and breathed deeply. A strong wind blew his hair in front of his eyes. He pushed it back, grinned, and took the napkin he held in his hand and waved it in the breeze.

"Good, the wind is from the northwest. This dry weather is perfect."

"For what, Papa?"

"Ah, that you will see, my child, for this is why we have come to Patna."

❧　❧　❧

Standing before the rickshaw, my father made certain I wore my *topee* to protect my head from the sun. He himself wore a cork helmet that snapped under the chin. Abdul handed up a leather box tied firmly with straps, and Yali slipped me a package containing fruit and cakes. We proceeded along a narrow but firmly packed path running perpendicular to the river. Soon we stopped amid a collection of mud huts clustered under tall shade trees, each with an untidy garden. Beyond them stretched miles of verdant fields that from a distance seemed to have been sprinkled with streaks of icing sugar. As we came closer I peered more intently, and I could see the whiteness was the petals of millions of gorgeous flowers undulating in the breeze.

"What are they?" I asked as Papa helped me down. I ran to the head of a blooming row and breathed in the lavish fragrance.

"Poppies."

"Poppies!" My hand brushed a cluster of fringed blossoms that were so ripe the petals flew off like frightened moths. They fluttered a long while in the air currents before settling on the reddish earth. Dazzled by the effect, I moved a few feet down the row and tried again. "Oh!" I cried in delight, running down the slender path between the rows, my fingertips jostling the feathery petals lightly, but having the effect of a scythe. "Poppies! Poppies! Poppies!" I shouted to the wind. A shower of white billowed up around me as I made my way back up a second row.

Breathless, I met up with my father again. I shook the petals from my hair and grinned. "Why have we come to see them?"

"Because these flowers are my business, the Sassoon family trade."

"You own these fields?"

"Not exactly. The government owns them, but we will buy most of the crop when it comes to auction in Calcutta later in the year."

"So you sell flowers?"

"Yes, Dinah."

"I don't see how you can get them to China before they die."

He threw his head back and laughed so hard he had to wipe his tearing eyes. "Today you will learn everything there is to know about poppies." He plucked a flower. "This is *Papaver somniferum*," he said in a reverential tone, "the most prized flower in the world. Not only is it beautiful, it contains a secret substance that eliminates pain, cures diseases, and makes men happy."

"Everyone must want it, then."

"Yes, and they will pay dearly for it." He twisted the stem, almost the thickness of my little finger, back and forth. The translucent petals vibrated prettily. "Our little secret is that it is quite easy to grow and process. We purchase it for a handful of rupees and sell it for baskets of silver."

My mother had told me tales of weaving straw into gold, explaining these were mere stories, but the idea of converting a plant to a valuable mineral was true! My father plucked the petals and held up the naked, unripened seed capsule. Its pale green flesh, the color of a baby frog, glistened with dew.

"Watch this." He took a knife from his pocket and made three vertical slashes in the fat bulb. "This is called 'lancing.' " A sticky milk, like white blood, began to ooze out. *"Lachryma papaveris."* He studied the droplets as though they were precious works of art. "The tears of the poppy. Every spring, when the petals begin to drop, the villagers cut the bulbs in the afternoon, leaving the sap to drip slowly out during the night. The next morning the congealed blackish fluid is scraped off before the heat makes it stick too tightly. This they do about ten times, until the head is exhausted and bleaches out. Later you will see what becomes of the residue."

Intrigued, I followed my father on his rounds. We passed through miles of fields. Large flocks of birds wheeled like hovering clouds overhead. "They are after the wheat or maize, which is alternated with the poppies," my father explained. He pointed out a distant platform raised upon poles to a height of twenty feet over the fields. When we came closer, I could see a small boy stationed there. After several birds began diving at the grain, the boy lifted a simple sling and selected a stone from a basket. With a graceful arch of his back, an unerring stone met its mark.

"Oh, no," I cried in sympathy at the plummeting bird.

"It must be done as a warning to the rest of the flock. Look." I followed Papa's gaze as the dark cloud looped up and back, away from the boy on the platform.

"Who cares for these fields?" I asked as we walked out to inspect an area.

"*Ryots*, or cultivators, lease them from the crown. The ryot plows his field, removes the weeds and grass before dividing it into beds with those higher dykes between them." He showed me a tank about ten feet deep, dug at one end of the field and pulled out a leather bucket attached to a rope. "Water is taken from here and used to irrigate the fields, which is necessary because most of the poppy cultivation is done after the monsoon. The seed is sown in November, the juice collected in February and March. Come, I will show you how that actually is accomplished."

At the far end of the field, dozens of women were scarifying the seed pods that had already been scraped that morning. A lady in a billowing pink sari greeted my father respectfully, her hands cupped in a triangle, her head bowed. My father showed me the instrument she carried. It had four two-pointed blades bound together with cotton thread. "This is called a *nutshur*. Only one set of points is used at one time as the capsule is cut vertically from base to summit."

He returned the tool to its worker and pointed to a collector who was working on another row. With swift, decisive movements the man used an iron scoop to collect the brown sap that had oozed out during the night, and as it became filled, he emptied it into an earthen pot strapped on his side. From time to time he wet the scoop and his fingers with linseed oil carried in a small jar tucked into his dhoti. "On dry days like today, he needs the oil to prevent the adhesion of the sticky juice. On moist days, his work is easier, but a portion of the sap is washed away, or worse, it becomes watery. That results in a lower grade, called *passewa*, for which we get less money."

"Can't you dry it to get the water out?" I wondered.

Papa beamed. "How your questions please me! You must have flowers in your blood. Come see what happens next."

The rickshaw-wallah spit out his betel juice and readied to take us. My father offered me water from a jug and gave me a slice of melon as we headed back toward the town by another route. On the outskirts of Patna we came across an enormous mass of brick buildings with red tiled roofs. A wonderful fresh-mown smell permeated the exterior, where men wielding wooden paddles stirred shallow trays of the tarry exudate.

"Here the gum dries in the sun for one to three weeks to remove the water content."

"So the drier the sap, the shorter the time it must cook in the sun," I said matter-of-factly.

"I shall have to put you to work," he said, grinning. He pointed to men bending over a table in the shade of a shed. They seemed to be kneading sticky rolls of black bread. "When dried, the opium is formed into three loaves."

Opium. This was the first time I had heard that word connected with the day's activities. Where had I heard it before? Mother . . . the trial. I recalled my mother's silver-and-ivory hookah that had been thrown on the pyre of her possessions. An image formed: my mother's languorous body stretched out on the chaise, her dimpled mouth sipping the fragrant smoke from the ivory mouthpiece. The smell of opium mingling with roses, clove incense, and her own particular musk could be recalled more readily than the elusive image of her oval face or shimmering eyes. The memory of Mama and the hookah mingled with the green of the scored poppy husk and ripe black sludge in the processing trays.

"Mama drank opium," I stated somewhat inaccurately, because I had confused the sipping sounds from the mouthpiece that led to the tubes with the inhalation of smoke.

My father stared at me with such cold fury, I knew I was right.

"Unfortunately, it caused her to be ill."

"Why? You said it cured disease and made people happy. Didn't you want Mama to be happy?"

"When you are older you will learn that it is possible to take too much of a good thing" was his perplexing response.

"Like eating too many jelebis."

"In a way."

"Or having too many friends."

"I don't understand . . ."

"If you have too many, you might not know which are good friends and which are bad," I dared, since I was still trying to sort out questions about Nissim Sadka.

"Some people are more easily fooled than others," he replied elliptically.

"I won't be fooled. I never liked any of them!"

"I'm sure you won't." My father's frown should have warned me off, but I only went back to the first topic.

"Why didn't you tell her to stop when she took too much opium?"

"That's enough, Dinah."

"But she would have listened to you."

"She didn't." He turned his back to indicate the subject was closed.

Since my mother always seemed to defer to my father, I found this difficult to comprehend, but said nothing more as we passed behind the guards who observed the workers, many of whom were young children. A man wearing a gun weighed out a quantity of the black mass and handed it to a man who carried a numbered ticket. Next down the line, a woman sat on a high stool in front of two basins. The first basin contained sufficient opium for three balls. The lower one held water. She lifted a brass hemispherical cup, into which she worked the ball, moistening it as she rolled it into a neat six-inch sphere. Then it was passed to a child who had a tray with two compartments, one containing thin pancakes of pressed poppy petals, the other a cupful of sticky opium-water. After rolling the ball in the water, the boy crunched it with the petals and a mixture of coarsely powdered poppy stalks, capsules, and leaves. The last man weighed the ball, adding to or decreasing the mass to make a consistent product. A young runner then carried the finished balls outside and placed them on pallets in the sun.

Our tour finished inside the godown, a cool, dark storehouse where the dried cakes were lined in frames. "They will remain here through the summer. The boys will watch to be certain they are not attacked by weevils, turning them to prevent mildew. By next October they will be completely dry, hard, and in condition to be packed into cases of forty cakes each. The cases will be auctioned in Calcutta, where the Sassoons will buy them for delivery to the Chinese market."

My heart pounded fiercely. "Are you going back to China?"

"Of course—" My stricken face alarmed him, and he put his arm around my quaking shoulders. "That's a long time off, after the auction in October. Let's not think of it now."

An Indian manager—a *gomastah*—dressed primly in a suit with a vest approached my father and handed him a sheaf of accounting papers. Papa loosened his grip on me and eased himself away. The two men walked off to a corner of the godown and conferred about the figures.

A tide of emotions swept over me. What would I do without a mother or a father? My stomach contracted. The air in the musty godown clogged my throat. I made my way to the nearest door—

opposite the one we had entered—feeling frightened and sorry for myself.

A muffled, almost animallike howl startled me.

I looked up to see, across the yard, a boy being beaten with one of the wooden paddles used to stir the raw opium. One worker held him down and tried to silence him while another struck his shoulders, his buttocks, and the back of his legs so forcefully I could hear the crack of the wood against his frail bones. Another boy heaved and sputtered as buckets of water were poured over him as he stood in a deep vat.

I ran for my father.

"Papa!" As I grabbed his arm, several documents fell to the mucky ground. Not caring, I urgently pulled him toward the yard.

"Dinah! What is—?"

"Come. A boy is hurt—"

"Hurt? An accident?" he asked as he let me lead him.

By the time we got there, the first boy was slumped against the wall. Huge welts were splayed on his back and chest. The thin skin around his ribs had burst. Blood trickled in rivulets, pooling at his waist. The other boy, still standing in the tub, was being brushed with harsh twig brooms. Everyone froze as my father looked at the injured children, then back at me. The brutality ceased. Now my father would punish the cruel bosses.

"That is enough" was all he said as he led me away. "It's not what you think, Dinah. Those boys are thieves. The workers are recovering what was stolen and making certain the culprits have learned their lesson."

Tears welled in my eyes. "But how—?"

"Listen to me, Dinah, those boys rolled around in the poppy residue, coating their bodies with opium. If a boy can escape unnoticed to the bazaar, bad men will wash him down to distill and collect the residue, paying him four or five annas. You would not object to someone being beaten for stealing my purse, would you? Well, that powder is almost as valuable as gold. Why, one godown alone contains more than ten lacs of opium. If we let one boy off lightly, the others will take the risk. By beating one, we prevent a hundred more crimes."

I trembled with exhaustion as much as confusion as my father carried me to the home of the gomastah, where we were given a simple meal of rice and fish. I slept the whole way back to our lodgings, awaking only when Yali prepared me for bed. I let her tuck me in, pretending to sleep until she snored rhythmically beside me on the floor. Then I got up and opened the door to my father's bedroom. He slept alone. I climbed in beside him and fell asleep. After that I spent every night with him until we made our way back to Calcutta and everything changed again.

6

❦ ❦ ❦

For several weeks my father and I made similar forays to inspect the opium operations as far west as Benares, as far east as Monghyr. This was the first time I felt my father entirely sympathetic to me and I made every effort to meet his expectations by being a good companion, which meant watching his signals for when he wanted to chat and when he wanted me to be silent. Almost every Sabbath we lit candles with others who shared our faith. Instead of living in Calcutta where there were two synagogues and about a thousand Jews, these enterprising souls were often the only Jews in their communities. Abraham Cohen in Bhagalpur, Samuel Duek in Dinapur, Hilali Moses in Ghazipur, and Yoram Moses in Gorakhpur each talked with my father about daughters or nieces who would soon require husbands.

The granddaughter of one of the Moses brothers was so attentive to his every whim, I asked my father, "Do you like her?"

"She is a fine young lady."

"Will you marry her?"

"No, Dinah. It is too soon for me to consider taking another wife."

"But you will . . . someday," I said, hoping this would not irritate him.

"Possibly, but it will not be the Moses girl, don't worry. Besides, you are such good company."

He could not have said anything that would have pleased me more.

The cyclical processes of the opium business began to lose their fascination, and as the Gangetic plain began to absorb the penetrating blasts from the sun, the days at my father's side wilted me to the point I moved sluggishly, my strength and curiosity drained like a much-scored poppy. I began to dream of my high, cool bedroom on Theatre Road, where the servants prepared fresh *tatties*, reed mats soaked with water and placed at the windows to cool air currents as they entered the room, and where there were new books to read. I missed my grandparents—even Aunt Bellore and the other Sassoons.

Sometimes we traveled overland on Grand Trunk Road, down baked, parched roads. A few trips could be made by railway, which, when it speeded along, were tolerable. I remember one car filled with pale, panting English soldiers in shirtsleeves who gave me sweets and seemed amused when I told them I was helping my father in "the opium business."

"Only one more place to visit and then we return home," Papa sighed. "Won't you like that?"

"Oh, yes! I cannot wait to see Jonah and Asher and—" I thought it wise not to mention my grandparents.

The day before Passover, we arrived in Monghyr, where we would stay the whole holiday week with the Josephs, a Jewish family who managed the Sassoon interests in the area. Monghyr was situated inside an old Moghul fort. Within the fort, a rocky spur projected into the river. My father and I climbed out on it to examine the temples. Across the river we could see carts drawn by bullocks with wide, curving horns and huge eyes, moving as though in a trance, and barefoot men with burdens on their heads, their dark limbs accentuated by their white garments. My father held my hand. I was content.

The morning of the first seder, my father asked if I wished to remain with the Josephs to help prepare for the evening meal.

"No, I prefer to be with you."

He seemed flattered by my loyalty. "Today we will ride in palanquins," he announced.

"What's a palanquin?" I asked.

"You must have seen the enclosed litters. They're mounted on poles carried by four bearers."

"Oh, those boxes with shutters. Why will we need them?"

"The track out to this refinery is too rocky and narrow for a carriage and too hot for the Josephs' horses," he explained.

I found I liked riding lying down. As we bumped along, I made a list of the ways we had traveled so far: by boat, by train, by elephant, by cart, by several types of carriages, by horseback, by foot, and now by palanquin. I thought about the seder table laden with the traditional foods and the familiar ritual, and I imagined returning to Calcutta with so many stories to tell. For that hour, at least, all was right with the world, I decided, and fell asleep.

This new gomastah—a tall Indian with squinty eyes—was not as cordial as most of the others had been. With a sullen expression he led us to the godowns. My father randomly selected four finished balls, took them outside, and laid them on planks in the sun. He poked, sniffed, weighed, and checked them scrupulously. From the distance I kept, I could see the manager fidgeting and wondered what might be happening, since my father had not behaved this way before. Using a pronglike tool, my father took a sample from four balls and prepared them in separate pots. Very slowly he measured water, mixed it with the opium, and set the combination over a small fire he had made on the earth.

The process took almost an hour, during which the opium samples were simmered, strained, and kept boiling until, by evaporation, each bowl was reduced to the thick consistency of syrup. The odor was reminiscent of something as soothing as the cleft of Yali's bosom. No, not Yali. Mama. I felt a wave of exhilaration, followed by a churning in my stomach. I backed away from the smoke and leaned against the scratchy plaster surface of a far wall while my father continued with his perplexing maneuvers.

From a satchel he lifted out a heavy tube with an elliptical earthenware cup at one end. He placed a pea-size sample into the bowl, bent over the flame, and drew a breath. His face turned red. He sputtered and coughed. After wiping his eyes, he cleaned the bowl and placed another hunk in it, repeating the process. This time he spat on the ground, wheeled around, and shouted, "Soo-er ka baccha," which meant something like "son of a pig." Anyway, his angry meaning was obvious. He took a long breath, then continued to chastise the manager in a gruff, slow voice. The gomastah quaked and apologized throughout his tongue-lashing. In order to increase the weight of the article—and consequently his profits—this processor had adulterated the juice of the poppy by mixing it with molasses. Later I learned that other swindlers used sugar, poppy seed, clayey mud, even cow dung for the same purpose.

At the end of his tirade my father swept the remains of the opium balls he had sampled onto the ground, then stamped them into the dust. "Men have been killed at Lintin Island for delivering excrement like this! I shall not risk my men or my name any further with you. Not only that, I will make a report, reminding every Calcutta merchant to avoid your chests this year—and the next as well."

Papa gathered up his gear and turned his back to the man, who continued to sputter excuses. As my father led me away abruptly, he muttered, "We are finished here. Might as well return to Monghyr and rest before the seder."

When we reached the end of the lane where we had left the palanquins resting in the shade of a banyan tree, he was vexed to discover one set of bearers had bolted. He threw up his hands and cursed the remaining palanquin-wallahs.

Not wishing to remain a moment longer than necessary, he placed me in the only sedan. "I shall walk alongside."

Traveling in the heat of the day, I soon dozed off, but awoke to the sound of conversation. Opening the curtains, I could see my father was now accompanied by five men who said they were making a pilgrimage to Hardwar, where hordes descended in April to celebrate the solar New Year with temple visits and river baths. One pilgrim said he hoped to see a depression in a stone that was supposed to be a footprint of Vishnu, the god of preservation.

"What is another name for the Ganges?" I called out.

"*Samsara-visa-nasini*, destroying the poison of illusion," the man nearest me responded.

Several others crowded around me, surprised to see a young white girl. "*Hansa-swarupini*, embodied in the forms of swans," a hefty pilgrim suggested in a funny, high voice. So pleased was I by this poetic addition that I repeated it twice.

Another man, whose face I could not quite glimpse because he was on my father's far side, called out, "*Ajnana-timira-bhanur*, a light amid the darkness of ignorance."

The man's hand lifted in a gesture I almost took for a blessing until, horrified, I realized he was about to strike my father. A flutter of my curtain blocked my view. My palanquin ceased moving; the bearers had frozen. "*Thugs!*" they shouted. For a second my body floated above my mattress as they flung away their poles. The hovering moment ended with a crash.

I must have been knocked senseless for a few minutes, for when I opened my eyes, my litter was jumbled with broken crockery and splintered wood. When I reached to free myself, a sharp pain in my elbow traveled down my arm. My forearm was no longer attached at the correct angle. The sight of it caused me to reel back until a trickle of water from a broken jug stirred me. I listened for any sound of the pilgrims or our bearers. There were only the squawks of crows, the shrill cries of mynahs.

Gasping with pain, I managed to sit myself up and push my feet outside. "Papa?" I looked over where I had seen him last. Only a dusty residue rose from the steaming road. In the distance I thought I saw a human figure, but it was just the wavy currents of heat. The bearers had dispersed. The pilgrims had vanished—and my father with them.

I crawled back into the wreckage of my sedan, propping the broken supports so they formed a rude shelter that would protect me from the blazing sun. An hour must have passed before the need to urinate overwhelmed me. My arm, if I held it perfectly still, throbbed, but did not shoot excruciating barbs down my left side. I thought I could get to the side of the roadway. The movement made the pain more severe, but I gritted my teeth and found I could tolerate it. Crouching in the high grass, I relieved myself, but as I stood up, a shooting pain caused me to lose my balance. I toppled to the left, slamming my arm into a clod of earth. The blow felt as if I had been impaled by a hot iron, and I screamed. A quiver shot up my spine as I waited to be saturated with pain again. The absence of the sharp sensations was even more unnerving. With a guarded movement I touched my elbow. As long as I held the arm to my chest at a particular angle, there was a deep soreness, but nothing like the searing torment I had felt before. I found a seat on a slight rise above the road and tried to figure out what I must do.

The bearers had cried, "Thugs!" What did it mean? Bewildered, feeling abandoned, I began to cry.

When I became thirsty I rooted around in the palanquin to see if any jugs had been spared. Remarkably, a small one had been cushioned enough so only the lip had cracked. A full cup of liquid remained, which I drank down at once. I debated pulling the litter to the embankment, but decided against it for two reasons: I would be harder to spot, and even more pressing in my mind was the thought that beasts lurking in the forest would prefer me under the trees than in the clear. Many times during the paddle-boat journey we had spied tigers along the riverbank, particularly in the twilight hours. They slipped between the trees, revealing a shock of tail, or glint of eye, or sinuous ripple of body, never the whole flank of cat. I recalled that tales of tiger shoots had been a favorite among the passengers, and I hoped they were lapping up the river waters and not foraging inland that night.

As I was trying to push thoughts of tigers out of my mind, a rustle in the bushes on the opposite side of the road froze me. A pair of enormous eyes glinted. "Missy-baba . . ." came the whisper. A terrifying moment passed before I realized that tigers did not speak. I focused on the short, muscular man who stood before me. He was one of the bearers who had bolted. He said he would take me back to the opium factory. I did not think the gomastah would be particularly pleased to see me again, so I pointed in the direction we had been going.

"Too far for *baba-log*, little people." He touched my sore arm, causing me to leap in pain.

"Ai!" I cringed.

He apologized, then scooped me into his arms, cradling me like a baby the whole way back to the refinery.

The bearer talked excitedly to the gomastah and his wife, boasting of how he had saved me from the thugs. The woman was wearing a pale violet sari that flattered her luminescent skin. Seeing me frightened and in pain, she caressed my hair and cooed to me as she would to an infant. When I was calm, she had me stand before her while she ran her fingers lightly down my dislocated arm. Delicately she pressed around the elbow joint, then walked her fingers down to my wrist and up to my shoulder. Then she went to the shelf over a charcoal stove and poured hot water out of a brass bowl. She filled this with an aromatic oil which she warmed over the coals. After dipping her hands in the glistening pool, she dabbed the back of my hand, my inner arm, my elbow. The pressure of her massage unexpectedly increased, but before I could back away in protest, her fingers worked in unison to crack and snap my joint. I felt as if I had been lifted from the floor by some unseen force, then lowered harshly. I blinked, gasped, and dared to glance at my injured arm. It looked normal! Tentatively I moved it to the right and left. I grinned at the kindly woman, who lowered me onto a mat and offered me a platter of steaming vegetables, puffed bread, and cups of sweet tea.

While I ate, the gomastah discussed what they should do. I understood enough of their language to realize they were anxious to be of service to me. With their tampered opium exposed, they faced ruin— not only for that season, but perhaps forever if they lost their license to process for the government. Here was a way to win my father's silence and gain back their good name.

Very quietly they questioned me about what had happened, the woman speaking to me, then relating my words to her husband, who remained at a distance so as not to frighten me further. They seemed agitated as I described the blow to my father's neck and shoulders and his swift disappearance. The gomastah called in the bearer to ascertain where the incident had occurred, then ran off to rally laborers for a search.

I sipped tea and watched the antics of a baby beginning to walk while the woman again massaged my sore arm with the warm, perfumed oil. I fell asleep on a *charpoy*—a rude cot—awakening to a familiar voice. Mr. Joseph had come for me.

"I became worried because I knew your father would not be late for the seder," he explained. He and his eldest son had ridden out by horseback and had become even more alarmed when they found my palanquin in the road.

"Papa is missing!" I sobbed.

"No, he is with my son David. The thugs left him only a mile from Monghyr."

"What is a thug?"

"They belong to the *thuggee* sect of religious criminals who are devotees of the goddess Kali. Posing as traders or pilgrims, they have been known to join wayfarers they intended to rob or—" He caught himself and did not explain that thugs almost always killed their victims, usually by strangulation with a knotted silk handkerchief.

"Is Papa all right?" I asked impatiently.

"He was hit with one blow and his satchel was robbed, but once he was free, he was able to walk toward town for help."

As the gomastah began babbling about the miracle of being spared by a thug, Mr. Joseph hushed him quickly, saying, "These men only wanted coins or valuables, and they got what they required."

After the gomastah's wife had bound my arm to my chest so it would not shake as we rode, one of her servants, a boy my size, brought over something swaddled in his arms. He unwrapped a cotton binding to reveal pointed ears and soft, trusting eyes. *"Shareef,"* he said, touching the animal's velvet black nose. "It's gentle." Holding it tightly, he lifted its arms to reveal a transparent membrane and grasping feet. It was a flying squirrel.

I dared to stroke its soft fur and was thrilled that it did not squirm away from me.

"For you," the boy said as he placed the bundle in my arms.

"Dhanyabad," I gasped in thanks. "I shall call him Shareef." I beamed up at Mr. Joseph, who seemed anxious to be on his way.

The gomastah's wife bent to me and whispered, "You please tell your honored father what we have done for you tonight so he will look upon us with kindness."

I nodded. She lifted me and my furry treasure into the saddle in front of Mr. Joseph. I waved farewell with my good arm.

When we arrived at the Joseph house, my father came out to greet me. His head was swathed in a bandage, his eyes bloodshot and blackened. "Dinah! Thank God you are safe!"

"The gomastah took care of me and his wife fixed my broken arm," I blurted in a burst of prompted loyalty. "And look what they gave me!" I held out Shareef for his approval.

"What is this?"

"A flying squirrel." I showed him the folded skin that stretched out to form its wings.

He shrank back.

"It is ever so quiet. Say I may keep it!"

My father's gaze met that of Mr. Joseph. The latter shrugged as if to say it would be impossible to deny me anything after what had happened. "I suppose so."

"I'll take good care of him, I promise."

As Yali took the animal from me, Papa folded me in his arms. "Come, now. You must wash up and get ready."

"For what, Papa?"

"It is Passover, remember?"

Even though it was late, the Josephs escorted us to the table, and the seder, the ancient celebration of deliverance from bondage, commenced.

In between the familiar courses there was hushed talk of what had happened.

"I bet they were surprised when they realized they had attacked a Sassoon," Mr. Joseph whispered.

"I think that was the point," my father replied. "They never meant to harm either of us. They were merely protecting the gomastah."

"How is that possible? There was not enough time to instigate a plan. You yourself said it happened less than an hour after you had words with the gomastah."

"The gomastah must have known the moment I selected out those four balls for testing that he was doomed. The boiling, refining, and smoking process took several hours. That gave him plenty of time."

The men nodded sagely at each other. The incident was part of the cost of their trade.

The lesson in panic, deceit, and retribution had been well-learned. I have never discovered—nor, so many years after, has it been possible to ferret out the answer—whether or not the gomastah's opium was boycotted that year or afterward. Somehow, though, I believe it was not.

7

By the time we entered Calcutta—this time by rail—I had accumulated only sixty-four names for the Ganges.

"I need forty-four more."

"Which is your favorite?"

"*Bhinna-brahmanda-darpini,* taking pride in the broken egg of Brahma."

"That is wonderful," Papa said, laughing.

"Now, how shall I get the rest?"

"Keep asking. Keep listening," was all he would say. He turned away, only slightly, but I remember feeling a chill come between us that I had not sensed since I had questioned him too closely about my mother.

Suddenly I did not want the trip to end. I moved closer to him on the seat and laid my head on his arm. Did I imagine him stiffen? Was this how it was going to be from now on?

Despite my sadness, the last minutes of our closest moments together drew to a close as, three months after the start of the journey, my father and I emerged into the chaos of Calcutta's Howrah Station. I was taller, browner, and in many other ways a changed child from the frightened, angry daughter who had walked up the *Lord Bentinck's* gangplank. The station's waiting rooms and platforms were smothered with humans engaged in every activity from sleeping to cooking to eating to wandering about in random patterns. Abdul organized a file of porters to carry cases of opium samples and our personal effects. The most precious souvenir, tiny Shareef, never left my side. The Josephs' sweeper had made him a home in a basket with a tight lid, which I insisted on carrying myself. Yali went ahead to locate a rickshaw for Papa and me. Once outside, I caught sight of Howrah Bridge, where a mass of men and merchandise in bullock-carts, buffalo-carts, gharries, rickshaws, and palanquins jolted over the humps where the pontoon sections were joined.

Soon my world would be narrowed to the houses in the Jewish districts bounded to the north by the old Jewish quarter around the synagogues—near my grandparents' house on Lower Chitpur Street—and the mansions of the Sassoons and the wealthier merchants who had established themselves along the opulent streets south of Park Street and east of Chowringhee Road. I didn't care. I was home.

The servants went to open Theatre Road while Papa and I were welcomed at Kyd Street.

"How dark you are," Aunt Bellore exclaimed. "Doesn't your father know about bonnets or topees?" She looked sternly at her brother. "How tall you've grown! You must be a head above Sultana already." She thumped Shareef's basket. "Let the bearer take that."

I grasped it tightly.

"What do you have in there?"

I looked at Papa with beseeching eyes.

"Leave her be. It is only a pet she received from a friend."

"*Bizzoonah!*" Aunt Bellore cried, using a superstitious oath. "It may carry the evil eye into this house."

"I did not know my sister adhered to the ways of the ignorant ones," he replied scornfully.

"I won't have a filthy animal in the house!"

"Bellore, please, after everything—"

"She cannot always have her way."

"Just this once," my father pleaded. "We'll be here only a few hours."

Bellore thrust her bosom forward and padded away angrily.

I ran off to the nursery, where I showed my brothers and cousins what was in my basket.

"Does he really fly?" asked Cousin Abigail.

"Not like a bird." I demonstrated by setting him on the top of the pole that held up her mosquito netting. Shareef glided halfway across the room and landed at my feet.

Jonah rushed behind him to see if he would fly up. "Don't scare him," I admonished. "He can't flap his wings, he just uses them like a sail." I picked up my pet and stroked him until the thumping in his breast diminished.

"Let me hold him," Cousin Sultana demanded. She plucked him from me and nestled him in her lap. "What does he eat?"

"Berries and nuts . . . insects too, but only if they are alive."

"Ugh!" Sultana and Lulu made faces. Abigail brought over a red grape and tried to shove it in his mouth. Shareef sniffed, but did not eat it. She kept pushing it until it burst and the flying squirrel began to lick it off her finger.

"He bit me!" she shrieked, causing her ayah to come running.

Seeing the finger dripping with the sticky grape juice, her ayah sent for Aunt Bellore.

"He will have to go," my aunt said when she saw Shareef quaking in his basket. "Your father has no sense allowing you to have an animal that carries diseases."

"He didn't bite Abigail." I looked pleadingly up at my father, who stood in the doorway surveying the scene.

In response, he came forward to examine Abigail's finger. "She's fine."

Aunt Bellore shook her head. "Benu, you should not indulge the girl."

Papa grinned conspiratorially at me and my fear for my new pet vanished.

It seemed his benevolence was extended the next day as well, when he permitted me to spend the afternoon at my grandparents' home. I was dismayed to see Nana had deteriorated. He barely spoke, and he hardly seemed to understand the tales I told him.

"Did you do your lessons?" Nani asked as we sat under the banyan tree in the small garden.

"Yes, Nani. I finished my books the first month."

"Now, what are we going to do to keep that mind of yours occupied?" she asked, passing me a dish filled with jelebis.

"Papa said I might go to a real school."

For a moment she looked doubtful. At that time there were no Jewish schools in Calcutta, although learned men in the community gave religious instruction to children, mostly boys. There were many British schools, but only a few Jewish families allowed their sons to attend these. "I'll see what I can find," she promised.

I can't recall spending more than a few minutes with my father in the subsequent days. He would rush off to his Clive Street offices or to visit friends, with no more than a brief farewell. Fortunately, the second week after my return, I was permitted to join the classes of Mrs. Hanover, a Christian missionary who had managed to attract more than a hundred students from the Jewish community by promising not to inculcate them with Christian beliefs. I found the lessons ridiculously simple, but enjoyed the companionship of the other children. Still, I was bereft that my father never returned home before I was put to bed. I was expected to take most meals with my brothers in the nursery and follow the same routine as before our journey together, but I resented having to eat with the babies. Even worse was having to sleep alone.

One evening, while my father was dressing for dinner, I sat in his chair, examining his collection of stiff collars. "Where are you going?" I asked petulantly.

"To your Uncle Reuben's house. It's his birthday."

"Why can't I come?"

"There will be no children."

"There were no children in Patna or Monghyr or—"

"That's enough, Dinah." He stared at me with a coldness I had not seen in many months.

I ran to my room, closed my door, made certain the tattie mats covered the windows securely, and let Shareef out of his basket. I lay down on my bed and allowed the flying squirrel to walk over me. Shareef crouched by my pillow and licked the tears that streamed down my face. What had I done wrong? Why didn't he like me anymore?

Yali tiptoed in to check on me. "What is the matter, Dinah-baba?"

I turned my back to her.

"Tell me," she pleaded with her soft doe eyes.

"Why doesn't Papa want me around?"

"He does want you here. Why else would we be living in this house?" she replied simplistically.

"He is never home."

"He goes to the office, he sees his family, his friends."

"But in Patna—" I sniffed.

"That was different. A man needs to be with other men and women."

And women! Patna! I remembered the woman in his bed. Was that what this was about?

My tears flowed even harder. "I wish we could go away again. Then he wouldn't need anyone else."

"Don't talk nonsense," she said in a distressed voice. "You are his little girl. Nothing can change that."

"Then why, when he is home, does he prefer to be alone?"

"A man needs to rest after work. You'll see, in a few weeks everyone will have their holiday and everything will be sorted out." Yali's tone was more wistful than convincing, but I tried to believe her.

Then, as if to prove her wrong, the first week of June my father left us at Kyd Street while he went off to Darjeeling to escape the heat. "Why won't you take us with you?" I had asked, since many families went to that hill station for the hottest months of the year.

"You would not want to miss school, would you?"

"We have a long break."

"The boys are too young."

"I could go with you."

"No, Dinah. This is a trip I must take alone."

I knew it was senseless to argue. He did not care how I felt. If he did—even the slightest bit—he would have made better arrangements than forcing me to stay with Aunt Bellore. I don't think she wanted me any more than I wanted to be with her, but she did her duty grudgingly. She had told my father that I could not bring Shareef to her house, but somehow he prevailed. The only condition was that I was expected to shut him up in the bathroom at night. On my third night, though, I awoke with a start. My darling Shareef was licking my face. I wrapped him in an end of the mosquito net and let him sleep with me the rest of the night. In the morning Yali showed me how he had broken a pane of glass in the bathroom, escaped into the garden, and back through the open window of my bedroom.

"How clever!" I said.

All the same, the pane had been broken, and Aunt Bellore surmised what had happened. The next afternoon I returned from the schoolroom to find Shareef's basket empty.

"Where is Shareef?" I sobbed.

Bellore shrugged her shoulders. "You can't expect he'd want to be cooped up forever. He must have escaped again."

I searched the house. There was no evidence of a broken window or open shutter, but he never returned. I knew that my aunt had taken him away, and I vowed I would never forgive her.

The summer heat in Mrs. Hanover's schoolroom was gruesome, even with the four punkah-wallahs, who worked ceaselessly. Still, I liked going, if only as a respite from Aunt Bellore's austere rules for my behavior, which varied from the ones her daughters were given. When I complained, all she would say was, "Somebody has to control you, and since your father shows no interest in the matter, the task has, unhappily for us both, been left to me."

Fortunately, Mrs. Hanover had taken an interest in me and was having me write short essays and do more challenging sums. If I finished my work early, she would give me a Bible verse to copy out in my neatest hand, and then illustrate.

Mrs. Hanover looked for verses that might have meaning to me. "You know about Passover, don't you, Dinah?"

"Yes, we had a seder in Monghyr."

"Good, then work on this one." She handed me the Bible, open to St. John, Chapter Six.

I read aloud, " 'And the Passover, a feast of the Jews, was nigh.' " After I had absorbed the idea of the story of feeding loaves and fishes to five thousand strong, I spent the rest of the afternoon drawing an elaborate picture of a crowd scene—with the people in saris and dhotis eating Indian breads and large fishes. Mrs. Hanover was extremely pleased.

Aunt Bellore was not.

Reading the verse, she became so furious she crumpled it. "Why won't your father ever listen? How many times have I told him that

Mrs. Hanover is only trying to poison your mind?" Her huge bosom heaved up and down. "You may not go back to that school."

"But Papa said—"

As an afterthought, she smoothed out my work to save as proof. "Once he sees this, he will understand I acted in his best interests."

I knew better than to argue with my aunt. I let my anger simmer for two days, waiting for the second Sabbath of the month. I was allowed to visit my grandparents every second and fourth weekend. Nani had made the original arrangements with Mrs. Hanover. She would stand behind me.

"I hate Aunt Bellore!" I announced moments after the Lanyado carriage deposited me at Lower Chitpur Road.

"I see," Nani said as she led me in to visit with my grandfather. She placed her finger over her mouth to warn me not to show my temper to him. I kissed him and accepted his tremulous pat before she led me away.

"So, you are unhappy at Kyd Street."

"Yes. Aunt Bellore is cruel to me. She does not permit me to do anything I wish."

"I am certain she has reasons for her rules."

"Her reason is to be mean to me. Besides, if it were not for . . ." I caught an idea forming. "Nani, you always said that Mama and Bellore were good friends and that Mama wanted Benu because she wanted to remain close to Bellore and the other Sassoons."

Her eyes shifted warily. "Yes, that's right."

"But Aunt Bellore was engaged to marry when my mother got the idea that she wanted to marry too."

Nani nodded cautiously. I sensed her considering how to explain the nuances of what adults thought and felt.

"When Mama married Bellore's brother, she made a better match, didn't she?"

"Your Uncle Samuel Lanyado is a fine man."

"Not as rich as the Sassoons."

"No."

"And Aunt Bellore's match was arranged for her, while Mama picked Papa." My voice rose feverishly. "Aunt Bellore must always have wondered if Mama was happier than she was. She was jealous!"

"That is enough, Dinah."

I was prancing maniacally around the room, oblivious of Nani's disapproval. "The whole time, Aunt Bellore only pretended to be my mother's friend. All the while, she disliked my mother for taking away her brother, for having more money, for marrying into a more important family. Why, Mama even had me first."

"I hardly think—"

"I am right, Nani, I know I am. It explains why Aunt Bellore is so awful to me and why she will not permit me to return to Mrs. Hanover's school."

"What? When did this come about?"

"I haven't been since Tuesday."

"Your father paid for the term."

"That's what I told her, but she won't listen to me. Will you talk to her? Please!" I implored. "Tell her I must go."

"Your aunt must have an explanation."

"Only that she didn't like a verse I had copied."

"What verse?"

I went over to the Bible that Nani kept on a shelf by her Sabbath candlesticks and leafed through it. "I can't find St. John. You are missing half the book!"

Grandmother motioned me to sit on her lap. She kissed my perspiring forehead. As she brushed back my bangs, she spoke kindly. "Dinah, Mrs. Hanover has broken her word to your father. As Jews, we believe only in the first book of the Bible; as a Christian, she believes in a second book as well, the one that talks about Jesus as the son of God."

"Why should one part of the Bible be true and the other not?"

"And the woman gave me her word." Nani sighed sadly. "I know you want to go to school. So do many other Jewish girls. That is why some good people in this community, especially Mr. Elias Cohen, have been working to begin a Jewish Girls' School. It should open after the October holidays. Do you think you could wait until then?"

I frowned. What choice did I have?

To divert my attention, Nani began discussing my father's return in a few weeks and how busy I would be with him.

"I can hardly wait," I admitted. "I want everything to go back to the way it was before."

"There will be many changes—"

"I don't want anything to change!"

"Nothing remains the same."

I was about to question her further when Nana was wheeled in to celebrate the Sabbath.

❧ ❧ ❧

The next day my grandparents took me back to Kyd Street, but we first visited the Jewish cemetery. As the carriage slowed, Nani took my hand. "Your grandfather and I have never been here because Ephraim was so ill. This is the first time we have come to see where your mother is resting. Wait here for us."

After my grandparents had walked away, I hopped down and followed them at a distance. Nani led the way. Her husband trailed behind. When she found the spot, she seemed to stare for the longest time, then bent closer to see if she had missed something. When it was obvious she had not, I heard a long, rumbling wail explode from somewhere deep inside her.

I ran up and studied the modest rectangle. I knew enough Hebrew to read: "The grave of Luna, daughter of Ephraim Rahamin, born on 4 Iyar 5614, died on 4 Tishri 5639." There was another sentence that I only deciphered years later that said, "May her soul be bound up in the bonds of life."

"What is wrong?" I asked my grandfather. He clasped my hand but was too overcome to respond. I looked around at the other stones. Their inscriptions carried the names of husbands, wives, and occasionally children.

"It does not have my name or my brothers'." I looked questioningly at Nana, but he merely shook his head from side to side. "Why doesn't it say 'Sassoon'?"

"Disowned," Nani spat. "How could he have done this to her—and to you?"

To me? What did she mean?

"He has left you motherless—in fact and in name."

⚜ ⚜ ⚜

A week later, Aunt Bellore took her daughters and me along when she went to Theatre Road to check that certain repairs were being made in preparation for my father's return. Someone had certainly been hard at work. The marble steps glistened in the sun. Lavish arrangements of flowers spilled from brass cache pots. The furniture had been polished and oiled. I scampered upstairs to find that my room had been repainted a jade green. My books had been placed in mahogany and glass cases, and the embroidered spread decorated with red and white poppies we had purchased in Patna was tucked into a new carved bedstead.

"Is this your room?" My youngest cousins were impressed.

"Of course it is."

"Green is an ugly color," Sultana said nastily.

"Well, I don't have to stay here if I don't want to."

"Where would you sleep?"

"Follow me." I thrust my chin in the air and led the way.

My father's old bedroom was still being refurbished. The walls were painted a pale coral. Two small beds—instead of a large one—were placed perpendicular to the place where the large platform bed in which my mother had died had been. They were covered with quilts appliquéd with a central lotus surrounded by mango trees, leaves, birds and stars. Matching armoires, carved with a border of fruits and flower garlands, stood in the old bed's place.

"This is where I will sleep," I said to my cousins.

"Really?" Abigail and Lulu gasped at the sight of a splendid white hibiscus plant growing out of a porcelain pot placed between the beds. Stuffed white doves were perched on the branches, and white silk ribbons shot with golden threads were sprinkled amongst the leaves.

"Yes, I always sleep with my father," I lied, since I hadn't since we had returned to Calcutta.

"No, you won't." Sultana wheeled around and faced me. "They will make you stay in your own room."

They? I had a premonition of disaster. "What do you mean?"

Abigail stared at her sister. "Hush, Sultana. Mama made us promise—"

"Promise what?"

Sultana folded her arms across her chest. "Can't say."

"Can't say what?" I shrilled. "Tell me!"

"You are getting a new mother, that's all." Lulu giggled.

"You're a liar!"

"She's not!" Sultana crowed. "You'll see, and . . . and you'll be sorry!"

I ran to my room and slammed the door. Sultana probably never spoke a truer word. Aunt Bellore was bad enough, but a total stranger! Now I was certain I had lost my father forever.

8

ozelle arrived with her mother—I was instructed to address her as Grandmother Helene—in tow. Because Mozelle's shoulders were narrow and her hips and buttocks rounded, she resembled an eggplant at first glance. At eight, I was exactly half her age.

After the formal introductions, my father bent close to my ear. "I've brought you a new mother and a new friend."

I looked at him warily, then at Mozelle, whose eyelids twitched. The poor girl was more frightened than I was. As Papa lifted Jonah and Asher and carried them inside, I seized my advantage and walked beside him. Mozelle followed behind docilely. We managed to get through an entire tea and tour of the house without the bride uttering one word.

The next day, every Sassoon came to inspect Benu's choice and to hear the tale of their marriage. The widowed Helene Arakie had been spending the season at the mountain home of her first daughter's family. The girl had married well, having the dowry to attract a man who traded cotton and silk. Helene's second daughter was so beautiful, her modest dowry had been overlooked by a wealthy trader in indigo. "All three of my girls have been fortunate," Helene said with more than a touch of smugness at having negotiated so well for her youngest.

"Youth is her only asset," Aunt Bellore whispered to Uncle Saul's wife, Rebecca, as they sampled the *rasamalai, rasagulla,* and the rest of the syrupy sweets.

"And when that wears off, what will Benu do then?" Rebecca tittered knowingly.

"So far my brother has proved himself more faithful than his wife," Bellore whispered haughtily.

Mozelle remained at my father's side, nodding when he spoke to her, shyly answering questions put to her with only a yes or no. I had been so prepared to dislike her, but how could I feel anything but sympathy for the poor creature?

Grandmother Helene was given the downstairs room where my grandparents had stayed. Within a short time she was supervising the household better than my mother or even my grandparents ever had. The Arakies had been modest storekeepers so she had no experience, just a natural aptitude. She had a sunny disposition, a love of beautiful flowers, a taste for rich, spicy food, and she adored children. Best of all, she liked animals. We were given kittens for the nursery, and a pony was purchased for the boys.

Since her mother was in charge, Mozelle had nothing to do. I offered to lend her my books, but was astonished to learn she could not read. Sometimes I would read aloud to her, but her attention drifted quickly, and she usually fell asleep after a chapter or two.

Aunt Bellore invited me to play with her daughters and was annoyed when I refused, preferring to stay home with Mozelle. "So you like your new mother, do you?" Her tone was probing, not pleasant.

"She's all right," I replied curtly. I was unwilling to give her the satisfaction of knowing I was accepting Mozelle, for in doing so, I might be seen as disloyal to Mama—something I suspected would gratify her.

Papa came to my room one evening to tell me how pleased he was that I was kind to his new wife. "When I go away, Mozelle will be company for you—and you for her."

An idea struck me. "Could she attend the Jewish Girls' School with me?"

"I don't think so."

"She doesn't even read," I confided.

"That's not important. In any case, that is not her desire."

"How do you know?" I challenged.

My father ignored me.

"Let's ask her."

"Dinah!" He looked exasperated enough to chastise me further, but he caught himself. I could tell he was mulling over his next words. He lowered his voice. "Mozelle must have quiet activities for the next several months."

Mozelle was sleepy most of the time. She napped more than my brothers. "Marriage must be tiring," I said.

Papa laughed heartily. "She has started a baby, so she must rest."

"When will she finish it?"

He chuckled even louder. "In May, I think. I will try to be home by then."

A pang reminded me that he would be going back to China in a few weeks, but I no longer feared loneliness. At least I would not have to return to Aunt Bellore's. I would be going to a new school, Grandmother Helene enjoyed my company and kept everyone amused, and the boys were older and more companionable. Mozelle and I would be together and, happily, soon there would be a new baby in the house.

❧   ❧   ❧

"What this house needs is music, laughter, people!" was Grandmother Helene's pronouncement a few days after my father's departure for China.

She was right. We had been a somber clutch ever since the date of his trip had been announced.

"I'm leaving you in good hands," he assured me. "Now, I want you to help Grandmother Helene take care of Mozelle. She will be your 'little mother.' "

"Yes, Papa," I agreed, finding the term "little mother" pleasing because it proved I was not as motherless as Nani had feared.

My father had acquired two women in the marriage contract: a nubile innocent to bear him children, and a sensible—at least that was what he thought—manager for his household.

Grandmother Helene was a big woman in body, in soul, in heart—and in requirements to sustain the three. The kitchen was the site of her first improvements. Our cook, a Muslim who was well-schooled in kosher laws, had until now brought little imagination to his task. Grandmother Helene had no qualms about rolling up her sleeves to work side by side with him until his creations met her exacting standards. Under her tutelage even the traditional *kooba*—stuffed rice dumplings—were more deliciously spiced. Specialties such as *pantras*, pancakes rolled with chicken, and *bamia khutta*, sweet-and-sour chicken and okra, were placed on the table several times a week. On the Sabbath, *muchli ka* curry, a tangy fish platter, and *hans mukmura*, duck with almond-raisin-and-spice sauce, appeared. No longer was only one dish offered for each course of the meal. Grandmother Helene insisted that a "taste of this and a taste of that" was best for her "Mazal-Tob," the Jewish name she preferred to call her daughter.

Indeed, in the early months, Mozelle felt sick if she went without eating for more than an hour. Tables in every room were laden with trays of fresh fruit, several varieties of *barfi* fudges, even my favorite, the creamy coconut candy, dol-dol.

"Bring me some figs. I want mango fool. I must have a turnover," she ordered in so docile a tone that she did not sound officious.

"Yes, yes, my darling," her mother cooed.

My brothers and I were no longer expected to take our meals in the nursery dining room. "This is one big family!" Grandmother Helene exclaimed. "We shall eat together."

Her concept of family stretched beyond us three children and her daughter to include her other children, their husbands and babies, her sisters' and brothers' families, her old friends from Calcutta, Darjeeling, and everywhere else. Rarely did only five of us sit down to a meal. Her hospitality became legion. The Arakie clan broadcast the news that her table was always set for twenty. We never knew who might appear at mealtimes.

The genial Arakies were the opposite of the staid Sassoons. They hugged, they shouted, they laughed, they cried—all in the space of a few minutes. Children could run freely through the mansion, racing, rolling toys, throwing balls. Father's Chinese porcelains disappeared for the duration. Other delicate objects were removed. The corridor runners were rolled and put away.

Quite soon Mozelle grew too large to frolic with the children, but she hated to be alone. "I am afraid here without Benu," she confided the first month after my father had gone.

Many a bride might have felt the same in so large a home, but few had as just cause as Mozelle. Her mother slept in her room at night, even though one durwan was posted outside her door and another in the courtyard below. If she rested during the day, I was expected to keep her company. Her body seemed to swell even as I observed her sleeping. Her chest grew as plump as pillows, her arms and legs thickened, and her belly, which held the venerable object, was that of a female Buddha. So awestruck was I by the metamorphosis that I vowed never to allow the same to happen to my body.

If I could not nap, I would slip downstairs to the terrace, where Grandmother Helene sat on a divan directing the malis to plant more flowers (especially the rare bicolor varieties of roses she adored), trim hedges to her specifications, and fertilize the vegetables and herbs she required for the table. Many afternoons, ladies would arrive about three for rounds of *nowta-hasthta*, a card game like baccarat. When my mother had entertained guests, I had been ordered to disappear, but Grandmother Helene included me. "Come, advise me on my play," she asked to flatter me after I had learned the basics.

Gone as well was the rule that I could visit my Raymond grandparents only every other Sabbath. Grandmother Helene declared this nonsense and said I might go whenever I wished.

"May they come here too?" I asked. "They hardly ever see Jonah and Asher."

She bit her lower lip. "No, your father was firm about that."

For the most part the Sassoons ignored us. We saw them at the synagogue, but they made a point of not calling at Theatre Road, and I was hardly ever asked back to Kyd Street. On one of the few occasions I did see them, at a Chanukah party at Uncle Saul's, Aunt Bellore questioned me. "Dinah, tell me, is what I hear true? They say that Helene Arakie has a crowd over for a big *tamasha* every night."

"Not every night," I demurred.

"She feeds a crowd at her table, doesn't she? Who visits? Anyone I would know?"

My guard was up, for I thought she was trying to discover if my Raymond grandparents were breaking my father's ban. "If you want the names, ask my Grandmother Helene," I snapped, and sauntered off.

Toward the end of her pregnancy, Mozelle retreated upstairs, no longer hazarding to transport her bulk—her width was nearly equal to her height—down the marble stairs. She spent her days propped against a mound of Persian pillows, her face as pallid as a new moon, her drooping eyelids giving her a perpetual sleepy expression. Her sausage fingers seemed forever grasping an almond turnover, and its crumbs littered the expanse of her enormous abdomen.

In the last weeks of her confinement, she contracted a severe case of prickly heat, and a filigree of pink welts laced her transparent skin. "Mama! I cannot tolerate it!" she cried out as her itch worsened toward midday. "Please, can't we go to the mountains?" Every one of her relations, except her mother, had fled to Darjeeling.

"You know you must not travel," Grandmother Helene chided.

As two ayahs patted their mistress's bulk with towels, one of them giggled and jumped back.

"What is it?" I asked.

The second ayah pushed on Mozelle's belly to show me that when the baby moved, visible bumps dotted the landscape of her abdomen. She started to dry Mozelle again, but Mozelle was so irritated at being poked from two directions at once, she lashed out and slapped the girl.

"Mozelle!" her mother admonished as she shooed the servants away. She draped her pouting daughter in a loose cotton sari.

I did not think any less of Mozelle for her outburst. People were known to go mad in Calcutta's heat. Out in the sun your brain would sizzle if you dared remove your clammy topee for even a moment. In the shade, your body bade you to do as little as possible. As the unrelenting heat blasted us, everyone was irritable, and at times we all were stricken with fits of bad behavior. My brothers whined and hit each other. I threw books against the wall, ripped up my drawings, even poured a pitcher of water over my head when I was wearing my fanciest frock.

At the apex of the cruel summer, we were allowed outdoor activity only in the early-morning hours before the sun climbed as high as the top of the rose arbor. My brothers and I were taken on sunrise walks in the Maidan, where we watched with astonishment as the British soldiers paraded in full uniform.

Yali shook her head. "Crazy men."

"Look"—I pointed—"they wear a different color uniform in the summertime."

Jonah studied the troops and reported, "They are the old ones soaked with sweat."

In the worst of the heat, we dozed on charpoys wrapped in wet sheets. The mattresses were removed from the string beds so that the punkah-wallahs could force the stagnant air to circulate around our burning bodies. Wakeful at night, we played quiet games on the terrace. This was the only time Mozelle seemed content. She talked sweetly about the baby, what she might name it, what it might look like.

"Do you think Benu will be back in time?" she asked her mother wistfully.

Grandmother Helene was hopeful. "He said he might."

"He won't," I offered from experience. "He is always away more than six months."

Mozelle sulked, but no one contradicted me.

In early June, Aunt Bellore and Uncle Samuel called on us after Saturday-morning services.

"How much quieter the house is than the last time I was here," Aunt Bellore said to Grandmother Helene. "It must be a relief to have your relations in the hills."

Grandmother Helene was not ruffled. "The children find it dull, but I am certain it is best for Mozelle." Her eyes gleamed. "And whatever is best for my Mazal-Tob is best for Benu's baby."

Aunt Bellore grimaced. Uncle Saul coughed as he reached for a letter in his coat pocket. "We've had word from my brother."

Grandmother Helene's dark eyes seemed to fill her round face. She staggered backward, as if in anticipation of a blow. An alert bearer rushed forward and took her arm.

"Didn't mean to alarm you," Uncle Saul sputtered. He helped her to a seat and handed her the sheaf of papers. "There are letters for you and Mozelle. Unfortunately, he doubts he will be home before September."

"Just as I said," I announced unwisely. My aunt glared at me.

"Would you like to see Mozelle?" Grandmother Helene asked Bellore.

"I suppose, if she wouldn't be disturbed."

"Of course not. Why don't you take her letter up yourself?" When Aunt Bellore had left, Helene offered Uncle Saul refreshment. A few minutes later she had settled him on the terrace and poured his tea.

She fluttered her eyes, gave a little sigh, and said, "Now, tell me, Saul, what exactly does Benu do in China that keeps him away so long?"

"It's rather complicated," he replied dismissingly.

"Then you will have to tell me the whole story."

Surprised by the intent gleam in her eye, he looked from her to me. Seeing I was just as curious, the eldest Sassoon brother, and head of the company, considered the matter for a moment and then shrugged. "Perhaps we should start with my Grandfather David, some forty years ago." He proceeded to tell us that as soon as the East India Company had opened the business to independent investors, David had begun to buy the raw opium grown in Rajputana in northwest India. His job was to transport it by clipper as far as Lintin Island at the mouth of the Pearl River, the pipeline to Canton, the only port the Chinese would open to Westerners. From there, smugglers with armed small craft called "scrambling dragons" and "fast crabs" would move the merchandise through a network of pirates, corrupt officials, and dealers to the masses who eagerly devoured the drug. Though he did a steady business, he became frustrated because he was almost always undersold by competitors, especially the Jardine, Matheson network. Still, who wouldn't be content with a profit that, although modest in this lucrative trade, was kingly in any other?

"Wouldn't the Chinese have made out better if they permitted the opium to be imported?" I asked.

My uncle ruffled my hair. "How can she follow this?"

Grandmother Helene beamed at me. "Well, Saul, if you don't give her an answer, she will pester you all afternoon."

"You're right," he chuckled. Warming to his role as family chronicler, he related that the prices of opium had remained inflated because the Chinese rulers refused to legalize it. "Then, in the 1830's, an official in the Forbidden City dared to suggest the laws against the drug did nothing more than benefit worthless scoundrels, and proposed legalization for everyone except state administrators, soldiers, and scholars. Not only that, he wanted to place a high tariff on every chest and forbid payment to the 'foreign devils' in any tender except barter merchandise. When my father, Moses, heard the news, he exploded, saying, 'If these regulations are strictly enforced, our opium will rot in our holds.' "

"Why?" I asked. "Wouldn't he sell more of it?"

"Well, it is more involved than that. He required silver, not trade items, to pay for the crop at the auctions."

"What happened?" Grandmother Helene prodded.

"My father was young and enterprising. He didn't think the restrictions would last. In the meantime, he suggested the Sassoons set up shop in Calcutta, a port a subcontinent closer to China than Bombay."

"That was wise," she said, nodding.

"Yes. Within a few months he heard they need be despondent no longer. A new crackdown was under way."

I was perplexed. "Then it was good that the Chinese said it was bad?"

"In a way, but the emperor was mistaken."

"Why?" I asked.

"He believed opium was an evil that wasted and killed his subjects."

"Doesn't it?" I thought of Mama and the hookah.

"Not always," he said, brushing aside my query with a wave of his hand. "Nevertheless, the emperor thought it did, so he appointed a kinchae—one of four so named in three hundred years—with the power to organize armies, to sentence to death, to take any extreme measure necessary to halt once and for all time the spread of the foreign devils' flower."

"That's the poppy, right?" I asked to check if I was following the complex tale.

My uncle nodded perfunctorily and went on to tell us that Lin Tse-hsu, the kinchae, barricaded the foreigners in their homes, holding them hostage for their entire inventory of opium—over half of India's crop that year. James and Alexander Matheson and one of my uncles were among the captives. When word of the Canton quarantine reached England, most patriots—those who realized the balance of trade for tea, silk, and spices could not be maintained without the lucrative opium trade—screamed for war.

Grandmother Helene poured more tea. "Some spoke against it, didn't they?" she asked in a hushed tone.

"A few moralists dared to differ. They believed that ordinary wars of conquest were somehow less wicked. But why? Most wars are fought out of greed—for land or goods or power." Uncle Saul's tone suggested he didn't wholly believe his own argument.

"Did they go to war?" I asked.

"Yes. Kinchae Lin confiscated and destroyed more than twenty thousand chests by crushing the balls one by one and dumping them into a creek that ran into the Pearl River."

"Was any of that Sassoon opium?" Grandmother Helene wondered.

"No. 'Fortune smiles,' my father wrote to his father. 'We have no partners in Canton, no stock in that foul harbor. The loss to Jardine is our gain.' He sat back and waited until the value of opium in his warehouses doubled. Then, avoiding Lintin Island entirely, he organized a small fleet to make deliveries into Macao, where daring captains were more than willing to sail into smaller ports for the premium paid for the scarce commodity." Uncle Saul took a long sip from the teacup. "Kinchae Lin could not hold back the flood of entrepreneurs that followed. His fury mounted further when British sailors in Macao were said to have killed a Chinese citizen. He put a price on the capture of English officers, soldiers, and Indian sepoys. The British reacted to this final affront by announcing that opium would continue to flow into China—this time in warships."

"That was the First Opium War," Grandmother Helene said to me.

Uncle Saul nodded. "Yes. After Admiral Eliot and his India fleet blockaded access to Canton, they made for Shanghai, leaving port cities along the way running with blood." His voice rose with enthusiasm. "Within a year a settlement, the Treaty of Nanking, was negotiated, forcing the emperor to compensate us merchants for the opium Kinchae Lin had destroyed and for the expenses of war as well. The most significant provision was that Hong Kong became a crown colony and the ports of Canton, Foochow, Ningpo, Amoy, and Shanghai were opened to trade. Opium was not legalized as such, but the treaty put blinders on the Chinese, who were forbidden to search British ships. By the middle of the 1840's, China was millions of pounds sterling in debt as the pressed cakes made from India's flowers flowed freely to satisfy the insatiable population of smokers." He leaned back and smiled smugly at Grandmother Helene. She returned his smile with a gracious nod of her head.

I stood up. "But it was wrong!"

"On the contrary, Dinah, it was not fair of the Chinese officials to deprive their people of a product that, once they were accustomed to, they could not relinquish without danger to their health. Don't listen to people who claim we addicted their citizens to opium. Every man makes that choice voluntarily. The Chinese complained we were draining them of silver, but had they not been draining us of silver for more than one hundred years?"

"But—"

"Hush, Dinah!" Grandmother Helene said with unusual severity.

Curious as to the change of tone in the room, Aunt Bellore had come to the door.

"Well, that's enough for now," Saul said, relieved not to have to respond to me any further.

But Bellore had her piece to add. She grinned as she boasted, "Of course, a ship owned by our family started the Second Opium War."

"Really?" Grandmother Helene asked with wide eyes.

"Yes. That was some ten years later," my uncle asserted. "The *Arrow*, a lorcha leased by the Sassoons, was attacked in the South China Sea. Her cargo was dumped and one of my cousins was kidnapped. The British took up arms, and soon the French joined the fray. After the two navies sailed into Shanghai and marched into Peking, the emperor was forced to negotiate, settling this time for twenty million pounds sterling—more than enough to balance the trade deficit. With the sweep of his pen, he legitimated our family trade."

"Tell me, what is Benu's part in this?" Grandmother Helene wondered.

"Benu has the aptitude for dealing with the Chinese. He learned the trading dialects and was able to balance the entire equation of the business so adroitly he could squeeze a positive position from almost any transaction." Saul caught his sister's eye. "For the last several years the Sassoons have been able to control almost three-fourths of the opium in India."

"That is very impressive. But what is Benu doing that keeps him away from his home—and his wife—for so long?" Grandmother Helene sniffed.

"Right now the Chinese are trying to grow their own flowers," my uncle continued in a level tone. "Benu must travel from port to port, trying to establish the higher-grade, more expensive imported poppy as the standard in the Chinese marketplace."

"Why can't you hire others for that task?" Grandmother Helene prodded.

Aunt Bellore bounded toward her. "How dare you interfere?"

Uncle Saul hissed a warning to his sister. "The child . . ."

Everyone stared at me.

"Go see if Mozelle needs anything," Grandmother Helene coaxed.

One look at the set of Aunt Bellore's tight mouth prevented me from objecting.

9

❦ ❦ ❦

I slept beside Mozelle on the afternoon that was to be the beginning of a beginning and the beginning of an end. Two punkah-wallahs fanned us, and from time to time Mozelle's ayah came in to bathe her face, arms, and legs with cool water kept in an earthenware jug. Sleepily I watched the ablutions. The humidity was so dense, the water did not evaporate. Rivulets formed on Mozelle's blistered skin. In the pastel light of the late afternoon she looked like a melon that had begun to spoil. She groaned as she tried to sit up. Her ayah assisted, to no avail, and I came around to the other side to help.

Mozelle stopped us both from lifting her, and fell back. "Ai, Mama!" she cried. She clenched her eyes and bit her lip. She did not seem to recover from the spasm.

"Mozelle!" I shook her. "Get the burra memsahib. Hurry!" I ordered her ayah.

Another tremor racked Mozelle, and her eyes flew open. She stared past me as though something horrifying had attracted her attention. I looked around. Nothing was there. I turned back too late to avoid the arc of vomit that covered one side of my body.

"S-s-sorry . . ." she stammered.

Yali bathed me in rosewater while Mozelle's sobs carried down the hall to the bathroom. When I was clean and dry, Yali had me drink a cup of tea in the nursery.

Grandmother Helene rushed in, her hands tugging at the folds in her dress. "Mozelle is so distressed."

I shrugged. "I suppose she couldn't stop herself."

"What a lovely, big girl you are. I will need your help with the boys tonight. Will you do that for me?"

"Yes, of course. May we have dinner on the terrace downstairs?"

"Dinah, tonight you are in charge of the household."

"Really?"

"Yes, and you may have your dinner wherever you like."

Such expansiveness was worrisome. People were rarely magnanimous with children unless they wanted to mollify them.

"Will Mozelle be all right?"

"Certainly. Having a baby is a perfectly normal—if temporarily unpleasant—state of affairs."

As I jumped up, the cup and saucer in my hand made an awful clatter. "Oh! I thought she had a summer tummy."

Grandmother Helene's laugh was a hearty rumble. "Well, it is certainly the biggest summer tummy I've ever seen."

"How long will it take?"

"The baby should arrive by morning, or tomorrow afternoon at the latest."

I could think of a dozen more questions, but she brushed me off with a brisk wave.

Elated by the news, I decided to organize a party on the terrace. To me the most enchanting Indian festival of the year was the Hindu celebration of Diwali, which commemorates the return of Rama from exile. Our pantry contained boxes of *divas*, small oil lamps the servants used to light up the garden on that special night. We were six months from Diwali, but since Grandmother Helene said I might do anything I wanted, I asked the servants to set out the divas. By dusk the gardens twinkled with hundreds of fairy lights, just the right atmosphere to make a baby want to appear, I decided.

When everything was set up to my satisfaction, I went to visit Mozelle, who seemed much recovered from the afternoon. She was sitting in a high wooden chair that had been lined with pillows, sipping lemonade. Her eyes were bright, and her cheeks more highly colored than in many a month.

I pointed to the window. "Can you see outside from there?"

Mozelle stretched her short, thick neck. "Just a bit. So many stars . . ."

"Not stars, diva lamps."

She didn't seem to hear me. "Again," she mumbled as her eyes crossed queerly and her hands clenched.

A lady with nutmeg-tinted skin emerged from the shadows. Long, slender fingers reached out from a white sari and skittered across Mozelle's abdomen. Nothing was said for more than a minute; then she spoke in a singsong. "It passes, it passes, it's gone." The lady retreated to where she had been sitting cross-legged on the floor. Mozelle's eyes fluttered open. She seemed to be coming out of a trance.

"I want to . . ." She gestured toward the open window.

Her mother and the other woman rushed to her side. Lifting her under the arms, they glided her across the floor until she could see the quivering lights outside. Jonah and Asher were singing an Indian nursery song they had learned from Selima:

> *Tali, tali bajao baba,*
> *Achcha roti haat banata.*
> *Thora mummy-ko do.*
> *Thora daddy-ko do.*
> *Jo baki hai.*
> *Burya ayah-ko do.*
>
> Clap, clap hands, baby,
> They make good bread in the market.
> Give a little to mummy.
> Give a little to daddy.
> What is left over,
> Give to the old ayah.

"How wonderful! Diwali is such a beautiful holiday. We always go down to the ghats to watch the lights floating on the river. Next time . . ." Her voice caught. I thought the sickness had clasped her again, but she recovered and said in a whispery voice, "Next time Benu will be with me and somebody else will see it with us for the first time." She patted her belly and gave a lopsided grin as she was helped back to her chair.

"Very nice, Dinah. A lovely thing to have done . . ." Grandmother Helene's voice trailed off as Mozelle started in again. The lady in white resumed her position, her movements, her words, mirroring the earlier ones.

"Who is she?"

"A midwife, a person who knows how to bring a baby into the world."

"What's wrong with Mozelle? Why does she act so strange every so often?"

"A baby comes in small steps, like an incoming tide. Each wave gives her a pain for a minute or so; each pain brings the baby closer. Better for you to leave now, Dinah. Come in again before you go to bed."

When I went in to say good night to Mozelle, she lay on her side, groaning like someone who had overeaten. I tiptoed over and touched her cheek. "Have them wake me as soon as the baby comes. I've never seen one that's brand-new."

As Mozelle stared past me, abstracted, her mother stepped forward. "Talk to Dinah, don't frighten her."

These words forced Mozelle to focus on me. She licked her lips.

"Yes, Dinah. I want you to be one of the very first." Her voice took on a command I had never before heard. "After all, you will be eldest sister of the family." A tremor seized her, but this time she fought through it. "It's not so bad, truly it isn't, and when it passes, it stays away for quite a long while. I can close my eyes and sometimes even sleep. How I wish I could wake up and find the baby in my arms!"

"I'm glad it isn't terrible. It looks so—"

Grandmother Helene steered me away. "You must get some sleep. Tomorrow will be an eventful day." Mozelle wailed, then moaned, sounding more like an injured cow than a person. I twitched in response. "Now, now, she'll be fine . . ." she said as I was ushered from the room.

The flickering elation at the spectacle of the diva lamps was obliterated by the quaking screams that punctuated the night. In spite of the heat, Yali closed the door to my room. Even so, it could not drown out the loudest wails, then—sometime after midnight—the gasps and screeches.

"Will she die?" I pressed against Yali's chest.

"No, no, she makes a fuss. If her mother would not pamper her so . . ." Yali sighed.

The intensity and frequency of Mozelle's complaints increased. Piercing shrieks and calls for help from God woke the boys, requiring both ayahs' attention to settle them back to sleep.

"Soon, soon," comforted Yali when she could get back to me. "They all cry out when the baby is about to come." An hour later Yali herself had run out of consoling words. Her mouth was pinched. Her eyes were glazed.

"Can't they get someone to help her? Why don't they call Nana or Dr. Hyam?"

Yali perked up. "*I* could not suggest this, but you could speak to the burra memsahib."

I ran down the hallway. A sickly perfume emanated from the darkened room. A husky breathing, frightening in its animalistic intensity, bellowed out into the hall. I located Grandmother Helene in the din without having to look upon Mozelle. She slumped over in the chair where her daughter had sat so regally that afternoon. "Mazal-Tob, Mazal-Tob," she muttered. Great, sagging pouches drooped below her eyes. Her silvery hair looked as though nesting birds had deranged it. One limp hand flopped over a pillow. "My poor Mazal-Tob . . ."

I touched her hand. "Is it time?" she muttered.

"A doctor," I whispered. "Call Dr. Hyam. My father would want Mozelle to have a doctor." When Grandmother Helene shook her head, I thought she was annoyed with me. "My grandfather is the best in Calcutta. Ask anybody."

"Hush, that's not the point," she said. A rising fury strained her voice as she went on, and the next words were cracked and halting. "This is your father's house, and he makes the rules."

"What rules?"

She seemed reluctant to speak, then sputtered, "Your grandparents are not to set foot here again."

I felt as though I had been slapped. Mozelle's cacophony floated in the background while I tried to make sense of this prohibition. Swirling visions of my mother's clothing and furniture on fire, of the final minutes in the courtroom, of my grandparents' sad eyes when they left the house for the last time, blurred before me. Mozelle's wind returned and her next scream seemed to split my spine. "What's wrong with Dr. Hyam? He is not a relative, only a friend."

"Your father would never approve . . ."

"Then somebody else," I sputtered. "Another doctor, please!"

"Yes, yes, we've sent for Dr. Basak at the hospital. He will be here shortly."

"Dinah!" Mozelle called pitifully.

I turned for Grandmother Helene's approval. She nodded so sadly I looked down. A few puddles of purple light illuminated the floor at my feet. I made my way to Mozelle's bedside, walking across them as gingerly as if I had been stepping on stones in a pond. When I reached the bed, I said, "Hello," without looking up.

Mozelle gripped my hand. "You are so cool."

The midwife lifted my chin and smiled at me, revealing a gold front tooth. "Talk to her, tell her a story, any distraction—"

I couldn't imagine what might be appropriate. Then a funny image came to me: Mozelle, hugely pregnant, riding an elephant. "Have you ever been on an elephant?" I asked.

Mozelle was so startled, she grinned. "No, have you?"

"Oh, yes, in Patna with my father. Shall I tell you about it?"

"Yes—" She broke off as her body jackknifed into a spasm. When it passed, I went on, embellishing the tale to make it more exciting and longer than it was.

The doctor, a very short Indian who seemed to be not much older than the patient herself, came into the room. Without taking notice of me, he began an examination, grunting as he reached between Mozelle's legs. I shuddered as most of his arm disappeared from view. When he finished, he spoke to Grandmother Helene. "All's well, the baby is quite satisfactory. She is young and small—inside, if not outside—and these cases take more time than most. There is no cause for alarm."

"Did you see the pads?" Grandmother Helene asked.

"Yes, no consequence there. A loss of blood is normal. There may be a few tears here and there. Nothing we can't stitch up later."

"But—" Grandmother Helene stopped. "Will you stay, then?"

"I regret I cannot. So many ladies wait for me." Nodding toward the midwife, he said, "You are in excellent hands." He washed up in the basin that Mozelle's ayah held for him, dried his hands perfunctorily, picked up his bag, and started to leave.

"Doctor!" Grandmother Helene's tone was pleading. "Isn't there something you could do for her?"

"There is laudanum, of course, but I was given to understand the husband did not wish her to have any."

"Yes, but that was before—"

"Do you think the gentleman could be persuaded to change his mind?"

"Yes, if he were here. Unfortunately, he is in China."

The doctor looked over at Mozelle. "Unfortunately for her, I can do nothing without the husband's agreement . . . unless someone else would accept the responsibility for him."

Grandmother Helene blanched. "She is *my* daughter."

The doctor shook his head sadly. "I require a gentleman, perhaps a close male relative—a father or a brother—before I could go against the expressed desires of the head of this household."

Grandmother Helene ran her fingers through her hair excitedly. "There is no father, and the brothers would never alter his instructions."

"A sad story. I know the husband thinks his first wife was given far too much opium during her childbirths, and this may have contributed to her . . . to her downfall."

"Do you think it did?"

The doctor shook his head. "That's doubtful."

I could see Grandmother Helene deliberating. "How would he ever know?" she asked, pleading.

Dr. Basak merely stared at me in reply. Grandmother Helene's shoulders sagged. The doctor bowed and backed out of the room.

After he left, Mozelle seemed calmer. Her shouts had changed to occasional whimpers. I know it was heartless of me, but the silence came as such a relief that I could not help feeling that she had been exaggerating her discomfort, as she had during her entire confinement. Also, the business of birthing the baby had gone on so long I was somewhat inured to her complaints.

When she closed her eyes and dozed off, Yali took my hand. "Come away now, Dinah-baba," Yali insisted. "You must take your chota hazri downstairs."

She served me on a lounge chair, and when I fell asleep after drinking my milk, she allowed me to stay there until the sun was quite high. When I woke in a sweat, she was ready beside me with a cool cloth and a bowl of sliced fruit. She tried to dress me in a lime-green frock with a frayed lace collar. "I don't like this one."

She grinned. "No matter. When you hold the baby, you might get it soiled."

The baby! I held myself perfectly still. There were no longer howls in the corridors. Nor were there infant cries. "Is it here?"

"Yes, Dinah-baba, she waits for you."

"A sister?"

"Yes, a sister-baba."

I flew down the hall. As I entered, the midwife and the ayah were busily tending a prostrate Mozelle. Selima sat on the other bed, the one I often slept in, with a baby to her breast. Grandmother Helene moved beside me. She was wearing a crisp blue gown and her hair was freshly washed. "Here comes Dinah. Ruby, look up and meet your big sister."

Selima turned the baby to face me. The infant was plump and pink, with damp tendrils of black hair that made her look much older.

"Ruby? Is that her name?"

"Yes, do you like it?" Mozelle said hoarsely.

I spun around. "She's pretty. A pretty little Ruby." I turned back to the infant and became transfixed by the alert expression in the dark pools that were her newly opened eyes.

❦ ❦ ❦

That night Ruby slept in the nursery next to my room. Mozelle was too weak to care for her own baby, but fortunately Selima had plenty of milk because she had given birth to a son of her own six months earlier. There were enough people rushing in and out of Mozelle's room—her mother, the doctor, the midwife, most of the servants, and relatives of her family—that I was content to stay away and watch the newborn's bathing and feeding and changing.

Perhaps I should have realized something was wrong, but it had been so long since Mozelle had been a normal part of family life that her absence at meals or her long recovery did not seem peculiar. I popped in for a wave or to bring her an especially lush flower from the garden or to tell her how sweet the baby looked sleeping, without noticing how weak she actually was. Since the heat was as awful as ever, nobody was lively, and her sweating and prostration seemed normal to me.

Only when the Raymond carriage pulled up the semicircular driveway did I feel the first frisson of fear. I rushed to greet them in the front hall. "I'm so glad you have come to see Ruby. I will never tell Papa, I promise."

Grandfather Raymond was walking with a cane, supported by Dr. Hyam. "You may tell your f-f-father anything you l-l-like," he stuttered.

"Wait till you see her. She is the biggest baby ever."

Nani's eyes lifted over my head and met Dr. Hyam's sharp gaze.

"Come, take me to the nursery, Dinah," she said while indicating the men should follow Selima to Mozelle's bedroom.

"Aren't you coming, Nana?"

"Later. I must see to M-Mozelle."

I proudly showed off Ruby, who lay on her tummy, her tiny rump poking up under several layers of netting. "She's sleeping."

Nani unfurled Ruby's tiny hand and placed a silver rupee in her palm. The sleeping infant clasped it.

"Why did you do that?"

"It's a charm against the evil eye."

"Shall I take you to Mozelle now?"

"Not just yet, Dinah. Let's have a glass of *lassi*." Turning, she handed me the cool rosewater-and-yogurt drink that was waiting for us on a brass tray.

I pushed it away, for the tension in her voice had terrified me. I flung my arms around her wide waist and held on fast. "Why did you come?"

"To see what could be done for poor Mozelle."

"What is wrong with Mozelle?"

"She has not recovered from the baby as well as she might. You know that."

"She's just tired," I protested, clutching at her even more tightly. When Grandmother Flora did not push me away, when she did not say I was being a silly girl, I knew that Mozelle was going to die.

Mozelle never rose from her bed. Racked with childbed fever, she was beyond the help of Dr. Hyam or Grandfather or any of the specialists they brought in. She was buried ten days after she had given birth.

The period of mourning for her had barely passed when I was told my grandfather had died in his sleep. Numbed by the birth and the events that culminated in losing my little mother, Nana's passing was but one more misery I added to my list.

10

❦ ❦ ❦

W
hat did I ever do to deserve two mothers-in-law?
Promise me you shall never join the conspiracy of
women who plague me," Papa said a few weeks
after his return home. We were walking in the gardens, which were more elaborate since Grandmother Helene had had
them replanted to her specifications.

I would have promised him anything if I had understood his request. Everything was so confusing. Everybody had been behaving
differently from the way I had expected. I had dreaded Papa's return,
thinking there would be a tumult similar to the aftermath of my
mother's death. Why was he so composed? Was a natural death less
upsetting than a murder? Or was it because my father had been with
Mozelle such a short time that his attachment was less than to his first
wife? Was this the conspiracy he meant? Was he asking me never to
grow up, never to leave him in life—or in death?

"You aren't angry with me, are you?" I asked.

He laughed lightly. "Should I be?"

"No."

"You shouldn't be angry with Grandmother Helene either," I said
seriously.

"I'm not. I was joking before."

"But Aunt Bellore and the other Sassoons are."

He ruffled my hair. "They were for a time, but they aren't anymore."

I bit my lip as I thought about the confusion during the four months
before he had returned. It had started when the Arakies gathered at
Theatre Road to console Grandmother Helene. For weeks the tables
sagged under the elaborate platters that were set out noon and night
for the Arakies' large circle of family and friends. I kept my ears open
for any news that might affect me.

"Two women in two years!" I overheard one Arakie say.

102

"At least Helene can enjoy some comfort," her cousin added.

"Unlucky house, unlucky children," another commented under her breath.

Despite these worrisome words, the clatter of the boisterous Arakies was a wonderful tonic. With a game or conversation or amusement always under way, there had been little time to reflect on the loss of my two mothers, my adored grandfather, my faraway father. Then one Sabbath afternoon—we had all attended services that morning, requiring eleven carriages, some making several trips—Aunt Bellore and her brothers Uncle Saul and Uncle Reuben arrived unexpectedly. Their interview with Helene was short and grim. By that evening I learned what had transpired: she had been ordered to leave before my father arrived a few weeks hence. The running of the house was to be taken over by my far-less-profligate Grandmother Flora.

I was so excited to have Nani back that I am afraid I did not show the proper appreciation or remorse I should have at Grandmother Helene's departure.

I have known indiscriminate women, have even been given that epithet myself by those who became jealous of my attainments, yet even today I believe Grandmother Helene was unfairly maligned by the Sassoons. Neither before nor after her daughter's death had she ever enriched her private purse. Her dress was modest and she took few personal belongings with her. If she fed too many people or overpaid at the market or purchased the finest food and beverages or indulged the servants with baksheesh or days off to visit their families, her motives had been benevolent.

"There is no point to life but to live," she had said when I had asked permission to resume classes at the Jewish Girls' School after the mourning periods for Mozelle and my grandfather had passed. "What did my Mazal-Tob have? Less than eighteen years. She barely saw her daughter. Her marriage was so brief she hardly knew her husband. Should she have eaten fewer sweets? No! She should have eaten more! Did I indulge her shamelessly during the time she carried her child? No! I should have given more selflessly. Was the doctor right in refusing her the comforts of laudanum? No! She should not have suffered for a moment if there was anything in God's power to spare her."

In the garden, I looked up at my father and wondered if Mozelle would be alive if he had been there. Seeing my tense expression, he took my hand and led me toward the roses. The older mali was clipping their stalks with shears while the younger lifted the thorny branches into the cart. "Papa, are you going to send Grandmother Flora away now?"

"Do you want her to stay, Dinah?"

"Yes. I am tired of people going away. Besides, she is lonely living by herself."

"I know, Dinah. I am lonely too."

He turned away and stared off into the distance, where Selima sat beside Ruby's carriage. Asher and Jonah were rolling a large ball on the lawn. "At least I have my children," he said, pleasing me enormously. Papa did not need any more wives or mothers-in-law. Everything he required, he already had.

❁   ❁   ❁

To prove this to me further, Papa did not return to China for the next two years. All his journeys to the opium fields were brief, and his brother Reuben went east in his stead. He took his responsibility as head of our household with utter seriousness. He did not revert to being the companion he had been in Patna, but he was in Theatre Road most every night. Grandmother Flora brought an order and peacefulness to the house that had never existed before. Grandmother Helene visited often, and the older children were permitted to go to her house whenever we wanted. I don't think there were better times for me, except those sublime moments in my mother's arms.

When I was almost eleven, Grandmother Helene prevailed upon my father to take us to Darjeeling. Though I was delighted not to spend another hot season in Calcutta, I was also a bit worried that our trip to Darjeeling might wreak new turmoil in our lives. For me the name conjured up the image of a bazaar where wives were bartered.

The carriage already had been ordered on the morning I woke with a rash. Nobody was allowed to see me until Dr. Hyam arrived. "Chicken-pox," he pronounced.

"But the high fever, the unusual spots . . ." Nani fretted.

"No, no. Come, look . . ." He waved her to my bedside. "With smallpox the vesicles are depressed in the center, much like a navel. These are flatter."

Nani sighed with relief. "I suppose she may not travel."

"Absolutely not. She'd be miserable, and she's infectious. The other children must remain behind, just in case."

"What about me? Am I in danger?" Papa asked.

"Did you have the pox when you were young?"

"We all did."

"Then you will not contract it again. Why don't you proceed to the hills? I'll look in on the children every day."

"No, don't go without me!" I protested, on guard against my father's meeting another woman.

They paid not the slightest attention to me. The heat at that ferocious apex of a Bengali summer caused my skin to swell and scab and itch in an agonizing succession of bumps. I spent days wrapped in a woolen blanket and covered by a linen sheet moistened with sulfur-brewed tepid water. My dreams were of soaring mountains, of fresh white snows, of climbing up and up, holding my father's firm hand. The Darjeeling of my febrile imaginings was a wonderland of jewel-tipped peaks, sugary frosts, peppermint winds, and nubile young girls being poked like melons by men searching for wives. When the fever broke and my worst complaint was the infernal itch, I was bound in a sheet lined with rice flour so I could not scratch. From a tray at my bedside I was dosed with an array of vile-tasting concoctions, including belladonna for headaches and aconitum for the fever. As I endured the cosmoline-lotion soaks and saffron-tea infusions, I berated myself for my lack of compassion for Mozelle's prickly-heat attacks. After the scabs began to form, then fall away, I was horrified to find the little pits that were left behind. Immediately my grandmother began giving me masks of mercurial plaster to avoid permanent pockmarks.

Grandmother Flora set amulets beside the pillows of the healthy children, but just when everyone thought they would be spared, Ruby came down with a horrid case. Pustules formed in her throat, around her eyes—which swelled shut—and spread over every inch of her chubby body. So sick was she that Dr. Hyam sent for Grandmother Helene, who tended her grandchild herself through two long nights of tantrums.

"At least I was quiet," I bragged to Yali.

"You take after your mother; she takes after hers" was Yali's reply.

At the end of two weeks, Ruby's fevers and spots receded. In the meantime, Dr. Hyam checked Jonah and Asher daily. Pale and skinny Jonah, whose nose ran continuously and whose tummy was the most sensitive in the family, was in high spirits and looked as though he was healthier than ever. "Maybe they will skip this bout," the doctor said as he left on Monday morning. "If the boys are clear on Thursday, you may leave."

Thursday morning Asher blossomed. Jonah frolicked during his brother's illness, not succumbing himself until three more weeks had passed. By then we had missed almost the entire season in Darjeeling, but we sent word to Papa that we would soon be on our way. Father posted a letter with a separate card addressed to me: "Dearest Dinah, do not depart. Give this letter to your grandmother and tell her to await our return to Calcutta. Your loving father."

Our return? I had expected it!

I knew what had happened when my father breathed the thin air of the high hills.

He had gone to the marketplace and had found himself another wife.

❀ ❀ ❀

"She's black!" Nani gasped as she and I watched my father's arrival. I had been ready to rush out to meet the gharry, but she held me back.

"No, Nani, that must be the ayah."

"Look," she hissed, "there is but one woman in the carriage. Anyway, what ayah rides next to the man of the house, eh? An ayah would be sitting on the seat with the children."

Any last hope crumbled as Father assisted the lady down with a tender maneuver. My stomach churned queerly. They paused together and took in the house, their eyes locked on the roof peak, then lowering—in unison—to include my grandmother and me. My father wore a gray suit. She was wearing a pale blue sari with a darker blue border shot with silver threads. Side by side they were the same height, both slender, with straight backs. They could have been brother and sister—if the woman's skin was not the caramel hue of the typical Indian. Gracefully she took his arm, and at the signal of her touch, he steered her toward us.

"Flora"—his face was impassive—"Dinah"—his mouth twitched—"I would like you to meet my wife, Zilpah."

"Zilpah?" Nani's breathing came in small staccato bursts.

"Zilpah Kehimkar Tassie Sassoon," said my father, as though he were making a point.

Unable to speak further, Nani merely nodded. I myself was unable to tolerate the sight of either of them and turned to watch the driver lift two boys out of the carriage. Their skin was a honey color—more like that of a Baghdadi Jew who had been too long in the sun.

My father beamed at the boys, waving them forward. Reluctantly they came and stood by their mother. "These are Zilpah's sons, Pinhas and Simon Tassie. Pinhas is almost the same age as Jonah, Simon as Asher."

A cart drew up, filled with dozens of trunks and cases. "Shall we go in?" Father asked as he guided his newest wife ahead of my grandmother, ahead of me. Even the skinny boys were over the threshold before I was.

Zilpah had not said a word. She glided in my father's wake through the downstairs rooms. Nani disappeared, while I moved in their shadow, trembling as though I had taken a chill as he pointed out the features of the mansion. ". . . I've had the gardens redone . . ." he droned on, crediting Grandmother Helene's designs as his own. From the glacial expression on the woman's face, I could not tell if she was impressed with her new surroundings or merely bored by them. We ended up in the hall.

"Bearer!" Papa called. "Brandy and soda, *burra peg*," he said, ordering a large shot. Then he leaned close to the woman's face. "Something for you, my dear?"

Her head tilted slightly, as though she was deferring to him.

"A *chota peg,* a little something to welcome you to your new home?" he coaxed.

Her black eyes glinted up at him as though he had offered her a jewel. I waited for him to ask what I might like, but he ignored me. When Abdul served them, my father saluted the woman. She raised her glass to his, all the while staring at him so raptly it seemed as though she feared that if she blinked, he might disappear.

I attempted to break this trance. "Papa . . ." My voice choked.

He turned. "Dinah!"

The warmth in his voice thrilled me, and I approached hopefully.

"Why don't you take your new brothers to meet the rest of our little family?"

Having not seen him in almost two months, I did not want to leave yet. "But . . ." I looked for a reprieve. He did not waver and the woman's eyes were filled with a determination that unhinged me. I fled from the room, not even looking back to see if the children were at my heels.

I found my grandmother prostrate in the nursery. Selima was bathing her face with wet cloths.

"Nani, have you taken ill?"

"No, no, Dinah-baba, don't worry yourself," Yali muttered.

Seeing the horrified expression on my face, Nani pushed herself upright. "Zilpah Tassie. I should have known. I should have remembered!"

"Why, Nani, is there something wrong with her?"

My grandmother started to speak, then stopped herself. She took the glass of coconut water Yali was holding and gulped it down.

"I hate her already!"

"No, no—don't talk like that—hush!" Nani gasped between each phrase.

I thought I had the answer to this new puzzle. Since the circumstances surrounding my mother's murder, I had kept my ears open to the secrets that adults barely concealed. To know that other people had strayed made my own mother's disgraces seem less horrifying. Why, even my father was imperfect. Hadn't I seen him in bed with an Indian lady in Patna? That was what this was! No wonder she was silent around my father. No wonder she made no comments on the house. Papa had not married this dark woman. And if he hadn't, she was not my mother. If she was not really my mother, she could not tell me what to do.

The tingling down my spine decreased. "Don't worry, Nani," I said brightly, "they are not really married."

"Pu!" She spat. "You heard your father. He said she was Zilpah Kehimkar Tassie"—she gagged on the last syllables—"Sassoon."

"Oh." I blanched. "What kind of a name is 'Zilpah' or 'Kehimkar'?" I bit my lip. "She's not Jewish!"

My grandmother shook her head. "I would agree, but some would not."

"Why?"

"She calls herself a Jew, but *we* know that the Bene Israel are impostors."

"I don't understand . . ."

Nani smoothed her dress. "After I see to the other children, I will try to explain."

Once she had satisfied herself the nursery tea was proceeding under the ayahs' jurisdiction, Grandmother Flora had our tray set up on a low table in the far corner of the room. Before she could begin, though, I blurted, "What does Bene Israel mean?"

"Supposedly 'Children of Israel.' " She twirled a spoon in her fingers, then dropped it with a clatter. "They only claim to be Jewish. There is no proof they are."

I bit into the buttery bread to keep her talking.

"These people tell a tale that has never been proved, something about Galilean Jews who came to India via Egypt. They contend a group of traders was shipwrecked off the western coast of India. They claim most of the travelers, and their possessions—including their Scrolls of the Law—were lost at sea. The seven men and seven women who survived came ashore south of Bombay, where they settled and began to press oil, a task they had done in Galilee."

"How long ago was this?"

Nani pursed her lips in scorn. "Supposedly before the Maccabean War and the rededication of the Temple. That's why they did not even know about the feast of Chanukah—something they only learned about from a Portuguese Jew from Cochin who tried to teach them something of their own faith."

I did some quick calculations. "Why, that's more than two thousand years ago. Maybe they aren't really Jews. Maybe they just think they are. She looks like any Indian lady to me."

"Exactly." Nani's tone was triumphant.

Suddenly the butter tasted rancid in my mouth, and several sips of sweet tea did not purge the acrid flavor. Had my father married an Indian by mistake?

"She must have been the wife of Jacob Tassie," Nani said, musing.

"There's a Deborah Tassie at school."

"The same family."

"She is not dark-skinned."

"No, they are also Baghdadis. I had almost forgotten about Jacob Tassie. I can assure you *his* mother kept the situation as quiet as possible. Jacob was an odd one from the beginning, always in some sort of trouble. Nobody was surprised he came to a bad end."

"What do you mean?"

"He went up to Darjeeling and met Miss Kehimkar there. We had heard that her father was a military man who had been killed in a skirmish with some hill tribes, leaving her mother a small house, which she opened to Jewish boarders. Jacob Tassie visited there, then stayed on to help turn it into an even larger guest house, which became very popular with the younger set and perfect for Jacob, I suppose, since he enjoyed drinking with his guests. They had some children"—her chin nodded toward Pinhas and Simon, guzzling their tea—"then one day he dropped dead in the street. Some say his heart failed; others said he was wasted from the drink." Nani grimaced. "At least he had the decency to keep her up in the hills and not try to make her the mistress of a house in Calcutta."

For a long while I thought about my abruptly changed status and the confusion my father had poured upon me. Ever since my mother's murder, we had lived on the fringes of the Calcutta Jewish community, hardly welcomed by even my father's own family. Now he had brought a new curse upon our heads, one my new friends would surely learn about. I squeezed my eyes shut. I hoped when I opened them I would find I was only dreaming.

Any chance of this was dashed when my father filled the doorway of the day nursery.

"My family," he said, waving his hand as though he was introducing us to an audience. I followed his proud gaze to where the four little boys sat tossing grapes at one another. Selima was holding a sleepy Ruby on her lap nearby. "Do you think we will need another ayah?" he asked the woman who pressed against his side.

She spoke in a voice that was so different from what I expected, it shattered me further. "Benu, my darling, six are hardly more than four," she said in a register almost as deep as a man's. "At least not when you have an almost grown girl who should serve her brothers and sisters, and four boys who will eat and sleep together."

"And what do you think, Flora?" Papa asked respectfully.

Nani stood up slowly, avoiding my plaintive gaze. Making her way to the door, she spoke so close to my father's ear I could barely hear. "I think I shall not be needed in this house much longer."

The woman in the sari stepped aside to let her pass.

※　※　※

"Don't leave us!" I begged Nani. "Besides, where will you go?"

"I have a home in Lower Chitpur Road."

"I thought it belonged to Dr. Hyam now." The doctor had married the previous year and had an infant son.

"I may stay there as long as I like."

"What about us?"

"Zilpah can manage on her own."

"You are leaving because you hate her too."

"I most certainly do not, and neither do you. What you dislike are the changes. Children are like plants—they can weather any amount of sun or rain or drought as long as the seasons are consistent. One day of downpour, another of broiling heat, can kill the most hardy shoot."

I pouted. "I'm not a child."

"That is another point. Your new mother is expecting you to be helpful to her and the other children."

I shrank from my attack position. "What should I do? She's ruining everything."

"Talk to her, tell her how you feel," Grandmother Flora offered weakly. "I cannot interfere."

As soon as Nani moved out, the alterations began. I never heard Zilpah voice an opinion or give an order out loud. By some subtle influence, the woman was manipulating my father and the servants to reorganize the systems, rearrange the furniture, turn our schedules upside-down. She floated about the house in one of her gossamer saris, surveying everything with a feline's smug expression. Since Nani had understood that we were happiest in a house designed for active children rather than sedentary adults, much of Grandmother Helene's jumble had remained. The very first week, Zilpah realigned the chairs in the hall into conversational groups, eliminating the large spaces for running and playing tag. Dinners became formal, with only one main course. The buffets of tasty treats, a remainder from Grandmother Helene's time, were banished.

"A waste of food," Zilpah declared, although anything the family did not consume went to the servants.

Even worse were her ideas about redoing the upstairs rooms. The bedroom where my mother had died was to be the boys' nursery. Mozelle's furnishings were removed at once. My father's dressing room, which had been enlarged to dispose of my mother's room after her death, was to be the new day nursery. My room was given over to Ruby, supposedly so she could have an ayah sleep with her, who also would tend the boys at night. Next came the second-best bath, which was reoutfitted for my father and his wife. The nursery bedrooms, although small, had the most beautiful vistas on the gardens, so they were combined into a new master suite. The guest bedroom became a small office and dressing area for my father. All that remained was a small room that had been used by servants and later for storage. This was to be mine. I was furious at being relegated to this far end of the house.

Never had I felt so alone. The four boys intermingled without difficulty. Jonah, the most daring and most likable, became their leader. Asher, a sweet boy who wanted to please everyone, refereed disagreements. Volatile Pinhas Tassie created the most disturbances, but his brother, Simon, wasn't a bad sort once away from Pinhas' conniving influence. I always felt odd-one-out, and the change in rooms did not help matters.

I told my father how I felt, which was a mistake, since he brought his wife in and asked me to repeat everything in front of her. I hung my head, but did not speak.

"Well, Dinah? Anything you can say to me you can say to Zilpah, especially anything about the house."

Summoning my courage, I explained my feelings. "I don't want to be so far from everyone. I am lonely—and sometimes frightened."

Zilpah pretended to listen, her mouth pursing and unpursing like a fish's. The rest of her face was immobile. Even her eyes hardly moved. With her usual economy of words she replied, "That is understandable. I will consider your concerns."

The next afternoon I came home from school to find Ruby's bed moved in with mine.

"The memsahib requires a dressing area," Yali explained nervously, "because when she is unwell, she needs a place to lie down so she will not disturb your father."

"I don't want to sleep with Ruby. She still cries out at night!"

"I will sleep by her bed so she will not wake you."

"I don't want to sleep with the baby!" Ruby was three, but barely spoke, and she did not toilet herself.

With my grandmother gone there was nobody who would stand up for me. Even after so short a time I knew it was useless to ask my father to support me against Zilpah.

That night I came to the dinner table in a grim mood. After the food was passed, I did not lift my fork. Nobody noticed for the longest time. My father wiped his chin and looked over at me. "Are you feeling ill, Dinah?"

I did not reply.

Zilpah waved to a servant, and my plate was removed. "Children must never be forced to eat. In time, the body will send a message of hunger that cannot be ignored."

My father tapped his fingers on the table, then proceeded to discuss a matter that did not concern me.

The next morning I sat at the table in the nursery reading a book that lay across my empty plate when my father stopped in for his usual greeting.

"Is that volume tasty?" he teased.

"Not really," I said without looking up.

He ruffled my hair. I softened in spite of myself and gave him a wide smile. He reached for some toast and offered it to me. I pushed it away. His nostrils flared. "What is this nonsense?"

"I'm not hungry, that's all."

"Fine, then go back to your room. You cannot go to school on an empty stomach."

I passed Zilpah in the corridor, but rushed by without speaking.

"Dinah!" my father called, seeing me ignore his wife. "Did you forget to say good morning to your mother?"

I held my head high. "She is *not* my mother," I shouted before turning and running to my room.

"Dinah, come back this instant!"

"Benu, let me—" was the last I heard before I slammed my door.

There was a pitcher of water in my room and some jelabis I kept in a brass box. Other than that I don't believe I ate anything else for almost three days. Nor did I leave my room. My father stayed away. Ruby slept in her old room. Only Yali stopped by to check on me. "I cannot bring you food. You must come out if you wish to eat. Please do so, Dinah-baba."

"I don't ever want to see either of them again."

"You may have kaka or baba or dol-dol or—"

"No!"

"What is this about? What do you want?"

This stopped me. I could not tell anyone that I hated my room, that I was lonely, that I didn't need another mother—least of all Zilpah—and I yearned for everything to be as it was before her arrival, so I remained silent.

The next morning I was so weak I could not sit up in bed. Dozing off and on, I heard someone enter my room.

Grandmother Flora bent over me. "What is the reason for this ridiculous behavior?" Her voice was harsher than I expected.

I burst into tears. "I want to live with you again."

"You belong in this house with your father."

"You don't want me either."

"Whether I want you or not is beside the point. You live here." Her chiding tone changed to a consoling purr. "You may visit me anytime you like, even after school each day, but this will remain your home."

The firmness in her voice alarmed me. "But I thought you agreed with me, that you—"

"Just because I don't believe Zilpah was born a Jew has nothing to do with this."

"She is against me."

"No, you only think she is."

"Why has she banished me to this closet? Why must I take care of Ruby? Why does she think I should not go to school anymore?"

Grandmother became indignant. "When did she say that?"

"I overheard her telling Papa." Zilpah had not used exactly those words, but she had wondered how long my father intended to humor me.

"I will talk to your father about school, *if* you will take your nourishment." Without waiting for my reply, she signaled Yali to bring in a tray. She fed me broth with a spoon as if I were a baby. I enjoyed her ministerings and wished she would never stop.

☙ ☙ ☙

As to religious observance, Zilpah was the most dutiful mother I ever had. We attended both Friday-night and Saturday-morning services, and she was much more strict about observing the Sabbath and the dietary laws than anyone else had been. Grandmother Flora was not the only person who thought a Bene Israel not as pure a Jew as a Baghdadi. Everyone doubted her Jewishness. Even a convert would have been accepted more readily. Nobody in the women's gallery of the synagogue even acknowledged Zilpah; nevertheless, she knew the prayers, every ritual, the most minute detail about how a holiday should be celebrated. When we were ignored, I felt as though she was an impostor and that I was her accomplice.

Aunt Bellore rejected her with the most vehemence. "Benu, have you lost your senses? How could you, a *Sassoon*, marry a Bene Israel!" she railed the first afternoon she had been introduced to his wife. I had been playing with Jonah on the terrace when Bellore dragged him outside to berate him for his mistake. Even though we were visible, she did not check her venomous tongue. "A nigger! My God, you've married a nigger! How could you do this to our family? To your own children?"

"I must ask you never again to speak that way about the woman who is my wife," Benu replied steadily.

Bellore modulated her tone to match. "Don't you see how unfair you have been to her? She will never be accepted in Calcutta."

"A Sassoon is always accepted."

She heaved an exasperated sigh. "Ever since you were a boy, you had to learn everything the hard way. It has taken all these years for people to begin to forget Luna, and now this . . ." she hissed. Her words became nastier as her volume decreased. "You may ignore the consequences, and your sons may not suffer from having a mother who was a profligate, an addict, an adulteress, but you have tarnished *that* child with every move you have made."

As her head tossed in my direction, I looked away. From where I sat, motionless, I could see my father's neck had turned crimson below his precisely cut hairline. He clenched both hands behind his back. Breathless, I waited for his response. He stared until my aunt slithered away.

A few weeks after my open rebellion was thwarted, I was asked to join my father and his wife after dinner, just the three of us. I would have been flattered if my father had not been so attentive to Zilpah. His eyes never wavered from her as he admired every gesture, every flicker of her long, curling lashes. Apparently he was not put off by her puckering mouth, which continued to unnerve me.

Zilpah offered me the chair right under the punkah. "Sit here, Dinah." She and my father sat on either side of me, observing me, as though I were a mounted specimen.

"How is school, Dinah?" my father inquired solicitously.

"Fine."

"Do your friends know about your new mother?"

"I suppose."

"Do they ask about her?"

I eyed him warily.

"What do you know about the Bene Israel?"

I shook my head.

"My people have a long and fascinating history. If you are questioned, it would be wise for you to have answers." Zilpah sat up taller. The folds of her sari aligned themselves in concentric drapes. Her immaculate hands remained clasped in her lap serenely.

"Don't you agree, Dinah?"

I shrugged.

Smiling, my father leaned back as Zilpah began speaking in that steady, clipped accent that was almost a parody of upper-class English. I decided to ignore her. But then, despite myself, I became intrigued with the tale.

". . . So word of these strange peoples, the members of the caste of Shanwar Telis, was heard far and wide. One day, about eight hundred years ago, a learned teacher came to India from Egypt. His name was David Rahabi. After talking to the people, he suspected the Bene Israel might be a lost colony of Jews. He asked many questions, but received confusing answers, for the group had been without scholars for centuries. Much knowledge was forgotten, but they kept the Sabbath, *kashrut*, circumcision rites, and—most important—they recited *Shema Yisrael* for every occasion. In order to test them, Rahabi brought a basket filled with many types of fish. 'Please cook these for me,' he asked the women of Shanwar Telis. Amazed, he watched as the women separated the fish into two piles: those with scales and fins in one, the remainder in the other. 'Why do you do this?' Rahabi asked. 'We use only fish that have scales and fins,' they replied. This convinced Rahabi to remain among them and to reeducate them about Jewish laws and life."

"Tell Dinah about your family," Papa coached.

"About a hundred years ago, my grandfather met a man who came to our district from Cochin. He became convinced we were authentic Jews. He taught my grandfather—along with several other community leaders—to be a *kaji*, the person who would officiate at services and ceremonies."

I knew this was supposed to impress me, so to keep the peace, I smiled thinly. Unfortunately, this encouraged Zilpah to ramble on about how important her father had been. "My father was a boy recruit in the forces of the British East India Company. Within ten years he was commissioned an officer."

My father's head bobbed enthusiastically. "Zilpah's father saw active service in the Second Sikh War and the Persian campaign. And in the Mutiny, the Bene Israel soldiers remained loyal throughout. Afterward Kehimkar was rewarded with the highest rank open to Indians in the military: subedar major." My father paused and stared at me.

I thought it wise to respond. "How did you end up in Darjeeling?" I asked, spitting out the name of the city with distaste.

"When I was about your age, my father was offered a position in Darjeeling. Unfortunately, that was where he was killed."

"How?" I wondered, this time with a keener curiosity.

My father filled in for her. "A party of murderous *dacoits* ambushed him on their horses."

"What's a dacoit?"

"That's what they called armed robbers, like the thugs, in that region."

"Oh!" I gasped as my sympathies moved in my stepmother's direction for the first time.

"After his death, Zilpah's mother managed a guest house and Zilpah assisted her."

"I thought you went to school."

"I attended one at Poona for a time. Even though you sometimes think I am against your schooling, Dinah, you can see I value education—even for girls."

Bristling at her last phrase, I stood up and formally thanked her for the explanation. Zilpah and my father gave each other self-satisfied smiles. I would not like her! I vowed. Still, when I found myself having to justify the Bene Israel, I passed on Zilpah's tale to friends at school. And though I determined she should not know this, over time I was finding fewer reasons to hate her.

11

For the next three years a truce was declared. Zilpah did not order me about and I did not cross her. When my father traveled—which was for shorter times than previously—we hardly saw each other. I was free to stay with my grandmother as much as I liked.

At fourteen, I was head girl in my class—quite a small class, since many of the girls who entered with me were removed at twelve or thirteen and kept at home to prepare for marriage. A wedding at my age was not uncommon, although I assumed this custom would not apply to me. The four boys attended school as well, the two youngest at the Jewish Boys' School, the two oldest at St. Xavier's. Ruby, who was six, should have joined the first class at my school, but although she was a darling butterball, she showed no readiness to concentrate on paper-and-pencil tasks.

After services on Saturday mornings, I would walk Ruby to her Grandmother Helene's. Though her house on Loudon Street was much smaller than Theatre Road, her guest list had not diminished. Her grandchildren, nieces, and nephews were closer friends to me than my own cousins. I especially liked her niece Masuda Judah, who was one class lower than me at the Jewish Girls' School.

Masuda had an older brother, Gabriel, who had thick reddish curls and emerald eyes. I would find any excuse to be near him. We had known each other for years, but suddenly I felt a tantalizing tingling when he was nearby, and a tremor of loss when we were apart.

Whenever we met at Grandmother Helene's home on holidays, we played *towli*—backgammon—which I usually won, and tommy-dot, at which he had all the luck. Unsure of how he felt about me, I hid my emotions behind a veil of intellectuality. When younger children tried to pester us, I had the idea to thwart them by using a secret language: Latin.

"*Cave, audiunt,*" I warned if they were listening.

"*Abite, molesti!*" we shouted to send them off.

Our private vocabulary was successful at annoying the others. Soon we began to write notes, innocent exercises to show off to each other. If we had passed them only at Grandmother Helene's, or even through Masuda, no harm might have been done. I was the foolish one who became entangled in my own web. And I was the one who paid most dearly for the escapade of the *tiffin-wallahs.*

Tiffin—the colloquial name for luncheon—was always prepared at home, not only in Jewish households where dietary laws were followed, but in almost every Indian household. Before eleven each school day, the tiffin-wallah called at our kitchen, where he received six tiffin-carriers—one for each of the five children at school and one for my father at the Sassoon offices. On the bottom of the five-sectioned tiffin-carrier was a bed of hot coals. The next two layers were perforated to keep the meal hot. The top two layers contained bread and fruit. The cook helped load these on a wide board, which the tiffin-wallah balanced on his head. He made the rounds to various other families until he had more than twenty of the stacking tin containers. Then he went from school to school and to the offices. Around three in the afternoon he reversed his order, picking up our empty tiffin-carriers and returning them to each scullery by the end of the day. I had always been impressed that he could keep the tiffin-carriers organized, since they were of a similar design. Somehow he did, for I never received okra, a vegetable I despised. Jonah always had an extra pack of *popadoms*, the crispy curry biscuit he adored. And only Father was given a helping of *achar*, the fiery pickle that none of us children could tolerate.

The first time I made my own use of the tiffin-wallah was the day I found one of Jonah's school books in my sack. "Tiffin-wallah," I asked sweetly, "do you go next to St. Xavier's?"

"Yes, missy-sahib."

"Could you please give this book to my brother Jonah?" I gave him one rupee along with my request.

The bony Bengali man grinned, revealing his betel-stained gums.

Jonah, who had been very upset that he did not have his spelling book, was delighted with my ingenuity.

A week later I copied out a Latin verse from the *Satires* of Juvenal I thought Gabriel would find amusing:

Si natura negat, facit indignatio versum.
If nature denies the power, indignation would give birth to verses.

"Do you deliver to Gabriel Judah?" I asked the tiffin-wallah.

"Yes, missy-sahib."

"Might I put something in his tiffin-carrier?"

He bent over, and with a free hand he pointed out Gabriel's tiffin-carrier on his board. I slipped my message on top of the bananas and biscuits.

Gabriel's reply, something he discovered in Horace's *Odes*, arrived with the pickup late that afternoon.

Tu ne quaesieris, scire nefas.
Pray, ask not, such knowledge is not for us.

I scurried to see what other nuggets Horace might have written and was thrilled to find amorous tidbits I had never known existed. Somehow I mustered the courage to respond with:

Persicos odi, puer, apparatus,
displicent nexae philyra coronae;
mitte sectari, rosa quo locorum
    sera moretur.

Boy, I detest the Persian style
Of elaboration. Garlands bore me
Laced up with lime-bark. Don't run a mile
To find the last rose of summer for me.

Gabriel's next find in Horace was even more daring:

Quis multa gracilis te puer in rosa
perfusus liquidis urget odoribus
    grato, Pyrrha, sub antro?

What slim youngster, his hair dripping with fragrant oil,
Makes hot love to you now, Pyrrha, ensconced in a
    Snug cave curtained with roses?

Makes hot love to you! The words burned in my mind for days. I could think of nothing else. I could not send back anything so wicked. Just knowing we were perusing the same passages was enough to stir feelings that were terribly new and wonderfully thrilling. How I adored the boy! I started to dream that we would find a way to be together forever and ever.

Gabriel sent me quotations about "Diana, keeper of the sacred hilltops" and I began to understand the meaning of translations like "By all the gods, why are you making him weak at the knees with love?" and "Come now, leave your Mother: you're ready to know a man."

Our game would have lost its amusement if we had not escalated the double entendres and hidden meanings. My gleanings through the steamier passages of Horace, Catullus, and Ovid had the added benefit of increasing my proficiency in Latin to the point that my teacher sent home a commendation for my diligence.

Proudly my father read her note to the entire family, concluding with, "It honors the family when you honor yourself at school." He bowed to me.

Even Zilpah congratulated me with unqualified praise. "Yes, Dinah, keep up the fine work."

Then I discovered the poems of Catullus. Even I did not have the nerve to copy the most titillating passages. "See XXXII and XXXVI" was all I dared.

Gabriel and I had not seen each other since the beginning of this correspondence. When we finally met, at Grandmother Helene's Purim party, he sought me out as soon as he could get away from his mother and sister.

"I am having difficulty with a translation. Would you be so kind as to assist me?"

I looked around furtively. "What seems to be giving you trouble?"

"The first and last lines of number thirty-six."

"It can mean only one thing," I giggled.

"No! It has to be something else."

"Why? Do you think men didn't have the same needs then as they do now?"

"But '*cacata carta*'?" He grimaced.

"Well, I think it means 'toilet paper.' What else could it be?"

Gabriel flushed a violet hue. I was laughing so hard I could not stop.

"What is so funny?" Masuda wondered when she saw us. "Tell me . . ." she begged.

"My Aunt Bellore . . ." I improvised quickly. "Isn't her dress hideous?"

"Yes," Masuda agreed, and joined in the laughter.

Relieved, Gabriel rushed off to be with the other boys.

"You like my brother, don't you?" Masuda asked after he had gone.

I shrugged. "He's nice."

"He likes you," she said with a conspiratorial smile.

"He just likes to beat me at games."

"You win at least half the time." She became more somber. "My mother thinks that is for the best. She believes a girl should be a boy's equal."

What was Masuda hinting? Were our parents considering a match? I wanted to ask more, but there were too many people nearby.

Just when I began to hope our parents might speak to each other, the tiffin-wallah slipped up. How did it happen? Did my meddling with his system cause him to deliver the wrong tiffin-carrier to the wrong person, or did I inadvertently move Gabriel's tiffin-carrier to the position on the board reserved for Pinhas Tassie's? Whatever the reason, it could not have fallen into worse hands.

Pinhas Tassie was as tall as I was, lean but surprisingly weak. Clothing, no matter how well-tailored, hung on him in awkward drapes. His feet were huge, as large as my father's, and he tripped often, walked into walls—in short, he was the clumsiest young person I had ever met. In sports, he invariably came in last or fell on his face. I suppose I laughed at him—we all did—but I do not think that was what formed the kernel of his resentment. There was something else, something about his character which distrusted me as much as I distrusted him. His cheeks were sunken and his heavy-lidded eyes seemed to be able to look two directions at once. Silent much of the time, he seemed to be observing everyone rather than participating. Just as his mother rarely responded to a situation, preferring to take action out of our sight, often days or weeks after the occurrence, I sensed that Pinhas toted up his score of inequities and slights, spilling them to his mother when they were alone. He had reason to be wary of me. I hardly had welcomed his mother into our household. My fasting, my coldness, my loyalty to my grandmother, had created rifts that had never healed. While I thought I treated Zilpah respectfully, my sullenness in her presence could have been interpreted differently, especially by her devoted son.

Most of the time Pinhas and I had the good sense to avoid each other. My brother Jonah was not so fortunate. Because the boys were almost the same age, it was expected they would do everything together, from sharing a rickshaw on the way to school, to studying, to sleeping side by side. Asher was a gregarious child who preferred to go along with a group's decision rather than invoke conflict by insisting on his own way, and thankfully for family harmony, Simon Tassie was almost as tractable as Asher. However, Jonah, who was accustomed to being first among the boys, resented Pinhas' interference. They frequently exchanged blows, with Pinhas receiving more than his share of the wounds. I always sided with my brother, which caused a further wedge between the two factions of the family, so it was my bad luck to have the most saucy of my tiffin notes fall directly into Pinhas' conniving hands. Even then, as I look back, I don't know how I could have risked writing:

Quem nunc amabis? Cuius esse diceris?
Quem basiabis? Cui labella mordebis?
Et tu, Catulle, destinatus obdura.

Where's the man that you love and who will
   call you his,
and when you fall to kissing, whose lips will
   you devour?
But always, your Catullus will be as firm
   as rock is.

When the tiffin-wallah did not deliver a reply that afternoon, I was unconcerned. I had searched for several hours before settling on this gem, and I expected it would take Gabriel a while before he located anything as audacious.

On Saturday I saw Gabriel for a few minutes outside the synagogue. "What did you think?" I asked, smirking.

"About what?"

"Gabriel . . ." I tilted my head playfully. "You know what I mean . . ."

He was perplexed. "What?"

We had so little time alone, I was becoming impatient. "You know . . ."

Shaking his head, he said, "Why haven't you answered me since last week? Didn't you like the one I sent you on Monday?"

"I wrote to you Wednesday!"

"I did not receive anything."

The back of my neck began to prickle with fear. "Weren't you in school?"

"I haven't missed a day this term. Don't tell me that ignorant tiffin-wallah put it in the wrong carrier?"

"I always place it on the top myself!"

"They look alike." Gabriel's voice rose in pitch. "Could you have put it in the wrong one?"

"Somebody else must have . . ." I gasped.

"Was it a mild one?"

"Not a good choice," I groaned.

"Don't worry. I never sign my name. Neither do you."

"Good, then nobody will know who wrote it or where it was destined," I nodded hopefully.

Gabriel was still agitated. "We eat in the courtyard. If somebody opened his tiffin-carrier and found a note, most likely he would have held it aloft and asked for its owner, especially if he knew any Latin."

"Somebody is keeping this a secret, maybe a friend of yours." I didn't sound optimistic.

"What if someone showed it to one of the teachers?"

"We would have heard by now. There would have been some sort of inquiry."

Pinhas strolled by and we naturally stopped talking. "What sort of inquiry? A Latin query?" he punned boldly. The smug expression on his face made me feel faint.

Gabriel saw my knees buckle. I would have fallen backward on the stone walk if he had not lunged for me, one hand clasping my shoulder, the other my waist. The sudden movement brought me upright, then flopped me against him. For a second or two I leaned on him, my head next to his, his arms supporting me. At that moment Zilpah came around the corner, holding Ruby's hand.

ꙍ ꙍ ꙍ

"This game must stop at once." Zilpah was not shouting. Her voice was soft, calm, controlled, but vehemence penetrated every syllable.

I faced her squarely. The two of us stood in the room my grandmother had once occupied, which now was a downstairs sitting room Zilpah used for working on the household accounts.

"A harmless exercise," I offered weakly.

"Harmless?" Her voice lowered an octave. The tight ball of black hair at the back of her neck seemed to pull her mouth into an obstinate line. The muscles in her gooselike neck lengthened until she towered over me. "Have you forgotten your position?"

"Nobody knows about it, except you . . . and Pinhas."

"You are fortunate somebody less discreet than my son did not find this." She waved the note in front of my face.

"Only a sneak like Pinhas would have shown it to you and told you what it meant."

Her nostrils flared. "For someone who is supposed to be a very intelligent girl, you are incredibly forgetful. Of course, we prefer to push past unpleasantness aside. Since I have come to the house, I have tried to establish order, peacefulness. I have been successful, at least with the younger ones and with your father." She paused. "I would think, for his sake alone, you would have wished to spare him anxiety by doing your duty at home, as well as in school. Frankly, I think it is possible the influence of your education has not been a healthy one. While I believe that girls must learn to read, do sums, to be educated so they can assume their proper roles in the Jewish community, after a point there is often a negative effect. I warned Benu that something like this might happen."

I felt close to despair. Zilpah was going to ruin everything. "What do you mean?"

"A girl who goes off to a fancy school every day is duped into believing she will go out into the world every day. At your age you should be home preparing for marriage. I have told this to your father, but since you have dazzled him with your good reports, he has taken your side."

I quaked under her scrutiny, but remained silent.

"Considering the past, considering what you—what you both—have suffered, I have acceded to him. Now he will see the wisdom of my words. I am only sorry it took so drastic an incident for his blinders to be removed."

"Are you saying I cannot finish school?"

"When a girl begins to behave as you have, the dangers are everywhere, especially a girl with your background. We can no longer trust you. We must watch you more closely or your reputation will be ruined."

"What do you mean, 'a girl with my background'? What's wrong with my background? *You* are the one everybody talks about. If they think badly of me, it is because my father married so low. The name Sassoon will never whiten your skin or give you a Jewish birthright!"

Zilpah did not seem to be provoked further. If anything, she was more quiescent. "Must I say it again? Must I speak even more plainly?"

"Yes, please do. I'm tired of your silences. You and Pinhas are alike. He tells you everything. You tattle to my father."

"All right, then." She stood and began to pace in front of me, the swish of her sari on the bare floor punctuating her words. "The time is coming, Dinah, when you must marry. This year would not be too early. I was betrothed before I was fifteen. Many of your friends will be married within the next few months."

She reached the end of the long, narrow room, spun around, and marched back, directly facing me. As she turned, the silk hem whooshed like a spill of water. "One of the reasons for having young girls marry is to protect them from themselves. No good family wants a girl who has any questionable character traits or who is thought to have compromised herself with a young man. Your indecent notes to Gabriel, your unseemly conduct at the synagogue, constitute the sort of behavior that give a girl a bad reputation and ruin her chances. Fortunately, nothing has come of this—yet."

Again she reached the boundary of the room. As she curved back, the sound—like a dragon's foul breath—warned she was coming closer. "Keeping you at home is the most prudent course. This will prove you have conscientious parents. Then, as quickly as possible, we will find you a suitable match. At least your dowry will be so extravagant you will have your pick, or at least that is what your father claims. Then there are other concerns . . ." I could see her deciding whether to check her tongue. My surly expression decided for her. "We still do not know if anyone will have you, no matter the dowry."

I froze, incapable of speech. A terrible unnamed feeling set my heart to beating wildly. On the far side of the room, Zilpah waited more than a minute before waving me to sit on a hassock. As she slid into the wing chair, her iridescent green sari draped into an obedient puddle at her feet. "You are the daughter of a woman who brought other men into this house while her husband was away. You are the daughter of a woman who could not control her need for opium. You are the daughter of a woman who neglected her family duties. You are the daughter of a woman of loose morals who was murdered in her bed by a jealous lover. Nobody has forgotten this. In this society, children are the products of their parents. Luckily, your father has an estimable reputation, so a case for you might be made, but only if no other taint touches you."

I felt as though a knife was being twisted between my shoulder blades. A sickness welled up inside me, causing me to bend over. Zilpah must have noticed my distress, but she pressed on. "Your beloved Baghdadi Jews are a superstitious clan. You and I know there is nothing wrong with walking under a tree after dusk—the spirits won't find us. You and I know cats and dogs are not going to bring demons into the house. You and I know this nonsense about the evil eye is ridiculous. But others do not. Even if they are not really believers, they see less harm in following the old ways than in the consequences that could befall them if they failed to do so. Do you understand me, Dinah?"

I lifted my head, but did not meet her gaze.

"Among these same ignorant people are the mothers of the men you might marry. They cannot forget you are the child who was carried out of her mother's bedroom bathed in her traitorous blood. They hold you no grudge. Indeed, they pity you, Dinah. But they do not want you to marry their precious sons. If I have been harsh to you in the past, if I am being harsh to you now, it is only to protect you, to keep you above suspicion to avoid any problems that might arise as your father and I attempt to secure your future."

At first I was furious she had dared to speak to me so forcefully, but then a fresh feeling welled up and diffused my anger. I was grateful for the clarity of my position. I saw what I now must do. I knew to whom I must speak. There was nothing more to say to her. Besides, I would not give her the satisfaction of knowing she had, in the queerest sense, done me a favor.

A *chick-chick*, a mosquito-eating lizard, skittered between us. I lifted it in my lap and stroked its knobby spine. It froze under my touch. I waited. I knew Zilpah was repulsed by the creatures. Eventually, I am not certain when, Zilpah left me alone. The chick-chick's tail twitched, its eyes caught the afternoon sun and glowed as if it too were on fire from the inside out.

12

❦ ❦ ❦

Your mother's speech may have been unnecessarily abrasive, but I cannot disagree with her," Nani said in a breathless voice I had not heard before.

I was stunned. Where were the words of consolation I had sought?

I concentrated on the banyan tree that curtained the Lower Chitpur Road courtyard in an embrace of shade. Once monstrous to me, the tree seemed diminished in size. Nani also appeared to have shrunk. So many things had changed. Dr. Hyam and his wife now lived here. My grandmother was more a boarder than the lady of the house. She would have been more comfortable at Theatre Road—that is, if Zilpah had not been in command. To have her defend the woman who had made it impossible for her to keep her place was a travesty.

I mustered my energies for the attack. "She is not my mother!"

Nani's expression—eyes rolling back, a snap of her head—was a rebuke meaning: Don't I know that better than you?

My expectation of a miracle crumbled. The indignation in my face dissolved. Unlike Zilpah, I knew my grandmother took no pleasure in my misery.

"How old are you now? Fourteen, isn't it?"

I nodded.

"My mother was married at thirteen. I was also married at thirteen, the first time."

"First time?"

"You may not have known your grandfather was my second husband. A few days after the marriage my groom took to his bed, and died within three months. I didn't marry again for sixteen more years. Why? Because of our superstitions. His family thought I had brought the evil eye to our union, which was nonsense. He was a weakling from the start. His parents thought marriage would strengthen him,

125

make him more of a man." She pounded her bony fist on the arm of the chair. "Afterward, I lived in his parents' house almost as their slave, which is why they were not interested in seeing me married again, and my first dowry had been so generous my family could afford nothing more."

"How could they—?"

She waved her hand to stifle my question. "That was a long time ago. Your mother—" She caught herself and began again. "Zilpah is only protecting your interests. If she spoke too plainly, it was because she believed that was the only way to reach you. You have not been easy to talk to, have you?"

"I suppose not."

"Marriage offers advantages." Nani gave me a few seconds to think about this. "You leave the house of your father and move into the house of your husband's family, or, if you are fortunate, one of your own. In your case, either might be welcome." She stared, her light blue eyes glinting. "You will have so generous a dowry you might be able to build a house, although maybe not one as grand as Theatre Road. And—"

"And maybe you could live with me!" I filled in.

She closed her eyes. "That is a lovely, if impractical, idea."

"Why?"

"The Hyams take excellent care of me."

"But—"

"Hush. I'm an old woman with few years left. Let's talk about your future."

"I do not want to marry."

"Never?"

"Not so soon."

"When might it suit you?"

"Two years from now I will be in the first graduating class of the Jewish Girls' School."

"It is that important to you?"

"Yes."

As she rubbed her chin thoughtfully, a breeze blew across the courtyard, scattering leaves. "The monsoon is early this year. It will rain all night." She sucked in a long breath. "What else haven't you told me?"

"About the Latin notes?"

She shooed my question away as the wind ruffled her long skirt, billowing up to reveal ankles that seemed too fragile to support her frame. "What are you afraid of?"

"Nothing." My hair blew into my eyes, stinging them.

She leaned close and smoothed my hair back. "You are afraid. Most girls are afraid of men; why shouldn't you be? After all, a man killed your mother."

"Why does everyone keep reminding me? It was a long time ago and she was different from me."

"A man killed Mozelle."

"Mozelle?" My voice sounded tinny, distant, as though I was not actually there.

"If she had not had a baby . . ." My grandmother's hand on my cheek was my only link with stability. "Stand up." I did not comprehend what she wanted. "Stand!" With surprising strength she pulled me to my feet. "Look, already you are taller than me, much taller than your mother when she was fully grown." She placed her thin hand on top of mine. "Your bones are more like a man's." She encircled my waist before moving her fingers down to rest on my hips. "You could safely have a baby tomorrow."

"I don't want a baby." I thought about Zilpah, who was expecting a child in less than a month. Unlike Mozelle, the pregnancy had hardly affected her. She was so tall the baby rode invisibly under her loose sari, not announcing her condition until the past few weeks. Even now she kept up with her duties, proving she could have a baby with little fuss.

"Eventually you might." Nani took my hand and led me into the house, where tea was laid out in the drawing room. Mordecai Hyam and his wife, Farha, were already seated.

I answered their initial questions about school and family; then, while Dr. Hyam started to tell Grandmother Flora about a recent case, I thought over my position. Marriage had never been a concern of mine until my gruesome interview with Zilpah. I was beginning to see that if I did not participate in the plans for my future, the adults would settle the issue between themselves. Not that a girl could choose the boy. Only a rare few like my mother and father had ever done so. And they were poor examples.

While I sipped my tea, I contemplated the possibilities. Gabriel Judah headed the list. More than ever I admired his pink, round face and his well-formed lips and especially his light hair, which most other Baghdadi Jews prized as well. I adored being with him, although since the tiffin-carrier escapade both sets of parents had made a point to keep us apart. We only glimpsed each other at the synagogue. I expected he would make me a good companion for life because he was more intellectual than most boys, but not so serious that he could not find jokes in Horace and Catullus. Thinking about how we had been embarrassed by the notes, I winced. I hoped the adults eventually would forget about it. Aunt Bellore was having a garden party in a few weeks. Surely Gabriel would be there, and we might be able to have a few words privately. Anticipating that day, I repressed a smile.

"Is something wrong with that pastry?" Farha Hyam asked when she saw the odd expression on my face.

"Oh, no," I stammered. "Just a sensitive tooth."

Reaching over, she poured cooler water into my cup and told me to drink it slowly. I went along with the charade, nodding that I felt better; then I went back to my musings of Gabriel. He was the first son from a jute-trading family that was not as prominent as the Sassoons, yet respectable. Zilpah and my father could hardly object.

An ayah was at the door. Farha Hyam waved her in and lifted her sleeping baby boy into her lap. As she stared at her infant with undisguised admiration, I thought about my grandmother's discussion, imagining myself in Mrs. Hyam's place. She was nineteen, just five years older than I was. Short, heavyset, Mordecai Hyam wore glasses and was already balding, even though he was only in his thirties. He had been too busy—first with his studies, later with my grandfather's practice—to marry sooner. I stared at Dr. Hyam, who always had been so concerned about me, and wondered what it might be like to be married to him. With some astonishment, I decided the idea did not repel me.

Soon the bearer announced the gharry had come to collect me. I stood to say good-bye to the Hyams. On my way past, I patted the baby's bald head.

Grandmother Flora struggled to her feet and followed me to the door. "Try to avoid upsetting Zilpah as her time nears. After the child arrives, I will speak to your father on your behalf, asking him to put off making a match until after you have completed your schooling."

Gratitude bubbled in my voice. "Oh, would you, Nani?"

Her voice lowered. "Remember, a betrothal might be arranged sooner. Only the wedding date would be delayed."

Feeling as though I had been rescued from an abyss, I kissed her forehead.

"Go, go home. This new baby will absorb them for at least half a year. Finding a partner will take twice that, the negotiations another six to nine months. There's plenty of time," she muttered as she pushed me out the door.

☙ ☙ ☙

Seti Sassoon was born while I was at school. The morning I left, there was no indication that Zilpah was feeling unwell. When I returned, Yali showed me to the nursery, where the honey-skinned infant rested peacefully. That a child could arrive with so little commotion was a revelation that perplexed me.

As Grandmother Flora had predicted, the baby turned Zilpah's attentions elsewhere. My father went to China for more than six months and I enjoyed whatever freedoms I was allowed, but since the disastrous tiffin note incident, I was circumspect, especially around young men.

For the next several years I immersed myself in my studies to the exclusion of everything else. When I wanted unconditional love, I visited Grandmother Flora. When I wanted a house filled with people and confusion, I went to Grandmother Helene. I kept my part of the bargain by behaving myself, so Zilpah had few complaints. Fortunately, there were no further mentions of marriage prospects, so I was content.

One afternoon shortly after my seventeenth birthday, Zilpah made an unusual request. "Dinah, would you accompany me on a walk in the Maidan?" She looked at me with her candid black eyes that offered me no chance of refusal.

I kept up with her fast pace down Theatre Road, along Queens Way, to the edge of the racecourse. When we arrived at the broad gravel lane—for some reason called Secretary's Walk—she slowed. Perspiration had formed a glassy patina on her face.

"Shall we sit?" I offered.

"No, no." She kept walking with a determined stride. "I did not want you to hear this news from somebody at school," she said without missing a step. I was curious, but not alarmed. "Your Aunt Bellore has kept me apprised of the negotiations. I promised not to say anything until they were final; she agreed not to make an announcement until you had been informed." She halted so quickly, the stones crunched under her heels. She spun to face me. With a sudden tender gesture she touched my shoulder. "Your Cousin Sultana is betrothed to Gabriel Judah."

I closed my eyes and exhaled loudly. Gabriel? No! How could he? And to scrawny little Sultana, who, even though she was nine months younger than I was, had hardly developed. He, by contrast, had become more attractive than ever. The sun had tinged his hair with bronze streaks, his brows and lashes had darkened, and his face had taken on a handsome definition. Even though I was almost his height, my figure was slim, and I thought that most boys would have agreed I was more alluring—and unquestionably brighter—than Sultana. How could Gabriel accept this situation? He abhorred girls as illogical and shallow as my cousin. In the years since our flirtatious correspondence, our friendship had deepened. I had always been led to expect we would be considered for each other, and now he was snapped up before I was ready, by my greedy aunt for her puny, mediocre daughter.

"But how—I thought—" I sputtered.

"Don't you think your father made inquiries there first?"

"Weren't they interested?"

Zilpah shook her head sadly.

"Why?" I watched her mouth twitch as she deliberated her reply. "What did they say?" I begged.

"Mrs. Judah said, 'We would not consider Dinah if she were the last Jewish girl in Calcutta.' "

"The dowry, wasn't it sufficient?"

"Sufficient for a maharajah's daughter, I would think." She took my arm and led me along much more slowly than before.

"You are thinking how stupid I was to object to an early marriage, aren't you?" I choked.

"No, in this case it would not have made a difference."

"Aunt Bellore would never have considered Gabriel Judah—his family is far beneath hers—if it hadn't been for the rumors about us. It is only because she thinks she is taking something from me that she has agreed."

"Dinah, Gabriel Judah is not the last fish in the sea."

"When will the wedding be?"

"In three months. Your aunt wants a very big show for her first daughter." Tears sparkled in her eyes as she turned for home. "I cannot tell you how sorry I am."

\\/   \\/   \\/

I did not yet realize the seriousness of my predicament. I wept for weeks, not just for Gabriel, but at the terrible truth of Aunt Bellore's perfidy. In the end, the bitter gall at losing him to Sultana was dissipated by Gabriel himself. A few days after the engagement was announced, his sister, Masuda, brought me a letter from him.

"Gabriel was going to tell you the news himself, but our mother wouldn't let him," she said sullenly. "I wanted you for a sister, not her!"

"We will still be friends, and now you will be part of the family," I said with more civility than I felt.

As soon as I was alone I read Gabriel's quotations from Horace:

Delicta maiorum immeritus lues.

For the sins of your sires, albeit you had no hand in them, you must suffer.

His message made me feel vindicated. I wished him well and wanted him to know this. Masuda was more than willing to give him my reply, a gem I found in Virgil's *Eclogue*:

Non equidem invideo, miror magis.
As for me I grudge thee not—rather I marvel!

This should have been the end of our private communication, but to my surprise, I found one last missive tucked under my door the morning of his marriage. Catullus was to have the last word:

Sed mulier cupido quod dicit amanti,
In vento et rapida scribere oportet aqua.
What a woman says to her ardent lover
ought to be written in wind and running water.

As Gabriel, flanked by his parents, made his way toward the *huppah* to consecrate his union, he caught my eye. With the slightest of gestures I acknowledged him, thrilled to be reminded I had been his first choice.

I was able to hold my head high through the agonizingly long festivities until late in the day. I remained on the outskirts of the circle of Sultana's friends, thinking if she did not see me, she could not gloat. All the same, I heard exclamations as Sultana showed off her wedding band and the solitary diamond at her throat that had been a gift from Gabriel's family. Then she held up her arm, and I caught sight of a double strand of pearls which formed a bracelet.

"Oh, that's lovely," Masuda murmured.

"My mother saved it for my wedding day," Sultana gushed.

I tried to get closer for a better look, but Sultana moved on to another group. My head began to pound. I was seething with curiosity about the bracelet's origin, for something in that flash of a wrist had triggered a memory.

❦ ❦ ❦

My last year at school was fairly dull. As the eldest student, I taught more than I studied. I began looking forward to the school's Prize Day. How proud I expected my family to be when they saw I would be honored with every top award.

The Sunday before school ended, a special luncheon was planned, to which both Grandmother Helene and Grandmother Flora were invited. After the meal, the other children—even Jonah and Pinhas—were sent away. My father and Zilpah had spoken little to each other across the table, but as soon as they were side by side on the way to the hall, they began whispering to each other. I saw nothing unusual in that; the intensity of their relationship had never altered.

Abdul brought everyone a brandy and soda, and nobody refused one, not even Grandmother Flora, who rarely took hard spirits.

"Would you care to try one, Dinah?" my father offered for the first time.

Reveling in my new adult status, I accepted immediately. The taste tickled, then burnt, but I determined I would finish it. Just then my father took his seat beside his wife—opposite me—and looked so grim my stomach contracted, almost rejecting the brandy. What was wrong? Then I thought I knew: they had discovered my last communications with Gabriel and were going to chastise me en masse. I clutched the stem of the glass and decided against drinking any more until the dreadful sensations subsided.

"As you know, your mother and I, your grandmother, and the others who care about your welfare have kept our word not to make plans for your future until you completed your studies. However, preliminary inquiries on your behalf were made, and the most influential *dilallas*—matchmakers—were consulted."

I watched Zilpah's face for a signal. When she dropped her eyes as he said the last words, I began to tremble. Whom had they chosen? Someone who would put Sultana's match to shame? I did not care; I only prayed it would be someone I could love.

"And so . . ." My father faltered.

My heart beat with happy expectation. I realized this was the moment I had been waiting for—that every girl waits for—my entire life.

Zilpah looked at him beseechingly. I could see they were both bursting with the news, but she was allowing him to be the bearer. When he could not continue, she looked up and said, "There are no prospects." Her face was blank. "None at all."

"Not exactly true—" my father started in a shaky tone.

"Please, Benu, those were insults, not offers," she spat.

"Well . . ." I began, thinking they were probably much too particular. "Who are they?"

Grandmother Flora shook her head, warning my father not to reply.

"Dinah has a right to know." He took a long swallow from his glass.

Before he could begin, Zilpah interrupted him. "Your father and I thought the most appropriate match for you, because of your maturity and your—shall we say—strong character, might have been a man somewhat older than yourself, a man of experience and substance. Not an easy category, since most men in our community marry young, but we thought we might find someone who had been educated abroad, or someone active in his trade, or even a widower. Unfortunately, nobody met our requirements," she said, lying, since I would soon discover these eligible men had rejected me flatly. "Next we looked at the young men your age, boys like Gabriel Judah and his friends."

My father shook his head. "Nothing. Nothing. Nothing."

I put down my glass and gripped the sides of the armchair. *Nobody* would have me? How could this be true? Wasn't I head girl at school? Wasn't I rich, with a dowry that would eclipse that of any girl of my generation? I thought of those boys they might have overlooked: the less attractive, the ones from poorer homes, the ones I would never have considered two years or even two hours ago. I listed the least desirable boys at St. Xavier's. "What about Aboodi Belilios, Ellis Silman, Immanuel Duek, Hayeem Arzooni?" After each name, my father shook his head pathetically.

"Not even Immanuel Duek? Who, then?" I staggered forward. "Who?"

Zilpah pushed me back into my chair. With her hand pressing my shoulder she kept me in my seat. "Do you remember Isaac Shooker?"

"I don't think so."

"You know," Grandmother Helene assisted, "the brass vendor at Barabazar."

"He's a cripple! He's—"

"The best offer." Zilpah's whisper grated.

"A generous Jew," Grandmother Helene offered.

"Younger than you might think—he's in his twenties," Grandmother Flora added.

Zilpah seemed grateful for the support. "His mother was from a good family."

I gave both grandmothers horrified stares. "How could either of you . . . ?"

Grandmother Helene threw up her hands. "Isaac Shooker makes the others look like princes."

"The others?" My head snapped back and hit the back rail of the chair. Stunned for a second, I rubbed my head and stared from person to person. Each avoided my eyes. "Who else, Nani?" I demanded, knowing she could not deceive me.

Grandmother Flora modulated her disgust. "The Tosters' idiot son and two men who have children older than you."

I gave an incredulous laugh. A cripple, an idiot, and two decrepit widowers?

Nani spoke to the hideous silence. "Don't worry, Dinah. We are not asking you to accept Mr. Shooker, or any of them. Better no marriage than a bad marriage."

Grandmother Helene forced herself to sound optimistic. "There will be other possibilities. When the parents of the boys have time to compare your dowry with the others, they will come around. Stupidity and superstition are the first response; reason will follow."

"Yes, yes," my father added. "Too many women are permitted to interfere with these arrangements. I shall talk to some of the fathers privately. They shall see the sense in my generous offer. They shall—"

I cut him off. "How long will this take?"

"I thought you were in no rush to marry." Zilpah's tone was a challenge I might have met if my status had been stronger. Instead I quailed.

"In the meantime, what would you like to do?" Nani wondered.

"I suppose I could teach. Already I tutor some afternoons. I'm certain I could get a position and—"

"Hush," Zilpah ordered. "You talk nonsense. Do you want to wear a signboard announcing: 'spinster'?"

"What else could I do?" I asked weakly.

"Hold your head high and continue to behave like a lady," she replied. "We have not given up yet. Your father and your grandmother have agreed to a plan of mine. There might be some possibilities . . ." She trailed off.

Under any other circumstance I would have begged her to tell me what she was thinking. At that moment, I did not want to know.

\// \// \//

There was a subdued celebration for my graduation. I knew my family felt that my academic honors—which had been handed out by the vicereine, the Marchioness of Landsdowne—not only did not make up for my unpopular status but also might contribute to my unsuitability, since I was better educated than many of the men who might have considered me.

Two of my schoolmates married within a few weeks. They did not invite me to their weddings. As the summer heat descended like a claustrophobic cloak, I retreated into the world of books while my father and his wife prepared for their annual return to Darjeeling. Ever since our aborted trip because of illness, we children had not been asked to accompany them to the hills. This was their time to visit Zilpah's mother ("My *third* mother-in-law," Papa groaned to me privately). For the past few summers I had resented this exclusive aspect to marriage, feeling as though they were escaping the heat at our expense. This year I was happy to be free from their disappointed expressions.

A week after their departure, Dr. Hyam sent a message asking me to call on my grandmother. Propped in a cane chair to permit air to circulate, she cooled her feet in buckets. A punkah-wallah worked double time to keep the stagnant air moving.

One look at her face, which was so swollen her eyes seemed mere slits in doughy flesh, and I nearly collapsed with fright. "What has happened?"

She barely moved her bloated lips. Her voice was distorted and mushy. "I'm an old lady, that's all. I can no longer tolerate the heat."

"You should go to a hill station."

"The altitude would make matters worse."

"What about Gopalpur, at the seaside, where many of the Sassoons go?"

"No, no, I will manage. Will you stay with me, Dinah?"

"There is nothing I would rather do."

If it weren't for Nani's miseries, the next weeks would have been pleasant ones. When my grandmother did not need me—which was most of the time, since servants tended her needs—I assisted in the dispensary. Finding the doctor's records and bills disorganized, I fashioned envelopes to hold the charts for his more frequent patients and combined the remaining by alphabet and then by symptom. I made lists of the accounts he had to pay and the receipts due him. To those who had not paid, I sent a reminder letter attaching a detailed list of dates and fees.

Dr. Hyam was amazed at how much money was collected in so short a time. "A pity you aren't a man, Dinah. You would do splendidly out in the world."

I had written my father that I was caring for my grandmother, and since he had not replied, I assumed he had no objections. Two weeks later, his gharry pulled up to the door of the Lower Chitpur Road clinic. When I saw him, I leapt to my feet. "Papa!"

"How is your grandmother?" he asked kindly.

"Better today. She slept well last night. At first we thought she was only suffering from the heat, but now Dr. Hyam thinks it might be her heart." I rushed to defend myself: "That's why he wants me here with her. I sleep in her room at night. He doesn't trust a servant to know if she needs attention, so—"

"Good, good . . ." He seemed distracted.

"Have you come to see Nani?"

"No. I mean, of course, later, when she can receive me. First, you and I must talk."

I led him into the office where I worked on the accounts and moved some papers off the extra chair.

"What are you doing here?"

"Helping the doctor." I tidied a pile of papers. "Nani says it keeps me out of trouble." I gave a weak laugh. "Do you want tea?"

"No, thank you. Must get home to the others soon. Zilpah's in Darjeeling . . . waiting for word from me." He stopped his choppy phrases long enough to wipe the perspiration from his face and rub the bump on his nose. "Dinah, my child. I bring good news." His eyes twinkled, and his mouth was creased in a smile. It felt as though a cool breeze had swept through the room. "Zilpah has found a possible match for you."

My mouth opened, but I did not speak. Nor did I hear him very well, because my pounding heart drowned out most of his words. "A fine man . . . son of a tea planter . . . Jewish family."

"Who is he?" I managed to blurt.

"Silas Luddy. His father was one of the first to try tea in that terrain. A rough beginning, but quite a success in the end." My father watched intently for my reaction.

I wondered what Mr. Luddy's flaw might be. "You say he is from Darjeeling?"

"Yes."

"Is he a friend of Zilpah's family?"

"Only an acquaintance."

A piece was still missing. Darjeeling, Zilpah . . . "Is he a Bene Israel?"

"No."

I exhaled with relief. "Does he know about me?"

"What is there to know? You are a lovely young girl."

"With an impressive dowry."

He waved his hand as if to dismiss that point. "Luddy has more than enough of his own. He just wants his only son to be happy."

An only son . . . someone who did not require a large dowry. I should have been thrilled, yet continued to be wary.

"Why does he want me?"

"Silas Luddy is an unusual man. He lives apart from the rest of his family in a house he built near Tiger Hill—a place with one of the most magnificent vistas in India. I have been told you sometimes can see Mount Everest from his veranda. However, his property is outside of the town, away from the social arena, for Mr. Luddy prefers the company of a few select friends who share his intellectual interests. Another woman might not be content in so remote a spot."

"Where did he go to school?"

"Between the ages of ten and twenty he was in England, but as he told me, 'A person's education ends only at the grave, or perhaps not even there.' " My father gave a hollow laugh before rushing ahead with his explanation. "They say Luddy's library is the finest in the province. That is what made Zilpah think of you. She thought a house filled with books would interest you."

"What is his profession?"

"He manages the accounts for his father's tea plantation—a substantial operation, I assure you."

I waited a few beats. "Does he know about Mother and . . . ?"

"Although we have not discussed that matter, I am certain his father has checked out our family—the facts are not secret—and has decided, quite rightly, that there is no hindrance to a match. Only the petty gossips of Calcutta would have let something over which you had no control ruin your chances here. Zilpah's idea to look away from that Park Street coterie was brilliant. The Luddys are as fine a Jewish family as you will find in India. Of course, Darjeeling has no synagogue. They worship among themselves on the high holy days, and there is *shohet*, a ritual slaughterer, in residence. But with the train, frequent visits to Calcutta are possible. Look at me—I've just come down to give you the news and will return with your reply in a day or so."

"I have always wanted to visit Darjeeling," I said, recalling my dreams of majestic mountains and fantastical snows.

"A splendid place." Papa beamed. "One of the loveliest on earth. I think you will be happy there."

"But I haven't decided," I protested.

"No, of course you haven't. Ask me anything you like."

My grandmother's servant had appeared beside me, and waited for my father to finish before bending and whispering that Nani had heard he had arrived and wished us to join her.

As we entered the Hyams' parlor, Grandmother Flora made her way toward us with small, hesitant steps. From across the room, the sound of her gasping breaths startled Papa. "Flora, how long have you been like this?"

She shrugged. "That's of no importance. Thanks to your daughter, I manage," she wheezed. "You haven't come to take her away from me, have you?"

Her servant propped her legs up. "Not immediately, but I bring you good news: a first-rate match for Dinah."

Nani coughed so hard she turned blue. The servant ran forward and placed cold cloths on her face and neck. "Shall I call the doctor?" she asked.

Nani shooed her away. "Don't be silly." She took a few deep breaths without coughing more violently, then leaned back on her chaise. "I'm too weak for these shocks, Benu. Start again and tell me what fish you have hooked."

Papa went over what he had told me about Silas Luddy.

"Luddy . . . I know some Luddys—the father must be Manasseh."

"Now he calls himself Maurice."

Nani closed her eyes. She was silent for so long, I became concerned she was having an attack. Without opening her eyes, she spoke in a slow, reminiscing manner, "A Chinese connection . . . they smuggled tea plants . . . very daring." Her eyes sprang open and she smiled triumphantly. "Am I right?"

"Very much so."

"Not bad for an old lady, eh?"

My father bowed from the waist.

She leaned forward. "There is something else . . . ah, yes, the wife. Something about the wife."

I was entranced by the changes flickering across my father's face: first a fleeting fear, followed by a relieved expression as he decided what strategy he would employ. "Her name was Hira. They say she was extremely beautiful. She was a Nepalese convert, not as dark as Zilpah by any means, perhaps more golden than you or I, but"—he rushed to reassure us—"the son is lighter than anyone in this room. His hair is black—handsome feature— and his eyes the same. His skin has an ivory cast. Trust me, his appearance will not disappoint Dinah."

Grandmother Flora seemed distracted. "She died in a fire. I recall that a child died as well . . ."

My father's voice was somber. "Yes. She was sleeping in a sick daughter's room on a very cold night. Coals from an overbanked fire spilled out, and the room went up in flames. She left two other daughters and Silas. He was away at school at the time."

"Poor child . . ."

"Maurice Luddy was devoted to his wife. He never remarried."

Grandmother Flora's chin bobbed. "Every match requires some commonality to bind it. Dinah and Silas both had the misfortune to lose mothers under tragic circumstances." She wiped away the moisture that formed on her forehead. "Yes, I see it might be possible."

I sat numbly, not knowing what to say or even think.

"Can't expect her to have an answer yet, can we?" She glanced at Papa meaningfully. "She must have time to absorb this. Still, she could do worse than a Luddy."

I found my voice. "When will I meet him?" came out hoarsely.

"Soon."

"Will you be taking me back with you?"

He dashed my hopes. "A girl does not go shopping for a man."

Unexpectedly I began to cry.

My father threw up his hands. "We are not barbarians. You shall have your chance to talk with Mr. Luddy when he comes to visit us. Until then the arrangements are preliminary."

"Why couldn't I return to the hills with you, just for a holiday and—"

"No." He was exasperated. "Much too far for you to come for that purpose."

"You said it was a simple matter to travel between Calcutta and Darjeeling."

Nani interrupted. "Your father already told you it would be unseemly, Dinah."

He took an envelope from his breast pocket and handed it to me.

"Silas Luddy has written you a letter to introduce himself. He said to give it to you if you were interested. You are interested, aren't you, Dinah?" He waited a beat.

As though she were in the room, I could hear Zilpah's voice saying, "You cannot afford not to be, can you?"

I sucked in my lip and opened the creamy, thick envelope. The smooth stock was embossed by a crest with a thunderbolt at its center. The ink was not black, but a custom mixture that created a rich brown. He wrote in a round hand with elegant capitals and perfectly formed letters. Rapidly I skimmed it, my heart thumping as I read a word here, a phrase there. I felt a peculiar pang at the closing and the florid signature, then began again more slowly.

15 August 1890

My dear Miss Sassoon,

How may I introduce myself to you? To point out my virtues would be an embarrassment, to state my failings would be foolhardy. Let me just say that I am a plain man with unpretentious tastes and requirements. My life in Darjeeling is quiet, with many hours of the day allotted for study and contemplation. Surrounded by the majesty of the snowy peaks and the daily transfigurations of lightness and darkness, I am a man of faith and constancy.

Though I would welcome a companion on life's journey, marriage has eluded me. Until this blessed time I have been unable to find a woman who would contemplate sharing the simplicity of my home. Darjeeling is distant from Calcutta, and Tiger Hill is remote from even that pleasant village. I do not want to paint a picture that is too austere. In season, when Darjeeling is the summer capital of Bengal, a delightful crowd ascends to these rocky clefts, and I, as much as the next fellow, enjoy the colors and temptations society offers. After the departure of the visitors, I readily admit I relish the peacefulness and the return to the solace of my intellectual pursuits.

If you could find it in your heart to leave the comfortable embrace of your loving family, I would like you to know that I would highly value your thoughtful attention to my proposal.

Your father has told me of his generous settlement on your behalf. While I am not a rich man, I have every comfort that I require. Further, as my father's only son, I will inherit the main interest in Luddy plantations, the proceeds from which should keep many generations secure. I expect you to keep the income from your dowry for your own requirements. You may wish to alter parts of my home to suit yourself, or to travel, or to provide for your family or friends. I do not expect to interfere with you in this, since I feel that we should live together as equals in every sense. I

*would take no liberties or freedoms for myself that I would not expect you
to take for yourself. In return, I ask you to make no pledge that I do not
make. If my philosophies offend you because they go against the customs of
this country or our religion, please forgive me, but my own interpreta-
tion of the Scriptures forbids me to accept happiness at the expense of another. As a wise woman, Miss Lucretia Mott, has written, "Then in the
marriage union, the independence of the husband and wife will be equal,
their dependence mutual, and their obligations reciprocal."*

*Your many fine qualities have been explained to me, but the ones that I
especially admire include your academic achievements that make you out-
standing among the young women in this country or any other, your high
spirits to overcome the sadness that has been a part of your short life,
and the devotion you have shown both the younger and older members of
your family. The surface aspects that so often attract a man to a woman
or a woman to a man are nothing but the perfume that leads the bee to
nectar; the deeper wells, hidden from immediate view, are what stand the
test of time.*

*With the hope you will consider me worthy to become your companion
through life's offerings of prosperity and adversity,*

I remain your devoted friend,

Silas Luddy

My eyes brimmed. "Have you read this, Papa?"

"Can't you see it was sealed?"

"Must I show it to you?"

Nani leapt in. "Of course not!" Then, more wistfully, "Only if you
wish to."

"Who is Lucretia Mott?"

Grandmother Flora shrugged.

"Nobody I know," Papa replied. "Why? Is she a friend of the
Luddys?"

"I don't think so," I said. Taking care not to soil the paper, I folded
the letter and replaced it in its envelope. "You may send word to
Zilpah that Mr. Luddy interests me," I said flatly before dashing from
the room.

❦ ❦ ❦

I could not sleep that night. The words of the letter tumbled together,
their meanings fragmented and exciting. As much as the letter introduced a man, it caused me to ask a hundred questions that would
never before have occurred to me. Should I blithely accept the man on
the faith of one letter and the recommendations of my parents? I was
too intrigued to say anything negative, too frightened by the sheer

force of a personality to know how to proceed. At dawn, drifting in my thoughts, the idea came: I would write a reply!

I took pen in hand and tried a few phrases. Everything seemed so stilted, so puerile compared with his felicity of expression. I reread his letter half a dozen times. The phrase "through life's offerings of prosperity and adversity" continued to intrigue me. Where had I heard that before? I pulled down my Latin books, leafed through them wildly, until the words lined themselves up for my approval. I began again:

24 August 1890

Dear Mr. Luddy,

My father gave me your letter and I will admit that, until I read it, I thought I could not even contemplate a union with a person I had never met. I continue to believe it impossible to make promises before we are able to speak to each other face-to-face, but at least your words have convinced me that many levels of compatibility might exist between us.

I have heard about your large library and your scholarly interests. I would hope we both might find more amusement in sharing these pursuits than in the more fleeting satisfactions of society. I have no qualms about living in Darjeeling. In fact, it is my fondest desire to visit the place I have heard so many people praise.

As Cicero wrote in Pro Archia Poeta, *"These studies are a spur to the young, a delight to the old; an ornament in prosperity, a consoling refuge in adversity; they are pleasure for us at home, and no burden abroad; they stay up with us at night, they accompany us when we travel, they are with us in our country visits."*

I look forward to the day when we shall meet.

Your friend,

Dinah Sassoon

I had copied the quotation from Cicero in Latin, but had torn up the page and begun again when I realized he might not be able to translate it. After I had rewritten the letter, I decided that a man educated in England probably knew his Latin and that he might think I was patronizing him by doing the translation. I began the letter again, halting to remind myself this was not some childish contest. Mr. Luddy's words had been in English; so my words should also be. I settled on the first, regretting my penmanship was not an equal to his, nor my quotation as original. Still, I had established myself as having an interest, without agreeing blindly; and I had given him a window into my mind.

The final decision was the most difficult: did I give the envelope to my father or did I post it myself? To hand it to my father would show I trusted him to deliver it unopened, but it could also indicate that my father had required I write it—a message that would cancel my attempt at independence. To post it would mean I dared circumvent my parents and might show too much initiative for a girl in my position. Which would Mr. Luddy prefer? I searched his letter for a clue. "I especially admire . . . your high spirits" meant he would like to receive a letter directly from me, yet he also mentioned "the devotion you have shown . . . older members of your family," which implied he liked a person to be respectful. My head pounded with the import of my decision, until ". . . overcome the sadness that has been a part of your short life . . ." popped out at me. This had to be his way of saying he knew about my mother and the disgrace, and he admired rather than thought less of me for it. I concluded I need not tread a line of prim propriety for his sake. Indeed, he might prefer me to act for myself. Eventually, and without total conviction in the soundness of my rationale, I sent the letter on my own.

13

S ilas Luddy and his father came for tea the fifteenth of September 1890. By that time we had written a dozen letters back and forth. I knew the names of his cats and servants; he knew the antics of my sisters and brothers. He told me about the system he was working on to catalog his library, which had resulted in a preliminary count of more than seventeen hundred volumes. I tallied the ones I had inherited from my mother, offering to add her hundred and fifty books as my contribution to his collection.

The arrangement between my father and his father was that after we met, the wedding date would be selected. Zilpah planned the day with military precision. At exactly three in the afternoon the gharry which had been sent to fetch them from the station appeared. From an upstairs window I watched as a slender man in a tall black hat, followed by a balding man, his topee in his hand, stepped out.

"Let me see. What does he look like?" Ruby pushed me back. "A mustache! Dinah, he will tickle you!" She ran off giggling.

Before I had a chance to wonder how I felt about the mustache, Yali was tugging me to the landing. I was to walk down the stairs and greet the Luddys in the vestibule. My sky-blue silk dress had full pagoda sleeves topped with large bows. The design had come from Grandmother Helene, who had asked if she might meet Mr. Luddy. "No," Zilpah had replied, "the man is not on exhibition. Her parents and her grandmother are enough for any man to face." However, when Grandmother Helene had asked to supervise my gown, Zilpah had deferred. What did she know of fashion? She wore only saris. Grandmother Flora would have been no help, since she still wore the traditional dress of the Baghdadi Jews. Because Grandmother Helene thought bustles were outmoded, her dressmaker had fashioned me a narrow bodice that fell smoothly without folds. "You have nothing yet to hide," she said, by way of a compliment. She also told the dressmaker to keep

143

the length demure but to be certain it cleared the ground, "since Dinah is apt to trip if she is excited."

Making certain my fingertips brushed the banister just in case, I made my way down the marble staircase in the manner I had practiced: head held high, looking forward, not down at my feet or at my visitor. I paused at the bottom step and glanced over at my father.

"Ah, here she is now," he said, trying to be nonchalant, but fooling nobody. "May I introduce my daughter Dinah? Dinah, this is Mr. Maurice Luddy."

I curtsied to the father. His sideburns were snow white and his skin leathery from the high-altitude sun.

"And his son Mr. Silas Luddy."

I turned in what I hoped was a graceful maneuver, but my heel caught in the crack between the tiles and I slipped slightly sideways. Catching myself in time, I offered my hand. Silas Luddy held it for a few beats—without either a clasp or a shake—before releasing it. His palm was cool. I concentrated on the length of his smooth fingers, the most elegant I had ever seen on a man. When I dared look up at him, I realized we were looking eye to eye. His gaze was riveted at the peaks in my sleeves, and his expression showed thinly veiled disgust. Suddenly I was as appalled by the frivolity of the dressmaker's concoction. Why, the bows were even higher than his shoulders! The color was garish next to the gray of his immaculate cutaway.

After we made our mumbled greetings, Zilpah led the tense group into the hall. She pointed us to our seats and we behaved as dutifully as children on the first day of school.

Immediately my father feigned a riveting interest in the history of the tea business. "Am I right that it was once believed that tea could never flourish in India?" he began.

"That's correct," Maurice Luddy responded cheerfully. "As you may know, the first trials were grown at low altitudes, resulting in such a poor grade we thought the experiment a failure. From my travels in China, I thought tea was essentially a hill plant. Would anyone listen to me? Absolutely not."

Zilpah interrupted long enough to offer him pastries. As he tasted several, he complimented her, "Splendid almond *sumboosak*, always my favorite. And may I say I heartily approve of the quality of your tea!" He winked before continuing, "Robert Fortune and I persuaded some Chinamen to assist in the—shall we say—quiet removal of several casks of seeds from Canton."

My father nodded respectfully, as one smuggler to another.

"In the first batch of seed, forty-two thousand plants were successfully raised, two thousand of which were allotted to the Madras presidency and forty thousand to Assam. I told them it was ludicrous to waste so many in those intemperate locations." Luddy guffawed loudly. "Eventually I was able to acquire twenty thousand for my experiment in the Himalayas."

While the older men dominated the discussions, I took sidelong glances at Silas Luddy. He hardly moved a muscle, even to take refreshment. I had not expected such a grave, unemotional man. His face seemed so flat, so without lines or movement, I wondered if he ever laughed or cried. I had expected someone pensive, someone of a serious demeanor, but not this sculptured coldness. Particularly prominent was his mustache, which was so tapered at the edges it appeared a waxen addition. I supposed he was trying to offset his extremely wide lips, but for me the effect was to draw attention to rather than detract from them. As I studied his individual features, though, I found nothing unpleasant about them. His forehead was high, and his hair, parted exactly in the middle, was cut with such precision it might have been painted on with thick strokes of tar. His nose was straight and of a moderate length. The whole face was slightly wider on the left than the right, but had a generally oval shape, with a tapering at the chin. The neck was thin, with a prominent Adam's apple protruding above the collar. More notable than anything else was his skin tone. My father had described it as "ivory," which was perhaps as apt a term as any, yet its cast had more ash in it—the color of stone.

I tried to imagine touching his face with my lips. An unexpected revulsion knotted my stomach. My mouth filled with saliva. Only a quick sip of warm tea relaxed my throat enough to prevent me from having to rush from the room.

The fathers continued endlessly discussing the specifics of tea cultivation, travels in China, and the difficulties in dealing with Indian laborers. I could not drink another drop of tea without the pressure on my bladder becoming painful, yet Silas Luddy looked as if he could sit in that same position the whole day without discomfort. The words in his letters had brought visions of someone taller, broader, pinker in flesh, softer in demeanor. I looked at his crumbless plate, the napkin folded neatly. How could I tolerate a man with so little animation, a man so pallid, a man who, if laid on his back, could be taken for someone dead? Once again I was struggling to swallow the bile in my throat, when the fathers rose in unison. As if pulled by an invisible string, Silas leapt up.

What was happening? Zilpah was saying something about the pleasure of meeting them . . . and my father was being told where the Luddys were staying . . . they were responding they would be seeing him the next morning . . . and then everyone was staring at me. I found myself standing as well, though I did not recall getting up. I glanced down. My dress was crushed and looked even worse than before. The color did not flatter me. I swore never again to wear blue.

Thankfully, the women were not expected to see the Luddys off. As soon as the door to the drawing room closed, I said, "I am afraid I drank too much tea." Using the servants' entrance, I made my way through the back of the house and upstairs to the bathroom. I splashed my sweating face with cool water, and without removing my dress, I fell upon my bed in a heap of hopelessness.

Nothing about Mr. Luddy appealed to me. Nothing! How could someone so charming on paper have had so little to say? Not ten words had been exchanged between us. And when he did speak, his voice cracked in pitch like a schoolboy's. Besides, I had looked preposterous in that frivolous dress. My movements had been jerky, awkward, and I had behaved like a mute idiot! Grasping the offending fabric in my hand, I twisted the slimy silk cruelly. By now he would be begging his father to rescind his offer. What would the elder Luddy say? The fathers had seemed pleased with the match. And Zilpah, who was thrilled to be getting rid of me, had glowed throughout the afternoon. What a victory for her to mate me with a half-breed whose only saving grace was a mind that—if I kept my eyes and ears closed—transcended his physical repugnance.

What could I do? What other choice did I have? Even Nani was sanctioning this union. I thought of myself isolated on some frozen Himalayan glacier, tormented by Silas Luddy's vacant stare, the howling wind my only companion, and I pounded the pillow in fury. Exhausted, I lay back and turned over on my side.

Zilpah peered in at the door. "Your grandmother would like to speak with you before she leaves."

I wiped my streaked face with the back of my hand. "I cannot come down, not now."

She replied in her most masculine register, "You are not pleased, is that it? Why? Doesn't Mr. Luddy speak as eloquently as he writes? Well, I am certain your letters must have flattered you as well." She noted the alarm on my face. "Did you think we did not know about your correspondence?" She tossed her head. "Dinah, you have a history of secret letters." Her reminder was thrust like a knife, and I flinched. "Your father encouraged Mr. Luddy to write to you the first time because we were certain you would reply privately—and so you did!"

She crossed her arms on her chest. "Don't look at me with those big cow eyes. We know you better than you know yourself. Unless you took the initiative, unless you participated in the game, we knew you would never accept our choice."

"Choice? You call that a choice?"

"Dinah, when you come to your senses you will realize we are not Brahmins who sell their daughters in infancy without a care for their feelings." She rushed on without taking a breath. "Through the difficulties in finding a husband, your welfare and your future happiness were paramount in every decision we made. You will never know how much it pained me when I had to advise you of the realities of your position in language you would never forget. Nevertheless, I did my duty. It is not easy to have to replace two mothers in a family. Nobody could have tried harder than I have." At last she paused, refilled her lungs, and continued even more forcefully, "Whose idea do you think it was to look in Darjeeling after searching the gutters of Calcutta for any man who might have you?" She came over to my bed and peered down at me. "Now, stop behaving as though you were the most eligible Jewish girl in India and come downstairs at once."

Traumatized by her outburst, I bolted up and backed away from her.

"Dinah, your grandmother is waiting." Her nostrils twitched and her lips made that fishy movement I found annoying. "In her condition she can hardly climb the stairs, but that is exactly what she'll do if that is the only way to reach you."

I felt as though I had been slapped. "I'm sorry. Tell Nani I'll be down in a moment."

I found Grandmother Flora alone out on the terrace, her feet elevated by a servant. One look at my face told her everything she wanted to know. "Dinah, you don't like him."

"It's not that . . . he was not what I expected—foolish of me to have had a picture in my mind . . . I suppose I'll adjust, but . . ." I broke out in heaving sobs and fell into her outstretched arms.

With my face pressed to her soft bosom, I could hear the uneven flutters of her heart. "Don't worry, I am not going to refuse him," I said without lifting my head.

"You think you should do as your father wishes."

"I must. You know that, Nani."

"*You* are the one who will pledge your life to him." She must have felt me shudder. Stroking my hair, she murmured, "He seems a kind, gentle, well-educated man. Already you have common interests. This glue will bind you more than any other aspect of marriage. Don't be afraid of the other, it is but a brief interlude between a man and a woman. If you took the time the average man and woman are married as an ocean, the moments of physical closeness are but a single bucket lifted from that sea. Most couples share so much more. Remember your Nana? I developed an interest in medicine and helped him in his consulting room. How much more we had to talk about then. If an association is limited to domestic matters, life becomes tiresome indeed. And I know you, my child—your active mind requires an intellectual companion. Didn't you tell me he was more than your match?"

"Yes, Nani, but I imagined there would be something tugging me toward him. If anything, I felt the opposite."

"What else could you expect under those circumstances? You were not alone together for even a few minutes. What one says in the presence of parents is bound to be stilted. You told me his letters were appealing. By himself he surely would be quite altered from the stiff young man trying to make no blunders, in the same way you were the cornered prey trying not to anger your captors."

I laughed at this image and sat upright. "I hope you are right." Nani smoothed back my hair. "He didn't like my dress, did he?"

She tweaked one of my shoulder bows. "I thought you charmed him."

"It was not to his taste," I said, fluffing up the skirt. "Not mine either, but I was too afraid to speak against Grandmother Helene, who is supposed to know much more about these things than I do."

"Further evidence of compatibility, perhaps?" Her eyebrows raised jauntily. "Both you and Mr. Luddy are practical people who are put off by frivolities." Her voice lowered to a more serious tone. "I understand why you did not speak out on the matter of the dress, but in the future, if you keep your own counsel, you will make fewer mistakes. Dinah, you are a sensible girl. You must do what you think appropriate in every matter, even this one. If you don't feel you can marry Mr. Luddy, then put an end to this right now."

I thought of the other possibilities—the cripple, the idiot, the old men. "How can I do that?"

"You think you have no choices. You think you must accept this offer because it is the only one you have had. Well, a few weeks ago there was no Mr. Luddy, and look what happened! Who knows what lies around the next bend?"

"Nothing, probably."

"And if you never marry? Would that be so tragic?"

She and I both knew that was not a realistic option, so her question required no direct reply. I changed the subject. "I don't want to be so far away from you, Nani."

"Pooh! It's foolish to pretend I will be around long enough to matter."

"Nani!" My tears welled up again.

"Besides, you won't miss the old gossips of Calcutta, will you?"

"No, I won't. Every time I go to the synagogue I feel they are watching me, thinking that somehow I am paying for my mother's sins. Any mistake I make, anything I say, every trifle, has been exaggerated. If I lived here, they would be waiting anxiously to see if I turn out like her. Why should it be any different after I am married?"

Grandmother gave a long exhalation. "Some water . . ." After a few swallows, she continued in a husky whisper that indicated she was having trouble breathing. "Who can read the future? Who would want to? Today I look back and remember when your mother came to us begging, 'If you let me marry Benu Sassoon, I will be the happiest girl in India!' and wonder what would have happened if we had forbidden it. Now I berate myself for letting her have her way, but at the time we could offer no objections. Benu was a fine young man from a good family. We wanted our daughter to be happy; every parent wants that." She noticed my pouting expression. "Yes, even Zilpah wants that for you."

"But—" I stopped when Nani's shoulders sagged and her eyes half-closed.

She struggled to continue. "We gave in to Luna. Who could have predicted how tragically it would turn out? Look what happened to me. When I met your grandfather, I was a woman almost thirty, with no dowry, one dead husband, and nothing to offer."

"Nana said you were the most beautiful girl in Calcutta."

She beamed, and for a moment the strain of her illness passed from her face. In the twilight I could almost imagine how she might have looked to a man who had become transfixed with the sapphire cast to her lively eyes. "My point has been proved. Anyone would have thought a girl like me would have had no opportunities, and yet I had many wonderful years with your grandfather. Anyone would have predicted that Benu and Luna would have lived as happily ever after as any storybook prince and princess . . ."

"Do you think I will live as happily with Mr. Luddy?"

She shrugged. "Part of it is what you each bring to the marriage, and part of it is luck. Let me finish by saying what I have said before: no marriage is better than a bad marriage."

Together we watched as the western sky took on an opalescence with streaks of flaming orange. "I wonder what the sun looks like as it sets over the Himalayas," I said, my voice more pliant than before.

Nani squeezed my hand. "Go to your father, Dinah. Set his heart at rest. Tell him you have agreed."

14

ψ ψ ψ

The next morning, after taking chota hazri in my room, I came down to find Zilpah in an ebullient mood. As soon as she saw me, she swooped up from the dining table and rushed to my side. "Come, sit beside your father." She led me to a place and removed the plates and silver herself. Clapping her hands, she called, "Bearer!"

Sedately Abdul marched in, carrying a silver tray so heavy the strain in his face was evident. As he set it before me, I stared at the silk cloth woven with golden strands that covered its mysterious contents. "What is this?"

"Your special gift from Maurice Luddy, in honor of his son," my father said, his fingers reaching for the tray. "Lift the cover."

I obliged at once.

"Oh, I have never seen anything like it!" Zilpah swooned. "Look, Benu! Can you believe it?"

The arrangement on the tray was so astonishingly lovely I did not want to touch it. Flower petals glued to a lacy cloth, like mosaics on a temple wall, were fashioned to create a scene of a peacock courting a peahen. Translucent sweets cut into jewellike facets lined the border of the tray. In the center, a brooch pinned to a blue velvet pad was surrounded by a garland of miniature white rosebuds. Its design was a peacock feather composed of sapphires, emeralds, and diamonds. As Zilpah's hand hovered above it covetously, I lifted the brooch, turning it in the stream of sunlight that poured into the room. After allowing me a few seconds, Zilpah swept it from me and brought it closer to her face. I could tell she was counting the stones.

"Very generous," she said as she passed it to my father. He did not examine it, but merely undid the clasp and pinned it to my blouse. "So, do you think your papa found you a good match?" He kissed my forehead.

The brooch was so heavy it pulled the thin batiste fabric down, and I checked to see if a rip was likely to occur. "Yes, Papa."

"Saturday evening we will host an official celebration. We must select a wedding date—not too soon, for we don't wish to seem hasty, and not too far in the distance, since we want to keep you the center of attention for a while. Your cousin Sultana's festivities will seem a pauper's compared with what we have planned." He pointed to the jewels above my bosom. "Nobody will ever forget the wedding of Dinah Sassoon."

Bypassing his wife, for perhaps the first time, my father enlisted the help of his sister and Grandmother Helene to plan my wedding. "Who knows more about a party than Helene? Who knows Calcutta society better than Bellore?" There were no arguments from Zilpah, who seemed so content to be rid of me she was willing to remain in the background until the deed was done.

My official *mileek* party was held in the hall, our largest drawing room. Fifty of the most important families arrived with only a few days' notice. Aunt Helene's dressmaker worked for two nights straight to fashion me a pale yellow dress with silk ruffles that gathered together at the scoop of my neckline, a design that was nothing more than a backdrop for the brooch.

Silas and his father joined our family for an early supper before the guests arrived. Even though they came together, I noticed that as soon as they were offered refreshment they moved to opposite sides of the room. I approached Maurice Luddy to thank him for his lavish gift. Then I crossed the hall and said the same words to Silas. For the first time I saw some animation in his eyes as he admired the brooch on my chest.

After the meal, we moved back into the hall. The furnishings had been rearranged into a semicircle, where the immediate family would sit to greet our guests. Silas and I were given seats side by side. His father started to take a seat in the audience, but Zilpah insisted he sit next to his son. My father was given the chair next to me. Grandmother Flora took the place that would have been reserved for Zilpah, who mingled with the guests. Given our choice of beverages, Silas selected the wine and I tentatively accepted a glass of cherry cordial. Grandmother Flora nodded that I might drink it. The cool, sweet liquid burned the delicate tissues in my throat.

As soon as the guests greeted us, a *dakaka*, a woman entertainer, entered the room shaking a *daff*, a tambourine, and carrying a *tabla* drum. Singing and playing her instruments, she created a pulse in the room. When she had everyone swaying and thumping to the familiar melodies, she stood in front of Silas and me and began her balancing tricks, first with a candy tray upon her head. Then she deftly maneuvered a filled wineglass from her crown, to her forehead, to her chin, to her chest, without spilling a drop. The assemblage, which finally had suspended its cacophony of chatter, broke into applause.

With a clap of her hands, the dakaka silenced the room. From her bosom she slowly withdrew a long silk scarf. Ruby and Seti were giggling. Next the entertainer seemed to pluck a gold coin from midair.

"How did she do that?" Ruby gasped.

The dakaka placed the coin in the scarf and folded it securely. Signaling for Silas and me to stand, she handed each of us one corner of the fabric and coaxed us to hold it aloft so everyone could see this symbol of our engagement.

"*Kilililee!*" the women screeched in spontaneous approval.

The Luddys' bearer came forward and held out a shiny black box. Maurice stood and accepted it.

Grandmother Flora had explained this part to me. "Silas may not place your engagement ring on your finger, for some believe this constitutes *kiddushin*, or betrothal. If either of you decided to terminate the engagement, you would have to get a bill of divorce once he had given you the ring."

Maurice Luddy managed to remove the box's contents without anyone seeing the gift. Solemnly he stepped in front of my chair. He smiled sideways at his son and took my hand. "Dinah, daughter of Benjamin, son of Moses, you would honor our family if you would accept this ring as a token of your promise to my son Silas." The ring slipped easily in place. He removed his broad hand to reveal a three-tiered setting: the first was a circle of diamonds, the second of emeralds, the third a sparkling sapphire crown a half-inch in diameter. I held my hand beside the brooch, thrilling at the even louder ululations of kilililees that echoed through the crowded hall.

Cousin Sultana was one of the first to push her way through the throng to admire my gifts. As she fingered my brooch, I noticed the pearl bracelet she wore, remembering I had last seen it at her wedding. My earlier suspicions were confirmed. A wave of fury enveloped me, canceling the elation I had felt seconds earlier. I was about to say something when her chattering sisters, who followed in her wake, pushed her aside. Sultana backed away to allow them and my other Sassoon aunts and cousins to have a closer look. In a fog, I grinned and nodded as everyone had his turn admiring my gifts. A few minutes later, when I realized it was Gabriel Judah's parents who were congratulating me, I forced myself to appear joyful. After they moved on, I spent a few seconds scanning the room, trying to decide how many of the guests also were parents of young men who had spurned me.

"Who was the matchmaker?" I overheard the mother of a girl two years behind me in school ask Aunt Bellore.

"One was hardly necessary," Bellore replied haughtily. What a change from my earlier position, when no matchmaker would stake her reputation on having to find me a partner! What I—and I suppose everyone else—had first thought was my "settlement" with the son of a convert from far off in the hills had instantly turned into my "catch." Swept away with my newfound status, I nevertheless was mindful that the glitter on my finger and bosom did not alter how I felt about Silas Luddy, nor would it mean much when we were alone together, alone for eternity.

Still, I was giddy with triumph. The people who had supposed I had no future were not laughing now. Many a myopic Calcutta mother was wondering why she had not thought to look for a husband at a higher altitude. All would have been perfect if I had not had the misfortune to overhear two snippets of conversation, each of which left a painful residue of doubt.

I had floated around that evening avoiding Cousin Sultana and happily accepting the well-wishes of people who once shunned me socially. Then Masuda grabbed my arm.

"He is very handsome."

I almost asked her if she really thought so, then stopped myself. "Yes, isn't he?"

"I love a mustache on a man, especially a thin one." She poked me and tittered.

"His hands, that's what I like most," I said, surprising myself. Nevertheless, it was true. Even from across the room I could see that when he spoke, his fingers moved more expressively than his face. I leaned against a post, trying surreptitiously to see how others were reacting to him, when another conversation, though hushed, could be understood.

A woman whose voice I did not recognize was chiding Grandmother Helene. "Bad luck to have done it that way," she clucked in mock sympathy.

"What do you mean?" Grandmother Helene asked.

"The ring, having the father place the ring on Dinah's finger."

"What are you talking about? You know the fiancé may not do it himself."

"Have you forgotten that if the father is a widower, someone else is to be given the honor—a brother, an uncle, even a near female relative on the man's side of the family—anyone who has not lost a spouse to death," came the smug response.

"I would not have thought someone as modern as you would be so superstitious. Besides, who else was there? The sisters are coming for the wedding, but not for this. There was no time to summon them."

The woman made an offended sound. "This child can afford not even the smallest amount of ill-luck. At least I hope the wedding will take place on a Tuesday."

"What's the big *tamasha* about a Tuesday?"

"I was married on a Tuesday because on the third day of creation, the Bible repeats twice, 'and God saw how good this was.' "

Grandmother Helene drew a long inward breath. "Of course she shall be married on a Tuesday. Most people must plan for a Sunday so everyone will come, but nobody will want to miss this party!" I smiled, knowing that she now would have to influence Zilpah to set that day of the week. Furious at the interferer who had found whatever fault she could with my happy occasion, I determined to support my grandmother's plea.

When I turned back to Masuda, her mother was leading her away. At sixteen, Masuda was the prime age to be paraded around. I was certain she would be married within the year. As it was, I would be wedded at eighteen, already ancient by the standards of the Baghdadis.

I took the opportunity to find a bathroom. Two women already occupied it. They had not closed the door tightly so I could hear their words echoing in the marble chamber. "Such a gaudy ring! Weren't you shocked by it?"

"Why? Sooner or later it will come out of Benu's pocket."

"You don't think the Sassoons paid for it?"

"No, no. Not the maharajah of Theatre Road!" Her laugh was harsh, metallic.

"The maharajah! Wonderful!"

"That's what he must think of himself to offer a dowry like that."

"The Luddys don't require the money."

"The old man may have debts, or he may want to acquire more land. Or pay his jewelry bills! Anyway, who knows? They keep to themselves up there. Had to, after Maurice married that woman who supposedly converted."

"I know for a fact she did. My aunt was at the *mikvah*. But I see what you mean. I wouldn't want a Luddy for my daughter."

"And I wouldn't want a Sassoon for my son. In fact, we turned her down for our Daniel."

"But that was when the dowry was half of what Luddy is getting." The woman chuckled. "Might you have reconsidered when you heard her price had doubled?"

"Absolutely not!"

"What about your Josiah? Could he have turned his back on fifty thousand rupees?" she teased.

"Fifty thousand! I thought it was twenty-five."

"Twenty-five, fifty, what is the difference? A scandal, if you ask me."

"What else is new in that family?"

"Ten years of it, and no end in sight. Trust my words. Bad luck comes in threes: Luna Raymond, Mozelle Arakie, and that black bitch he parades around as though she was one of us. I tell you this: they have never banished the evil eye from this household."

"Did you notice she has her mother's huge eyes?"

"Yes, the same queer color of tea."

"If she's anything like her mother, this blushing bride is going to be a handful. Good thing they are shipping her to the hills so we won't have to hear about her so often." As the door moved in my direction, I ducked into the pantry until the two horrid women were gone.

Fifty thousand rupees! I had never been told the exact amount, but now I was appalled. Even though Silas denied he required my money, by the terms of our marriage settlement he could make use of it without my permission. Could I trust him? I sat down on a stool, shuddering at what else had been said about me. Only a few moments earlier I thought I had silenced the wagging tongues. Would there never be an end? Could I never conquer the rumors that I had not engendered? I halted that line of thinking when I recalled my own stupidity with Gabriel. Twisting the ring on my hand, I decided it was not unlucky that Maurice Luddy had placed it on my finger. "Superstitious witches!" I muttered. I would not let them plant seeds of doubt. Of course I could rely on Silas. He had promised me in writing and I was certain my father would never have concluded the negotiations without the proper documents, so I would have the last laugh as I determined where and how I would spend my fifty thousand. Comforted, I stood and smoothed my dress. I was about to become a wealthy woman in my own right. The crones of Calcutta might not know this now, but they would eventually. I would see to that.

At the end of the evening, when most of the guests had departed, I noticed Silas and his father together for the first time. Maurice Luddy's expression was tense. Silas seemed to be only half-listening to his words of counsel. Then I noticed an odd occurrence. When Maurice reached out to mollify his son by touching his shoulder lightly, Silas rebuffed his father with a sharp swipe of his hand. Maurice's expression soured and he turned away. For a moment I worried about what was the matter between father and son, but as Silas made his way toward me, I dismissed the exchange as a typical misunderstanding, not unlike those I had had with Zilpah in the past.

Although we were observed from across the expanse of the largest room in the house, Silas and I could speak alone for the first time.

"A wonderful evening," he began tensely.

"Yes, everything went very well," I agreed formally.

"Are you pleased with the gifts?"

My hand clasped the brooch, and I flushed with embarrassment for not mentioning them at once. "Oh, yes! So much more than I expected, or required. And while I think they are exquisite . . ." I paused. How could I say this without giving offense?

His eyelids twitched. "Yes?"

"I admire the ring and the brooch, as any woman would, but what astonished me more was the way the brooch was presented—the flower petals, the arrangement—and that something so beautiful had been created for me."

"I am pleased you noticed." His eyes widened and brightened.

"Who does such lovely work?"

"A friend of mine, but the idea was my own."

Something stirred inside me. "Thank you," I murmured.

We fell silent until we noticed we were being observed. Both sensing the need to breach the gap, we began again in unison. I deferred to Silas.

He cleared his throat. "However much I respect the tenets of our faith and traditions of our community, I also believe they can be modified to suit the individuals. I hope my saying so does not give offense."

"Not at all, but would you mind if I wore a Baghdadi wedding dress? More and more of the girls are selecting European gowns, but I wanted to honor my grandmother," I said, leaving out that I did not want to make the same mistake by wearing something frivolous that he might find displeasing.

"That is entirely your choice," he said gallantly, then grinned. "But it is one that would gratify me, as I myself prefer the traditional to the fashionable."

"I suppose everything else will be left to our parents."

"Not quite everything. Since you have expressed your wish concerning your dress, I have one preference." He looked around to be certain we were not overheard; then he made a quarter turn to the wall. I pivoted to match him. "After the ceremony and the celebration, I would like us to return to Darjeeling directly."

The request puzzled me. Usually newlyweds observed a seven-day period in the home of the bridegroom's parents. During seven nights the couple joined their families for *sheva berakoth*, special prayers. I had assumed that since the Luddys lived so far away, we would spend the first week at either their lodgings in Calcutta or possibly at Theatre Road. But wanting to accommodate Silas, I replied, "It is only proper that we return to the house of your father."

"No, not my father's, nor your father's house. I wish to take you to my home. Your father will think I am asking this because I am not a boy of sixteen and I have lived alone for many years. However, that is not why. I am concerned for your feelings. They make the first night a nightmare of publicity. Do you know what a *mashti* is?"

I shook my head.

"She's the inspector of virgins, who waits with the family outside the door to collect the *byadh el wech*—the sheet that should be 'white with blood.' " He shook his head with disgust. "Traditions that dishonor women should be discarded."

I appreciated his sensitivity, but I was not certain how to respond. Probably he knew more about the embarrassments that merry wedding guests could inflict on a couple than I did. I knew my virginity was not in question, so he was not protecting me from disgrace. Besides, I was not afraid of leaving home—I welcomed it. Not having Zilpah preside over my postnuptial days would also be a relief.

I lowered my head demurely. "Does your father agree?" I asked, thinking this must have been what their earlier encounter had been about.

Silas nodded.

"Then ask him to discuss the matter with my father. I have no objections either way." The last came out in a rapid burst, for I could see Aunt Bellore bearing down on us, her huge bosom bouncing with every step.

❧   ❧   ❧

Ever since I had overheard the discussion of my dowry, I had become more and more unsure about the match. I knew brides went through a period of doubt, but this was something more. Perhaps the answer lay in the relationships between the members of the Luddy family. If I could discover why the father and son were alienated, maybe I would understand the undercurrents that were so worrisome.

"Tell me more about the Luddys, Papa," I asked him as we waited for Aunt Bellore and Grandmother Helene to arrive on the day we were to make the final preparations.

"What do you want to know about them? Their family? Their homes?"

"No, their business."

He lifted his eyebrows for a moment, then beamed. "Luddy is a clever man. Not only did he have the foresight to see the Darjeeling region as ideal for tea cultivation, but he developed his fields more effectively than most of the other growers. Even more important, he has organized his family's assets with superb foresight."

"In what way?"

"As you know, he has two older daughters and Silas. He gave each of the daughters twenty-five percent of the holdings as a dowry. Both their husbands work in the enterprise. From what I have heard, it is an amicable situation, with the sons-in-law following Maurice's instructions. Wisely he realizes that eventually every family has its jealousies, rivalries, and feuds. To prevent these from crippling the firm, Silas was given a quarter of the business now, and will inherit his father's share. This means that Silas will retain control and will make settlements if disputes arise. Even more astute, Silas does not live on the plantation, nor does he participate in the daily operations. His responsibility is twofold: first, he manages the fiscal aspects of the family's wealth; second, he is in charge of developing new blends and markets for the tea. Both jobs give him a perspective the others do not have. This Luddy is a shrewd man."

"Do you think they require my dowry?"

My father seemed vexed. "We have been through this before, Dinah."

I repeated my question. "Do you think so?"

"No, I don't," he said with finality, punctuating each syllable. He looked out across the glistening lawns. It was after the heaviest period of the monsoon season, but rain poured in sheets, turning the paths into muddy streams. "The carriages will be late in this weather." He sighed and leaned back in his chair.

I wanted to ask what he knew about any problems between the father and son, but felt unable to do so. An hour later, when the ladies finally arrived, there was little small talk. Aunt Bellore had lists. Grandmother Helene rambled on and on with ideas for everything from food to flowers to the shoes I would wear with every outfit. Zilpah either agreed or disagreed with each point. My father refereed. I spoke my mind only once, in reference to my wedding dress.

"Are you certain?" Grandmother Helene asked. "Nobody has worn a Baghdadi gown in many a year."

"Grandmother Flora wore one," I said, "and so did my mother."

Nobody spoke for a long moment, until Zilpah, who had long been criticized for her refusal to wear anything except a sari, said, "As you wish, Dinah."

"What is this nonsense I hear about there being no full week of sheva berakoth prayers?" Aunt Bellore added to stir the stew.

"Mr. Luddy's only request," my father said to curtail that discussion.

"I would not permit that with my daughters," she said haughtily. Eliciting no response from Papa, she pressed on with a hint of annoyance in her tone. "So have you definitely set the date for Tuesday, the twenty-eighth of October?"

My father nodded. "It suits everyone."

With a wave of her long arm, she presented the scene outside the window as though she was introducing a visitor. "Except the monsoon."

Grandmother Helene spoke in the singsong voice she usually reserved for children. "It came early this year. Now it is running its course."

The old enmity from the time when Aunt Bellore had removed Grandmother Helene from Theatre Road infested the room. "Well," Bellore snapped, "I can remember many a ghastly day in November. That is why *we* never plan outdoor parties before December."

"The Luddys want Dinah to enjoy the end of the Darjeeling season and to settle in before winter," my father replied soothingly.

"Also, we had many calendars to consider," Zilpah said, giving me a meaningful stare. I recalled how she had quizzed me about my monthly flow, counting forward and backward as she made her calculations.

"I think Zilpah has made an excellent choice," I chimed in, publicly taking my stepmother's side for the first time.

Zilpah's mouth trembled slightly, an indication that I had pleased her.

"The date is settled," my father said to close the subject.

Zilpah opened a drawer in an inlaid table and pulled out a wooden box that held a stack of wedding invitations. "These arrived this morning." She passed around copies, giving me the first one. The ivory-hued card was about eight inches long and three inches wide.

"Very lovely work," Aunt Bellore said in a brittle voice.

"Yes, my dear, the color was a splendid choice," complimented my father.

I fingered the glossy surface, repeating "Dinah Luddy" to myself.

For the next few weeks I found myself entangled in a coil of customs organized to prevent either the bride or the groom from thinking about what was soon to come.

The Thursday preceding the marriage ceremony, Silas' sisters, Gala and Gracia, and their husbands marched up our drive in a procession led by the traditional Baghdadi dakaka musicians plucking their kanuns; drumming their tablas, dimbahs, and zirnas; and shaking their tambourines. This was the night for the *khadba*, the "night of the red color" ritual. A chorus of women entertained with songs praising the bride and groom, lauding our families, and wishing us good luck, while Grandmother Helene and her daughters painted first my fingernails, then Silas' with green henna, which, when dry, turned a gruesome shade of orange that was supposed to repel the evil power of demons.

After our fingers were wrapped in silver paper, Silas' elder sister came forward to present me with a bracelet that matched the other pieces I had already received. The women danced about us and sang out choruses of *Afaki-Afaki*, concluding with a piercing round of kilililees.

Two days later, on the Sabbath, Silas was called to the Torah as *Li'heyoth Hathan*, the groom-to-be. From the women's balcony I listened to his gentle, melodic reading of the Scriptures, noting how much better his voice was in song than speech. In the interval following his reading, the women tossed sugar-coated almonds and caraway seeds down on him.

When we returned home from the service, Zilpah said, "Yali will give you your meal in your room this afternoon. You will need to gather your strength for tonight."

"I wish everything was over already," I moaned as I contemplated three more days of festivities.

"Your father and I are as exhausted as you are, but he is determined you shall not be denied a single celebration."

"I hope I never have to go through this again," I said, forgetting that Zilpah had been married twice, my father three times. At last I understood why he had opted for two quiet weddings far away from the drawing rooms of Calcutta.

That night came the *toowafah*. I received several more elaborate gift trays. The balance of the presents were the customary molasses and candies.

Dutifully, lacking enthusiasm, Silas and I went through the rituals. We both were tiring of the demands we had to follow for each rite. Obedience might not have been so difficult if family members had been in agreement about how each event should proceed. As it was, Silas and I were pushed here and there, told where to sit, when to stand, what to say by a variety of people who recalled their parents had done it a certain way and their instructions were the only ones to be followed. Although I never dared mention it to him, I was grateful Silas had insisted on leaving the city after the reception. Another week of being ordered about would have been unendurable. We shall have our way in the end, I repeated to myself, to make it through the last confusing days.

Since no activities were planned for my final Sunday in Calcutta, Grandmother Helene invited me to bring Ruby for a visit. I leapt at the opportunity to be away from the preparations at home, rushing my sluggish sister to be ready. At ten, Ruby was a sweet, chubby girl with shiny pink cheeks, long black curls, and huge round eyes fringed by sweeping lashes. She was the sort of child strangers could not help patting on the head and proclaiming, "What a pretty one!" She had learned to smile modestly in response, which was the sum of what she had managed to master. She had just begun at the Jewish Girls' School and was in the first year, at least three years behind the others her age. Even then, she struggled to learn to read and could not manage any sums.

"The difficult birth," Grandmother Helene explained. "She'll catch up with herself in a few more years."

In our household Ruby was lost in the shuffle between me, the four boisterous boys, and the demanding wiles of Seti, who at age four continued to absorb her mother's interest more than the rest of us combined. Quick and wiry, Seti had almost equaled Ruby in academic achievements and probably would surpass her older sister within the year. To prevent Ruby from being neglected by Zilpah or intimidated by Seti, Grandmother Helene had taken her motherless granddaughter under her wing, having her to visit as often as she could.

On that Sunday, we arrived in a downpour.

"How can it continue to rain every day?" she sniffed.

"Everybody thought the rains would have been over by now," I replied, glancing out the window in the hope that a miracle might occur even as we spoke.

She ran her hands through the knot of gray curls that capped her wide head. "I am sorry to say that Bellore Sassoon may have been right."

"If so, then it is for the first time." I laughed gaily to let her know the weather was neither a concern of mine nor a responsibility of hers.

A servant took my cape and then bent to assist Ruby. Grandmother Helene tweaked one of her long sausage curls. "Just like mine when I was your age. Your Auntie Badra has a surprise for you," she said, turning Ruby over to her eldest daughter. "Dinah, come up to my sitting room and I will show you what I am planning to wear to your wedding."

Once there, she lay down on a loosely stuffed chaise covered in a flowery fabric and organized the pillows under her back and arms until I thought she would never be satisfied. There was no mention of dresses. I took the wing chair and waited for her to settle herself. At last she was comfortable, but her fingers continued to fondle the lacy trim on the pillow she clasped in her lap. "Are you going to leave for the train right after the reception?"

"That is what Silas wants."

Her eyes sparkled merrily. "So, you will cheat the mashti out of her job."

I turned my head so she would not see me coloring.

As she clasped her hands together and cracked her fingers, the sound jolted me to attention. "Good for you. The night I was married, my young husband—Bension was only fourteen—was not quite certain what to put where." She threw her head back and laughed. Ripples of flesh wiggled on her arms and legs. "The mashti knocked on the door and asked what was taking so long. Without even waiting for us to reply, she burst in and"—she pressed the pillow to her abdomen to control her amusement—"and assisted Bension, if you follow my meaning." She watched me closely. When I did not blink, she asked, "Has Zilpah spoken to you?"

"What about?"

"About the marriage bed."

I shook my head.

"As I expected." She flexed her neck from left to right, trying to shake out a kink. "The task is left to me." She seemed more pleased than annoyed.

She thought I knew nothing of what went on between men and women, but hadn't I found my father in bed with a woman in Patna? Hadn't I seen Indian women massaging their infants' genitals to stimulate them? And hadn't I lived my life in India, where holy cows and bulls and stray dogs mated in the streets, where every aspect of life from birth to death could be viewed from a carriage seat?

Actually, the Indians themselves were modest in conduct. I had never seen a Calcutta boy and girl openly walking hand in hand or even married people kissing, yet Yali—without shame—had taken me to a shrine where young girls worshiped a phallus in order to get a good husband, thinking it would help my predicament. I had visited Hindu temples, which contained huge representations of the female pudenda with a penis penetrating the center. Even so, I was more interested in—and furtive about—studying the temple friezes that depicted the union of those mortal lovers made divine: Krishna and Radha. In fact, any image of a couple in close embrace, even a man's hand touching a lady's cheek, caused queer sensations to shoot down my spine and created more of a longing for something I could not fulfill than any explicit view of disembodied genitalia.

As I matured, I compared my body to the physical ideal of the Hindu deities, who had thick thighs, broad hips, tiny waists, and large melonshaped breasts. After I had grown taller than any other woman in my family, remaining slender with broad shoulders, narrow hips, and disappointingly small, pointed breasts, I knew I was never going to look like a goddess. I only hoped that Silas would find me to his taste.

Waiting for my reply, Grandmother Helene twisted the lace so forcefully that it ripped. "I know a little about it," I answered to cover the gap.

She ran her tongue along her lower lip as she fashioned her words. When she was ready, she spoke in the most ordinary of tones. "I do not know exactly what you have discovered on your own, so let me just say that most women do their daughters a disservice—as my own mother did to me—by moaning that the union between a husband and wife is unpleasant. On the contrary, the whole process is meant to be pleasurable, but like most worthwhile activities, practice and patience must be brought to the task before the rewards may be reaped. Otherwise, why would anyone bother?" She chortled.

I leaned forward, anxious for more.

She grinned at my eagerness. "May I offer some practical advice?"

"Yes." I nodded and gripped the arm of the chair and listened, entranced, as she made certain I understood the Jewish laws regarding clean and unclean days. ". . . So this not only fulfills the sacred obligations but also separates the man and the woman so each will have increased hungers for the other. During the days when you must be apart, you may continue to enjoy each other's company. Look to those times to share your worries. More troubles come from hiding feelings than releasing them. And never, never go to sleep angry with one another." She stared with softhearted, benevolent eyes. "Any questions?"

"How soon might I expect a baby?" I dared.

She shrugged. "Most girls who have attentive husbands receive one within the year."

"Does it hurt?"

"Yes, especially the first birth, but when the pain ends, there is joy."

I blanched. "I meant the other—what comes first."

"From what I have seen, I believe Mr. Luddy will be a gentle, considerate man. You are well-mated physically and he should not overwhelm you. If anything displeases you, tell him and I am certain he will do his utmost to keep your comfort in mind."

With a creak and a groan, she stood up and made her way to her dressing table. From a bottom drawer she removed a small brass chest. "A gift for you." She opened the lid and showed me the three glass jars fitted inside. "To prevent babies, if that is your choice at first, use this one before and this one afterward"—she held up the last jar— "and this one for any soreness." She unscrewed each top, took a dab, and wiped it on the back of my hand as she described the salves in more detail.

"What if . . . ?"

Patiently she waited for me to gather my thoughts.

"What if the man does not appeal to you?"

Her moon face glowed. "Dinah, my child, don't rush ahead with all sorts of assumptions. The attractions you are anticipating do exist between some, but hardly most men and some women when they first meet. Already you may have experienced that sensation with an acquaintance . . ." The words hung for a long moment. "Those are transitory glimpses into the powerful feelings that will be unleashed by a marriage. Today these sensations lie dormant, like sparks waiting to be ignited when touched to straw. Unless your partner is cruel, unpleasant, or unusually distasteful—and your Mr. Luddy is none of these—time together will stoke those fires." She sniffed and straightened her skirts. "Now, is there anything further we should discuss?"

"There is another matter, not on the same subject, but . . ."

She came up behind me and rubbed my neck and shoulders. "Come, now, there are no secrets between us today."

"For my wedding day, I have been wanting to wear my mother's jewelry. It cannot be found."

"Have you spoken to Zilpah?"

"Yes, she says nothing was ever given to her."

"And you don't believe her."

"Well . . ."

"The fire . . ." Grandmother Helene prompted softly.

"No, I don't think so. The furniture and clothing were burnt, but I was in Mama's dressing room when everything was being removed. I saw Yali take the jewel boxes away for safekeeping."

"Have you asked Yali what she did with them?"

"Yes."

"And . . . ?"

"Because she did not want to anger my father or upset my grand-mother, she—" I stumbled.

Grandmother Helene leapt to the wrong conclusion. "She sold them!"

"No! Yali would never—" I protested. "She gave them to Aunt Bellore."

"What is missing?"

"I do not know exactly what my mother owned, but I remember a long necklace with pearls as big as marbles, and a matching bracelet with two strands, Grandmother Flora's ring with one huge pearl in the center surrounded by smaller ones, a gold tiger brooch—it had emer-alds for eyes—and I might recognize some other pieces if I saw them." I ground my teeth in frustration, then shouted, "Cousin Sultana was wearing the same bracelet on her wedding day. I am certain she was!"

"That doesn't surprise me." Grandmother Helene began rearranging the pillows on her chaise.

"Can't you do something about this?" I wailed.

"I can't speak against anyone in your family when my half-witted granddaughter requires their protection."

Her strong characterization of Ruby shocked me, and I almost rose to my sister's defense before I was hushed.

"Let's not deceive ourselves. Ruby will never be as clever as you or Seti. At least she's a pretty girl who can be trained to run a home."

I swallowed past the rising lump in my throat. "What about Aunt Bellore?"

Grandmother Helene paced the room, now and then tugging the draperies to make them hang more evenly. "Everyone thinks your aunt is a pious woman." She picked up a cloth and began to polish a silver candy dish vigorously, while I mulled over her reply.

"She was my mother's closest friend . . ." I offered in a voice that trailed off as I recalled a much earlier discussion with Nani. "No. She was not her friend. No friend is jealous of another's happiness." I flushed with the fury that boiled up under the surface. "She hated Luna and she hates me!"

I must have looked as though I would explode, for Grandmother Helene held the silver dish against her chest like a shield. Trembling with rage, I realized the evidence surrounded me. From the hour of my mother's death, Aunt Bellore had led the group that treated me as an outsider. She refused to accept her role as the most appropriate maternal substitute. She made me feel unwelcome in her home. She protected her daughters from my company. She might even have been behind my father's initial distrust of Grandmother Flora, and she certainly had instigated Grandmother Helene's departure after Mozelle's death, leaving her brother's children adrift again. Her vehement prejudice against Zilpah had fueled the other women of the community. Worst of all, she had matched her daughter to the only boy in whom I had shown any interest. Why? I did not know enough of men and women, of passions and jealousies, to sort this out then, but the door to this sordid labyrinth had flung wide open.

And what of Zilpah, the woman I most resented? What proof did I have that she had ever tried to harm me? None! Since the first days, she had struggled to manage our untidy household. With firmness she had reined in my two unruly brothers and had achieved peace among the four disparate male siblings. She had coached the backward Ruby and had, as a parent should, adored her own Seti, but she had never neglected me. I had met each of Zilpah's attempts to win me with petulance at best, disobedience at worst. As though a curtain had opened, I saw that I had been covetous of my father's love in the same way as his sister, Bellore, had been envious of her brother's love for Luna. Zilpah's desire to find me a husband when I was younger derived from a fear—a very realistic one, as it turned out—that the task would not be easy. She must have sanctioned the lavishness of my dowry even though she knew it meant less for Ruby, less for her own Seti, and diminished her own fortune considerably. Yet when every man in Calcutta turned his back on me, she was the one who had found Mr. Luddy.

Shaking with the terrible truths that coursed through my mind, I held Grandmother Helene's firm hands until I could speak again. "I have been wrong about so much," I gushed. "I should never have trusted Aunt Bellore. I was so awful to Zilpah."

Grandmother Helene frowned. "This is supposed to be a happy time for you and the family, Dinah."

I fought back a new volley of tears. "Bellore is a thief, isn't she?"

She pointed to my brooch, bracelet, and ring. "I realize you feel as though you have been cheated, but why not look at how much you already have? You are marrying into a fine family. You will have the dowry of a princess. You do not need your mother's unlucky baubles to weigh you down. I know a girl is sentimental at a time like this, but if you or I raise this question now, a tumult will break out and everyone will take sides."

"But they are mine!"

"I am not certain about that. From what I understand, your mother did not have the most methodical of minds. She made decisions on the spur of the moment. Her necklaces and bracelets belong to whomever your mother promised them to. And she may very well have decided to give them to her 'best' friend."

"Aunt Bellore did not really like my mother, not after she married her brother. I think she was jealous that Luna's match was better than hers."

"So now she has the jewels and the last laugh."

"Yes, and it is not fair."

"Do you want to know what *my* mother would have said?"

I waited with fists clenched.

"*Khallil kaskeen yikser kirrabetu.*" Grandmother Helene wrapped her arms around me. "That means 'strong vinegar will break in its jar,' or in other words, your Aunt Bellore will do the greatest harm to herself in the end."

"B-but—"

She squeezed me harder. "You must put this out of your mind for the present. Maybe later, after you are settled, your husband could make a request through legal channels to acquire what rightly belongs to you—and to him."

"I see." I felt as though a mist was lifting. "Aunt Bellore would have to fight the Luddys then."

Grandmother Helene nodded sagely. "In this world a woman lets a man fight her wars—at least on the front lines." She winked. "You and I know women organize the battle plans."

I hugged her back, hoping she could read my gratitude in the wordless salute.

15

At dawn of my wedding day the rains had ceased, but the humidity made even the doorknobs seem mushy. Across the lawns the vapors hovered about a foot off the ground in a static layer—an illusion children adored. I looked out to see Asher and Simon using small shovels to lift a "cloud" pile and carry it to a new place before any zephyr dissipated it.

"Do you think Aunt Bellore's weather predictions will come true?" I asked my father when I saw him downstairs.

"No. This wind will push the clouds out to sea by late morning," he stated confidently as he selected the carpets to be laid outdoors. "You should try to rest now, if you can."

"Wish I could." I yawned. Because it was believed that it was bad luck for the bride and groom to sleep the night before their marriage, our friends had kept both Silas and me up all night. "I'm too excited, and too hungry!"

Everyone who had lasted the night—except me—was served a chota hazri. Zilpah ordered me to fast. While everyone ate, I went out on the terrace. The skies were the color of slate, with streaks of red that looked like wounds. Low clouds, like bloody bandages, hovered above in the manner of a threatening army.

Papa was now supervising the setting up of the marquee on the lawn. "By the time we return from the synagogue, the sun will be burning on this canvas," he said with as much sincerity as he could muster. I thought we would be lucky to get through the day without at least one downpour, but I did not dash my father's hopes.

Yali came and led me upstairs for bathing and dressing. My gown followed the Baghdadi design that a bride of Shalom Cohen or Sheikh Sason might have worn, except the fabrics were more elegant. The inner layer was a gossamer white silk caftan with hundreds of sequins sewn into the bodice and rippling across the winglike sleeves, which were bordered with two inches of embroidery. Over this garment was a wrapper cut from a gold-purple-and-black-striped Chinese brocade. It laced down the front with golden braid. Underneath everything I wore baggy trousers of the finest gold silk. My headdress had a wide band of glittering stones that came down low on my forehead, covering my eyebrows. Grandmother Helene's clever dressmaker had managed to tailor the ordinarily shapeless costume to flatter me. The layers were cooler than I had expected and more comfortable than a European creation.

When I was almost ready, Zilpah came to my room. "You look very beautiful." After a long pause she continued. "The time has come to speak to you as a mother to a daughter." I expected she was going to launch into something about the physical side of marriage, a subject already covered by Grandmother Helene, but I did not stop her. "Dinah, you have a will of iron. It has not always been easy living with you. Considering everything, who am I to say you would have grown up strong and whole without that trait? These last years have been difficult—for everyone—but now the time has come to bend to another person's wishes. There is no place for obstinacy in a marriage."

I felt a release, as though I had been tensed to protect myself from a blow and had managed to avoid it entirely, but no words would come.

She started to leave.

"Wait! Please, would you walk me down the stairs . . ." I paused to swallow my tears. ". . . like a mother would."

❧   ❧   ❧

On the way to the synagogue in the gaily decorated phaeton, I began to wonder what Silas would wear. Knowing I was in traditional dress, he might have selected a *dagla*, the Arabic long coat, but he looked so handsome in a cutaway that I thought that would be my preference. This and other mental diversions kept me calm until, rounding the bend in the road, I caught sight of the steeple of the Maghen David Synagogue. My face flushed. I gasped for air. Zilpah leaned toward me and fanned me as we pulled up to the building that was the pride of the Jewish community of Calcutta.

The synagogue, the largest Jewish house of worship in the East, was an enormous Italian Renaissance-style building with a massive facade of ornamental stonework. At the last moment, the architect had added an imposing steeple. Nobody in the Jewish community objected. In fact, they were pleased that the architect, in his ignorance, had managed to comply with the talmudic injunction that a synagogue should tower above the other structures.

I felt too weak to step down from the carriage. "I cannot—"

"Take a few deep breaths," Zilpah coaxed. "You will be fine in a moment."

I could not comply. I felt as though submerged underwater, fighting my way to the surface. A breath would be fatal. Just before my head burst, I gasped, panted, gasped again. I was drowning, drowning with the knowledge that this was not a passing fright. All the preparations, all the parties, all the commotion had hidden the fact that I did not know this man. My absorption with the dress and Aunt Bellore and Zilpah had muted the truth that I did not care for him. All Grandmother Helene's promises that I would feel differently later, all the lies I had told myself to get me to this moment, crashed about me like waves, plunging me into the swirling depths. The humidity pressed from every side. My garments stuck to my skin; perspiration matted the hair under my headdress. Zilpah pumped my arms, bringing a gush of wind under my sleeves.

My father blotted my face with his handkerchief until my eyes seemed to focus.

"Can we go in?" he asked, trying to mask his impatience.

"I think so . . ."

After he helped me down, I felt rooted in place. Zilpah pushed me forward. I could not take a single step on my own. With each parent bracing an arm, they walked me up the stairs. I kept my eyes forward to prevent feeling dizzy. Crossing the entrance, the first person I saw waiting to greet me was Aunt Bellore. She wore a green silk dress with my mother's strand of matched pearls, each the size of a small onion, draped like a medal across her bosom. Like a fireball, the anger swelled inside me and propelled me without assistance. I felt as though a rod supported my spine. I determined not to do or to say anything that would give this woman the satisfaction of thinking me unhappy on my wedding day.

Zilpah and Aunt Bellore climbed to the balcony. Papa led me into the sanctuary. He helped me up onto the two-foot-high *hekhal*, or platform. Silas waited under the *huppah*, the nuptial canopy. I did not look directly at my groom until we stood together. Silas looked resplendent in a formal black frock coat and gray striped trousers.

The *hazzan*, Sholom Aaron, was not an ordained rabbi—there were none in India at that time—but a learned community member who acted as the *mekkadesh* who officiated at weddings. He had expressive eyes that riveted first on Silas and then on me, giving us each a silent promise that we were under the care of a friend. With a glass of wine in his hand to begin the betrothal, he said, "Blessed art thou, Lord our God, king of the universe, who has made us holy through thy commandments and has commanded us concerning marriages that are forbidden . . ." He droned on, but I could not follow him, for again my head was spinning. The time came for the ring. Silas placed a gold band on the index finger of my right hand. As he repeated the ancient words which consecrated me unto him according to the laws of Moses and Israel, his firm clasp minimized my trembling.

Next the *ketuba*, the marriage contract, was read out to the assembly. This marital settlement included the amount of my dowry, plus what the Luddys offered us, with the addition of the biblical "two hundred *zuzeem* for a virgin," which, when said aloud, was mortifying. Our witnesses came forward and signed the ketuba, as did Silas, before it was handed to me for safekeeping. My first view of this beautifully illuminated version of the marriage contract written in Hebrew cheered me. The border was a trellis of leaves interspersed with red poppies. In the center, between the pledge of the bride and the pledge of the groom, were a peacock and peahen with beaks pressed together. I suspected Silas had seen to this detail.

Further benedictions were read over a cup of wine, from which we both took sips. The hazzan, his merry eyes crinkling at the edges, took a small china cup and held it aloft. He reminded us this would serve as a recollection of our grief at the destruction of the Temple, adding, "You are about to commit an irrevocable act. Once the cup is smashed, it is gone forever. So, too, may this marriage be permanent for infinity."

He handed it to Silas.

With as much force as he could muster, Silas dashed it to the floor, shattering it at once—a good omen at last! The women in the balcony rained a chorus of kilililees on us as we were led to the Ark chamber where the Scrolls of Law were kept. There we made *zoor*, respectfully kissing each Sepher Torah and privately dedicating ourselves to follow God's laws. Finally Silas and I emerged to the congratulations of the assembled guests.

We rode alone back to my house in the ornate open victoria his father had hired for the occasion. "You were so right to choose that gown," he said as we drove away, waving to our family and friends.

"Thank you, Silas." I smiled uneasily, adding with an exaggerated sigh, "The commotion is over. Well, almost."

"What a relief," he agreed. "I was so worried about breaking the cup the first try, I told my father to be certain it was made of the finest porcelain."

"You didn't break it, you pulverized it," I said, making him laugh much harder and much more naturally. "I was lucky to remain standing. They kept me up all night, and Zilpah made me fast today."

"I managed a short nap this morning, but I have also fasted. In fact, I am starving."

"Me too," I said, thinking: This is the first thing we have in common.

❀ ❀ ❀

The carriage took a circuitous route back to Theatre Road to give our guests time to assemble and greet us. Together Silas and I entered the house and inspected the breathtaking flower arrangements. A platter of delicacies was waiting for a servant to carry it outside. Silas took two sandwich points, popped one in his mouth, and handed me the other. "Quick, nobody is looking."

I pointed to the horizon. "We had better join everyone before it rains."

As he looked out at the fast-moving clouds, the wind rustled the canvas of the marquee. "We can always have the party in here," he said uneasily as he led me to the transformed garden.

"Oh, no!" I pointed to the center of the lawn, near the fountain, where a canopy supported by poles sheltered the wedding cake. "It's wobbling!"

"Bearer! Bring some men," Silas shouted to the nearest servants. In a few minutes the workers who had set up the canopies were at work securing the ropes and stakes.

When we stepped forward with our parents, the seven blessings over the wine were recited and the food was served. Silas and I took our places in the area demarcated by Oriental rugs, where the immediate family was to receive the guests. Everybody milled around admiring my dress, my ring, and chattering about how splendidly everything had gone. With several hundred people to greet, Silas and I had only a few moments to eat and drink. I was happy we had taken the chance to steal a few bites earlier.

Before we had chatted with even half the crowd, Aunt Bellore came up behind Zilpah's chair. "This weather will not hold off much longer. You had better get Dinah to cut her cake."

Zilpah pretended to take no notice of the breeze that whipped Aunt Bellore's taffeta skirts. Her own silver-and-white sari was firmly tucked in place while she remained seated. "Not everyone has had the opportunity to help himself at the refreshment table," she said crisply before turning to say a few words to the next person in line.

Aunt Bellore moved behind Grandmother Flora, who was propped with cushions so discreetly she seemed to be managing to sit upright on her own. By nodding her head and saying little, her shortness of breath was not noticeable to any but those who knew her intimately. At Bellore's touch on her shoulder, Nani shivered.

"Flora, are you cold? Your lips are blue," my aunt bellowed so everyone could hear.

"Just a bit. The air has changed."

Zilpah stood to signal Grandmother Flora's servant. "Get her a shawl."

"Thank you, Zilpah," Nani said hoarsely.

Aunt Bellore remained beside her. "Don't you agree, Flora, the time has come for Dinah to cut her cake?"

"Well . . ." Nani did not want to upset either woman.

"Yes, yes," Zilpah capitulated. She walked down the circle of chairs to the Luddy section, took Silas' hand, and led him to me. "Children, go to the wedding cake. Your fathers and I will meet you there."

In the few minutes it took for everyone to comply, the sky blackened with alarming speed. Even I could smell the mossy promise of rain. Silas and I approached the seven-layer cake set into a horseshoe of chrysanthemums.

"It weighs more than a thousand pounds!" Grandmother Helene triumphantly displayed the masterpiece she had ordered—and paid for. "Look, each layer is in the shape of a Star of David." The sides were decorated with an intricate latticework entwined with garlands. In order to reach the top layer, which we were to cut open for good luck, we had to climb a staircase lined with a Persian hall runner.

I mounted the first step, the silver cake knife in hand, and looked for Silas. The crowd pressed into a tight wedge, pushing him back. I could see his hand waving in the center of the group. "Go ahead, Dinah, I'm coming."

Just then there was another gust of wind. The poles of the canopy jiggled, causing me to hesitate on the third step.

"Dinah, you'll have to climb to the top to cut the cake," someone called.

I looked down in time to see Aunt Bellore push Silas away as he reached the bottom step. She pressed her bulk ahead of him and climbed up. Suddenly her hand was on my wrist, poking me toward the cake. I struggled free from her clasp, for I knew what I was to do. The cake's top layer was false. Beneath the icing was a box containing doves. The tip of the knife was to be used to rip the thin paper that held the birds in place.

I reached over, trying to figure a way to make the largest possible cut swiftly so the birds could escape at once. The complicated design of sugar icing looked too lovely to spoil. Unexpectedly she again clamped her hand on my wrist, forcing the knife straight into the center of the layer. I felt something resist the blade and jerked my hand upward. Her grip fell away as she cried in horror. Two inches of the blade had impaled the breast of a white bird. Its spasmodic screeches pierced the air. The other birds flew into the swirling wind. Blood spurted across the cake. Looking down at my chest, I found it splattered with tiny crimson dots as well. I looked up at Aunt Bellore. Her face was running with repulsive red streaks. Silas had sprinted up behind us and was easing her down. He grabbed the knife and, with a deft stroke, managed to get the twitching bird back into the cake before too many guests realized what had occurred.

Aunt Bellore turned.

Then everyone knew.

Exactly what happened next is uncertain. The wind snarled in sharp gusts and ripped the canopy in several places. Some frightened guests backed into the poles. In any case, the canopy was brought down on our heads, almost tumbling the cake, which managed to stay upright only because it was buffered by the floral horseshoe.

Silas and I ducked down and sat on the stairs until servants removed the mangled tent. All the while, we could hear Aunt Bellore's howling that this was surely a most inauspicious omen for a marriage.

The rain began with drops so large they could fill a teacup in a few minutes. The servants rushed about carrying carpets, furniture, food. Quicker than everyone could find cover, the plump tears melted together into sharp sheets like a vertical river. Wells of mud formed in every depression. Running feet churned it into vile slush that licked at the hems of the last sets of trousers and skirts to make it indoors. Even with Silas' attempt to shield me with his jacket, my beautiful gown became soaked.

Grandmother Helene followed me up the back stairs.

"Where is your brooch?" she asked as Yali rushed to undress me.

I reached for the spot at the cleft of my bosom where it had been pinned. "Oh, no!" I choked.

Yali wiped my tears and dressed me in my traveling clothes as though I were an injured child.

"Yali," I mumbled, "I am leaving you."

"Yes, missy-sahib."

"Silas said I might take a servant, but I did not think you would want to live so far from your family."

"You are my family, my first baby."

"Would you have come with me?"

She lowered her eyes.

"Would you come to care for *my* baby?"

She looked up at me—I was more than a foot taller—her large black eyes becoming glassy. "If you wish it."

There was a knock at the door. My father filled the doorframe.

"Come in, please."

He waved his wife forward. Zilpah opened her clenched hand to reveal the peacock. "The servants went down on their hands and knees until they found it."

"How can I ever thank you?" I looked from her to my father and back again. "For everything you have done for me, when I have—"

Zilpah raised her hand to silence me. "You must hurry. You have a train to catch and the roads will be slow in this downpour."

The next minutes of farewells passed in a blur. Outside, the rain poured off the verandas like spools of gray silk. A closed landau rolled up, a black ribbon of water trailing each wheel. The torrent began to overrun the curb. Silas boosted me in so I would not get my shoes wet. The *syce*, or groom, was about to close the door when I realized I had not kissed Nani good-bye. I climbed over Silas, splashed down into a deep puddle, and ran to the door where my bent and tired grandmother stood quivering.

"Be . . . happy . . . Dinah," she said, taking a shallow breath between each word.

Mindless of the ankle-deep water, I stepped back into the carriage. Silas took my hand in his. "Now I will take you home."

PART II

❦ ❦ ❦

The Drought

But to that second circle of sad hell,
  Where 'mid the gust, the whirlwind, and
    the flaw
Of rain and hail-stones, lovers need not tell
  Their sorrows. Pale were the sweet lips I saw,
Pale were the lips I kiss'd, and fair the form
I floated with, about that melancholy storm.

—JOHN KEATS, *A Dream, After Reading
Dante's Episode of Paolo and Francesca*

16

❧ ❧ ❧

Darjeeling, 1890

Staring at each other as the train carrying us into the next phase of our lives pierced the twilight, we were two strangers with only the most surface knowledge of each other, who were thrust together from that moment onward. As I shivered in the dampness of the miserable afternoon, I looked to my new husband for solace.

"What I despise most about this trip is the dust," Silas said. His tone was so serious I would have believed him if the glass of the rattling railroad car was not being battered with relentless rain.

Relief flooded through me: humor might be the key to getting to know him better. Fanning myself, I played along. "And this heat. I thought we would find relief in the hills."

Grinning, he rotated to face me. "Perhaps we should have remained in Calcutta for a few days." He tilted his head apologetically. "The storm has made us several hours behind schedule already. We can't possibly reach Darjeeling until late tomorrow."

"Yes, you are absolutely right." I put on my most imperious accent. "Please *do* ask the train to turn around." I shuddered in the draft.

"How have you managed to be such a good sport about everything?" Silas took my icy hands in his. "You are cold."

"I soaked my feet leaving Theatre Road. They say if your feet are cold, the rest will never warm."

"Who are 'they'?"

"Yali and Selima, my ayahs."

"One doesn't argue with one's ayahs."

"Never!" I giggled.

Silas was agreeable to be with, even under these uncomfortable circumstances. When we had arrived at Sealdah station, he had been furious that the lower berths he had reserved on the Eastern Bengal Railway had been filled. Our first-class day carriage might have been comfortable enough for a short journey, but after five hours of jolting on the hard benches, we both wished for a few more amenities.

After a few hours of trying to rest with my head upright, I longed to lie down, and drooped toward Silas. With the gentlest of touches he arranged my head on his shoulder, which was so bony it did not offer the most comfortable of perches. I dared not pull away lest he think I was rejecting his kindness, and somehow I drifted into an intermittent slumber as we rolled across the flat, melancholy stretches of the Bengal plain. Then the train halted rudely.

Silas tightened his grip on my hand. "The Ganges crossing. Follow me. My bearer will tend to everything else."

Blinking, I stepped out on a muddy siding by a riverbank amid clamoring torch-bearers. Men carrying umbrellas guided us to a flat-bottomed stern-wheel river steamer that reminded me of the *Lord Bentinck* and that trip long ago—in fact, the last journey I had taken—upriver with my father.

Once we had settled inside and the boat wheezed toward the Sara Ghat on the opposite bank, Silas asked, "Dinah, are you more awake now?"

"Yes, quite."

"Good, then listen to what I am going to do. After we land, I will leave you here with my bearer. Take your time and follow him up to the platform. I am going to bound ahead."

He caught my startled expression. "Not a very civilized place. If our reservations did not get through in 'well-organized' Calcutta, surely my wire for a berth on this leg will have been mangled by the Anglo-Indian Railway clerks. So, my girl, possession is left to the swiftest. I shall race up the bank, over the railway ties, and stake our claim!"

"I'll come with you," I offered limply.

"No, it would be most unseemly." He looked at me sternly. "You would beat me up the hill and I would be the laughingstock of the coolies from here to Bombay." He squeezed my hand. I felt my heart plummet. I did not want him to leave me, even for a few minutes. Not that I was afraid. The new sensation of being tied to him warmed me as though I had been plunged into a steaming bath. I smiled at him gratefully. He touched my cheek.

There was a change in the sound of the engines. Since it was too black and foggy to see anything, he took this for his signal. "Follow the bearer. I'll shout for you once I have secured our position."

The rain had receded to a strangulating mist. The torchlights along the route up to the platform illuminated bronze faces with high cheekbones and flat Mongol features. A world of loose-sleeved coats and high cloth boots had replaced draping dhotis and bare feet.

"Dinah! Over here, Dinah!" I heard Silas shout, but the mist swirling amid the engine's clouds of steam hid him. His bearer led the way. Coolies, who hefted our trunks and cases, traipsed at my heels.

At last I recognized Silas' pale hands waving at me. "Silas!"

"There you are!" he cried, lifting me up to the compartment. The bearer had already prepared a tea tray, and Silas poured cups of sweet tea. "Have some buttered bread." We sat on opposite upholstered benches and ate greedily. "Gulliver will make us eggs whenever you like. Until then, this should restore our strength."

"Gulliver?" I asked. "What sort of a name is that?"

"From Swift. I rename my servants. 'Bearer' or 'mali' is so anonymous as to be disrespectful; the Indian names are too personal and invade privacy. I give each servant a name I think suits, and also one I choose to repeat—like Gulliver. The syllables roll off the tongue and have a summoning quality about them, don't you think?"

"Does he mind?"

Silas shrugged. "Would he say so if he did?"

"I suppose not, but—"

"You object?"

"No, it's only that the idea is . . . unusual. Why does he wear that curved sword?"

"Gulliver is a Gurkha from Nepal. He never is without his *kukri* in his scabbard. Perhaps you know that the British have trained many of them to be superior mountain soldiers? Well, they also make the most trustworthy guards and companions. He's as brave as a lion and he would not hesitate to sacrifice his life to protect me—or you."

I stared at the short man in the blue cap. He had fine, almost feminine features that contrasted with his fierce, darting eyes. Although he was impassive, I sensed he heard and remembered everything.

Silas leaned his head back on the linen headrest. His lips curled pleasantly as the train lurched forward. We were on our way again. We both stretched out on the berths and slept for an hour or more. At the next stop—Haldibari Station—I sat up and looked out on ruddy-faced mountaineers in Tatar hats and unveiled women with necklaces of silver, turquoise, and coral.

After we pulled away, Silas moved from his window seat. "Sit here."

"Why?"

"Because a wife must do as her husband says," he said with mock sternness. I had been facing backward, so he took my hand and settled me in the seat he had relinquished. A while later he tapped my shoulder. "Close your eyes," he ordered. "No, not yet. Wait, wait . . .

we are going around a curve . . . not yet—Gulliver, wipe the window." I sensed the servant leaning across and heard the swish of linen on glass. Gulliver backed away "Ready? Now!"

I blinked as I caught my first glimpse of a roseate line of parapets and battlements far above the lazy ridges of blue mountains. I pointed to the flashes of white at the very top of the landmass. "Clouds or snow?"

"Mirrors for the sun," Silas replied. "Watch them change color as the sun rises higher."

Entranced, I observed their transmutations from pale pink to burnished gold to silvery white as we sped toward that greatest of natural barriers: the Himalayas.

Silas allowed me to drink in the scenery in silence. At last he began in a husky voice, "They rise up twenty-nine thousand feet from the base of the Siliguri Plain. Some people think it is the end of the world, the highest, the coldest, the most inhospitable place for people to live. Others believe it is the beginning of the world—where streams and rivers and oceans are formed, where pure air is created into clouds which revolve around the planet, where the gods dwell, where the human spirit is refreshed and renewed."

"Which do you believe?" I murmured.

He shook his head. "Each person decides for himself."

At last we arrived at Siliguri—six hours later than expected. The rough grass of the foothills was sheeted in a glassy coating of water, but the shining sun made everything glimmer as though veiled in a decorative frost. The natives working in the fields wrapped scarves around their heads as if they had toothaches. On the other side of the platform was a dumpy little toy train that, compared with the monstrous iron engines across the way, did not appear as if it could manage a tour around a garden, let alone a climb of thousands of feet.

Suspiciously I eyed the open trucks covered with flimsy awnings. "Is that the Darjeeling Himalayan Railway?"

"The views are better without a glass barrier." Silas guided me by the arm. "At least it has stopped raining."

The difficult journey, the cold, the lack of sleep, had left me weakened, and I did not feel secure on my feet. Nor did the tiny train inspire confidence. The gauge of the track was a mere two feet, though it was said the engines could pull the train uphill four feet for every hundred as it ran through the foothills of the steepest mountains on earth.

A man with a gilt cast to his skin walked alongside the train banging a gong. The waiting passengers filed into the six easy chairs per section—three on each side, facing each other. A whistle screamed.

The little blue engine began to pant and sputter as it warily pulled us forward and upward and into the sky.

After the first hour, I became more confident the perambulator-size wheels could support the carriage. Then two men who sat on a small platform on either side of the engine's prow began throwing something onto the tracks. "What are they doing?"

"Spreading sand on the rails for better traction."

"Will we ever speed up?"

"No. It chugs along at about ten miles per hour, but remember, we are gaining a thousand feet an hour."

"How many miles will we travel?"

"Fifty."

I calculated how long the trip would continue: three more hours. Sighing, I settled back and watched as the long views across the yellow plains to the shining Teesta River became lost in the hazy distance. Soon a jumble of paddies and palms and banana forests surrounded us.

"We are entering the Terai," Silas said in an irreverent tone. "Here they grow inferior grades of tea."

The higher we climbed, the more the vegetation became unfamiliar to me. There were the monstrous leaves described only in fairy tales, undisciplined bushes as high as trees, huge stalks of tufted grasses, stands of yellow straws that bent over the tracks and rudely flicked our arms as we passed by. Banks of ferns lurked in the crevices of the moist rocks. And over everything, luxuriant creepers knotted the jungle as though weavers had competed to cover every last inch of soil.

"The higher we climb, the smaller the leaves become," Silas commented as we passed under a bower of purple bougainvillea and chugged along beside the scarlet blossoms of a tulip tree.

The sturdy train bored through the greenery like a resolute mole. Suddenly it lurched around a curve so tight I could look back into the next carriage. Silas reached out and plucked a fat pink hydrangea from an embankment. He handed it to me as the train stopped dead.

"What is happening?" We started to zigzag backward.

"Now you see why the wheels are so low." Silas explained how the switchbacks enabled the train to gain height efficiently. "My mother never trusted the train," he said softly.

Just then the train jerked and heaved. "I can see why," I replied, thinking: This is the first time Silas has mentioned his mother. "You know something?" I struggled to control my voice. "I have no idea whether my mother ever was on a train." I thought about this for a few seconds. "She must have been . . ." I swallowed. "But when?"

"Do you think people who have lost their mothers are different from others?" Silas asked in a thin voice.

"I do," I responded without elaboration.

"Me too." With a fingertip he touched the tear that formed on the inside corner of my eye, and in a most remarkable gesture, he pressed the moisture to his lips.

The train gave another tremulous shudder that echoed my jumbled emotions. We were clamoring across a bridge above a point we had passed half an hour earlier. I leaned against Silas while the train twisted, backed, circled, and dodged in a crazed attempt to inch higher and higher, as though it were unwinding a tangled skein whose beginning was lost somewhere between where the snows left off and the clouds began.

"Here it comes, the Batasia Loop, perhaps the most famous phase of the trip." I held on tightly while the train appeared to be a snake tying itself into a knot, its engine whistling impatiently for its own guard's van to clear the track. After two complete spirals the train continued on the last leg into Darjeeling.

\\/ \\/ \\/

Sinking clouds shrouded the town. Vapors trailed into the valley as though they were flowing into a cup. Peeking through the veil, I could see scattered settlements perched on ridges enfolding a large basin. A slate sheet moved ominously in our direction, threatening to drench us.

Gulliver commandeered a whole line of *tongas*, brightly painted carts, to transport my tin trunk, two canvas hold-alls, three dressing bags, two tiffin-carriers, a teapot in a basket, a tin bonnet box, and six large crates. Silas lifted me into the first tonga and vaulted in beside me. The driver raised the hood over the tiny pony-cart. With a sprightly gait we trotted up a steep road, harness bells clanging.

"I should have arranged to be met at Ghoom. The road to Tiger Hill is closer from there, but I wanted you to see Darjeeling properly for the first time. I apologize, since it was hardly worth the trouble today."

I was about to say something consoling, but a sneezing fit caught me by surprise.

After we pulled off the narrow trail, I thought we were heading up an even more remote mountain lane, when the tonga halted at the edge of a forest. Huge cryptomerias dripped in the rain and shrouded the dark wood of a mysterious structure. A man in a bright robe appeared to emerge from nowhere. I stopped sneezing long enough to see he was opening a wooden gate set between the trees. A covered porch jutted out to the path like a long wooden tongue. Silas hustled me into the shelter. A high, thin door opened at our approach. The man dressed in the saffron cloak bowed.

"Welcome to Xanadu Lodge, Mrs. Luddy," he said.

My response was a renewed volley of sneezes.

"Thank you, Euclid," Silas replied for me. When we had stepped inside, he said, "Welcome home, Dinah," and swept his hand to reveal the most astonishing room I had ever seen.

We had entered on a higher level, then stepped down into a room sixty feet across and twenty feet wide. The far wall, which vaulted up to a thirty-foot peak at that end of the house, was a succession of arched windows the full height of the room. At the base of the high center windows were veranda doors. In the center of the room, a fire in a round stone hearth blazed out on three sides. Semicircular benches covered in red and purple cushions surrounded each of the fire beds. The mullioned panes were splattered with rain that reflected the tints from the flames inside.

Silas steered me in front of the crackling logs in the hearth. Gulliver removed my cloak and wet shoes. The man in the strange robe had disappeared. Numbly I sat down on the thick, soft cushions and gazed out the window wall. A gust blew the fog aside and revealed the pointed top of a Japanese cedar, then closed it off as though snapping a curtain into place. "What is out there?"

"The whole world," Silas offered with a self-satisfied smirk. He must have noticed I was too tired to joke with him, so he backpedaled. "You must wait to see it for yourself. My description might destroy what you have come so far to view."

The mountains, I supposed, and let it rest, since I had already had several views of the peaks that day. "What are those?" I pointed to a sheaf of thunderbolts carved above each of the arched windows.

"Darjeeling means 'place of the thunderbolt.' "

"Oh, yes," I exclaimed, recalling the crest on his stationery. Once again one of Silas' details impressed me. Even as weary as I was, I realized a man of talent had designed this house. Knowing nothing of architecture, I could not decide what it was about the room that made it special. There was a satisfying balance between the height and the width, something about the proportions of the hearth, the line of the windows, the contrast between dark wood and bright cushions, even the hue of the young man's saffron robe and Gulliver's snowy jacket, that fit like pieces of a puzzle.

Gulliver carried in a silver tray and laid it on the table beside us. As he began to ladle soup into lacquered bowls, Silas asked, "Will you have some of this? It's *gya tuk*, a Tibetan noodle soup."

"Later perhaps."

"You need to warm yourself from the inside out." He handed me a bowl. "Besides, your ayah would want you to."

I managed a few sips before my trembling increased. I put it down before I spilled it.

"A mountain chill sets into your bones. Perhaps you should have a bath. I do not have any women servants, but the cook's wife has agreed to tend to you for the next several days. She's a simple woman, and not as accomplished as someone in your home in Calcutta, but she has a good nature and will try to see you are comfortable. The season here ends in a few days, and after that you will have your pick of the girls. Until then I hope you will manage."

"Thank you, Silas. I take care of most of my own needs anyway." I tried the soup again. Tasting of egg and garlic and vinegar, it was too spicy for a tender stomach that had not yet settled from the poundings inflicted by three trains, a steamboat, and a pony-cart.

"What else would you like?"

"I'm mostly sleepy." I yawned, but the strain caused a pain somewhere deep in my chest. I gasped for air, and when I could not draw a nourishing breath, felt frightened.

"You are at over eight thousand feet. The air is thinner. Everything, even standing and walking, will seem difficult until you are acclimated. In a few days you'll be romping the hills like a native." He looked at me tenderly. "I think you should have that bath and rest as long as you like. There will be plenty of time later to see the house and also to . . . to become better acquainted."

I smiled in gratitude, and he called to Gulliver. "Have Seneca's wife come up."

"Seneca?"

"My name for the cook. I prefer three syllables, remember?"

"Who was the other man, the one in the robe, who greeted us?"

"Euclid. He's my assistant. He helps in the library and with the accounts. That's why I've given him a more mathematical name."

"Not three syllables."

"No. He's an educated man from a fine Bhutanese family. I could not classify him as a servant."

"I understand. He's your *babu*—office clerk."

"Not quite a babu, and please, for my sake, do not ever let him hear you say that word. It would insult him."

The contortions of Silas' logic were not penetrating the fog of my weary mind. I'll sort it out tomorrow, I promised myself as a wide-faced woman with a ruddy Oriental face bowed to me and babbled something I didn't understand.

"She's from Sikkim," Silas explained, "and mostly speaks Rong."

"What's her name?" I asked.

"Don't know. Why don't you name her?"

Three syllables, I thought. The one that popped into mind came from Silas' first letter. "Lucretia, after Lucretia Mott. Is that all right?"

Silas nodded his approval. Gulliver came forward and spoke to the woman. She grinned at me, revealing a gold tooth between two gaps.

"Are you ready for your bath?"

I shivered.

"We don't take cold baths here. I'm sure you will find it will be most pleasant."

"A warm bath, yes, and a bed—" I stopped. This would be our first opportunity to be alone together, and he had every right to join me in that bed. Still, I should not have been the first to mention this.

"We both need to sleep for a few hours," he said, as though reading my thoughts. "I am planning to go to my own room and lie down. If you awaken, there will be a supper served in your room. If you do manage to sleep through the night, we shall meet again tomorrow." He stood up. "Follow Lucretia—she'll show you the way."

I faced him. "Thank you." I thought I should have added something, but what? For marrying me? For bringing me here? For permitting me to rest?

He touched my cheek with the back of his hand. "Sleep well, Dinah."

A cheerful, bowing Lucretia led me to a huge room at the southern end of the house, with four windows, which were actually doors, along the wall opposite the bed. Pressing my face close to the glass, I could see they led out to some sort of veranda. Books from the floor to the ceiling lined the rear wall. A square that could have slept four people end to end or side to side was draped with a rose coverlet inset with what seemed to be two jackets embroidered and appliquéd in gold. The floor was first covered with a Tibetan carpet, then dotted with woolly white rugs. A collection of Indian paintings was hung across every bare space of wall. At my first glance, they blurred. I would have to ask Silas to tell me about them.

Lucretia opened a door at the far side of the room. I walked into a paneled chamber. A wooden tub brimmed with steaming water. Tins with additional hot water were set against the wall. On the side wall, a porcelain sink was flanked by baskets of vermilion poinsettias. At the far end was a water closet set behind a frosted glass door. More small lamb's-wool rugs formed furry islands amid the sea of frigid tile.

Lucretia made motions indicating she would undress me. Nobody except Yali had ever done this since I had grown, but since I could not manage the buttons down my back alone, I gave myself up to her, and in a few moments I found myself soaking in the warmest, deepest water of any bath, dried with the largest, fluffiest towels, and tucked into the softest bed I had ever known.

Exhaustion fell upon me and pinned me down. My mind struggled to grasp where I was and what had happened. I was close to the top of the earth, far, far away from my family. I was married to a strange, unfathomable man, and as yet I had not shared his bed. Did he mean what he said about not coming to me tonight? Did men always do what they said? Maybe I had misunderstood him. The idea caused me to fight sleep like a victim of a drowning. What would I do if he did? Perhaps he would wait until tomorrow . . . perhaps he was as fatigued as I was . . . perhaps . . . I mused as waves from Morpheus engulfed me and submerged my cares.

❀   ❀   ❀

I did not wake for supper. In fact, I did not move that night or, so it seems, the next morning. Sometime around midday I stirred and found my way to the bathroom. Perspiration soaked my gown and there was a painful contraction in my chest. I wiped my hands and face with frigid water in the basin, but found no relief from the heat that burned within. Staggering, I managed to get into bed before falling back into a tumultuous sleep. When I next opened my eyes, there was a ruddy glow in the room. My unsteady vision caught the movement of a person sitting by a fire. I opened my mouth to speak, but was overcome with uncontrollable spasms of coughing. The figure moved to my side and placed a cool palm on my forehead. She took my hands in hers and rubbed my knuckles as if she could divine a secret from the bones. A lamp was lit by my bed. A cup of syrupy tea was pressed to my lips. I tasted a bitter spice, but did not reject it since the effect was strangely soothing. I slept. I awoke and sipped more tea. I was fed cubes of tart melon. I was assisted to the bathroom and back to bed, but before I was covered, a hot compress was placed on my chest. I slept. I burned. In my dreams I steamed up the flood-swollen Ganges, climbed icy peaks, lay exposed on blistering plains, was surrounded by stinking tides, floated on airy clouds. . . .

I awoke. Shafts of light spread out across my coverlet like a blessing. I lifted my eyes to the windows. Shimmering glaciers appeared to lie just above the oaks and cedars. From my prone position the view was truncated, a tantalizing taste of what must lie even higher. With an effort I managed to sit upright. While I considered whether I had the strength to stand, there was a gentle tapping at my door.

"Yes?" I rasped.

The door opened a crack. "May I come in?"

Without considering my appearance, I agreed. Silas slipped through the opening and shut the door behind him. "Did you sleep well?"

"Very. I did not realize how tired I was. I suppose I missed you at supper last night."

"And the night before that too."

"What do you mean?"

"Today is Friday. You have been ill. The best course was to let you sleep it off. You do look so much brighter, even though Lucretia thinks you still have a touch of fever."

"Friday!" My mind struggled to grasp where I had been. Tuesday . . . the wedding and starting the journey . . . Wednesday . . . the long night of travel, meeting the Darjeeling toy train in the morning, climbing all day, and arriving here in the late afternoon. That meant I had slept from Wednesday night through Thursday and into Friday. "I am sorry, I—"

He stepped closer to the bed. "No, I should never have attempted to bring you here in that horrid weather. Forgive my stubbornness in demanding to have events go my way."

"You could not have known."

"Even with the most favorable conditions, it is a grueling trip. I am accustomed to going without sleep for days at a time and to withstanding the wide shifts in temperatures and altitudes. I subjected you to this thoughtlessly when I might have—"

I raised my hand. "Please, Silas, I don't blame you. I feel so much better now, really I do. I will bathe and dress and be out in an hour. Then I hope you will show me the house."

He backed away. "I'll send Lucretia in."

The high steeping tub that surrounded me with warm water, from my toes to my chin, eased my aches. After drying and powdering me, Lucretia wrapped me in a long woolen robe and tried to untangle my hair. Realizing my usual upswept hairdo was too complex for her, I directed her to braid it in one long plait, just like hers. Giggling, she complied.

A tray set out on a table by the window offered a tempting array. The most appealing were various dumplings and a bowl of sliced fruits. Lucretia held up several of my frocks for me to choose, but she frowned at the thin fabrics more suitable for the heat of the plains than the changeable hill clime. I settled on a mauve skirt and matching three-quarter-length coat with wide revers and full sleeves over a linen blouse. Lucretia struggled with the unfamiliar buttons and hooks, then clucked her tongue as she felt the stiffness of the blouse's heavily starched collar. I smiled to myself as I wondered what she would think of Aunt Bellore's solution to the perennial limp collar. Determined to maintain a crisp appearance even at the end of a Calcutta afternoon, my aunt kept her collar erect by inserting a band of metal cut from a food can between her neck and the fabric. Horrified at the idea, I had hoped I would never be required to be as fashionable. Here in the hills, even the simplicity of my tailored outfit seemed out-of-place. I was anxious to meet other women in Darjeeling and see what they wore.

The effort of dressing proved to be almost too much. I had to take another cup of tea and splash water on my forehead and wrists before I dared join Silas. What would he think of his weak wife? He had been most considerate, but surely the delay of our honeymoon must have been disappointing. I wondered what I could do to make it up to him.

Silas stood as soon as he heard the door to my room open. "Ah, how much better you look. The flush at your cheeks becomes you. Soon you will have the complexion of a mountain woman." He led me to a chair set by the center windows. "Would you like to sit?"

I noticed that a door to the terrace was open. "Could I see outside?"

"Yes, of course." He guided me onto the long veranda solicitously.

The porch, which extended the full length of the house, seemed suspended in space. The hill fell away in a long plunge to a valley below, where the metallic roofs of small houses glinted in the distance. Above, as far as the eye could see, enormous mountains loomed, their heads wreathed in clouds.

"Chomolungma, the Goddess Mother of the World, is shy this afternoon. Usually she greets us only at dawn. With the weather clearing to the north, she could show her face tomorrow."

I looked at him quizzically.

"Chomolungma is what the natives call Everest. Because of her status as the mightiest of them all, one cannot help being impressed by her. To me, though, she is too benevolent, too serene. I worship the one with the double peak: the fierce Kanchenjunga."

Once again, the odd language he used intrigued me. I could not imagine any civilized man—let alone a Jew—worshiping a mountain.

"This air is too brisk for you. Come inside."

I turned and scrutinized the house. In the full light of day it seemed more a Buddhist temple than a home. And in a sense, it was a shrine to the mountain, for every effort had been made to blend into the hillside forest, yet make available the spectacle that pierced the sky. Silas showed me his bedroom, a match for mine down to the steeping tub in the bathroom. Instead of a table, an ornate desk filled the cove by the glass doors.

"How beautiful!" I gasped.

He puffed with pride. "It is made of rosewood inlaid with ivory and mounted with silver."

"Where did it come from?"

"I believe it was part of Clive's haul when he defeated the Nawab of Bengal at Plassey."

Reverently I ran my hand over the embellished surface.

"Do you really admire it?"

"It's the most exquisite piece of furniture I have ever seen."

He clapped his hands. "Gulliver!" The bearer appeared and bowed with his hands together. "Have the Clive bureau moved to the memsahib's room at once."

"But . . . I did not mean—"

"What belongs to me belongs to my wife."

I was too stunned to say anything more. Silas pretended not to notice my shock and went on to show me some of his favorite paintings. "This watercolor is attributed to Baswan and is called *Anvari Entertains in a Summer House* . . . and here is a design by Tulsi the Elder, *The Construction of Fatehpur-Sikri*, the finest example in my collection of work done during the period of Akbar . . ."

"My ignorance appalls me. You will have to teach me about art."

"Another duty I shall anticipate."

We walked back into the arched main hall, where a table had been placed by the center windows. A snowy cloth was set with golden plates for two.

"Where is the kitchen?" I asked.

"On the lower level, along with the storerooms. There are outside steps at either end of the house, and inside stairs at the center. The servants have pleasant quarters there as well."

I pointed to a narrow hall to the left and right of the entranceway. "What is down those?"

"On the left, there is a large empty room I use to hold the furnishings I haven't yet been able to place. I am afraid I am quite incorrigible when I see something that catches my fancy. I hope you have a more practical bent to balance my impetuousness."

"I've never been able to investigate that side of my nature, so you could steer me in either direction."

"What a conundrum for a husband!"

Why did my pulse quicken when he said either "husband" or "wife"? "What is down the other corridor?"

"A room I use for an office. Euclid spends most of his time there, though his own quarters are downstairs so he can manage the staff. Either front room could be converted to a nursery someday."

Discomfited, I looked away.

A long-haired cat rubbed against Silas. "Which one is this?" I asked, recalling the mention of his cats in his letters to me.

"Ek. It means the number one in Nepali. The number two, Dui, is the shyer of the pair—and the male, I might add."

I patted the cat's long chocolate tail that arched away from the creamy body. At my touch the animal bolted.

"She'll warm to you in a few days."

"I hope so. I haven't had a pet since I was given a flying squirrel when I was seven. However, he caused many problems."

"Why?"

"You know how most Jews are about pets and the evil eye. How glad I am to be living in a more—" I caught myself.

"Yes?"

"I was going to say a more rational place."

He beamed and gestured to the table. "Would you care to have tiffin now?"

I followed him to the table. So we both could enjoy the view, Gulliver had set our places side by side. The billowing clouds alternately covered and revealed the bare escarpments, but resolutely hid the tips of the elusive peaks. The light shifted minute by minute. The tints of the view constantly changed.

"I could sit here the whole day," I said as I tasted the soup.

"Often I do that myself. Do you like it? It's *faktu*, a soup with radishes, said to be an aid to recovery."

"You have a very good cook."

"He'll make anything you want, from your favorite Baghdadi dishes to his native specialties."

As the rest of the meal passed with only a few congenial phrases bantered between us, I hoped he would think my reticence the result of weakness from my illness. Several times Euclid passed by carrying papers and books. I could sense the pause in his footsteps. It seemed as if he were listening in for a second before he moved away. Servants had never concerned me before. Even Gulliver, though strange in his ways, did not invade my consciousness the way Euclid did. I could see I was not alone in my discomfort. Silas also glanced in whatever direction Euclid had gone, and seemed tense until he was out of sight.

After we had tea and a spicy rice-and-raisin dessert, Silas spoke. "I have some papers to examine this afternoon."

Now I understood the difficulty. His attentions to me had been keeping him from his work. For a moment I resented this interference, for I was beginning to enjoy his company, but the lapse was momentary. I managed to smile gracefully and said, "I wouldn't mind a rest in my room."

Once I was alone, I wondered what I might have said to displease my husband. If he wanted to join me, he could have knocked on the door. Was there something I had done to put him off? Or was he waiting for the evening? So far we had hardly touched. What would happen when he approached me? I hoped he would not find me wanting.

That evening was the Sabbath. I lit the candles and we said prayers together. After that, there was a repeat of the afternoon, with polite chatter about the weather, some of the art objects I noticed placed around the house, and the chef's ability to make a delicious *kofta* curry, not unlike one that Grandmother Helene might have served. And then Silas suggested I might like to retire early.

I returned to my room, sat at the silver desk, and waited. Lucretia appeared and wanted to know if I would bathe. I sent her away. Surely Silas would come to me soon. I waited by the windows until I heard no other sounds in the house. Then I undid my buttons, let my clothes fall where they would, washed quickly, and crawled into bed. Perhaps Silas was biding his time until the servants retired before he crossed the long expanse between our rooms. I remained upright, the cushions tucked about me, the covers smoothed, my hair falling prettily around my shoulders. It was difficult to read in the shadowy light, but I felt more at ease with a book in my hand. I closed my eyes, imagining what would happen when he would ask to join me in the bed and a whole new phase of my life really would begin.

He never came.

17

᭙ ᭙ ᭙

A knock jolted me from an unsettled slumber. The door opened. "Dinah, may I . . . ?"

"Yes, Silas." Was this the moment? In the pellucid light I could see he was wearing a long caftan. He held out a matching one for me. "Put this on, it will keep you warm." I obeyed. The smooth wool muffled the chill. "Come with me." He took my hand. "The mountains are out."

He positioned me in the center of the carpet by the parlor windows, my feet precisely in a red circle in the design. Pinks and purples slashed the sky. I had to strain my head back to see the snows. At the very top, three white peaks barely showed themselves above the mist of mountains in the foreground. In the middle the tip of Everest glistened in a ruby halo.

"I feel as if I could almost touch it."

"A trick of light on snow. In fact, it is over a hundred miles away. This morning there are no clouds over six thousand feet—that is why we see each snowy peak with such clarity."

"Do they have names?"

He listed them as though he were singing a hymn. "In the background there are Chomolungma, Lhotse, and Makalu. In front come Kang, Jannu, Kabru, Dome, Talung, Kanchenjunga, Pandim, Jubonu, and Narsing."

Below, a sea of clouds alternated from white to gray to hues of blue and red as they passed over the ridge into Darjeeling like a tidal wave.

"A splendid show, isn't it?" he sighed as the whole range revealed itself like a wanton woman, but Mount Everest, which loomed behind the more proximate peaks, was coy, and after the first half-hour, disappeared.

"Is she gone?"

"For now." He came around to face me. "Are you disappointed?"

192

"Yes." Bravely I raised my eyes to meet his. He started to stammer something, but changed his mind and kissed my forehead. I held my breath as he kissed each cheek. Then, cupping my chin to tilt it upward, he kissed me on the lips with a touch so quick the only sensation was the bristle of his mustache brushing past.

He moved his hands to my waist. "I think we becoming friends. Do you agree?"

"I do, Silas."

"Good, for I believe that love begins as a refined mutual relationship based on the sharing of the mind as well as the body. Otherwise men and women are nothing more than animals who inflict their passionate natures on each other for selfish reward. That is why I objected to the traditional rites that follow marriage. That is why I brought you here, where we can come to know each other—on all levels—at our leisure."

The sound of padding feet caused me to turn slightly. Euclid carried a stack of books to the far end of the room, where papers already covered a long trestle table. He looked away as soon as he saw me glance at him.

Silas dropped his hands from my waist. "Shall we dress and have chota hazri together?"

"Yes." I smiled at his intense gaze. "Do you hold services here?"

"This time of year it is impossible to gather a *minyan*. On the holy days we make the effort; otherwise we worship simply in our homes. I thought you would appreciate a quiet day, so I have gathered some books you might like." He waved and Euclid came forward with three volumes, one of which was by Lucretia Mott.

I opened it. *"Discourse on Women,"* I read aloud in an inquisitive tone.

"An original thinker. I am interested in your opinions on her theories."

"I'll read it today," I said, thinking I was more curious to explore his kisses than his philosophies.

☙ ☙ ☙

I spent the day at the Clive bureau, as Silas called it, reading passages from the *Discourse on Women* and starting a letter to Grandmother Flora. "It's difficult to believe that five days have passed since Silas and I were wedded," I began, then put down my pen. Five days and still he had not come to my bed. There had been the journey and my illness, but even so, I wondered why I displeased him. When we were together he was friendly, even kind, but there had been several opportunities he had neglected. The curious thing was that he seemed more interested in my mind than my body, and though I was pleased he took me seriously, I was anxious to discover the secrets of marriage.

That evening we played three games of backgammon. Silas seemed delighted that we were evenly matched. "I shall have to teach you chess," he announced, but did not begin my lessons. Yawning, he suggested it was time for us both to get our rest.

With a smattering of Hindustani, the cook's wife and I managed an efficient bedtime routine. That night as I again waited in vain for Silas to visit me, I wondered what she thought of a husband and wife who did not share a bed.

In the morning, I heard Silas' knock. Expecting that he would want to show me the mountains again, I sat up as he placed a cup of Chinese tea in my hand. I took a few swallows and handed it back. He placed it on the table, bent and kissed my forehead, then kissed each of my eyelids. A tremulous wave tumbled from my breast to my toes. So, this was the beginning! His hands explored my face as though he were a blind man memorizing my bones. My fears dissolved. He had been right to wait until we were friends . . . it seemed so easy, so natural.

He spoke in a hoarse voice. "There is a book attributed to the sage Vatsyayana in the Gupta period, called the *Kama Sutra*. *Kama* means desire of every kind and its fulfillment, and like the English word 'desire,' it discusses passion between men and women as well as how to elevate that passion to the purest levels of attainment. For instance, it says that during the first three days of a marriage the husband and the wife should sleep on the floor and abstain from intercourse. For the next seven days they should bathe to the sound of music, adorn themselves, dine together. Then, on the tenth day, the husband should speak gently to his wife to give her confidence, yet restrain himself until he has won her over, for women, being gentle by nature, prefer to be wooed in this way. It suggests that if a woman is forced to submit to rough treatment from a man whom she scarcely knows, she may come to detest the act, or to revile the whole male sex, or worst of all, to discard her respect for the man she has married."

He was quiet for a few minutes. I calculated rapidly: this was Sunday morning and if I counted the marriage day as the first, six days had passed since the ceremony. At least four more would be necessary to follow these conditions.

He kissed me again, this time alongside my ear. The place burned from his touch. I wanted him to continue, not to speak, yet he whispered, "The *Kama Sutra* speaks of sixteen types of kisses . . ."

He stood up abruptly. "Good morning, my sweet Dinah," he said as he departed, leaving me bitterly disappointed.

W W W

On Monday morning my first thought was: This is the seventh day of my marriage. Then I chided myself for counting. After breakfast, Silas asked if I would like to drive down to Darjeeling with him, returning by way of the Luddy Tea Company offices. I agreed at once.

The syce brought a gaily painted tonga to the door, and Silas decided to drive it himself to save the space for packages from town. We pulled away at an aggressive trot. At the end of the drive I noticed a sign that read Xanadu Lodge and remembered Euclid's words of welcome.

"Why is it called Xanadu?"

"From *Kubla Khan*, the poem by Coleridge. Don't you know it?"

Once again I felt ignorant.

He tightened the reins as the tonga turned a sharp bend. On the straightaway he began to recite:

> "In Xanadu did Kubla Khan
> A stately pleasure-dome decree:
> Where Alph, the sacred river, ran
> Through caverns measureless to man
> Down to a sunless sea."

Along the hills, workers were heading out to the tea gardens, which formed a verdant quilt up and down the sharp flanks of the mountain. He made a turn at a sign for the Auckland Road and continued:

> "That with music loud and long,
> I would build that dome in air,
> That sunny dome! those caves of ice!
> And all who heard should see them there,
> And all should cry, Beware! Beware!"

A bullock-cart crossed the road in front of us, causing Silas to pull up sharply at such a timely moment in his oration that we both laughed and laughed. "Now, where was I?" he asked as he regained control.

"Beware! Beware!"

"Right," he continued, finishing with:

> "And close your eyes with holy dread,
> For he on honey-dew hath fed,
> And drunk the milk of Paradise."

"What is the 'milk of Paradise'?" I asked.

"You should know," he teased.

Again I must have appeared obtuse to him. "Wine or spirits or ambrosia or . . ." I offered in a rush.

He grinned pleasantly. "Some would suggest the milky sap of the poppy."

I swallowed hard. "I see."

"If you had read Coleridge, or knew more about him . . . Well, no matter, I'll have Euclid bring you some books this evening."

As we approached Darjeeling, a file of women porters plodded uphill past us, carrying burdens on their backs supported by straps wound around their foreheads. Silas began speaking rapidly. He wanted me to absorb as much as possible, including the history of the town, which was started as a sanatorium for heat-prostrated soldiers of the East India Company: "And they were not unaware there was strategic value in having a hill station at a key pass into Nepal and Tibet." He explained the differences between the Himalayan people: ". . . and he's a Buddhist from the monastery at Ghoom, she's from Bhutan, he's from the Teesta Valley, they are Sikkimese . . ." He pointed out the sights: ". . . St. Andrew's Church . . . Lawn Tennis Courts and the Shrubbery, the grounds of Government House, where the business of Bengal is conducted in summer . . . Eden Sanatorium . . . and here we are at the Chaurasta, the center of Darjeeling."

A short while after the bandstand, we turned down the Lebong Road and pulled up at a whitewashed building with a red tile roof that housed the Luddy Tea Company. Silas' brothers-in-law, Harold Ezekiel and Israel Cohen, greeted me curtly. Then Silas led me to a tidy office and had a servant bring tea and cakes.

"I'll have to go over the accounts and sign some documents," he said.

"Don't worry about me," I replied.

"I apologize for taking so long," he said about an hour later as several leather cases were loaded into the tonga.

"I didn't mind," I answered sincerely, for I had enjoyed the change of scene. "I was sorry not to see your father today."

"He prefers to stay at the plantation house."

"Does Euclid work in Darjeeling?"

"Mostly at the house. Tonight he will assist me with these." He thumped one of the cases.

"Is Euclid a Buddhist?"

"No, he's a Christian. Why?"

"His robes. I thought he looked like a monk."

"He's far from a monk." Silas laughed congenially. "He thinks the color suits him." He chuckled for a few moments, then stopped the cart. "Would you like to return home or see something more of the town?"

The air was turning colder, but I was not ready to end the day. "I'd like to go on."

Silas tucked the blanket over my knees. "I have just the spot." He headed into the village of Bhutia Basti and up to a gaudily painted temple with huge prayer wheels on both sides of the doorway. The lama, a friend of Silas', was very pleased to show me the hundred-volume Buddhist canon and three gilded wooden Buddhas in a glass case that formed an altar.

The one in the middle looked familiar to me. At first I could not place the flattened face with the chubby cheeks, until I noticed a resemblance to Euclid.

"What wonderful painted eyes! They seem to follow you wherever you stand," Silas said. I saw what he meant, and again thinking of Euclid, shuddered.

❀ ❀ ❀

The next two days—the eighth and ninth, including my wedding day to my silent count—passed quietly. I read a book on Indian art of the Moghul period, a subject that did not engage my full attention. After tiffin on Wednesday, I asked Silas if I might see a book of Coleridge's poems. "I would like to read *Kubla Khan* for myself," I said.

A shadow crossed his face. "I thought I asked Euclid to put the book in your room the other day. I'll remind him now."

Silas was gone longer than I had expected, and he returned agitated. "I did not bring home all of the documents I need, so Euclid and I will have to return to the town."

I would have enjoyed another excursion, but only replied, "I'll be fine. Don't concern yourself about me."

Euclid brought the book to me as I sat out on the sunny veranda. I thanked him, but the surly expression on his face did not change.

"Do you like Coleridge?" I asked, to see if I might get a warmer response.

"Silas is the one who cares for poetry," he replied, backing away.

I took a deep breath and looked up to the snows, which had receded into the line of clouds for the afternoon. Contenting myself with the purple ridges of the foreground hills, the swaying cedars, and the bright pots of geraniums that bloomed on the posts, I read and reread the poem, trying to discover what Silas had meant about opium. The words were seductive and wonderfully evocative of the setting in which I now lived. Xanadu Lodge was a splendid name for the house, yet I could not understand why the poem seemed disjointed, almost as though it had two separate parts with different rhythms. A good question for Silas, I thought, pleased I would have something to discuss at dinner.

Scanning *The Ancient Mariner*, I mused about something else altogether. Silas and Euclid had been gone less than an hour. They would just be arriving in Darjeeling . . . so there was plenty of time. I strolled around the house. The servants were downstairs for their afternoon rest, and nobody would bother me unless I pulled one of the silken ropes that rang their bells.

I opened the door to Silas' room. I had been inside only once, when he had showed me the house. Otherwise, when he closed that door, he was in his private sanctum. I felt a momentary twinge that I might be trespassing, until I reminded myself this was also my home. The books on the shelves were arranged by a system I had not yet deciphered. Small cards lettered in flowery calligraphy stuck out at various points to indicate sections: classics, poetry, art, history, flora, fauna, and so on. The book for which I was searching fitted in none of these categories. I was about to undertake a volume-by-volume check when I saw several books on the table beside the bed. I glanced at the titles on the spines: *The Bhagavad Gita; Narrative of a Journey Through the Upper Provinces of India, from Calcutta to Bombay*, by Reginald Heber; *Titian's Son*, by Alfred de Musset; *Treatise on the Remedies of Good and Bad Fortune*, by Francesco Petrarch; and there, on the very bottom, was a slender blue volume: *The Kama Sutra!* Tucking it under my arm, I rushed to my own room.

The index itself stunned me. It extended from the "Arrangements of a house and household furniture" and "The classes of women fit and unfit for congress" to "The kinds of love" to "On kissing" to "On pressing and marking with the nails" to "On biting." Biting? I flipped the pages forward, eagerly reading the eight styles:

> The hidden bite
> The swollen bite
> The point
> The line of points
> The coral and the jewel
> The line of jewels
> The broken cloud
> The biting of the boar.

The boar? "The biting which consists of many broad marks . . . with red intervals . . ." I should have found this distasteful, even frightening, yet I was stirred as I wondered why a man and a woman might find this appealing.

The next chapter, "On the Various Ways of Lying Down, and the Kinds of Congress," offered practical advice. I figured out that *yoni* referred to a woman's private parts and *lingam* meant the man's, but how they went together was more perplexing. "When the legs of both the male and the female are stretched out over each other, it is called the 'clasping position.' " Giving this and other possibilities some thought, I could imagine how the act might be accomplished, but later in the chapter some suggestions were beyond me. "When one of her legs is placed on the head, and the other is stretched out, it is called the 'fixing of a nail.' " Realizing the time was growing short, I skipped a few chapters—to my eternal regret, for if I had read the few pages under the title "Auparishtaka," I might have saved myself much confusion and pain later. Instead, I studied the section "About the Acquisition of a Wife," with particular emphasis on the first days after marriage, to see what Silas might have in store for me. There were elaborate instructions for gaining a girl's confidence, leading up to the "shampooing of the thighs" before the actual congress. I was hoping that Silas would not be trying to duplicate this millennium-old instruction guide too faithfully, when words in the last paragraph captivated me:

A man does not succeed either by implicitly following the inclination of a girl or by wholly opposing her, and he should therefore adopt a middle course. He who knows how to make himself beloved by women, as well as to increase their honor . . . becomes an object of their love. But he who neglects a girl, thinking she is too bashful, is despised by her as a beast ignorant of the working of the female mind.

Did Silas' neglect mean that he thought me too bashful? Was he "an ignorant beast"? I felt more confused than before. Suddenly I noticed that only a mauve light streaked in through the window. What time was it? I clasped the book and tiptoed into the hall. Gulliver was lighting the lamps. I almost hurried back to my room, until I asked myself what harm might there be in letting a servant see me enter my husband's empty chamber when all I was doing was returning a book. With my head held high, I completed my errand. As I came out into the drawing room, I heard the rattle of tonga wheels on the pebble drive.

❧ ❧ ❧

Euclid was laughing. As I went to meet my husband, his assistant's smile dissolved. Without a word of greeting to me, he ducked downstairs. Kissing me on the cheek, Silas handed me a packet of letters. "There are several from Calcutta for you, and for us both, an invitation to the last ball of the season at Government House. Would you care to attend?"

"Would you?"

"When I was a bachelor, I was needed to round out the numbers, but I have never found much stimulation at such events. Frankly, I'm a bit of an outsider in these parts."

"I have always been an outsider as well."

"There are two types of outsiders, though. Some, like my Nepalese mother, are immediately outsiders by birth or circumstance. Her solution was to get in the middle and eventually wind up running the show. Others, like me, who are born in the limelight, choose to distance themselves and remain on the sidelines."

"We do not have to go on my account," I replied, masking my disappointment with an uneasy grin.

"You would have no objections?"

"Not if you would rather stay at home."

"Usually I would, but not this time. I have spent so many years disappointing my hostesses, they are most eager to see the young lady who finally won my heart." He winked. "Funny, after all this time, the 'fishing parties' never figured out I would only marry a Jewish girl."

"What's a fishing party?"

"Oh, you know, those girls who come out from England—especially during the hot weather—to 'fish' for a husband. They flock to the hill · stations, where the men are so lonely—or shall I say so desperate? —that even a lady who has no grace or wit can be transformed into the belle of the ball."

"What I do not understand," I began, hoping he would catch the sarcasm in my tone, "is why, with so many 'desperate men,' they would need to drag in a reluctant partygoer."

"Ah, but you see, the poor blokes who man the hill stations are drab soldier boys who do little to fuel the fantasies of the fisherwomen." His lilt blended in with my tease, so I was confident he had not taken my words amiss. How I was enjoying this easy banter!

"Did you break many hearts?"

"A few, I suppose."

"Then, if we go to the party, I shall have to watch my back."

"Would you like to go?"

"Yes, if you would."

"The end of the season is worth a celebration. It is always a relief when Darjeeling reverts to the natives. Besides, it's an excellent opportunity for you to find yourself a good ladies' maid."

"Lucretia suits me, if she is willing."

"Are you certain?"

"Absolutely."

I could tell he was pleased as he accepted a drink from his bearer's silver tray. "A brandy for you this evening?"

I shook my head.

"A lemonade?"

I nodded to Gulliver.

"Did you read the book?"

The *Kama Sutra* came to my mind, and I flushed.

"The Coleridge," he prompted.

"Oh, yes!" I gasped with relief.

"And . . ." He waited for my reaction.

"I am still perplexed," I said, trying to sound intelligent as I questioned him about the oddness of the poem.

"I agree the rhyme scheme is neither like a stanza nor an ode," he began, relaxing as he lapsed into a pedantic lecture. "In fact, the poem creates conflict among scholars. Almost everything about it is known, except what the damn thing is about!" He chuckled, taking a sip of his drink. Standing in front of the center window, he stared up at the mountains. In the lilac twilight, a few snow streamers spewed out from Kanchenjunga. The other peaks were glowing crimson wisps.

"The milk of Paradise . . ."

He grinned. "What about it?"

"How did Coleridge know about opium? I thought that mostly the Chinese took it and . . ." I was reminded of my mother and stumbled. ". . . others in the East."

"Many artists of his day spent a considerable part of their lives in a cloud of poppy smoke, dreaming the dreams they so brilliantly reproduced for us, so it is not surprising that Coleridge would herald opium as 'a spot of enchantment, a green spot of fountain and flowers and trees in the very heart of a waste of sands!' " His voice rose with an ecstatic ring that alarmed me. No matter what anyone said about the benefits of opium, I could never forget the part it had played in my mother's downfall.

"I am surprised that so eminent a writer as Coleridge would have taken opium—and more surprised he admitted it."

"What do you know about opium, Dinah?"

"Quite a bit about the plant, its cultivation—I've been to Patna—and something about the trading difficulties."

"I meant its usage."

"For pain . . . it cures diseases . . . also may make men happy . . ." I parroted my father's words from long ago, although I had never understood how the poppy plant managed these congenial alterations when it had the opposite effect on so many.

"They say Coleridge wrote the poem in a dream. However, one cannot write while one sleeps."

I took the tall glass from Gulliver and drank a few long swallows while Silas went on.

"So the 'dream' is said to be the visions Coleridge had during an opiate trance." He stared at me. "You know nothing of why men take opium over and over, do you?"

I shook my head.

"Have you ever seen someone smoking?"

"Yes."

"Your father?"

"No! He never does."

Silas waited.

I hardly remembered my mother, except filmy images. Mostly I recalled her on the chaise, the beautiful inlaid hookah, the laxness in her mouth, her eyes half-closed, her gown hanging in sleepy folds, her limp hand stroking me, and the smoke . . . the sweet smoke curling around her head.

"When I was very little . . ." I mumbled. "I saw some people use it."

"How did they seem?"

"Quiet, sleepy, somewhat confused. I didn't like the smell of the smoke."

"Have you tried it?"

Alarmed, I spilled my drink. "Never." I let Gulliver mop the floor, but waved him away when he asked if he should replace my glass. I felt a chill and drew nearer the hearth.

"Why are you shocked? What do you suppose supports your father and his entire family?" He held up his glass. "A vice, to be sure, but so is this brandy or a pipe of tobacco or the betel or *pahn* the natives take." He threw his head back and gave a throaty laugh. "Not to mention the addictive allure of delicately brewed tea leaves."

I raised my voice and asked, "Have you?"

"Drunk tea?" He made a crooked grin, then sobered. "From time to time, as a means of relaxation, but not as a routine. Would you like to puff a pipe with me one of these days?"

"Of course not. And—" I caught myself.

"What is it?"

"Nothing." I hung my head.

"I would prefer if you wouldn't keep your concerns from me," he said gently.

"And I would prefer it if you would not take opium either." My heart beat wildly as I waited for his response.

Silas was quiet for a long time. At last he spoke in the same measured way as before. "You are sensible. A clear mind and a good book are more to my taste in any case."

The tingling in my spine subsided. At least that was one worry I would not have.

Silas paced the perimeter of the carpet in front of the fire. "However, there is one point neither of us can afford to disregard. Men of commerce look to control commodities the rest of the world cannot do without. Men of art, who sometimes are dependent on those same commodities, offer visions and dreams, images and stories to enlighten, glorify, nullify the grim tedium of trade. Ideally, one can play both sides, as I do. The tea business supports my artistic and literary interests." He blinked several times and added as an afterthought, "And the opium business supports my lovely wife."

Supported. I emphasized the past tense in my mind. I could not renounce the origin of my dowry, but I would not be dependent on the poppy enterprise any longer. Relief that I was married and away from that part of my past suffused me.

Silas must have sensed that he had pressed the point too hard. "Shall we try a round of chess?" he asked.

ꕥ   ꕥ   ꕥ

A banging sound woke me. Sweat beaded on my forehead. I threw off the comforter, my heart pounding. Bang! Then another: Bang! A shutter? Was someone dead? I rushed to the door and opened it. Bang! There it was again. Somebody had forgotten to bolt one of the glass doors leading out to the veranda. The wind rising from the valley had pushed it open and it fluttered in the gusty air. As I locked it, I wondered: What time is it? The clock over the mantel was almost at three. My hand was on my doorknob when I thought I heard noises. They came from Silas' room. Two male voices, muffled so I could not separate them, were speaking in short angry bursts. My heart, at last quiet after being awakened so rudely, began to pound again. Why would Silas be arguing with someone at this time of night? What could possibly be wrong?

At bedtime we had parted amicably. He had complimented me on my first chess lesson. He had held my hand and kissed my fingertips— with teeth pressing slightly, as the *Kama Sutra* had suggested—and kissed the soft flesh inside my elbow, then the cleft of my neck, before reaching my lips and pressing much harder than ever before. I had thought he might ask to follow me to my room, and when he did not, I took especial care of my toilette. If he came to me later, I would be fresh for him. For a long while I had remained awake, thinking that if Silas were counting the same way, tonight was the ninth day; and tomorrow would be *the* day.

I heard the lock turn on his door and jumped behind the post. Euclid, fully dressed in his saffron robe, stepped out and slammed the door behind him with a firmness that was an indication of disrespect. To reach the stairs to the lower level he did not have to pass me, and fortunately, he had no intention of remaining upstairs. I waited until the only sound was the ticking of the clock, then made my way back to the vastness of my lonely bed.

I got up early, scrubbed my teeth, and wiped myself with a cloth dipped in cold water, since no servants had been asked to bring hot water this early. I checked the snows—they were hidden behind a solid wall of mist—reclosed the draperies, and went back to bed. I had learned that Silas liked to come to me in the morning. This had to be the tenth morning. It would not be long now. . . .

At eight, Lucretia appeared and asked me if I wanted a tray. Nettled to see her and not Silas, I indicated I would dress and join my husband. She shook her head and tried to tell me something I did not understand. Still irritated, I took my place at the breakfast table beside the center windows.

Gulliver poured my tea before pointing out that he had not set a place for Silas. "The sahib is unwell this morning." He backed away before I could ask what he meant. I assumed Silas was sleeping in because he had been up late arguing with Euclid.

As I finished my toast, Euclid appeared. "I will be going down to Darjeeling in an hour. Would you like me to post any letters or might there be anything else you require, Mrs. Luddy?"

"Nothing, thank you, Euclid, but could you tell me what is the matter with my husband?"

"One of his usual headaches."

"Is there anything I can do?"

His thin mouth formed a stern line, and he shook his head. "What he requires is quiet, a dark room, and to be left to rest, although the pain is such that he cannot find any respite in sleep."

"Is he ill?"

"Not with a disease, if that is what you mean. This is the sort of sick headache called a migraine that some people suffer routinely."

"Has he seen a doctor?"

"Yes, but they can do nothing for him. Many important men have been similarly afflicted—Caesar, Paul, Kant—so Silas is in fine company."

"How often does Silas have them?"

"Once or twice a month."

My bad humor was not improved by the realization that this man knew my husband far better than I. "How long have you known Mr. Luddy?" I asked sharply.

"For more than ten years, since I was fifteen."

"Has he had these headaches all that time?"

"As far back as I can remember."

"Why did you come to this area, Euclid?"

He informed me that he had come to study at St. Paul's School. He had met Silas through a teacher who was one of his friends, and began to assist him on holidays. "And he has made a place for me ever since," Euclid concluded.

"I am certain you have made a place for yourself, Euclid. Silas speaks highly of you."

His feet shifted. I could tell he wanted to be away, yet I continued to command his attention. "Do you play chess?"

"Yes."

"Mr. Luddy is teaching me. I wondered if you would be kind enough to play with me later, if he is still unwell. I would like to learn a few moves that might impress him with my prowess after only one lesson." I tried a little laugh, but it sounded as unnatural as I felt in this man's presence.

"As much as it would honor me to assist you, Mrs. Luddy, my duties lie elsewhere today," he said tensely.

"Of course. Forgive me for even suggesting it. Perhaps some other time." As I stood up, Gulliver came forward and pulled out my chair. I looked across to Silas' closed door. "I had better see what I can do for him," I said, making my way in that direction.

Euclid moved to block me. "He must have absolute quiet and no light of any kind. Even a narrow ray from the door hurts his eyes—like a knife blade, he says."

"Who tends him when he is sick?"

"Gulliver and I do."

"Then you must teach me how you manage without opening and closing doors. Invisibility is a skill most women would be pleased to master."

❦ ❦ ❦

Silas was turned toward the wall. A thin cover draped his legs. The dim light that stole from under the draperies illuminated his face, which glowed a waxy white. Beside his bed there were two bowls. One held a soaking cloth; one was for sickness. At my approach he groaned, and without opening his eyes he lifted the cloth from his forehead and held it up for a replacement. Silently I took it from him, wrung out the one that floated in the water, folded it lengthwise, and laid it on his brow.

His skin was dry, not feverish, as I might have expected. His utter stillness, though, was what concerned me the most. Even his breathing was so shallow his rib cage hardly moved. His arms were bent across his chest with hands curved rigidly, like claws. At first I had suspected he was only recovering from his disagreeable confrontation in the middle of the night. Now I realized a true torment afflicted him.

"Silas," I whispered. "What else may I do for you?"

One eye opened, tearing as it squinted to focus on me. "Din . . . ah . . ." The two syllables were an effort. "Where is . . . ?"

"Euclid has gone down to Darjeeling on an errand. Gulliver is waiting outside. I heard you were ill and wanted to tend you myself."

"Kind . . . thanks . . . just my usual headache . . . need to rest . . .

but . . ." His speech came in garbled bursts, his mouth wincing with the effort.

"Hush. I am sorry to have disturbed you. Ask Gulliver to send for me if there is anything I can do."

"Gulliver . . . yes . . ." His color darkened as he held his hand over his mouth.

I waved his bearer in. There was no time to close the door as Gulliver rushed to Silas' side and held the bowl while he was sick.

Finding Euclid had left, I decided to take some fresh air. Emerging from the lush woodland, I made my way along a lane guarded by spreading cedars, tall waving bamboos, hemlocks, and *sungri katus*— oaks with large pale acorns. My walk took me down the mountain road that passed our house to a widened area by a curve where I noticed travelers often stopped. From the tonga I had not understood the reason, but from the path I could see a lane that led to a small clearing in the underbrush. In the center rose a simple altar of stones under a stand of prayer flags, cloth strips painted with black characters and nailed by one edge to bamboo poles. A group of Tibetans was making offerings to the God of the Mountain. My eyes lifted across the blue waters of Lake Senchal to the spurs and peaks above.

I knew the Indian custom of taking *darshan*, having seen them making a pilgrimage up the Ganges to the holy city of Benares or to a palace, temple, or house of a famous seer, in an attempt to absorb some greatness or beauty into their lives. The most devout dedicated their lives to escape the cycle of being reborn, but most took a few weeks to satisfy a hunger for something loftier to illuminate their modest existences. At that moment I felt as though I too was but a pilgrim in those hills. No, I reminded myself, this is your home. I walked back up to Xanadu Lodge feeling more peaceful and more settled than before.

Just past sunset, Silas emerged from his room. After asking Gulliver to dim the lamps, he turned to me. "My symptoms will be gone in the morning. They always are."

I remained as quiet as possible while he sipped broth from a lacquered bowl.

"Have you seen Euclid this evening?" he asked after a while.

"Gulliver said he did not return from Darjeeling, but he sent the tonga back with the post." I offered him the packet. With much agitation Silas shuffled the envelopes until he found what he had been searching for. He read the brief note, then crumpled it in his hand.

"Is anything the matter?"

There was a long pause. "Euclid has decided to return to his family for a few weeks."

"So suddenly? He did not mention anything to me about it when I spoke with him—" I stopped myself. This was none of my business. Besides, I knew they had quarreled and that Silas would not have wished to explain what had occurred, at least not now when he was feeling so wretched. "I hope his absence will not place more of a burden on you."

"I shall manage. Dinah, if you will excuse me . . ." He stood up, almost losing his balance, but steadied himself long enough to get to his room with a modicum of dignity.

18

❦ ❦ ❦

So much for the tenth day—and the eleventh. Silas spent that Friday as a convalescent, sipping tea and nibbling dry bread. At first he appeared as if he had been ill for weeks instead of less than a day, but by evening a rosy glow replaced his pallor and his despondency transformed into an ebullience that I found disturbing by contrast.

We lit the Sabbath candles and said our prayers together. "You cannot know how wonderful it is to have a Jewish woman by my side." He smiled and his teeth glinted in the candlelight. During dinner he was more loquacious than ever before.

"What are you planning to wear to the ball tomorrow?"

"Are you well enough to go?"

"Of course. Do I look like an invalid to you?"

"No, you don't, but—"

"My headaches are a trial, but at least they always end within a predictable length of time. Otherwise I might go mad. The odd thing is that once the pain has left me, I feel more energetic, more alive than in the weeks that preceded the attack." He stretched his arms above his head. "Ah, I am so happy to be without the pain. It's humbling. Unless one suffers, the misery of the wretched people on this earth cannot be understood properly. My agony is a cruel, exacting professor teaching a lesson that can be mastered no other way." He patted my hand. "Now, what will you wear? How about that blue dress you first wore in Calcutta?"

"Oh, no!"

"Why not? With a shawl you will be warm enough."

"I was certain you did not care for it."

He tilted his head and raised an eyebrow. "Well, the design is fine, the color suits you, and I know it is the height of fashion this season—

just the sort of gown you will feel comfortable in at Government House
and the other ladies will envy. Only . . ."

"Yes?"

"With some minor modification it could be even more sublime."

"What would you suggest?"

"The bows at the shoulders and in the back are unnecessary—they
clutter the line. And though I do not know much about the underpin-
nings, if you carried less bulk underneath, the skirt would fall more
flatteringly and you could move more freely."

How much he recalled about one dress stunned me. Moreover, I
agreed with his suggestion. The next morning I set Lucretia to work
removing the offensive fillips.

We rested during the afternoon, breaking the Sabbath with prayers
and a light meal of dumplings and fruit. When I was dressed, Silas
came to inspect me. Beaming, he had me spin around and around as
he admired the narrower silhouette and the cleaner lines of the
gown. "Wait," he said, holding up his hand so I would not move. A
few minutes later he returned, hiding something in his fist. "Close your
eyes." I felt him move behind me and clasp something around my
neck. It was a string of pearls centered with a jewel suitable for a
maharajah's turban: a huge pink pearl teardrop. As I hugged him in
thanks, he held me close, rubbing the small of my back. "You are so
beautiful, so beautiful," he murmured in my ear.

And beautiful I felt as I entered Government House on his arm, as
he squired me around, showing me off to the officials of the Bengal
government, the leaders of Darjeeling's hot-season society, and the
permanent residents who saw this night as the passing of the baton
back to them for the next six months.

I looked around for Maurice Luddy, whom I had not seen since the
wedding, and asked Silas' sister, Gala Ezekiel, where he was.

"Ever since Mother died, he has avoided most social occasions," she
replied, and clasped my hand. "I do so hope you and Silas will be
happy together."

I smiled shyly. She seemed satisfied for the moment.

I danced every dance, saving every other one for my husband, who
waited on the side when I was engaged. At supper my place was on
the governor's right, which I suspected was due more to my status as a
Sassoon than as Mrs. Luddy. The only difficult moment came when he
asked me what I was reading. Under the influence of two glasses of
champagne, I almost blurted: "The Kama Sutra," but caught myself to
change "Kama" to "Kubla," so it came out, "Kubla Khan, by Coleridge."

During the ride back to Tiger Hill Silas regaled me with gossip about
the people I had met. The names and faces and tales were hopelessly
muddled, but I did not care, since I would not have to sort most of

them out for half a year. Gulliver and Lucretia waited at the door to serve us. I was so giddy that Lucretia had to follow me about picking up my shoes, stockings, and gloves and unbuttoning me as I whirled around the room babbling about my success to a woman who could not possibly understand me. At last I sensed her frustration and sent her off, saying I would take care of myself. I dabbed my face, splashed water on my body, only rinsed my mouth, and slipped into bed coiled much too tightly to unwind into sleep.

When the door opened—without a preceding knock—I did not start. And when Silas moved to the side of my bed, I welcomed him with outstretched arms. The twelfth day, I thought, liking the number very much.

❀   ❀   ❀

For a long while Silas kissed my face from the tips of my ears to the hollow at my throat. He licked at my eyes, brushed my lips, then pried them open with his tongue. I tried—not too unsuccessfully, I thought—to return each in kind with the modesty of a virgin, yet with enough enthusiasm to encourage him to press forward.

To this day I recall every detail of what happened next. Many a bride might make the identical claim, of course, but I doubt many have experienced the same results. There were two starkly remembered moments: before my mistake, and after. Perhaps a doctor of the body or of the mind would soothe me by claiming one momentary lapse could not have influenced the outcome, that under normal circumstances we would have recovered. And a doctor might have gone on to reassure me the circumstances were *not* normal. There is good sense in that tact, but I do not speak sensibly. I speak from the authority of having lived through the moment. Nobody else was in my position. And I know—logic aside—that at that instant I was at fault.

We kissed and kissed until Silas began to stroke my arms, my hips, lightly touching my breasts with his right hand. I angled myself to face him slightly, and his other hand reached toward the hem of my gown. I was wearing a white lawn shift with embroidery around the neckline. A sheaf of ribbons formed the shoulder straps, and more were twisted into a sash that tied behind my back. I did not want to frustrate him as he blindly worked to free me. His breathing was rapid and I felt his lingam—that was the word that came to mind—swelling against my leg. Knowing exactly where to pull to loosen the girdle, I reached behind me, untied the ribbons, and slid the gown over my hips. The movement so startled him that he pulled back on his elbows to see what I was doing. Cheeks burning, eyes flashing, he seemed entranced as I kicked the gown away from my feet and onto the floor.

I lay on my back, like a gift. Silas, still wearing an undergarment, hovered above me on his haunches. I thought he was pleased, but no! what I had taken for desire became an outbreak of the most acute anxiety. Sweat poured off his chin. He gasped as though he were drowning. His teeth ground and muscles bulged in his neck. He bent his head to my chest and laid his cheek on my breast. He kissed its underside, moved up to the nipple, then sucked like a baby. "Do you mind?" he mumbled.

My reply was to stroke his fine hair to coax him to continue. The sensations emanating from my breasts and flowing down to my thighs were oddly pleasant and might have been even more so if the strain between us had not been foremost in my mind. Let it be over, I prayed. Let us just get past this point.

As though answering my prayers, Silas tensed. He rocked back on his knees and pulled off his covering. I closed my eyes. He knelt on either side of my legs. With a few quick thrusts he poked his sex at me, hitting a bony arch far off the mark. Using one hand, he tried to aim it more precisely. Expecting pain or some other sharp sensation, I held my breath. Once, twice, a third time I felt myself parting, yielding; then everything became easier. The hardness had melted. Was he inside me? I felt nothing except the weight of his body upon mine. Could it be this simple? He groaned and moved his hips in a shallow circle. His body was slippery with perspiration. He ground against me for several long minutes before sliding off and turning on his back.

"Sorry, too much drink at the party. Never a good idea to overdo."

I was so ignorant I did not realize what had—or had not—occurred. "No, it was fine, didn't hurt a bit."

He must have suspected how confused I was, but his own humiliation was so intense he did not care to correct me. Moving away, he said something about going to sleep. I reached for him, pulling his arm. "Please, don't go back to your room tonight."

He refastened his underwear. "A long day, we need to rest."

"I do not want to be alone." The yearning in my voice delayed him. He lay next to me. "The bed is so large, there is plenty of room." I lifted the cover and he crawled in beside me.

He kissed my cheek. "Dinah, I—" I hushed him with a strong press of my finger on his lips. "Good night, Dinah." He turned his back to me and curled like a baby.

Watching the nape of his neck, I could determine when he drifted off to sleep. When I thought he would not notice, I crept out of bed and made my way to the bathroom. Reaching between my legs with a soft facecloth, I checked for bleeding. Nothing. I touched myself for soreness. There was none. I tried to recall each detail of what had happened. Everything had changed when I had removed my gown and exposed myself lewdly. Hadn't I been warned that my body was not exactly the feminine ideal? I was too tall, too bony, my breasts (especially when I lay on my back) were flat cakes, not the juicy globes that men preferred. And what was admirable about the flatness of my belly or that mound of tangled hair?

After a long while I returned to the bed, finding a spot as far away from him as possible. For hours I lay there worrying how I had offended him, wondering what I had done wrong. Eventually I fell into a fitful sleep.

When I opened my eyes, Silas was at the window looking up at the snows.

"Silas?"

"Sorry to have bothered you."

"Do you always check them so early?"

"Yes, a custom since the day I came to this house. I need to know which of the mountains are out. If they are closed in, I find I can get back to sleep. Otherwise this is my best time for quiet contemplation."

From the bed I could not see the view. "What are they like today?"

"Come, you must see . . ." He held out his hand.

I moved beside him and looked up and far away. In the foreground all was blackness. The first light of day was outlining the peaks in red. A wisp of a moon hovered over Kanchenjunga, which, as though in homage, sent snow streamers blowing out in the direction of the celestial presence. Together we watched in awe.

"Is it never the same?"

"Never. The sight compels me. I could live nowhere else." He placed an arm around me protectively.

I would have liked to make a similar affirmation. I did not, sensing that once words were said, the picture was framed. Instead I shivered in the morning air. Silas pulled me closer and kissed my forehead. I bent my head shyly and, to my surprise, I noticed that his underwear stood out like a tent. Gently he pushed me back to the bed. With the curtain open I saw what he looked like as he unveiled himself. My images, derived from the exaggerated Hindu carvings, made his lingam seem modest in size. He placed my hand on it. I did not recoil. As I touched it, I watched his face. His eyes were partially closed. His mouth twisted in something between a painful grimace and a wry smile. His secret flesh was dry, smooth. He put his hand around mine to encourage me to hold it more tightly than I would have dared. He slipped my fingers up and down the shaft. The skin slid as though it were unattached. He lay back and his eyes clenched. He groaned. I stopped.

"No, faster," he gasped.

In a few seconds I watched as he moaned, writhed, and spilled his seed. As he rolled over on his stomach, I touched his back. "Do you want to sleep?"

"Yes."

I pulled the cover over him and busied myself in the bathroom until he was lost in a deep slumber. Then I took my turn beside the window, watching the theater of the snows.

꽃 꽃 꽃

Two hours later, when the light completely filled the room, he called to me from the bed. "Dinah, darling girl."

I rushed to him. He pushed me down beside him and lifted my gown, but did not remove it. Now I was convinced he did not find me pleasing. By stripping myself I had disgusted him. Better not to show my ugliness; better he should grope in the dark. I lay back. He parted my legs. I could see he was as ready, as he had been earlier, and I knew he would have to remain that way for us to continue. He had liked it when I touched him, so I reached for him, stroking as I had before.

"Yes, that's it, yes . . ."

He aimed for me and I lifted my hips, guiding him to where I thought he should go. I tried to receive him. My hand closed on the stem, but the diameter diminished until he shrank into a soft little pod.

"Too soon. We need to have our chota hazri."

We separated to dress, and met timidly at the table. I wondered what Gulliver and Lucretia thought, for by now they knew we had spent the night together. They were, of course, expressionless. I was thankful Euclid was away, for I would not have wanted to think about his musings on the events of the night and morning we shared.

We both pretended to be famished. The meal proceeded in silence until Gulliver poured second cups of tea and went to stand at the far end of the room.

"What are your plans for the day?" I asked as Silas began simultaneously, "What do you wish to do today?"

We laughed uneasily. He indicated I should go first. "I suppose, with Euclid away, you will be very busy."

"The monthly accounts must be completed this week."

"Silas . . ." I began, without thinking through the idea that was crystallizing. "Couldn't I help you—just while Euclid is gone? I am very good with sums, and my writing is tidy. I used to assist Dr. Hyam with his accounts, and I trust I could learn yours. Or I could write letters for you or organize your papers. I would feel so much better if I could be useful."

He was thoughtful for a moment. "I don't see the harm, if you will follow my instructions. Euclid has attempted to make 'improvements' on my systems, but I have firm reasons for setting out the columns and notations as I do."

"Your obedient servant," I said with a twinkle.

We set to work in the next hour. I did not tell Silas, but his system was so simple any fool could have mastered it within the day. With only thirty lines per page, there was never need to tabulate more than thirty figures. The only challenge was to carry over the totals on the bottom of the page to the top of the next without transposing a figure. When I could not achieve a balance at the end, I went back to a previous page and found that just such a mistake had occurred in the work Euclid had completed earlier.

"Here's the difficulty," I said, showing Silas the error.

"How did you find that so quickly?"

"There is a trick with nines that will disclose a transposition error," I told him.

"How did you know that?"

"They do teach girls some useful methods in school," I said lightly, but the sarcasm in my voice was impossible to hide.

He examined my work. "Very nice, and you did it amazingly fast. I thought this would take the entire day. Would you like to go down to Darjeeling after lunch? It's market day, the best time of the week to go to town."

۷/ ۷/ ۷/

Clusters of people thronged around us as soon as we began our way on foot through the crowded lanes of the market. Most people recognized Silas and showed a quiet curiosity about his memsahib.

"Why do they stare at us?"

"They are surprised we are walking. Most sahibs ride about on ponies, their women in rickshaws or *dandies*. Look." He pointed to a hillside where two men were pulling and two were pushing a fat Englishwoman up the side of the hill in a rickshaw. "And over there." Four men were carrying a lady in a dandy, a strong cloth slung like a hammock to a bamboo staff.

"How uncomfortable that looks! How do you sit in it?"

"Sideways, or you can lie on your back. We often use them for treks in the high hills."

I shuddered, recalling my horrible palanquin experience. "I would rather walk."

Silas made his way down the rows of tea sellers who had come in from the most remote plantations high in the hills. "They offer leaves of the rarest grades," he explained. Between his thumb and forefinger he rolled, then broke a leaf and sniffed it. This he repeated over and over at each stall. A few samples seemed to please him. "Some of these independents have lots they tend better than their children. Just the right amount of rain or shade or a more loamy soil can make all the difference in a leaf. I will pay a premium for small flavorful amounts to include in my special blends."

"Where do these people come from?" I asked as I surveyed the crowds of mixed races.

"Most are pickers who come down to purchase and show off their finery."

I pointed out some Oriental-looking women. "Where are they from originally?"

"Those are Lepchas from Sikkim. Their women wear those heavy ear ornaments, and both men and women part their hair in the middle."

"And who are those pretty women?" I indicated two girls who were wearing necklaces that dangled silver charm cases.

"Bhutias. Their men also wear long braids."

"And that woman?" I pointed to someone with a large carved necklace, a silver headdress, and nose ornaments that hung to her chin.

"She's from Nepal," he responded as we pushed through a crowd of coolies who carried huge loads on their backs supported by a wicker band across the forehead. We had to move out of the way for a milkman riding a pony, who balanced his pails on bamboo poles.

A shopkeeper showed us a drum made from two human skulls. "From the Dalai Lama's palace at Lhasa," he claimed. Another tried to interest us in a set of temple bells.

A man who specialized in weapons offered a *dao*, or hill knife, for one rupee or a brass Buddhist scepter with prongs at the ends for two rupees. While Silas examined the pieces, I fingered some Chinese gilt buttons next door. The seller, a young woman dressed in a padded jacket, striped skirt, high felt boots, and a mass of jingling jewelry, moved gracefully as she brought out other treasures to tempt me, but my eye had roved to a stand where a white-haired man with a bronzed face offered iridescent butterflies.

I looked around for Silas, not wanting him to become impatient with me. He was neither to my right nor to my left. I turned around and saw a thin boy with long black hair to his shoulders whispering in Silas' ear and pointing. Silas followed the line of the boy's finger to a house at the end of a staircase cut in the hillside. Silas shook his head doubtfully. The boy's gestures signified he was certain of his words. A cloud passed over Silas' face as he moved beside me.

"Let's go," he said, disappointing the man, who had hopes of making a butterfly sale.

"Is something the matter?" I asked as we pushed our way to the edge of the crowd.

"I am more tired than I expected . . . the long night . . ."

I nodded amicably. "Shall we start for home?"

"Yes, after we have some tea in the market. Or would you prefer to go to the Planters' Club?"

"Something here would take less time."

He led me to a café that was nothing more than some upturned crates covered with goatskin rugs. The tea seller poured two steaming cups and offered us a plate of spicy candied apricots. Silas joked with the man in his native dialect for a few minutes; then, glancing again at the hillside, he hurried me to the tonga, tied to a hydrangea bush.

As we made our way uphill, I focused on the peasants, who scaled the inclines with an enviable economy of action. With their thickset physiques and short limbs, they seemed a special breed, more animal than human. I turned around to watch a line of lithe bodies hugging the sinuous paths, when a familiar spot of yellow caught my eye.

I blinked. We were on the edge of a field dotted with green and golden patches. A darker spot moved in the distance, as though following our progress. We came around a bend, bringing us momentarily closer to the man.

Now I was certain.

It was Euclid. He had not returned to his home after all. He was staying in Darjeeling.

I looked over at Silas. His gaze was riveted to the road. Wondering if I should direct his attention to Euclid, I reached for his sleeve, then recoiled. In front of us, gigantic spiderwebs like ghostly curtains hung down from the abundant foliage that draped over the road. Behind us, the corrugated tin roofs of the town dazzled in the late-afternoon sun. My mind spun with questions. I felt suspended between the two places. I did not wish to go forward or backward. I would have burst into tears if I had not looked up, up, and been soothed by the creamy sameness of the snows.

19
❦ ❦ ❦

S ilas did not object when I told him I wanted a bath, a light
supper in my room, and an early bedtime. If anything, I
sensed he was pleased not to have to entertain me through
the evening or feel he had to come to me in the night.

In the morning, I woke to find my monthly flow had begun. After
we had chota hazri, my husband asked me how I was feeling.

Looking away, I tried to be offhand. "Not as well as I would like . . .
a bad time to be a woman."

He understood at once. "Then you must rest. I need to go to the
company offices this morning. Is there anything I can do for you?"

The rapid way he made plans to go off without me put me on guard.
"I would prefer to come with you." When he did not respond, I filled
in the yawning gap. "If I knew more about your business, I might
understand the account books better and . . ." What else could I say to
convince him? And why was it so important that I do so? I had not
sorted out the muddle, but I sensed that if I did not remain close to
Silas during the next few days, while I was indisposed, and the following week, during which I remained unclean by Jewish law, he would
rush into Darjeeling alone at every chance. And if he were alone, he
would meet Euclid—a thought which infused me with an amorphous
anxiety.

I decided to be forthright. "You do not want me to accompany you."

"That's not it." He shifted his feet. "My errands are boring. Besides,
my family will not understand your interest."

"I should have known my place," I said, exaggerating my facetious
tone. "I am just a woman. Nothing proves that more than my current
predicament. Until you wrote me those letters, introduced me to Lucretia Mott, told me about the freedoms that awaited me, I did not
question my lot." I modulated my voice. "I am not angry with you,
Silas, because I know your beliefs conflict with those of society—and

217

possibly with those of your own family." I stood up, as though I were going to retire to my room, then turned and spoke. "What disappoints me most is to be disillusioned. The unique way your father organized his business and family affairs impressed my father. I suppose I was expecting that Maurice Luddy would sanction your philosophies on other matters."

"Dinah . . ." His voice warbled with anxiety. "Your health is my only concern. Nothing would please me more than to have your company. In fact, I planned to show my brother-in-law Harold your accounting work today."

"How soon will you be ready to leave?" I asked.

"Can you be ready in half an hour?"

"Certainly, Silas. I am not one to make a fuss."

❀ ❀ ❀

After two days of office work, Silas and I went out on ponies to inspect the tea gardens. "Garden," which conjures a tidy plot, is both an apt and an incorrect term. The huge plantations, employing fifty thousand workers in the Darjeeling region, covered every inch of slope that had enough soil to hold roots fast. These were not rude patches, but tidy sections with plants laid out in such geometrical precision the hillsides looked as though they had been combed.

Every time we left the house, I kept a lookout for Euclid's saffron robes. I had not seen him on the last two treks to or from Darjeeling, and he eluded me that morning as well. As I sighed in relief, a spicy odor reminiscent of ginger root mingling with the acrid smell of hay—the combination creating the tannic scent of tea—assaulted me. "I wonder if vineyards smell of wine."

Silas laughed aloud. "What a thought!" The he turned serious as he mulled over the idea. "I think not, because the chemical changes in making tea are less drastic than those in fermenting wine."

"How logical you are!" I grinned back at him, deciding I was right to stick close to him.

From a distance the green patches of tea plants seemed like velvet squares. Up close the leaves were broader and coarser than I expected. We rode our ponies up and down the rows, and once in a while Silas dismounted to check the base of a plant, smell the leaves, and search for pests. "The manufacture of tea begins in the field," he explained as he picked a few leaves and showed them to me. "Good cultivation multiplies yield; careless plucking modifies price. You see, only the first flush of the new shoots is taken. The younger, more succulent the leaf, the finer the tea. And it is important to take care during the picking not to bruise or crush the tender leaves. That is why we do not pay our pickers by weight, but by the day. Otherwise they would rush and the whole crop would yield less at market."

"May I try?"

He helped me down and held the reins in his hand. "You pick two leaves and a bud: that's the golden rule of tea plucking."

"Two leaves and a bud," I said as I attempted to grasp the stalk and break it cleanly without injuring the leaves. The job was trickier than it appeared. I tried again.

Silas laughed. "It is said the Chinese emperors would not accept tea bruised by rough or impious hands; thus the leaves for the imperial brew had to be plucked by young virgins by moonlight."

When I scowled at the fact that I still was qualified to pick tea for the emperor—and might be so for some time to come—Silas looked at me quizzically. I managed to avoid his gaze and ask, "Once the tea is picked, what happens next?"

He snapped off a leaf and rolled it in his hand. "You can take the leaves of one of these bushes and come out with three different results: black, green, or oolong tea. Most of the world prefers black tea—which is completely fermented—so the bulk of this crop will end up in that state. Green tea is not fermented, just steamed to make the leaves sufficiently pliable to be rolled and to stop fermentation. Then we alternately dry it and roll it until it turns too crisp to be handled. After it is fully dry—in a state that kills the start of any fermentation process—it is ready to be shipped."

We remounted our ponies and made our way down a steep grade, with Silas leading and me following. Thinking we might slip at any moment, I concentrated on the animal's footholds more than the words of Silas' explanation of the oolong tea process: ". . . bruised by manipulation . . . sets fermentation going . . . stopped by roasting." On a piece of flatter ground I drew alongside. "The Chinese prefer the oolong, but the Europeans have not acquired the taste, which is good for us, since the full process is elaborate and expensive."

"So you primarily produce black tea."

"Yes. Now, I believe the area to develop is the highest end of the spectrum: the rare-tea market. I will call my newest blends Emperor and Imperial. What do you think?"

I reined in my pony. This was the first time he had asked my opinion, and I did not want to blandly agree, nor sound ignorant with a careless remark. "I see the necessity for both, like gold and rice," I said slowly, choosing my words. "On one side of the scale, there will always be people who want gold—a small quantity for a large price. On the other, there will be more who require rice—a large quantity for a small price. I suppose the fluctuations in the market might balance each other in good times and bad, but . . ." Silas was staring at me queerly, so I stopped myself.

"Go on, please," he urged.

"Well, even though there must be a large market for something very inexpensive and a small market for something very dear, the most stable market most likely would be the middle ground. You know, the government worker, the civil servant, the army major, the professor. They would want the finest quality they could afford at a price they thought was fair but not cheap. Do you understand what I mean? They certainly do not want the same brew their servants drink."

"What a mind you have! You have set out the question more exactly than anyone else I have ever heard. What we are attempting to do is to arrive at three grades of leaf tea: one which produces the lighter, less intense tea the lower classes select; a broken grade, which gives the brisk liquor the Continentals prefer, for the middle markets; and a fancy line of expensive blends, for the upper classes. I expect to do a brisk business from brisk tea." He rambled on about how his father had reservations about his idea to combine the body of an Assam with the fragrance of a Darjeeling and a touch of the pungency from a Ceylon leaf, but at the moment I was too flattered to follow the details.

Later, as I lay in bed that night, I thought about Maurice and wondered again why I had not seen him yet. I was more certain than ever there was some difficulty between father and son—the cause of which I had not yet discovered. Putting those distressing thoughts aside, I concentrated on my husband's complimentary words and went to sleep more content than I had been since seeing Euclid skirting the path.

❦ ❦ ❦

Over the next several days, winds buffeted Xanadu Lodge around the clock. I was learning that it howled from the west and whined when it poured through a gap in the hills to the east. Then, three nights later, a storm blew up the valley, lashing the house with dry, violent winds. The windows that brought us the snow views were shuttered and locked with iron bars. As there were but small high windows on the entry side of the house, I felt as if I were being encased in a coffin. "Better than a shower of glass," Silas replied when I complained. "If this subsides in the night, Gulliver will have them off before you awaken." Seeing my distress, he had reached out to touch me. I pulled back as a reminder that I was still unclean. He did not persist.

I understood the laws of *niddah*, the days my husband could not come to me, but did not know how to signal him when he again might do so. Grandmother Helene had explained that sexual contact was prohibited from the moment I discerned blood, and continued at least five days or until every trace of the menses had disappeared, plus another seven clean days thereafter—always a minimum of twelve days. I expected this would mean two weeks away from Silas. This was the eleventh day. I had a few more days to find a way to tell him, although I was both anticipating and fearing our next intimate encounter. I hoped he would find me more desirable the next time, especially if I made no more foolish mistakes, but what if the time apart had muted his interest in resuming our marital relations?

On that turbulent night, as I lay awake listening to the high-pitched screeching that rolled up the ravine, then dissipated somewhere far in the distance before beginning again, my mind churned with the possibilities. During the lulls, I slept lightly. A new clatter brought me to my feet. Voices. I opened the door a crack. Gulliver and Silas were speaking. Other servants were moving around. More storm protection, I assumed. I closed my door. Soon the house was quiet except for the wailing through the treetops in concert with the tattoo of branches slapping on the roof.

Because the protective boards were not removed before dawn, I had no sense of day and night. I was awake through the fiercest hours of the tempest, asleep when the winds diminished to a dull roar. Lucretia did not arouse me until after one in the afternoon. My head was pounding, my stomach weak with hunger. I took my meal in bed, then dressed in a loose dressing gown and went out to find Silas.

Gulliver stood by the hearth as I entered the room. I looked for Silas in his usual chair or by his writing desk. "Where is Mr. Luddy?" I asked.

"He went to Darjeeling, memsahib."

"When?"

"Last night."

"In that storm?"

"On an urgent matter, memsahib."

I thought at once of Maurice Luddy. "Is someone in his family ill?"

"He left you a letter." Gulliver handed me an ivory envelope like the ones I had received in Calcutta in what seemed like another lifetime.

I sat on the hearth bench to read the few scratchy sentences.

I did not want to disturb you, but a friend has had an accident. Do not concern yourself about me. The roads are dry and pose no problems downhill. I will return in time for supper tomorrow. Forgive my haste. Silas.

A friend? An accident? Euclid! I called for Gulliver.

"Yes, memsahib."

"Who has had the misfortune?"

"I do not know."

Yes, he did. "Euclid?"

The bearer's impassive face twitched imperceptibly.

"That will be all, Gulliver," I said, dismissing him.

In the late afternoon, the winds whipped up once more. Accompanying them were claps of thunder that reverberated across the ravines and echoed off the cliffs in eerie volleys of dwindling booms. Anxiously awaiting Silas' return, I called for Gulliver and ordered an elaborate tea to be readied. "Certainly, memsahib," he said, bowing.

I did not want him to leave yet. "Gulliver, what is your given name?"

He blinked, then replied, "Jetha."

"And what is Lucretia's?"

"Namgal."

"Jetha," I repeated. "Namgal." I liked the way they felt on my tongue far better than Silas' affectations. I wondered what Euclid's real name was, but sent Gulliver away without asking.

The rest of the afternoon passed without a sign from Silas. At last, only moments before darkness fell, he rode up to the gate in the tonga. I opened the door for him myself. Gulliver stepped forward to close it, then took my husband's cloak.

"Bring the tea at once, Gulliver."

Even in the murky light I could see his pallor. The skin under his eyes was gray. His mouth was drawn into a tight line that puckered his mustache into a terrible grimace. Only once before, when he had been in the throes of his headache, had he looked so miserable. I knew something terrible had happened to Euclid—and though it pains me to admit this, I could not help feel relief that the disagreeable little man was out of my life.

"Here, drink this," I said, serving Silas a cup of tea and adding a chota peg of brandy without asking if he wanted any. He clasped the cup with a wooden gesture. I poured myself the same, but with a burra peg to fortify me for whatever was about to come.

I waited for him to gather his strength, which at that moment was a feat of great restraint. As a lightning bolt struck close to the house, its sharp flare flashed through the cracks in the wood battens and illuminated the bolts carved above the windows. Next came the thundering crescendos, each one stopping my heart.

"Darjeeling deserves its name," I managed between the bursts. Seeing my distress, Silas finally spoke. "Don't be afraid, Dinah. There are always storms like this at the start of the cold weather. They clear the air, and though the temperatures fall, the views are splendid and the climate is exceedingly healthy."

"I have never feared natural phenomena," I replied firmly. "My concerns are for you. Something awful has happened."

"Yes, Dinah." His voice broke. Almost a minute passed before he could begin again. "Euclid—he . . ."

"Is he dead?"

"No, thank God, no!"

I hoped he took my shocked expression as confusion, not disappointment. "What happened?"

"He tried to kill himself."

"How? Why?"

He shook his head. "So much to explain . . . Dinah, please forgive me. If I had known the consequences, if I had known any of this could have happened, I would never have . . ." He trembled so violently I darted for his cup and placed it on a table.

Looking around, I saw Gulliver standing ramrod straight in the shadows. Lucretia was at her post by my doorway. "Could we talk about this in your room?"

Silas did not protest as I led him by the arm. I glanced over my shoulder as a warning for the servants to leave us in peace. Silas propped himself up on his bed. I brought a chair to the edge, but he took my hand and pulled me to his side. Leaning back on the fur pillows, we both stared across the blank boarded wall, which flickered with the eerie reflections of the one lit lamp.

After a long while he spoke in a singsong voice that assisted his untidy confession to roll off his lips. "I met Euclid when he was a boy of fifteen. Ever since I can remember, since I was a schoolboy, I found that I preferred the company of men. When I was in England, I met other like-minded friends who helped me to see there were many who felt as I did. I dreaded the moment when I would have to come back out to India, especially to the closed society of the Jewish community, where they would never tolerate my difference. The first year I lived under my father's roof again was a terrible strain. We fought most of the time. I do not think he discovered my secret, but he guessed I was not like the others and blamed my education for giving me lofty, elitist ideas." He closed his eyes. "It was then I knew I would have to live on my own and thought of building a house near Tiger Hill." His face firmed into an impenetrable shield.

Ignoring the fact I was unclean, I stroked his cheek, much as he often had done to mine. This act of tenderness crumbled his shell. He gasped and blurted, "When I met Euclid, I found happiness in India for the first time. He was a gentle, sweet boy who looked up at me as if I were a prince. I encouraged his studies and invited him to live in our home. My father never liked him. He thought Euclid was only using me to further himself. And then . . . then . . ." He turned toward me, sobbing.

Perhaps I should have been thinking how this affected me, but I was so lost in his pain that I worried only if I had the means to comfort him. "Silas, Silas, please do not cry. Please, I only want to know the truth . . ."

"Then he discovered me . . . with Euclid."

"Who did?"

"M-my father."

That explained the estrangement between Maurice and his son. The long silence was punctuated by the sudden torrent of rain that drilled on the roof. I took his hand in mine. "So you built this house and came here to live with Euclid."

"Yes."

"And you were happy together for many years."

"Yes."

"He was your assistant, your confidant, your closest friend—but never your babu." I gave a weak laugh, showing that I had understood his warning not to use the title of "clerk" with his friend.

"How wonderfully understanding you are."

I understand nothing! I wanted to scream, but all I said was, "So, that is why Euclid resented me. I did not realize he was jealous, but now everything makes more sense, except . . ."

Silas filled in. "Why he left and why he—"

"What did he do?" I interrupted. "And will he recover?"

"Belladonna and ground glass, a common rat poison. The symptoms began much like dysentery. He told the family he was staying with—an old professor from school—that he was having stomach troubles, and they left him alone. When the storm began, a servant sent to close the shutters found that Euclid had fallen into a stupor. If the doctor had not come at once, if he had not treated a child who had mistakenly tasted the same poison only weeks before . . ."

"And now?"

"The doctor is unsure of the damage caused by the glass—bleeding continues internally—but the effects of the belladonna have been counteracted."

"Then he is not out of danger."

"They think he will survive, but he might have done some permanent damage."

"All because of me."

"No, not you. You are entirely innocent. Everything is my fault. I was crazy to believe I could work out something that would satisfy everyone. I did not want anything to change between Euclid and me. Through the ages, other men have managed to have families as well as their male friends. I thought that if I lived more normally, Euclid and I could preserve our way of life forever. And it might have worked out that way, if he had not been so demanding, wanting me to himself, expecting me to ignore you. Euclid's own selfish stupidity led to this crisis!" Silas stopped himself. "No, *my* selfish stupidity. How could I have believed I could balance everything? Worse, I deceived you from the first."

As he spoke, I was devastated by a confusing galaxy of feelings, as though a mirror had broken and I was gazing into thousands of reflective fragments of my life. I understood everything. I understood nothing. Yet underneath the layer of distress ran a river of relief. The trepidation I had felt since the first day in Calcutta, when I had thought Silas had found me repulsive, the apprehension that had festered during the first days of our marriage, when he had not approached me, and had culminated in our unsatisfactory intimate encounters, when I was certain he found me undesirable, were melting in the glare of his confession.

"Why did you choose me?"

"I always had wanted a wife, a wife who would prove my normalcy to the outside world. I even believed I wanted children. And you seemed the perfect choice. Most Calcutta girls would not have been happy in Darjeeling, let alone on this godforsaken hill. The remoteness frightened any my father approached on my behalf. One or two candidates became available, but I rejected them as unsuitable, as they lacked any education. I knew that if I were to tolerate a woman's presence, I would have to meet my intellectual equal. When I heard about you, I became enthusiastic. I thought: Here is a possibility! You were the most brilliant woman I had ever heard about. And, as my father so shrewdly saw, you had good reason to want to leave Calcutta, and also to be content at Xanadu Lodge. He said, 'She will be grateful for a man like you and will turn a blind eye to your . . . your faults.' "

"You assumed I would accept Euclid, and you required Euclid to accept me!"

"No. It was my intention you should never know about Euclid. I believed we could be discreet. Nothing worked out as I had imagined. Since meeting you, I honestly had begun to lose interest in Euclid. You kept me enthralled—you were so curious, so humorous, so pleasant to be with. I was beginning to feel very close to you, and Euclid sensed this. I explained it was only right that I devote myself to you for the first few months. I told him I would approach you slowly, try to make you my friend before making you my wife. The moment he supposed I was attempting to meet my marital obligations, he went crazy with jealousy. We fought. He left the house, saying he was returning home to Bhutan, but going only as far as the town. Then he badgered me with messages, begging me to join him for a few hours. I refused, out of loyalty to you. And so he took a drastic course."

"Now what shall you do about him?"

"What can I do?"

"Bring him back here?" I offered without sincerity.

"Impossible, now that you know."

"I agree. Unless . . . I went away."

"Where would you go?"

Where could I go?

Silas sat upright and swung around to face me. With the lamp behind his head, he loomed like a blank, expressionless ghost. "I want you to stay with me."

My face was illuminated; thus he must have seen the cost to me written in my eyes as I spoke my version of the truth. "No, you are only saying that because you feel duty-bound. I cannot be what you want. I am a woman. You never wanted a woman, did you?"

"I was not certain. Believe me, Dinah, I did not know if I did. I prayed I would find you appealing. After ten years of looking—oh, forgive me for saying this now—but I thought I could be attracted to you because your body is not too encumbered with curves. I liked touching you, being with you. And it might have worked if Euclid's questions and threats had not infected me. Every time we were alone together, he grilled me about what had occurred. He warned me it would never work, that I could never make love to a woman. No matter how I tried to shake his predictions, they loomed in my mind, rendering me unfit. But, Dinah, if this terrible accident had not happened, if he had left me in peace, I think we could have come together as man and wife. With your kindness, I would have overcome my . . . my difficulties." In the long pause, he swallowed audibly. "We could still try again—"

"No." I moved to the far edge of the bed. "I suspected something was the matter. I thought it was my fault, and some of it was. Still, out of ignorance I persisted. Now that I know, I would rather have no man than one who comes to me with a natural aversion."

"You do not understand. I am committed to you, tonight more than ever before. I want to find a way to earn your forgiveness and make you content. Your situation was not good when we met, and I admit it is not greatly improved now, but with me at your side you can have far more than you could alone. If you want, we both can forget the physical side of marriage. You can have me to lean on, and have your freedom besides. I admit it was thoughtless and selfish to marry you, but you must believe me when I say there was never any concern for your dowry. It is inviolate. Everything else I own or will possess is at your disposal, so you may live the life of your choosing. Can't you see that if we remain together, we both may lead a life of dignity? I would treat you like an honored sister. You would have more freedom than any other married woman—or any single woman—and if a child should ensue, I would claim it as my own."

I was too stunned to respond. I felt as though I were caught in a cage. The options were merely keys dangling on an unreachable hook. We were married—for life—and I would have to tolerate his terms and learn to live with them. His offer was more than generous, yet a prison of gold is as permanent as one of iron.

After a long silence, he began to speak in an entirely different manner. It was as though a new person had walked into the room and taken his place. "When I was younger, I went on summer treks to the barren wastes, where the green line of trees ends, but before the snows begin. Up there, in the last high place that men may walk on this earth, huge boulders the size of houses—like the marbles of giants— litter the landscape." His voice took on the compelling timbre of a master storyteller. For a moment I was able to forget my torment and listen.

"During the day, the rocks are so close to the sun they heat to fiery temperatures. Then at night, when the peaks spill cold air into the ravines, they explode, as if they were eggs dropped from the sky." His final mysterious words hung in the air. What did he mean?

At last he explained. "Even the hardest granite will be crushed by extremes: too much heat, too much cold—the love for a man, the love for a woman." Silas leaned back with his eyes closed and spoke very slowly. "To survive, I must choose one over another. Now. So I will make another promise: I will never, no matter what he says or does, see Euclid again."

A searing pain, as though I had drawn it like a lightning shaft, shot from his heart to mine. Just then I loved Silas as one loves someone who has leapt through a ring of fire to save her. Just then I also knew the hopelessness of our position and that his sacrifice was unendurable.

"No, I cannot ask you to make that choice."

"I make it freely."

"Next time Euclid might actually kill himself. Then how would you feel?"

"He cannot intimidate me with threats to harm himself."

"Silas, I don't want to coerce you to stay with me either."

"It is my decision."

"No, you are merely accepting your duty."

"I already know the horror of living a life on the fringes. If we do not stay together, we both will suffer. Is that what you want?"

"No, but I do not want to live with a man who does not want a woman."

"Dinah, we could make a decent life together. We could travel. We could have friends to visit. Besides, there are fewer alternatives for you than for me."

Yes, I know! I wanted to scream at him, but I marshaled my emotions as I began to realize that if I returned to Calcutta, my worst fears would come true. The gossips would be vindicated. "Her mother's daughter!" they would shout from the rooftops.

"You say that if I stayed here I could have my freedom. You meant with other men, didn't you?"

"Yes. We could both be discreet."

"There are always complications . . ." I omitted saying "like Euclid." I took a long breath and continued, "Do you know the Indian proverb about the profligacy of Calcutta women?"

He shook his head.

"They say that if you put a bag of Calcutta dust under the bed of a good woman, she will be corrupted. Can't you see that is what they will say about me?"

"Who cares? I would protect you. Your position as my wife would armor you further."

I closed my mind to his arguments. How could I live out a charade for the rest of my life? Even if Euclid did not return, there would be others like him who would complicate our lives. And even if I could not imagine the men who might tempt me, I could see the futility of loving another under these odd circumstances.

Yet Silas was accurate about one point: what other choices were there? Nobody else would marry a woman who had lasted less than a month with a perfectly respectable man. My father would want my dowry back. I would be a prisoner in his—and Zilpah's—house. My stepmother's graciousness to me in the past months had been predicated on the fact I would soon be married. And her response was likely to be benign compared with the vitriolic tongue of Aunt Bellore.

These terrible thoughts churned and fermented until I could not think sensibly another moment. "I cannot stay with you!" I burst out. "I don't want to live like that for the rest of my life!" I fell upon him, and he did not resist as I pummeled pillows and flesh in a blind fury that soon dissolved into heaving, exhausted sobs.

When my rage was spent, we lay side by side in the darkness. Somehow my head found its way to his chest and I slept for a few hours. I woke when he got up and left the room. I heard a scraping and banging as he himself removed the storm protection. The winds had settled into a modest blow. An icy patina covered the valleys. In the early light the world sparkled with the glow of pearlescence.

Silas brought me a cup of tea. I started to get out of bed. "Not yet. The mountains are asleep, but the atmosphere is so clear they will show themselves today." He took a seat by the window, keeping watch.

We were lost in our private deliberations. All I had ever wanted was to be a virtuous wife and not to tread the path the society ladies of Calcutta expected me to take. No matter how I tried, I had failed. Had Grandmother Flora's advice been right? Was no marriage at all better than a bad marriage?

"Come see," Silas called in a faraway voice.

I stood beside him and saw that massive Kanchenjunga was haloed in purple light. Now at last I understood his obsession with the flowering of the snows. Each day at dawn he had the vision to look up and far away, his mind cleansing itself of petty details, daily conceits, the banality of everyday life, even the serious difficulties such as those we faced that day. Compared to the heights, our concerns were minuscule. No wonder he lived in the world of his mind, always striving toward nobler thoughts. Why did I always look down and across the enticing spaces of blue sky? Why did I prefer the wide and distant plain? Why did I long to return to the riverbank, to a passage to the sea?

What would my mother have done? She would have stayed here and led her own life. But hadn't I determined not to be like my mother?

"Silas," I said as gently as possible, "I cannot remain here."

"I wish I could persuade you," he said morosely. "I feel like someone who sees a person he cares about setting out on a perilous journey on an uncertain ocean. At the same time, I realize why you must do so. You are far too young, too intelligent to waste your life with me."

"No, that's not it. It's because of what happened to my mother—"

He touched his hand to my lips. "Hush. Listen to me. I will go to Calcutta with you. I will assume the entire responsibility for the failure. I will explain my inadequacies to the leaders of our community so they will dissolve the marriage."

"Your reputation will be ruined."

"My reputation is nothing. How can they hurt me? I live perched on this hilltop. I will have the majority interest in the Luddy gardens. I care nothing for society. Certainly I shall never again attempt to marry. I will dedicate myself to clearing your name, no matter the expense to me. To the best of my ability I must protect you. You are the one who was deceived. You are flawless. You are intact. Your reputation must be restored."

Poor Silas had never before stormed the bastions of Calcutta's tight Baghdadi society. "What you suggest is chivalrous, but impossible. I have been here almost a month. No matter what we say, they will never believe us."

Instead of responding, he pointed to the mountains. "I told you the haze would lift." I watched with him as the invisible hand of twilight peeled away the gloomy mist. "All the peaks are out. Kang, Jannu, Kabru, Dome, Talung, Kanchenjunga, Pandim, Jubonu, and Narsing are anointed by new day's light. They bore into the sky, those emperors of the earth. Here, from this room, we are as close as any mortal to the top of the world. Here we can forget so much of the baseness of this life. Wherever you go, Dinah, I hope you will remember the eternal snows that were here before we came and will be here long after we have left."

I shivered in the draft. As he placed his arm around me, I encircled his waist. Ironically, we were joined in a common purpose at last. I lifted my eyes as the sun illuminated Kanchenjunga. As a final blessing, the pinnacle of the world, the great goddess, the all-seeing mother—Everest—glowed golden as she rejoiced in the dazzling newness of the day.

20

❦ ❦ ❦

How did word reach you so quickly?" Yali asked when she greeted us in the vestibule at Theatre Road.

"What do you mean?" I stammered.

Silas placed his arms around my shoulders as he saw Yali's expression change from confusion to fear. "You do not know? Then why have you come?"

"To visit with the family," he replied evenly. "Who is here now?" Yali shook her head. "Nobody is in?" He turned to me.

I shrugged. "Zilpah always insisted the family gather for Sabbath prayers. By this time on a Friday we would always be together . . ." I had ignored Yali's mournful eyes as long as I could. "Papa!" I cried. "Has something happened to him?"

"No." Yali opened her arms and gathered me in. "Everyone is in Lower Chitpur Road."

"Nani!" I sobbed as Silas and Yali supported me. "How bad is it? Maybe I am not too late—"

Then my ayah whispered the sad truth. Grandmother Flora's frail heart had faltered sometime between Wednesday night and Thursday morning. Nobody knew the time for certain.

"Have they buried her already?" Silas asked.

"Late yesterday." She bowed her head.

Yesterday, while Silas and I had been working on how to break our news and trying to anticipate the various reactions. I had been steeling myself to face Zilpah, Aunt Bellore, Cousin Sultana, not to mention Papa, and now all my anxieties were sucked into a void in the pit of my stomach. Nani was gone.

On the way to Lower Chitpur Road, Silas spoke in a monotone that he hoped would penetrate the fog of pain that had enveloped me. "We cannot tell anyone why we are here, at least until the mourning period is over."

231

"A charade will make it worse in the end."

"What charade?" He held up our clasped hands. "Nobody is watching us and we are still friends. Friends care for each other during times of loss."

"If only my grandmother were here. I wanted her advice."

"If you wish to change your mind, my offer stands."

I shook my head.

"Dinah, your grandmother had been ill for a long time. I do not mean to sound unsympathetic, but people we love do die. The legacy they give us is the strength to go on and make our own choices. They did not lead blameless lives and neither can we. Even though I may disagree with you, I admire your courage to try for a better life than I could offer. Part of that courage must have come from your grandmother."

"Oh, Silas, what if nobody believes our story? What if we cannot get a divorce?"

He closed his heavy eyelids and lowered his head. "Leave that to me."

🌾 🌾 🌾

After the period of mourning passed, Silas wanted to speak to my father alone. Thinking he would be more understanding if I were present, I insisted on being by his side. However, I had not anticipated the roar that accompanied Silas' initial utterance.

"You have not what?" Papa shouted so loud the brass tables in the hall vibrated.

Silas hung his head.

"I do not understand what you are saying." My father's voice deepened and he strung his words out in long, menacing syllables. "The marriage took place more than a month ago. What have you two been doing this whole time? Playing backgammon?"

"Only a few games," Silas said with a shaky laugh. Seeing this only infuriated my father further, he continued earnestly, "You must believe me. I have not been able to apply my conjugal rights."

Papa stared at me darkly. "Dinah, what do you have to say about this? Have you refused him? Is that what this is about?"

"It is not her fault," Silas interrupted.

"Of course it's her fault! You are two perfectly healthy and capable people. Or, Mr. Luddy, have I overlooked something obvious? With all your high-and-mighty book learning, have you too many brains and not enough balls?"

I felt a wobble in my knees as my father's eyes burned into me. "Papa, it won't ever work out. We have tried, honestly we have." I hated my squeaky voice. "The last thing I ever wanted was to return to Calcutta, but this is a matter of life or death."

My father cocked his head. "Life or death?" he said with disbelief. "Has this man beaten you?" I shook my head. "Or harmed you in any manner?"

"N-no. Someone else—"

"Someone else has threatened you?"

I looked beseechingly in Silas' direction, but his eyes were riveted on a spot on the Kashmir carpet. After a long interval he gasped, "There is another man . . ."

Like a spring released of an enormous pressure, my father leapt forward and grasped my shoulders. "You little hussy!" He shook me so violently I thought my neck might snap. "The fruit doesn't fall far from the tree, does it?"

I almost welcomed the pain as his fingers dug into my flesh. With enormous effort Silas pulled him back. "No, you are not listening to us," he gasped. "I am in love with someone else. I was living with this person before I met Dinah, and continued the relationship afterward. Because of his jealousy, he almost killed himself and—"

"*He* almost killed *him*self?" My father's eyes began to twitch uncontrollably as he backed away from both of us.

Silas plunged on. "Since I was quite young, I have preferred the company of men. I thought I could change, I *wanted* to change, but even with your daughter's kindness and patience we could not . . . I could not—"

"You are one of those," Papa said with sneering contempt. "And knowing this, you married my daughter!" His face twisted into an ugly leer. "You money-grubbing perverted coward! Get out of my sight! Both of you! Leave my house at once!"

Somehow Silas and I found ourselves on the portico. No carriage was in sight. We stumbled down Theatre Road to Chowringhee Road and waved down the first rickshaw-wallah we saw.

"Where to, sahib?"

"I don't know, the Maidan, I suppose."

"Where in the Maidan?"

"Anywhere. Just get on with it." The two of us were not as heavy as a corpulent man, but the rickshaw-wallah could not pull us rapidly. No matter. The sound of the wheels grinding out their protest against the uneven tarmac in concert with the wheezing regularity of the rickshaw-wallah's tubercular chest drowned out the roar of our wildly beating hearts.

After an hour of wandering the Maidan's roads, we decided to go to Grandmother Helene's out of pity for the rickshaw-wallah. The exhausted man spit a red clot—was it blood or betel juice?—and grinned at receiving triple the number of rupees he had requested. "Lovers," he muttered as he jerked his rickshaw into an alley where he could rest.

Grandmother Helene listened more calmly as we described our predicament. There was a long pause. Then, without expression, she began to ask a series of sensible questions. "Where will you live while arrangements are being made for a divorce?"

Silas shrugged.

"Should we live apart?" I asked.

"It depends. If you do, the whole community will start talking. If you don't, they will later question the validity of your claims."

"We are damned no matter what we do," I sighed.

"Not necessarily. I propose you both should come to live with me. You can trust I will not gossip about who slept where or when."

Suddenly she noticed that I was shivering in the light dress I had worn that morning. December often brought a swift change of temperature when the sun went down, but my anxiety was probably more responsible for my shakes than the weather.

"Poor child," Grandmother Helene said under her breath, and handed me her shawl. She took my hands in hers and rubbed them. "So it is settled, then. There's no need to return to Theatre Road tonight. I'll send for your things. Tomorrow, when your father has thought this over—or rather, when he has talked it over with Zilpah—he will come around. He's more sensible than you think, unless he feels he has been double-crossed." She stopped abruptly and gave Silas a piercing glance. "About the dowry . . ."

Silas rubbed his hands as though nothing would ever warm them. "Yes?"

"Have you touched it?"

"Not a single anna. Dinah and I agreed she would administer her own funds."

Grandmother Helene made a clucking sound, as though she either did not believe him or thought that his modern ideas on this matter were no longer of any consequence. "Then Benu Sassoon will stand by your decision. In the past he has always been reasonable where you were concerned, Dinah. Remember when others thought you should have been married off long ago?" Her words hung in the air for several seconds.

Without warning I began to cry. My grandmother did not attempt to calm me, and when Silas started in my direction, she waved him away. "Let her be. She needs to mourn."

"Her grandmother . . ." he agreed with tenderness.

"Yes, that too, but also the death of her expectations. You have defeated her."

"I did not know we were in combat."

"Dinah had such high hopes—we all did. You should have known better than to marry her."

"I tried. I thought if only—"

"You have done an injustice to this girl, Silas. How deep the scars from this will be, I cannot predict."

"Dinah knows how dreadful I feel."

"Your repentance will not protect her future."

"What can I do for her?"

"A payment would not be out of the question."

"No! I don't want Silas' money. I have plenty of my own."

"I am not certain of the terms of your marriage settlement, but surely your dowry will be returned to your father." Grandmother Helene gave Silas a meaningful stare. He nodded his assent. "It may never revert to you, Dinah. Even if you remarry, your father is under no obligation to offer the same amount again. Remember, he has two other daughters to provide for as well. And if you never remarry, you might need to have some security that does not depend on the good-will of your father . . . or his heirs."

Silas cleared his throat. "I would be willing to assist Dinah. Although I do not control any capital right now, I could make a regular contribution."

I stared at them both numbly. "This is not a financial issue! Why does everything come down to ounces of silver?"

Grandmother Helene stared at me as though I were the most igno-rant girl in Calcutta. "At least your husband has not lost his senses. Take it from a woman who is alone in the world, you need to protect yourself."

I felt numb. "You do not think I will ever have another chance to marry."

She ran her hands through the tight curls in her hair, but did not reply directly. "I can't blame only you two poor lambs. Benu and Zilpah must accept their part in this. Your father was so anxious to see you settled that he did not examine the facts more closely. Surely others in Darjeeling might have hinted at Silas' . . . tastes." She gave him a steely stare. "How did you hide this from your own father?"

I studied his tragic face and wished he would not reply. "I was so unhappy with how miserable I made him," he began with surprising dignity, "I told him the other times had been boyish mistakes. I promised him I had reformed. My father wanted so much to believe me that he never said anything to the Sassoons." He sighed wearily. "If only I could make everything right again."

Grandmother Helene turned from us and studied a portrait of her late husband on the mantel. When she rotated back, her face glowed with a renewed serenity. "I have no logical reason for saying this, my children, but I have a sense the future is nowhere near as dark as it seems at this moment. So let us not waste energy on blame and fretting. There are too many practical problems to surmount." Somehow she managed a conspiratorial grin. "The first of which is, what shall we have for supper?"

❦ ❦ ❦

The next afternoon Grandmother Helene arranged to have one of the elders of Calcutta's Jewish community explain divorce law to us.

"Are these children certain they cannot be reconciled? You are more fortunate than you think," began Hayeem Elazar Barook, who was wearing the same sort of dagla, the long Baghdadi gown, that my Grandfather Raymond had.

The four of us sat in Grandmother Helene's drawing room. Most of the space was given over to tables groaning under Grandmother Helene's generous version of tea. The visitor and Grandmother Helene were the only ones who partook.

She shook her head. "No, Hayeem, there are special circumstances . . ."

"Yes?"

Silas and I remained mute.

Sighing, Grandmother Helene filled in. "As you were telling me earlier, the grounds for divorce include the presence of a physical defect in one's spouse."

"Only if the defect refers to the inability of one member of the union to cohabit or procreate. Of course, a woman who is incapable of bearing a child, for instance, would not be considered defective as long as there was prior knowledge of the problem before the marriage."

"Dinah," Grandmother Helene asked in a hoarse voice, "were you aware of his problem before the wedding night?"

"Of course not," Silas intervened.

Grandmother Helene silenced him with her eyes. "Dinah?"

"No."

"When did you notice it?" she prompted.

"After we tried to . . . He just could not manage to—"

"This is unnecessary," Hayeem Barook said, looking away. "No one is on trial here. Let me just say that any defect, no matter how serious, if it does not preclude the possibility of cohabitation, will not suffice to demand a divorce. As I understand it, these young people have been together only a short while. During this period there has been a move to a strange location and the death of a beloved family member." He winked at Grandmother Helene. "I suggest that with more time . . ."

"I am convinced they will never be married in the eyes of God," she replied firmly.

The old man's white brows arched with surprise. "Such a sad business." He shook his head. "However, if matters stand as you say, Helene, I will do everything in my power to assist you both. It is only too easy to commence and complete a divorce under Jewish law. That is why any reputable member of the community attempts to procrastinate. Men and women change their minds, circumstances are altered, unforeseen things happen every day. I would not want either of you to regret this decision."

We both nodded solemnly.

"The only requirement is a sufficient reason for the marriage's dissolution and, most important, mutual consent. If at any time prior to the giving of the *get*, the bill of divorcement, either of you reconsiders, your marital obligations will remain in effect."

"There is no other choice," Silas replied.

"And you agree with him?" Barook asked me.

"I do."

"All right, then. I will make the arrangements with Hakham Sholomo tomorrow."

"Won't you need to speak to my father?"

"He is not a party to this matter," Barook replied.

"He is already so angry. Don't you think that—?"

"This is something we should handle on our own, Dinah," Silas insisted. "Don't you see it will be better for everyone if we don't inform him until this business is over?" Silas continued earnestly, "He will have to accept a fait accompli. Otherwise he may try to manipulate us into doing something we do not want."

"But tomorrow?" I gasped.

"Is that too soon?" Hayeem Barook asked pointedly as he suppressed a smile. He probably was thinking we still might work out our difficulties.

I thought I could use the excuse I was still in mourning for my grandmother, but what would be the advantage of prolonging the matter? I clutched the peacock brooch that clasped the collar of my jacket and gazed directly into the old man's molten eyes. "No, tomorrow would not be too soon."

❀ ❀ ❀

Hayeem Barook took us to the home of Hakham Sholomo Abid Twena, where witnesses were already assembled in a library bursting with books stacked on shelves, tables, even in the corners.

Hakham Sholomo began the proceedings in a chilly voice. "A divorce is effected by the simple means of the writing of the *get*, the signing of the *get*, and the delivering of the *get* by the husband to the wife." He pointed to the tiny man who waited expectantly with dark eyes gleaming. "May I introduce my *sofer*, or scribe, Samuel Musleah."

Hayeem Barook broke in and explained further. "The *get* must be written in Aramaic, and only a trained sofer can prepare it so it meets the peculiar requirements. For instance, the words must fit on one page and fill exactly twelve lines, no more, no less."

"Why is that?" Silas asked.

"An old custom. The *gematria*, or numerical equivalent, of the word *get* is twelve."

Silas' lips were pursed thoughtfully. For him the tension of the moment was dissipated by his curiosity. What I wanted was for the whole matter to be finished.

"Shall we begin?" Hakham Sholomo asked gently.

Silas nodded. He reached for my hand. The hakham's bright eyes followed the movement, but he did not comment.

"Do you, Silas Luddy, son of Maurice, give this *get* of your own free will without duress and compulsion?"

"Yes," whispered Silas.

"Perhaps you have bound yourself by uttering a vow or by making any binding statement which would compel you to give a *get* against your will?"

"No, I have not," he responded to that and several similar questions.

There was nothing for me to do, since it was the husband's responsibility to order the *get* be written. Even though the day was cool, the room soon became oppressively hot. No refreshment was offered during this transaction, which dragged on for several hours while the scribe tediously scratched out the traditional form, making some letters very tiny, others so they spread out over a wide space to fill the requisite twelve lines. At last he called the witnesses to place their marks on the document.

After Hakham Sholomo had asked if I would receive the *get*, to which I replied yes, he read it aloud. When he had finished, he looked at me and then at Silas and spoke solemnly. "Ordinarily, once the next step is taken and the *get* is delivered from the hands of the husband into the hands of the wife, the divorce is completed. However, in unusual circumstances the *get* may be written and delivered conditionally. That means it will not take effect except on fulfillment of a stipulated condition. I do not wish to embarrass either of you further, but I feel I must offer protection to any innocent party. Therefore, to be certain no issue has resulted from this union, the condition of this *get* is that it will not become final for eleven months from this date."

I gasped and looked over at Silas. His face had taken on the impassive mask I remembered from our first meeting.

Hakham Sholomo then reached into his pocket for a pair of scissors and cut the four corners of the parchment. "This is to ensure that no paper can be substituted. I will keep the pieces as proof of what has occurred here this morning. You will both receive written statements that certify that your marriage has been dissolved according to the requirements of Jewish law, but these will not be delivered for eleven months, as I have already explained."

No pleasantries accompanied our departure. Outside, our carriage was waiting, and as we stepped up into it, I thought: How odd for us to be driving off together. "Do you think we should have planned for two carriages?" I asked, half-jesting.

"Symbolic perhaps, but not practical. After all, we don't dislike each other."

"There was hardly time to get to like each other!" I laughed, not meaning any offense.

Silas also seemed amused, but his response was more serious. "I will never forget you, Dinah. I hope we can remain friends."

"I have no hard feelings."

"May I write to you?"

"I will always welcome your letters."

"And may I help support you?"

"You have no responsibility for me any longer."

"Helene Arakie's argument was sensible, and they tell me that many men do."

"I can understand it being necessary if there were a child or if the woman had no place to go, but not in my case."

"It is considered a *mitzvah*, a good deed, and it would help me repent for marrying you when I never intended to leave Euclid."

"I do not want to feel beholden to you."

"All I ask is for you not to be too hasty in turning me down. Your father has not been appeased, and now you will have almost a year before you can change your situation. Besides, he may be even more upset once he hears we did the deed behind his back."

I puffed up righteously. "You are the one who insisted he had no say in the matter."

"He may see it differently, at least at first."

"Perhaps, but he would never throw me out."

"Just leave the option open. I will always be there if you need me. The eleven months hardly matter in my case. Certainly I shall never marry again." He looked at me steadily. "I hope the delay shall not be a hardship for you."

"Have you seen any suitors lining up at Theatre Road?"

"You may be surprised."

The carriage was pulling up at Grandmother Helene's gate. Silas helped me down and spoke close to my ear, "So, it is over."

"Yes," I murmured.

"And it was not so awful as you expected."

"No," I agreed, wondering why I felt no different than I had this morning. I entered the vestibule and smelled the familiar ginger and lemon scent. Grandmother Helene stood at the top of the staircase, wearing the same blue gown she had worn to see us off. Silas gave her a modest wave while I stood numbly by his side, thinking the world had not changed either. It was the same huge incomprehensible sphere that spun on its axis and revolved about the burning sun despite what had happened to me that day or would happen to me the next.

21

❦ ❦ ❦

In the span of a few months I had gone from daughter to wife to
. . . what? Living with Grandmother Helene, I lacked an identity. Worse, I seemed an outcast. To my surprise, redemption
came from an unlikely quarter.

Zilpah, for all her faults—or the faults I attributed to her in those
days—lived by a religious code which defined for her what should and
should not be done in almost any circumstance. This comprised more
than the primary aspects of ritual, dietary proscriptions, and prayer.
Above all was family harmony.

I do not know what she said to my father. In fact, I do not know
exactly how he learned of my divorce. All I remember is that on the
day Silas left for Darjeeling, she arrived at Grandmother Helene's
house and told me she had come to fetch me home. My adopted grandmother, who probably conspired in this reconciliation, slipped from
the room after a few minutes of polite chatter.

"Zilpah, I appreciate your offer, but perhaps if we give my father
more time . . ."

My stepmother's face was unusually pliant. "As you know, your
father sometimes reacts first, thinks next, regrets last. Perhaps I understand him because he reminds me of my own father. The trouble is,
those characteristics benefit a soldier more than a parent."

"He has never admitted to me that he has regretted anything."

"Parents feel they must be above confusion and error so their children will feel secure."

I wanted to turn from her gaze, but her dark eyes flashed with such
intensity I forced myself to meet it.

"Maybe this is the time I should admit my blame in the choice of
your husband," she continued. "I was the one who suggested to your
father that he look for a match away from Calcutta. I introduced the
Luddys to him. Though I did not know Silas very well—he always kept

to himself—I had heard rumors that he was an odd sort of fellow with unconventional ideas. When he built that strange house near Tiger Hill, the town gossiped for a year. On the other hand, I too was an outsider—first as a Jew, second as a Bene Israel. Neither the Indian nor the Jewish community accepted me, so that may be why I was sympathetic to someone whom society might have scorned unfairly. Just because someone preferred to live independently, just because someone's tastes were more scholarly than social, was no reason to condemn the man. For your sake, I should have explored some of the rumors—rumors I hastily attributed to bigots—but I was convinced that we had stumbled upon the perfect man for you. And if it had not been for his . . . peculiarity, you might have agreed with me."

"Do you think I should have stayed with him?"

"You had no other choice." Zilpah spoke with the elegant diction that humbled me. "After he thought the matter over, your father came to see your side. You accepted the match with the expectation that you would do your utmost to make it a success."

"What will become of me?" I said, trying to cover my plea with a brave smile.

"The worst days are behind you. In the meantime, I would be pleased to have your company, since your father is about to go off again in a few months. Together we can explore what might be over the horizon."

"I don't know—"

"You would be much more comfortable at Theatre Road."

"No, that is not what I meant. I would like to live with my family again, but I am not certain I could enjoy being inactive."

"Then we shall find something for you to do," she promised warmly.

For the first time in my life I believed her.

☙ ☙ ☙

"You will have to look farther than Darjeeling to find someone who does not know of either calamity" was Aunt Bellore's comment when she paid a house call the day after I returned home. She came dressed in a shiny black satin suit with flounces at the wrong places, and a slippery sound accompanied her every movement.

"Thank you for the advice," my father said with the hint of a sneer. He showed his sister into the smallest of our drawing rooms, where Zilpah and I had been teaching Seti and Ruby a card game. Zilpah hurried the younger girls away so they would not hear whatever might fall from her sister-in-law's venomous tongue.

"I am only thankful that our parents have not lived to see the day when someone in this family would be a party to a divorce. Zilpah should have known better. After all, she knew about the Luddys."

"That's not true," I said defending Zilpah. "Nobody guessed his secret." I astonished myself by standing up for my stepmother, and my father's eyes shone with gratitude.

Aunt Bellore sat herself in the place Zilpah had been sitting, her dress swishing like a burst of steam as her bulk settled down. "And what is this business about having to wait a year?" She stared at me coldly.

"Eleven months," my father corrected.

"There is something fishy about this whole business, but who cares for my opinion?" She glanced back at her brother. "Eleven months or eleven years, you had better start combing the bushes, because this girl isn't getting any younger. My Sultana will make me a grandmother in a few months, and my Abigail will be wedded before Dinah gets another chance."

Zilpah, who had just returned, remained standing in the doorway. "Bellore, please, why can't you think of the child's feelings for once?"

"Well, then, Dinah," Aunt Bellore said to me, "what do you feel about this?"

As my father raised his hand to silence his sister, I jumped in with a reply coated in honey: "I feel fortunate to have the support of my family. Besides, I am not anxious to contract another marriage."

"At least, considering everything you went through, not immediately," Zilpah said with an exaggerated sympathy that she hoped would defuse my aunt's vitriol.

When Abdul arrived carrying a tray of tea, even I noticed the pot was of china, not silver, and that bread and butter were all that accompanied the beverage. He began to arrange the plates on the small table in front of Aunt Bellore, a space far too small to lay out a proper spread. Normally Zilpah would have suggested we retire to the hall to eat, but she seemed determined to go on with the clumsy arrangement. The conversation did not continue until Abdul, after doing his best to find a place for everything, had taken up his station in the vestibule.

"Now what will you do with yourself?" Aunt Bellore prodded.

"I thought I might teach at the Jewish Girls' School," I answered stiffly.

"What are you trying to do, make yourself completely unmarriageable?" Zilpah opened her mouth, but Aunt Bellore's next volley silenced her. "Not many women in your position would stand by such a difficult stepdaughter the way you have, Zilpah, but it is time Dinah came down off her cloud. Unless she becomes an observant young woman with modest habits, she can look forward to being a spinster who is always pitied and lives off the charity of first her parents and later her brothers."

"No daughter of mine need fear that end!" my father bellowed. "She is richer in her own right than you are, my dear sister."

What did he mean? Aunt Bellore lived in a mansion that was easily a match for Theatre Road. She had inherited more jewels and fine furniture than the brothers. Her husband had a key position in the Sassoon enterprises. Even so, she sputtered, then whitened.

I pretended not to have noticed. "Aunt Bellore is right, Papa. If I worked at the Jewish Girls' School, everybody would be reminded of my predicament. My first duty is to the family."

"That is better," my aunt replied in an artificially soothing tone.

Zilpah and my father exchanged puzzled glances.

"We will talk about your future later." My father stood up. "Now I must return to work."

"Good, for I have an idea that shall please each of you," I said enigmatically to his back as he left the room.

❂   ❂   ❂

Several days passed before I had the opportunity to present my plan to my father. For some reason he was away before I came downstairs in the morning and home either so late that I did not want to approach the subject or too surrounded by the other children for me to have him to myself. I might have hinted that I wished to speak with him privately, but my goal was to catch him off-guard. The thought that he might have been avoiding me did occur, but I was not daunted. The important factor was to present my concept in a businesslike fashion and, no matter how provoked I might be by his response, to counter his concerns with logic, not emotion.

The seed of this idea had germinated ever since I decided I could not remain in Darjeeling, yet I had not been certain how the shoot would develop until Aunt Bellore's vile attack provided the fertilizer. My first plan, to teach school, was flawed, for there would be many obstacles to overcome for little gain. My second, which had congealed as Aunt Bellore fumed and scoffed, had layers of possibilities. The only difficulty lay in convincing my father to agree to set it in motion.

After five days of waiting, I finally caught him at breakfast.

"Good morning, Dinah," he said, beaming. "How pleasant to see you up this early."

"Good morning, Papa," I replied, trying not to let on that he knew that I knew we had been playing a cat-and-mouse game. "Ever since Darjeeling I have found it difficult to sleep late."

"Why is that?"

"Silas had a custom of awakening at dawn to see the snowy peaks."

Papa crunched his toast nervously. Any mention of Silas was more discomfiting for him than for me. I busied myself with my fruit cup until he wiped his chin and asked, "Well, what is on your mind, Dinah?"

"I would like to discuss my prospects for the future."

"Of course, whenever you like," he said, shifting in his seat as though he were about to rise.

"Now would be convenient for me."

"Well . . ." he demurred as Zilpah glided into the room. He smiled at her, then glanced back at my frown. "I have a splendid idea," he said, glancing up at his wife. "Would you object if I took Dinah to lunch, my dear?"

"Not at all, except you promised I could have the phaeton."

"If you don't mind, Dinah, I'll send the office jaun at noon," he said, apologizing for the common vehicle he used for getting around the city.

"I'd like that," I said buoyantly. "You know the funny poem, don't you?"

"I don't believe I do," he said, rising to his feet.

I grinned up at him, and quoted, " 'Who did not know that office jaun of pale pomona green/ With its drab and yellow lining, and picked out black between.' "

My father laughed. "You are in a fine mood today." And before I could ask where we would be going, he hurried from the room.

The syce drove me to meet my father at the Castellazzo Brothers' restaurant, a place I had heard about but had never been to before. I shivered with anticipation when I saw my father waiting in front of a colonnaded building that later became one of Calcutta's most famous restaurants, Firpo's.

"Good afternoon, Mr. Sassoon," greeted the burly man who opened the door. "Your usual table, sir?"

"Today I would prefer something on the veranda, Mario," Papa said under his breath.

We were led upstairs to the corner table nearest the Grand Hotel. Without even asking, a bottle of Scotch and two glasses were placed before us.

"Does he expect you to drink the whole bottle?" I asked.

"See this mark on the label? At the end of the meal the waiter will measure the difference with his thumb, you'll see."

"Do you come here often?"

"My brothers and I frequent the place. I have never brought Zilpah here," he said, knowing this would please me enormously. I hadn't felt so close to him since our trip to Patna, more than half my lifetime ago.

"Where do you usually sit?"

"Downstairs, in the front section. I like to see who is going and coming." He opened his menu and suggested omelets and potatoes. Then he straightened his back and gave me his full attention. "Now, where were we? Oh, yes, we were talking about how you might occupy yourself during this, ah, awkward period. Knowing how much you like school, I was thinking you might like to go off to one near Simla and—"

I cut him off. "No, I have had enough of the hills."

He leaned back and rolled his neck as if to relieve some stiffness. "We might consider England. More and more young ladies your age are continuing their studies, and as you know, some British young women go to school abroad."

I shook my head. "I don't want to leave India like a dog with its tail between its legs. After all, I have not done anything wrong."

"No, you haven't," he agreed somberly, "but you always liked your studies."

"I want to be more useful."

"That is not necessary, my child. Just be kind to Zilpah and the others, and all will work out."

"But I feel so ineffectual," I said; then, realizing my voice had become too strident, I cleared my throat and continued quickly before my father could offer another platitude, "I would like to be able to assist you more directly."

"And I would like nothing better than to have your charming company."

"I could help with business."

He patted my hand. "That is not your place, although I appreciate the thought behind the offer."

"If I were your son, wouldn't you be preparing me to follow in your footsteps?"

"Yes, certainly, but you are not a son. Soon you will have a family of your own."

"That is unlikely, at least for a year. What am I to do until then? You don't know what it's like to be married and independent one moment and then find yourself back in the nursery."

"Dinah, I want you to know something . . ." He swallowed hard, then continued, "I admire what you did. Another woman might have lived with a man like that to have the comforts he could provide. It took courage to come home."

Tears blinded me momentarily, but they did not betray me as I said softly, "Thank you, Papa."

"Flora Raymond would have been proud of you as well."

The mention of my grandmother's name caused my spirits to deflate further, but my father pretended not to notice my glum expression and prattled on. "She was a generous person, as was your grandfather.

They helped support the synagogue and took on many charity cases. We'll never know how many people he treated without payment or how many others he assisted financially after he cured their health problems. He used to say that the worst disease is poverty." My father shook his head and sighed. "There is not much left besides the Lower Chitpur Road house and clinic. Dr. Hyam is paying off his debt, so there will be additional income for a few years. Not including that, you and your brothers should clear almost five thousand rupees each."

Five thousand! Now I would finally have some capital of my own, without even considering the dowry that was under my father's jurisdiction now.

"I thought that would cheer you up," he said, winking at me.

"Nevertheless," I began cautiously, "that doesn't occupy my time. I still want to work for you, Papa."

"Now, Dinah, let's be reasonable," he said with a benign smile.

I am being reasonable! I seethed silently, using the energy that bubbled under the surface to force my voice into a lower, more masculine register. "When I was in Darjeeling, I helped balance the Luddy Tea Company ledgers. I found errors the previous man had made and tidied them up in short order."

"Where did you learn how to do that sort of work?"

"Don't you remember I also once assisted Dr. Hyam with his accounts?"

"Yes, but—"

"It is only simple mathematics with a dose of common sense. I know the Sassoon books would be much more complex. That is why I thought I might commence with your personal ones—or even the household accounts. Mostly, though, I would like to assist you. I could write out your correspondence and do little services to give you more time for matters of greater consequence." I took a quick breath that did not give him time to intervene. "The best part of my plan is that nobody need know about it. I can work at home, and so it will not be a public position like teaching would be."

The waiter served us large oval platters each containing an enormous omelet swimming in a tomato sauce. Vegetable florets decorated the top, and a bowl of crisp potato sticks wrapped in a white napkin was served alongside. I cut into the spongy yellow egg. "How thick it is! And yet so light!"

"I thought you would find this enjoyable." My father had a bemused expression as he watched me. Ignoring his own plate, he took several more gulps of his drink. "Dinah, I do not want to disappoint you—and I want you to know the generosity of your offer impresses me—but I just cannot think of a place for you."

I swallowed my mouthful and said in a flat voice, "When Jonah and Asher have finished school, you will find places for them, won't you?"

My father attacked his omelet with an exaggerated gusto that prevented him having to respond. I did not mind, for I knew it always took a few minutes of contemplation before he could change his mind. In the meantime, the fashionable gentlemen who had filled the room fascinated me. Most were British officials or businessmen. There were only a few women scattered about.

My father put down his utensils with a clatter that startled me from my reverie. "I suppose I cannot expect you to sit on a shelf until the next opportunity arises, can I?" His eyes twinkled as he watched my face melt with disbelief. "As you know, I am preparing for a trip to China. Do you have any comprehension of what that entails? The crates purchased at auction this autumn must be graded, priced, and accounted for. Shipping preparations must be made for the different batches being allocated to different destinations. Accounts from last season must be reconciled, so when I meet the brokers face-to-face they can remedy any shortfalls. Of course, we have employees who manage these duties, and I oversee the ledgers. Still, if you are as good as you say with figures, an extra eye might ferret out a mistake that another has overlooked. Also, some of our systems have become clumsy as the business has grown. We need to develop more efficient methods. I am looking forward to your contribution." He framed his last words in the form of a challenge.

All at once I was not so certain I was doing the right thing. The family trade both perplexed and intrigued me. Why had I pushed my father so hard? Was it out of boredom, a desire to win my father's approval as an adult woman, or was I merely curious as to how Sassoon and Company functioned? With the typical impetuousness of youth, my deliberations lasted only seconds, and I replied energetically, "When do I begin?"

"Calcutta is not Patna and you are no longer a young child so I cannot take you with me everywhere, but next week I will begin by having you accompany me whenever possible so you can see the flow. After that, you can complete your paperwork at home. You may use the desk in my study, but—"

The waiters began clearing our plates, so he broke off and finished his second scotch until they had finished. I was imagining myself working at the Clive desk when I remembered ruefully that I would never see it again.

"Please allow me to explain this to Zilpah," he said, bringing me back to the matter at hand.

"You do not think she will approve."

"She will if she is approached correctly."

A few years ago I might have resented that she needed to be consulted, but now I could see that my father knew what he was doing. Zilpah had a stern and unyielding demeanor, but she was not mercurial or unfair, so I was certain he would be successful. More important, my brief association with Silas had taught me something about the union between a man and a woman. In our few weeks together we had begun to develop a feeling for when the other might be receptive to an idea. As soon as Euclid had sensed that Silas was developing a tie with me, he had feared his own would loosen. Now I realized that I had understood Euclid's position so keenly because when Zilpah first entered our household, I had resented her bond with my father.

Leaning back against the cane chair, I was suffused by the pleasure of rational thought triumphing over childish emotion. I should be glad for that time with Silas, I decided. Not many girls had that sort of firsthand education. I only hoped its price had not been too high.

"I really am glad to see you so happy today," my father said with relief in his voice.

I looked at him with luminous eyes. "You have made me happy, Papa," I said, meaning every word.

22

〰 〰 〰

Coincidences delight me. I feel that if I have thought about something, and then it happens, that I have somehow pulled the mystical cords that control the weave of the universe. A few days after our lunch at Castellazzo Brothers', a huge crate was delivered to Theatre Road.

"Come see, Dinah. It's for you," Ruby called merrily.

I could not help but stare at my little sister. She was not yet eleven, but in the short time I had been with Silas, her body had matured with alarming speed. Her high, round breasts bobbed as she jumped with excitement, and her skin had taken on the oily texture of a much older girl. Even so, she was not the mental equal of Seti, half her age.

I allowed her to take my hand and lead me to the stableyard, where the syce and bearer awaited my instructions. "It comes from Darjeeling," Abdul said. "Do you want us to open it?"

I nodded. They pulled the metal bands apart. What could be inside? Half of Silas' library could have fitted into the box. A panel fell away to reveal a mysterious object wrapped like a shroud in long lengths of bright Nepalese fabric. Ruby and Abdul worked together to unwind it. As soon as sunlight illuminated an edge, I realized it was the silver-and-ivory desk I had been thinking about when I imagined working for my father.

"Oh, Dinah!" Ruby cooed. "It is the most beautiful thing I have ever seen in my whole life!" She brushed her hand across the inlaid-rosewood top, then tugged on the intricate pull of the top drawer. "What is this?" She held up an envelope with Silas' distinctive thunderbolt crest.

25 December, 1890

My dear Dinah,
 On this day when people of the Christian faith exchange gifts, I wish to

return what properly belongs to you. I trust you will not begrudge me the pleasure of envisioning you sitting beside this bureau now and in the future. From time to time, if you think of me, please write to tell me where your life leads you.

As William Wordsworth writes, "Every gift of noble origin Is breathed upon by Hope's perpetual breath."

> *As ever,*
> *Your friend,*
> *Silas*

For a moment I felt a longing for him, and as soon as the Clive bureau was placed in my room, I took pen in hand first to thank him for his generosity and also to tell him of my chance to work for my father. In less than a week he replied with an enthusiastic commendation.

A month later I responded.

> *15 February, 1891*

Dear Silas,

My father, who thought his bookkeeping systems were so complex, has been surprised—as you were as well—to discover that I have not had any difficulty deciphering his papers. At first I was tempted to explain there are few mysteries in recording and reconciling figures, but some hidden sense warned me not to belittle my contribution. Don't you agree that if one does not make what one knows seem inscrutable, one's work has less worth?

With the beginning of the new year I was able to review last season's ledgers, thinking how to refine or simplify the systems used. I offered suggestions to my father, and he gave me a free hand to organize them. While I appreciate his trust, I am concerned that something might happen that I cannot anticipate now that will ruin my plan. On the other hand, if I blindly copy the old methods—even after its weaknesses have been revealed to me—I would not be doing my job conscientiously.

I would value your opinion as to the above.

> *Yours,*
> *Dinah*

I had struggled with the opening and the closing, deciding simplicity was best, yet after I had posted it, I worried whether I should have confided in him in the first place. Silas' reply came by return post.

> *19 February, 1891*

My dear Dinah,

Every novice in every field asks the same questions as you have asked of me. Do not revile me for bringing this to your attention, but accept my observation as though you were a stranger, then suddenly realized you were among friends.

Already you have shown an insight into the minds of employers and their workers that far surpasses the brief experience you have had. If you will trust those same stores of good sense and basic knowledge, you will succeed beyond anyone's, even your own, expectations. Do not hesitate to contact me with any question, serious or trivial. Be assured I will respond as thoroughly as I can; and as promptly as the vagaries of the post permit.

He went on for several pages detailing current difficulties in the tea business and solutions he was considering. Before closing, he returned to my situation.

I hope you will not think it impertinent of me to wonder if your father is offering you remuneration that in any way equates with your worth.

Wages? I had never thought to ask for payment for my work. Thinking the matter over, I decided not to discuss this with my father, who continued to provide generously for me. If anything, I saw my efforts as a small recompense for the difficulties I had caused him. Yet I knew that Silas, who held the most modern notions of equality between the sexes, would not agree with my point. Deliberating how to explain my feelings, I waited awhile before responding.

1 March, 1891

Dear Silas,

Thank you for your continuing concern about my financial situation. I thought you would be pleased to learn that my Grandmother Flora Raymond left me a bequest approximating five thousand rupees, with additional income from Dr. Hyam being paid toward his purchase of the Lower Chitpur Road property and clinic. This should relieve your mind, since you always felt that I would be more secure with money in my own name. I have no use for the principal now, but might apply a bit of the income to purchase my own clothing or books, if my father approves. In any case, you no longer have to feel as though you should contribute to my upkeep, although I will never forget the goodness inherent in that offer.

About the other matter you raised: I have sound reasons for not wishing to accept payment for my labors at this time. First, I have yet to understand the scope of the Sassoon family shares. Presently, my tasks involve only those accounts that my father controls and his personal ledgers. My father admired how your father organized his enterprise. Now I see this may be because of the complexities the Sassoons have propagated at every level.

I can hear you suggesting that I merely walk up to my father and ask him to explain the matter to me. This I shall do, but in small doses and over a long period. You do not know my family well, but suffice to say that my uncles, and especially a certain aunt, would not be content to have me knowing their business. However, my father leaves for China in a few weeks, and some of my questions—the ones that will provide linking verbs in the grammar behind the activities—will be asked so I can be more useful while he is away.

I closed with news about the family, including in postscript an announcement of the birth of the daughter born to Cousin Sultana and Gabriel Judah.

I had thought that while my father was abroad my workload would increase. On the contrary, he kept most of his documents in the Sassoon offices and there had been no instructions to forward them to me. I suspected that Uncle Saul, the clan's titular head, did not know the extent to which I had assisted my father. He knew I came around to the offices now and then and that my father had indulged me by making it appear as if he included me in his affairs, but Saul had assumed this had been either to mollify me or to help me forget my most recent disgrace. Certainly he saw no reason to divert me himself. Also, since the godowns were empty and the new crop not yet ready for processing, a natural lull in the business had occurred. Zilpah had not resented my takeover of the household accounts, so these I completed with an inordinate attention to neatness and detail. After that I kept busy with the stacks of old receipts that needed to be entered in the final journals and reconciled. With nothing more to occupy myself, I decided to fashion a series of reports, using the old records to compare the past several years with the current one.

These tasks engaged me for only part of each day, and I also was finding it gratifying to read or spend time with my sisters and brothers. At five, Seti had been promoted to the second class at the Jewish Girls' School, the same one in which Ruby languished for the third year. I enjoyed working with them both on their schoolwork—Seti because she was so quick to learn and eager to move ahead; Ruby because she did make progress, even if the increments were tiny. And when she did succeed, her joy surpassed her little sister's.

Pinhas and Jonah still clashed, unfortunately. Jonah had never accepted that Pinhas, who was six months older, had moved into his place as the eldest boy in the family, and besides, in many ways they were too much alike. Asher, who was thirteen, and Simon, who was twelve, were more compatible, equally interested in anything that involved kicking or throwing a ball. The person who had changed the most was Zilpah. With my father away, she had lost both her brittleness and her sparkle. It was almost as if she had been a top that had split a seam so she could no longer spin without wobbling.

One morning she sat at the table lost in her own thoughts while I tried to draw her out. "Wouldn't some *aloo makalla* make a nice tiffin tomorrow?" I suggested, since I had tired of the dull menu she had organized recently. "I know you like roast duck."

"Why don't you ask the borchi to make it?" she replied lethargically.

"Would you prefer something else?"

"No."

"We could also have *tomato khatta* and *pulao*."

"That sounds lovely."

Thinking of how often I had needed to tell Silas of what was on my mind, I could understand the loss she felt when my father traveled. And if strong, resourceful Zilpah could react like this, my own mother's withdrawal was even more understandable.

After she excused the other children, we found ourselves staring at each other from the opposite ends of the table. I gave my stepmother a shy smile and she returned it with a salute of her teacup. For the first time I felt as though we had finally become friends.

❧ ❧ ❧

Several weeks passed, during which I worked to create the reports I thought my father might wish to see. Long before he would review them, the final tallies had an unexpected impact on me.

	Number of Chests		Average Price Paid Per Chest		Total Average Rupees Received
Grade	1	2	1	2	
1887–88	21,508	18,421	1,720	1,654	67,360,223
1888–89	22,789	19,943	1,690	1,595	70,187,310
1889–90	28,811	20,214	1,543	1,498	74,542,512

Grade 1 Li Yun   *Grade 2 Fuk Lung*

More than seventy-four million rupees in one year! The totals astonished me. In the past, I had been working with the fragmentary bits of inventory and shipping, but by moving figures from different ledgers and combining them, I gained an overview of the vast extent of the Sassoon enterprises. I wrote the calculations in *lacs* and *crores*—words that broke down overwhelming amounts into figures people in India used to describe the value of huge figures. More usually they expressed the purses of governments and potentates, not families. A hundred thousand rupees equaled one lac, which meant the Sassoons had spent over 745 lacs this season. The crore of the maharajahs was the equivalent of ten million rupees, or a hundred lacs, and that meant an intake of seven crores, forty-five lacs! This did not describe the profits of the company, only how many chests of opium were shipped to China and what price they had cost at the Calcutta auctions. What did an investment of this magnitude yield? I wondered. Ten percent? Fifty percent?

I began to search for clues of opium's market value. All I could discover was that a can of smoking opium fetched between 7.75 and 8.20 Spanish dollars in Canton. How many cans were in a chest? A hundred? I selected the lower dollar figure and worked on the conversions, which came to less than a thousand rupees for fifty cans of the lower grade. If the chest price was around fifteen hundred rupees, something was wrong, for we could not pay ourselves back at that rate. Finally I realized that in my ignorance I had been imagining tins the size that held Darjeeling tea. Only the tiniest amount of opium was ever used at one time. What size tins did it come in? One would need to have more than seventy-five tins to break even at the auction price. Then there were shipping and other costs. Since I could not begin to estimate these, I saved my questions and parceled them out—one to an uncle—the next time we were together as a family.

A week later, we attended the Passover seder at the home of Aunt Rebecca and Uncle Saul. I first approached Uncle Ezra, who found my interest in the family trade amusing.

"I see you enjoyed spending time with your father."

"Yes, there is only so much I can do at Theatre Road," I said, grinning, "before I start climbing the walls." An unexpected ugly image—a ladder placed against the wall outside my mother's bedroom— flashed before me. I hesitated for a moment as I imagined Sadka and Chachuk climbing up, murder weapons and chloroform vial in hand . . .

My uncle, who did not notice my momentary distress, prattled on. "Do you really miss counting crates at the warehouse?"

"Well, maybe not." I laughed uneasily. "Too many crawling bugs."

My uncle scratched in sympathy. "You would never catch me there."

"After seeing those crates, though, I wondered in what size tin the product eventually is delivered."

"Oh, something very small indeed," he replied, delighted that I had not asked anything too taxing. He made a circle of his thumb and forefinger. "Even smaller than that—an inch in diameter and a half-inch deep."

"That is even tinier than I expected," I said, and drifted off to join my cousins.

The second uncle with direct experience in China was Reuben. An hour later he had drunk too much wine to be curious as to my reasons for the question, but sober enough to give an accurate response. I began again by mentioning that I had been to the opium storerooms, then asked how many tins one of those crates could make.

"Somewhere between six hundred and a thousand tins." Uncle Reuben stroked his thick, wiry beard. "The smaller figure, if they do not dilute the stuff."

Recalling the dishonest gomastah in Patna, I said, "I thought the Sassoons prided themselves on the purity of the product."

"We do." He threw his arms up in the air in a gesture of supplication. "Unless you challenge a lot at the auction, though, you are stuck with what they sell you."

"Don't we break it down into tins ourselves?"

"No, we have factories that contract to us. Then Chinese dealers take over local distribution." He scratched his head as though he was trying to free gnats from his hair. "This business is too complicated for a girl to follow. What would you know of captains who require bribes to unload the cargo so they won't 'accidentally' drop some in the sea, or of wily customs agents who have ways of extracting extra fees for their own pockets or— ?" He stopped when he saw Aunt Bellore coming our way. I took the hint and moved on.

Uncle Jacob, who spent most of his time in the Patna region, did not even know of my work with my father, so this was the uncle I targeted with my most daring question. The most prolific of the brothers, he had sired ten children. Holding his youngest, a girl of less than six, he welcomed me with an easy grin. "Here comes your most beautiful cousin, Simha."

"Don't listen to your father," I said, flushing. "Check out your cousins Abigail and Lulu before you believe him."

"Don't distract Simha's attention from her father's opinions," he said with mock seriousness. "I am training her to penetrate the surface values and look into the heart."

His compliment flustered me further, and it was a while before I could organize my thoughts to query him. "Do you remember when I was not much older than Simha and my father took me to Patna?"

"Yes," he said without comment on that turbulent period.

"I have always wondered about what happened to that raw opium. I know you ship it to China, but how much does a chest sell for to the factories that repackage it there?"

Jacob seemed startled by my question. His green eyes glinted as he thought of how to phrase his answers, yet his voice did not hesitate. "There is no easy answer, Dinah. The values change constantly. We base our price fluctuations on the auction cost, the shipping amount, the duty paid in port, labor, and other numerous expenses. Besides, the Chinese have a thousand and one ways to bleed us. We must be ever vigilant." He looked up to see if he had satisfied me.

"I had no idea it was so complicated," I said in a breathy voice. "Let me put it this way: if a chest of opium is worth, say, a thousand rupees on the wharf at Calcutta, as an average, how much more will you sell it for? Ten percent?"

"Hardly ten percent." He chuckled. Simha tugged at his lapel and he placed her on the floor. "Now, Dinah, what is this about? A school assignment?" Simha said something about requiring a bathroom. "Sumra!" he called to his wife, and pointed Simha in her mother's direction.

I tossed my head so the wisps of hair fell prettily around my face and shoulders. "I don't attend school any longer, but I enjoy calculations."

I could almost hear his thoughts. My very inaccurate estimate of a thousand rupees for a chest and the allowance for so little profit must have disarmed him. He sighed and said, "About three times the Calcutta auction cost. We figure one-tenth for shipping and related fees, forty percent for Sassoon handling and expenses, and eighty percent for duties and other unofficial payments.' Then we add on a hundred percent for the raw cost of the chest. That comes to . . ." He waited for me, to see if I had been listening, as well as to test my arithmetic skills.

"That is two hundred and thirty percent, leaving a floating seventy percent for which you have not yet accounted."

"A 'floating percent'!" He guffawed. "Where did you ever hear a term like that?"

I shrugged.

"I shall have to remember that," he said, not unkindly. "Anyway, we call it our 'margin,' or the amount we have to work with as we set up different deals. The less of that margin we spend in getting the opium to its last destination, the more money the family receives."

On the way home that evening, Zilpah filled in the last piece of the puzzle.

"Not an especially handsome baby," she began as she mentioned the affair's center attraction: Sultana's baby, Miriam.

"She was not at her best," I agreed. The baby had howled most of the time. "Anyway, I do not know how one evaluates an infant."

"The shape of her head is uneven, although it will round out eventually, and her color is too yellow for my taste. If I were her mother, I would find a different dai." Her tone changed. "Did you hear the news that Gabriel Judah is being given a higher place in the firm in Saul's department?"

"Really?" I said, masking my surprise with a yawn. "I would have thought he would have gone into the office of his father-in-law, Uncle Samuel."

"I suppose there was some wisdom in the choice. Would you want to work for Bellore's husband?" She gave a sisterly laugh.

"Will he ever receive a share of the Sassoon company?"

"No. Only the brothers have shares."

I remembered my father saying that I had more than my aunt did. "And Aunt Bellore doesn't either?"

"Her settlement was her dowry, which, if you recall, included the inheritance of the house in Kyd Street."

"That means Uncle Samuel doesn't get a portion either."

"That's true."

"Why is that?"

"It is never wise to bring into a business someone who is not a family member."

"But he married into the family and she's a sister."

"Of course, women cannot control a business, and not every marriage works out." She did not have to elaborate on that point.

"How is he compensated?"

"I imagine he gets wages and other considerations. I have never asked. It is not my concern."

As the carriage pulled into Theatre Road, my sisters were asleep on our laps. The boys were following in a second carriage. The driver opened the door. "Fetch the ayahs for the girls. We'll wait here for the boys," Zilpah said.

A huge moth flew into a nearby torch. I watched as it flared and was consumed. "So, the brothers share everything equally," I summed up.

"It is not as simple as that. As with any business or any family, there are often arguments, but who is complaining? There is more than enough to go around."

In the bustle of unloading a weepy Seti and a stubborn Ruby, plus four rowdy boys who had drunk freely of the ritual wine served throughout the seder, I had no time to follow up with mental calculations. Once I was in bed, though, the figures began to rush around in my head. Giving in to the whim to settle this once and for all, I got up and went to my silver desk that I affectionately called "Clive."

"Now, Clive, where shall we begin?" I pulled out my first report table and multiplied the average number of rupees the chests had cost, times the three hundred percent that included the Sassoons' profit. The figure was a staggering 223,627,537.50, or almost 2240 lacs or 22 crores! I remembered that that included the expenses, so I went back and worked out the profit, using the seventy-percent margin of three times the auction price and estimated the profit at almost twenty-five percent. That still brought five crores, sixty lacs into the Sassoon family *each* year! After I divided it among the five brothers, there was almost one crore, twelve lacs per family. Poor Aunt Bellore! I smirked. With her high-and-mighty ways, she was not included and never would be.

Satisfied by both the scope of my discovery and that Aunt Bellore could no longer terrify me with her puppetlike powers, I crawled back into bed. My head pounded as I struggled to comprehend the grand scale of this fortune. A few weeks ago I had thought myself flush because of the five thousand I had in my own name from Grandmother Flora, but that was insignificant compared to the amounts that swirled in my mind. To think my fifty-thousand-rupee dowry once had embarrassed me or that I had worried I had been taking too much from the family purse! Why, my dowry was a tiny fraction of last year's income. Surely there were times when the crops were meager or the prices kept low or the Chinese created expense difficulties or . . . No, any way I viewed it, this was a colossal fortune.

What could it purchase besides grand houses and jewels and luxuries for the family? I asked myself as I wandered around my bedroom in a daze of figures. And how did it compare to the average man in Calcutta? From the household accounts, I knew the highest-paid member of the staff was the bearer, Abdul, who received sixteen rupees a month, or less than two hundred rupees a year; the ayahs made about one hundred and fifty a year; while the sweeper and the *mate*, or cook's assistant, received only six to ten rupees each month. The staff of twelve hardly amounted to two thousand rupees per year . . . I scratched out a rough ratio of the servants' wages to our income and came up with a figure so minuscule it couldn't be possible. There had to be something the matter with my figures, or if not, with the world. Otherwise, how could one family have amassed such richness while so many had so little?

Once I understood the scope of our wealth, more questions followed. The knowledge that I was one beneficiary of this wealth had made me giddy with excitement. What would I do if it were mine to manage? "Women cannot control a business," Zilpah had said. Well, if I could, would I hand it out to the beggars or build a school or lavish it on my children? Would I expand my empire with more investments or struggle to keep what I had by following in my father's footsteps? No, I mused. If I were in charge, I would invest the profits from the opium in other enterprises.

No matter how anyone explained away the family business, an undercurrent of unease never had been assuaged. No matter that Silas had equated opium with brandy or even tea as a substance voluntarily used, or that he had lauded its effect on the creative mind. No matter that Dr. Hyam and others used it for medicinal purposes or that few cared what happened once we shipped it to China. The word, the smell, even the money, were reminders of my mother's ruin. Yet now, as I contemplated the immense sums, I understood why my family had turned a blind eye to the flower's faults. And I wondered—if the decision ever became mine—if I might do the same.

What nonsense, I told myself. The closest you will ever get to the Sassoon assets will be as the wife of an employee. Then I realized how much I would loathe being in the same position as the wives of Samuel Lanyado and Gabriel Judah. The man I marry won't have anything to do with opium, I vowed silently, as I climbed into bed for the second time.

"If only I have a choice," I hoped out loud.

23

❦ ❦ ❦

The next morning, after redoing some of the figures to make certain a calculation or a faulty assumption had not fooled me, I put some of my confused feelings into words. I knew better than to share a single figure from the family ledgers with an outsider, but I did tell Silas that the disparity between the coolie and the merchant was so cavernous, God's design obviously did not include the equality of men.

I suppose that same polarization occurs in nature. Witness the ant and the anteater, the mouse and the lion, the eagle and the fish.

I wrote three more passionate pages before ending with a quote from Shelley.

"The rich have become richer, and the poor have become poorer; and the vessel of the state is driven between the Scylla and Charybdis of anarchy and despotism."

Instead of receiving one of the philosophical responses I expected, I found only a note included in a package of books.

22 March, 1891

My Dear Dinah,
    You probably have read Nicholas Nickleby *or* Oliver Twist, *so instead of the obvious I send you some of the lesser-known works of Mr. Dickens. I am rather keen on* Our Mutual Friend *and* Dombey and Son, *and also suggest you join me in trying to decipher the ending Dickens might have planned for* The Mystery of Edwin Drood, *which he kindly had not finished at his death to permit the amateur sleuths of the world to invent our own solutions.*

*I will share mine with you, if you will do the same for me. Let me know
if you see any references that relate to the Indian cult of the thuggee.*

He went on to say that his father had been ill, thus I could not be
upset with him for preferring to solve the Dickens story rather than the
mysteries of the universe during that trying time.

I put his package aside since the hot weather had brought on an
irritating stomach ailment. When I was recuperating, I found the books
amusing. *Our Mutual Friend* had me comparing life along the Thames—
bodies floating in the river, murderers and thieves, mercenary young
women, and other grisly characters—with that along the Hooghly.
Once the scheming Wegg was dumped into a garbage wagon at the
end, I was ready for another satisfying read and plunged into *Edwin
Drood*.

*An ancient English Cathedral tower? How can the ancient English Cathe-
dral tower be there!*

I was whisked away from steamy Calcutta at once, but the second
page brought me a rude shock.

*. . . Lying, also dressed and also across the bed, not long-wise, are a
Chinaman, a Lascar, and a haggard woman. The first two are in a sleep or
stupor; the last is blowing at a kind of pipe, to kindle it. And as she blows,
and, shading it with her lean hand, concentrates its red spark of light, it
serves in the dim morning as a lamp to show him what he sees of her.*

What was this? What had Silas sent me? How was it that I was
sitting on the upstairs veranda cushions, the very place where my
mother had entertained Nissim Sadka and so many others, reading
about the hideous reality of an opium den?

*"Another?" says this woman in a querulous, rattling whisper. "Have
another?" . . .*
*She blows at the pipe as she speaks, and occasionally bubbling at it,
inhales much of its contents.*
". . . It's nearly ready for ye, deary . . ."

The grimness caused my skin to crawl, and I read on with horrified
fascination.

*". . . I see ye coming-to, and I ses to my poor self, 'I'll have another
ready for him, and he'll bear in mind the market price of opium, and pay
according.' "*

Closing my eyes, I saw the darkness of the cellar, could almost smell the sweat and dampness blanketed by the cloying, fruity breath of opium smoke, the breath that had wafted from a lady's inlaid hookah in this very place.

"Ah, my poor nerves! I got Heavens-hard drunk for sixteen year afore I took to this; but this don't hurt me, not to speak of. And it takes away the hunger as well as wittles, deary."

I remembered how little my mother ate. Had opium dulled her sense of hunger? If only I understood more about the substance, maybe I could find the keys to unlock the rest of that secret past.

"What visions can she have?" the waking man muses, as he turns her face toward him, and stands looking down at it . . . what can she rise to, under any quantity of opium, higher than that!

Visions? Did my mother have visions like De Quincey and Coleridge? I thought about her dreamy face, her incoherent babble—but that might be my weak recollections. After all, I had been a child. Still, my memories had not clouded over time. If anything, they had become more distinct.

The words blurred as the choirmaster of the cathedral at Cloisterham left the opium den.

That same afternoon, the massive gray square tower of an old Cathedral rises before the sight of a jaded traveler . . . Then the Sacristan locks the iron-barred gates that divide the sanctuary from the chancel, and all of the procession, having scuttled into their places, hide their faces; and then the intoned words "When the wicked man—" rise among groins of arches and beams of roof, awakening muttered thunder.

"And he'll bear in mind the market price of opium," I read again, thinking about the reports in the Clive bureau drawer and my notes on the market price, the tiny tins of Patna's finest grade that must have made its way to London as well as Canton. "I got Heavens-hard drunk for sixteen year afore I took to this; but this don't hurt me, not to speak of," the hag had said to defend her vice. There was that same excuse again! Would I have felt better if my father was off selling Scotch or Bombay gin? What about turnips or rice or bread? Every hunger was an addiction. True, one could live without Scotch or opium and one did have to fill the belly with wheat or rice, but someone had to provide for the need. My father believed it was unfair to deny people who were desperate for their dose of poppy juice. Had he also been unable to deny his wife's need for her dose?

I closed my eyes at the picture that flickered before me as though it was a part of my own past rather than the imagination of Dickens. I slammed the book shut. Here was the bleak side of the opium equation. Somehow it had been easier to imagine the chests going off to China as though they were dumped into a chasm on the other side of the world or that the Chinese people required opium much as the English required tea. In fact, wasn't that the exchange: opium for tea, tea for opium? I thought of the clean, tidy world of the Darjeeling tea gardens. Their sweet smell was not so different from the sweet smell of the Patna flower fields. Then my doubts resurfaced as I contemplated a gentleman—a British choirmaster!—sinking into the filth of an opium den to satisfy his cravings before rushing off to church. It wasn't only my mother! There were men and women in every stratum of society who were enslaved by the flower. My mouth filled with sour saliva. The book fell from my lap as I hurried to the bowl and disgorged my tiffin.

1 April, 1891

Dear Silas,

Figures cannot lie. Tidy digits have a logic that may confound the uninitiated, but once their key is revealed, they soon march to one's command like crack troops. And as soldiers do not question their superiors, numbers do not confront their purpose on the page.

One of my regrets at leaving you has been the severing of so many interesting dialogues, although you manage to make your voice heard with unique methods. If you divine that the tone of this letter might have been inspired by the reading you encouraged, I shall permit you, this time only, the pride of having landed your arrow at the target's center. A particular dialogue that we began—the exploration of Coleridge and his vices—was incomplete. Did the poet ever wonder from whence his "milk of Paradise" came? Did he ever picture the peasants who plant the poppy, score the husk, bleed the sap, and scrap the residue? Did he think about the bullock-carts that carry the crates or the musty storerooms where they are stacked? Did he consider the clerks who tally the weights and grades and prices, or the well-dressed gentlemen who buy port with the profits?

Or does the ryot or the gomastah or the fine gentleman of commerce never wonder how the precious silver comes to line his pockets? Who offers the customers their first taste of smoke? Their second? How many puffs before one cannot turn away? What about those men and women whose craving for the sweet smoke surpasses their interest in life itself?

I raved on for several pages, then posted the letter with a sensation of release. The next morning I berated myself for carrying on so selfishly. Hadn't Silas written that his father was ill? I had completely forgotten to mention it. I hurried to write a second note to ask after Maurice's welfare. Either Silas was too busy with the tea business, which was very consuming that time of year, or was working on a thoughtful response to my diatribe, or my insensitivity to his family had angered him. In any case, I did not hear from him for several weeks. And during that period my father returned to Calcutta.

❦ ❦ ❦

At first I was not anxious to show him my reports that described our family's complicity in a revolting commerce. Then, after he had been home for more than a week, he invited me to have lunch with him at Castellazzo Brothers'. Already in the throes of the hot season, the restaurant at noon had six punkah-wallahs stationed around the veranda to keep the air flowing. Unfortunately, the breeze also carried the scents of the alley. The barrage of foul odors—garlic and fish, melon rinds and burnt sugar—caused my stomach to twist.

"Could we sit inside?" I asked.

"Yes, certainly," he said.

This time he ordered Italian noodles instead of an omelet, red wine instead of Scotch. When a glass was poured for me, I merely pretended to like the vinegary drink for the first few sips, then discovered it was tasting better and better.

In an excellent mood, my father told me how well his trip had gone. As he spoke matter-of-factly about his commerce, the feelings unleashed by *Edwin Drood* seemed less consequential. If I only paid attention to the figures, not the people behind the figures, I could avoid the unpleasantness. Besides, months had passed since he had been so accessible to me, and I was anxious to demonstrate my utility.

"I did some reports while you were away," I mentioned casually.

"What sort of reports, Dinah?" he replied with an air of indulgence.

"Well, I discovered that the figures in different sections of the ledgers told a fraction of each story, but if I combined them in various ways, an interesting narrative emerged."

He threw his head back and laughed. "Stories? What an idea!"

I folded my hands on the table, not showing any offense.

"All right, tell me what you discovered."

"I compared various aspects of the last three seasons, and two facts developed. Since 1887, the total number of chests has gone up by seven percent the first year and by fifteen percent the next, but at the same time the prices have gone down, first by three percent and then by seven percent."

Papa leaned forward. "Yes, that is interesting. What do you make of it?"

"I do not know enough to give an analysis. I can only ask questions."

"And what would those be?"

"First, why is the crop yield higher? Has the weather been especially favorable? If so, weather is a risky element, which means one should not expect a bigger crop each year. Is it because methods are more efficient? If this be the case, these methods might be expanded until greater yields are brought out from every ryot, for if the increases continue and the price does not go down substantially because of it, your profits should increase consistently. On the other hand, if the price at market is lower, there are several facets to discuss. Is this the result of supply and demand? If so, the percentages I mentioned are not in line. All the same, this is not worrisome in itself, since the margin continues in our favor."

My father, who had been tapping his fingers on the tablecloth, stopped. His fingers danced in the air. "Margin? Where did you hear a word like that?"

"Was that the wrong choice?"

"No, on the contrary, it was a very precise one." He shook his head. "You never cease to amaze me."

I tucked his compliment away and pressed on. "Could the increased production be creating poorer grades, or even worse, could the increased number of chests be because of a dilution in Patna? I remember that concerned you when I was a child—"

Papa waved his hand to cut me off. "That is not a factor. Well, perhaps a small factor. We are ever vigilant for impurities." He raised his glass but did not drink. "Your analysis is quite provocative. I am very proud of you, my dear. Now, is there anything else?" He raised one eyebrow.

Sensing his patience was waning, I spoke in a rush. "That is only one of my reports. I have several others you might want to look over. The figures are too complicated to memorize."

"I should hope so." He beamed and set down his glass. He opened his mouth to say something else, but I jumped in.

"Before I finish, I think you will be pleased that, with the fifteen-percent increase in the number of chests and the seven-percent decrease in price—and if the costs of selling have remained constant—there was a six-percent increase in profits last year."

My father's smile vanished. "May I ask how you calculated profits, my dear?"

I looked down at the snowy tablecloth, which was now stained by drips from wine and red sauce from noodles. The grisly patches blurred as I blinked back tears. "I used a textbook figure of one hundred and fifty percent of the cost of sales," I said, skirting the specific figure I had heard from Uncle Jacob, "so I could put the increases and decreases into perspective, and I kept our costs the same from three years ago, after checking there had not been any significant changes from the shipping or tax ledgers."

My father laughed obligingly. "That is one textbook I would like to read." I dared to look into his eyes, and found them without judgment. "Anything further?"

For a moment I felt as if I had been untruthful with him—and myself. I swallowed hard. "Do you ever . . . ?"

"Yes?" He was drumming his fingers again.

"Do you ever worry that people will stop needing so much Indian opium?"

"There are ninety million Chinese opium users, and few ever give it up once they start," he said, the tautness around his mouth increasing.

"What if they grow their own?"

"Even if they plant half their fields with poppies, they will require more and more. Of course, Patna is the finest grade in the world. You mustn't concern yourself about ending up on the street someday."

"That wasn't what I was thinking about."

"What is it, then?" he said with a hint of impatience creeping into his tone.

"Don't you ever . . . ?"

"Yes?" His expression was somber, yet soft. This was the moment to ask what was on my mind.

"Do you think there is anything wrong with selling opium?" I blurted out.

"Whatever brought this on?" he asked benevolently.

"Some people may not benefit from the product," I gulped.

My father diverted his gaze from mine. "As I said before, there are millions of opium users." He tapped the bottle on the table. "And millions of wine drinkers. Certainly we would be healthier if we drank only spring water and breathed pure air, but that is not the nature of the beast." He poured himself some more wine and took a lingering sip. "Besides, my brothers and I are not any more accountable for the weaknesses of others who indulge in too much of our smoke than one of the Castellazzo brothers is if I am foolish enough to belt down this whole bottle. What we are responsible for is the thousands of workers— from the peasants in Patna to the merchants in China— who depend on our business to feed them and their families. One doesn't halt growing a crop or dispense with a whole trade because of the stupidity of some abusers." Unexpectedly he reached across the table and clinked my wineglass with his own. "Oh, Dinah, I shall be so sorry to lose you again."

What on earth did that mean? I held my breath while the waiters cleared our plates and served fragile pastry cornucopias filled with lemon pudding. Half-moons of mango dusted with pink sugar decorated the plate. At any other time I would have been enchanted with the treat, but now I began to perspire with dread.

Papa pulled his hand back and poked at his dessert. He did not lift the fork to his lips until he muttered the beginning of his explanation. "I may have found another possibility . . ." With his attention focused on me instead of what he was doing, he took a hesitant bite, and flakes of pastry crumbled down the front of his waistcoat. He did not brush them away.

"Who?" was all I managed to utter.

"A young man from Cochin. You know where that is, don't you?" He pressed back some damp locks above his ears with his manicured fingertips. "A most agreeable port south of Bombay."

"Have you ever been there?"

"No, but it has a fine reputation, especially among Jews. The Jewish community has been there far longer than in Calcutta. Many families date themselves back to the 1400's, when they came over to escape persecution in Spain."

How could I tell him I did not want a black Jew for myself without insulting him and Zilpah? Or, considering my predicament, was that the only alternative?

"Now, these Jews are not Bene Israels," he said, as though he had been reading my mind.

"How did this come about?" I asked as the first clutch of fear brought on by the unanticipated news lessened its grip. My abdomen relaxed and I was even able to let a cool mango slice slip down my tight throat.

"How did the first Jews get to Cochin?" he asked, confused.

"No, how did you hear about this man?"

"In Hong Kong I became reacquainted with someone who handles some Sassoon business in that region. He is primarily a spice merchant," he said as an afterthought.

Poking at the pastry, I waited for him to continue.

"Anyway, this man—his name is Elisha Salem—has a nephew who he says would consider a Calcutta girl."

Especially someone with a dowry like mine, I thought to myself. Before I could wipe away my scowl, my father continued deliberately, "I assumed you would be more intrigued with my news. You do want to remarry and live a normal life, don't you?"

I forced a weak smile. "I hadn't expected anything so soon, since . . . well, since I am not yet free to marry, and—" Another odor from the kitchen, something incompatible with creamy puddings, wafted past. Perspiration dotted my brow, and I had to lower my head.

"Are you all right?" he asked with tender concern.

"The heat," I mumbled.

"Not a smart idea to bring you here today, was it?" He rolled his napkin, dipped it in his water glass, and wrung it out on the spattered cloth. "Here, place this behind your neck. Let some drip down your back as well. Nobody will notice." The coolness did relieve me to the point I could sit upright again. "Better?" he asked.

"Yes, I think so." A few sips of water revived me further.

"Good. The red wine didn't help matters. As I said, we should stick with water!"

"Have you told Zilpah?"

He blotted his own brow. "I thought you should hear the news first. If you had any serious objections, I would not pursue the matter, thus there would be no point in getting Zilpah's hopes up. You know how anxious she is for you to be settled and happy, especially since she blames herself for that unfortunate Luddy business."

"Thank you for speaking to me first," I said evenly. "I can only think of one objection, Papa. Darjeeling was far away, but I could return to Calcutta in a few days. Cochin is the other side of the subcontinent."

My father looked at me with a profound sadness in his eyes. "I know, my child," he sighed with despair. "Life is often both the closing and the opening of doors."

"Yes, if you shut one to block out an unpleasantness, the next one opens a whole new group of problems," I said with a rueful laugh.

"Have you considered the possibility that happy surprises may lie behind one of them?" He had forced a lilt in his voice, but it sounded strained.

"You are right, Papa. In my position I would be unwise to say no without hearing more about the man. What does he do? How old is he? What is his family like? Is he handsome? Might he wish to move to Calcutta?" I asked in a rush.

My father shook his head and rubbed the bump on the side of his nose.

"He wouldn't live in Calcutta?"

"No, that is not it. I know almost nothing about the young man except that he had a good position in the family spice business until his father died, leaving many debts."

Ah, that was it. They were desperate for money—my money. "At least do you know his name?"

"His name is Edwin Salem."

"Edwin?" I almost shouted. "Like Edwin Drood!"

"Who is that?"

"A character in a book I just read, a book I did not like very much."

"What sort of bloody rubbish is this?" My father's face reddened. "You won't consider this man because his name was in a book?"

"I did not mean it that way," I demurred.

"I am glad you did not, or I would have to stop trusting that good sense you have shown working with my accounts." He stood and gave me his hand. Two waiters came and moved the table so I could get out more easily.

"Then it is decided," my father said as he helped me into the office jaun. "I will contact this man's family and begin preliminary discussions."

I sat in my seat and closed my eyes. I did not dare respond, for I was afraid the noodles and the cream, the smells and the heat, combined with the shock of the news and the man's unfortunate name, would cause me to be sick again.

24

❧ ❧ ❧

Your Aunt Bellore came running to me with the news about the possibility," Grandmother Helene said when I next saw her after my lunch at Castellazzo Brothers'.

Stepping around the array of boxes and trunks that littered the first floor of her house, I ignored the remark and asked if I could be of some assistance. Fanning herself, she groaned, "I wouldn't know where to tell you to begin. Since there are no hotels in Madhupur, I must take my crockery, cutlery, and linens, besides clothing and everything else."

"Seems more like work than a holiday," I said as I helped her prepare to leave for her annual vacation. My father's family preferred Darjeeling, while other Calcutta Jews selected the seaside fishing village of Madhupur. Even though Grandmother Helene had a modest income from her late husband, everyone believed my father was the main contributor to her sustenance, and ever since the Sassoons had accused her of extravagance after her daughter died, she had attempted to live frugally.

"Once I arrive, I do nothing but give orders to the cook. Provisions are wonderfully reasonable there. Why, I can buy pigeons for two annas, a seer of tomatoes is even less, and the sweetest papayas in the world grow on a tree just outside the door of Myrtle View—the cottage I take each year."

"It sounds lovely."

"Since this is not the most crowded season, the rent is less than my monthly expenses would be here. This will be Ruby's third time with me. Why don't you join us?"

"Papa wants me to remain in Calcutta in case he hears from Mr. Salem again."

A strange look crossed her doughy face. "Let's sit for a while." Stepping across bundles of bedding, she kicked a path into the parlor.

271

"I cannot bear to think about this mess until I have had a drink of lime water. It's so much more refreshing than lemonade, don't you think?" Without waiting for a reply, she summoned her bearer and placed her order.

"So where was I?" she asked after she had downed a full glass of the pungent liquid mixed with a spiced-honey syrup. "Your Aunt Bellore . . ."

"She cannot know any more than I do at this point." I shrugged to make light of the encounter, but a wariness in Grandmother Helene's gray eyes put me on guard. "Or has my father told her something he did not tell me?"

"I would not want you to hear this from anyone else. Would you pour me another glass, *abdalak*?" she asked, using the tender expression for a loved one.

I had to steady the silver pitcher with both hands. "Please tell me," I urged.

"Apparently this man, the father of the boy—"

"His father is dead. Elisha Salem is the uncle who spoke to my father in Hong Kong."

"Yes, whatever," she said, fanning herself more quickly. "Anyway, there was some sort of dispute about an amount of money he owed your father. The man says he never received the shipment in question, your father claims he did. Even if Benu Sassoon is wrong, he can refrain from doing business with the man in the future, or worse, persuade others not to deal with him. Never forget, Dinah, that a Sassoon can ruin a lesser man with a mere implication."

I felt chilled despite the cloying heat. "What does that have to do with me?"

"Bellore claims that Benu promised to forgive the debt if the uncle arranged this match for you."

I shuddered. "I wonder what is wrong with the boy."

Grandmother Helene seemed to shrink back into the cushions on her chair. "We don't know much yet. He's from Cochin, but this you knew, and is from a modest family. The second son of a spice trader, he hardly seems destined to become the Croesus of his community, but you will never want for money. Take it from me, Benu is the most generous of the Sassoons."

"If there was anything terrible, like one eye or one leg missing, don't you think my aunt would have mentioned it?"

"You are right about that." Grandmother Helene sighed with relief. "Now, what am I to do about all this?" She gestured to the boxes and bundles.

"Why don't we make a list?" I suggested, and I began to organize her baggage.

❦ ❦ ❦

A few days later, when Zilpah and I were arranging roses in baskets on the terrace, I told her what I had heard, stating firmly that it did not alarm me. "My dowry would interest any man. Even Silas, who claimed the money would be mine to manage, was impressed at having a Sassoon for a wife."

"What a sensible viewpoint," she commented, stepping back to study her creation. To my eyes, two long stems ruined the symmetry. She glanced at my mass of pinks, whites, and oranges and said, "I would never have put those colors together, but the way you did it is splendid. They look like saris in a Hindu procession. I picked only reds, but they won't even stand up for me."

I assisted her by cutting the stems off at a steeper angle and inserting them more firmly into the clay pressed at the bottom of the bowl. "There, is that better?"

She nodded her thanks, then looked over my shoulder while I filled in my own basket with greenery. "We have been making more inquiries about the Salems," she began evenly. "I feel it my responsibility to know everything about this man before we invite him to visit."

"What have you learned?" I asked without halting my work.

"When his father died, his mother returned to her family with enough money to live simply. They gave the eldest son a small stake to establish a business—something having to do with a shipyard that repairs fishing boats—and two years ago she married off her middle child, a daughter, to another Cochin Jew. The youngest, this Edwin, has a reputation as a mischievous lad who was always up to pranks. Because he often was in trouble with his teachers, his mother—at no small sacrifice—moved him from school to school. We know that he spent some semesters at St. Xavier's in Calcutta."

"When was that?"

"He was there for two years, around the ages of thirteen and fourteen. He was born in 1872, so that would have been in—"

"You mean he is my age exactly?"

"Yes. Your Uncle Saul checked the records at the school."

I thought of the boys my age who had gone to St. Xavier's after the Jewish Boys' School. "Gabriel Judah might have known him," I said in an offhand way so Zilpah would not notice the pang I felt. "By now Aunt Bellore has probably spoken to him . . ."

"Gabriel does not recall a Salem boy."

"Where did he finish school?"

"He left before his formal education was complete, probably because his mother could no longer afford the fees, and went to stay with some relatives in Singapore. That's where he learned the rudiments of trading. He's been back in Cochin for a year or so."

"What does he do there?"

"I believe he was assisting this uncle—the Elisha Salem your father knows—while he was in China." She turned to gather the ends of the stems and plucked leaves in her cutting basket before she asked warily, "What do you think?"

I found it easier to respond to her back. "His mother sounds as though she has done everything she could for her children. The uncle is more peculiar, but I won't be marrying him. Best of all, it doesn't seem as though Mr. Salem is tied to Cochin." My voice rose enthusiastically. "Maybe he would move to Calcutta and I could be closer to everyone."

"Ow!" Zilpah cried as a thorn dug under her nail. She sucked on her finger, then replied firmly, "A girl goes to the family of the husband. Mr. Salem has a widowed mother to care for. His trading connections are with Singapore, a port convenient to Cochin, and he has a job with his uncle."

"I guess you are right," I replied without rancor. Resigned, I decided that unless there was something monstrously wrong with this Edwin Salem, I would accede to their wishes.

❧ ❧ ❧

As far as I could tell, only a few letters about the match were sent back and forth. The Salems were not the correspondents the Luddys were. I did not care, for experience had taught me that letters revealed far less than one glimpse, one conversation, one hour together would.

"It would be our pleasure to consider Miss Sassoon," Mrs. Salem had written. Zilpah had followed with an invitation for the Salems to visit Calcutta at their convenience, but delicately suggested they wait until after the hot weather, after the monsoon, and after the High Holy Days. This brought us to the end of October, within a few weeks of when I would be free to remarry. Mrs. Salem agreed to wait until then, and announced that we could expect them on the first of November.

Over the next few months my father indulged me by giving me documents to copy and books to balance. If my delight to be hard at work had not been muted by my ruminations on the morality lesson in *The Mystery of Edwin Drood* and my mind not muddled with thoughts of the intriguing Edwin Salem, I might have extrapolated from his sales figures and refined my analyses. As it was, I did the rote work competently, but without enthusiasm. Perhaps sensing my diffidence—as well as expecting I might be leaving—my father began to turn my duties over to his clerks. By the time Rosh Hashanah and Yom Kippur had passed, my sole responsibility was to prepare my wardrobe. This time I did not want any frivolous blue dresses, so I undertook the ordering of my own clothing and proudly paid the durzi myself from my little legacy.

I selected fabrics in *crépon* and silk with the most simple yet eye-catching details. One of my favorites was a shirt ornamented with three silver star-shaped buttons. The slim godet skirt flattered me with curves in the right places, and the short basque jacket minimized my height. Another costume, cut from a crisp green sailcloth, had mother-of-pearl buttons and a white collar and cuffs. Its dignified look was more suitable than flounces and frills.

"Why is Dinah getting new dresses?" Ruby complained when the durzi came for the second fitting. "Mine are also too tight!" She pushed out her expanding chest to prove her point. Since returning from Madhupur, she had lengthened and blossomed, and had shocked us by becoming a woman. Zilpah was perturbed because Ruby, who barely understood what was happening to her, had been frightened and could not manage the rags without Selima's assistance. Also, Ruby was often pouty and difficult, so to keep the peace, Zilpah agreed she might have some new clothes as well.

"Why is Dinah able to pick the designs and I am not?" Ruby whined as Zilpah and the durzi settled on her fabrics.

"Because you are too young," Zilpah said with a firmness that sent Ruby rushing from the room in tears. Lying, Ruby told her ayah that Zilpah had said to take her to visit her Grandmother Helene. When Zilpah discovered that Ruby had left, she decided to let it pass, saying, "This is a difficult period for her."

That evening, after Grandmother Helene brought her back to Theatre Road, Ruby boasted, "Grandmother Helene said she would have some dresses made for me."

"How nice, Ruby, I am certain they will be very lovely," I replied on my way past her. In the small drawing room I found Zilpah and my father discussing Ruby with Grandmother Helene. Nobody asked me to leave the room.

"Tell me, Helene," Zilpah said, holding her hands out in supplication. "What am I to do with a girl who has the sense of a baby and the body of a woman?"

"She's a pretty thing," Grandmother Helene said with a touch of pride in her voice. "Doesn't she remind you of Mozelle?" she asked Benu.

"I suppose so," my father responded gruffly.

"You might consider finding *her* a husband, someone mature, who would look after her."

Zilpah was shocked. "That's ridiculous. How could she manage on her own?"

"There would be the family of the husband, her dowry, servants . . . and I always would be there for her," Grandmother Helene replied earnestly.

"It's barbaric," Zilpah sniffed.

Aware of the resistance, she did not push the issue. "Well, there's plenty of time to plan for Ruby. May I suggest you keep your minds open? You never know when the right opportunity might present itself. We have learned the folly of waiting too long in these matters." She shot me an apologetic glance.

The preparations had left me feeling hopeful, so comments about my situation were no longer like barbs pressed under my skin. I had lived with the facts long enough to have accepted them; and I also had realized the dire predictions of my elders often proved false. Hadn't Silas come along? And now this Mr. Salem was a new mystery: *The Mystery of Edwin Salem*. I ached to know what he looked like and whether he would find me attractive. Nothing could have been worse than my first reaction to Silas, and if it had not been for our insurmountable problem, I might have carved out some happiness there. Or maybe I was going about this all wrong. I should have rejected Silas because my first reaction had been the most accurate assessment of the man, but was it fair to judge the next man by that standard? I could be content with a good man who did not dazzle me. After all, the chance that I could interest a marvelous match had long ago been lost.

❀   ❀   ❀

Because my parents had not yet met the Salems, Zilpah decided they would have a preliminary discussion with the boy and his mother without me.

"You can't exclude me. I must see him! How else am I to know—?"

"Of course you will see him," she replied smoothly. "My scheme should please everyone. Edwin and his mother will arrive at the front portico, and your father and I will escort them into the hall for refreshments. If, after we become acquainted with them, your father and I are in agreement that the boy is suitable, I will suggest a tour of the rose garden. You will be on the upstairs veranda assisting your sisters with their studies. From there you may contemplate the boy—and he may contemplate you—without the awkwardness of a direct encounter."

"When would I meet him?"

"If you like what you see, formal arrangements will commence. A few days after that we will introduce you to Mr. Salem. You would then have at least a week to become acquainted before contracting the engagement."

"And if I do not care for him . . ."

"Dinah, nobody will force you to marry against your will."

With resignation I accepted Zilpah's plans and tried to occupy myself until November. Since responding to *Edwin Drood*, I had been taking more time before replying to Silas. I had deliberately decided not to tell him about Edwin Salem until we arranged a marriage. Otherwise he would worry that he had ruined my chances. I kept occupied by tutoring my sisters, although my mind drifted as I imagined the possibilities. *Let his faults be obvious!* was my most fervent wish.

On Sunday morning, the first of November, I woke to what seemed to be the sound of a tabla drum. After a few confused semiconscious moments, I realized it was the fierce, anticipatory beat of my heart.

Seti popped in. "Aren't you coming downstairs?"

"No, not today." I was expected to join my parents for breakfast, but could manage no more than a taste of tea and a few slices of fruit in my room.

"When is he coming?" Seti asked after her own meal in the nursery.

"Eleven o'clock."

"Why aren't you ready?"

"There is plenty of time."

When Seti next bounded in, she chided, "You still aren't dressed!"

"I haven't had my bath."

"What if they are early?"

"They will not be," I replied peevishly. "It would be rude to be early."

"Maybe they are rude people." Seti stuck out her tongue and ran away.

Her visits were punctuated by Ruby's, who kept inquiring about what she might wear. "Shall I wear a pink dress?"

"Pink would be lovely," I said distractedly.

A few minutes later she was back. "What about the blue with the white stripes?"

"That is a very suitable dress. Wear it if you like."

"What do you want me to wear, Dinah?" she said in a whining voice that unnerved me.

"Ruby, I do not care what you wear. Have Selima help you dress, and leave me in peace!"

When she ran off sulking, I was so pleased to be alone as I buttoned myself into my green-and-white outfit that I did not regret my snappish remarks.

At half-past ten Jonah came by to announce that he and Pinhas were off to a friend's house and wished me well. "They've banished us from the territory."

"Thank goodness. If the Salems took one look at either of you, my chances would be ruined," I said, forcing a smile.

"Listen, Dinah, if he's a frog, forget it." My brother gave me a supportive grin. "For your sake, I hope he's a prince."

"Frankly, I rather like frogs, if they stay in their original skins. It is those princes who turn out to be frogs that are more alarming." I pointed to my green skirt. "Besides, a frog would match rather nicely, don't you think?"

Jonah bent over—he was taller than I by a foot—and kissed me on the cheek gently so as not to muss my hair. The gesture caught me off-guard, and tears welled up at his unexpected empathy. "Don't worry, Asher is on duty today," he mumbled as he rushed off.

"What?" I called after him. He must not have heard me, because Seti pranced through the open door, speaking excitedly. "Wait till you see Ruby!" I heard Ruby giggling in the corridor. "Come in and show her," she prodded.

"No, I don't want to." Ruby's tone was petulant.

Curious, I came to the doorway and was confronted by an astonishing sight. Instead of a short child's frock, Ruby was wearing a blue-and-pink dress with a tight-nipped *cuirasse* bodice. Her sleeves were elbow-length and ended in ruffles. The frilly yards of dark pink ribbons, bows, and laces amused me until my eyes riveted on the mature, square-cut décolletage. Ruby had pushed her breasts up so two mounds protruded past their lacy shield.

"I do not remember you being fitted for that dress," I sputtered. "Where did you get it?"

"A gift from Grandmother Helene."

"And who did your hair?" Her lush black curls had been drawn on top of her head, with long spirals draping to her shoulders. The front had been crimped into tidy rows that emphasized her large eyes. "You are far too young to wear your hair up."

"I am tired of everyone treating me like a baby."

"I think she looks almost as old as you do," Seti said, fueling my concern that Ruby had added five years with the transformation. "Selima worked on it for an hour. Isn't she beautiful?" Seti crooned enviously.

"Has Z-Zilpah seen her?" I stammered.

"No, it's a surprise," Seti admitted.

"Don't you like it?" Ruby sniffed.

"Well, Ruby . . . I don't think it is a good choice for this particular morning," I began. "Why don't you change into that yellow dress you look so pretty in?" Large drops cascaded down her round cheeks. "You could leave your hair up, though," I added to soften the blow.

"You don't like it!" she wailed as she rushed from the room with Seti dashing behind her.

The upstairs clock chimed eleven. Before I could calm myself, Yali signaled that the Salems had arrived. From Zilpah's plan, I knew how the encounter would proceed. First there would be greetings near the portico. Zilpah would lead the way, followed by Mrs. Salem, Edwin, and Benu as they moved into the hall. They would stand about for a minute or so to take in the long view of the garden, admire the Chinese objects, then sit down to refreshments served by Abdul and his son, Hanif, who was learning to assist him. The clock struck the quarter-hour. I visualized the strangers seated in the leather chairs opposite my parents: she was short, round, with chubby cheeks and a docile smile. He too was short—shorter than I, but that was all right— with a stocky, muscular build and a likable face. Nothing flashy, but pleasant, friendly, easy to live with. I could be satisfied with a man like that . . . he would be a good father . . . like Uncle Jacob . . . My mind wandered as I thought about the amiable chatter of no consequence that was covering the next thirty minutes.

At the half-hour chime, I sat at my dressing table, moistening capricious strands of hair and pushing them back into place. The reflection in the glass mocked me. Compared with Ruby's naturally peachy skin tone, mine seemed sickly. Compared with Ruby's succulent globes, my breasts were barely discernible under the sensible jacket. Next to her youthful ribbons and laces, I looked like a spinster in a man's waistcoat.

The three-quarter-hour bells chimed. My father should be taking Mrs. Salem on a tour of the downstairs rooms, while Zilpah would be trying to draw Edwin out.

Twelve o'clock. Now my father and Mrs. Salem must be in the parlor. This is when Papa would ask pointed questions about Edwin, as well as explain about Silas. If that went well, the four of them would reunite in the garden at a quarter past. The moment had come for me to go out to the veranda. I tiptoed down the hall.

"Dinah!" someone called in a husky hush.

I clutched my throat with surprise. "Asher! You frightened me."

He grabbed my arm and said breathlessly, "I saw him!"

Simon stumbled behind him. "Yes, we both did."

"But how . . . ?"

"Didn't Jonah tell you what we were going to do?"

I had forgotten Jonah's mentioning Asher and shook my head.

"On purpose, we left some balls on the terrace table just outside the hall. Then, while we pretended to look for them, we caught a glimpse through the window."

"Well?" Though I could see Asher's mouth moving, I could barely hear his reply because a rushing sound, like a cyclonic wind, blocked my ears. "What?"

"He's a splendid-looking fellow, really he is. Much better than that Judah boy you liked, and Silas is a toad compared to this guy."

Toads and frogs . . . I almost laughed, but the muscles in my jaw

were so tense I could barely force my lips to function. "Really? Is he
. . . fat?"

Asher's cherubic face glistened. Dimples winking, he went on, "No."

"Short?"

"Not at all. He might even be taller than Jonah, but I can't say for
sure because he was sitting down."

"What else?"

"You'll see soon enough, but I didn't want you to brood."

I studied his expression for any hint of deception. Asher's face was
open and filled with good tidings.

The clock struck the quarter-hour.

I was late!

❀ ❀ ❀

Crouched down, Seti peered through the veranda's stone balustrade.
I hung back in the doorway. "Are they in the garden yet?"

"No, but I can hear them talking underneath, so they must be
outside," she said in a voice that seemed to boom in my ears.

"Shhh!" I warned as I took my place next to Ruby, who was still
dressed in her ridiculous flounces. Infuriated at her disobedience, I
flushed, but could not say anything. Below us I could hear my father's
bass laugh. I pretended to read. "Seti, your lessons," I hissed.

"I can't see out if I stand up," she protested. "Look, here they
come!"

The four of them made their way down the path farthest from us.
My father led, with Mrs. Salem close beside him. Only their backs
were visible. Contrary to my expectations, Mrs. Salem wore a slim
black dress that fell to the ground in a bell shape. The sole decoration
was a hem and collar trimmed in a mouse silk. The fine taste of the
widow's gown won my admiration, and I was hopeful that what I had
worn would appeal to her in turn. Next came Zilpah in a lavender sari
which swirled around her in the light breeze. A few years ago I might
have wished her to have worn a European dress, but today I was filled
with pleasure at how gracefully she moved, even floated, out into the
dappled light of the palm-shaded walk. Edwin, or the shape of a man
who could have been nobody else, walked ahead and slightly to the
right of her. The wind was blowing from the left, so the folds of the
fabric that wafted out from Zilpah left my prospect hidden behind an
infuriating curtain.

At the end of the garden that faced the house—the place where my
mother's furniture pyre had been built—was the most prominent of
Grandmother Helene's legacies: the rose arbor. In the distance I could
see Zilpah pointing to the rare blooms, and Mrs. Salem's nodding

admiration. My father stood behind the women. At last Edwin turned away from them and faced the house.

My first glimpse of him is as vivid to me today as it was then. He appeared in a sparkling circle of midday sun that glinted off his high brow, yet left his face in shadow because his head was tilted slightly down. Then, as if he knew he was being observed, his back straightened. His wide, clean-shaven face and chiseled chin glinted in the pool of golden light. A sheaf of long hair had fallen over one eye. With a gesture that caused me to tremble with excitement, he brushed back the straight sheaf of brown locks with spread fingers.

The two men started forward down the center path, directly toward us. The ladies lingered behind. Seti stayed at her post, but Ruby, who could not contain herself, stood up and leaned over the balcony for a better view. I caught a glimpse of a breast even more exposed than before, but had no time to chastise her, since any movement of mine could be seen. With my book propped on the table I managed to sit facing the end of the veranda, but twisted my neck so in my periphery vision I could follow every one of Edwin's long-strided movements.

Seti could not contain herself. "Here they come!"

I gave her a kick to silence her. She winced, but took heed.

My father was speaking to him. "Your mother and I have come to an understanding. The only thing you have to do is make your choice."

Make your choice? That was an odd way of asking him if he wanted to consider marrying me or not.

"What do you mean?" Edwin replied. His head was lowered as though he were watching his step. I saw a delicate pink tinge at the nape of his neck, then that gesture again: the fingers slicing through the hair, with every strand falling into place like obedient slaves. He was not ten feet away from where I was sitting. He did not look up at the veranda, but had turned three-quarters of the way around to face my father.

My inner tabla again threatened to drown out the voices. I felt as though I was pushing walls of water away from me as I fought to hear my father's muffled words. "In good faith you have come a long way, so your mother and I have agreed to permit you to choose between either of my eligible daughters. Dinah is the elder of the two and Ruby is the younger one. They are very different young women, but either would make you a fine wife."

Either! Was this his response to the problem about Ruby? Was he going to marry her off to *my* Edwin, to that glorious man, who at first sight seemed as unpretentious and candid as Silas had been refined and impenetrable? The invisible flood rose up and threatened to crash on me as I leaned back away from the railing without a thought for how my recoiling might appear. As if responding to a very different set of phenomena, Ruby leaned forward and waved.

How free and young and pretty she looked! How much smaller and more pliable she would seem! There were no Silas, no Luna, no difficulties in her past. How long would it take before Edwin realized how hopelessly slow she was? Or would he even care? Men liked women who did their bidding without question. What must I have looked like at that moment? Certainly I was pale, frightened, and shaking from the shock of my father's betrayal. Even more discouraging, I was dressed like Ruby's mother instead of her sister. I could not look at him to see how he was reacting to Ruby's insouciant glee. It was all I could do to sit upright and go on breathing through the next hideous minutes.

"Yes, that's my little Ruby on the right." I imagined that Edwin's eyes had riveted on her moist cleavage. "And Dinah on the left."

I kept my eyes down at my book until a force from somewhere outside my body seemed to be lifting my head up and shifting it to the side. For one long, impetuous second I met Edwin's upturned gaze. The intensity of his profoundly confused expression caused my left eye to twitch. I turned away abruptly.

When I again pivoted around, Edwin had vanished.

25

♈ ♈ ♈

Zilpah was by my side, holding my hand. I was oblivious to anything more than her presence. If she spoke, I did not hear her. The crashing of cymbals, the deeper clatter of the *pakhawaj* drum, joined my insistent tabla.

The music diminished, as though a procession had moved off into the distance. Zilpah spoke close to my ear. "Dinah, he wants only you. Mr. Salem spoke to your father. He said: 'I choose Dinah.' "

I stared into her coal-black eyes, desperate for them to be clear and true. She could not meet my gaze. "What else?" I dared.

"His mother did have the last word. 'Mr. Sassoon is being most generous,' she said. 'He has told me about the two fine young women. We will return to our lodgings and talk this over together.' "

"Then it is not decided."

"As a mother, I can understand her reluctance to stand by her son's hasty remark."

"Why did Papa do it?" I cried in anguish. "Why did he mention Ruby when the man was supposed to be for me?"

Zilpah shook her head. "I don't know what Benu was doing. He never mentioned it to me beforehand. I am afraid he made the decision on the spot. You know how concerned we all have been about Ruby lately. Her own grandmother was encouraging us to marry her off in the next few years, and of course, even if we found a match tomorrow, I would never permit her to leave this house until she was thirteen or fourteen."

"Why would Mr. Salem want her?"

Our glances met again, but this time I looked away first. "Apparently Edwin's mother voiced concerns over your marriage to Silas. You must admit, Dinah, the story does not tell very well. She was finding it difficult to believe in your . . . your purity, and hinted that she thought it a pity you did not try to work out your difficulties awhile longer.

Because your father thought Edwin looked like a most promising young man and because he did not wish to lose him entirely—and since the mother's interest in you seemed to be waning—I suspect he decided to add Ruby to the bargain."

"Did Papa inform Mrs. Salem about Ruby's faults?"

"Certainly. Your father and I have seen enough of the pain that deception can inflict. Benu explained that Ruby has not progressed rapidly in school."

"That is putting her in the most favorable light."

"He did not prevaricate, Dinah. He went on to explain more about her weaknesses in arithmetic and reading."

"And what did Mrs. Salem reply?"

"That did not change her mind. Even I must admit that Ruby did look like a luscious fruit ripe for plucking. Did you see her smiling and waving? From that distance she looked like a merry little addition to any household, as well as much older than she truly is. When Mrs. Salem saw Ruby, she said, 'I can teach her to be a proper wife and—' "

"What else?" I demanded.

"—and she said something about it being a man's job to train a wife to his tastes in other matters."

"Edwin doesn't want her!" My voice rose to a squeaky pitch. "That's what he said, isn't it?"

"As I explained, Dinah, his mother tried to dissuade him, at least from committing himself today. Even so, the boy might have his way. He replied to his mother forcefully, as though nobody else had been standing beside them, and said: 'If I take the younger sister, I will hurt the elder sister's feelings.' "

I could imagine Edwin's hand raking his hair back from his brow to the nape of his neck and his deep-set eyes narrowing as he stood up to his mother. I would have preferred his declaration for me to have included something about how much more intelligent and beautiful I was, but at least he was a man who could make an honorable choice. "What did she say to that?"

"Nothing."

"And Papa?"

"If you could have seen the sour expression on the mother's face, you would understand that at that moment Benu could not consider the boy's word alone. What your father said was that he would look forward to hearing from them both when they returned for dinner tomorrow."

"So, as I said before, nothing is decided."

"I believe the boy has made up his mind."

"His mother might influence him."

Zilpah was shaking her head. "No, not that man. He's a stubborn one. Actually, in many ways he seems to be very much like you." She laughed without hostility.

"Maybe Mrs. Salem will not want either of the Sassoon girls. What then?"

"Now, Dinah, don't let your emotions transport you from reality. I agree with you, Mr. Salem is charming, and I can see from your response you liked him very much—at least at first sight. Remember, that is all it was. You have not exchanged a single word with the boy. As I recall, you were infuriated because you and Silas barely knew each other. Now it seems you are ready to rush into this stranger's arms."

I bowed my head. Zilpah was right, but for some crazed reason I did not care if we ever spoke. If they had ordered me to stand under the huppah and pledge my life to Edwin Salem that very evening, I would have rushed down the aisle without a second thought. Never in my life had I ever wanted anything more ardently.

Zilpah patted my shoulder. "I can understand why you feel desperate to have him. Everyone wants you married off happily, and you have not had many opportunities. This one seems to meet your standards—your physical standards, anyway. Nevertheless, if the Salems change their minds about you so early in the discussions, it will be for the best."

"No, please, Zilpah, please don't let that happen!" I clutched at her sari so roughly the draping fell away from her body.

"Dinah, I have never seen you like this! What has come over you?"

I scanned the ceiling as though the filigree decorations would provide an answer. "Didn't you ever feel this way? When you met your first husband . . . or Benu?"

Her face took on a soft glow. "Yes, Dinah, I know the sensation. Perhaps I felt it when I first saw Benu having dinner at our boarding-house. It can be frightening, overpowering, and wonderful if everything works out. Or, if it doesn't—and this is what frightens me for you, because so often in life our hearts' desires are thwarted—the pain can be dreadful." Suddenly she was sobbing. I watched, amazed, for I had never seen her cry. The twists of her serene face, the puffiness around the mouth that pursed but did not smile, the utter disruption of her tranquil demeanor astonished me. "I don't know what came over me. Your father must have shocked me as much as he shocked you." She refolded and tucked in her sari, and as she did so, she looked at me in bewilderment.

"Please, Zilpah, just do what you can for me."

"I might have some influence over your father, but I doubt that Mrs. Salem would listen to me. In any case, I will speak with him tonight and with her tomorrow."

"I promise that Papa and you—and Edwin—will never regret this."

❦ ❦ ❦

The next morning I heard that Ruby was moping in her room. Selima was running back and forth trying to encourage her to eat. Zilpah paid a brief call and left in disgust. I managed to dress and be downstairs for breakfast because I did not want my father to think I was behaving childishly.

"I won't be joining you today," Papa said in a rush. "I am already late for an appointment. I am looking forward to our dinner this evening." He gave Zilpah a pat on the shoulders, indicating that she should not stand to see him out. "Now you ladies can spend the entire day making preparations without worrying about me."

After a second cup of tea, Zilpah cleared her throat. "I have decided we should not overwhelm the Salems tonight. It might be preferable if only Pinhas and Jonah ate with us and then Asher and Simon joined us later in the hall."

"What about the girls?"

"Considering the events of yesterday, I think it would be more diplomatic to keep Ruby in the background." As she studied my reaction, I tried not to show my satisfaction at my sister's exclusion. "Besides, Ruby is not on her best behavior. I will personally supervise what they both wear and allow them to come down for a brief hello for, say, a half-hour toward the end of the evening."

I grinned with relief. "Which do you think I should wear: the pearly silk or the pleated mauve?"

"They are both lovely, but—" Just then an agitated Abdul came into the room carrying a silver tray and handed Zilpah a note. "What's this?" she cried, puzzled that the post had been delivered so early.

"From the lady who was here yesterday, memsahib."

My heart plummeted. The Salems were canceling their plans to return tonight. They had rejected us both.

"Who brought this?" Zilpah said with alarm as she read the words that I could not see.

"The memsahib and her son."

"Are they waiting in their gharry now?" Zilpah added excitedly.

"Yes, memsahib."

"Dinah, this is most extraordinary. Mr. Salem requests a meeting with you this morning. I presume he means immediately, since he is sitting in front of the house this very instant." She looked me over. My skirt was ordinary white linen with no decoration save a few piped gores and my chemise was a practical one with simple tucks down the front.

I looked behind me and realized I had forgotten the jacket that had tight wrists with rosettes on the sleeves and on the closures. "My jacket is upstairs," I said nervously, and patted my hair.

"You look fine, my dear. It is wise for a man to see a woman as she might appear at breakfast instead of wrapped and packaged as a gift." She clapped her hands. "Have Yali bring Miss Dinah's jacket from her room," she said to the ayah, who was passing. "And, Abdul, we will require pastries and tea for four. Set the table for Miss Dinah and her guest on the terrace and for me and Mrs. Salem in the small parlor."

"Won't we be together?"

"No. Yali will sit on the far end of the terrace and work on some mending or whatever, and I will take this opportunity to speak with Mrs. Salem alone."

I felt trapped in a crosscurrent of conflicting emotions. "What if he has come to give me the unhappy news himself?"

"Dinah, he probably wants a chance to meet you. If they were rejecting you, his mother would convey her regrets to your parents. Or if he wanted to be a perfect gentleman, he would speak directly—"

I cut her off. "What if you are wrong?"

Yali came rushing in. She handed me my jacket and went to work pinning my hair more tidily. Annoyed by her fluttering, I pushed her aside and primped in front of the sideboard mirror.

Zilpah started for the door. "We can't leave them in the carriage any longer. Yali, go sit on the terrace with Dinah. Dinah, you may take him for a walk in the gardens if you like, but do not come inside the house until we come out or send Abdul to fetch you."

❦ ❦ ❦

Zilpah was alone when she brought Edwin to me. She must have asked Mrs. Salem to wait in the parlor. I stood on trembling legs.

"Mr. Salem, I would like you to meet my stepdaughter, Dinah Sassoon. Dinah, this is Mr. Edwin Salem of Cochin. I believe you two would prefer to talk in private." As she backed away swiftly, I focused on the silk fringe of her sari as she closed the glass door and left us to ourselves.

"Miss Sassoon, you are so kind to have agreed to see me. My mother tried to deter me, but I could not wait until this evening. I had to see you again immediately. If this offends you, please understand that I meant the opposite, to honor you."

His voice! I had heard it from a distance yesterday, but here under the wooden eaves of the terrace it took on a resonance that vibrated my bones. In the beats before I could respond, I saw his hand reach up and brush back his hair, not as forcefully as the day before, but more gently, only moving the fringe that drooped near his exquisitely tangled eyebrows. My knees felt so weak I had to sit down. I prayed that my momentary silence, my gesture for him to be seated, and the few seconds I took to rearrange my skirt looked like the graceful movements of a self-assured woman in command instead of a girl clutched by a desire to throw herself into his arms.

"Thank you for coming, Mr. Salem. In doing so you have saved me the terrors of an endless day." I gulped at my forthright words, but did not regret them.

"My thoughts exactly," Edwin boomed. "Why do parents want to draw everything out?"

"Because they have nothing else to do. It fills up the time they are yearning to waste."

"You do not like to waste time, do you?"

"No, Mr. Salem, I abhor it . . . and most other frivolous endeavors," I went on effortlessly.

"Could you call me Edwin—perhaps not if Mother is around, but now that we are alone?"

"Oh, yes, Edwin, I would like that. If you will call me Dinah."

"I hoped you would say that, Dinah. I do so love doing what I am told I must not do." He winked conspiratorially and shifted until his back was entirely turned from Yali. I swiveled about as well so we were more side by side than face-to-face.

"This whole procedure is barbaric, don't you think?" he asked.

"Well, one cannot expect to find a wife in a bazaar, so what other choice is there?"

"I almost had that feeling yesterday."

"What is that?" I wondered, not following him for the first time since we had begun to converse.

He glanced away. "When I was given the choice between two girls."

"I did not know about that until afterward."

"It came as a jolt to me too."

"My sister is much younger than I."

"I came across India to meet you. How could I have selected her?"

"If you do not prefer me, then you should not be forced to accept me."

"Nobody forces me to do anything against my will. They never have and they never shall!" he shouted. When he lowered his voice, he did so without apology. "My mother has had a hard life and has sacrificed much, especially for me. I cannot blame her for wanting me to be happy. She should give you a chance. Just because she has heard rumors and just because you have an unusual past does not mean you are not the right wife for me. You have traveled to places like Darjeeling. You have been to a good school. To me you are much more interesting than the young women I have met around Cochin."

"What rumors are you talking about?" I gave him what I hoped was a steady gaze.

"About your first marriage and your mother's death." There was no hesitation in his voice as he spoke. "My mother, like so many of her age, is superstitious. She knows you descend from the Cohen who founded the Jewish community here, and she reminded me of an old saying . . ."

"Yes?" I asked, wondering what he meant.

" 'The tears of a Cohena—the daughter of a Cohen—bring bad luck,' she warned me." He shrugged. "I pointed out to her that we had known those facts before we ever left the Malabar Coast and that we had made a promise."

"Only a promise to consider me," I added, not thinking I could be hurting my chances. Any concern that this young man did not like me or that I might not feel the same way after we had met had been dissipated in the first seconds of our encounter.

"Well, then, I will consider you if you will consider me."

"Consider me considering." I laughed.

"All right, then, consider me considering you giving me your consideration."

"My considerable consideration."

"You win that round!"

A small breakfast had been placed on the table beside us, but neither of us showed any interest in the food. Nor did I offer to pour the tea. Suddenly I realized that my arm lay on the edge of the chair and his rested on the same place on his chair. If the gap had been an inch narrower, we would have touched.

I leaned closer to him. He bent toward me. I spoke softly. "Is this a match with winners and losers?"

"No, this is the one game in which there are only winners."

"Does the game have rules?"

"Oh, yes, thousands."

"How do I learn them?"

"We invent them as we go along."

"Fine. Rule number one: the game begins when one team member shows up by surprise and declares the play is on."

"Rule number two: the game may be played by only two. No more, no less."

For a long while we stared at each other, completely absorbed and not requiring speech to be comfortable together until "Well . . ." was spoken in unison and accompanied by mutual laughter. The next moment his hand folded across mine. I felt as if a bolt etched a jagged line in my heart. Only his pressure on my wrist kept me from surging toward him.

"Dinah . . ." How euphonious my name sounded when he said it!

"Edwin," I attempted, entirely forgetting *Edwin Drood* or any other association except that of the moment, when his light brown eyes with flecks of gold bore into mine.

There was nothing more to say and everything more to say. Staring at him as if I had just been granted the gift of sight, I knew that everything was going to be all right.

"There they are," Zilpah said loudly as a warning.

We slipped our hands into our respective laps and struggled to our feet. Zilpah noticed that we had not eaten. "You weren't hungry?" she asked. Not waiting for a reply, she went on, "Did you sit here the whole time? I would have thought they would have wanted to go for a walk, wouldn't you, Mrs. Salem?"

"Yes, especially since there is a breeze on this side of the house."

"November is one of Calcutta's better months."

"You were so right in suggesting it," Mrs. Salem replied smoothly.

"Well, then"—Zilpah looked at me for some sense of where she should go—"I certainly hope this pleasant morning visit does not preclude your return this evening. My husband is looking forward to having you join us."

"We would not miss it, Mrs. Sassoon." Edwin spoke for his mother.

Somewhat flustered, Mrs. Salem nodded. "Yes, eight in the evening is the time I believe you mentioned."

"Why don't you come at seven?" I added to show that I was keeping up my part of that particular round. "Papa is usually home by then, and that would give us more time for you to meet my brothers."

"Very well," Zilpah said as she brilliantly masked her shock. "Seven would be excellent."

* * *

That evening Edwin got on splendidly with Pinhas and Jonah. During dinner they discussed teachers they knew in common at St. Xavier's, and from time to time Jonah beamed at me to let me know he approved. When Asher and Simon were invited in, Edwin turned his attention to the younger boys, effortlessly changing the topic to cricket and tennis and whatever else interested them. The whole while I worried how he would react when he saw Ruby, and I was even more apprehensive to see how she would behave.

Just before their bedtime, Selima ushered the two girls into the hall. Ruby wore a cream-colored frock with a rose sash. A large lace bib covered her chest. Her long raven curls fell around her shoulders. She had a matching bow in her hair. Seti wore an identical dress, but with yellow and green ribbons.

"How many more brothers and sisters do you have?" Edwin asked me.

"That's all, we're all here!" Seti blurted.

Edwin bent close to her. "Are you certain? Every hour or so, two more come out of a secret door. Maybe there are dozens more waiting their turn."

"No, there aren't!" she giggled.

"Oh, dear." He made a sad face. "I did so hope there were a few more beautiful sisters. Are you the last of your line, then?"

"Yes."

"You could not find one more?"

She shook her head.

"Not even one?"

She had caught on to his joke and teased him back: "Well, maybe one."

"How could you?" Ruby asked in alarm. "There aren't any more of us. You know that, Seti."

Edwin studied Ruby to see what new twist she had added to his game. When he saw the earnestness in her expression, his mouth twisted for a second; then he recovered and spoke with an exaggerated sigh. "Then, if there are no more Sassoon girls, I shall have to wait and hope that someday I have a daughter that is an equal to any of you three." He turned to me and winked.

From the rustle of activity on the parental side of the room, we sensed the evening was about to end. Edwin drew me aside and whispered, "I do not want to go."

"I don't want you to leave either."

"I must see you soon."

"Tomorrow. I will ask my father."

"I don't care what your father says."

"Edwin!" I admonished.

"Rule number twelve: your father shall not rule my life."

"Rule number thirteen: your mother shall not rule mine."

"Touché." He looked at the gilded clock on the mantel. "It is half-past ten. I cannot wait any more than twelve hours. No, even that is far too long."

"You will be sleeping most of that time."

"Perhaps you shall sleep. I shall lie awake talking to you."

"And I shall respond, but in my dreams." I pretended to yawn, even though I had never been less tired in my life.

"I will come tomorrow, as early as I dare."

As soon as he left, I felt a dreadful pulling in my chest. I wanted to be beside him, close to him, touching him, and any separation was almost more than I could bear.

"He is coming back tomorrow morning," I told Zilpah after they had departed. "Do you think Papa will mind?"

"No. Your father and Mrs. Salem have agreed you both should have a week to become acquainted with each other."

I beamed, but did not mention that we were already acquainted.

"We are pleased you both seem to be taking our match with remarkable amiability," she said with a conspiratorial grin.

26

⚜ ⚜ ⚜

The following morning Edwin arrived at nine o'clock without his mother, who would be "coming later." He and I assumed our position on the terrace and talked for several hours without stopping.

He asked me about my schooling, the courses I had preferred, the authors I had read. Anything I replied was met by a welcoming nod, as though I had expressed his exact preference, or if I had not, that he understood why I felt as I did. With Silas, I had always been on guard, concerned that any moment I might seem puerile or my reasoning faulty. With Edwin, I believed I had just made the most marvelously brilliant point and he was waiting expectantly for the next.

"I heard you went to many schools," I said, curious as to why someone like him would have had any difficulties learning.

"Yes, they kept sending me away."

"What did you do wrong?"

"Wrong? I did everything right." Seeing that he had perplexed me enough, he explained, "Schoolwork is simplicity itself if you have a tidy mind. Thousands of compartments fill my brain. I merely open a door, pick a subject, then shovel in the information. When it is full, I close it. Whenever recall is required, I only must remember which drawer to open. It is both a gift and a curse."

His singular description of learning left me speechless. At last I managed, "You never have to study?"

"Oh, I have to study—that is the shoveling part, and shoveling is hard labor—but after that I rarely forget anything."

"That is impossible."

"Try me."

"The date of Clive's victory at Plassey."

"Seventeen-fifty-seven, but that's too simple."

"When did Marco Polo visit India?"

"In 1295."

"*Caput mundi.*"

"The Romans thought of Rome as *caput mundi*, literally the head—or the capital—of the world."

"Who wrote 'Gather ye rosebuds while ye may'?"

"Robert Herrick. '. . . Old Time is still a-flying . . .' " His expression taunted me to give up.

I worked hard at thinking up a more challenging question. Finally I had it. "The rules of the game. Our game. Recite them."

"Rule number one: the game begins when one team member shows up by surprise and declares the play is on. Rule number two: the game may be played by only two. No more, no less. Rule number three: speaking the same word at the same time entitles me to a kiss—someday." He went on right down the list to the most current ones. "Rule number twelve: your father shall not rule my life."

I had forgotten most of them, except the third, which had thrilled me the moment he invented it. He probably knew exactly how many kisses I owed him. "I give up. You know everything!"

He shook his head. "I don't know everything. I only know what is in the compartments. That is why I went to so many schools. Once they had nothing more to offer, I moved on. It is true I did not complete the program, which really means going for so many years and taking so many courses and meeting the requirements to pass each of them. I had more than enough to my credit by the time I was sixteen, so there was no point in wasting my mother's money to have me warm a seat for several more years. That is why she sent me to Singapore. And just because I did not sit in a dusty classroom doesn't mean I did not continue my education. Whenever I want to learn something new, I open up a fresh compartment and get to work."

"Am I in one?" I asked in a shaky voice.

"No."

I flushed.

"You are in every one," he said in a voice that sounded like water rushing over stones.

In a few moments we were called into the house because his mother had joined us for tiffin.

After the meal, Zilpah spoke tensely. "Mrs. Salem, I thought we might show you some of our fine city." She went on to describe an excursion she had organized.

In the landau the two women faced forward, while Edwin and I sat on the same seat and faced backward. Neither of us cared much for where we were going. Since Edwin had attended school in Calcutta, he had no interest in sightseeing. However, with both mothers watching our every twitch and straining to overhear our every whisper, we dutifully pretended to be watching the promenades of the Maidan as we made our way up the Red Road and back down to the racecourse, where little men curried horses that glistened in the sun.

On several occasions, Zilpah asked the driver to stop. Edwin and I would wait until the ladies were out, then alight from the opposite side of the carriage and stroll away from them so we could finally say all the ideas that had welled up in the interval.

I had never before heard anyone who could talk as fast as Edwin. In less than a minute he expressed more than the average person did in an hour. I already knew he had an extraordinary memory, yet he did not flaunt his education, not even the way Silas might have. Everything about Edwin was a fusion of mind, of body, of spirit, of knowledge. Best of all, he could communicate without words, a skill that was essential as Zilpah and his mother chatted stiffly in the background.

"Where shall we go next?" Zilpah asked gaily as we headed out of the Maidan at last.

"The river," I suggested. "It is always lovely just before nightfall."

"Perfect," Edwin murmured into my ear.

"What is perfect? The river?"

"You . . . you . . ."

After several hours, we returned to Theatre Road. "Please join us for a light supper this evening. Nothing formal, just the family," Zilpah offered graciously.

"No, you have gone to far too much trouble for us today." Mrs. Salem looked over at her son and gave him a warning glance. "Don't forget, you have been entertaining Edwin since dawn."

"I know you both must be tired, so I will not insist—at least not tonight, but you must allow our driver to see you to your lodgings."

"That is most kind, Mrs. Sassoon," Mrs. Salem said.

The moment they had left, I was miserable. "Couldn't you have made them stay?"

Zilpah looked at me with deep concern. "Dinah, this is only their second day in Calcutta. We cannot rush things."

"Why?"

"It would be unseemly," she replied testily.

I burst into tears.

"I thought you two were having a wonderful time. What happened? Did he say something unkind to you?"

"No, no, it's not him, it's you." I gulped. "Not you, I mean it is you and his mother. We need time to be alone, to talk together."

Zilpah's shoulders sagged with relief. "You do still like him."

"I have never liked anyone better in my whole life."

"Your father and I want you to be happy with him, but we cannot let you spend time together unchaperoned."

"I know, but couldn't we go out with someone else?"

"Who?"

"Yali?"

Zilpah gave the matter some thought, then shook her head. "Ayahs have a reputation for letting girls twist them. I don't think that would satisfy Mrs. Salem."

"I am not her daughter. Why should she care?"

"Propriety concerns her. Believe me, she has not forgotten about the problems you present. This match has not been finalized. You must see the sense in not doing anything that would cause her to question your worthiness."

"I suppose you are right, but couldn't you get rid of Mrs. Salem for a day and supervise us yourself?"

"She is alone here. How can I do that?"

"What about Grandmother Helene?"

Zilpah's lips pursed a few times before she replied. "I don't see any objections to having a woman her age attend to you. Besides, it would do her good to get out, since she does not have her own carriage. Perhaps you two could even assist her with some errands."

I threw my arms around Zilpah and gave her a loud smack on the cheek.

The next morning she convinced Mrs. Salem to permit us to go off with Grandmother Helene. As soon as we were out of sight of Theatre Road, I shifted in my seat so Edwin and I touched at several points. Wordlessly I tried to convey that he could relax, but he misinterpreted my expression and stiffened.

"Now, children, why don't you pretend I am not here?" said Grandmother Helene blithely, aware of every nuance.

Our first stop was a fruit market in the Tiretta Bazaar, where Grandmother Helene strolled more as an amusement than a purchasing expedition. She sniffed the figs, tasted the pistachios, poked at the apricots, before selecting a large quantity of almonds. "Look at those grapes! Like black pearls! The first of the season. I must have some of those." She bargained without enthusiasm, for she had to have them at any price, and placed her treasure in the basket a market boy carried on his head.

Edwin and I followed several paces behind. "What a wonderful grandmother," he said as he admired the heavyset woman's bouncy step.

"She's not really my grandmother. Both of mine are dead. She is Ruby's."

"Oh, my mother doesn't realize that."

"Would it make a difference?"

"It should not, but she walks a narrow path between what she thinks is right and wrong. The problem is that she lets others determine her path, not her own judgment. If she would only do what she thinks is right, if she could be more flexible . . ." His voice faded off as Grandmother Helene waved us to follow her into an alleyway.

Just when it seemed that she must go down every row and check out the delicacies offered at every stall, she stopped abruptly. "Enough. Let us go back to my house and eat almonds and grapes and maybe some tiffin besides."

After a light luncheon in the dining room, she served coffee in the parlor. Only two cups arrived. I began to pour and handed her one made with extra milk and sugar, the way I knew she liked it. "No, I won't have any. You two have exhausted me. I hope you will forgive an old woman, but I must go upstairs for my rest." She looked around the room. "Oh, it is far too bright in here. The sunlight bleaches my upholstery." She went to each window and closed the draperies. "That is better. It will stay nice and cool in here this afternoon." She made her way to the vestibule doorway. "Now, Dinah, as you know, my servants take a good long rest themselves in the afternoons. If you require anything else, you shall have to find it yourself. Nobody will be available for several hours." Without another word, she closed the door.

Edwin spun on his heels and stared at me for confirmation of what had occurred. I was grinning. He held out his arms. I leapt up and managed to fly across the room and into his enfolding embrace without my feet touching the floor.

"Oh, Dinah! At last! My darling."

I craned my head back and looked up at him as his warm hands cupped my face. "How many?"

He blinked. "What?"

"How many kisses are we owed?"

"Ten thousand and one."

I pushed him back firmly. "No, how many?" I demanded.

"Thirty-two."

Sensation left my legs, but his arms were so strong that I lost my fear of falling and let the tide sweep me toward him. I reached up and placed my hands at the back of his neck, caressing his hair, which felt like thick bands of silk. He placed one leg between mine and twisted me around so he could bend over and reach my mouth. His forelock brushed my cheek. "One," he said as he touched his lips to mine so lightly I felt as though he had blessed me. "Two," he said as he pressed harder. "Three." His mouth opened. "Four," he said without moving his lips away from mine. Five and six I counted to myself, and after that, silence gripped us. There was nothing but the tender and the hard, the tasting and probing, touching and pressing, as we thoroughly investigated the sublime nature of the kiss.

\/ \/ \/

We spent the next day, and the next after that, and even one more after that, in Grandmother Helene's parlor. There was no more talk of bazaars or shopping chores. Grandmother Helene merely came for us at ten each morning and delivered us back at Theatre Road every evening at six.

We never expressed our gratitude, but she knew that nothing she could have done for us would have pleased us more. As soon as we were alone, Edwin and I would fall upon each other like starving animals and devour each other with kisses. After an hour—maybe longer—we would be satiated enough to speak. Our words would tumble in an avalanche. We had to share every detail of our lives since we were last together. A broken perfume bottle, a funny story of a servant, a sight on the street, an unhappy thought alone in the night bubbled out until the well of individual experience was drained and our memories blended with the moment. Only then did we dare take refreshment, move about the room, and speak of more abstract ideas.

There were no secrets between us. One day I told him he must not touch me, and he was infuriated, thinking my feelings for him had altered. When I tried to explain about the time of the month, he grabbed me, plunged his tongue into my mouth, then said, "Now I have sinned. So what?"

"You don't mind?"

"Mind! Do you expect me to remain apart from you for half my life?"

"You don't like rules."

"Only the ones I invent." He gave me a lopsided grin. "You probably have never done anything naughty in your life."

I told him about the notes I had sent to Gabriel Judah in the tiffin-carriers. He told me about pranks he had played. Then he recounted his adventures in Singapore.

"Why did you leave?"

"Without any money of my own, I realized I would have to follow the orders of my dictatorial uncle the rest of his life. They only wanted an errand boy. How horrid it was to be an outsider in that tight clan! My cousins could do no wrong. They blamed everything that went awry on me. Is there anything worse than being an outcast in your own family, particularly when you have done nothing to deserve your treatment?"

"No, I agree with you." I explained how I had felt after my mother's death, how I had been treated by the Sassoons, and especially Aunt Bellore, and then how dreadful it had been when I returned from Darjeeling.

Soon it was apparent there was nothing we could not say to each other. After dozens of final kisses we parted reluctantly.

That evening, I confronted Silas' unanswered letters. Even though our parents had not set a wedding date, Edwin and I had promised ourselves to each other. I had to crumple three attempts before my announcement satisfied me.

7 November, 1891

Dear Silas,

I hope it will please you to learn that my parents have found a most suitable young man from Cochin, who has shown an interest in marrying me as soon as they can conclude arrangements. His name is Edwin Salem and fortunately bears no resemblance to Edwin Drood!

I have come to think of you as my spiritual brother, and as a brother I believe you would approve of Mr. Salem, who is well-educated and extremely kind. Even more important, he has spent the last week in Calcutta and we find our sensibilities mesh in uncanny ways. Sadly, though, I realize that it might prove difficult to convince a new husband of the unique regard we have held for each other through complicated times. Thus, I can see no option but to break off correspondence once my parents have settled my marriage plans. I hope you will agree to the necessity for this sad surgery.

I assure you that my good fortune pleases me and hope this will relieve you of any sense of responsibility on my behalf. Even if we never write or meet again, I shall think of you often and with fondness.

Your friend,
Dinah

At the end of the week Zilpah felt secure enough about our intentions to have the Salems join the family at the synagogue. From where I sat on the balcony, I could not see Edwin clearly until Aunt Rebecca leaned back. Even then all I could glimpse was his back gently swaying and sometimes his hand reaching back to smooth his hair. For the first time I resented not being able to worship with the men. For the first time I understood the reason for the separation, for who could keep one's mind on religious matters if one's beloved were by one's side?

Outside, Edwin joined his mother. There were a few pleasantries before they drove off.

"Aren't they coming home with us?" I asked Zilpah.

She steered me toward our carriage. "They have other plans for the afternoon."

"I have hardly spoken to Edwin today."

"The Sabbath is a day for rest and contemplation" was all Zilpah would say.

Sunday the Salems came for tiffin with the whole family. My brothers and sisters each had to have their time with Edwin, so I was consigned to sit with his mother and Zilpah. We hardly had a second alone together. By the end of the day I suffered a pounding headache that only his kisses could have relieved.

On Monday the plan was for Edwin and me to spend the morning with Grandmother Helene and then to arrive toward the finale of Zilpah's tea party to introduce his mother to the Sassoon women.

Throughout our private tiffin—Grandmother Helene had insisted she preferred taking hers in her room—Edwin had pouted. "Must we leave so early? I don't like being cheated out of two whole hours alone with you."

"Edwin, after our wedding, you will be clamoring for two hours *away* from me."

"Never!"

"Most men enjoy leaving the house. Many enjoy returning as well, but husbands and wives were never meant to be together day and night."

"That is nonsense. After the past two miserable days, I do not want to be apart from you ever again."

"What will we do each day? Spend it in bed?" I clapped my hand over my mouth. "I didn't mean *that*, I meant *sleeping*."

"I know exactly what you meant." He winked. "But, no, I want you to be at my side all the time. If you could assist your father, you could certainly assist me."

"With what?" I knew Edwin had something to do with the exportation of spices and his uncle had some connection to the Sassoons, but the financial side of this alliance had been obscured by the sheer force of our mutual attraction. The issue of the importance of my dowry had loomed large in relation to Silas. With Edwin it had seemed inconsequential—until that moment. Was Edwin expecting to live on the income from my capital? If we invested it properly, I supposed we could manage in Cochin. Even so, we could never approach the lavishness of Theatre Road or even maintain a modest establishment like Grandmother Helene's without a significant contribution on his part.

He did not respond, but stared off with a moody expression I found both infuriating and intoxicating. I kissed his cheek to bring him back. "I could help you with what?" I reminded him.

"With everything, with anything, what does it matter so long as we are together?" He gave me one long fervent kiss. "There is a much more serious issue that cannot wait."

As I studied his face, I could see the intense glimmer in his eye. Something was troubling him deeply. "What is it, Edwin?"

"I cannot tolerate this situation." His voice had a nasty edge.

"What is the matter?" My voice cracked.

He glanced around with the wild expression of a caged animal. "We must arrange for the wedding immediately."

"We only met each other one week ago yesterday."

He looked at his watch. "One hundred and ninety-four hours ago to be precise."

"Is that all it has been?"

"Yes. And I feel as though I have wasted every minute of my life until now, and I refuse to discard much more, following the insane rules of proper behavior." He had let go of me entirely and was striding about the room like a troubled toddler looking for walls to kick, toys to smash.

"What can we do about it?"

"We can marry, that's what we can do about it."

"I am certain our parents will make the arrangements."

"But when?" he shouted. "When?"

"Edwin!" I admonished him, with a gesture that someone might overhear us. "We can't wed with one day's notice."

His face darkened, and for a second I worried that he was directing his anger at me, but then he rushed to my side and held me around the waist. "Why shouldn't it be tomorrow? When you told me about your last wedding, you said you never wanted to go through that rigmarole again."

Placing my hands behind his slender neck, I looked into his flashing eyes, awestruck that this perfect man was so anxious to be joined to me. "No, I surely don't want any more big tamashas, torrential downpours, or dead doves . . ."

Edwin, who noticed every nuance, had heard a drop in my voice. "There is something else, isn't there?"

"I am not free to marry you until the twentieth of November."

"Why? The date of the month? You already know that does not matter to me."

"No. There is another reason. When I left Silas, Hakham Sholomo, the man who prepared the *get*, did not entirely trust our story. In case I might have conceived a child, he said the divorce would not be final for eleven months."

"That is ridiculous! What baby ever took eleven months?"

"I suppose he added in a safety margin," I said lightly.

Edwin was not amused. "Did he mean eleven months on the Jewish calendar or the European?"

"Would it make a difference?"

"If they go by the Jewish calendar, it might be sooner."

"Will our parents agree to rush into this?" I asked with a new wariness. Why was Edwin so anxious to seal the bargain? I wanted him with all my heart, but a few weeks did not matter.

"Why shouldn't they?" he said, shrugging his shoulders.

"Moving too quickly can hurt reputations, or so they tell me."

He threw back his head and laughed. "People hurry to get married when they have concerns about a baby. Nobody would think that was our problem when we have known each other little more than a week." He stroked my brow, then pressed my eyelids with kisses so exquisite I melted in his arms.

"Don't you want to marry quickly?" he asked with a warble in his voice that touched me deeply. He clasped the sleeves of my dress and crushed me to him.

"Edwin," I chided without pushing him away, "don't muss me. We'll have to greet my aunts soon."

"I shall place our case before them. I shall ask them to help me wed you tomorrow."

"Oh, please, not my aunts. Speak directly to Papa, but not to my aunts." I was so overcome with the idea of him confronting Aunt Bellore that I began to weep.

"Don't . . . I was joking . . . don't . . ." Caressing away my tears, Edwin became so engrossed he missed the opening of the door and Grandmother Helene's quiet entrance.

❦ ❦ ❦

Tension greeted our arrival at Theatre Road. Zilpah's face was set into her tightest mask. Mrs. Salem stood to greet Grandmother Helene and to thank her for once again chaperoning us. "You have been so kind to the children," she said stiffly.

"It has been my pleasure. If I am any judge, you have made a fine match. In fact, they are most anxious to do their duty," she added with a hint of gaiety.

As Mrs. Salem's expression soured, I felt that Grandmother Helene might have gone too far, but before I could ascertain the damage, Zilpah steered me away. "Let your aunts meet Edwin on their own for a few minutes."

"But—" Zilpah's grip tightened and I found myself in the servants' corridor, the place where I once had eavesdropped on conversations in the hall.

"Dinah, there is a small difficulty—"

"What do you mean?" I asked evenly, though my legs began to wobble.

"Mrs. Salem has been speaking with your Aunt Bellore, and—"

"No! Aunt Bellore would not try to ruin this for me!"

Zilpah was shaking her head, but I could not tell if it was in agreement or to mollify me. My eyes blurred. "All she did was listen to Edwin's mother's concerns about your marriage to Silas, about whether or not . . . well, you know what I mean."

I leaned against the wall and waited for Zilpah to tell me the worst.

"Earlier today I reminded Bellore there was no way any of us would ever know what went on between you and Silas, but you could not have remained with a man who could never love any woman. Then I asked her to assist us in arranging this marriage for you because you were becoming very attached to Mr. Salem."

"You should never have told her that. Now she will do something to make certain I cannot have him."

"That's unfair. She said she wanted to help us out in any way she could."

"And you believed her?"

"Now, Dinah, Bellore is not going to hurt you."

"How do you know?"

"Because she agreed with me. She said the way to put these rumors to rest once and for all—and at the same time to satisfy Mrs. Salem— would be to have you examined."

"What are you talking about?"

Zilpah looked away and whispered, "To have someone check to see if you are intact."

"Can they tell by looking?"

"Perhaps, or by feeling."

"Who would do this?"

"A doctor, I suppose."

"What if Mrs. Salem did not want to take the doctor's word? What if she thought the rich Sassoons bribed the doctor to lie for me?"

"I understand why you would not want to submit to this. Nobody will force you."

I was silent for several moments as my thoughts clarified. "Edwin and I would like to have a quiet ceremony here at the house."

"That could be arranged, if Mrs. Salem agrees to the match. I can see why you would not want to go back to the same synagogue where—"

"No, that is not what I meant. We want to get married right away."

"But, Dinah—"

I cut her off again. "I will not permit a doctor to check me. If I am to satisfy Mrs. Salem, she must do it herself. She may look to her heart's content, if I may marry her son before the next Sabbath begins."

"This week?" Zilpah asked, shocked. "How could we make the preparations that rapidly?"

"We do not want any fuss. We only want a mekkadesh, a ring, and a huppah."

She peered at me as though she were trying to diagnose my illness. "I do not know what Benu will say about this."

"Men like to get things over with as quickly as possible. Edwin wants the same. In fact, he's the one who cannot wait. You'll have to convince his mother, that's all."

"Dinah, aren't you afraid of the examination?"

"No. Not if it will settle the question."

"Aren't you concerned about what Edwin's mother might find?"

"You never believed me, did you?"

"Your descriptions about what happened were so . . . well, vague. When Silas tried . . . was there any bleeding?"

"No, Zilpah."

"No pain?"

"No, just a pressure on the outside."

"How do you know he never was inside, even for a few seconds?"

I shook my head. "I believe that nothing happened. And besides, no matter what Mrs. Salem finds, it will not make a whit of difference to her son."

"How can you know that? And even if you are right, what if she forbids the marriage? What then? Isn't it better for me to say that I refuse to put you through the embarrassment?"

"No. I shall take my chances, Zilpah. Besides, Edwin would defy his mother on this. I know he would."

"Your father would not give his permission if she withdrew hers."

"Then I would defy my father."

"Dinah!" She shook me so hard, pins fell from my hair. "You have lost your mind over this boy."

As from a faraway place, I could hear Grandmother Flora's voice telling me about Luna begging her to marry Benu. Now I knew how my mother had felt. Despite everything I had done to be different from her, I was walking in her shoes once again. I straightened my back and pulled away from Zilpah. "Tell Mrs. Salem I will do as she says whenever she wants, if Edwin and I may marry this week. Now I will go out and thank Aunt Bellore for her kind assistance and invite her to my wedding."

27

🌱 🌱 🌱

ate in the afternoon on Tuesday, the day after the tea party,
I waited for Esther Salem. Yali had bathed and perfumed me
like a maharani.

"Nobody is to tell Edwin about this," I had warned Zilpah.
"Surely his mother will mention it."

"You must instruct her she must not."

"This concerns him as much as his mother."

"No, he could not care less. Any man who feels for a woman as he
does about me would refuse to permit anyone to shame her. If he
learns what we are doing, he will forbid it."

"Then why not let him put an end to this? Your father and I are
reluctant, and—"

"I am the one who will have to live with Mrs. Salem. If I do not
satisfy her, the question will trail me like a foul wind."

Zilpah had seemed baffled by my argument, but she acceded and
arranged to have Edwin occupied with a visit to the Sassoon offices
while Mrs. Salem visited Theatre Road.

As I waited, I lay back on my bed and tried to concentrate on a book
Silas had recommended, Zola's *Nana*. I don't know whether it was the
significance of the moment or the book itself, but I found the story
distasteful and never finished it.

There was a knock on the door.

Zilpah came into my room first. "Are you ready?"

I placed my book on the bedside table.

"Do you want me to stay?"

When I shook my head, Zilpah waved Yali in. I signaled for the ayah
to go.

"But, Dinah-baba—"

I pointed firmly for her to leave.

Mrs. Salem came into the room and stood by the door. For a long

305

moment Zilpah hovered behind her; then, after one lingering glance, she closed the door softly. The click of the latch resounded in the room.

This was not an act of submission. The contrary was true. My insistence to have the question settled was one of the most aggressive acts of my life. Edwin and I both wanted to marry at once—not that a week or two would have mattered—but it was our way of wresting control over our fate from the adults who until that moment had juggled our lives like crafty carnival performers.

Anger is the leash that keeps other emotions, like fear and shame, in check. Anger braced my spine. Anger hardened my expression into a stolid grimace. And anger bred a freshly wrought sense about how to conduct this rite that transcended any experiential knowledge that I might have had.

Tentatively Mrs. Salem approached the foot of my bed. I stretched my legs out under my dressing gown and folded my arms across my chest. Let her decide what to do next, I thought, and said nothing.

For a long time she fixed her eyes above me. The more she fidgeted, the more superior I felt. Then, as if she had found a reserve well of resolve, she gazed at me shrewdly. "Let us get this over with, shall we?"

I drew my legs up to my chest.

"Yes, that's better. Why don't you hold your knees and spread your legs?" Her hand was on my thigh, gently insisting I follow its lead. "Take off your undergarments."

I already had, so I said nothing.

"Well?" The question came as a whine.

"I did that before you arrived."

She waited a beat and lowered her head. "There's not much light. Turn toward the windows," she ordered.

With an awkward twist of my buttocks I shifted to my right. Edwin's mother stood up and walked around to that side of the bed. A hot ray of sun beamed across my mound. I pretended I was a stone temple goddess carved on a frieze: unfeeling, impenetrable.

"My aunt was a midwife," she said to put me at ease while she stared between my parted thighs. "Nothing can be seen on the outside, as you must know." Her voice was that of a strident teacher. Anger checked my instinctive reflex to kick her away. Anger helped me to keep my eyes open and my mouth closed while she reached out with her left hand and peeled me like an unripe mango.

How thankful I was that Edwin did not know what was happening! Tears stung my eyes. Mustn't think of him, not now. Her other hand pressed in a way that made my stomach churn. Oh, Edwin, it will be worth it if we have our way. The price is small compared with what will happen in a few days. Then you will be the only one to do this to me for as long as I live. Another queer, slippery poke and then a firm hand pressed my knees together. I glanced up. She tucked one hand behind her back. With the other she smoothed her dress. Her face had blanched, and with the sun illuminating her from the back, she looked like the bright center of a flame.

I fumbled with my gown, trying to tie it while prone, then inched to the bedside and dangled my legs.

She backed away from me. "I don't know . . ."

Every restraint broke loose. I leapt up and toward her, shouting, "You are lying!"

She held out an arm stiffly to keep me from grabbing her. "No, that is not what I meant."

I fell back on my bed with a thud. She took one step in my direction and stood there, one foot in front of the other so she could retreat with an economy of movement.

I gasped. Something was wrong with my throat.

"I don't know what should be there or should not be there." She turned away from me. "It is more complicated than I had imagined," she whispered. "The other women I had seen were having babies . . . I should have asked someone else, someone with more experience, like a *mashti*."

"Nobody else." My voice broke into fragments. "Please."

Her bosom heaved. "That won't be necessary. I should not have insisted. If your own aunt had not suggested this would be the only way . . ." She looked straight ahead. "From your willingness to submit, I should have known you were telling the truth, but I am a mother and . . ." She faced me slightly. "When you become a mother, you may do things to protect your children that you find distasteful."

I barely listened to her confession. My mind raced on. "We will marry this week." I tried to catch her eye. "That was the—"

"Yes, well . . . I always planned to have the ceremony in Cochin."

"Have you discussed this with Edwin?"

"Of course. My other children were married there, and he promised he would also be married in our synagogue in the traditional Cochini way."

"Have you talked with him this week?"

"Not about the wedding, and certainly not about this." She looked at her hand, obviously wanting to wash it off. "That was what you wanted, wasn't it?"

"All Edwin and I want is to wed this week, whether in Calcutta or Cochin or China!"

"We could leave for the west in a few days . . . you could marry a week or so after we return." Her eyes darted like a trapped animal's. "I don't see why you must rush." When I did not reply, her hands twisted in her lap. With wonderful clarity I realized she was floundering.

"Friday morning would be best."

She stood up and looked at the door as if it would open by desire alone. "If your father agrees, I will not stand in your way," she said, and left me alone. I fell back onto my pillows, wondering: How will I ever be able to live under this woman's domination?

❦   ❦   ❦

Bliss is winning. Winning brought an exhilaration I had never felt before, because I had never won before. That evening my father brought Edwin home with him. Both were beaming.

Without asking permission, we left our parents and went out onto the terrace. When we rounded the corner, Edwin clasped my hand and gave me a flurry of moist kisses that could have been considered discreet only by their placement below the elbow.

"Well, what did he say?"

"What did your admirable, generous, adorable father have to say?"

"My father may be generous and admirable, but adorable?"

"Don't you suppose Zilpah thinks of him that way?"

"Edwin!" I tugged my hand away.

"He said yes, so nothing else is of any consequence."

"Yes to what?"

"Yes to everything. Yes to our marriage, yes to making the arrangements regarding your *get*, yes to doing it as soon as you and the family can organize everything."

"Did he discuss my dowry?"

"That is supposed to be between him and my mother, but the subject was mentioned. In fact, I referred to it first." Edwin stroked his hair back, something I now realized he did more frequently when he was anxious. "I told him that I did not care what your settlement might be, because now that I had come to know you, I would take you if you had not a single rupee to your name."

"What did he say to that?"

"At first he was silent; then he showed true insight. He said: 'Many a young man would say that to a prospective father-in-law to impress him with his sincerity. Unfortunately, you are following in the footsteps of another fellow who courted my daughter and who made similar protestations to me. The tragedy is that I might have understood had he been a rotter after only her fortune, but his motive was more obscure and in the long run potentially more damaging.' Well, what could I respond to that?"

"I suppose you could have called his bluff . . ."

"How alike we are!"

"You didn't?"

"I did."

"What did he do?"

"He was flustered at first; then he asked how I would support you. I explained that we could live in my mother's house and that my family's trading business had potential. My Singapore cousins will buy directly from me. Merchandise that I acquire from China as well as India should interest them. Also, in the Kerala region we grow splendid sandalwood trees, and sandalwood is one of the few commodities, besides opium, that the Chinese import from India. I asked for his assistance in developing my network, as a businessman, not as a father-in-law."

"Do you want to sell opium?" I asked warily.

"Not especially. Why?"

Flooded with relief, I couldn't reply for a moment. "I just wondered. What else did he say?"

"He said that he was a man of his word and that he could not permit one of his daughters to leave home without a settlement to ensure her comforts, now and in the future."

"I see why you both are so cheerful tonight."

"No, you know why he is. I am able to smile only because once again I bask in the glow of my beloved."

I made a sour face. "A poet you are not."

"That may be, but you have not told me about your day. You must account for every second since we have been apart, or have you forgotten rule number twenty-two?"

I looked around as I attempted to cover the interlude with his mother and saw my four brothers coming across the lawn toward us.

Edwin's arm, hugging my waist, did not fall at their approach.

"Hello, Edwin," Asher called.

He waved at him.

"My day was much quieter," I said under my breath. "All I did was arrange our wedding date with your mother."

"Your father said we would settle that this evening."

"I have settled it already."

Pinhas and Asher overheard the last sentence. "What is settled?" Asher asked.

"These two think that between them they can conquer the problems of the world," Pinhas teased.

"Only one," I replied. "The only one that matters."

With a fierce tug Edwin drew me closer to him. "When?"

"Friday morning."

His hands shot into the air to pull back his hair. "You are joking!"

"What is happening on Friday?" Jonah asked.

"We are getting married," I announced as I hugged him and Edwin both.

"That's the day after tomorrow," Asher said in the squeaky range of his changing voice.

"How did you . . . ?" Edwin gasped. "My mother wanted us to have the wedding in Cochin. She never would have agreed—"

"We had a nice chat and I convinced her this is what would make you the happiest. A good mother wants her child to be happy, doesn't she?"

"What a darling you are!" Edwin said, kissing me on the mouth in front of the boys and whoever else might have been looking.

☘ ☘ ☘

Negotiations form the core of human commerce, whether the currency is money or trade goods or time or love. Over the years I have found that major setbacks come from minor points that have their roots in the pride of people who wield power for the sake of power itself. Even marriage, which should be a refuge from the tussles of the larger world, is often a miniature battleground where sides are taken and wars are waged. Looking back at that evening, I see that even without a plan, Edwin and I—I in the bedroom and Edwin in the boardroom—had prepared our troops for the treaty session that took place that night. Disarmed by the affection Edwin and I were demonstrating for each other, our parents capitulated to each other like a domino train.

"Nobody gets married in the morning," Zilpah began.

"Well, we can't very well be married Friday evening," I said smugly.

"Can't you wait a few days longer?" she added weakly.

"No." I smiled and waited.

"I suppose I have no objection to Friday," Zilpah began, "so long as we keep the celebration simple."

"Only the Sassoons and the Salems," Papa said.

"And Grandmother Helene," I added.

"Of course," Zilpah replied, "that goes without saying."

"Do we have to invite Aunt Bellore?" I asked.

"How could we not?" Zilpah countered severely, then gave a rueful chuckle. "Besides, don't I recall that she was the first one you wanted to ask?"

I backed down.

"When do you want to leave for Cochin?" my father asked Mrs. Salem.

"As soon as possible."

"Last time we permitted Dinah to leave directly after the wedding, but I now regret that decision," Zilpah said with a pointed look in her husband's direction.

"Absolutely," he replied to gain a second to gather his thoughts. "We must have the seven nights for feasting and the sheva berakoth prayers observed here. They may leave anytime after that."

Esther Salem glanced at her son, but his eyes were locked with mine. "Whatever you wish," she said in a silky voice. "Perhaps when we return to Cochin, the children will indulge me by having a ceremony at our synagogue according to our customs. They are quite ancient and beautiful."

"I would marry Edwin a dozen times," I said to the collective sigh of the three adults in the room.

"I will arrange for a hazzan tomorrow," Papa offered.

"Could we have a huppah in the rose garden?"

"Yes," Zilpah cooed. "A lovely idea."

"And some wine and cake afterward."

"There isn't time to prepare much more than that," Zilpah agreed. "Will that satisfy you, Edwin?"

Everyone looked to Edwin. "I believe a marriage is a contract, and as such it should be serious, not frivolous." He turned to face me on the settee, where we had been sitting side by side holding hands. "Please, could you wear that green suit you had on when I first saw you sitting on the veranda?"

"That is hardly what a bride would wear," his mother hissed at him.

He squeezed my hand and I knew what he was thinking. Rule number nineteen: all traditions began the day we met.

"There won't be time to have a new dress made," I answered calmly.

Zilpah smiled tightly. "Dinah, there are several lovely new—"

"I shall wear the green outfit."

My father stood and stretched. "What else is there to discuss?"

Edwin rose to his feet, pulling me up beside him. "Only that I will always be grateful to you for giving me your daughter."

Papa took a step toward us. "If you can say the same ten years from now, I will be content."

Edwin rearranged his hair. His mother, who had been at Theatre Road since her appointment with me earlier, seemed relieved she could finally retire. The five of us walked to the portico, the parents striding ahead, Edwin and I touching each other in the shadowy background.

"I'll see you in the morning," he said as he helped his mother into the cab of the carriage.

"No, Edwin, you will see a tailor in the morning," his mother called over her shoulder.

"Until tiffin, then," he said, waving as the carriage pulled away.

We followed my father into the house. At the bottom of the staircase he shook his head, and I hastily asked, "You do like him, don't you, Papa?"

"I am not the one who must like him."

"But you do, I can tell."

"A *pukka* chap. A very clever boy, I'll tell you that. First class, if he is what he seems," he said, starting to climb the stairs.

I followed right behind and called up, "You don't trust him, do you?"

"Experience kills trust, Dinah," he said as he reached the landing. "To be practical, we have little information about the boy or his family. I do not know what he told you about his prospects, but he has no capital. Only the goodwill of some kindly relations has protected him thus far, and the uncle who has introduced him to us does not have the most savory reputation. If there was an honorable way for me to protect your dowry, I would. As it stands now, he will control your fortune after the wedding."

I gripped the banister. "You think that is why he is in such a hurry."

"I did not say that, Dinah, but it is a possibility, one of many."

"You are the one who selected him."

"I invited him to visit, that is true, but the two of you have usurped my authority on the matter."

"You are wrong about him, Papa."

"I have no reason not to trust him and no reason to trust him, but it is to your credit you have embraced this union with such confidence." My father kissed me on the cheek and retired to his dressing room.

Zilpah, who had been standing behind me the whole time, accompanied me to my room. "Good night, Dinah."

"Good night, Zilpah, and thank you."

She shook her head. "No, I did nothing. You did a good day's work. I am proud of you."

"Do you think she will tell Edwin?"

"No, she could barely look me in the eye throughout the evening. She felt more shame than you did."

"At least it is over." I put my hand on the doorknob. "A small price to pay for Edwin."

"He is a good man. Even your father is convinced."

"He did not sound convinced to me."

She patted my shoulder. "If he had grave doubts, he would never have given his permission."

Yali came up behind us and handed me a package.

"Thank you, Yali," Zilpah said. "I almost forgot. This came for you this afternoon. It is from Silas."

I turned it in my hand. "Probably another book."

"Dinah, don't you think—?"

"I already wrote him last week and told him about Edwin and that I would never write again. He may have sent this before he received my letter, or this could be his response."

Zilpah sighed. "I should have known you did not require my advice any longer, but sometimes I forget you are not the same person you were when I came to this house."

After closing the door to my room, I placed the package on the Clive desk. I was so weary I allowed Yali to put me to bed. I closed my eyes, but the moonlight that fell through the shutter bothered me. Groaning, I got up to reposition the slats. As I walked past the desk, the package caught my eye. Curious, I decided to open it. The book had been wrapped in a second binding of silver foil and embossed with an intricate rangoli design. Taking care to keep the exquisite covering intact, I slipped out the volume. Because Silas often tucked his letters inside a book, I held it upside down and shook. Nothing fell out. I opened the flyleaf and, holding it up to the moonlight, looked for an inscription. There was none. I turned to the title page. In the pale shaft of light, the letters of the title glinted like tiny iridescent flies. Silas had sent me his copy of the *Kama Sutra*.

28

♦ ♦ ♦

Everyone could see that Edwin and I were linked in mind and spirit long before the culmination of the marriage ritual. The scene under the huppah hastily draped in jasmine and hibiscus is a blur I can barely recall. Surrounded by family, with my brothers and my sisters by my side, I saw no one else but Edwin. I sipped the wine and repeated the words when required, but any knowledge of those events has been superimposed by one lasting memory: Edwin's eyes riveted to mine.

After the breaking of the cup and the rounds of kilililees, he clasped his arm about my waist and never, never let go. Everybody talked about us. "So happy! Have you ever seen a bride and groom as jubilant?" they murmured as we passed, beaming.

Aunt Bellore pushed forward and gushed her congratulations. "I have never known a bride to appear so content," she said to us both. "At least not since Luna married Benu," she added in a tone that would have anyone, even Edwin, believe that she was praising us. Only I knew she meant her words as barbs to break the perfect bubble that until that moment had surrounded us.

Sensing my mood had changed, Edwin steered me away from the guests. "Dinah, my darling, what is wrong?"

"Nothing." I shuddered. "Just chilly."

"You must tell me. Rule number fifteen: there will be no secrets between us."

"I hate her!" I seethed.

"But why?"

"Didn't you hear what she said about my father and mother?"

"I thought she was complimenting us." His eyelids drooped with concern. "You told me your parents were a love match."

"Yes, but . . ." I could not go on. Silently I mulled over my turbulent thoughts. My mother had adored my father. Together they had pro-

314

duced three children they both had cherished. What had gone wrong between them? I could not recall any angry words ever expressed. The practical problems inherent in my father's long absences and my mother's overreliance on her friends had brought her into contact with other men. Now I had come to know the enormous power of a physical attraction. With my father away, with the privacy of her own house, with nobody watching over her, she had succumbed to her instincts. The evil force had been Nissim Sadka, not my mother.

And what of my father's love for her? Had it ever diminished? I thought not. Whenever he returned, the relationship had flourished. And what of my father's fury when he came home after her death? What of the burning of her possessions? What of his refusal to mention her again? Were those the actions of a man who did not love his wife? No, they had been the violent responses of a man whose lover had been taken from him cruelly. I gripped Edwin more tightly. What if anything happened to him? How would I go on? Could I take even one more breath without him?

Finally I spoke. "Aunt Bellore thinks happiness is an illusion that cannot last."

Edwin stared as my aunt's bustle moved across the garden like a load on the back of a bullock-cart. "Vinegar comes from spoilt wine. Unhappy people try to inflict their sorrows on others in the hope they will experience some relief. In fact, all that ever happens is they sour further."

"Why do you think she is unhappy?"

"From the first time I saw her, I thought her one of the most pathetic women I had ever met."

"But she has so much."

"She has nothing compared to us, for she has never in her life felt as you and I do this day."

A surge of feeling so intense and so physical that I thought I could no longer stand upright coursed from my toes to my neck. I leaned against him. He gathered me around and pressed me to him. In front of everybody he kissed me on the forehead. The assembled guests began to clap and shout and fill the air with kililees that were carried on the wind halfway across Bengal.

Sabbath prayers were said at the long tables set up in the hall as the Sassoon clan, along with Edwin and Esther Salem, sat down for the meal. After the final blessings, the guests left early. And then, at long last, Grandmother Helene and Zilpah put us to bed in the study downstairs.

When the door closed behind us, Edwin and I stood facing each other, standing farther apart than we had been since before he had slipped the golden ring on my finger. Walking over to an arrangement of blossoms in a Chinese urn, he plucked out a vermilion rose and handed it to me. A few loose petals that had burst open in the heat of the closed room fluttered to the floor. He untied the white velvet ribbon around the urn and pressed the nap to his cheek. "This is you," he said obliquely. He pointed to a matching vase opposite, filled with white roses and decorated with a red ribbon. "Give me a flower and untie that ribbon for me."

After finding him a tighter rose, I fumbled with the knot and gave the ribbon over to him as well. He held up both ends in his hands. "Like these ribbons, our lives have been a straight line since birth"—he tied one end of the red to the white—"until now." He flicked the far ends. "But look, two free ends, each flapping away with the belief they can go their own way." He handed me the white end and held on to the red himself. Then he gave a tug and my end flew toward him. "See! I caught you unawares, so you yielded to me. Another time I could fall in your direction. However, is this how we wish to live? Will the constant strain on the knot tighten it or break it?"

"Tighten it."

He gripped the knot. "Indeed, it is firmer for the moment, but perhaps the fabric will weaken, then rip when we least expect it."

"Edwin!" I laughed at his solemn expression. "What in the world are you talking about?"

"Wait. Let me show you something wonderful." He wrapped the ribbons around his hand. "Watch what happens next. I could take the obvious approach by tying the loose ends together into a circle, a symbol, like the wedding ring, of the symmetry of marriage. But, with a simple twist we become unified within the curve of time." He rotated the ribbon, then knotted the ends together. "Now find the end." He placed my fingers on top and showed me that no matter how long I traced the track, it went on and on and on. "Now do you understand?"

"Yes, Edwin."

"Do you understand that I have suffered during my life and in my previous lives for this moment of perfection? The ends are tied, first by the vows that joined our minds and second by the act that joins our bodies. From this moment on, you and I are united in perpetual rapture." His mouth pressed mine while his hands moved across my body with an insistence I had never felt before.

"Nobody lives in ecstasy forever."

"Why not? You know about Buddhism and the Noble Truths," he said, finding the hooks at my waist. "Suffering may be universal, but it can be prevented and overcome. For as every drop in the ocean has the taste of salt, so does every word carry the flavor of Nirvana."

My skirt landed among the petals and flowers on the floor. Then

Edwin calmly undressed as well. We let our hands drop from each other long enough to facilitate removing our own undergarments. Edwin's muscular body shone in the light from the candles. I felt no shame as he cupped my breasts, then slid his hands across my hips and down my abdomen. I felt sorry for a bride who was fearful at this most exquisite of moments, and had a fleeting thought of gratitude for having been with Silas long enough to know what a man was like.

"Oh, Dinah, my most beautiful Dinah." He placed the twisted ribbons over our heads. The circle or curve of time—or whatever—bound us at the shoulders. He pressed his loins against me and eased me toward the bed. "Now I will prove to you that we can live in ecstasy forever, or I will die in the attempt."

❀ ❀ ❀

Salt . . . salt in the sea and in tears and in the taste of Edwin's flesh. Salt . . . as in the waves that crashed over me the second time we coupled, this time with me pressing down on him and Edwin sucking my nipples hungrily while kneading my buttocks and pressing up into me with a thrilling, gentle probing that was quite different from the insistent plunging an hour earlier.

And then again, side by side but still as joined as the endless ribbon, we rocked back and forth and gave each other little nibbles and bites until the flurry of spasmodic bursts surprised us both. Perhaps we slept a few hours or perhaps the next hours only felt like a dream as we touched and licked and kissed and found new ways to elicit the same terrific trick of galloping pleasure.

Sunlight crept under the shutters. Blinking, I opened my eyes to see how we looked with my legs placed over Edwin's shoulders. His eyes were bolted closed. His fine jaw was set as he concentrated on his task. Distracted by how beautiful he looked, I watched with fascination as his hair draped across his face.

He kissed me and murmured, "I am not hurting you, am I?"

"No, no . . ." I lied a little, for I was becoming sore.

He collapsed on me. "Well, then you have outlasted me."

I stroked his hot, moist back. "I wouldn't mind a rest."

"We don't have to master every chapter the first day."

"What do you mean?"

"You know, the 'twining position,' the 'mare's position,' and what you just attempted, 'the rising position.' "

"Edwin!" I pummeled his buttocks and rolled him off me. "What are you talking about?"

He turned on his side and ran his fingers through my hair, spreading it like a fan on the pillow. "Do you think you are the only one who has ever read the *Kama Sutra*?"

I turned away from him.

"How lovely and pink you are!" He traced his finger along the lacy pattern on my chest as I attempted to hide my face under a pillow.

There was a knock on the door. "Yes?" he called gaily.

"Chota hazri, sahib," Abdul said softly. "I shall leave it outside."

Edwin pressed his ear to the door, and when he heard the steps retreat, opened it.

"Edwin!" I chided, for he had brazenly stepped out naked.

"Hungry?" He placed the tray on the table.

"Hungrier than I have ever been in my life!"

He poured the tea and smothered marmalade onto my toast. "That's good. You must gather your strength for what I have planned for today."

❧ ❧ ❧

"Where are we going?" I asked Edwin as we dressed each other before joining my parents and his mother in the dining room.

"I won't tell you even if you torture me."

"I wouldn't know how to torture you."

"Oh, yes, you have the ultimate power over me. Even one rejected kiss would be like a whiplash," he said as he finished buttoning the back of my blouse.

"I could not refuse you even one kiss, so I suppose I shall never know."

Side by side we ate at one end of the table. Deliberately we ignored the questioning glances of our parents. Benu worked hard to keep Esther Salem's interest in his conversation, while Zilpah concentrated on the other children. Fortunately, Abdul announced that our carriage had arrived before we had to join in any small talk.

"Are you going to the synagogue today?" my father asked.

I looked at Edwin for a response, but he gave an enigmatic smile.

Zilpah shot Benu a withering glance. "I'm sure the children would prefer to be alone," she said, and told everyone not to bother to see us out.

The high step up to the carriage caused me to wince, but fortunately, Edwin did not notice.

"Where are we going?"

"You will see soon enough."

"Anything will be better than having the entire community observe us. Besides, I could not bear the thought of you having to sit so far away from me today."

"I know." He kissed my neck, and a flash of pleasure shot through me like an arrow.

The day was cool and dry and sunny, the most favorable possibility in Calcutta's stifling repertoire. The mansions that gave the City of Palaces its name gleamed in their fresh white coats of *chunam*, or lime, that erased the creeping green damp deposited after the monsoon. The boulevards were dry and sweet-smelling. The street sellers walked with a bounce in their step. The lawns of the Maidan stretched like an enormous green felt with strollers, sportsmen, and military marchers looking like pieces played out on an enormous game table.

The carriage turned to follow the banks of the Hooghly. Just past the walls of Fort William, a forest of masts came into sight. The flags of many countries rippled in the breeze like a flock of mismatched butterflies. There were Chinese ships with an eye painted on either side, clumsy country boats heaped with jute bales, and huge ironclad freighters with gaping holds devouring lines of freight-carrying coolies.

"Here we are," Edwin said mischievously as we drew up to a budgerow wharf, where several barges were tied in a row. "Four o'clock," he said to the syce, then took my hand.

We stepped over two barges to the one farthest from land. A turbaned man stripped to the waist bowed to us with his hands pressed together. "I bid you welcome, sahib, memsahib."

I stood on the creaking deck, looking around with astonishment as two sailors cast off their lines and, wielding their huge oars, pushed us out into the current.

"Come see." Edwin motioned toward the cabin that covered the back third of the boat. He pushed aside a curtain to reveal a large room surrounded by Venetian windows. Inside, silk carpets covered with huge pillows lined the room's perimeter. Bowls of fruit and flowers filled small tables nailed fast to the floor. Several large tiffin-carriers were set on hot braziers. Aromatic scents of cardamom and turmeric and clove mingled with the ripeness of the muddy ghat.

I reopened the curtain that served as the door and watched as the oarsmen's movements in unison with the flow of the river propelled us swiftly downstream. "Where are we going?"

Edwin gathered me to him. "To the end of the world."

I looked at the curtain flapping in the breeze. "But the men—"

"Don't worry about them. They face backward, and I warned them that if they turned around, even for a second, I would not pay them. Besides, lying down, nobody can see in."

In the wake of a steamer, the barge lurched, causing me to fall back onto a mound of cushions. In a split second Edwin was attempting to unfasten the tight buttons at my collar. "Bloody hell," he growled when he could not undo even one.

"Your fingers are too thick."

"Your clothes are impossible. I shall force you to wear saris from now on."

"The Indians are much smarter than we are about many things," I said as I hurriedly removed the blouse.

"Like the *Kama Sutra* perhaps?" He winked. "Now, where did we leave off?"

How swiftly he found his mark and how easily I found the rhythm! Now I understood everything: why men and women were kept separated, why young girls were married off, why parents did not trust their children, why chaperons were necessary. I marveled that a few vows had released me from the shackles that bound an unmarried girl and permitted me to embrace a sparkling world of pleasure. Was there ever anything so arousing as flesh pressing flesh? Dry flesh, moist flesh . . . my soft inner thighs next to his downy flank, his taut belly grinding against my softer one, his rippling shoulders and the long cords of his neck arching above me, his dazzling high brow, his warm mouth smiling, kissing, probing me in places I had never imagined I would find stimulating, let alone rapturous.

Later, we remained joined, with legs entwined like Hindu icons, and fed each other cool slices of fruit. We might have paused, but then a huge hull passed by. As the barge rocked in its turbulent wake, our satisfaction intensified and we made love once again.

At last we uncoupled. Edwin propped himself up on his elbow and peered out the window. "We are heading back to the dock."

"Already?"

"It must be close to four. Anyway, it is not too soon for me."

"Are you tired of me already?"

"I would need medical attention if we went on for another hour."

"Me too," I admitted shyly.

"Do you want to come back here tomorrow?"

"Can we?"

"I have hired the boat for the week."

"Maybe we should rest at home for a day," I said seriously.

As Edwin frowned, I suddenly had a flash. Before my marriage to Silas, Grandmother Helene had given me some salves that might help us in our current predicament.

"No, let us return tomorrow. And this time I will have a surprise for you."

PART III

❧ ❧ ❧

The Sowing

In the beginning the Lord of Beings (Brahma) created men and women, and in the form of commandments in one hundred thousand chapters laid down rules for regulating their existence . . .
—*The Kama Sutra* of Vatsyayana

29

❦ ❦ ❦

Cochin and Travancore, 1891–1892

At every platform, from Calcutta to Cochin, the dramas of farewells were reenacted for the audience of passengers inside the steamy train, who had taken part in a similar tableau and now watched with wearisome detachment as others took leave of their loved ones.

"You can tell a person's caste and religion from the manner in which he says good-bye," Edwin told me in Kharagpur, the first stop en route to Madras.

We were looking down from our private salon, a luxurious and unexpected gift from my father. Usually leased to foreign potentates or to carry the wives of maharajahs, our private car had a large sitting and dining room, two bedrooms, a bath with a gilded tub; and at either end of the car, berths for servants.

"What do you mean?" I asked Edwin, wondering if he was like Silas in his desire to fill me with the knowledge he had accumulated about where we were and where we were going.

"Europeans pump hands, like those chaps over there." He came over from his armchair to the sofa where I was sitting and pointed to an army officer and a gentleman in a white suit. A steam valve hissed and a momentary fog blanketed them. "Those must be Muslims, for they always embrace bosom to bosom," he said, indicating an animated group at the far end of the platform.

"What about those two kissing?" I tapped the glass so he could see two women, probably mother and daughter.

"Hindus would never kiss in public, so they must be Anglo-Indians." His last words were muffled by a whistle. The farewells, called out in a plaintive gabble of Hindustani, Tamil, and Telugu, became more frantic.

323

"What do the Hindus do?"

Edwin pressed his hands together perpendicular to his chest and bowed. "The *namaste*, what else?"

"Who cries?" I asked, recalling the many tears my six brothers and sisters, Zilpah, Grandmother Helene, and my father had shed at Howrah Station.

"Everyone cries the world over. No matter what caste, color, or race, humanity is the same at the core."

Until that moment I myself had remained dry-eyed. Did that mean I was less humane than most, or did Edwin offer insulation from loss? Was I so content to be in his arms that I could shed my attachments like a snake slithering from its skin without looking backward? I clasped Edwin's hand and massaged his fine hairs with a deep circular movement. Next to his pink skin my hand seemed dark. I marveled at our differences, loving each one of his.

Bowlegged Hanif came into the room carrying a basket of fruit he had purchased on the platform. Esther Salem lifted a piece, sniffed it warily. "I suppose it will do."

After he took them to the pantry, Edwin grinned. "What do think the chances are of Hanif getting together with Yali?"

Since Edwin had no servants of his own, my father had arranged for Abdul's son to accompany us to Cochin. And Papa had asked Yali to remain with me. "Last time I sent you off to Darjeeling without anyone to look after you. I will not make the same mistake twice," he had said crisply. Even though I knew Yali could not have helped my problems with Silas, I was comforted to have her by my side.

I understood what Edwin meant. He wanted the romance that bound us to infect the whole world. He had decided that Yali and Hanif could do nothing else but fall in love because they spent so much time in our proximity.

"Be sensible, Edwin. Yali is Hindu, Hanif is Muslim."

"I will be pleased if they don't squabble all the time," his mother interjected.

Edwin ignored her. "I refuse to be sensible, at least not until our honeymoon is over."

"When does a honeymoon end?"

"When the children start arriving," Esther Salem replied.

Edwin and I chuckled together. His mother had said: "Pretend I am not here," but she was always interjecting comments into our conversations. Sometimes I felt she was waiting for me to loosen my guard and reveal something that would prove my perfidy. Remnants of suspicion, like sinews caught between the teeth, remained to be probed, but I determined to foil her at every turn. As the train lurched forward, we could see the outstretched arms and the yawning O's of the final cries of a few miserable wretches for whom the farewells had not been sufficient.

"How are you feeling?" Edwin whispered.

"Better," I said with alacrity. The grind of metal on metal of the accelerating train made it harder for his mother to overhear us. "I hope I can tolerate it."

"What? The train trip?"

"No, following Dr. Hyam's prescription."

"Me too. All I have to do is look at you and—"

I hushed him with my hand when I saw his mother turn in our direction. As he kissed my palm, I wriggled away from him and crossed my legs primly.

"You winced."

"Did not."

He patted my thigh. "Maybe we should hold off altogether for a few days."

"Are you looking for an excuse?"

"Remember what the doctor said."

I blushed at the thought. Dr. Hyam and his wife had been invited to one of the last sheva berakoth dinners. When I greeted him on the terrace, he said, "Your grandparents would have been pleased with your young man."

I beamed at this pronouncement. Then, because nobody else was nearby and there was no one else I could confide in, I asked, "Is it usual for a girl to have some difficulties?" His kind hooded eyes closed momentarily. I realized he must have been thinking that another problem, perhaps one similar to what had occurred with Silas, was distressing me.

"I would rather discuss this in my consulting room tomorrow," he said, relieving me of an explanation when so many ears were nearby.

He was surprised when Edwin and I both arrived, and even more astonished that Edwin followed me into the consultation room.

"Now, Dinah, you had something you wished to ask me about—in private."

As he waited for Edwin to excuse himself, Edwin cleared his throat. "Dinah and I are worried," he began shakily, before his voice firmed. "You see, by the third time, we find it difficult to ignore the pain." He bowed his head.

"The third time since the wedding?" Dr. Hyam asked.

"No, the third time each morning," Edwin replied, smoothing his hair.

"Each morning?" Dr. Hyam echoed. "And what do you do when the pain persists?"

"Sometimes we cannot begin again until the evening," I filled in with a whisper.

"You do not have to force a lifetime of love into the first week."

"I suppose we will need to build up stamina," Edwin replied stiffly.

"Any difficulty urinating?" Dr. Hyam asked him.

"Some burning, actually."

"And you?" Dr. Hyam looked at me. I nodded. "Any embarrassment when you cough or sneeze?" I nodded again. The doctor stroked his beard. "I really should examine each of you, but your symptoms are typical. All I can say is I am glad you came to me now, or you would have had a most unpleasant journey." Shaking his head, he went to the next room, where he kept his medicines.

A few minutes later he handed me a tin of powder and instructed me how to mix the solution. "Dinah, you are to take this three times a day; Edwin, you are to take it morning and evening. Continue until the symptoms have been absent for three days in a row. At the first sign of recurrence, begin taking it again." Then he gave us several salves. "Avoid spicy foods, peppers, curries, and the like. Have fruit as often as possible, and juice with meals. At least ten glasses of liquid a day." He grinned at us both before pursing his lips and adopting a serious tone. "Most important is to give those delicate tissues a rest before you do permanent injury."

Edwin blanched. "I did not know . . ." His chin dropped and he looked at me apologetically.

"Now, then, don't worry. You have not harmed each other yet, but from now on"—Dr. Hyam waved his arms as if he were conducting a symphony—"*andante sostenuto*, slowly, yet sustained."

Edwin shrugged in my direction.

Dr. Hyam explained, "Once a day, until you are both completely healed. And . . ." He hesitated, then decided to speak forthrightly. "For the duration, remain in positions in which the husband and wife face each other. Do you understand me?" He looked at Edwin, who nodded that he did. "The female bladder is under too much strain if the man approaches the woman from behind. If either one worsens—and you must be honest with each other in the matter—you must refrain for at least three days. After that . . ." He threw up his hands. Seeing Edwin's rapt expression, he realized he had to be specific. "Twice a day—and by that I mean once in the morning and once in the evening—is the pace I recommend. Many happily married men and women find satisfaction with only a few such occasions each week."

When we were alone in the carriage, Edwin asked me if I believed the doctor.

"I suppose we should follow his advice."

"About everything?"

"Until we are healed."

"But not that nonsense about once or twice a week."

"Of course not!" I protested, unable to imagine such a drought.

A few miles out of the station, Hanif served the slices of melon the doctor had ordered. Side by side on the sofa, we sucked on the sweet fruit, sipped several cups of tea, and watched the world drift by in a verdant blur. The train sped through a land that seemed to stretch to eternity. Now and then the window became a canvas for a sudden stand of trees silhouetted against the beige earth.

As the world darkened, the window mirrored the interior of the railway car and showed less and less of the outside world. Still I was mesmerized.

"What is so interesting?" Edwin asked when I seemed intent on a monotonous landscape glowing under the light of an almost full moon.

"I see us," I said, pressing my head next to his and admiring our double portrait. Just then a group of regular shapes emerged, as though they had been dropped by a child playing blocks behind the clouds. "What are they?" I pointed to the pyramids.

"The old Dutch tombs."

"Where are we?"

"Balasore," Edwin replied with a chuckle. "That makes three of us. You're sore, I'm sore, and Balasore!"

We both doubled up with uncontrollable spasms of laughter.

"What is so amusing?" Esther asked as she peered around from her seat.

"N-nothing, Mother," Edwin sputtered, and fell into my lap with a contorted clutch of his sides.

❀ ❀ ❀

Two days later we arrived at Shoranur, terminus of the rail line. The platform seemed to be nothing more than an island in a leafy sea. Buffalo-carts were hired for the grueling journey to Trichur. After that, there was an easier road to Ernakulam, across the water from Cochin.

While we waited on the ghat at dawn for Hanif to unload my trunks and cases, Esther Salem rubbed her back and groaned, "Isn't it time they extended the railway to the sea?"

"I didn't mind any part of the trip," I said to Edwin.

"Nor I," Edwin replied, kissing my cheek.

"What do you young lovebirds know of pain?" she asked crossly.

Edwin stifled a burst of laughter and went to arrange for the boats. When he returned, the sun had brightened to reveal the harbor. "That's Cochin." He pointed across a wide canal. A few minutes later, the punt carrying the three of us pulled away from the loading wharf, and Edwin said, "Now you will see why they call Cochin India's tropical

Venice." As we moved out into open water, he continued, "It's no wonder my family are traders. For thousands of years, this port has welcomed vessels from all over the globe. Traders following the monsoon winds across to India came from Rome and Greece, from Egypt and Arabia, and landed in Cochin, which was the hub of the spice trade and the easterly routes to China. Eventually it became the first Portuguese establishment in India."

As the boat glided on the placid bay, I watched the gulls career in the pink sky. "You do like boats, don't you?" I asked with a private wink.

"Some boat trips are more pleasurable than others," he mumbled into the wind.

"What?" his mother called.

"Dinah was just wondering where we lived," he replied.

"Our house is on Mattancheri, a district on the southern peninsula," my mother-in-law explained. "It is faster to travel by water than to go around by land."

"Are there ferries?" I asked to be polite.

"No, but there has been talk of establishing a regular service," Edwin replied.

"Yes, and there has been talk of putting down a railway to the sea too," said his mother sarcastically.

Turning down a less-populated canal, where the backwater banks were a thick tangle draping the water's edge, I felt as if I had entered a strange new land. Screw pines bordered the water. Rich green foliage formed a dense backdrop, and a belt of pendulous coconut palms fanned the sky. Here and there whitewashed houses dotted the shoreline. Fruit trees offered shade at many of the doorsteps. Gardens were demarcated in tidy squares. A strong breeze whipped kites and clotheslines. I knew the Salems were not wealthy, but I supposed they owned one of these pleasant dwellings beside the sea.

By the time the boat came to a rude jetty, the sun had baked my arms and head. Dizzy, I stumbled ashore and followed Edwin into a narrow lane blocked by a barricade of horns. An odoriferous flock of rams, goats, even oxen swarmed to greet us. Mosquitoes circled ravenously about my ankles.

Edwin noted my slow progress. "It isn't far now."

As we rounded another corner, the brightness and color of Cochin faded into the dun of ancient plaster. A few shafts of light spilled down a street so constricted two carts could not pass each other. A long row of three-story buildings made an enclave unto itself. The narrow windows of the stone houses, like those designed to retain heat in a colder country, gave the impression the inhabitants had something to hide.

In front of almost every doorway, bronze-tinged women sat on stools, sewing and gossiping while children played. Several of them had legs the size of tree trunks. At our approach the chattering stopped. Edwin waited for me to catch up and took my hand. To each woman he gave a small bow, greeted her in an unfamiliar tongue, and said something that included my name. Each woman rose and bowed to me. I nodded quickly and moved on. Esther Salem lingered at each doorway as she accepted the comments from her neighbors with a satisfied smile on her lips.

Just before the bottom of the dead-end street, Edwin indicated a building with a Dutch-style clock tower. There were Hebrew, Roman, and Indian numerals on the dial of the clock. "That is Paradesi Synagogue, where we worship. It was built in 1568," he said proudly.

Compared to the splendid temples of Calcutta, it was a disappointment, but I said nothing.

Another woman with grossly distended legs braced herself against the wall of a gabled house across the street. "Welcome home, Edwin," she said, kissing him.

"Thank you, Aunt Reema."

"And this must be Dinah." She reached up and patted my cheek before I had time to recoil. "What a beauty," she gasped to Edwin.

"Yes, isn't she?" he gloated.

We waited in front of a dingy house with a large Star of David on the door. "Well, aren't we going to go inside?" Esther Salem asked when she arrived, panting.

Edwin kissed his fingers and touched the mezuzah before opening the latch. The thick wooden door grated against the tile floor with a teeth-jarring screech. His mother stepped forward, followed by his lame aunt, who had to hold on to the walls to remain upright. Then Edwin placed his arm around my shoulder and guided me into my new home.

30

O h, Dinah-baba," Yali wailed, "you cannot stay in this place!" She surveyed the small second-floor room that Edwin and I would share. One slender bed was draped with torn mosquito netting. Although the walls were freshly whitewashed and the floor matting new, it was less pretentious than Yali's quarters at Theatre Road. "What would your father say?"

I stepped into the hall and peered into Esther Salem's room. "I suppose she will offer us the larger bed," I replied, my voice more tremulous than I would have liked.

"She will not," Yali said with a finality that surprised me.

"Then Edwin will provide something else," I responded hopefully.

"I will provide what, my darling?" Edwin asked from the top of the steps, where he was directing the coolies to stack my belongings.

I gestured to the dark furniture in his mother's room. "Are we supposed to sleep here?" I pointed to his old bed. "Or there?"

He placed his arms around my waist and hugged me to him. "We could fit anywhere."

Yali turned her head.

"Edwin!" I pulled away, but his clasp tightened.

"Dinah will sleep in the room of your mother," Yali said with as much authority as Zilpah would have mustered.

Edwin cocked his head to see if he had understood her Hindustani correctly. "Yes, a splendid idea." He grinned like a schoolboy as he reflected on how this could be done.

"She won't like it," I whispered.

"She will follow what I say in the matter," he said in a testy voice I had not heard before.

How would the three of us live in such a tiny house? I wondered as I wandered around my new home. Downstairs there were three rooms: a modest living room, the size of the smallest parlor at Theatre Road, a dining room, and a pantry combined with a kitchen. The furniture was of bulky teakwood carved with flowers, birds, and animals in what I learned was the Indo-Portuguese style. Over the camelback sofa was a portrait of Mrs. Salem's father, a heavy-jowled man.

On the second floor were the two bedrooms, one primitive bath, and a sitting room under the gable that faced the street. Two sulky servants lived in a small godown at the far end of the courtyard garden.

"Where will our servants live?"

"We did not expect them," Esther Salem replied irritably. "Arrangements are being made for Hanif to board with neighbors. Yali will have the attic bedroom where Hanna stayed as a child."

"Isn't it hot up there?" I asked.

"It was not too hot for my daughter," she retorted.

Esther Salem moved into her son's room without a word of protest, but her groans and sighs of the next few weeks were ample reminders of how inconvenienced she felt.

☙ ☙ ☙

The first morning I awakened to a tapping on the window.

"The shutters! Close the shutters!" I cried in terror.

"Hush, there are no shutters."

"What is that sound?"

"Look, darling." He showed me the window, which had several wires pulled taut along the top of its frame. Wooden balls suspended from the wires trembled in the wind.

"Is that a decoration?"

"No, a practical way to keep the crows from flying into the room. We use swaying balls to confuse them." He stroked my back. "Poor darling, do you feel better now?"

"I suppose so," I said, kissing him to blot the dark sensations.

His hand flew up. "What's this?" he asked with alarm.

I looked down at my skin. Welts had appeared over my whole body. "I've been bitten. Insects adore me."

"How clever they are." He kissed a bump between my breasts. Then he pointed at a gap in the mosquito netting. "I didn't fasten my side tightly enough."

"Do you think I could get sick from so many bites?"

"Dinah, really. You've lived in India all your life."

"Never in Cochin. What if I become sick . . . like your aunt?"

"That's unlikely."

"What is wrong with her and those other women with those huge legs?"

"It's called 'Cochin leg' here, but its medical name is elephantiasis because of the way it swells the extremities."

"How do you catch it?"

"Some think it hereditary, or it might be acquired from impure water."

"Not insects?"

"Who knows for certain?"

"Is there no medical treatment?"

"Nothing that cures it permanently."

I shuddered.

"Now, don't worry yourself," he said, and blotted my concern with kisses.

"What shall we do?"

"About what?"

"How shall we spend our days?"

"We do not have to decide everything the first morning. First things first."

"What comes first?"

"We must get married," he replied. "Cochin style. And then we shall see about the rest."

After breakfast, we were summoned to his mother's bedside. "The trip exhausted me, and one never can sleep well in a new bed." Edwin didn't comment. "I shall require help to arrange the ceremony."

"When shall it be, Mother?"

"Next Tuesday. Reema will attend to everything."

"Shouldn't Dinah have a say?"

"What could she know about our traditions?" She lay back on her pillow and stared at the mosaic images with Hebrew inscriptions on the ceiling.

"I will be happy to follow your mother's wishes . . ." I said sincerely, then added a tag, ". . . in this matter."

I saw her mouth twitch.

"What is it, Mother?" Edwin asked as impatience crept into his voice.

"I would prefer Dinah to call me Mother too."

Edwin looked at me with a hopeful expression. My stomach churned, but I did not want to disappoint him. "Of course I will . . ." He mouthed the word, but I balked at having her replace my mother in any way. Steeling myself, I said the word "Mother," then hurriedly added, "Esther. Is there anything else?"

"Could Yali attend me for a few days? Just until I feel better?"

I looked away in case she could read my selfish thoughts. "Of course, Mother Esther."

That afternoon Edwin took me for a walk around Jew Town. "Cochin's Jewish quarter was established shortly after the Dutch conquest in 1661, but the first Jewish settlement in this region was actually down the coast at Cranganore."

"Oh? How long ago was that?" I asked.

"If you can believe the tales I heard in childhood, the first Jewish merchants were members of Solomon's Phoenician fleet almost three thousand years ago. Others believe we arrived at the time of the Babylonian captivity. At any rate, we know the group was well established when the King of Cranganore granted the Jews possession of Anjuvannam—the village mentioned in the copper plaques in the synagogue across from our house."

"What are those?"

"I'll show you them on our way home. The point is, the king gave Joseph Rabban, head of a Jewish family, hereditary ownership of this territory and we have thrived here ever since. To my knowledge, the only time the Jews were treated miserably in India was under the Portuguese conquistadors."

We had made our way down to the end of the street and were standing in front of an ancient building that looked like a square fortress. After Edwin tapped the gate, a durwan appeared and let us in. "Would you like to see the palace?"

I followed Edwin inside a dank entryway, wondering if I would ever accustom myself to the smell of moldy decay that permeated this ancient section of town.

"The rajahs of Cochin and Travancore always protected their Jewish citizens. That is why the Jews of Cochin settled close to the palace. Ah, here we are." He pointed to a long flat wall painted with tapestrylike frescoes of entwined nude forms. "What do you think of that?" He slipped his arm around my waist and rested his hand on my hip.

I supported my weight against him as I took in the dizzying sight of animals and humans intermingling in sexual encounters. Smooth female flanks, furry haunches, protruding horns, moistened lips, drooling muzzles, arched backs, tumescent organs, swelling breasts, gaping legs, groping arms, rosy nipples, pleasured smiles, and lustful sneers competed for space on the wall.

"Edwin!" I gasped.

"Aren't they superb?" he said under his breath. "The frescoes are scenes from the *Ramayana*. They were painted with vegetable colors about two hundred years ago. Isn't it extraordinary how they have retained so much of their brilliance?"

"But—"

He pivoted so he could kiss me on the lips.

The sound of footsteps broke us apart. We followed the durwan down a back staircase to a courtyard, where, hand in hand, we paused to admire several ornate palanquins, which Edwin explained were still used on state occasions by the Maharajah of Travancore.

"I went to school with his son."

"Which school?"

"La Martinière in Lucknow."

"How long were you there?"

"Two years."

"There is so much I do not know about you yet."

Stepping into a dark passageway, he took my hand and pressed it to the bulge alongside his inner thigh. "You know everything important."

The next doorway led to the synagogue. Edwin explained, "These buildings share a common wall." As we passed through the vestibule and into a bright hall hung with silver lamps, he continued more somberly, "From darkness to light."

In contrast to the grim palace next door, the room's milky walls gleamed in the sunlight. Unexpected touches of color caught my eye: green doors painted with flowers, red and gold trim around the tabernacle, and hand-painted blue-and-white Chinese floor tiles. Edwin slipped off his shoes, and I followed his lead, for the willow-patterned tiles were too beautiful to scuff.

He half-opened a silk curtain to reveal Torah scrolls and a golden crown. "This is our Ark of the Covenant." Pointing to the scrolls bedecked with tiaras set with gems, he went on, "One of the maharajahs of Travancore gave them to us." He opened the curtain farther to show me the most important relic. "Here are the copper plates I told you about. They are the oldest records of Indian Jewry, recording the privileges which usually were reserved for princes, but extended to the Jews."

I stared at the crude Tamil inscriptions. "What does it say?"

"It specifies the rights given to the Jews 'so long as the world and moon exist.' "

"What are they?"

"There were seventy-two gifts, including the rights to collect tolls on boats and carts, the revenue from and title of Anjuvannam, the lamp of the day, a white cloth spread in front of your path, a palanquin, a parasol, a drum, a trumpet, a gateway, a garland, among others."

"I can understand the part about tolls and revenues, but why the rest?"

"Some were symbolic, some had military implications. If you allowed people you did not trust to build a defensive barrier like a gateway, for instance, rebellion was more difficult." He gave me one of his most glorious smiles. "We flaunt our privileges on ceremonial occasions. You'll understand more after our wedding."

As we left the synagogue, I was reluctant to cross the street and return to the closed walls of his mother's home. "Could we walk on for a while longer?"

In the twilight, we watched fishing boats gliding out from the fingers of canals and converging in the palm of the harbor. On a pier built out from the shore, fishermen wearing conical straw hats were working a large triangular net suspended on poles. "Those are the Chinese nets."

I watched as a primitive arrangement of pulleys raised and lowered this ungainly contraption. "How can they lift those huge boulders?"

He pointed to the counterweights. "It balances perfectly. Like a child's seesaw."

"How clever, but they don't seem to be catching many for all that work."

"They rarely land more than a couple of fish at one time, yet thousands of men make their living at it." He clasped my hand. "We should go back."

The sound of water lapping against the seawall filled me with an undefined longing. "Not yet—" My voice caught.

"What is it?"

"Couldn't we find a house to live in—a place just for us?"

"You cannot be happy in my mother's house." It was a statement, not a question.

"I always wanted a home of my own, and we have the means to find something very nice."

"I don't want to spend your dowry."

"My father wanted me—wanted us—to be comfortable."

Edwin hung his head. "I should never have expected you to live in Cochin."

"I am willing to live in Cochin, Edwin. I just don't like your mother's small house." My voice rose to a tense pitch that humiliated me. I took a breath and whispered, "There is no rush to make a change. I only wanted to tell you my thoughts."

Edwin stared out across the water, even though the blackness which had swiftly descended in the tropical evening prevented his eyes from focusing on any particular view.

"Edwin . . ."

He did not respond.

"Edwin, let's go home."

We walked back at the fast, clipped pace he set. What had I done? When we were almost at the end of the street, I said, "Edwin, I didn't mean to upset you."

He took my hand in his and gave it a squeeze. My heart leapt in appreciation for the reprieve and kept beating at that faster pace for a long while into the evening.

♨ ♨ ♨

The next time we returned to the synagogue, it was to say our wedding vows. Until then the tiny house bustled with preparations.

"A pity that we cannot have everything the way it was meant to be," Esther Salem griped as certain ceremonies were truncated because they had no meaning to a couple who had lived together for several weeks.

The Tuesday morning of the wedding itself, Edwin's sister, Hanna, came early to prepare me. First she tied a *tali*, a local Indian marriage symbol, around my neck.

"Thank you, it is lovely," I said. "Where's Edwin? I want to show it to him."

She giggled at my enthusiasm. "You cannot see him."

"Why not?"

"His brother and uncle are giving him a bath and shaving his head."

"No!" I shouted.

Hanna giggled again. "You will see."

I was not permitted to eat at midday, which for me was more of a relief than a purification. After the other women had finished their pungent meal, they dressed me in the traditional Cochini bridal dress called a *marante deldpud*. Aunt Reema showed off the lavish embroidery of the shirt and the cords of gold braid on the blouse. "This is the one Hanna wore for her wedding. Pity there was not time to make you one of your own. The skirt alone took a year to complete."

I smiled to myself. The idea of having to wait a year to marry Edwin was ludicrous, when we had been unable to wait more than a few days! The system was backward, I realized. First should come the wedding night, and then if the partners were compatible, the rituals that would unite the couple for eternity could commence. In my case, having the liturgy first—as when I married Silas—was a formula for disaster. Having an abbreviated courtship—like mine with Edwin—followed by this panoply was more sensible. Now we could say our vows with conviction.

"Here they come!" a young cousin called from the gable window.

A white carpet was stretched out a third of the way down the street. A band of musicians led a large procession. After them came Edwin, wearing a large pillbox skullcap embroidered with gold thread and a white satin shirt also covered with intricate designs. A breeze rippled his long cloak and revealed white silk pants. From the second story I could not tell how much hair remained, for he was draped in masses of jasmine garlands that covered the back of his neck.

"Have you been to the synagogue and heard the story of the copper plates?" Hanna asked.

"Yes."

"Good. Now you will see them come to life, for in our weddings we use the rights given to us so long ago. You and Edwin will walk on the white carpet, you will wear garlands, the men will carry parasols and lamps that are lit by day, and drums and trumpets will play for you."

Hanna led me downstairs and placed ashes on my forehead. "A sign of mourning for the destruction of the Second Temple."

"In Calcutta we break a cup," I offered, but nobody was listening. Garlands were lowered over my head, women circled me, coins were tossed into the air. Just before we stepped outside, they covered my face with an opaque veil. The white carpet became my guide as I looked down and followed it to the synagogue door.

Inside the temple, I was seated on a chair under a hoop from which a long drapery was hung. The fabric enveloped me, and all I could see were blurred shadows of people moving about me, then a flare of light as candles were lit.

Unexpectedly Edwin's voice sang out, "By your leave."

The congregation responded, "By leave of heaven."

The strange chanting between Edwin and the guests continued. "O give thanks unto the Lord, for he is good," Edwin said.

"For his mercy endureth forever."

"May joyous occasions multiply in Israel . . ." Every time I heard Edwin's voice, so strong and firm, my heart soared. If only I could watch his expression, look into his eyes, and see what they had done to his hair! ". . . Blessed are thou, O Lord, who sanctified Israel by means of the nuptial canopy and wedlock."

At last I was released from the drapery for the betrothal, but still could not tell how much of Edwin's locks they had shorn because I wore the veil.

My ring, which had been made from a coin used at a ceremony on the previous Sunday, was dipped into a gold chalice by a white thread with seven strands. After tasting the wine, Edwin placed the cup in my hand and spoke in Aramaic, *"Ba kiddushiki."* He slipped the ring onto the forefinger of my right hand and repeated the phrase.

The congregation called out, "May it be a good sign."

The marriage contract was read, several unintelligible songs were sung in Maylayalam, and at last my face was uncovered. We shared some wine, and the service was complete. As we stepped down from the pulpit, I reached up, as though for balance, and tipped Edwin's hat. Lovely dark locks peeked back at me.

"I thought they shaved you," I mumbled.

"They did." He grinned. "They shaved my face."

Unexpectedly, tears streamed down my face.

"A lucky sign!" Aunt Reema cried. "They will be blessed with many children."

"Make way for the bride and the groom," a woman called from the rear.

"The street is closed," someone in the front shouted back.

There was a buzz of voices. "What is this?" Edwin boomed. A new sound, like a tuneless trumpet, splintered the air. "It's Amar!" He rushed ahead, leaving me behind.

Stepping outside, I faced the flank of an elephant arrayed in Moghul splendor. Beside it was a troop of red-turbaned soldiers who saluted us with fife and drum. Looking up to the height of the roof, I saw a golden howdah cosseting a young gentleman. He wore a scarlet coat with diamond buttons and a turban of white silk set with the largest, most dazzling ruby I had ever seen.

I clasped Edwin's outstretched hand. "Come meet my friend, Prince Amar of Travancore," Edwin said as the elephant once again brayed his congratulations.

❦ ❦ ❦

There was not one elephant. There were five. Each took up half the breadth of Jew Street. Tail to trunk, they stretched almost to the square. After the prince descended, the entire wedding party flattened themselves against the walls of the buildings or ducked inside doorways while the prince's *mahouts* turned the massive beasts around and led them to a grassy intersection near the fishing jetties. Ten sweepers followed behind the beasts, scouring the street, a necessary procedure, since they obviously had been waiting there for some time.

The prince embraced Edwin and said something to him privately. Both men laughed. I was surprised to see that the Indian, who had seemed enormous atop his elephant, was a head shorter than Edwin. His face was as round as a moon and had a greenish pallor. He wore wire-rimmed spectacles and had cultivated a curlicue mustache that seemed pasted on his smooth face. Small dark eyes like onyx gems darted back and forth as he surveyed the effect his arrival had on the guests.

"You did not expect me, Winner, did you?" he said in a voice that was so slurred it was difficult to understand.

Edwin playfully punched the prince's diamond buttons one by one. "Of course I did, Lover," he said, grinning. "Didn't I make it to your wedding—*sine magnis elephantis*."

They continued to trade quips with each other until Edwin took notice of my inquisitive expression. "Isn't this a wonderful surprise?"

"Yes," I said a bit dubiously, "but why does he call you 'Winner'?"

The prince grinned broadly, causing his mustache to tilt. "It is a nickname we gave him at La Martinière because 'win' was in his name and also because Edwin won many prizes." He pursed his lips. "And I suppose you will want to know about my name also."

"The prince became 'Lover' or 'Lover-boy' because his name, Amar, sounds like 'amour,' " Edwin explained. "And not because he has a way with women."

"I doubt that is true, Edwin."

The prince's eyes shone their approval of my comment. "After you, bridegroom," he said, indicating that Edwin should lead him across the street.

Edwin hesitated, but finally went ahead after Amar insisted.

Esther Salem stepped forward to greet the prince. "An honor to have you in our home again, sir," she said with her back straight, her eyes fixed on his ruby. "It is our custom that today the bride and the groom are king and queen in our household. For a week we call them the *manamatee* and the *manamarlen* and not by their proper names. Anyone who makes a mistake will be fined." She pointed out Edwin's uncles, brother, and brother-in-law. "Prince Amar, do you see those men dressed in red?" He nodded. "They are the *shoshbinim*, the groom's men, who will guard the honored couple and punish any lapses."

The prince hung his head respectfully. "I understand completely." He turned to Edwin. "Now, Winner, will you be kind enough to introduce me formally to your beautiful wife?"

Edwin's brother, Julien, approached the prince. He shook his head sadly, like a father about to reprimand a foolish son.

"Hello, Julien," the prince said jovially. "What have I done now? Surely merely saying one little 'Winner' doesn't make me a loser, does it?"

Julien's chin bobbed solemnly.

The prince sighed and threw up his hands. "What is my punishment?"

"Usually a few coins," Julien said with a touch of embarrassment. He held out his hand.

The prince reached deep into a pocket and brought out three large silver coins. Julien seemed stunned as they clanked one by one into his fleshy palm. "B-but . . ." he stuttered. Mother Esther took them from him with a sly smile.

The prince licked his pink lips and turned back to me. "Now, where were we? Oh, yes . . . so this must be Dinah . . ." He cocked his head to see if Julien had heard him use my name.

The flustered brother held out his hand again. Prince Amar reached into the same pocket and came up with four more coins. Julien made a clumsy attempt to give two back, but Amar protested, "Surely one

'Dinah' is worth more than a 'Winner.' Oh, now what have I done?"
He hit his head and allowed the coins to go singing across the tile
floor, then reached into his other pocket and pulled out a handful of
smaller coins. They were, however, gold. "Now I suppose I shall have
to pay double."

Esther Salem passed around a brass bowl to collect the fines while
Edwin laughed and laughed. Guests who had heard of the prince's
prank were pressing forward trying to find out what would happen
next. I was appalled by the garish display, but forced myself to keep
smiling.

Musicians began to play in the courtyard and the street, prompting
the dancers. As the guests approached us, they wished us luck, using
our names deliberately, then proffered a few rupees or a bottle of
whiskey to pay their fines. A table was soon laden with a variety of
liquors and the bowl clinked with coins.

"What will happen to the bottles?" I asked Edwin.

"What we do not drink tonight will be used during the week of
celebration. After that they are given as favors in the card games that
everyone enjoys in the evenings."

The more the drinking and dancing increased, the farther down the
street the party progressed. We should have moved along with our
guests, but Edwin and I were trapped by the prince, who wanted to
know more about me. Edwin politely told him where I was from and
who my father was.

"Ah, yes, my father knew some Sassoons from Bombay. How would
a scoundrel like Winner come to marry into such an esteemed family?"

"An introduction from my uncle," Edwin said without seeming to
take offense.

"Tell me more about Calcutta—I have never been there," the prince
demanded.

"A city of palaces, or so they say," was all I could offer.

"Palaces?" He chuckled. "Wait until you see Padmanabhapuram!"
He stroked one of what must have been two dozen pearl necklaces that
filled in the short space between his collar and his chin.

"Is that where you live?" I inquired.

"No, that's where my uncle, the maharajah, resides. I have my own
humble quarters on the palace grounds."

" 'Humble' is hardly what I would call them." Edwin turned to me.
"The principality of Travancore is even grander than Cochin."

"Travancore is a nineteen-gun state," Prince Amar added.

I glanced over at Edwin to see if this was of importance. "Cochin is
entitled to only seventeen guns," he filled in.

Listening to this interchange, I felt a pang that the descendants of the great dynasties had been reduced to petty bickering for favor in an empire where foreign rulers handed out titles like so many pieces of confetti.

The two men continued bantering as if there was no raucous party or patient bride nearby. Despite the prince's apparent concentration on the discussion with Edwin, he managed to fix his gaze in my direction. Edwin did not sense the distraction. The other guests hovered a safe distance away, not daring to interfere with the prince's right to occupy the attention of the wedding couple. I longed to join the others, if only to remove myself from the odd man's scrutiny.

The sun went down behind the high facades on the street of the Jews, and purple shadows soon bathed the pavement. A chain of women dancers came for me. I clasped the hand of Julien's wife, Gladys, and danced for a few minutes until I reached the Salem house. There I broke off and took a much needed break in the bathroom.

"Dinah?" I heard Edwin's voice on the stairs. He knocked at the door. "Will you be long?"

"No."

"I have something to show you. I had hoped to do it while it was light, but Prince Amar's visit changed my plans."

"Will he leave now?"

"No, he will come with us."

"Come with us where?"

"I cannot say." He led me back outside into a glittering world of flickering torches and brilliant stars. The guests, many of whom had drifted back to their homes, formed a pathway down the street. Additional torchbearers from the prince's retinue lit the way to the plaza, where the elephants waited. Edwin and I were assisted up into the howdah on the elephant just behind the prince. In the darkness, the torches below formed an eddying current of light, which we followed like ships adrift on a rolling sea. I recalled the first time I had been on an elephant, with my father in Patna, and wondered what he would think if he could see me now wrapped in Edwin's arms atop a royal elephant, breathing the moist, thick air of this tropical night in this faraway coastal town on the other side of India.

I was uncertain which direction we were taking, but the pungent smell of low-tide muck suggested we were approaching the waterfront.

"Stop here," Edwin called to the prince.

The mahouts poked and shouted at their lumbering charges. I was lifted down with the assistance of the prickly musculature of the elephant's trunk. After Edwin gave some instructions in Malayalam, torchbearers ran forward and made a ring of fire around a small house with a Dutch tile roof.

"What is this?"

Edwin bowed. "Your new home, my darling Dinah."

The door opened. His sister, Hanna, was silhouetted in the glow of candles. I walked forward, knowing, from the telltale odor of sandalwood, that the prince was directly behind me. A flickering glow on the whitewashed exterior made the walls seem higher than they were. One square room was furnished with heavy carved pieces of furniture similar to those I had seen in Jew Town. Windows on the far wall reflected the light of the many glass lamps that hung from the ceiling on long chains. Three large silver candelabra glowed in the center of a round table, where platters of delicacies were laid out. A cut-glass decanter was filled with wine and two large glasses rimmed in gold were nearby.

"Where are we?"

"A mile south of Jew Town. From the garden you can see across to Ernakulam."

"There is a garden?" My voice rose with excitement.

"A small one with coconut palms bending to the sea."

Hanna pointed to a doorway on the left. I followed her to a small bedroom, where there was a bed even larger than the one we had borrowed from Mother Esther. A cool buff stone covered the floor. A tile shelf contained a simple copper basin.

"There are only three rooms," Edwin said apologetically, "but on the other side are a kitchen and an exterior entrance to godowns for Yali and Hanif."

Hanna crossed her hands high on her pregnant abdomen. "Do you like it?"

Before I could respond, Prince Amar spoke in his sloppy manner. "A charming place to spend a few nights, I agree, yet hardly a place for a woman of this fine lady's background."

"Everyone cannot live in a palace, Lover," Edwin said without rancor.

"Ah, my dear friend, forgive me," he continued in that honey-coated tone that was beginning to irk me, "but from what you said, your bride is accustomed to luxury."

"I think it is wonderful." I was so happy to have a place of our own that my voice reflected my honest pleasure. "It is exactly the sort of house I wished for when I first saw the island." I beamed at Edwin, and his evident pride prompted me to muddle on, as if a quantity of compliments could override the prince's insult. "Besides, as I told my husband, any room where he and I are together is heaven to me." I had spoken without realizing how appalled Hanna and the others who had accompanied us would be at the intimacy of my statement. At their startled expressions, I flushed. Suddenly I felt as foolish in my wedding garb as a child caught playacting. After all, I was no more a bride than Hanna!

There were awkward attempts to cover the uneasy silence. Hanna passed a platter of food. Julien began to pour brandies. Then the prince's voice boomed out over the babble. "Mrs. Salem, my dear friend Edwin Salem, once again I say your names aloud in the presence of these witnesses." He patted his chest. The diamond buttons twinkled in the lamplight. "Having no more coins in my pockets, I hope you will permit me to defer my fines and accept my word as my credit."

Edwin tried to gesture this was unnecessary as a crooked smile crept across the prince's pasty face. His mustache wobbled. "My dear friends, on this joyous and most auspicious occasion you must grant me the opportunity to tell you and everyone present that it would give me the greatest honor if you would accept as my gift to you both the residence that we call 'The Orchid House' to be your home in Travancore, now or later, tomorrow or the day after, from this day forward, as long as the world and moon exist."

31

♦ ♦ ♦

I n the morning Edwin and I sat up in bed and stared out on a
silvery channel at crossing boats. A long-legged bird walked on
the grassy bank, trying to swallow a fish too large for his gullet.
We sipped tea from the tray Hanif had delivered and crunched
the toast Yali had prepared. For a long while I tried to sort out the
sensation that coursed through my veins. My bones felt so light that if
I had not been holding on to Edwin, I might have floated. Then the
word came to me, the meaning of which I had never before known:
contentment.

"What did you think of Prince Amar?" Edwin asked lazily.

The mention of the name dissolved the perfection of the moment.
"He surprised me. Why didn't you ever tell me about him?"

"There has not been time to tell you about every one of my friends,"
he said, kissing me hard on the mouth. "You keep my lips so busy,"
he mumbled between light pecks on my cheeks.

With a friendly shove I pushed him away. "I would have thought
the son of a maharajah might have been at the top of your list."

"He's not the maharajah's son, he's his nephew. And besides, one
never brags about one's friends."

I searched Edwin's face for his usual grin, but he had spoken the
words with utter seriousness. "So, you met him at Lucknow and have
been pals ever since."

"He was one of the few boys from this region, and we traveled
together. Amar is one of the most brilliant men I've ever met, a true
genius with figures. He was to continue his studies in England."

"Why didn't he go?"

"Amar was the third in line to the throne of Travancore. 'The prime
position in the world,' he claimed, 'for I have every privilege and no
responsibility.' Then both his brothers died and everything changed. As
heir, he must be available to his uncle and the court."

"His uncle is the maharajah?"

"Yes."

"Doesn't his uncle have any sons?"

"Yes, I believe he does."

"Then why won't one of them become maharajah?"

"Travancore is one of the few places in the world where inheritance is passed through the maternal line. That means the eldest son of the current maharajah's eldest sister or aunt succeeds, not the son of the ruler. Amar's mother is the maharajah's eldest sister, so Amar will become the maharajah someday."

"How lucky for him."

"Not really," Edwin said sadly. "He is a simple fellow who prefers the world of ideas to the machinations of ruling."

To me, Amar's display of elephants and troops, the immodest way he had tossed coins about, and his grandiose offer of a house—which I saw as nothing more than a way to belittle Edwin's gift to me—belied my husband's explanation. However, I decided this was not the time to contradict Edwin, who then would feel pressed to defend his friend.

"What is this business about the Orchid House?"

"You heard him as well as I did. He gave us the house."

"We aren't going to live there, are we?"

"It is ours to do as we wish."

"I want to stay here."

Edwin patted my hand. "I am pleased you like this modest dwelling, but I never intended it to be our final home. I could see it was impossible for us to be ourselves under my mother's roof, and that is why I brought you here."

"What would we do in Travancore? Isn't your business in Cochin?"

"The time has come for me to reevaluate my position. As you know, I have been working with my uncle. Although he has been kind to me, there have been some difficulties . . ." He pushed himself around until his feet were dangling off the edge of the bed. "Anyway, this is a good time to consider other options." He went to the washbasin and splashed water on his scratchy face.

Fascinated, I watched the tightening and relaxing of his naked buttocks as he lathered his shaving brush and wielded his razor. The composure I had felt moments before dissolved as my mounting desire mingled with new apprehension.

Edwin buttoned his shirt. "Aren't you getting up?"

"Why should I? Don't you think it would be simpler if I spent the day in bed to be ready for you whenever you wished me?"

"I wanted a wife, not a courtesan," he said without smiling.

"What's the difference?" I asked lightly.

He shifted his feet impatiently. "A wife helps make decisions; she gives as much as she takes. A courtesan is a mere receptacle. After the man has filled her, she is worthless."

I regretted the tense turn of the conversation. These sudden shifts in Edwin's mood were never nasty, but they often caught me unaware. When his face darkened or brightened, when he turned a serious discussion into a joke or vice versa, my flesh tingled, my brain reeled, as I fought to keep up with him. My new husband was like a weather system, bringing stormy winds or gentle breezes without warning. I felt like the captain of a ship who had to be alert to maneuver his craft under variable conditions.

"Tell me more," I asked evenly as he fastened the tiny buttons at the back of my frock.

"About what?"

"The Orchid House. Have you ever seen it?"

"Yes. It is the house where Amar's mother lived when he was young."

"Where does she live now?"

"As the first princess, she has a wing of the palace. She will be the next maharani."

"Do you mean that Amar's wife will not become queen?"

"Yes. The mother takes that role."

"Why?"

"It's part of the wisdom of the ancients. Consider the Jews. A child is not born Jewish unless his mother is Jewish, because while a father's identity may be shrouded in mystery, the mother's is always known. Thrones that rely on paternal inheritance can be questioned. Those through the mother are inviolate. At least in Travancore a purity of line is guaranteed."

"Who lives in the Orchid House now?"

"Probably some relations."

"Where would they go if we took Amar up on his offer?"

"How should I know?" He sighed loudly. "Why don't we visit and find out? The countryside is very appealing and the journey through the backwaters would make a wonderful holiday." As he started for the large central room of the house, I followed behind and watched him pluck a banana from the bowl and eat it rapidly.

He handed me a banana, but I replaced it. "I hardly think we need a holiday. We have not yet begun to live any sort of regular life together. Every day has been different so far."

"Is that a complaint?"

Tears rushed into my eyes. I turned my head from Edwin and walked outside to the waterfront side of the house. Along the far shore, warehouses with tiled roofs glistened in the morning sunlight.

"Dinah!" he called after me.

I blinked, hoping he would think the glare had caused my eyes to water. "If we had remained in Calcutta, you would have gone to an office and I would have managed a household and visited with family and friends. I would have known what was expected from me, and you would have known what was expected from you. People are happiest when they have markers to follow, at least from day to day. Nobody knows what life may bring, I realize that, but they should live their days in a pattern of constructive deeds."

"Who says that should be our course?" he asked gently. "You are describing the acceptance of a sort of slavery. The pathetic rickshaw-wallah is chained to the yoke of his vehicle in order to feed himself and his family a few grains of rice. For twelve hours a day, through drowning monsoon and scorching summer, he carries his burden until at last he succumbs, a broken old man before thirty. Great fortune has been showered on us both so we might break from such binds, whether brutal like the rickshaw staves or benevolent like familial duty. We have been given the luxury of living each day different from the last, to expand our horizons, to make discriminating choices."

"How shall we live?" I asked in an edgy voice. "On my dowry?"

He straightened his back, and his mouth puckered with displeasure. "Certainly not. We must keep that intact until we have determined the best possible use for the money. We must analyze investments. If we went to Travancore, we could look for opportunities in that land—it's a frontier ripe with possibilities. Also, I have several ideas to pursue in Cochin."

"For instance?"

"I could represent the Sassoon interests here. I know most of the opium goes east to China, but there is a steady trade to the west. Cochin might be a port of call."

"You said you didn't want to do that," I said with alarm.

He looked at me queerly. "Why does that worry you? There is hardly a commodity with more profit than poppies."

"Well," I demurred, since this was hardly the time to bring up my mother or *Edwin Drood*, "I would prefer to be independent of my family—and yours."

"I see your point," he said gently. "I didn't mean to upset you. Many other possibilities exist. There hasn't been time to discuss everything with you. If I had known how anxious you were . . ." He trailed off.

I reached over and clasped his shoulder. "I am sorry, Edwin. Everything has happened so quickly that I felt adrift. When I woke this morning and found myself in yet another bed, it took a few minutes before I even knew where I was."

His mouth curled at the edges. "You were beside me. Nothing else should matter."

I nodded. "Sometimes I fear that when I wake, you will have disappeared."

"For me, Cochin is home. I forget how foreign everything must seem to you. I can understand why you wouldn't wish to go somewhere new again. We shall remain here as long as you like. Only . . ." He paused. "I would not like to insult Amar."

"We might visit him someday."

"Of course, we shall visit him whenever you like."

"If we did, we would not have to live in Travancore, would we?"

"No, certainly not. However, once you see it, you may decide Travancore is one of the most enchanting places you have ever seen."

Dimly at first, then with ever-increasing clarity, I saw how masterfully Edwin had managed my distress. He had listened to me, he had acceded to my wishes, and somehow in the process he had maneuvered me into a new comprehension of his position. Even more astonishing, now that I had the assurance I had craved, I wanted to give him what he desired.

"Sahib!" Edwin and I turned and saw Hanif running toward us in some agitation.

"What is it, Hanif?" Edwin shouted before we met up with him.

"Your mother is ill."

"Oh, Edwin!" I said in alarm. "What could be the matter?"

"Don't worry." He patted my hand. "This is her way of making me pay attention to her. Mother was not pleased when I told her I bought this house for you. Since I was the youngest, she always expected me to remain by her side."

I thought he sounded unsympathetic and I worried that his mother really might be ill. My concerns faded somewhat when we visited her an hour later. Esther Salem had moved back to the larger bedroom and was propped up on pillows. The room had a sour smell.

"Good morning, Mother," Edwin said without much emotion.

"At least you two look as though you slept last night. I couldn't close my eyes, not for a minute."

"What seems to be the trouble?" he asked. "Is it your back again?"

"No, that pain has subsided." She clutched at her chest and spoke with a loud intake of air between syllables. "I fear there is something the matter with my heart."

"Oh, Mother." Edwin grinned. "More than half the population of Jew Town must be suffering from overindulgence. I saw you sipping the wine." He went to the window and threw open the shutters. "It stinks in here. What you need is some fresh air and a walk in the sunshine. Dinah and I have already had a long stroll along the banks, and it cleared my head considerably."

His mother shielded her eyes. "No, the light bothers me."

Edwin sighed and adjusted the slats to direct the light to the ceiling. "Now, Mother, if you get out of bed and come downstairs, Dinah and I will take tea with you."

Esther Salem pouted. "I don't know if I have the strength, Edwin."

He turned to me and shrugged.

"May I be of assistance, Mother Esther?" I asked in my most amenable voice. "Perhaps some mango juice would soothe you, or—"

"I cannot abide mango juice!" she shouted so unexpectedly that I shrank back into the doorway.

Without another word Edwin turned from her, took my arm, and escorted me downstairs.

Aunt Reema was waiting for us in the parlor. "Don't be too hard on your mother," she said in a gravelly whisper. "If that prince hadn't shown up and—"

"What does this have to do with Amar?"

"What would your mother do if you left Cochin?"

"Is that what this nonsense is about?" Edwin's tone had a seething edge I never had heard before.

"Edwin!" His mother sounded like she was in pain.

He stepped out in the hall and looked up the stairs.

"Edwin!" Now she seemed frightened.

I watched as he climbed several steps, paused to deliberate whether to continue up or not, then, changing his mind, hurried back down and out the door.

"What shall I do?" I asked Aunt Reema.

"Let him be. This has nothing to do with you, or at least not directly."

"What if it is her heart?"

"No, it isn't."

"Maybe it would ease her mind if she knew I do not want to go to Travancore."

"Oh, yes." Aunt Reema seemed relieved. "Tell her that, please."

With reluctance I climbed the stairs in Edwin's stead. I pushed open the door to her room slowly to avoid flooding her with light.

"Edwin . . ." Her face was turned away. "I was afraid you had gone out. Was that Reema leaving? She hasn't been very helpful. She thought you and your wife should have the day together. Your *wife*! I have to admit the word sounds strange to me, but I suppose I will have to get used to it. Besides, it is not as though you haven't had enough time alone with that girl—" She stopped, for when she glanced behind her to see her son's reaction, she realized she had been talking to me. Her face blanched momentarily, but she recovered rapidly. She pushed herself back into a sitting position and stared at me with weary eyes, the green color of a stagnant lagoon. "You weren't happy here, were you?"

I was too shocked by her vitriolic tongue to respond.

"I suppose this humble house had nothing to offer after the grand way your family lives in Calcutta. Even the pretty cottage Edwin bought with the meager amount his uncle owed him for his third of the business doesn't please the likes of a Sassoon."

"The house is perfect," I said slowly.

"You are only saying that because you are planning to take off for Travancore." She paused and baited me. "Aren't you?"

"I told Edwin I thought we should remain in Cochin. I did not know he had sold his stake in his uncle's business to buy the house."

"That represented the sum total of the money his father was able to leave him, a loan from his brother, *and* his earnings in Singapore."

"I did not know," I repeated, swallowing any mention that my dowry had to be worth fifty times that amount.

"Where is Edwin?" she demanded.

"He has gone out."

"Where? To see Amar?"

"The prince left this morning."

"You liked the prince, didn't you?"

I had not, but I did not want her to know this. "Any friend of Edwin's is a friend of mine."

"Someday you might reconsider that statement. I have never approved of that alliance." She rearranged the pillows behind her head. "What can Amar do for Edwin? He is a frivolous man who uses Edwin to amuse himself. Any time Edwin has spent in Travancore has been a waste. Keep your husband here. Mind my words, or you also will lose him. You cannot imagine the tales I have heard. The women of Trivandrum are the most immodest in the subcontinent. Of course, Amar can have any woman he likes, but also, there are many who offer themselves to friends of the prince as a way of gaining proximity to power."

I had been about to tell my mother-in-law we were on the same side and that I would do anything to dissuade Edwin from taking the prince up on his offer, when her last words were like a slap across the face. I clenched my fists behind my back and willed myself not to respond.

Esther Salem closed her eyes. "I thought I could trust you, Dinah. I thought we could be friends. Now I am not so certain. Already you have driven my son from me. Any other time he would have rushed to my side. Because of you, he hurried out the door. That pretty little sister of yours—what was her name?—she would have listened to me without question."

I fought to control the fury that boiled within. "What do you want?"

"Only what you want, my daughter. Edwin is a complex boy. I have known him far longer than you. Let me guide you as to how to make him happy. He was miserable in Singapore. He does not like to be off on his own like many men. He needs a guiding hand. Together we can care for him."

I don't require any assistance taking care of him, I said to myself as my spine stiffened in resistance. My only weapon was silence.

She opened her eyes and gave me a look so penetrating I was certain she could read my mind. "You never have told Edwin of our time together in your bedroom in Calcutta, have you?" I willed myself to remain motionless, as she continued. "Neither have I. We each had our reasons. But remember this: just because I gave my permission for the marriage does not mean that I was entirely convinced by your . . . condition."

Confident that Edwin would be more upset to hear what she had done to me than about question of my purity, I curled my lips in a half-smile.

My refusal to subjugate myself melted her accusing stare. She turned away and closed her eyes. 6I think I can sleep now," she muttered.

I left without another word.

🌼 🌼 🌼

If Edwin's mother had not really been ill the day after the wedding, she managed—if only by sheer force of will—to develop a fever later that week. Although I did not say so aloud, I thought she had poisoned herself with her selfish thoughts. Even kindly Aunt Reema was at the end of her patience.

"Do you think your Yali might come back, if only for a few hours a day?" she asked.

"Of course," I said, relieved I could send someone as my substitute, for other than a short dutiful visit accompanied by Edwin, I had refused to be alone again with my mother-in-law in that festering room.

His sister and brother also took turns, and together we weathered the episode. Even after the fever passed, though, she rejected any nourishment except bread and broths. By my third week in Cochin, Esther Salem had begun a routine of spending the morning in bed, coming downstairs for tea with relatives, and retiring again before dinner. Yali reluctantly attended her at night, and we hired an additional servant to assist during the day. Unfortunately, her moods did not modulate, and her tongue was as brittle as ever.

One afternoon Yali greeted me in tears. "What is the matter?" I asked.

She shook her head and would not speak.

"Did you get any sleep last night?" I asked. Mother Esther was always calling for Yali to bring her special drinks and treats in the middle of the night.

"A little," she said, wiping her eyes with the corner of her blue sari.

"Yali, if you are tired, or are ill, or—"

"No, no, missy-baba," she said, using my baby name as she sometimes did at intimate moments between us.

"You can tell me, Yali. Please." I put my arm around her and felt the boniness of her bent shoulders. "Go home now and rest. I will tell the memsahib you cannot work for her any longer."

"No!" Yali clasped my hand. "Not today, maybe later, but not today."

Hearing a note of fear in her voice, I exclaimed, "Yali, what are you afraid of?"

She kept her eyes downcast. "If I leave today, she will think I have told you what she said, and she will—"

"What did she say? You must tell me."

"Last night . . . she was not well . . ."

"All right, I will take that into account. What did she say?"

"She . . . she . . ."

"Yes, Yali . . . ?"

"She said that it was a pity her son had not taken her advice and married missy-Ruby. She said your sister would have made the sahib a better wife and her a better daughter . . . that she should have listened to what they said about you and forbidden the marriage, and that . . ." She choked on her tears.

"What else?" I urged, and then was both sorry and grateful that I did.

"She accused me of aiding you in the deception."

"What deception?" I asked before I realized what she meant. "About what happened when I lived with Mr. Luddy?" I answered for myself.

Yali nodded sadly.

"She thought that I did something to help you the time she came to check you. She told me I must tell her what tricks I used. When I swore I had done nothing, she became very cross and she . . ."

"What?"

"She struck me." Yali turned her head so that I could see a faint purple bruise at the edge of her chin.

Seething, I insisted that she gather her things and follow me home. Once there, I told Hanif that nobody was to disturb Yali for three days. "A holiday," I explained.

"What holiday, missy?" he asked, hoping he might enjoy one too.

I looked on the calendar. There were only two more days to the year—the same year I had lived in Darjeeling, divorced Silas, learned about my father's opium business, met and married Edwin, and moved to this godforsaken stretch of earth. "The new year, Hanif. She shall have the three days off before the holiday and you shall have the three after."

"Oh, yes, missy-sahib," he said with delight.

❧ ❧ ❧

Edwin took Yali's reappearance as a sign that his mother had recuperated. A veil of normalcy fell over our lives for the first time. For about a week we rose together, had a leisurely chota hazri in bed, followed by a walk along the waterfront, and then Edwin would take a boat to his uncle's warehouse, returning in time for tea. While he was away, my own day was a pleasant mix of organizing my little household, light reading, and reverie. How enchanting it was to know that Edwin would return to me in a few hours, the next day, the next week, and for all imaginable time after that.

On New Year's Day, 1892, a cabin boat flying the royal elephant flag of Travancore pulled up at the wharf nearest our dwelling. A minister dressed in a blue turban with silver lace entwined into the folds, followed by a retinue of six courtiers, arrived at our doorstep. Edwin welcomed them respectfully.

The minister stepped forward and read from an official document: "Hail and Prosperity. Greetings of the New Year are sent by His Highness Sir Padmanabha Dasa Bala Rama Vanji Kulashekara Kiritapati Munne; Suhan Maharaj; Maharajah Rama, Rajah Bahadur Sir Shamshar Jang; Knight Grand Commander of the most exalted order of the Empress, Maharajah of Travancore, on behalf of his nephew and heir, Amar Rama. Your gracious presence is requested in the capital city of Trivandrum. A humble vessel is placed at your disposal to transport you at your convenience." He stepped back and saluted. One of the escorts marched forward carrying a polished ebony box. Another aide opened the box and lifted out a rolled letter and handed it to Edwin, who broke the seal and read it, chuckling.

"What is this about?" I asked.

"Amar sounds lonely. He sends you his compliments and promises you will have every comfort, including 'the company and consort of your husband.' "

"What does he mean by that?"

"The prince is quite astute. He probably sensed your reluctance to share my attentions. He wants to assure you that you will be as welcome as I at his palace, his table, and so on. He reminds us this is the most delightful time to travel south. The weather is mild and the monsoon is months off. What do you say?"

Loath to discuss the matter in front of the daunting line of royal retainers, I turned back into the house while Edwin dismissed the visitors.

"This will impress Mother," he said, waving the document the minister had read. "It's from the maharajah himself."

"What sort of a man is he?"

"I've seen him a few times, but I've never spoken with him. The maharajahs of Travancore are educated men with progressive ideas. This is another result of the matrilineal system. You see, when a man picks a wife, he is often stirred by a vacant beauty or the desire to consolidate his power. On the other hand, women tend to select men for their intelligence and kindness. Which do you think will thrive better over centuries: a state ruled by the vain and proud or one managed with grace and thoughtfulness? Amar's father was a talented man, if a commoner, which explains his son's intellectual gifts."

Suddenly court life did not seem so daunting. "I suppose we cannot refuse without insulting Amar."

Edwin was elated. "We need stay only a short while. Besides, you will like his mother, the first princess." He rushed on without taking a breath. "Wait until you see the benefits of having the inheritance pass through the women. Of course, the present ruler is an older man, but when Amar takes over, the state will have a monarch with the energy of male youth tempered by the ripe mind and good sense of a mature woman."

On the other hand, I thought to myself, the throne could be held by a good man like Edwin with a selfish woman like his mother in the background, but I held my tongue and only nodded as Edwin raved on about a system he admired. Noticing an unsympathetic expression on my face, he blinked at me. "What's bothering you now? You still do not want to go, is that it?"

"On the contrary," I said as I realized this petty business with his mother had made me more than ready to get away from Cochin. I smiled at my husband. "Of course we shall go. I can be ready as soon as you wish."

32

❦ ❦ ❦

Two days later we departed Cochin at dawn in a boat propelled by ten stout men whose well-oiled mahogany skin seemed impervious to sun or rain. The slim craft cut through the water with the sinuousness of a snake, but seemed more suited for speed than sturdiness.

"How shall we fare if the seas swell?" I asked Edwin as I reclined on a rose silk cushion.

"We will never face the ocean."

"We are traveling down the coast, aren't we?"

"Yes." He gave me an enigmatic smile, then explained, "We will remain on a maze of inland backwaters called the captive sea."

"The whole way? It must be a hundred miles."

"More." On a map he showed me how this mysterious weave of waters ran parallel to the ocean all the way to Travancore. "Isn't it curious that the state is shaped like a conch, as if echoing its link with the sea?" He went on to describe the area as walled in on the eastern side by the Great Western Ghats, which rise to eight thousand feet, and bounded on the west by the ocean. "Thus Travancore is coddled in an embrace between the hills and water," he concluded lyrically.

"You make it seem like a magical world."

"In a way it is."

I stared up at the dappled light spilling through the emerald fronds and listened to the intermittent splash of the oars, which sounded like a huge fish pulling us forward like some tonga pony of the waves. Just before nightfall of the next day, we arrived at Quilon. Except for brief stops to relieve ourselves, we had eaten and slept on the boat for two days and nights, so it surprised me when we pulled up to a quay.

"We'll stay here tonight," Edwin announced.

Almost hidden behind draperies of palms and cashew trees on the bank of Lake Ashtamudi, the town was a primitive waterfront trading post.

"But where?" I asked, surveying the shabby wooden houses along the winding canals.

"We are to be guests of the British resident. He lives up on that hill."

I followed his hand movement and saw some more substantial dwellings and then the residency. In the setting sun its crenellated red roof glowed like a torch. Intricately carved balconies glinted like white birds.

Word that the maharajah's launch was at Quilon reached the British resident before Edwin and I could climb the hill. We rejected the offer of a palanquin, wanting to stretch our stiff legs. The resident and his wife met us at the gate and introduced themselves.

"Hello. I am Dennis Clifford, the resident of Quilon. It is my pleasure to welcome you to our little outpost," said the tall man, whose clothes hung on him as though they were tailored for someone with more flesh. At first I thought the climate might have disagreed with him, but then after studying his bright eyes and florid cheeks, I decided he preferred loose garments, a practical solution in this humid land. "May I introduce my wife? This is Jemima Clifford."

I shook hands with a winsome lady whose voluptuous chest dominated her slender frame. She wore her auburn hair in ringlets that framed her heart-shaped face.

"Delighted to have you with us," Dennis Clifford said with an aristocratic accent. "Not often do we have the opportunity to have a guest so recently out of Calcutta," he said to me, surprising me with what he already knew.

"I am certain you will be wanting a proper tea," his wife said, steering us to a table on the veranda overlooking the town.

I warmed instantly to our hosts. They had the gift of making a visitor feel like the most important person in the world.

After making sure my plate was filled and my cup of tea mixed to my preference, Dennis Clifford pointed out the sights of his domain. "In the distant clearing is the temple, and over to the right is the fruit-and-vegetable market. I am afraid that except for our central location in the state and the ruins of the Portuguese fort at Tangasseri, Quilon has little to offer." He grinned conspiratorially. "Why have I accepted a post in this backwater? Is that what you are wondering? A low mark on the ICS examination? A political disgrace?" His high forehead crinkled.

"Well . . ." I shrugged slightly, hoping that that minor acknowledgment did not give offense.

"Quilon may seem sleepy, but it is a strategic location—the sole location south of Cochin suitable for a port."

"That sounds promising."

"Indeed. However, the maharajah is a provincial fellow who cannot see beyond his own navel. He is well-matched by the British resident to Trivandrum, a kindly old codger, but one whose fondness for the past has clouded his vision for the future."

"How frustrating for someone with progressive ideas."

Mr. Clifford's eyes widened. "You are very perceptive, Mrs. Salem. What do you think would be the way to relieve the difficulty?"

"I suppose the solution would be to move from the sidelines into the center of power."

"You think I belong in Trivandrum."

"Forgive me if I spoke out of turn."

"Not at all. I asked for your opinion. I was only wondering how you knew so much about politics. Is your father involved in Calcutta's raj?"

"No, he is a man of commerce."

"Then what would you know about sitting on the sidelines?"

"Why, Mr. Clifford, that knowledge is every woman's birthright."

His lips twitched with amusement, but he did not laugh at me. "Then, from one bench-sitter to another, let me just say that at the moment, life in Trivandrum is an exceedingly tedious round of pompous rituals. Distasteful moments of intrigue punctuate the doldrums while a few delicious bites from the apple of privilege sweeten the pot."

I looked confused.

"The maharajah is old, sickly, and set in his ways—some of which are difficult for anyone with European sensibilities to appreciate," he said with a touch of disdain. "Sir Mortimer Trevelyan is old, but in perfect health and as wily as they come. He is an old crony of the former governor of Madras, and he will remain in place until the maharajah's successor takes over. After that—"

"Now, Dennis, after two days on the water these young people would probably prefer lighter conversation," his wife said. "Mrs. Salem, forgive me, but I am hungry for news from the outside world. I hear you are recently out from Calcutta."

"You know more about me than I do you," I said good-naturedly.

"When the young prince passed this way a few weeks ago, he told us about you both."

"Of course," I said with relief, and settled back on the settee. As the tropical darkness enveloped us, I found it surprisingly easy to tell Mrs. Clifford about how Edwin and I had met, and our two weddings. "There is no way out," I concluded. "Two ceremonies in less than a month have sealed my fate."

"Poor darling, is that a complaint or a boast?" Edwin interjected in a husky voice that caused my pulse to leap.

"Sounded like a boast to me." Dennis Clifford chuckled. "Now we had better adjourn inside, or instead of dining as guests of the residency of Quilon, you will be the feast for the carnivorous winged beasts who crave visiting delicacies."

As he spoke the words, I became aware that some of my romantic sensations might have been the result of an insect attack. Swatting my arms, I followed the Cliffords' lead.

"After the journey, I thought you might like to bathe," Mrs. Clifford suggested.

"Oh, yes."

"Baths have been prepared in the room adjacent the nursery."

"How many children do you have?"

"Seven at last count," she replied. "And one more on the way. Tomorrow you might allow me the honor of introducing you to them. They do so like to see a fresh face now and then."

"I'd like very much to meet them."

"That's good, because the house is too small to hide them from you."

Side by side Edwin and I bathed in a room with two large metal tubs in the center. On the pegs lining one wall hung sacks embroidered with the children's initials and containing their toiletries. Slippers, from the smallest on the left to the largest on the right, were placed underneath the sacks.

"Isn't that adorable?" I said. As I lathered myself, children's calls filtered through the wooden walls. "I am beginning to admire Mrs. Clifford."

"Would you like a house filled with so many children?"

"I wouldn't mind. I've always lived in a large family. There were three of us, then came Ruby, then Zilpah's boys, and finally Seti."

"What do you think of the resident?"

"Awfully nice. Do you know anything about him?"

"I seem to recall Amar saying that he is the nephew of the former viceroy, the Marquis of Ripon, and I believe his wife is the daughter of an earl. Makes one wonder why they are stuck in this corner of the empire."

"He thinks Quilon is about to boom."

"That hardly seems likely," Edwin said with a laugh. He stood up and poured a pitcher of water over his head, then shook himself off like a dog, spraying me.

"Edwin!"

With a fluid gesture he stepped out of his tub and into mine.

"Edwin!"

"Hush." He bent over and kissed me, and soon his intentions were clear. He knelt over me.

"Edwin . . ." I whispered. "The walls are too thin. There are children running about." He paid me no mind and proceeded to lick my nipples. Sloshing water over the side of my tub, I propped myself up slightly as he maneuvered above me. Just then we heard a creak.

He started and leapt out of the tub, banging his ankle. "Ow!" He rubbed the spot and looked at me dolefully.

I shook my head. "Bad boys get punished."

He pouted as he wrapped himself with a towel.

"Later," I promised.

※ ※ ※

The table gleamed with silver. Jemima appeared in a yellow gown edged with coral silk ribbons around the bodice, waist, and hem. Her husband wore a white dinner jacket with a frayed cuff.

"What a joy to have you with us," Jemima said, clasping my hand as she led me to my place.

"Indeed, indeed," the resident added, smiling broadly in my direction.

The servants placed bowls of a clear broth in front of us. "I must warn you, the soup is not only hot, but quite spicy. I am a firm believer that chilies protect against tropical disease. Most of the cooking here is my alteration of home recipes with local condiments."

I took a tentative sip. At first I tasted only a chicken stock. Then an assault fired the roof of my mouth. Another sip seemed smoother to the tongue, but then I was accosted with a second volley that caused boiling tears to form. I blinked, but not before Dennis noticed.

"My dear, I do think Cook has overdone it this time."

"No, it's delicious, really," I protested.

Jemima passed me a plate of rolls. "Try one of these with it."

The bread was superb, soft and yeasty, with a touch of sweetness that was the perfect foil to the broth. "You must tell me how to bake these," I said.

"Do you have a cook?"

"No, not yet. Yali and Hanif do almost everything for us."

"I counsel many new girls just out from England. They expect to have everything as they did at home, so that is the hardest adjustment. For you, the most important step will be reconciling to the peculiarities of the Malabar climate. Would you mind some counsel from a veteran?"

"I'd welcome it."

With my encouragement, Jemima launched into advice covering everything from molds to fevers to training servants. "I have never had any difficulty. Just remember that an untidy mistress has untidy servants; a weak mistress has idle servants. I know some may think me cruel, but I keep back a portion of my servants' pay, partly to prevent them from running away at the least difficulty, and partly so I may dock small amounts in fines for various transgressions. At the end of a year, my good servants thank me, for they have a nice sum set aside."

The serving of a large fish distracted her attention. With an astute eye she watched her bearer remove the bones. I turned my attention to the discussion the men were having.

"Since the opening of the Suez Canal, there has been a veritable explosion of interest in the resources here," Dennis said as he brushed back the tufts of hair that bristled above his ears. "Quilon is exceptionally well-situated to be a transit point for Ceylonese goods to be shipped to Europe."

"Do you think more ships will be calling here?" Edwin asked earnestly.

"Absolutely. Mostly the ships come into Bombay, or, as a second port of call, Cochin. Nevertheless, the harbor of Quilon has splendid possibilities."

Edwin leaned toward our host. "Really, sir, that is quite interesting."

The resident had noticed that I was no longer occupied by his wife, so he turned to a new topic with me. "I understand this will be your first trip to Travancore, Mrs. Salem."

"Yes."

"When Prince Amar passed through here a few weeks ago, he mentioned you would be coming this way soon. And, of course, when he sent the royal launch, his men alerted us when to expect you. May I say how pleased I am you have offered the prince your friendship at this time."

I looked at him quizzically.

"Then you do not know," he said slowly. "I thought that might be the case. I should have guessed Prince Amar would not want you to feel obliged to accept his hospitality."

"Is something the matter?" I asked nervously.

"Don't you know why Amar was in Cochin last month?" his wife interjected.

"I supposed he was seeing the Maharajah of Cochin," Edwin offered easily. "They have such close ties."

"Exactly so. The prince had come for advice about the transfer of power in case his uncle's health worsened."

"Is the maharajah ill?" I asked.

"The man has had a weak heart his whole life. There was an episode before Christmas when some claim his heart stopped and his lips turned blue. They revived him with cold water and brandy."

"It sounds serious," I said, recalling Grandmother Flora's illness.

"Yes, quite." The resident folded his hands and peered at Edwin thoughtfully. "The prince confided he has high regard for you, Mr.

Salem. He told me he was hoping you would become one of his advisers someday. I must admit when I met you and your enchanting wife earlier today, I was a bit dismayed to find you so youthful. Now I realize you have much to offer the heir. May I speak frankly?"

Edwin nodded respectfully.

"Travancore is like most Indian states, with factions broken along religious and caste lines. Among the Hindus, there are several castes of Brahmins who are wealthy and contentious; the Nayars, the largest and most important section of society, from which all the royalty descend; the Iravas, who do much of the agricultural work; and the Shanars, who are the Tamil-speaking laborers. There is also a large colony of Syrian Christians, a smaller group of Muslims; several despised slave castes; and the odd Englishman like me—not necessarily in order, mind you."

"And the maharajah must make decisions that satisfy everyone," his wife added.

"I do not know if he ever satisfies anyone. At best, he pacifies. In any case, as a Jew you stand outside these factions, giving you a neutral position. When the new maharajah takes the throne, everyone will plead his own interest and Amar will lose perspective. Where will he turn for advice? To a prime minister, who may have been corrupted . . . to his mother, who will have ideas of her own . . . to the resident, who must represent the crown above all? No, a man looks to his friends, often his boyhood friends. Who better than you, especially since your friendship began when there was little chance he would ever be maharajah?" He stared at Edwin with eyes the hue and toughness of steel.

"That may be true," Edwin replied carefully, "but my wife and I have no intention of making Trivandrum our home. This is merely a trip to introduce Dinah to Travancore and to spend time with an old friend."

"I thought the prince gave you the Orchid House," Jemima stated bluntly.

Edwin's hands waved in the air as if he was dismissing the idea. "Merely a gesture, part of a wedding game."

"That's not the way I heard it," she replied crisply.

"Well, my dear, we have been told only Prince Amar's version, and we both know how impetuous a young man he can be. Just let me say I believe it is possible you will be on the scene when a transition takes place." He hesitated and watched the effect his words had on Edwin.

"Then, sir," my husband replied somberly, "would you have time to speak with me tomorrow and advise me on the particulars?"

The waiters removed our plates and served a pudding. "Yes, let's leave this business until tomorrow," his wife suggested earnestly. "Remember, Dennis, these two are on their honeymoon."

"I don't know how long a honeymoon lasts," I said. "Edwin's mother says that it ends when the children come. Do you agree?"

"Certainly not," Jemima exclaimed. "Or I would not have had quite as many."

❦   ❦   ❦

In the morning, while Edwin met Dennis in the resident's study, his wife introduced me to five of her children.

"Paul and Mary are away at school. I am considered a renegade, since I would not permit them to leave before twelve, but I believe a child needs his mother until then and the rest of the world is wrong-minded on that score. Besides, I am perfectly competent to tutor my own."

"I am certain you are right," I replied with conviction, since I could not imagine having to leave home at five or six and not see my parents for some years, like many of the English girls I had known.

A toddler climbed on her lap and pummeled her chest. "Mooky, mooky."

"Oh, Sebastian." With a demure shrug she put the boy to her breast. "If you will permit me one more piece of advice, may I suggest you feed your own children when the time comes? I have not lost a single child, and this is because my own sanitary habits are far beyond what one can expect of any native ayah. Besides, a child should have but one mother. That is not to say I don't have help with the children. We employ two ayahs at present and I'll bring on a third for the new baby. Someone else can wipe its bottom or wash its clothes, but only a mother can nurture and educate."

My thoughts turned to my mother dozing on the veranda at Theatre Road, the mouthpiece of the hookah cupped in her hand. "Not every mother is as skillful as you, Mrs. Clifford."

"You will be a fine mother, Mrs. Salem."

I heard footsteps behind me and turned. Edwin and the resident were standing in the hallway. "We must get ready to depart," Edwin called softly.

With her free hand Jemima clasped mine. "I wish you could stay longer."

"We will pass through Quilon on our way back to Cochin," Edwin said.

"You must plan to remain longer next time," Dennis insisted graciously.

At the wharf, the men had a few final words together while I rearranged the cushions and told the porters where to place the baskets of fruit we had purchased.

"Don't forget my suggestions," the resident said as he shook Edwin's hand. "And remember to advise me if the situation changes. I would rather not wait for official tidings."

"Don't worry, sir, I am most happy to oblige."

The next section of our journey took us through a series of tunnels carved in the mountains that crept close to the waterways, and in a few hours we came to Varkala. The village sat quietly at the foot of red hills streaked by water spurting from sharp clefts.

"Above here are three springs of sanctity and purity that have always attracted pilgrims," Edwin pointed out. "Once I climbed that hill, called the Mountain of Shiva, for the splendid view. Sometime I will take you there, and also to see the *math*, the hermitage where a Hindu mystic they call Narayana Guru presides. Amar is quite taken with his preachings, which declare that Hindus should break free of the caste system. 'One caste, one God, one religion' is his motto."

"Doesn't that sound familiar?"

"Exactly. I'd say he was the Moses of Malabar. Actually, the guru is attempting to open the temples to all Hindus and abolish idols. To set an example, Amar has replaced the statues in his own home with mirrors to remind everyone that 'As we are, so are our gods too.' When Amar becomes maharajah, I would not be surprised if he enacts laws to that effect."

"Is the maharajah really dying?"

"That is Dennis Clifford's opinion, but who knows? He has dozens of doctors and healers who attend his every breath."

"Did Amar give you any hint of this?"

"No. If I had known the situation, I probably would not have brought you here."

"Why? Don't you agree it would be good for Amar to have a friend nearby?"

"Situations involving power are complicated. I am no expert in royal politics, but I have heard enough to guess the intrigue is exceedingly unpleasant. Amar has dreaded this for many years, ever since his brothers died."

"How did they both die at the same time?"

"Cholera. There was an outbreak in Travancore before the monsoon floods."

"I still don't understand why you would not have come if you had known."

"Because if the old maharajah dies, anything we do or say will be deemed suspicious. Everyone will think we have come for personal gain."

"The prince sent for us."

"We know that. Others might think we manipulated him into giving us the Orchid House or that we are vultures hovering outside the palace walls."

"Is that what the resident suggested?"

"No, but even Clifford wondered if we knew the situation before we arrived in Quilon. Now he does not believe those are our motives. However, he wanted me to see how we would be perceived. He gave me suggestions on how to proceed if the worst happens. Let's just hope it doesn't."

33

♦ ♦ ♦

Trivandrum, the capital of Travancore, unfolded like a mysterious flower.

I was asleep when we docked, and moved in a daze to the litter that carried me through the silent nighttime streets. Without fully awakening, I passed through a lofty gate, up stone stairs, and into a gaslit chamber where the walls had a golden glow. Yali attended me and soon I was asleep in the arms of my husband.

In the morning, as we lay in bed sipping tea served by Hanif, I hardly knew where I was. "Could you open one of those compartments in your mind and tell me what you know about Trivandrum?" I asked Edwin.

"Well, its Indian name is Tiru-Ananta-puram, meaning the 'sacred city of the snake Ananta.' You know about the snake on which Vishnu—whom they call Padmanabha in Travancore—reclined. He's a very important deity here."

I rolled out of bed. "I want to know more," I said as I peered out the narrow windows.

"We'll spend the day looking around," he said lazily.

Even before he was ready, I padded in my bare feet down the stone corridor to an arched doorway. Stepping outside, I saw our dwelling was one of many along a street bordered by twin stands of regal palms. Two women in flowing white gowns bent over the red soil paths, tracing patterns with white powder. Working rapidly, guided by almost invisible marks, they fashioned geometric arabesques that flowed from their fingers like ribbons. From a distance I admired the variations. Strolling closer, I admired the intricate workmanship. Just before I approached, a graceful lady had finished her design by adding a hibiscus blossom at the main intersection of her lines. As she stood up, turned, and smiled at me, I gasped. The gauzy drapery of her garment did not even attempt to cover her chest. Confused, I gave a jerky bow and rushed back to the Orchid House.

I bumped into Edwin at the doorway. "That woman—her breasts are completely exposed!"

He gave a wry smile. "That's how the Brahmin women dress here."

I stiffened. "Is that the fashion for everyone at court?"

"Wish that it were," he said with an admiring glance at the woman's back.

Just then a breeze whipped up, destroying the ephemeral patterns in the dirt. I shook my head. "What a waste."

"Not at all," Edwin countered. "The pleasure was in the preparation, not the glory."

"Don't you believe they feel a pang of regret?"

"Perhaps those who live from moment to moment rest more easily."

"That is merely the excuse that has kept Indians slaves to the caste in which they were born."

Edwin shrugged. "While you may think an immutable caste restricts potential, others believe the system offers freedom. Look at our predicament: you and I have so many choices, we do not know what to do, not even where we should live. But if I had been born a sweeper in Trivandrum, I would die a sweeper in Trivandrum. I would not question my lot. I would make the most of every day."

"Until you actually are a sweeper in Trivandrum, you cannot possibly know what they feel or think," I replied with a sniff. "For instance, if I were the sweeper's wife, I might hope that my children might do better than their father. And if I knew this was impossible, I might despair."

He gestured to the smudged remnants of the white patterns on the red earth. "Does that look like the work of despairing women?"

"Obviously they are not the wives of sweepers," I replied.

"You are right. This is the royal garden area. However, that doesn't alter my argument." Edwin led me inside, and I sensed the discussion was over.

"Will we see the prince today?"

"He will have been informed we are here. I expect he will greet us as soon as he is able."

⚘ ⚘ ⚘

A cow-drawn cart driven by a syce in a black turban was waiting when we left the Orchid House, which I soon realized was the grandest dwelling in that walled section of the town.

"Who else lives here?" I asked.

"The extended family of the maharajah: children, sisters, and court favorites."

Passing a street bordered by humbler clay houses, I asked, "And who lives in those?"

"Other high-caste Brahmins."

We rolled along sandy avenues laid out in a regular fashion. The quantity of sturdy buildings surprised me. Edwin pointed out two hospitals, several banks, various ministries that one would expect in a capital, and dozens of schools.

"I have never seen so many schools so close together."

"Remember what you said about the longings of a sweeper's wife to better her child? Travancore has the highest literacy rate in India, which is the result of having a woman sitting beside the throne."

My resistance to Travancore began to melt. "I would like to meet the maharani."

"There is none. Remember I said the maharajah's mother is dead. Amar's mother is the first princess. She will become queen when his uncle dies."

"Will I meet her?"

"Certainly. She was very kind to me when I was last here."

After passing churches and chapels for the Protestants, Catholics, and Syrian Christians, we came to the Street of Merchants, which was filling with men whose faces had high, noble brows and wide almond eyes.

"What do you think?" Edwin whispered as we passed a group of Brahmins.

"They are very handsome," I replied.

"Indeed." Edwin chuckled. "You can see so much of them!"

My gaze shifted from their honey-glazed faces to their clothing. "I would hate to be a tailor in Travancore."

"Yes, the higher the caste, the less they wear. Do you see those men?" I glanced at a group who had ivory cloths around their loins and only a cord draped around their shoulders.

"Yes."

"They are dignitaries."

"Why do they have that cord?"

"It signifies rank. They get them from the priest at birth and wear them until they die. The cords are their sacred link between birth and death."

The men wore their hair in long knotted tresses that hung over their shoulders, giving me the impression they were female, but when they turned, it was clear they were not. "Why are there no women anywhere around?"

"The wives and daughters of Brahmins don't walk about until after sunset."

"And I know why." I giggled as we moved on behind the bazaar, where copperware glinted in the sun among fruits, grains, and printed cottons that flapped in the breeze. Edwin held my hand discreetly. "Where is the palace?"

"We'll go by it before we head back to the Orchid House. I don't suppose we should be away too long, in case Amar summons us."

The cart came to a stop after we rounded an archway guarded by armed soldiers on horseback. "Only the royal family may pass underneath," Edwin explained. "We won't go any farther today."

I looked over a low wall to see an immense tank in which hundreds of Brahmins had plunged to their waist in water and were making ablutions and praying. With their dripping hair and glistening chests, they looked like golden gods emerging from a sacred sea. "Why are they here?"

"Some sort of ritual or festival—I do not know." Gesturing more than speaking, he conferred with the driver. Turning to me with a somber face, Edwin said, "They are praying for the health of the maharajah."

"So, it is true," I said softly. "Maybe that is why there has been no message from Amar."

Edwin nodded. "We had better return to the Orchid House."

During the morning we had seen clusters of soldiers wearing the large red turbans of the maharajah's guard. Now they were marching in formation toward the palace. The dust from their boots blew across the cart and covered us with a burnt-sienna mist. I gave Edwin a searching stare. He smiled slightly to console me, then gave clipped instructions to our driver.

The sky crowded with swift-moving clouds. More and more people milled about. Large droplets began to spatter the road intermittently. In the distance, we heard a rumble that I first thought was thunder, until I recognized the regular beat of drums and then the long wail of a fife. The driver halted the cart, and we strained to listen. Now a burst of booms drowned out the music. Another volley came in rapid succession, and many more followed.

"What—?" I asked Edwin.

"Rifles," he replied as a lightning flash illuminated the taut cords of his long neck.

"Does that mean he is dead?"

"Yes, I think so."

I looked down at my trembling hands. The rain had dissolved the red dust into scarlet streaks.

"Now I wish we had never come," I moaned.

"Dinah, my darling, don't worry."

"Why are so many soldiers on standby? Will someone contest Amar's succession? Why were they shooting?"

"It was a military salute. The old maharajah had been sick for a long while. His time had come. Amar's hour is here. Just think, we are about to witness something few people ever see. This should be wonderfully exciting."

With renewed admiration I watched the raindrops running off my husband's chiseled chin. "Yes, Edwin," I said, lifting myself to kiss his shining brow.

❦ ❦ ❦

The wails of the women of Trivandrum and the piercing sound of the death horn echoed in the streets of the capital as everyone prepared for the cremation.

"When will it take place?"

"This afternoon, I believe."

"We will remain in our quarters, won't we?" I asked in a thin voice.

"That would be a grave insult to our friend."

"Thousands will gather here. He won't know where we are."

"Eventually he would be told."

"Edwin, I do not want to see it."

"You don't have to watch. I doubt we shall get closer than a mile away."

"Edwin . . ." I pleaded.

"Surely you could not have lived your life in India and avoided the sight of cremations."

"I cannot . . ."

He saw my distress, but it puzzled him. "We shouldn't have walked so far in this heat. After you have a nice tiffin and—"

"No, Edwin, I shall not change my mind on this!" I snapped in a brittle voice.

He opened his mouth, then closed it without replying. I could not explain that every flaming pyre reminded me of the gruesome night my father burned my mother's possessions.

"I suppose you could be ill," he said, backing down.

As we arrived at the red path to the Orchid House, we saw Hanif waiting at attention. When he caught sight of us, he waved wildly. Edwin hurried to see what the commotion was about.

"You just missed him," Hanif said breathlessly.

"Who?"

"The sepoy sent by the British resident." He handed Edwin an official envelope.

"Is that from the Cliffords?" I asked.

Edwin turned it over. "No, the resident in Trivandrum—the bloke Clifford told us about."

"You did send word to Clifford, didn't you?"

"Yes, late last evening."

"Do you think this man knows what you did?"

Edwin tore open the envelope and read it rapidly. "No, that is not the problem. This is an invitation to sit in the distinguished visitors' enclosure." He stared at me.

There was no choice. Now I would have to attend the funeral.

\\/   \\/   \\/

If there was ever a man who could be described as "doddering," it was Sir Mortimer Trevelyan, who had been resident to Travancore under three maharajahs.

"My last state funeral," he said with misty eyes as he greeted each of his guests.

When I was introduced, he clasped my hand between both of his trembling ones and said, "Ah, the Sassoon girl. I knew your grandfather in Bombay. Quite a fellow! Quite a rich fellow." He winked at Edwin.

"My wife is from Calcutta," Edwin offered politely.

He cupped his ear. "What's that?"

Edwin dropped the point and steered me to a seat behind a velvet rope as a noise rose from the crowd, signaling something was happening.

"Here comes the body," exclaimed a voice from behind.

"Why is it being pushed through a hole in the wall?" I asked.

"Probably so as not to pollute the sacred gate," Edwin replied. "Afterward they will rebuild the wall to prevent the departed spirit from returning to trouble the survivors."

"Do you believe that spirits return?" I asked in a solemn whisper.

"Of course not."

"I do."

Edwin gave me a wondering glance, and, indeed, I was surprised at myself. I had not thought about my nightmares of my mother's ghost for years. It came back to me now: my mother lying in a section of the cemetery reserved for outcasts; my mother with a grave marker that denied her marriage and motherhood; my mother, who could not possibly be resting in peace. And all because of her murderer, Nissim Sadka. Why did the awful face in that courtroom suddenly flash before my eyes now?

"Dinah . . ." Edwin tugged at my sleeve. "Are you all right?"

Concentrating on the spectacle of the mortal remains covered with garlands of flowers in order to blot out the past, I clasped his hand. Small guns that gave a "pop" rather than a "bang" were sounded for each year of the departed prince's life. By the time I counted to sixty-nine, the specter of my mother had faded into the waves of undulating dust that churned in the wake of the procession.

Bareheaded bodyguards marching on foot were followed by their riderless horses. Next came a band that played a muffled version of the Dead March on the drums. After them marched a brigade carrying their muskets reversed and flags furled, then British officers in full uniform with strips of black crepe attached to their shoulders. The officers of state filed in a double line. Then, walking entirely alone, Amar strode with long, purposeful steps, trailed by his tiny nephews, two of whom were but babes carried in their mothers' arms. Behind him came a tall woman swathed in a filmy fabric that billowed in the wind like a vertical cloud.

"That is Amar's mother, the new maharani. Do you know why she is covered up?" He did not wait for my response. "To hide her happiness." As I shot him a warning glance, he lowered his voice and spoke into my ear. "At last she has her chance to rule. Nobody in Travancore will have more influence than she has."

"Where is Amar's wife?"

"Somewhere in that crowd of women to the rear. The wife has no status at court, remember."

The dignitaries were led under an inner canopy, while the body was borne around the pile three times before being placed on the pyre. Three last volleys of musketry were fired. Amar stepped forward as the smoke dispersed.

"What is he doing?" I asked my husband.

He shrugged. A gentleman behind us replied, "He is to put some rice and money in his uncle's mouth and break pots of water."

"And who are they?" I indicated the noblemen who took over from Amar.

"The Brahmin priests." I kept my eyes forward as our informant continued his explanation. "They are saying the *mantras*, prayers delivering the body to the five elements."

As the first licks of flame from the torches ignited the wood, I turned away and looked into the kindly blue eyes of the gentleman.

"You do not have to watch, my dear. Even the relations turn away out of respect." A piercing wail rose from the women, chilling me. "Now they are adding the ghee. Once the fires burn as high as the sheds, we may leave. The pyre will burn for at least two days."

"Thank you," I whispered, my gaze having discovered the face below the gentle eyes to have been ruined by smallpox depressions. Only one spot, the size of a child's palm, was an unblemished field upon his right cheek. This eerie smoothness seemed more of an anomaly than the disfigurement.

A tap from Edwin brought me around. "We can go now, but since we were his guests, we will have to make a brief appearance at the home of the British resident."

I coughed as the wind blew some acrid smoke our way. Edwin hurried me in the opposite direction, but the crowd surging toward the flaming pyre cut us off.

"Oh, Edwin," I choked, "I can't breathe!"

"I know a shortcut through a back street," said the man who had sat behind us.

We threaded our way behind him and soon found ourselves at the door of the residency.

"Thank you," I sighed gratefully.

"I am Percy Dent," he said, holding out his hand and pumping mine forcefully. "And you must be the young couple from Cochin."

"There are no secrets in Trivandrum," Edwin said with a gracious smile. "Yes, I am Edwin Salem and this is my wife, Dinah."

"I am very pleased to make your acquaintance, Mrs. Salem. Your husband does not seem to recall that I knew him many years ago."

"Have you been here long?" I asked.

"That depends on your definition of 'long.' I date from after the arrival of Sir Mortimer Trevelyan, but before Amar was born. I was brought in to tutor the new maharajah's eldest brother, and have remained as a royal educator ever since."

Edwin gave a respectful bow. "As I recall, you also taught Amar."

"Amar was not a boy one instructed. I provided the food for the mind; Amar devoured it."

"Of course, it comes back to me now. We called you 'Professor P.' Am I right?"

"Yes, yes," he said, letting out so great a sigh, his barrel-shaped belly expanded to a point that jeopardized his waistcoat buttons. "In those days, you and Amar were boisterous lads with more on your mind than books. I am surprised you took any note of me. Shall we go inside?"

I would have preferred to go directly back to our rooms, but I knew we had to make an appearance. Sensing my anxiety, Edwin guided me gently.

At the door, we greeted the resident again. Sir Mortimer did not recall who we were until an aide whispered "Sassoon" in his ear.

"I knew your father in Bombay," he said.

"Did you?" I replied without missing a beat. Looking past him into the foyer, I saw a welcome face. "Mrs. Clifford!" I called. Immediately I felt better than I had in many days.

"Hello, Mrs. Salem. I'm afraid we arrived too late for the ceremonies."

"Where is Mr. Clifford?"

She gestured to where her husband was talking loudly to Sir Mortimer Trevelyan. "Did you meet the resident of Trivandrum?"

"Yes, for the second time today, but he did not remember who we were."

"If you spent thirty years bowing and scraping in a native court, you too might have lost some of your sensibilities. Now you see why we prefer Quilon."

I nodded politely, even though I sensed that Jemima would not be entirely averse to exchanging her house above that buggy backwater for this airy marble palace.

"How did you find the prince?" she asked in a silky voice.

"We haven't seen him yet. We arrived the evening before the old maharajah died."

"A pity your timing was not better. I am certain he was told you were in residence. Is there anything you require?"

"No, we have everything we need."

"Poor child," she said, patting my hand. "A sad way to begin your holiday here."

"I don't like funerals," I said softly.

"No, they are never pleasant," Jemima said, looking at me carefully to see if she could discern what else might be the matter.

Edwin moved alongside me. "I hope you will excuse us, but it has been a long, hot day."

"Of course. If you don't mind, I will call on you tomorrow."

"I would like that," I said sincerely, but at the moment I was relieved to be able to leave.

No carts were available. Everyone in Trivandrum was on foot. By the time we reached the Orchid House, I wilted into my husband's arms. He began to pull off my clothes like a mad dog who had slipped loose of his collar. "This is what you need, what I need," he said as he knelt above me. I closed my eyes. Fiery images swirled in my mind, blocking any sensation but heat and horror. I forced myself to focus on Edwin's face. His eyes were half-closed, like a man at prayer. I stroked his taut back. My fingers explored each knob of his spine until I clasped his buttocks. He shuddered and plunged deeper, faster, harder. My mouth locked with his. All other visions were shattered by the insistent sensations. Once again pleasure triumphed over pain.

34

W W W

I had no quarrel with Edwin. I had no quarrel with Amar, the new Maharajah of Travancore, or even Travancore for that matter, and yet those first weeks were trying for me. Edwin may have found the rituals that surrounded the death of a ruler intriguing—and I might have thought them so for an hour—but over days and days they became tedious indeed.

One afternoon I sat reading *The Moonstone* in the pleasant nook that looked out on the bathing tank in the gardens, while Edwin stared at our Hindu neighbors taking their ablutions.

"Is that a good book?"

"Yes, you would like it."

"I don't know how you can read when so much is going on. If you would only take more interest in what is around you—"

"There is quite some difference between seeing and being part of something," I snapped.

"Unless one studies a situation, it is foolhardy to become involved in it. I can barely figure out the relationship between Dennis Clifford and Sir Mortimer, let alone whom Amar will appoint as his prime minister or how we might help Amar. At least I am keeping my eyes and ears open."

"And I am not?"

"You rarely leave the residency."

"What shall I do? Tell me and I shall do it."

"Now is certainly not the time. I have been married long enough to know that," he said as he stormed out of the room.

For a few minutes I brooded. What did he expect from me? With a sigh I opened my book, grateful that I had a good tale to engage me, and read: " 'Cheer up, Rosanna!' I said. 'You mustn't fret over your own fancies. . . .' " The irony pulled me away from myself and I felt silly for having upset Edwin. Just remember, you could be half a wife in Darjeeling listening to Euclid's jealous banter, or a spinster drifting about Theatre Road, or married to some old man that nobody else would have, I reminded myself. I resolved to be cheerier, and went to apologize.

"Where is the sahib?" I asked Hanif.

"He has gone to the fort to see the last ashes removed."

"And Yali?"

"She is in her room. Shall I summon her?"

"Yes." I went back to my quarters with a sigh. I would bathe and dress in something fresh. When he returned, I would follow his lead and not turn his words into an argument.

Edwin appeared again before I had dressed completely. I dismissed Yali and put on my own shoes. His amiable expression made me feel reprieved.

"You went to the fort."

"Yes, and the air is cool and breezy." He tugged my hand. "Come for a walk with me. You need a change."

"You're right," I said as I allowed him to pull me from the seat. Arm in arm we strolled the red paths within the walled enclosure. "My problem is that I feel as though we are looking out the panes of a foggy window. Our view is always clouded and we are unable to wipe away the dew."

"I am not certain I agree with your allusion, poetic though it may be, but if I go along with you, I would say the sun burns more brightly every day and soon the mist will lift and all will be revealed."

"But when?"

"The official mourning period is almost over, after which Amar will liven up the court. You do not know him as I do. Yes, he has his serious, his academic side, but more than anything he likes to enjoy life. Why else would he have us here?"

"So we are to be court jesters?" I said with annoyance, then regretted I had gone back on my resolution.

Edwin's brow lowered. Even his scowl was endearing. "Now, Dinah—"

I cut him off. "This waiting is frustrating. We have both seen those Indian families waiting on railway platforms. They sleep there, cook meals. Sometimes I wonder whether they are ever going anyplace at all. Well, that is how I feel living here."

"I realize these last weeks have been tedious for you, but I feel as if we have been granted the privilege of being witnesses to history."

"You have misunderstood me," I replied shakily. "Ever since we decided to come here, I have felt I was moving away from the center of my own life."

"You have felt that way from the hour we left Calcutta."

There was a scolding tone to his voice and I bowed my head. "Perhaps I have too much ambition for a woman."

He threw an arm about my shoulders, and his fingers drummed a protective tattoo on my back. "Now, darling, that is what I adore about you. Only there is a difference between ambition and impatience. Hasty decisions cause expensive mistakes. You may think I have been wasting my time here. On the contrary, I have watched and listened and have decided the time may soon come when together we can profit handsomely from our sojourn here. I share the resident of Quilon's belief that it is more rewarding to be in an area poised for growth than reap the harvest of a place past its peak."

"What are you planning?"

"I have several ideas."

I tugged at his sleeve. "If you do not include me in your thoughts, I feel even more useless."

"Well, then . . ." He cleared his throat. "From what I can tell, Travancore is married to the sea, yet Trivandrum does not have a decent harbor. The consequence has been the lack of progress in transportation. This fertile spice coast, which has been cut off from the rest of the subcontinent by the natural impediment of the Western Ghats, could increase its trade a hundredfold across the Indian Ocean."

"What would you do?"

"I was thinking in terms of shipping."

"What do you know about boats?"

"Not a great deal, but as one thought leads to another, experience builds upon experience. My uncle in Singapore may be a crass man and difficult to admire, but he is a smart businessman. He used to say that trading was like a tree. The root of his profession was buying and selling, and everything else branched from there. As long as you could follow an idea to the root, it was an acceptable investment, but he warned against making leaps into areas that did not come from the same source." He gesticulated excitedly as he described his apprentice- ship on the wharves of Cochin, his family's trade in spices, his work with the shipping agents of Singapore, and his dream of someday owning a fine vessel.

I could not follow everything he was saying, but was elated to have a light shed in the dark corner of our future. If he wanted a ship, I would do everything I could to help him.

ψ ψ ψ

By dawn the next day the populace of Trivandrum, who were to witness the ascension-to-the-*musnud* rites, crowded the courtyard of the pagoda of Patmanabhan. Brahmins filled the first ranks, while the others filed behind. The first members of the royal family to climb the temple steps were a retinue of women. "The ranis are the custodians of the keys of the temple while the god is absent from it," Dennis Clifford explained. "This ceremony is the receiving of the subsistence allowance. It is the maharajah's way of showing that he is subservient to the god and his representatives, the priests."

After Amar solemnly accepted sacks of rice and bolts of cloth, the priest gave him the first of his official titles.

The resident's wife nudged her husband. "What is happening?"

Dennis Clifford whispered, "With obedience he accepts the title of hereditary sweeper. In this way the highest ruler of the land takes on the mantle of the sweeper caste, the lowest in the Hindu world, and thus he also accepts the mantle of religious humility."

The crowd surged in front of me. I was able to make out the stooped figure of the new maharajah sweeping the temple steps with a crude straw broom. From then on, the rites became more complex. One after another, Brahmins came forward and prostrated themselves on the steps, then circumambulated the pagoda. The sun rose to its apex, but no umbrellas were unfurled. Edwin discreetly fanned me while the maharajah was anointed with consecrated water. Finally the high priest handed the sword and belt of state to Amar.

The new maharajah then marched around the pagoda and returned to announce his first order. "I hereby grant an additional five thousand rupees per annum for the repair of the temples."

A cheer rose from the citizens, who had wondered if Amar would retain the religious fervor of his uncle. "A clever boy," Clifford murmured. "Now his people's suspicions will disappear and he will have more freedom."

The sepoys escorted us to the old Audience Hall in the fort, where European officials and friends waited to welcome the maharajah. The room was a long, narrow upper chamber furnished with red carpets, velvet sofas, ten-foot mirrors, and lamps that hung from long brass chains. Paintings of former rulers lined the ocher walls. The colonnaded room opened onto a large open veranda that looked down at a vast square where troops were drawn up, richly caparisoned state elephants with bells about their necks carried bejeweled howdahs, and thousands of citizens waited expectantly.

We watched as a trembling Sir Mortimer Trevelyan, helped by two sepoys, made his way into the maharajah's presence and took a seat to his left. Next Dennis Clifford and his wife came forward.

"I suppose our friend will become the new resident to Trivandrum," Edwin murmured.

"How can you tell?"

"Look where he has been placed, right beside Amar's mother."

"Mr. Clifford said he did not want the position."

"On the contrary, he covets it."

"But—"

" 'He doth protest too much, methinks.' "

I watched the expressions on both the Cliffords' faces and decided they were more confident about courtly duties than they had led me to believe. "Amar would get on with Dennis better," I added in a whisper.

"Absolutely."

Suddenly I noticed there were no other women on the podium. "Isn't Amar's wife here?"

Edwin discreetly pointed to the far right side of the gallery, about ten rows back from the front. "Over there." I saw the profile of a plump girl who could not have been more than seventeen. She wore a simple white gown and a thick golden collar.

When the time came for us to approach the ivory throne, I began to quiver. Edwin took my arm and led me along. To calm myself, I kept my eye on the glittering canopy supported by pillars of silver. At the foot of the throne, I had no other choice but to look up. Amar was wearing an ornate turban adorned with an aigrette of diamonds, emeralds, and two pendant pearls that looked like enormous teardrops. Six bird-of-paradise feathers drooped across one eye in a sultry pose. As I curtsied, I lowered my gaze, but when Amar raised me up, his eyes locked with mine.

"My dear friends, may I welcome you to Travancore at last and beg your forgiveness for not being able to offer you the hospitality I would have under other circumstances." He attempted to enunciate each word, and the effect was stilted.

"Sir, it is an honor to be here, and thank you for the graciousness you have already extended us," Edwin said, his formal words lightened by a subtle glibness that echoed their friendship.

Amar's intense stare in my direction did not extend to include my husband, even as he replied, "Next week, when I can properly receive you, I shall compensate for the inconvenience." He turned to the next guest, cutting off any possible reply, and we backed away.

We were not placed near the other foreign visitors on the left, but were given a prominent aisle position behind some royal children and ahead of Amar's wife. After I took my seat, I smiled to show my pleasure at the honor. Amar nodded regally. From the corner of my eye I saw my husband's chest swell as he accepted the silent appraisal of the dignitaries, who must have wondered who we were.

❀　❀　❀

The following evening we were invited to the state dinner at the British residency. Edwin and I arrived early to watch the procession as the maharajah, this time atop the largest of the state elephants, followed native musicians whose strange flutes piped a high-pitched tune.

The maharajah was greeted first by Sir Mortimer Trevelyan, next by the Cliffords. After a nod to some minor British dignitaries, he clasped Edwin around the shoulders. "Winner! What do you think of your old Lover-boy now?" His pale face seemed to light from within. "My dear Mrs. Salem, I hope your new home pleases you." He took my hand.

"Yes, thank you."

"How might I make you more comfortable?"

"We lack nothing," I replied nervously, for he continued to hold my fingers in a tight squeeze.

"I am certain you are being polite, for there must be some little amenity that would be a welcome addition."

I shook my head, hoping he would move on.

"Now, Winner, your charming wife is too modest. She does not understand how much pleasure it would give a newly minted maharajah to snap his fingers and have her wishes gratified." He gave a childish pout that again reminded me of someone else. "Give me a hint. Does she have a particular flower that is her favorite? A particular color? We could have the gardens replanted to suit her. Does she miss the foods of Calcutta? I could send for a Bengali chef. Does she find the climate too hot? I could install more punkahs. There must be something I can do to make up for my inability to welcome you properly."

Edwin gave me an anxious glance. From Amar's behavior at our wedding party, I knew he was both flamboyant and determined. The maharajah would persist until we offered a suggestion.

"Read," I mumbled. "I like to read . . . perhaps I could borrow some books."

Amar pulled his hand away and thumped his chest. "Of course, the little scholar!" His lisp had returned. "I had forgotten. Tomorrow morning you must visit my library and take whatever you want."

"Thank you, sir."

He stepped closer to Edwin. "She will come, won't she?" He spoke like a worried child. "If she doesn't," he said, wagging his finger, "I will send my entire library to her." Then he whispered something in Edwin's ear before moving on.

Edwin patted my back. "That wasn't so terrible."

"What did he say to you?"

Edwin grinned sheepishly. "Nothing."

"Something about me."

"No."

"Then tell me," I coaxed.

Seeing my worried expression, he confessed, "What he said was: 'Now let us have some fun.' "

"What did he mean?" Mother Esther's admonition about Amar corrupting Edwin echoed in my mind.

"I suppose it was his way of letting us know that we were not going to spend the rest of our time in Travancore in mourning."

"Did you notice he referred to the Orchid House as our home? He doesn't think we are going to live here for the rest of our lives, does he?"

"I do not know what he thinks."

"We are not going to, Edwin," I insisted.

"Travancore, Cochin, Calcutta—what difference does it make so long as we are together?"

"You wouldn't remain here," I said, unable to control the rising pitch of my voice.

Edwin gave me a sharp look.

"But you said—" I whispered.

"I know as much about tomorrow as you do, no more, no less. Together we will decide everything, but for some reason you will not take my word for that. Maybe you would be content if I permitted you to decide everything for us both from now on."

"I did not say that," I choked, and looked around, hoping no one could have overheard our dispute. Just then Jemima Clifford caught my eye and came over to us. "Hello," I managed with a forced smile.

"Tonight the maharajah officially begins his reign. Already he is making his mark," she said in her silver-toned voice.

"What do you mean?"

"His uncle was austere—at least in public—yet there was a side of him few ever knew . . ." Glancing around at the other guests who strolled by, she dropped that train of thought. "Anyway, it seems our young ruler will have a more lighthearted style."

"I thought you did not care for court life."

"I didn't . . . until now," she said, shaking her head prettily so her reddish curls gleamed in the light from the brass lamps.

"Is it true, then?"

She tilted her head questioningly.

I formed my words carefully. "My husband believes the old resident might be retiring in the near future."

"Ah, here comes Amar's mother," she said, ignoring my remark. "Have you met her?" I shook my head. "Then you must. She speaks English more beautifully than I do. Shall I introduce you?" Without waiting for my reply, she led me to a woman flanked by saffron-turbaned soldiers.

I curtsied to the new maharani. When I raised myself before her, I discovered she was equal to me in height. Mrs. Clifford began the introductions, but the maharani fluttered her hands for silence. "I have heard much about Mrs. Salem." Then, to me, "I remember your husband as a schoolboy. Since there were so few who could be considered my son's intellectual equal, I always encouraged Amar's interest in him." I noticed the stress she put on "intellectual," with the intimation that this was the only area where the men shared a commonality. "What a comfort it is for my son to have his good friend beside him during these trying times."

"It gratifies my husband to be of service," I replied stiffly.

With an elegant wave she dismissed my comment. "I have been informed you are Edwin's dearest asset," she said with a silken smoothness.

"Thank you, your highness." I forced a smile, hoping she would not detect I had taken offense. Ever since I had overheard people gossiping about my dowry, I had resented any reference to my monetary worth.

"I look forward to having you visit me in my part of the palace, so I too may partake of your rich mind," the maharani continued graciously.

I was so ashamed that I had mistaken her meaning, I gushed, "And you must visit mine—I mean, the Orchid House—"

The maharani raised her long tapered fingers in the same gesture she had used to silence Jemima. "I know the Orchid House well, for that is where Amar and his brothers were born."

"Oh, yes," I stammered, then looked up into her large eyes and saw she was observing me with an empathetic expression.

A few seconds earlier she had seemed formidable. Now I admired her regular profile, her noble brow, the deep cleft at the delta of her throat, and the elegant way her black hair spun with silver wound around her forehead. A gauzy vest that some of the noblewomen wore when associating with the British covered her breasts, yet their outlines could be glimpsed. Enormous rings of diamonds and rubies hung from her earlobes, and her long, naked arms were entwined with spirals of gold encrusted with glittering jewels of every hue.

Her fingers moved like sinuous sea grasses, calling me closer to her side. "My son is very young. He was not raised to rule. He did not choose this course. Do you follow me?"

"Not really," I said aloud, wondering why she was confiding in me.

"At the moment, my son wears his power like an ill-fitting suit. Every mother knows it is better to have a tailor cut the cloth a few sizes too big rather than a few sizes too small, because a boy invariably grows into his garments. Until then we must overlook his awkward appearances and make allowances for his immaturity. He trusts you and your husband because you have few favors to ask."

"He has been too kind already, and—"

A mere curl of her wrist cut me off. "Would you do me the personal kindness of assisting my son in the coming days?"

"Of course, your highness, but I am uncertain how to help."

"A woman can temper his—shall we say—tendency to excess better than a man."

"But—"

She held up that authoritative hand. The enormous diamonds set into her rings caught the light, blinding me momentarily. "Friendship is the only requirement. Everything else will come with time. Mothers, even wives, bring too many complications . . ." Her voice trailed off as she caught the eye of a man in a white uniform. "Ah, the *dewan*," she said. The old maharajah's prime minister moved toward us, and I backed away.

Dennis Clifford waved me over. "You know how to impress the right people, Mrs. Salem."

"She is a very lovely lady, isn't she?" I offered.

"As smooth as a tigress."

Just then Amar's wife walked by slowly with her legs wide apart and a white drapery billowing ahead of her like a Genoa sail. I realized she was enormous with child.

"Have you been introduced to Rukmini?" Dennis asked.

"Not yet." I looked at the girl's round face and ascertained it was also swollen due to her pregnancy. Even with those changes it was apparent she had never been an attractive girl.

"You are wondering why Amar would have chosen her," Dennis said in an uncanny echo of my thoughts. "She is from the Kilimanoor family, which regularly infuses the royal house with their bloodlines. The point is that in Travancore, the *woman* selects her mate, even when she marries someone in line for the musnud."

"Do you mean she was able to pick a future rajah and he had to accept her?"

"The process is more complicated than that. Family members do most of the choosing, although she decided on him many years ago, when his brothers were alive and she did not expect to become the wife of a maharajah."

"Edwin attended their wedding only last year. By then she had to know Amar was next in line."

"The point is that she hardly matters. She will never be maharani. Her sons will never rule. Her husband may consort with anyone he chooses. The poor girl is really a nonentity."

"I would like to meet her. May I approach her? Or will she come up to us?"

"We can do nothing without an introduction from her husband, nor can she."

"What if Amar does not choose to have us meet?"

"Then you shall not meet." The sternness of his tone surprised me.

His eyes roamed the room before he continued, "May I speak frankly, Mrs. Salem?"

"Of course."

"Nobody would have taken notice of your residence at the Orchid House if Amar had remained a prince. Now many suspicions have arisen. 'Who are these Jews from Cochin?' they ask. 'How will they influence the maharajah?' If your husband offers advice or opinions, they will affect Amar's appraisal of an issue. People who desire to predispose Amar will seek out Edwin and try to cultivate him as a way of getting to the maharajah."

"What can we do about that?"

"Be cautious." He gave me a penetrating stare. "When you were in Quilon, you made this seem to be a post-wedding journey of a temporary nature. Now I understand you may be settling in Trivandrum. Is that true?"

The change from pleasant advice-giving to direct interrogation put me on edge. I struggled to give a noncommittal reply. "My husband wants to extend his friendship in this difficult time."

The resident did not press me. He slipped his right hand into his pocket and rested his weight on that foot. "The esteem the maharajah has bestowed upon Edwin impresses me. Others must have noticed as well. I have the sense that much of his generosity has been aimed in your direction."

"I am very grateful for his favors."

"And how will you express that gratitude?" he asked in a slippery voice that caused the skin on the back of my neck to crawl.

I glanced around, hoping someone would catch my eye and come over, but no savior appeared. "The maharajah is Edwin's friend. I shall follow my husband's lead."

"Well said, my dear Mrs. Salem. You are a clever young woman. But remember this: cleverness is not needed if caution prevails."

His words hit me with the force of a physical blow. My discomfort with Amar, which I had felt from the first moments of our meeting in Cochin, had been put into words by an unbiased party. More than ever I felt I had to arrange matters so that we would not dally in Travancore. How, though, could I convince Edwin to leave?

❀　❀　❀

"My library contains over ten thousand volumes. Among them you might find something to suit your fancy," the maharajah said. "During my reign I hope to triple the collection."

We were standing in a rotunda lined with shelves from the floor to the top of its glass dome, which spilled a beam of light into the stone chamber. The atmosphere favored the maharajah, who seemed younger and more approachable—until he spoke again.

"Here is one place you can be Winner and I can be Lover-boy again." Amar winked at me. "Don't you agree?"

"To be truthful, I can't imagine Edwin ever calling you that," I said, forcing myself to underline the statement with a laugh. Instead of becoming more at ease in the maharajah's company, I was finding his mannerisms increasingly disconcerting.

"Now, why ever not?" He batted his thick lashes like a bashful boy. "Am I so ill-suited to my nickname?"

Edwin rescued me. "My wife has never seen you relaxing in your private quarters. Since our arrival we have attended more state occasions than most people do in a lifetime."

Amar walked toward me, then halted a few inches shy of my folded arms. "I never dreamed of becoming a ruler," he said, his words becoming more jumbled as he continued. "Yet here I am. The chosen one. I must accept my fate. I must meet every obligation." His hands fell to his sides in a dramatic gesture. "Yet I *must* retain some of my own life—something purely personal—or I shall never be able to fulfill my duties with enthusiasm." He gave us an imploring look, like that of an animal who wishes to be rescued from a trap. "Winner understands, don't you?"

When Edwin nodded, Amar focused on me. "And you will try to, won't you?" He tilted his head provocatively.

I could think of no reply, for I was trying to determine exactly what it was about his appearance that had been disturbing me. Something about his long, curling eyelashes that looked inappropriate on a man, and his jutting lower lip made my stomach churn.

"Ah!" Amar jerked his neck upright. "Now I understand the problem. She feels left out, and why shouldn't she? What is the first thing we would do when someone new came into school? We would give him a nickname! I admit I have never felt comfortable addressing your wife as Dinah or Mrs. Salem. So what shall it be?" He shot a glance at Edwin.

"I call her 'darling.' " He chuckled.

"That will never do," Amar groaned. "The point is to make her feel like one of the boys."

"What do you suggest?" Edwin asked.

"Let's see . . . Dinah . . . Diana . . . the huntress . . . hunter . . . hunt . . . no, I do not care for any of those. What about something to do with Sassoon? Nice sounds to that one, don't you think? Sasso, Sooner, Sassy . . . Sassy! Ah, that's not bad. Quite suitable even. A sassy person says what she thinks. A sassy woman is both spirited and smart."

"A sassy person talks back, and that certainly suits my wife."

"Well . . ." As Amar waited for my reaction, I tried to quell the confusion I felt. I welcomed the maharajah's effort to make me feel more at ease in his presence, but his vigorous application of his point seemed ludicrous. "Do you object?"

I found the name insulting, but dared not admit it. "I suppose not . . ."

"Then that settles it. Winner, Sassy, and—"

"Come now, Lover, have your feet turned cold?" Edwin gibed.

"We could just use the initials L. B.," I offered hesitantly.

"Brilliant solution, Sassy." Amar touched his turban in a salute. "A jewel, your most treasured asset, a woman fit to rule! I wish she was mine," he said in a tinny voice, then cleared his throat. "However, so long as she is yours, that is the next best thing. Now, Sassy, have you found something to read?"

"Do you have *Lorna Doone*?" I asked in a burst of nostalgia, as well as a desire to stump him.

"I have no recollection of anything past the scientific sections. Why don't I send for Professor P.? He has a system to locate everything in the collection. Until then, allow me to show you my private chambers. I would like to ask your opinion about them."

We followed the maharajah through several winding passages that led into courtyards filled with pools of water: some ovals, others hexagonal honeycombs. When we reached a series of three circles looped together with bridges as part of the linked circumferences, Amar gestured extravagantly. "This would be a lovely place to bathe if the water was not hotter than the air. Someday I will bring in tubs of ice to cool them. Wouldn't that be amusing?"

Edwin rolled his eyes at me.

A gate with a wrought-iron pattern of two peacocks opened before us. The maharajah's guards saluted him by lifting ceremonial silver spears. In this inner garden, we heard the soothing pulse of water trickling down stone steps. Just beyond, we entered apartments inlaid with blue-and-white tiles in so many patterns and variations the eye would never tire, and yet from a distance they formed a harmonious whole. In the center of the room, a mattress covered with a blue silk carpet was tucked under a sky-blue canopy held up by silver poles.

"This is the sitting room, but you see the difficulty, don't you?"

"It is gorgeous," I said as I surveyed the silver tables, silver spittoons, and a giant hookah encrusted with silver and sapphires.

"Ah, but where in this sitting room does one *sit*?" Amar gestured to the bed. "Only the ruler may lounge, the others must stand." He bounced onto the mattress and leaned back on his arm. "Would you come sit beside me, Sassy?"

I was uncertain whether this was a test or an order. "I see your point, sir."

"What's the matter?" He sulked. "Are you angry with your friend L.B.?"

"Don't forget I know what the initials stand for!" I giggled to defuse his annoyance.

"Why am I starting to worry that your nickname was a mistake on my part?" He sighed loudly. "Anyhow, I want to do away with all this." Sweeping his hand in dismissal, he knocked the hookah over onto the bed.

Edwin ran over and righted it. "What do you mean?"

"I want to replace this array with furnishings from the palaces of the kings and queens of Europe."

"Do you want to remodel this room or your entire apartments?" I speculated.

"The whole palace, and perhaps some of the other dwellings. My mother is in agreement. Her home shall be one of the first to be renovated, and then the first princess and her sons will need to live in new surroundings to prepare them for their future. The Orchid House and other dependencies must be brought in line. By the time I am finished, Travancore will be the most stylish state on the subcontinent. What do you think?"

Edwin had a peculiar glazed expression, so I filled in. "There are many beautiful aspects to what is here. Surely you will not dispose of the treasures you possess."

"I plan an intermingling of East and West, a blending of comfort and utility."

"Do I understand you are planning on acquiring thousands of pieces of furniture which will be of enormous value and require transportation from a vast distance?" Edwin asked slowly.

"Yes, Winner, but ships sail to these shores every day."

"What sorts of ships, L.B.? Vessels carrying oils and spices and cannonballs will hardly transport your precious cargo safely. What you require is a special boat with padded compartments to handle delicate objects in violent seas."

"Then I shall have something built to my specifications."

"That could take years, but one could be refitted—if the right ship could be found."

"You know more about these matters than I. What do you think?"

"I see no difficulty, provided you could find an owner willing to do the modifications. It might take several passages to transport your furnishings, then afterward it could be reconverted for more ordinary cargo."

I felt as if I were inside Edwin's mind as he laid the groundwork for the offer I expected would come. In a few minutes, after a discussion of how to locate the furniture and whom he might send to Europe to do the buying, he did not disappoint me. "You may not have realized this, Amar, but I was considering entering the shipping business in Cochin. Dinah and I have already discussed establishing a regular ferry service between Ernakulam and Cochin and the islands."

The maharajah hopped about in his excitement. "Then you are the man for this enterprise, aren't you?"

"Perhaps. I must consider what sort of investment to make and how I can reuse the holds to transport spices and fine woods to Europe and then return with your order. After meeting your requirements, I could locate commodities to import for the Indian market."

"A ferryboat might be too small for the task."

"Our capital should finance a cargo ship, and a firm order that would ensure profitability from the start would convince me to make the investment."

I hardly dared glance at my husband, but finally did so surreptitiously. His eyes were gleaming, his hands gesturing happily as he and the maharajah deliberated the venture. This is what we both had been waiting for. For the first time since we had left Calcutta, I no longer felt Edwin was drifting aimlessly. At last he had something to occupy his mind, a purpose to pursue. Even if this meant we would remain in Travancore for quite some time, I looked at the prospect with fresh eyes. I should have believed him from the first, I reminded myself as I basked in the glow of his enthusiasm.

35

♦ ♦ ♦

ll I had been waiting for was happening. Edwin was stirred to a fiery heat as he contemplated owning a great ship. After the maharajah's furnishings arrived, we would not be bound to live in Trivandrum. In fact, since the capital of Travancore was not a decent port, Cochin was a more likely base. Despite the splendor of the Orchid House, the waterside cottage where we had spent so few nights alone was the place where I dreamed of returning, and all that seemed within my grasp. Even so, at the moment I could not see beyond the fact that Edwin was planning to leave me in Trivandrum while he went to search for a ship.

Edwin, who could have chided me for my shortsightedness, held me close as we lay among the cushions on our wide, low bed. "I shall not stay away any longer than necessary."

"How much time will it take to find a ship?" I asked, trembling.

His eyes gleamed with expectation. "I can't say."

"Why can't I come with you?"

"You could, as far as Cochin. I am certain it would please Mother to have you."

"To fetch and carry and listen to her complaints."

"Where else could you go?"

"The cottage."

"It would be unseemly for you to stay there alone."

"Why can't I accompany you to Bombay?"

"The shipyards are no place for a woman, you know that, and I could not do the job properly if I had to worry about your welfare." He kept stroking my neck as he spoke. "I would have to be out at all hours. By spending the evenings with merchants and traders, I might gather an inside tip. A distressed situation, an anxious seller, that is what I am after." He punctuated his last words with a kiss at the nape and muttered, "Nothing better than an inside tip."

"How soon?"

"Not for several weeks. Professor P. must first complete his lists and calculations. Until we know how many cubic feet of space the furniture will take in the holds, I cannot leave."

A pain, like a weight crushing my chest, caused my breath to come in short bursts. "I cannot let you . . . I will not . . ." I choked. Tears streamed from my eyes.

"What are you afraid of?"

I nestled against him and wept. "Since our marriage, we have hardly been apart for more than an hour . . . and you once said we would manage our lives side by side."

He stared into my eyes with vast tenderness. "And so we shall. This will be the briefest of interludes. I will work night and day and rush back as soon as I have located something."

"Do you think you will find a ship in Bombay?" I asked in a steadier voice.

"The chances are excellent. I might be lucky enough to locate something in Cochin." His voice dropped. "At worst, I might have to go to Singapore."

"That could take months!"

He placed his finger on my lips. "I doubt that will be necessary, but I wanted to prepare you. I would never hide anything from you, my darling Dinah." His eyes glistened when he saw he could not console me. He turned away to compose himself in a movement that gave me pause.

I reached out and touched his arm. "Edwin. Just think, a ship of our own."

He flexed his arms. "I hope I shall find something we can afford. Fifty thousand won't exactly buy the *Great Eastern*."

"What will it buy?"

"Something serviceable that should not require too much overhaul belowdecks."

"Do you plan to spend it all?"

"Not if I can help it, although we don't want a tub of rust, do we?"

"Do you really think it will be profitable?"

"Who are some of the richest men around? Shipowners. There must be a reason. Besides, how many start with a commission that pays for the entire first voyage? With that advantage, our profits should tumble in. With them we shall buy another boat." Contentedly he sank back on the pillows. "Wouldn't a fleet of three . . . or even four . . . be fine?"

I sensed he was imagining himself striding the deck of one of his ships, shaking hands with the captain, examining his crew as they lined up for inspection. I saw myself at his side in a white dress and wide-brimmed hat. The harbor in the background was Calcutta, and on the quay marveling at the gleaming ship were Aunt Bellore and Cousin Sultana, Zilpah and my father, my brothers, Ruby—

A knock on the door disturbed my reverie. Hanif brought in a silver tray with glasses of lemonade, water biscuits, and a letter from the palace.

"What does he want from us now?" I wondered peevishly.

Edwin broke the seal. "He has asked me to visit this evening."

"Am I not invited?"

"Not this time."

I felt both solace and disappointment. While I had no desire to see Amar, I did not want Edwin to either. But was that fair? I had pushed my husband into actively pursuing a profession, and now that he was doing my bidding, I wanted him to remain by my side.

"Do you have to go?"

" We *are* his guests, Dinah."

"I know. We are his marionettes, who must jump when he pulls our strings."

"There are strings everywhere. A child is controlled by his parents; a worker is managed by his employer. What is the difference?"

"I suppose you are right," I said sweetly, even though I did not want him to agree to do whatever Amar wanted. "What does he have planned?"

"He probably just wants to talk or play chess."

"I play chess."

"Do you? Who taught you, your father? I bet he's a pukka player."

Thinking it better not to mention Silas, I said, "An old friend taught me, but I am not very good."

Edwin stood and stretched. "Neither am I, at least not compared to Amar. With his mathematical mind, he's a wizard." He went to the basin and began to wash.

Wizard. What an odd term, I thought to myself. In some ways, though, it was apt. There was cunning behind Amar's lambent eyes. And a razor-sharp mind underneath his sloppy speech. Again I sensed there was something else—something odd and mercurial that frightened me. Ever since I had met him only minutes after my marriage in Cochin, he had seemed too friendly. Anytime he came close enough to me for even our clothing to touch, I felt annoyed. I had never voiced these feelings to my husband, for it was wrong to make a man choose between a friend and a spouse. Nevertheless, when Edwin went away, Amar would be the maharajah with supreme power over his dominion and I would be his beholden guest. Absurd as it was to think he would ever do anything to harm his friend's wife, I suspected he was not beyond using me to amuse himself. I hated the name "Sassy" and now I was stuck with it. His protestations that he only wanted to include me, turning their boyhood duo into some sort of a triumvirate, had been ludicrous. Why couldn't Edwin see through Amar? Even his own mother saw through his "ill-fitting suit."

"What shall I do if Amar invites me to the palace while you are away?" I said to his back.

"You cannot refuse him, unless you are unwell."

"Then I don't see how it is unseemly for me to live in the cottage in Cochin and proper for me to remain at the Orchid House without you."

As Edwin spun around, soap from his face sprayed out. I thought he was going to contradict me, but he stared at me with wide, worried eyes and said, "I see your point. Let me give it some thought."

My heart soared. In his own way, Edwin was realizing he could not leave me here alone. I was confident he would figure a way to take me with him. If I could only be less demanding and more clever, we would not have to chafe against each other. Most of the time, my first response was to argue or complain, while his was to try to understand my position. How lucky I was to have him! With a burst of feeling, I jumped up and hugged him.

"Ow!" he groaned as the razor nicked his chin.

I pulled the cloth from his waist and blotted the scratch. "Sorry, darling."

"Kiss it," he ordered.

I licked the ruby globule obediently. He found my mouth and gave me a fierce kiss. Together we stumbled back to the bed.

"You'll be late for the maharajah."

"The hell with the maharajah," Edwin said as he labored to make the pain in my chest float far, far away.

☙ ☙ ☙

"I have settled everything," Edwin announced the next morning.

"What time did you come in last night?" I asked sleepily as Yali placed a teacup in my hand.

"Must have been more like morning. I saw the sunrise."

"What did you do?"

"Talked about old times mostly. You would have been bored." Seeing himself in the mirror, he brushed his hair, which stuck out over his head like bristles on the back of a water buffalo.

"You shouldn't have got up so early."

"I didn't want to wait to tell you the good news."

He was going to take me with him!

"You won't have to be alone in Trivandrum."

My heart beat in anticipation.

"Dennis Clifford was there, at least for the first part of the evening.

Since the maharajah's made no move to have him become the resident in Trivandrum, he mentioned he might be returning to Quilon. I don't think he can abide living with Sir Mortimer Trevelyan much longer. On the other hand, though, it would be a mistake for him to disappear or he might lose his chance to be seen as Trevelyan's obvious successor. Then I thought of a way he could help us and we could help him. I mentioned that you needed a companion while I was away, and he graciously offered to move into the Orchid House—with Mrs. Clifford, of course."

"Of course," I muttered, not at all pleased with this solution. "What about their children?"

"You won't mind if they come down from Quilon, will you? You could help with their Latin and other studies. You once told me you liked to teach."

"I do, but . . ."

Edwin cocked his head. "Yes?"

I tried to swallow my disappointment and reminded myself that the Cliffords would insulate me from Amar's whims. "I suppose there is plenty of room here," I offered meekly.

"You do like Jemima Clifford," he added hopefully.

"Yes, darling, I like her very much."

Relief flooded his face; then he grimaced.

"What is the matter?"

"Too much wine."

I shook my head. "Were you naughty boys last night?" My voice was light and teasing, but when his face darkened for a moment, my pulse quickened. Mother Esther had warned me about Amar's adverse influence. What did she know that I did not? At least if Edwin was away, the maharajah could not sway him. I would stay with the Cliffords, protected by them. Once Edwin bought the ship, we would return to Cochin for good. After a few brief weeks of separation, all would be well.

☙ ☙ ☙

The moment the maharajah's launch disappeared into the mists of the captive seas of the backwater, I burst into sobs.

Jemima Clifford comforted me as though I were an injured child. "Now, now, he will be coming back soon . . ."

Something terrible was happening to my throat. I choked, coughed, sputtered, and then was grasped by the fear that I would never be able to breathe again. My panic must have worsened the condition. As I slumped to my knees, even sanguine Jemima became alarmed.

"Boy! Come here!" she yelled at Hanif, who at Edwin's insistence had remained behind to assist me. "Your cap! Take it off! Fill it with water." He bent down and scooped up some brackish water. She splashed my face. "There . . . there, Dinah." My hysterical sobs diminished to sputtering gasps. "Ah, your color is better. We must get you home and cool you off properly," she said as she continued to dribble water across my forehead.

I sat up and wiped my face with the back of my sleeve. I must have been a horrid sight with my hair mussed, my face streaked with tears and muddy water. She helped me stand. I thought I could manage until my gaze followed the turn in the river where I had lost sight of Edwin. Once again my legs felt like jelly.

"What am I to do?" I mumbled as she seated me in the cow-cart.

"You will go on," she said firmly. "I know this seems like a tragic moment, my dear, but Edwin is alive and well and will return in a few short weeks. You must do him credit by holding your head high and making certain everything is in order when he returns. Dennis and I both know you are not some silly sprite who will require coddling. Give yourself a day to recover and organize a new routine, and you will be fine."

"What do you mean by 'a new routine'?"

"It's never smart to become set in one's ways, for if you do not alter your habits, life has a way of altering them for you."

My mind was far too flustered with the loss of Edwin to comprehend what she meant, but the next morning she put her words into motion.

Much too early came a knock at my door. "Hello, Dinah. It's Jemima."

"Come in," I said as I sat up in bed. "What time is it?"

"Half-past six. Won't you join us for breakfast in the garden?"

"I rarely get up before eight and I usually eat in my room."

"Now, remember what I said about making a change? The mornings are so cool and pleasant in this season that I thought we might take a walk together with Vicky and Teddy. They adore the women who draw the mandelas, and want to decide which is the most beautiful. Won't you help mediate with me?" Her children had arrived the day before, but I had been too preoccupied by my last hours with Edwin to see them.

After we had admired the designs, Jemima suggested we sit on a bench while the children raced down the paths. "You are fortunate to have such healthy children," I said.

"Aren't I?" Jemima glowed. "I seem to have had my children in clumps, two years apart with a break to catch my breath in between."

"How old are Vicky and Teddy?"

"Twelve and eleven. And over there are Alexandra, who is seven, and Norman, who was just six. Then there's the last set: Sebastian is two and . . ." She patted her swelling abdomen. "Number eight. I wish you could meet Mary and Paul. You remind me very much of Mary. She's the brightest of the lot, although Alexandra may prove to be her equal. It's my view that girls are so much better at studies than men. What a pity they can never go as far, at least in public life."

"I'm not half as bright as Edwin, and I understand the maharajah is brilliant."

"Now, now, your husband's told us about your considerable achievements, but you have made my point for me. There is no way for you to gain recognition for what you know. After all the school prizes are handed out, girls fade into the background." The resident's wife mopped her brow with a lace handkerchief. Her blowing curls softened her tired face. "Will you help me with the two oldest and possibly Alexandra? We could have lessons every morning around this time and finish before tiffin."

"I'll give it a try."

She smiled and the gap between her front teeth winked at me. "Thank you, Dinah. The children do find the same voice tiresome after a while. Besides, it will be good practice." She gave me an affectionate glance. "How long have you been married?"

"Five months."

"You are fortunate to have some time to yourselves before the babies start. Even though they take nine months, once they take hold inside your belly, nothing is ever the same again." Thinking about how quickly Mozelle had changed, I shuddered. Mrs. Clifford took my reaction wrongly. "There is nothing to fear," she said, patting my hand. "Even the birthing is not as horrid as some women make it seem. Of course it hurts—I'd be doing you a disservice to say otherwise—but the pain is temporary, and the moment the babe is born, you feel it was worthwhile."

"I want to have a child," I muttered.

"Of course you do. Who knows? Maybe your Mr. Salem will come home to a little surprise of his own."

I shook my head. "Not this month."

The resident's wife flushed. "There'll be plenty of opportunities once you are reunited."

Thinking of Edwin's welcoming arms, his breath hot against my neck, his long, lean bronzed body pressed to mine, brought too many tears to blink away.

"What's the matter with Mrs. Salem?" asked Alexandra, who skipped up to me, her long golden braids flopping under her topee.

"Too much sun," her mother said. "Call the others, it's time to go inside."

❦ ❦ ❦

The next afternoon Jemima proposed a cultural hour, when we each would prepare something to read to the other and then we would discuss the points. Jemima was a clever woman. By keeping me occupied with her children and a round of obligations, she was staving off any chance of my collapsing into despair. Indeed, when I was alone for more than an hour, loneliness washed over me like a rogue wave and I had to struggle to keep my head above water.

The first week Edwin was away, I did not see the maharajah, but Dennis Clifford reported on his activities each afternoon. Mostly Amar was embroiled in tedious affairs of state. There was one curious ceremony, to which only the highest Brahmins and British officials were invited, that I was sorry to have missed after Dennis reported to us during a tea in the garden.

"As you know, one of the maharajah's titles is 'Slave of the God of Wealth.' As Maharajah of Travancore he receives a revenue of more than thirty-seven lacs each year for his personal treasury. Thus the avaricious Brahmins invented the custom of ceremonial rebirth for their master and their slave in order to obtain a share each time there is a new ruler."

The Quilon resident paused dramatically and bit into a cucumber sandwich lathered in chutney. Jemima and I were so captivated by the story, hardly a cup rattled. At last he continued. "This morning we gathered in the audience hall. Amar sat himself on one end of a gigantic pair of scales. Gold was placed on the other end until it balanced."

"I thought that sort of thing happened only in fairy tales," Jemima commented.

"He is not a light man," I said, laughing. "It must have taken quite a load."

"Gold is very dense. Still, the amount was impressive."

"What happened next?" his wife asked.

"As I understand it, the gold will be formed into a large hollow cow with space enough to permit the maharajah to pass through it, and in doing so, be spiritually reborn. That will take place sometime next week, and only the Brahmin priests will attend, for the cow will later be divided among them as one of their perquisites."

"It never ceases to amaze me that while we are different from others in many ways, the likenesses shine through," Jemima said in a wistful tone. "One cannot help recall the Christian doctrine that 'unless a man be born again, he cannot enter the kingdom of heaven.' "

"My dear," Dennis said kindly, "the new birth of the Christian is a far different thing from the new birth of a heathen prince. The latter is the work of man; the former is the work of God. The new birth of the Christian is that the soul becomes alive to God."

"What else is happening at court?" his wife said to spare me digression into Christian theology.

"Oh, yes, we all are invited to a musical soiree at the palace tomorrow evening," Dennis said, getting his wife's message.

She smiled at me. "Dinah, that should take your mind off Edwin for a few hours."

Gulping ever so slightly, I glumly agreed.

Once I learned it was to be an event attended by Sir Mortimer Trevelyan and other members of the European community, though, I had no concerns about how Amar might behave. I dressed in a pale violet tea gown and took special pains with my hair. During the dinner preceding at the British residency, I was seated between Sir Mortimer Trevelyan and Percy Dent. After initial pleasantries Sir Mortimer engaged two Portuguese visitors from Goa in a discussion on currency exchange. I was more comfortable chatting with the professor.

"Were any of the books I sent over suitable, Mrs. Salem?" he inquired. "I admit they were not exactly 'light reading' in the line of *Lorna Doone,* but you did say you wanted food for discussion."

"The essays were perfect. Mrs. Clifford thought we should concentrate on poetry as a start. Last week I presented James Henry Leigh Hunt's *An Answer to the Question: What Is Poetry?* while she discussed Shelley's *A Defense of Poetry.* Next week we will tackle what Matthew Arnold had to say in *The Choice of Subjects in Poetry.*"

The professor leaned back and crossed his arms above his protuberant stomach. "If you would like to elaborate any points with me, I would be most happy to act as your sounding board."

"Thank you. Perhaps you might have an opinion on—"

"You shall form your own opinions. You have a perfectly capable mind of your own. All you need is to be steered in the right direction, if you slip off course."

"You sound more like a sailor than a teacher."

"I am hardly that. I've had only one trip out that was the opposite of 'posh.' You know what that means, don't you?"

"No, I don't think so."

"Port outbound, starboard home, the placement of the more expensive cabins so you avoid the sun. Well, one taste of baking in starboard on the way to India poisoned any affection I could have had for the sea, which also managed to be as ghastly as possible. Some think I stayed on in Travancore to avoid the return passage." He gave a charming smile that made me forget his pocked face.

"That can't have been the only reason," I said sweetly.

"I was orphaned whilst I was at Oxford. Here I have found a true home."

"You will be going to Europe to supervise the acquisitions, won't you?"

"Yes, I am afraid there is no other choice."

"I hope the voyage won't be too dreadful."

"I am mustering my courage even as we speak."

"How long will it take to locate everything?"

"At least six months." He went on to tell me about the letters of inquiry he had sent to European dealers.

Six months! If he took our ship over, that meant the boat would be idle at the wharf until he was ready to leave. A ship should be sailing, not waiting like a syce at his master's beck and call. As I made a mental note to talk to Edwin about the advisability of this plan, the professor explained he would have to leave for Europe before our ship could be ready.

"That makes sense," I said, camouflaging my commercial concerns. "Tell me more about what you will be looking for."

Delighted at the opportunity, the professor prattled on about his preference for Regency over Louis XIV. "The pieces made for Versailles set the standard. The veneer techniques of Boulle cannot be surpassed, and I want some superlative examples for the maharajah's private suites. Our collection must also include a few of the solid silver pieces of that day, although I believe the swirling curves, the asymmetrical designs, and carvings in the form of rocks and shells of the Régence will blend in with the native workmanship in Travancore more harmoniously."

"Come now, Percy, you shall put Mrs. Salem to sleep," Sir Mortimer Trevelyan chided. "Have a cheroot with me on the veranda while the ladies take this opportunity to freshen themselves."

The professor stood and gave me a deep bow. "I apologize if I have humored myself at your expense."

"Not at all. The decorative arts are of particular interest to me."

Trevelyan tugged the professor's arm and whisked him away.

The women, including Jemima, the wives of the two Portuguese diplomats, and the daughter of a Dutch trader, retired to an upstairs room to primp.

"I don't know if I ever will accustom myself to the manner in which the ladies of Travancore dress," one of the Portuguese women said as she adjusted her corset.

We giggled about the thin draperies that barely covered the breasts of the Brahmin women, until Jemima, patting her own lace-bordered décolletage, said, "Men are much more curious about what they don't see than about what they do. They want precisely what they are not supposed to have."

The second Portuguese lady fluttered her thick lashes. "As for my Manuel, I tell him that living in India is like visiting a marketplace. One checks out the merchandise in the stalls, but eats at home."

We laughed until tears came to our eyes, and our ebullient mood lasted as we made our way to the palace. Dennis Clifford walked with his wife on his right and me on his left through the Courtyard of the Sun. In the center was a huge circular stone surface. "The prince of sundials," the Quilon resident explained. "With its thirty-foot-high gnomon, it is able to measure in units of fifteen seconds."

"If you come during the day, I would be delighted to explain it to you" came the familiar mushy voice.

I spun around. "Thank you, sir."

"Now, Madam Salem, may I escort you into the Hall of Pleasure?" Amar offered his arm. I could not refuse. He led the way through an arch inlaid with ivory and sandalwood. "Here is our little Shish Mahal, a copy of the Mirror Palace in the Agra fort. My illustrious ancestors opened it for only one night each year, for diwali, the festival of lights. I am told my uncle gave private parties here, but he never invited me. As soon as I knew I would be the next maharajah, I vowed to use it as often as possible."

Two fifteen-foot doors opened at our approach. Coming from the torchlit darkness of the marble hall, we were assaulted by a thousand circles of light. Dizzy, I leaned against Amar. He paused and slipped his arm about my waist. I might have thought the gesture was meant only to steady me, but then his hand brushed down and over my buttocks.

"Have you ever seen anything so gorgeous?" Jemima's high-pitched admiration gave me the chance to take a step away from the maharajah.

The Hall of Pleasure was designed to refract and reflect light a thousand times over. Candles and torches were set in niches lined with convex mirrors and then banded with faceted colored stones. Every imaginable surface, including the panels on the curvilinear ceiling, was inlaid with silver. The room was alive with twinkling and blinking and glittering. If anyone moved, a flash occurred somewhere in the room, followed by an odd undulation that made one feel as though the structure had swayed. When Amar led me to a seat, I had to feel it below me before I dared sit. I kept my eyes fixed on my lap until I felt my balance was restored. When I looked up, the maharajah was taking his place beside his mother at the front of the room. Shifting around, I could see the guests were arranged in a semicircle. No special situation had been given to me. Again, I must have misconstrued everything. The reason the maharajah himself had seen me in was that I was the sole female visitor without an escort. As the music began, my concern at his fleeting intimacy faded.

The native instruments of Travancore were an unfamiliar assembly of strings, pipes, drums, and small basin-shaped cymbals that produced a tinkling tone. As lyrical *ragas* echoed in the shining room, I wished Edwin were beside me. After an hour the musicians seemed to be gathering strength, while I had to concentrate to keep my eyes open to the dazzling spectacle. Another hour must have passed before the maharajah stood. Even though the *vina* player continued with an elaborate solo that had begun slowly but escalated into a poignant plea, the audience followed the maharajah's lead. Servants wearing both red and white turbans carried silver goblets and platters of refreshments around the room.

I took a glass of pungent fruit punch. I felt a burning sensation as the last taste lingered in my throat, and accepted a second glass to quench my continuing thirst.

"That can be quite intoxicating," Professor Dent warned.

"I did not realize . . ." I said as I tried to swallow past the pain.

I handed the empty glass to a passing servant. The professor waved to someone else carrying a pitcher. "Try some coconut water to dilute it," he suggested kindly. At the maharajah's approach, he stepped aside.

"I hope you have enjoyed the evening thus far," he said with an exaggerated politeness.

Perspiration covered my brow. My mouth filled with thick saliva. I managed to nod my head, but words would not form.

"Do you require anything?" Amar asked with more concern in his tone.

"I suggested coconut water," the professor replied, and placed a glass in my hand.

Something wavered in front of my eyes. I was becoming transfixed on the ruby streak of light that played across the maharajah's white robes and illuminated his diamond buttons with a rosy hue.

"Yes, very refreshing," Amar said. He gestured for me to drink. Mechanically I took one sip. Amar's face was pink, his dark eyes like melting chocolate, his mouth moist and fleshy. "What do you think, Madam Salem? What do you think of my pleasure dome?" Not concentrating on his speech, he had slurred "Shalem" and "pleshure."

My swirling mind recalled Silas and "the stately pleasure dome of Xanadu." I stared into my chalky glass of coconut water and thought of "the milk of Paradise."

The maharajah's head tilted. "Well . . ."

"I wish Edwin could see this room."

"Oh, Winner has been here with me. He's the one who first suggested I open it more often. When we were young the two of us used to—" He halted as the maharani approached. "Ah, here is my mother. Mrs. Salem was telling me that her husband would have enjoyed our little gathering."

"He shall return soon," the maharani said firmly. "Until then I would like you to visit me from time to time."

"I would be honored."

"You will come for tea tomorrow." It was a statement, not a question. With the barest flicker of her feline eyes, she concluded our encounter and drifted off, much as a swan turns and skims across a lake.

"My mother likes you," Amar replied.

I could think of no response as he edged closer.

"She always liked Winner too. For centuries our family has felt an affinity for the Jews of the region." Amar was standing with less than an inch of space between his crossed arms and my breasts. He spoke in his softest, mushiest voice. "There has always been a sympathetic bond with your people, which transcends the boundaries of our caste system and our fear of foreigners."

Again no retort could find its way through my muffled mind.

"I have never seen you so silent, Sassy," he said into my ear. "Are you unwell?"

My knees shook. "It's late . . ." I blinked to stop the lights from threatening to immolate me. There was a commotion, an echoing sound, and the high ping of metal strings vibrating against hollow wood. I crumpled into a heap at the maharajah's feet.

I heard the maharani speaking softly from a long way off. "Do you think she might be . . . ?"

Jemima gently sat me up. "No, I am fairly positive she is not."

"She had a large glass of the punch." Professor Dent's voice echoed hauntingly.

I opened my eyes, ready to close them to the glitter if necessary, but found I was in a darkened room lying on something cool and slippery. "Where am I?" I asked as I searched for Jemima in the gloom.

"In the place where my wife and her friends were listening to the music," the maharajah explained.

"Jemima?"

"I am here, don't worry," came her reply from a shadowy corner.

"I have ordered a palanquin to take you back to the Orchid House. Mrs. Clifford, would you be so kind as to direct it here?"

I heard a shuffling and reopened my eyes. In the spilled river of light from the doorway I could see that for the moment Amar and I were alone. I was too apprehensive to think to ask why his wife had not been invited into the public room or wonder where she had gone.

"Almost everyone enjoys a taste of my toddy, which is fermented from our palms, but obviously you are unaccustomed to spirits."

I managed to sit up and slide away from him, but his hands had reached behind me as if to give support, then lingered on my back and kneaded my shoulders.

"I didn't know what was in it . . . I had two."

"Two?" he roared. "No wonder." I heard a sucking, then a gurgling sound. "I prefer a pipe myself."

For a moment I did not follow his meaning. "If I can sleep, I shall be—"

His hands pressed against my forehead. "You are cold. You may be ill. I shall send my physicians and—"

"No, please." In trying to stand, I was relieved to find my balance restored. Turning around, I realized he was taking puffs from his hookah. His eyes squinted at me in the darkness. My stomach churned. Now I knew whom Amar reminded me of: Nissim Sadka.

Amar lurched toward me. "I feel sick," I said, holding him off. The doorway framed a familiar silhouette. "Jemima!" I called.

As she came forward, I waited for the maharajah to back away. Instead he moved closer, his hands supporting my sides so it seemed he was holding me upright. Only he and I knew the edges of my breasts were being squeezed.

"She requires assistance." Once we were out in the lighted hall, his hands guided the small of my back. "She should lie down." Amar allowed Jemima to guide me into the gilded palanquin, and then he spoke close to the lattice slats. "Good evening, Mrs. Salem, I hope you will recover quickly." His hot breath felt like a fog on my face, and his smell—a combination of the sulfur of a burnt match and something cloyingly familiar—lingered even as I was carried out from the sparkling world of mirrors and under the welcome canopy of the misty, moonless night.

❀ ❀ ❀

Other than my mortification at having become inebriated and having given the maharajah the opportunity to touch me, I suffered no ill effects from the evening. Perhaps he had been trying to assist me and in my confused state I had imagined the intimacies. As a precaution, I vowed to avoid any opportunity to be alone with him again. At first I thought to excuse myself from tea with the maharani—after the previous night, it would have been a simple matter to send regrets because of illness—but then I decided my best protection might lie with her.

Soldiers wearing scarlet tunics guarded the entrance to the maharani's quarters in the central section of the palace. I passed through a hibiscus garden into a reception room where the maharajah's mother waited in front of a carved ivory panel. Her black hair, shot through with silver streaks, was entwined so intricately I wondered how long it took to arrange it. She wore a white silk robe draped under her breasts, with the thinnest gold cape covering the upper part of her torso, out of deference to my sensibilities. Even so, I could discern her large brown nipples. Since breasts were never concealed here, I wondered if Amar had thought touching mine was as natural as shaking my hand. Or did the fact that mine were hidden pose an irresistible temptation for a man accustomed to seeing women's chests bared?

The maharani's musical voice brought me back from my musings. "Thank you for coming to see me, Mrs. Salem. I trust you are feeling better."

"Only my pride stings today."

"I was told you had too much of the toddy."

"I had two glasses before anyone warned me. I hardly ever drink spirits."

"No one has criticized you. We were concerned."

"Thank you."

The maharani took a seat on a padded stool and waved for me to do the same. In the sunlit room, her arms gleamed with bands of diamonds and rubies. "There is a time in a woman's life when she is apt to be more sensitive," she noted, giving me an appraising stare.

I felt I should reply, although I resented being forced into an intimate confession. "I am not that fortunate yet."

"One of these days you will be," she replied with the smoothness of warmed honey. "I myself am one of the most fortunate women. I have given birth not only to boys who were next in line for the musnud but also to girls who will rule after me. I have survived to see my son become the maharajah. And I have lived to see my daughters give birth to boys. This ensures that one of my grandsons will also become maharajah, although it would be no blessing for me to live for that day."

Sipping my tea, I was perplexed by this remark until I realized she was saying that she would have to see Amar dead before his nephew could reign. That would mean she would have buried all three of her sons. "What happens if no sister or aunt of the maharajah had given birth to sons? Would the maharajah's own son then inherit the throne?"

"No, the musnud can pass only through a woman. Your question is most interesting, however, since this situation happened in recent times. The sister of one maharajah died in childbirth, which also took the life of her only daughter. There were no other women heirs. Application was made to the British government for permission to adopt a princess from a branch of the family in which maharajahs usually find their spouses. Her caste was impeccable and the community accepted the adoption. I am descended from that line."

I put down my cup. "Do you think the women of Travancore fare better than women elsewhere in India?"

"Yes, we can pick our husbands and we can rid ourselves of them, yet that rarely happens. Don't you find it interesting that with the woman in control, there is apt to be less friction in a marriage? And if there is, well, we have a way for the man and woman to separate so each may find a more suitable companion without anyone feeling wronged or having to do an unkindness to the other."

"What if only one wishes to leave?" I asked, hoping the question was not impertinent.

The maharani did not seem offended. "It is my experience that if one is unhappy, he or she has a way of making the other person miserable. But again, the woman has the last say. If she leaves, the children go with her so they are not uprooted. Here, where women are taught and teach, they are more responsible for the welfare of the people than the men."

Surely life was not as idealistic as her pretty portrait, but I was in no position to challenge her. I thought of a way to turn the conversation. Looking around the room, which was mostly filled with Indian pieces inlaid with ivory and silver, I asked if the professor was to purchase anything for her.

"Yes. I want fewer chests and tables, softer chairs in hues of yellow and gold, more color and light."

"Until last night I never realized there was such a thing as too much light," I said with a laugh. "My eyes must be too sensitive."

Two aides simultaneously replaced our cooled teacups with steaming ones. "Did Amar have an opportunity to speak with you last night?" she asked with a sudden change of mood.

I froze in the motion of reaching for my next cup. "About what?" Could she have known about our moments alone in the darkened room?

"Anything about elephants?" she hinted coyly.

"Not that I recall."

"Good. I was to invite you, but when I saw him approach you, I supposed he had decided to do it himself." My puzzled expression spurred her on. "We both know you are lonely with your husband away. We decided you might benefit from a diversion. That is, if you are well enough . . ." She paused to give me an opportunity to fill in an explanation. ". . . for this is apt to be a strenuous journey."

Intrigued, I reassured her I was in the best of health. "What sort of trip is this?"

"Amar is arranging an elephant hunt. He has wanted to have one for some time and has had his scouts out searching for a herd ever since the coronation."

"Who else will attend?"

"His retinue and the honored guests of the state."

"Will you also be going?"

"Certainly. In my brother's reign, we had hunts infrequently. He much preferred a life of what he called 'contemplation.' His predecessor, the uncle who had no sisters or aunts, was quite a sportsman."

"Do they kill the elephants?"

"Oh, never! Or at least not unless somebody's life is endangered. The purpose is to capture a wild herd and bring them in for taming. Without elephant labor, much of the forestry and building around the state could not be accomplished."

"And Mrs. Clifford, will she receive an invitation also?"

"Of course. Sir Mortimer has declined. His weak back cannot tolerate the rough terrain. Mr. Clifford will take his place on the second howdah."

"How long does it last?"

"That depends on the elephants. We should be away for a week or more. May I tell Amar you will join us?"

The idea of leaving the confines of the court and the cloister of the Orchid House appealed to me immensely. "Yes, I will, but how I wish Edwin was here!"

36

❦ ❦ ❦

I rode to the hunt with Professor Dent. We sat side by side on a swaying howdah shaded by white umbrellas. The long journey was uncomfortable, but I found the professor's explanations distracting.

"If we don't thin the herds, they multiply rapidly. The last hunt was more than five years ago; therefore we are overdue, for already there are reports of the destruction of sugarcane crops in the south."

"Can't fencing or walls control them?"

"My dear Mrs. Salem, no field can be fenced against a herd of determined pachyderms."

"Determined pachyderms? I like that."

The professor puffed with the compliment. "A curious thing about the elephant is that he seems unaware of his strength when working with humans. We coexist because of their tractable nature. Once captured, an elephant seems to thrive as man's muscular assistant, felling trees, hauling logs, lifting timbers." The professor trilled the R in "thrive," then glanced at me for approval. I gave a little laugh at having caught him in his mock pomposity.

He chuckled in return. "Soon, my dear lady, you will experience a *kheddah*, the roundup in which they capture the beasts. The *shikarris* located a wild herd months ago and by now have provoked the beasts in our direction."

"How do they do that?"

"During the day they stalk the herds, and at night they maneuver them with torches. Fire is one of the few things elephants fear."

"How do they capture them?"

"Geography assists this endeavor. There is a wide waterway on one margin of the territory, and the high cliffs of the Western Ghats on another, which narrow the elephants' choices."

We had reached a bluff from where I could view the long line of

trained elephants, followed by more than fifty carts laden with supplies. The professor explained that many more had gone to set up
before us. "Do you see that bend in the river?" He pointed to the
horizon. "That is where we are heading. You'll find the camp comfortable enough."

After more than ten hours of traveling, with a brief stop for tiffin, we
arrived at a lakeside clearing. More than a hundred tents were already
in place. A large marquee in the center was garlanded in flowers and
lined with thick Persian carpets. Shelves cleverly rigged from bamboo
and wire housed a small library. Desks around the perimeter were
available for the maharajah's staff, and in the center, soft armchairs
formed circles around a platform topped with a silver-and-ivory throne.
Amar was nowhere around, but his musicians were already playing
raga after raga. The sweet sounds of the strings trailed into the blustery
wind and were quickly dispersed by the commotion of the arrivals.

I was taken to my tent, where Yali awaited me with a basin of tepid
water and a fresh frock. I washed away the dust, sipped my favorite
tea, ate a few pastries, then lay down for a short rest.

My ayah woke me after dark. "Dinah-baba, you must be ready for
dinner soon."

Disoriented, I sat up. Candles in silver holders cast long shadows on
the undulating surface of the tent. Stiff with aches from the journey, I
dressed with Yali's assistance. Outside, a guard in a white turban
escorted me to the maharajah's marquee. Hundreds of fluttering lamps
lit paths and demarcated doorways. Beyond the perimeter of the encampment, blackness loomed. We could have been on an island in the
midst of a vast sea.

My seat at the long table was next to Dennis Clifford and across from
his wife. Fortunately, Amar was more than ten places removed. The
most prominent positions were given to the men who were jockeying
to become the next dewan, or prime minister. The current dewan had
remained in Trivandrum to handle the affairs of state. The maharani
sat on the ruler's right. To the soothing strains of the music and the
tinkling of fine crystal, a meal with more than a dozen courses was
served. In the palace such luxury was taken for granted. In this wilder-
ness it was astonishing.

Afterward we were escorted into a smaller pavilion, where chess-
boards were set up on camp tables. Cheroots and Madeira were served
around as Amar greeted each of his guests. When Jemima stepped
forward, he asked after her children, then turned to me. "What do you
think of my little diversion? I realize it hardly makes up for not having
Winner by your side, but perhaps it will return the bloom to your
cheeks?" While he had made every attempt to be precise with his
words, they came out stilted.

"You know as well as I do how disappointed Edwin will be to have missed this," I responded formally.

The maharajah drew his mouth into a thin line. His heavy lids were half-closed. He did not seem to have heard me. The trip must have exhausted him as much as me. "Do you play chess?" he slurred.

"Only a few games with my first husband."

The maharajah's eyes snapped open. He stared at me for a long moment, then spoke with elaborate politeness: "A refresher course must be in order." He gestured to the chess table set up on a platform.

I cringed at the idea of having to play in front of the courtiers and guests, but there was no chance of escape. I had made no claims to proficiency at the game, so I could not be embarrassed by my playing. In fact, my naive moves should lead to a game so boring, I expected that Amar would release me after the first defeat. I took a long breath and moved my white king-pawn forward. The maharajah moved his matching black pawn.

"The game of chess is a battle; the chessboard is the battlefield," Amar began to pontificate. "Diagrams for combat, like Hannibal's plan for the Battle of Cannae, could have been represented on a chess-board." He prattled on while I made predictable moves to his gentle leads. "Good development of that knight," he complimented.

Nodding absently, I concentrated on the game. Amar's physical presence no longer worried me, since observers surrounded us. I had no hope of winning, but perhaps I would avoid looking foolish.

"Ah, an aggressive move!" He lowered his voice. "You are showing real promise, Sassy."

"You could win this game," Professor Dent said as he moved closer to me.

"The maharajah has been very generous to a novice."

"Only until now." Amar's eyes gleamed in the torchlight, and he rubbed his hands together. "Professor P., why don't you assist her? The professor is the one who taught me the game, and he has not lost his touch."

"That would be very kind," I said, hoping this would bring the evening to a swift conclusion.

When Amar pinned my knight on his next move, Professor P. said softly, "Do not fear, we have a plan of our own."

I smiled playfully. "We do?"

The professor made the next move for me, checking Amar's king on the diagonal. There was only one move Amar could make. His eyes blazed. "You should have considered the pawn at white's queen-bishop two," Percy Dent chastised with a smirk.

Assisted by the professor, three of my white pieces had maneuvered Amar into a checkmate. For a second the maharajah was confounded.

"At least the king is never physically taken," he said in a jolly tone. He stood and stretched.

I took this as the cue that I might rise.

"Sleep as late as you wish. Our beaters will work through the night to bring the herd closer to us. There are three possible places we might corral them. This camp has been set nearest the most likely spot. If all goes well, we should have an easy ride late tomorrow, then a few exciting hours."

"I'm looking forward to it," I said, and retreated as swiftly as I could.

☙ ☙ ☙

The next morning the valley filled with a thick fog. Bearers brought chota hazri to our tents. The thick, damp air made the world outside so uninviting, I lay on my charpoy and fell back to sleep. It was almost noon before I strolled through the encampment. After a few minutes of looking for someone I knew, a downpour began. I ran to the largest marquee, where I found Jemima having tea with several fashionably attired ladies and the few gentlemen—mostly older fellows like the professor, who remained in camp.

While the rain poured off the canvas in silvery sheets, we munched on freshly fried popadoms dipped in hot sauce, and drenched our throats with steaming cups of sweet tea. Aides ran about tightening ropes and resetting poles as pockets in the roof filled with water.

"The poor men will be soaked," one of the ladies said, more out of politeness than concern.

"Men love that sort of thing," another added. "They're like little boys when it comes to mucking about."

"I hope they don't do the job without us. I have heard the final corral is quite exciting and rarely seen," Jemima said, turning toward the professor. He had been standing by an open flap smoking his cheroot. "Isn't that right, Professor?"

"Yes, yes. I remember one in particular, Amar's first, when he was about twelve. You must ask him to tell you about it this evening."

The rains diminished by late afternoon and we were treated to a radiant sunset over the river. The men had trekked into camp well-splattered, but pleased to have stirred the elephants in our direction, even though they had not gained as much ground as they would have if the weather had been clearer.

After the formal dinner, Dennis ushered us to cushions clustered around the maharajah's makeshift throne. Musicians played plaintive ragas in the background. Amar sat cross-legged at the throne's base, leaning his back against it. The men were smoking cheroots. A hookah was passed among some of the courtiers, and I recognized the perfume of opium. I tried not to react when I saw Amar take some puffs of the gilded pipe. Fortunately, it was not proffered to the ladies.

"An excellent smoke," someone murmured.

Jemima remembered the professor's suggestion and asked the maharajah to tell about his first hunt. "Ah, yes, of course," Amar said, launching into his tale with enthusiasm. "My great-uncle—this was the Rama Varma, who came before the late maharajah—had an elephant called Jummo that he claimed was more than a hundred years old. The beast had served three maharajahs before him and was always decked in gold, from the plugs in his tusks to the paint on his legs to the gold tassels that swung from the silk cloths that covered his flanks. Even his forehead was painted with golden sunflowers. On the occasion of my first hunt—and on that occasion only—I was invited to ride in the maharajah's howdah atop Jummo. That was when my two brothers preceded me in line for the throne, so nobody had paid much attention to me. Anyway, this elephant had a son, a huge tusker even bigger than himself known as Ganesha—after the god with the elephant head, Mrs. Clifford." When she nodded in understanding, he went on, "Ganesha led us as we journeyed throughout the night. By then we had been on the road for over a week to cover the hundred miles to the hunting grounds on the eastern trail toward Madurai, and the maharajah was impatient to get there. Ganesha must have picked up the scent of a tiger, for he stopped with such a violent lurch that his mahout was shaken out of his perch and landed under the bull's feet. Unfortunately, he was crushed to death. Now, as most of you are aware, a bond between a mahout and his beast lasts a lifetime. My great-uncle warned the shikarris to expect the bull to act unpredictably until he had recovered from the loss. Ganesha was taken to the end of the line, where two dousing mahouts were employed to keep him cool in hopes that his mind would not wander to the loss of his friend."

"Do elephants really have such deep feelings?" the Dutchman's daughter asked.

"Anyone who has worked with an elephant is captivated by their uncanny sensitivities," Amar stated firmly, then continued. "While the maharajah and his party were scouting for the elephants, word came into the camp that the shikarris had sighted three tigers. An elephant had to be dispatched to find out if the maharajah wanted to turn back for some sport. Ganesha was one of the few remaining in camp, and the new mahout in charge assured everyone he was behaving quite normally. I suppose the lad was trying to distinguish himself as a man worthy of being assigned to this noble beast. To prove his point, he jabbed the elephant with his *ankus*. Ganesha tossed his trunk in the air, trumpeted a hideous bellow, and plowed into two shikarris. One was trampled under the massive feet, another ran to climb the nearest tree.

Other servants rushed in every direction. In the mayhem the rampaging beast seriously wounded two more."

"How horrible!" Jemima cried. "What did they do?"

"He had to be put down, of course. My great-uncle himself pumped more than seventy bullets into his thick skull. I cannot remember ever weeping more in my life. Curiously, back in Trivandrum after the hunt, faithful old Jummo died in his sleep. Some say he died of a broken heart, for he had been in perfect health."

The mood at the table was somber. Determined not to let his party sour, Amar hastily added, "Nevertheless, that is not what I recall most from that hunt. You know my Shankara. She was the youngest of the animals rounded up that very week. When I saw her she looked at me with those wonderful warm eyes, and I will admit, she was the first female to steal my heart. 'Do you like her?' my great-uncle asked. I told him she was the most beautiful elephant I had ever seen. 'Then I shall give her to your eldest brother. It shall be his elephant.' You can imagine how disappointed I was, yet what could I say to him? My brother was thrilled, of course, and like most children with a special possession, he did not permit his next brother or me to touch her." Amar looked at his guests with a downcast expression. "As much as it pains me to admit this, when my brothers died, I had little concern for what it might mean to someday assume the musnud. I thought only of Shankara and that now she would be mine."

With shining eyes he stared at the far end of the tent, where his mother sat. The guests waited for her response.

"Amar is being a bit melodramatic. Too much water on the brain today, perhaps?" she said, arching her eyebrows. "All the children rode about on Shankara, and Amar took little interest in her until he was much older."

Amar cocked his head in deference to his mother while everyone else sensed the time had come to chat among themselves.

Several ladies stood to leave, and each bid a good-night to the maharajah. He waved them off with a cordial word. Seizing the chance, I made my way to where he was lying with his head propped up by his hand. "Good night, dear Mrs. Salem."

"Good evening, sir."

"Why not stay for a while longer? I am in a philosophical mood tonight. We might share our views on marriage, for instance."

"My views are that of my husband, and my husband is not here to share them," I replied elliptically.

"What a profound statement you have made. Come and enlighten me some more." He reached to pull me down beside him.

I resisted, pretending he had been trying to get to his feet. "No, don't bother to stand on my behalf, sir."

He slumped down. "We are both alone. My wife is about to have her child. Your husband is off on an exciting mission." He was slurring again. "I wonder which shall be delivered earliest—the boat or the baby?"

"Is your wife well?" I asked, hoping that a diversion to this subject would safeguard me.

He ignored the question and waved to the hookah. "Would you like some? A fine, light grade. It will help you sleep."

"No, I never do."

"Yes, yes, Winner told me that. Not good for ladies anyway. They sometimes become irrational. Nothing worse than an irrational woman . . ."

Unwilling to be drawn into a defense of my sex, I merely backed away.

I had almost reached the entrance to the marquee when he whined, "Sassy, please . . ."

Just then Dennis appeared from the shadows. "I'll escort Mrs. Salem back, sir. Don't worry about her." He took my arm and I felt safe at last.

❦ ❦ ❦

"You mustn't mind Amar when he gets like that."

"What am I supposed to do?" I asked with a quaver in my voice.

"Exactly what you did. Be firm. Be polite. Be a lady."

"Sometimes he frightens me." I mulled over my next question, then dared, "Do you think his pipe influences him?"

"Except to make his speech impediment worse, I doubt it. Perhaps it might affect someone less accustomed, the way two toddies might affect a woman who rarely drinks." He winked. "Not someone who takes a small amount on a regular basis. To me, the boy is a lamb who has suddenly been awarded giant horns. He hardly knows what to do with them, yet cannot resist taking a few stabs to see what sort of power he possesses."

I could have taken the ram analogy further and asked what I should do if he directed those stabs at me, but held my tongue. "Thank you and good night," I said as he delivered me to where Yali was holding a lamp.

"Good night, Mrs. Salem. Sleep well. Tomorrow is bound to be an exciting day."

I was exhausted even though I had done nothing more strenuous than stroll around the encampment. Just being in the maharajah's presence was a strain. The more I was near him, the more I was reminded of Sadka's vile presence and saw myself in my mother's role. Yali unpinned my hair, helped me undress, then stepped outside to call for hot water. She gave a little cry. Thinking she had confronted a snake, I rushed to the tent flap.

"Amar! What are you doing here?"

"I like it when you call me 'Amar,' Sassy."

"Pardon me, sir. I suppose the name came to mind because that is what Edwin uses when he speaks of you to me."

"Don't worry, Mrs. Salem, we do not hand out fines here." He stood inches from me. "As I said before, I would like to talk with you."

Not expecting anyone, I had appeared in only my thin lawn chemise. I crossed my arms to cover my chest and shivered. "Please, not now and not here. Someone might see us."

Ignoring my plea, he stared at me. My hair was cascading down my shoulders and blowing in the breeze. He touched the long tendrils and wound them around his hand, pulling me outside the tent. "Such beautiful hair, a shame to bind it. So soft, like silk strands. Our women's hair is thicker and coarser. But this, this is like threads of beaten gold." He touched to his cheek the hand that bound my hair. "So soft . . . so soft . . . I have never met a woman like you: a woman of education, a woman of the city, a woman of wealth, a woman of virtue who has known more than one man."

"But I haven't," I protested.

"You said you were married before."

"That was a mistake."

"The marriage—or telling me?"

"Both, I suppose."

"Does Winner know your little secret?"

"Of course! And it is not a secret. My parents arranged a match with another man about a year before I met Edwin. He turned out to be very unsuitable—he had an illness, something incurable he had not mentioned. This led to the dissolution of the marriage before it was consummated."

Amar seemed disappointed by my explanation. "You intrigue me, Sassy. I cannot help myself. Even Winner would understand my fascination. Yes, Winner would." He reflected glassily for a moment, then murmured, "Winner. Was there ever a more apt nickname? Didn't the poor fatherless boy win the prize?" With a swift gesture he wound another turn of my hair. My feet refused to budge, so my head strained toward him.

"Please, Sassy, I do not wish to harm you. Please, I only want to converse with you. I do enjoy our little chats. They stimulate me. Pray, think of me. Think of how alone I am. My wife gives birth any day now. I have not considered taking any more wives. I have no permanent mistresses. Now that I am maharajah, I suppose I should have some, but they do not amuse me." He loosened my hair and stepped back. "I did not wish to be maharajah. Everyone knows that." He gave a slight moan. "Now that I am, everybody wants something from me.

How shall I know my true friends? At least I thought I could trust Winner and his wife—and that they could trust me."

"I would not be here if I were not your friend. I would not be here if I did not trust you." I rubbed the spot where my hair had been tugged at its roots. "I shall forgive you because you were carried away by your inquisitiveness, but if you touch me again, I shall leave Travancore and never return, and neither will my husband." I fought back tears.

"Now, now, Sassy. The hour is late. We are both tired."

"Indeed." The voice was that of Amar's mother. She appeared out of the blackness, her white gown a shimmering column in the moonlight. I could not make out much of her face beyond a reflection of her eyes and the flickering of some jewels that seemed suspended in midair as her dark arms blended into the obscurity. "Are you all right, Mrs. Salem?"

"Yes, thank you, your highness."

"Good. I was afraid you might have caught a chill this morning. How kind of my son to check on you. He worries about his guests, especially ladies unaccustomed to this sort of hardship."

"I am very comfortable."

"I am glad for that. I think you will find tomorrow's events to be quite remarkable. Please join me on my howdah. We can share the adventure together."

"I would be honored. Good night, madam. Good night, sir."

"Good night, Mrs. Salem," the maharajah said thickly. "I wish you a good rest."

❦ ❦ ❦

The maharajah had done me a favor. At last I knew that my concerns were not the idle speculations of a neglected bride. I fascinated Amar and he was used to having whatever he wanted. The British raj usually allowed native rulers a free hand with their states. If anything happened to me, it might be made to appear an accident, unless the Cliffords had some doubts. Amar was not stupid. Because of this, he could never force his hand with me. Nevertheless, terrible things could happen. He could pursue me to the point of scandal. There was little that went on in this camp that every servant, every guest would not soon know. If I were embarrassed, Edwin and I would have to leave Travancore. Our investment in the ship would be in jeopardy. And this might stir trouble between Edwin and me. I had no doubt that Edwin would come to believe my side, but I could not bear having to defend myself. I saw our marriage as being as perfect as an egg. The smooth white shell was the sturdy encasement of our love. If Amar managed to tap that shell, he might not break it, but he could inflict a hairline crack. Nothing would ooze out, yet the structure would be weakened. Forevermore, we would have to take care not to damage it further.

These thoughts prevented me from sleeping. As the night wore on, they became even more convoluted. Where was Edwin? What was he doing? When would I see him again? Every sound from the jungle, every footstep near the tent, every creaking of a rope or flapping of a canvas caused me to jump. Amar wouldn't dare come back, I consoled myself, but that did not calm my pulse. A pinkish light tinged the brass basin and lamp: dawn had come. I was safe. Only then could I fall asleep.

❦ ❦ ❦

Yali wiped my face and hands and feet as though I were a baby. I looked like a mess, I knew. I could not have slept more than an hour. As she brought me tea in bed, a heaviness weighed me down. What was I doing here? How could I escape? And if I did, where would I go? Back to Trivandrum and the Orchid House? Back to our cottage in Cochin or to Mother Esther's claustrophobic room on Jew Street? Back to Calcutta and Theatre Road? That is exactly where I would have been, if not for Edwin. Or I might have made the choice to remain in Darjeeling with Silas. Yes, I could still be under the spell of the snows, with Euclid padding around morosely, Silas laid up with his headaches, and the eternal wind battering the exposed walls of Xanadu. I took a deep breath. The smell of oil frying popadoms filled the air. Sunlight streamed under the tent. Elephants trumpeted. I remembered my visit from Amar's mother and reminded myself I was not alone. The kindly Cliffords, the gentle professor, and the second-most-powerful person in the kingdom were on my side. As Yali slipped my gown over my outstretched arms and handed me my topee, I smiled.

With my head held high, I joined the party congregating outside the marquee. Everyone was munching crisp breads passed from silver trays and drinking cups of dark tea. The elephants were decked out in full regalia. A shikarri blew a brass horn, and the elephants trumpeted their reply. Amar was lifted into the royal howdah. Into the air the elephant-crested banner was lifted. The hunt was on.

37

✾ ✾ ✾

The trap was a four-sided stockade constructed of split boards supported by rough logs that were bound with hide rope to the sturdiest trees. Though the barricade appeared flimsy, the very flexibility of the structure enabled it to resist the pounding of a captured beast by yielding to its onslaught. A curve in the river on one side and sharply rising cliffs on the other bounded the area. Beyond, on a hill overlooking the corral, all the guests, except the younger men participating in the roundup, were atop elephants—four or five to a howdah to spare as many beasts as possible for the work ahead. I sat behind the maharani and her attendant.

"What if the wild elephants notice us?" I asked Amar's mother.

"They say that elephants rarely look up. I suppose that is because they are already so tall they doubt anything higher is of interest to them." Although I didn't reply, I realized she might have been describing herself and the maharajah.

After an hour we heard the distant shouts of the herders. The elephants were coming! The galloping of their heavy hooves thundered through the forest. Leaves trembled like warning rattles. Coconuts fell from swaying palms. Their tamed brethren swayed restlessly. Then a leading family of tuskers came into view. Halting at the riverbank, the largest squirted trunkfuls of water over his back. A cow lifted her baby. Blissfully unaware of their impending fate, two older calves pranced in the water.

"The one in front is a female," Amar's mother explained, as more elephants arrived. "As in Travancore, elephants are a matriarchal society."

"The large ones on the outskirts must be the males," I commented.

"Right. Their function is to procreate, not to lead." She grinned slyly. "As it should be, don't you think?"

Trumpets blared forth, announcing the maharajah's approach from

415

behind the advancing horde. Once across the river, Amar directed a line of *kumkis,* his trained elephants, into a flank formation to prevent escape. Scenting danger, the lead cow bellowed madly. The others in her herd charged to the right, then to the left, looking for a breech. Seeing none, they lunged into the kumkis. For one terrible moment it appeared the herders could not prevent the marauding elephants from breaking the line. Prodded by their mahouts with the iron-tipped ankuses, the trained beasts held their ground. The confused wild herd reversed direction, and this time the line followed them toward the stockade and formed into a funnel shape as they advanced. The enclosure was well-camouflaged with fronds and bamboo, giving them the sense they were heading into acres of jungle.

When the herd was almost beneath us, the lead cow paused to sniff the air. A bull trumpeted. The maharani and I gasped in unison. From every side the beaters and clappers converged. Coolies with flaming torches formed a wide outside band. The kumkis stood firm. More than forty elephants passed through the narrow mouth of the funnel, and in so doing, crossed the line between freedom and captivity.

A drawbridge closed in the compound, locking inside a dozen of the most experienced kumkis and their mahouts. When the dust cloud from the stampede subsided, I could see Amar and some of his favorite courtiers in the center of the ring. Dennis Clifford and the rest of the guests who were assisting formed the next ring of protection. Darting eyes and excited grins betrayed their feelings, but they did not speak.

Because I had been told that elephants were never killed, only roped for taming, I was unprepared for the violence that followed. Mahouts furiously jabbed the heads of the wild elephants with their ankuses. Blood poured down the wrinkled faces, blinding the beasts even as they lunged at the rickety fences. The yelps of the animals mingled with the mahouts shouting, *"Maro, Maro!* Strike, Strike! *Dant do!* Spike him!"

Kumkis worked in tandem as monitors on either side of each newcomer. Leaning with their full strength, they impeded the struggles of their wild brothers while the ropers crept forward with their nooses of oiled hide and slipped them on the hind legs of the captives. Each time a roper managed to hobble an animal, onlookers on the other side of the fence shouted, *"Arre! Arre! Hai-yai!"* partially to congratulate their coworker, as well as to distract the wild elephants while the roper clambered back up the hindquarters of his kumki to avoid the murderous feet of the hysterical tusker.

The choreographed dance of lithe men who leapt in and out between the massive moving columns of stamping flesh proceeded until the largest male vented his outrage. One powerful kick snapped his foreleg stay as if it were twine. The nearby kumkis stumbled backward while any mahouts on the ground scrambled to safety. The furious animal swung around, looking for an exit. As he did, something caught his eye and he looked up. Perhaps the bright clothes of the ladies or their perfumed scent riled him further, for he lunged into one of the main supports of the corral. Three or four poundings brought logs tumbling like twigs. They snapped beneath his feet. A wall crashed forward. Six kumkis moved into position to prevent the rest of the structure from collapsing, while the ropers rushed for ladders, gateways, and tree branches. Our own mount trumpeted and stamped, as did several more on the hill, but with tender words and familiar prods, our handlers calmed them.

The maharajah, who had been positioned on the far side from where this event was taking place, thought quickly. Rallying the mahouts in his area, he directed a frontal attack on the brute. His kumkis sensed the severity of the situation and moved to check any movement of the monster while the maharajah's troops drove him back with blows and spear jabs in his face and flanks. The circle tightened around him. He backed away until his hind legs became so crossed, he lost his balance and crashed to the ground. Thankfully, nobody was crushed under the heaving body. Once the rogue was down, brave men roped his neck and feet with double and triple bands.

"Amar was wonderful!" I said to his mother.

"He always has to be in the middle. He was never content to sit on the sidelines. That's why I believe he will make a good ruler."

"I thought he did not want that job," I said before realizing I might have spoken out of turn.

The maharani stretched her sinuous neck proudly. "Everyone wants to be the first. It is human nature. It is what helps us survive." Her hands finished her words as obviously as her voice did.

Shouts rose in the visitors' gallery. "Look, someone is coming!"

"It is a palace courier," the maharani said as the messenger galloped up to Amar and handed him a document. He waved to his mother and sent the courier in our direction.

In a few minutes a panting man bowed before us. "Joyous news. The wife of the maharajah has just given birth to a daughter." The ladies on their elephants applauded.

After a slow descent on the slippery rock trail, we were back in the valley and a safe distance away from where the last captives were being bondaged. I transferred to Dennis Clifford's howdah.

"What will happen now?" I asked the Quilon resident.

"No doubt the maharajah and maharani will return to Trivandrum ahead of their guests."

"Oh, that is too bad" is what I replied, while I thought: How wonderful! The festivities would continue, but Amar's attentions would no longer intimidate me.

❦   ❦   ❦

Two days after our exhausting journey back to the capital, a messenger arrived at the Orchid House with a letter from the palace. Amar was requesting me to meet him in the elephant stableyard to see how the captives were faring. Jemima, who had not recovered from the ordeal entirely, had been advised to remain in bed. Her husband had returned to Quilon to attend some urgent matter. Other than Yali, there was nobody who could accompany me. I knew I could not refuse Amar's invitation without a good excuse, but I thought if I might find his mother, she once again would be my ally.

I sent a message to the maharani that I would be visiting the stable later that afternoon and wondered if I might stop by to see how she was feeling. The return response was affirmative.

Gardenias and camellias scented her walled garden, where we drank cool fruit drinks from coconut cups. Laughing like old friends, we compared aches and pains from the hard ride home. I shared my concern for Jemima's health and she promised to send her physician over.

"It must be time for me to view the elephants," I said warily. "Would you care to accompany me?"

"No, thank you. I saw the captives this morning. They are adjusting well."

"Even that rebellious tusker?"

"He is in a separate enclosure." Her mouth curved upward without smiling. "In the end, he may turn out to be the finest specimen of the lot." Her piercing eyes bore into me. "All true princes must have high spirits that resist initial attempts at taming. It will take an experienced mahout to gentle him without ruining his temperament."

Was this also an explanation for her son's behavior in the camp? If so, who would tame him? Wasn't the Maharani of Travancore supposed to be the wise reins for the impetuous prince? No answers were forthcoming, and I left her presence dreading a reunion with her son.

As my cow-cart entered the stableyard, I noticed that many of the guests of the hunt also had assembled. Once again I had misinterpreted the situation. Amar had not summoned me for a private interlude. My imagination had taken hold because of the repugnant way he had touched me. Perhaps my uneasiness had made me too vigilant. After all, what had Amar ever done but try to please me? Even The scene at the tent could have been innocent. The lonely maharajah said he desired to talk with me. Was it so terrible that he had wanted to touch my fine hair, which was so different from that of his race? Had my own resistance irked him into behaving as he did? I sighed as I joined the others. Everything was so much more difficult on my own. Surely when Edwin returned, my worries would be set right.

Whereas many of the smaller elephants roamed the pens with loose bindings on their hind legs, the larger tuskers were bound on all four legs, and two large bulls were tethered between trees by neck and leg ropes. Kumkis strode freely through the herd to keep them calm. Mahouts sauntered about, speaking softly to their charges. Keepers offered buckets of *gur*, or raw sugar, to two mothers and youngsters. Even the most reluctant cows found the flavor irresistible.

Up close, the animals were quite distinctive. Their faces ranged from alert to curious to angry to dull. Here and there some troubled types stood off on the side, sullen and depressed. A small sugar-swilling female was quite lively. While she was occupied with her gur bucket, a wizened old mahout climbed up behind her head and gave her a few gentle prods. She flapped her ears, but he was not unseated.

"She'll be the first out on her own," predicted a knowing voice behind me. "Just like a woman to make the best of a bad situation."

I turned and smiled at the professor. "Hello. How nice to see you here, Professor Dent."

"And you, Mrs. Salem. I take it you have quite recovered."

"I hope so."

"Well, it shall not be long now before your cure arrives."

"My cure?"

"Your husband, madam. If my calculations are correct, he should return this week, or the next at the latest."

"How could you know?"

"I don't. It is an educated guess."

"Since nobody around here is as educated as you, I certainly hope you are right," I said, grinning.

The mahouts urged six of the kumkis to the edge of the corral and goaded them to raise their trunks in a royal salute as Amar appeared on the elephant I recognized as his beloved Shankara. She was decked out in a saffron garment with a crimson fringe. Resplendent in a cream satin tunic with ruby buttons, the maharajah rode around the outer circle greeting his guests.

"In less than a year, almost every one of the newcomers will have mastered more than twenty-five commands and will have become useful citizens of the state," the professor explained.

"Why do they do it? Why don't they rebel?"

"Elephants are intelligent beasts who find pleasure in service. They receive excellent rations and accommodation, they may live in family groups, they are never mistreated. Where would you prefer to live? Wild in the jungle, where you must forage for your food and fight for survival, or in the comforts of the Orchid House, where servants minister to your every need?"

I was about to say something about the Orchid House being another form of captivity, but I caught myself and replied, "I am not an elephant, thus I cannot speak for them."

"Indeed you are not!"

The professor and I were laughing the moment Amar approached us. As we greeted him respectfully, I found the sunlight hurt my eyes. I had to shade them as I answered Amar's questions about my health and the welfare of the Cliffords.

Amar signaled his mahout to lift me up into his howdah. "So you won't strain your eyes," he explained. I wanted to resist, since I did not wish to be singled out in front of this group, but before I managed an excuse, I was atop the elephant. "Now, isn't that better, Sassy? Come, let me show you my favorite acquisition." We plodded around to the far side of the stables, where the mammoth rogue tusker was bound to the wall with four strands of chains. "He's coming around. Certain herbs are being added to his feed to make him more docile. By next week he'll be hobbled with ropes. We are certain he will respond quite well. The recalcitrant ones who refuse to eat are the ones who may never adjust."

"Is he your favorite?"

"No, look over there!" In a far pen, a single female was sitting in a deep pool, showering herself with arcs of water. "Some of the mahouts think she may be expecting a calf. In any case, she is a magnificent specimen. Young and yet fully grown, and with the sweetest face I have ever seen. What do you think of those adorable eyes? She was very balky at first, but I think we can win her over."

"She is splendid," I agreed. I thought the creature emanated an eerie understanding of her position as she stared back at us.

He patted his mount's flank. "She reminds me of old Shankara here. That is why I have decided to give her to my nephew, the boy who will become the next maharajah." Amar turned to me as if his decision required my approval.

"Your nephew should be thrilled."

"He's too young to understand, but my sister will be pleased. Mothers . . . sisters . . . they keep a man busy, don't they?"

Once again he had not mentioned his wife or his new baby. Then it occurred to me the maharani had not said anything about the birth of her granddaughter either. Had I made an error in etiquette by not offering my congratulations first? I could remedy that now. "How is your daughter?" I asked.

"A scrawny child who hardly sleeps."

"Has your wife recovered?"

"I believe she has."

His flatness disturbed me. "I would like to see the baby. Is that permitted?"

"Yes, if that is your fancy." He saw my confused expression and tilted his head. "You must remember, this little girl has no status. She is not a princess, which is really a blessing. In Travancore a maharajah's daughter has all the advantages and none of the responsibilities."

"Then you are happy about her birth."

"Of course, why shouldn't I be?" He seemed distracted by something the elephant in the pen did, then turned his attention back to me. "Now, I require your help on an important matter. What am I going to name her?"

"How can I help with that?"

"Surely you have some ideas for names. Most women do. I wanted something different. What would be a good Jewish name for a female?"

"You would not want the daughter of a maharajah to have a Jewish name, would you?"

Amar roared with laughter. "I am not talking about the baby. I am talking about the elephant!"

The switch stunned me. When I recovered, I spoke evenly. "We use mostly biblical names like Ruth, Esther, Hannah."

"Who was Dinah?"

"The daughter of Jacob and Leah."

"Does it have a meaning?"

"In Hebrew, it means something like 'vindicated.' "

"That hardly sounds suitable for a lovely woman. What would you have to resolve or avenge?"

My heart pounded. I had never thought of my name having anything to do with my life. It was pleasant, euphonious, went well in both the English and Baghdadi communities. It had the same lyrical ending as Luna and Flora, tying me into the female line of my family. Could my name have been an omen for the future?

The maharajah was still speaking to me, but I stared at him without answering, again unsettled by his resemblance to Sadka. At that moment, riding atop a maharajah's elephant across the subcontinent from Calcutta, I realized how far I had come from my childhood pledge to search out Nissim Sadka and make him pay. How ridiculous that cry of revenge seemed now. Men like Sadka and Amar did as they pleased, and no one ever punished them. All I could do was avoid people like them in the future.

Amar's voice became more insistent. "I could name the elephant Dinah."

"Oh, no!" I shouted so loudly that Shankara flapped her winglike ears.

"I was not serious."

I blanched.

"Any other suggestions?" As I shook my head, he persisted: "Who was the leader of the Jews?"

"There were Abraham and Moses . . ."

"Did they have wives?"

"Moses was married to Zipporah."

"Zipporah. I like that. A proud name, a strong name. Thank you for the idea."

My head was beginning to pound. I wished I hadn't come after all. Even though the maharajah's behavior had been gentlemanly, once again I had ended up feeling agitated in his presence.

"I am pleased I could be of assistance. Now I must return to see how Mrs. Clifford is faring."

"Yes, of course. My mother told me she was not well."

I was amazed how quickly my message had been passed on. Amar must have been told of my visit to the maharani moments after I left her wing of the palace. I reminded myself not to assume that either kept secrets from the other.

The maharajah signaled his mahout to cajole Shankara onward. When we came around to the side of the building, one of his red-turbaned guards gave a peculiar salute that Amar acknowledged with a cheerful bob of his head. I had expected we would return to the others by the central pen, but instead we headed down a slope that led to the riverbank. Was this another trick to get me to himself? When a second soldier raised his arm, I looked at Amar for an explanation. He kept his eyes resolutely forward. I was a prisoner on his howdah. He could take me anywhere he wished, for any purpose. My panic mounted as the elephant stopped at the top of the embankment, where stone steps led down to a ghat.

"I thought you would prefer to be alone now," he said in a voice so low and garbled I did not understand him at first.

Alone? With him? Here by the water? What was going on? Fully aware of my confusion, he watched me squirm before he gestured to the riverbank, where the launch we had traveled in from Cochin to Travancore was tied to the bank. Two of the same oiled oarsmen stood about on the wharf. As if on cue, they parted to reveal a tall, solitary figure.

Edwin!

Edwin had come back!

38

※ ※ ※

The ship is glorious. She is everything I had hoped to find and more," Edwin was saying after we had been reunited a few hours. The agony of the weeks he was away dissolved as easily as a lump of sugar in a cup of boiling liquid. He smelled the same. He tasted the same. He loved me as never before.

Naked and unashamed, I stretched out beside him and stroked his arms, his chest, his face. "I have never been so happy."

"No? I shall have to go away more often, since reunions please you so much."

"One doesn't inflict pain to experience the relief at its cessation."

"Maybe that is what being a *fakir* is about."

"Buy me a bed of nails and I will lie on it, if you will promise you will never leave again."

"You missed me."

"Horribly."

"Didn't the Cliffords do their part?"

"Nobody can do your part."

"I hear Amar staged an elephant hunt to keep you occupied."

"Having scores of elephants overrunning plantations might have had something to do with it."

"I am sorry to have missed it." Edwin sat up abruptly. "You haven't let me tell you about our ship."

"Tell me about it." I sat up and faced him. "How big is it?"

"Two hundred and ninety-one feet in length, a little more than thirty-seven feet in breadth, and twenty-seven feet in depth."

"That large!" I pressed my bare chest against his. "How old is she?"

"She was built in 1882 in Newcastle."

"And of what is she made?"

"Iron. She's a sturdy craft."

"Iron. Hmmm." I reached between his legs and stroked him.

423

"Dinah . . ." He made only the thinnest protest as I pushed him onto his back and straddled his flanks.

"I like big, hard ships . . ."

"Poor darling, I do not think I dare ever leave you again," he said, clasping my buttocks and pinning me to him. I marveled at how quickly the sensations returned. The lightest touch of a nipple, the wetness of his tongue on my neck, the press of his pelvis joining with mine, and I fell into a swirling vortex, falling, falling beyond caring if I ever reached bottom.

Afterward, his deep eyes blazed with the most tender of emotions as he slipped out of me. I thought he was about to cry. "What's the matter?"

"I do love you beyond reason. While I was away, I thought of nothing else but this."

"Nothing matters as long as we are together." I flung one leg over his and moved to press myself against him.

He pushed me away slightly. "We don't want to get sore again, do we?"

At that I loosened my grip. "All right, you win. Tell me more about our vessel."

"She's wonderfully suited to our task. She has one main deck and a spar deck. The balance is devoted to cargo space."

"Where did you find her?"

"In Bombay. She is—or shall I say, was—owned by a man called Ong Ken Ho of Singapore. He ran into some difficulties and hadn't paid his fees in Bombay. That is how I heard she was for sale. I met his agents and they accepted my second offer."

"What did it cost?" I asked gently.

"Forty thousand."

"That much!"

"Initially I offered thirty and bought her for thirty-five, but she had work done on her boilers recently and I had to pay off those debts before the shipyard would release her."

"Does she need further repair?"

"Nothing besides the conversion for our purposes."

"How much will that run?"

"Maybe another five thousand, less if we're lucky."

"That means we'll have five thousand remaining, plus my grand-mother's money," I said as I calculated our financial position aloud.

"Don't forget we have to get her over to Europe and back."

"Won't Amar be paying those expenses?"

"We cannot charge for the journey over if we won't be hauling anything for him."

"What a waste for the ship to travel empty all that way."

"I won't let that happen. On my way here I spoke to Uncle Elisha about investing in wood and spices to sell on the other side. That means an additional risk, since we don't have purchase contracts yet."

"If we buy the goods right, we surely can profit."

"My feelings exactly, but I have to look into the matter more carefully. This is rather new to me."

"And to me," I reminded him. "No matter what, we are in this together."

"Good. I hoped you would say that. We can go over my preliminary figures later."

"How much will Amar pay for the return trip?"

"He wants the entire space for himself and special padding and crating. After talking to other shipowners, I've determined that a fair price—including a premium for the additional services—would be about twenty thousand rupees. And he's offering a five-thousand-rupee bonus if the ship returns ahead of schedule."

"Even without the bonus, that would be an excellent return." I smiled serenely. A few moments later I had thought we were down to zero. Now our imaginary balance sheet contained a small fortune in silver in one column and the deed to a huge ship in the other. What a clever man I had married! I gave him a wet kiss and jumped up.

He pulled me down and held me fast. "Wait, I haven't told you about the engines."

"I have to go—talk quickly."

"It's a beauty. A three-hundred-horsepower, ninety pound, two-cycle steam engine from Glasgow."

"Sounds lovely. Now I must—" He loosened his grip. I really did have to make my way to the bathroom, so I rushed from the room.

"Don't you want to know her name?" he called after me.

After I had relieved myself, I replied, "Of course. What is it?"

"The *Normanton*."

"That doesn't sound very exciting."

"I did not think so either. That is why I have rechristened her."

I paused in the doorway of the room, thinking that I might have enjoyed selecting the name with him. I forced my voice to sound neutral. "What did you choose?"

"I wanted to honor you." He beamed at me expectantly.

What a coincidence! Amar had almost named an elephant after me, and now I would have my name on a ship. "You didn't call her 'Dinah'?"

"No, I hope you don't mind. Your name is too precious to plaster on a ship and send it off to sea." He watched my reaction closely. "I picked the next-best one."

"Yes?"

"I named her the *Luna Sassoon,* in memory of your mother."

"Oh, no!" I gripped the doorway.

Perplexed, he stared at me. "What is the matter? Did I do something wrong?"

"No, I . . . I am overwhelmed . . ."

"You never mention your mother. I supposed that is because her death was such a terrible shock for you as a child. Don't you think the time has come for her to live on as a noble memory?"

Beyond the veil of my misting eyes, Edwin sat among the white sheets like a magical guru who could dispel bad dreams. When he stretched out his arms to me, I stumbled into them and began to cry.

"You are pleased, aren't you?"

"Oh, Edwin!" was all I could reply until I sorted out the conflicting feelings that tumbled inside. A few hours earlier, Amar's query about the origin of my name had unleashed churning emotions. Was this the salve to soothe the wound?

He stroked my hair and with each long, firm sweep of his gentle hand calmed my fears. First he had healed my heart when he came into my life and rescued me from the disaster of Silas and my predicament as my mother's daughter. Now he had brought an even more precious gift: a chance to right the wrongs against my mother, if not as direct vengeance on her killer, then as a way to give her memory esteem. There might not have been a grave marker with the words "Luna Sassoon" on them, but a great ship would carry her name halfway around the world.

"Then you approve?"

I squeezed him more tightly, hoping he would take that for his answer.

This did not satisfy him. "Well?"

"A noble gesture . . . I adore you for thinking of it."

"She will make our fortune," he said confidently.

I closed my eyes and willed his words to be true, and yet . . . and yet I could not stop thinking that anything named Luna Sassoon had to be doomed.

※ ※ ※

After Edwin's return, the maharajah seemed to lose interest in us. Perhaps our passion annoyed him, or his own wife's recovery from childbirth had made her more appealing. Perhaps his official duties consumed his time. Whatever the reason, we were not summoned to the palace more than once a week, and our seats were no longer among the most favored. Even the Cliffords, who continued to live with us since they had not been invited back to the residency, were relegated to very minor positions.

One evening after a light supper at the Orchid House, Dennis explained that the political situation was not going as he had predicted. "I thought Amar would have replaced his uncle's dewan with one from his own younger set. Now I percieve that if Amar changes the guard now, he will have to concentrate on reorganizing his government. The easier course of maintaining the status quo gives him time to pursue his own diversions."

"Would those be mathematics or astronomy or elephants or . . . ?" Edwin winked and waved for Hanif to pour more wine.

Dennis shot a glance toward his wife. She tasted her freshened glass of wine and smiled knowingly. "Dennis, darling, do you think palace gossip stops at the smoking-room door?"

"Not at all. Perhaps you could enlighten us?" Her husband chuckled.

"I have heard there is a mysterious woman who takes much of his time and leaves the maharajah fewer hours to entertain people like us," Jemima replied in an offhand manner.

"You sound envious," her husband teased.

"Only because the Shish Mahal is going to waste."

"Has Amar been entertaining there?" Edwin asked with a tinge of trepidation in his tone.

"We went once. The place is dazzling!" Jemima said breathlessly.

"The lights made me ill," I replied testily. "He and his new friend, whoever she may be, are welcome to it."

Dennis drained his own glass before steering us back to his point. "Frankly, it comes as a shock to me. Not even the professor gave me so much as a hint."

"Now, Dennis, affairs of the heart are hardly matters of state," his wife said to break his sullen mood. "At least Amar was discreet until the child was born."

"I can see this comes as a bit of a jolt," Edwin offered sympathetically. "When I returned, I expected the viceroy would have retired Sir Mortimer in your favor. I suppose he and the old dewan have worked together for so long that if one stays, the other will also."

"That appears to be the position."

"Are you disappointed?" Edwin asked.

Dennis stared at his empty glass. "Life in Trivandrum does have its charms, but as you know, I have always been keen on the possibilities of Quilon. That ship of yours could find it a comfortable berth for a home port."

"And speaking of port . . . or would you prefer sherry?" Edwin waved for Hanif to serve the fortified wine.

Jemima and I went to check on the children while the men launched into plans to have a pier built as a way to attract larger ships to Quilon.

The following week the Cliffords decided to return to their residency. After they left, we made plans to visit Cochin for a few weeks, then Edwin would make a final trip to Bombay to approve the conversion of our ship. I had long ago decided I would rather be at Mother Esther's beck and call than the maharajah's. Before leaving Trivandrum, we visited the maharani, who thanked us for our kindness "during our difficult time of transition," and the maharajah, who called us "Winner" and "Sassy" with affection, but seemed distant nevertheless. We agreed we would return in time to welcome the *Luna Sassoon* to Travancore and to oversee the unloading of her cargo. Then we departed for the north along with Percy Dent, who was going to sail for Europe to acquire the furniture. After supervising the packing, he would return on the *Luna Sassoon*.

"Posh both ways," I promised the professor. "You'll have your choice of any cabin on our ship."

"I'm looking forward to it," he said, his eyes twinkling at the prospect of his great adventure with the maharajah's bottomless treasury to spend.

After our arrival in Cochin, we were pleased to find Mother Esther in robust health. She insisted the professor be her guest while in Cochin. Edwin and I took up residence in our cottage, where we were blissfully happy because it was ours alone.

When Edwin had returned from his journey to Trivandrum, he had brought a packet of letters from my family that had been delivered to Cochin and never forwarded because Mother Esther claimed, "I expected you to return at any moment." Sitting in the Orchid House garden so far away from Calcutta, I was comforted to learn that nothing much had changed. Grandmother Helene wrote that she was well and that the family had lost interest in marrying off Ruby, at least for the moment. My father discussed sending the four boys to different schools ". . . so each might find his own way in the world. Zilpah and I would welcome Edwin's ideas of where might be most appropriate for each, since he has had experience at so many." Zilpah had filled in with the tidbits that women like to know, concluding with the news that Cousin Sultana was expecting again. I had written to everyone and told them about Travancore, the maharajah, the elephant hunt, and Cochin, but, following Edwin's directives, omitted anything about the ship.

"Not until she returns from her first voyage and the venture proves profitable."

I saw his point and kept the secret.

On our arrival in Cochin, I found a second packet with responses to the letters I had sent. A school had been found for Jonah and Pinhas, Seti had won the same prizes at school that I had when I was her age, my father sent along the figures on the current opium crop, which he knew would be of interest to me. The single bit of sad news was the loss of Sultana's expected baby in her sixth month.

Immediately I responded with condolences to my cousin and Gabriel. As I wrote, I thought about what might have been if I had been matched with Gabriel, the first boy I believed I could not live without. How young and silly I had been! I looked across at Edwin as he read *The Moonstone*. His lock of hair covered one eye. He was too engrossed to push it back. Sunlight pooled at his back. Concentration was etched on the elegant planes of his face. The cords in his long neck rippled in the dappled light. His physical beauty was matched by his gentle nature and lively mind. I marveled that this man loved me and was pledged to me for a lifetime.

He looked up. "What are you thinking about?"

"My cousin who lost her baby."

"Isn't she the one who stole your jewels?"

"That was her mother's doing."

"Justice comes in curious ways."

"Edwin! How could the death of a baby have anything to do with someone else's greed?"

He shrugged. "If you were Hindu you'd say there's karma to consider. Everything will tie together. You'll see. Someday you'll have those baubles back and everything will be put right."

"I certainly don't need some pieces of rock and metal to put my life right. Everything that is important to me is made of flesh and blood and is here in this room."

He beamed. "I was afraid you would always be yearning to return to your family and Calcutta."

"I am content with you, darling, but I do hope to see them again soon."

"And so you shall."

"When?"

"After our ship returns. Then we can have as long a visit as you like."

I didn't reply then, for it was unnecessary. He turned back to his book and I stared off into space, wondering why I felt no pressing need to visit my family. Were most women so fulfilled by one man that they required nobody else in their lives? I knew everyone was wondering when I would have a child, and though the idea was appealing, I felt no urgency to have one. Edwin was sufficient. If I didn't have him . . . The thought made me gasp.

He looked up, worried. "Darling?"

I forced a little cough and shook my head to let him know I was fine. He blew me a kiss and went back to his reading.

❧ ❧ ❧

Only a week later the latest letter from Calcutta brought grim tidings. Fortunately, Edwin was there when it arrived and had come to listen to me recite the news. I could not get past the first lines, written in Zilpah's fine hand:

My dearest Dinah,
A terrible tragedy has fallen upon Calcutta and the house of Sassoon. The Bombay plague has struck. The first to perish was poor Sultana's daughter, Miriam. How she will handle two losses coming so close together is a worry to us. Her house is under quarantine, since three servants have also succumbed. Even our household has not been spared . . .

The paper fell from my hand. Edwin called for Yali to assist me and for Hanif to bring brandy and water. Then he took the letter from me and read on in silence.

"Who is it?" I choked at last. "One of the children? Papa?"

"No, no. Nobody in your immediate family."

"Who?"

Edwin stared at our servants. "There were two. An ayah called Selima, and . . ." He walked over to Hanif and took the boy by his shoulders. "I am sorry, Hanif, but your father has passed away." The boy's eyes widened, but his face remained stony.

Yali and I hugged each other. "Selima!" We broke down in tears for the woman who had been my milk mother and Yali's closest friend.

I managed to calm myself while Edwin assisted the servants to their quarters. I retrieved the letter and saw that Edwin had relayed only the news of the second paragraph. My heart pounded and legs rattled as I rushed to take in the devastating list. Edwin returned to find me numb with shock. The oldest of the Sassoon brothers, Uncle Saul, and his wife were gone. Also Uncle Jacob and four of his ten children—including my favorite, little Simha—had perished. Eight Sassoons felled by one scythe! Was that the final total? Or was the contagion spreading? My mind swirled with a chilling fear that more were to come.

The next hours and days are blank in my mind. Edwin brought me to Jew Street, where his mother and aunt administered to the bereft servants and me. I cried for Simha and Sultana's Miriam and for the other children, for my aunt and my uncles and for Abdul and Selima, and then I composed ghoulish lists of those I begged God to spare and those I was willing to sacrifice. When I reconsidered my vile thoughts—of wishing I could trade Aunt Bellore for Grandmother Helene or Zilpah for my father—self-hatred turned to sickness. No food would stay down and I thought I would never stop vomiting.

"I must go back to Calcutta . . . I must see everyone . . ." I begged Edwin.

"Impossible. I would never take you to a plague-infested city. I was ignorant of the scourge until I was in Bombay, but there it was confined to the most destitute. To think it has spread to homes like yours . . ."

Every day I would ask Edwin if the post had arrived and every day he would assure me that it had. A week later my father wrote a brief account of the funerals. There were no further reports of illness.

> We have joined with the government in a voluntary effort to halt this devastating disease. Whole areas of bustees near the Hooghly, where there have been the largest number of cases, have been evacuated and the worst dwellings set afire. Our disinfecting program has halted the spread in the homes of our families and friends. In Jacob's house the scourge was passed by alarming conditions where the food was prepared. We have had to fight ignorance everywhere. In our case, Selima became ill while staying with her family for several days. Please be assured there has never been contagion at Theatre Road. Abdul has lived with his family for more than a year now. Both servants died in hospital. We all have accepted inoculations, thus you should have no further cause for concern.

He went on to commiserate with how I must be feeling so far away, although he added that he was content to know the distance meant I was out of any danger.

The pain of the losses eased, but my physical reaction did not. A doctor was consulted and my pregnancy was confirmed. Delighted, Edwin used this as an excuse to cajole me to eat more. Yali fed me broths, mild rice dishes, mashed bananas, and coconut milk, and my strength returned by degrees. When Edwin announced, though, that the time had come for him to return to Bombay to inspect the final work on the *Luna Sassoon* and see her off on her maiden voyage, I protested vehemently. The plague had started in Bombay! He could not leave me now! The spells of vomiting returned. Edwin was racked with indecision.

His Uncle Elisha offered his services. "You must remain with your wife. I can see that the construction meets your specifications and pay off the contractors. Also, I can supervise the goods that are shipped. Who knows that business better than I do?"

"Shall I let him go in my stead?" Edwin asked, hoping I would insist he do it himself, since he had not always trusted his uncle in the past.

"You have prepared everything admirably. The orders are finalized, the export documents complete. The ship is ready to sail," I replied in the practical tone I knew would have more authority than a hysterical one. "I know how much you want to be there to see the ship off, and if it weren't for the contagion . . ." Despite my resolve, I broke down.

"I wish I could put your fears to rest, but I cannot, not after what has happened in Calcutta. And even if this was your imagination, the anxiety could harm you."

"Will you stay with me?"

"Of course I will. Nothing is more important than your welfare."

"Oh, Edwin!" I said, bursting into tears again. "I do not deserve you."

"Nonsense. This is the most sensible course."

❀ ❀ ❀

I passed through the difficult first months of my confinement and began to bloom with expectation. The word came from Calcutta that the disease had been conquered. Edwin and I discussed whether I should make the trip to Travancore when the ship was due. I had vowed never to be apart from him again, and convinced him I would be well enough to make the trip. "Jemima went on an elephant hunt when she was further along than I will be."

"If the doctor agrees" was all Edwin would promise, but I was feeling so energetic I was confident he would.

I looked forward to seeing Jemima in Quilon, for this time her child-rearing advice would be more pertinent. And I was content to visit with Amar and his mother once again, since any threat the maharajah had posed in the past would vanish with Edwin at my side and my child growing inside me. Hadn't the maharajah shunned his own wife during her confinement?

Thankfully, Edwin did not share that repugnance. Indeed, my changing shape fascinated him. I found my reactions to lovemaking more intense than before. After the *Luna Sassoon* unloaded in Travancore, we would have the perfect excuse to return to Cochin, where we would wait the final weeks until the birth. Our long-range plans included a trip to Calcutta as soon as the baby and I were able. My father had offered another private train car for that journey. The future, which only a few months before had seemed at the mercy of a lascivious maharajah and the death-dealing plague, now loomed rich with possibilities.

39

~~~~~~~~~~~~~~

T he *Luna Sassoon*, her holds laden with more than two thousand pieces of the finest of Europe's furnishings, was due to arrive in the port of Quilon no later than the third week of September 1892. If she made it by September 1, we would receive the bonus. Without consulting Edwin, Uncle Elisha had made a deal with the captain to receive half the five thousand rupees if he met the deadline.

"Isn't that an exorbitant amount to share?" I had wondered when Edwin told me about the arrangement.

"At first I too was shocked, but my uncle has good business sense. The entire matter of making the date is in the captain's hands—and God's. Weather permitting, the captain is the one who must spur his crew to keep the boilers stoked day and night. Besides, this will be a further incentive for him to remain on the *Luna Sassoon* and continue to do a good job for Salem Shipping Services."

"Salem Shipping Services? Where did that come from?"

"I've been toying with it for some time. Do you like the three S's?" He reached into his pocket and showed me a design of the three initials entwined with waves.

On our way to Trivandrum, we rested in Quilon for more than a week. In my seventh month of pregnancy, I was carrying the baby high and experienced few discomforts, but I had been warned to take this break in the water journey.

Jemima wanted to indoctrinate me with everything she knew about raising children, and had even written out notes to guide me later. "Yali will be in charge of the child, but you will feed it," she announced.

"Yes," I agreed.

"Good. Do not listen to anyone who tries to persuade you that you have not enough milk or that it is poor in quality or that 'hardly anyone does it now.' The class of women who substitute for you are

433

more prone to disease, and one must trust one's own hygiene in the end." After my scare with the plague and Selima's fate, she did not have to convince me. The resident's wife seemed relieved. "I knew you would be sensible. Now, should you experience a sense of thirst— what we mothers call 'sinking'—do not resort to malt liquor or any stimulants. To my mind, there is nothing better than a cup of barley water cooled with new milk, or in hot weather, milk and soda water. Another point I must stress is the importance of keeping the infant with you at night. Your ayah can sleep by your bed and take it away for washing and changing. However, the baby must be warmed by the mother's body and comforted by the mother's heartbeat. If you require some time to sleep soundly on your own, there is no problem in handing the baby over after chota hazri or going back to bed anytime during the day. Will you remember that?"

I promised I would, then went over her notes on how to handle crying fits and rashes and weaning. "In Calcutta, you must stock up on Paget's Milk Food, which is concentrated and keeps indefinitely. However, you must supplement it with orange or grape juice, fresh bananas, and raw meat juice to keep the blood healthy. Now, as to the clothing, let us go over this list . . ."

Jemima's requirements were daunting. I dutifully asked questions even though it was difficult to imagine that an infant would require so many vests, flannel petticoats, yoked frocks, and nun's veiling. While we women contented ourselves with these necessities, the resident brought Edwin current with Travancore's political situation.

When we were alone, my husband confided to me that our plan to make a hasty exit after the ship arrived was prudent indeed. "It is more worrisome than I would have suspected, at least to hear Dennis tell it."

"Do you think he might be bitter?"

"He never wanted the Trivandrum post."

"And Amar never wanted to be maharajah."

"You might be correct, but from what he tells me, the maharajah has shown more and more of an inclination to follow his uncle's habits."

I had heard ominous rumors about the previous maharajah ever since we had first gone to Travancore, and I decided to have the matter clarified finally. "I thought he was supposed to have been a devout Hindu."

"He was, but he had a weakness for the flesh. He had some—shall we say—peculiar habits."

"What do you mean?"

"Must I paint a more vivid picture?"

"What is the deep secret?" I said, exasperated. "I'm not exactly an innocent whom you must protect from the truth." I patted my abdomen and grinned.

"The old maharajah became a devotee of the tantric cult of Hinduism. Have you heard of it?" he asked warily.

"Yes, it has something to do with a quest for knowledge, but how does it apply here?"

"Part of the belief system worships the human body as a microcosm of the world. They attempt to arrive at an ecstatic state through spiritual and physical intoxication. Some devotees use sexual rites to achieve this state. I suspect the old maharajah perverted the laws to allow him to do whatever he wanted."

"There's nothing abnormal about maharajahs having many women."

Edwin's face contorted. "When we were young, Amar and I hid on the balcony of the Shish Mahal and watched one of the rituals. Young girls and boys were brought in naked. Wine was poured on their bodies. The maharajah and his priests licked them clean. Then some animals were slaughtered and blood was poured on the children before they were used to satisfy the men's lust."

My stomach churned with revulsion. "They did not harm the children, did they?"

"That depends on how you define 'harm,' but no, they did not kill any." Edwin turned from my stricken face. "Now you know. You wanted me to tell you."

"Amar did not partake, did he?"

"No, not while I was there."

"Did you . . . ?"

"Of course not, Dinah!" His eyes blazed. "They would never permit me to participate in a Hindu ritual, and besides, I was a boy."

"Did they smoke opium as part of the rituals?"

"Maybe they did. I cannot recall. Hookahs were present. What difference does that make? Wine and opium have their place."

"You think of them in the same breath!"

Edwin shrugged. "I don't defend excesses of either."

"I think Amar's personality is altered when he smokes his pipe," I said before I could catch myself.

"In what way?" Edwin asked curiously.

Not wanting to divulge anything about what had happened outside my tent during the elephant hunt, I demurred. "I don't know. It's a feeling I have had . . ."

"Well, even if that is true, there is nothing we can do to change him."

"So you think Amar has been involved in tantric rituals like his uncle?"

"No, but I think he hasn't been an angel either. All Dennis Clifford

said was he heard that a whole flock of royal babies are expected
during the new year."

"I suppose that every time he gets one woman pregnant, he has to
take on another."

"Why do you say that?"

"He rejected his wife when she was expecting."

"How do you know that?" Tension filled my husband's voice.

I backpedaled. "I guess I don't. It only seemed that way to me."

"I am sorry I saw what I did, and even sorrier you forced me to tell
you." Edwin was taking pains to steady his voice. "Do me a favor,
Dinah: don't try to understand what is happening with people whose
customs are different from ours. On one level we can socialize, on
another we can never participate. Even people like the Cliffords are
foreign to us. Do you think they know what it means to be a Jew? Of
course they don't. The differences fascinate everyone, which makes for
interesting friendships, but in the end we can only rely on our own
people."

"That is why I never wanted to live in Trivandrum," I added smugly,
ending the conversation.

❦   ❦   ❦

By the time we left Quilon, I had begun to think our return to
Travancore had been a mistake. The late-summer heat was unbearable
for a pregnant woman. I languished in the coolest part of the Orchid
House, taking hourly sponge baths. Seeing I lacked the energy even to
lift my head, Edwin would sit beside me and read aloud for hours on
end. And when a messenger came to summon him to the palace one
afternoon, I was thankful the invitation did not include me, for I could
not have tolerated having to dress in finery.

That night I slept soundly and did not realize that Edwin had not
returned until the next morning. When I awoke, he was getting undressed, but I thought he was dressing. Confused, I watched him
bathe, then dress again. "Were you away the whole night?"

"Yes, I was."

The color drained from my face as my mind flashed to an image of
one of the old maharajah's rituals. Edwin knew at once what I was
thinking. "Oh, don't be silly, it was an ordinary party. Well, perhaps
not so ordinary," he said, laughing.

After he coaxed me into the circular breakfast room, he continued,
"Amar had some huge blocks of ice added to the water tank behind the
palace. They were so enormous that young ladies in transparent gowns
floated on them and served whiskey and snacks while we swam
around in the cool water."

My teacup clattered as I tried to set it on the saucer but missed. "Did you spend the night in the tank?"

"Just about."

"And not in a hammock?"

"Dinah, I would never—"

I stared into his eyes for the truth. They were reddened and drooping, yet there was no hint of deception. I looked down at my own swollen body and began to cry. "I should have come with you."

"No women—or rather, wives—were there, but I remained in public view throughout the evening." He poured himself a cup of tea, leaned back in his chair, and closed his eyes.

"Did you ever expect Amar to become this . . . ?" I searched vainly for the right word.

" 'Dissolute'?" Edwin offered. " 'Vile'? 'Wicked'? 'Sinful'?" Preoccupied, he stirred three lumps of sugar into his tea.

"So . . . so consumed with his sex."

"I suppose he sees no reason he should not have anything he wants." He took a sip, made a puckering face, but continued to finish the cup.

"Why does he want to tempt you?"

"He doesn't tempt me. You tempt me."

"I don't mean *him*. I mean his consorts."

"Dinah, you have nothing to fear. Amar and I may have been boyhood friends, but he knows nothing of our ways," he stated, beginning to peel an orange. "Just as we find some of his practices confusing, even detestable, he does not understand ours."

"I'm sorry we ever came here!"

"Hush, Dinah. We must take the bitter with the sweet." He handed me an orange section and popped one into his mouth. He chewed for a long time while he gathered his thoughts. "If you hate it so much, we need never return. In a few days our ship will be in port. We will receive payment and probably the bonus. Then we can leave."

"You are confident, aren't you?"

"Reports have indicated fine weather. The ship left Marseilles three days ahead of schedule . . ." He grinned. "I don't care about the bonus—it would be just the icing on the cake. In any case, Amar is grateful for what we have done. He told me so last night. All he wanted was for everyone to enjoy himself. He paraded about with a few young ladies, but frankly, I did not see him touch one. He does it to demonstrate that as maharajah, he can have anyone he wants. I haven't seen this harem, nor this special lady friend, that Dennis Clifford hinted about. There was more drinking and smoking than anything else."

"How was his mood?"

"Frankly, Amar did not even seem happy. The first months of his reign were devoted to ritual, then he tried to satisfy his whims, and now that has become tiresome. I think his serious nature will prevail. If we stayed on, we could do more business here. Amar would always pay the top rate."

"No. We should move on. Besides, we no longer need him."

"We didn't come to Travancore to make a fortune from our friendship."

I felt I had been slapped. "You are right, Edwin," I said with remorse. "But I think we should be independent. Court life does not suit me."

"Nor me, if the truth be told. We can leave anytime we want. Poor Amar has a life sentence."

"I don't mean to be critical of Amar. He has always been kind to me."

"He admires you and worries about you as well. Last night he asked how you were managing in this heat. He offered to move you to a part of the palace where cool water flows under the stones."

"You didn't say I would go, did you?"

"I put him off. If you say no to Amar, he will take it as a challenge to change your mind." Edwin caught my eye and blew me a kiss. "Come now, you know I am right."

Unexpectedly, tears ran down my cheeks. "I am sorry to be so sensitive. Jemima warned me this could be a difficult time." I sucked a second slice of orange, trying not to think about what had occurred the night before.

Hanif stood in the doorway. "Yes?" Edwin asked.

"Someone from the palace, sahib."

"Not again," I moaned.

Edwin waved Hanif to let the man in, but Hanif shook his head slightly to indicate that Edwin should come with him. With a tired sigh, Edwin stood slowly and lumbered out. In the distance I could hear loud words reverberating along the marble corridor. Was that Edwin shouting? Someone was arguing back. Supporting my lower back with my hand, I rose and went to see what was happening.

By the time I caught up with Edwin, he was on his knees on the floor, staring at a document and shaking his head.

"Edwin! What's the matter? What's wrong?"

"Gone! All gone!"

"What is gone?" More news about a plague? "Who has died this time?"

"No . . ." His arms covered his head. When I bent beside him, though, his flailing hands pushed me off.

"Is someone ill? Did someone die? Your mother? Edwin!" I screamed for his attention, but his misery had made him oblivious.

Hanif reached down, picked up the paper, and handed it to me. I read the news: the *Luna Sassoon* had been lost at sea.

"Who wrote this? Where did it come from?"

"How should I know?" Edwin said in the most pathetic voice I had ever heard.

I waved for Hanif to assist me, and in a few minutes we had Edwin lying on a low sofa. I offered him a brandy, and he took a few gulps. Hanif wiped his brow with a moistened towel. Two small punkah-wallahs fanned him. I read the report, which had been sent by the harbormaster of Goa, more carefully.

> *To the owner of the vessel* Luna Sassoon:
>
> *It is my unfortunate duty to inform you the steamship* Luna Sassoon *foundered approximately 150 miles due west of Goa on the twenty-fifth of August 1892. Three members of the crew survived and were rescued by the sailing ship* Anglia Castle, *which brought them to this port. The ship's master was not among them and the first mate perished from his burns the day after his arrival.*

The paper went on to give latitude and longitude and other navigational aspects of the disaster, then concluded:

> *An initial inquiry was made as to the cause. Weather conditions were fair and seas were mild. Winds were twelve knots WSW. The crew reports an explosion belowdecks in the vicinity of the boiler room at 0400. Fire spread rapidly throughout the ship and all hands were ordered to abandon at once. Only two lifeboats were lowered in time. The one on the starboard side was engulfed in flames from flying debris. By the time the other boat was able to make it around the sinking ship, no other survivors could be located. A copy of this report is being forwarded to the attention of the Lloyd's agent in our port . . .*

"The professor . . ." I gasped. "They don't mention him. He must have died as well."

"Yes . . . yes . . . all my fault . . ."

"How could it be your fault?"

"I should have gone to Bombay. I should have inspected the boilers. I told you they required repairs. Somebody may have installed inferior valves . . ."

"But the ship made it to Europe and almost the whole way back. She was ahead of schedule . . . she . . ." I faltered as I remembered the captain's incentive to bring the ship in early. Had he pushed the machinery beyond its limits?

I glanced back at the report. "Lloyd's," I read aloud again. "That's the insurance company. How much was she insured for? How much was the cargo insured for?"

Edwin did not respond. His eyes were empty. All substance had been sucked from his strong frame. If he had not been leaning against the wall, he might have crumpled. At last he spoke in a hoarse, shaking voice. "Uncle Elisha was supposed to see to it when he was in Bombay. There were some problems in arranging a survey. He made the usual inquiries and discovered something I had overlooked. In *Lloyd's Register*, the book I had studied before making an offer on the ship, there were many kinds of symbols and markings to certify ships. I missed one detail. Under the date of the last survey, a small red line had been drawn. The other information was in order; therefore, I did not realize the red line meant that—as of that date—the vessel had been withdrawn for noncompliance with the Society's rules."

"I don't understand."

His voice became louder and shakier. "That means the goddamned ship had serious structural or engine problems that had to be conformed to before they would recertify it."

"But you did have the ship worked on," I reminded him calmly.

Edwin took a long inhalation, blew it out tight lips, and continued haltingly. "My alterations were to prepare the holds for the furniture . . . and to tune up the engine. I did not know . . . about the certification problem at the time . . . and no special work was ordered to bring the boat into compliance."

"But why didn't your uncle—?"

He jumped up. "Why didn't he indeed!" He spun around with clenched fists shaking. "He said that he thought the work the previous owner had done on the boilers would suffice, and when he found it wouldn't, he said there was no time . . . he said I didn't authorize it . . . he said the ship looked fine to him and there would be plenty of time to do the work later. 'Why spend money until you've made some money?' It made sense to me." His face began to redden alarmingly. "The ship seemed in fine shape. There wouldn't have been a problem if that wretched bribe hadn't tempted that covetous captain. What did he care if he burned out the engine, as long as he made it in ahead of time? Foolish man! It cost him his life and it cost us . . . ."

Everything. I realized we had lost my entire dowry. Nevertheless, the maharajah had lost far more. The value of the cargo was greater than the worth of the ship.

"Does Amar know?"

"He must. The news came from the palace."

"We must go there at once."

"No," Edwin said slowly. "No, he will be too furious. We must give him time to think sensibly."

"Isn't it better to face it at once?"

"You know how impetuous Amar can be. Give him time to gather his thoughts. He may have lost a great deal, but the cost will hardly put a dent in his treasury, and . . ." His reddened face became covered with pale blotches. "My God! Did you hear what I just said? Dent! The professor! He loved the man like a father."

"We must go to Amar, if only because of the professor. We shall talk of that loss, not the other."

Edwin bowed his head. "Yes, you are right. We must go." He rushed toward me when I stretched out my arms. Trembling, we clasped each other while our child kicked and squirmed between us.

40

♥ ♥ ♥

Amar was calm, too calm. On the turquoise bed, under the sky-blue canopy, in the blue-and-white-tiled room, he leaned against the satin bolster. His hands were folded serenely across his diamond-studded belt buckle. He took slow puffs from the large silver hookah.

At last he spoke. "We were the only family the professor had. Travancore was his home. He leaves no wife, no children . . . I carry his legacy: not here"—he pointed to his scrotum—"as a son carries for his father, but here"—he pointed to his head.

"He was a brilliant teacher . . ." Edwin mumbled.

Amar did not reply. The lone sound was the ominous gurgling of the pipe.

"He was very kind to me," I began hesitatingly. "He introduced me to marvelous books, he taught me about . . ." I was about to say "French furniture," but caught myself in time and slipped in "chess."

The maharajah's eyes glimmered. "Like me, he thought you showed promise," he said mushily. "Come now, Sassy . . ." The maharajah pushed his bulk away from the cushions and stretched out to me. "Don't back away from me, not now, not when I need you most. We still have each other, don't we? What are friends for?" He came toward me and touched my shoulder. My swimming eyes refracted the turban's dazzling jewel as it approached me. Where was Edwin? What was he doing? I craned my neck around. Yes, Edwin was nearby. I extended my hand to my husband, but he was out of reach. The maharajah continued to speak in his sloppiest manner. "Yes, what are friends for? Friends help each other in their hour of need." He licked his lips. "I will not say I am not disappointed to lose the furniture. Each piece was priceless . . ." His hand stroked my upper arm carelessly. "Did you know that the French did not want to let some of the finest ones

442

go?'" He gave a rueful laugh. "Or was that their way of inflating the price?" He threw up his hands.

I was enormously relieved to have his touch released. I eased myself nearer to Edwin. His arms clasped me from the back and held my waist tightly. Could Amar tell he was bracing me? Probably, because Amar did not advance. The maharajah's eyes circled the room, where a few retainers watched for any sign of an order. Amar waved them away. We three were alone.

Amar adjusted his long tunic. His stubby fingers wrapped around the thick pearl rope that looped past his waist. "No . . . nothing that is lost can ever be replaced—nothing made of iron, nothing made of wood and silk, nothing made of flesh and bones—and yet the world goes on." He gestured to my belly. "In the midst of everything that is lost, a new life comes forth. Think of the child that carries your seed, Winner. What a mind it will have! And you shall have the duty to fill it with many of the treasures the professor taught us. In that way he shall live again." Amar's face hardened. His dark eyes were suffused with a disoriented glaze.

The atmosphere in the room had changed. Tears fell from my eyes. This time they were not as much for the professor as for our predicament. I watched the maharajah's face for clues.

"You are a noble man with noble ideals."

I wanted to kick Edwin for trying flattery, which was obviously the wrong tack. The moment he saw Amar's face twist, he realized this too.

"How generous of you, my old friend," Amar said silkily. "Even noblemen must be treated fairly. When something is taken from them, they should be given something in return. Don't you agree?" His tone softened further. "Now, I know you could never repay me for what I have lost with silver, even if you pledged a lifetime of earnings to the cause. Therefore, I would never consider having you undertake that sort of debt. Yet if I forgave the matter entirely, I would not be doing you a favor either. For the remainder of your days you would carry the burden of your responsibility. Just as a child welcomes a swift, fair judgment when he has made a mistake—to turn his little wronged world right—so you must be yearning to balance this obligation."

As Edwin's grip tightened around my waist, I had a crazy hallucination of the fairy tale Rumpelstiltskin. Imagining Amar as the ugly gnome who would demand my firstborn child as payment, I crossed my hands protectively on my abdomen.

"What do you have in mind?" Edwin's words rang out sharp and clear against the tile walls.

Amar stood in front of us, massaging his pearls. "You know what I want." He paused and grinned maddeningly. "I want Dinah."

Curiously, that statement, which should have been shattering, came as a relief—at least to me. What I had always suspected had been true! It was as if I had become a coin that had been flipped in the air between the men. For the briefest second I felt infused with the flattery inherent in the toss. Then the reverse emotion of extreme loathing welled up. Caught midway, I was like a wild animal stunned by a bright light.

Edwin, however, was able to react. Letting go of me, he approached the maharajah with a crooked smile. "Amar, come now, this is no time for one of your jokes."

"Why don't you call me Lover-boy? You were the one who gave me that name. Is it any wonder I have tried to live up to it ever since?" Amar's thick lips twisted evilly, annihilating any hope that he had been jesting.

Edwin moved quickly to stand between the maharajah and me. "My wife is expecting our child. Why would you want to shock her after what she has been through already? You know she lost many loved ones to the plague a few months ago, and now she feels this loss as deeply as we do." His tone was firm, yet conciliatory. I admired my husband's control under the circumstances. If I had had the strength, I would have pummeled the bastard.

"We both have appreciated your hospitality," he continued. "We both have admired you. Amar, after everything we have been through, don't kill that now."

"My dear Winner, why won't you admit when you have lost? I cannot take your prize away forever, but she could be shared. Now might be the most propitious time. Her mind is as exquisite as ever. Even her shape—like a perfectly ripe pear—appeals to me. A few nights are all I ask. I would be gentle. And then she would have the child. After that she could spare me a few hours every month. Is that so much? I realize I cannot dissolve your union—unless that should be her choice someday. In Travancore the rules permit the wife to make the decision."

As his hideous demands escalated, the more rational he tried to sound. "Winner, don't look so shocked. Sassy is a worldly lady—she has been married two times already, and who knows what occurred before that? Come now! Didn't she tell you about what happened during the elephant hunt? She didn't? Dinah, why weren't you truthful with your husband? Why didn't you tell him about that time I came to your tent? What are you ashamed of?" He lunged forward and patted my belly. "Now you can understand why I am so anxious to see that child. There are some things that cannot remain hidden."

"You are insane!" I screamed as I shrank from him. "Nothing happened, Edwin! Nothing! He visited my tent. Yes, he did! But I would not let him inside. I stood outside and tried to get him to leave, until his mother came along and ended it."

"Dinah, who would believe you?" Amar continued in his exasperatingly level voice. "That is not the story my mother tells. Who else could speak for you? Your servant, who has been paid to protect your honor since the day you were born? I know everything about you, everything about your high-and-mighty family, and the mother they say you take after." He took a long breath and gave a slippery grin. "Nobody's perfect, my dear Sassy. Even your husband can be corrupted if the pipe is filled with something sweet to smoke and the woman who wants him is persistent enough." He turned his outrageous accusations on Edwin. "In the past, my friend partook quite freely of the delicacies offered at the palace, and this visit was no different. Didn't he tell you of our escapade last night with hot opium and cool women? Can you imagine the pleasure when one's brain is fired with Patna's finest and one's throbbing organ thrust into a fleshy tunnel filled with icy flakes? Ah!" The maharajah closed his eyes and rolled his head back. "Men and women are not very different. You and Edwin can both enjoy the pleasures of this life. I will find him some suitable companion, and when you have delivered your burden, we shall taste some of these more exotic delights together, Sassy, and then you will see why it is better to yield to life's glories than to refuse."

I fought to prevent this perverted image from searing into my consciousness. I preferred Edwin's innocent explanation of the previous night's revelries. What Amar said could not have happened! And yet hadn't Mother Esther warned me that Amar would corrupt Edwin? Why had I ignored the warnings? I glanced at Edwin. His eyes were bright and steady as he met my gaze. I heard his thoughts as though he had been screaming: Don't believe him! He has lied to me about you and now he's lying to you about me. Don't you see what he is trying to do? If we allow him to divide us, we will be lost. With all my will, I tried to convey the same message to my husband. We never turned from the other as Amar poured out more of his venom.

"My uncle had a Swedish woman, a British countess, and a Portuguese maiden. However, he never had a Jewish woman from Calcutta. How I yearn to taste that forbidden flesh for myself! And now I shall have my chance, won't I, Winner?"

A crazy thing happened next. Edwin did not protest. I watched my husband's face set into a stony mask. Did he believe the maharajah's disgusting lies? How was I going to prove myself? After the baby was born, he would see it would not look anything like Amar, but even so, would Edwin ever trust me implicitly again?

He spoke, sounding as though he was a long way off. "Sir, we are both upset and tired. My wife is in no condition to be reasonable. I know you mean her—and me—no harm. Let me talk to her. Let me prepare her. I will return in the morning and we will review an arrangement that will be fair to everyone."

The world turned on its head. What was going on? There was no up or down, no left or right. I had nowhere to turn. I dimly heard the maharajah say elatedly, "I knew you would want to save your honor. Women need coaxing, but I am not worried about Dinah. She is a very bright, a very sensible woman. Besides, she has always liked me. Sometimes I think the biggest mistake I ever made was not introducing myself to her a few minutes *before*, instead of a few minutes *after*, your wedding. Things have a marvelous way of sorting themselves out in the end, don't they?"

"Yes, sir, they do," Edwin muttered. "Now I will take her home to rest."

"Don't wait until tomorrow," the maharajah demanded. "I want you here tonight. Let us talk about it then, shall we?"

"All right. I will not bring Dinah."

"No, no, of course not. Give her time to recuperate and to think. There is no rush. Tonight we will share another pipe . . . and whatever suits your fancy. We both need to blot our sorrows. Until then I, for one, plan to get some sleep." He gave a wide yawn and clapped his hands. Guards bounded inside each of the six doorways. Three rushed to attend the maharajah. Two others were directed to escort us home. I felt myself half-carried, half-pushed from the room by Edwin, and somehow, without any will of my own, I found myself back out in the festering midday heat of the hideous Travancore summer.

❦   ❦   ❦

The next hours were a blur. Edwin would not speak until we locked ourselves in the bath at the Orchid House. He sketched his plan slowly, to be certain I understood each aspect. "I will go to the maharajah tonight. I will tell him we have spoken and will make him a counteroffer. You will come to him once a week for a month. You will satisfy him in any manner which will not require penetration, as even we are having difficulties in that area."

"But . . ." I sputtered. "That is not true!"

"Hush, darling, listen to me. Nothing will ever happen. We will leave Trivandrum tonight. I am only trying to explain how I will pacify him. I will tell him we will go to Cochin for the birth, returning here to live. Once we are back, I will offer to share you for a year. With that we will agree the debt has been repaid, and you will determine what happens after that."

"He'll never believe you."

"Yes, Amar will be fooled because I have asked for conciliations and you will be given the final decision at the end. He will suppose you would have demanded that. Then, after we have made our bargain, I will sit with him while he has a few pipes."

"Is anything he said true?" I gasped, wondering if Edwin had partaken of the opium or the women.

"Did he tell the truth about you?"

I shook my head. "All lies."

"Then I won't believe him if you won't."

"Of course I won't," I cried fervently. "But can we get away?"

"Listen, I know how Amar reacts. By midnight, when he dozes off, I will slip away."

"Amar will have us followed."

"Not quite that soon. I know the way he thinks. He has the curious capacity to reduce everything to the lowest common denominator. He truly believes that his loss can be repaid by having you. In his convoluted mind, if this simple solution can meet his need for retribution, he does not see why we would object."

"He is not stupid."

"No, he is nearsighted. Even with his considerable brains, he cannot fathom a love as encompassing as ours. What does he know about us? Our union was arranged, in much the same way his was. He recognizes how he feels for his wife. He assumes our relationship has the same basis. I pity him as I pity every man who has never experienced the sublime joy of a love like ours. From the hour we met, I have never doubted you; you have never doubted me. There is no one else in my life. Nothing that anyone could say about you could change that. Some men may have lapses because they remain unsatisfied at their core, but I feel as complete with you . . . as I hope you do with me."

"Yes!" I was mesmerized by every word. The shell of our perfect egg was inviolate. Every sense became more alert. "Tell me what I should do."

"I have sent Hanif to find a suitable small boat—a boat for four. We will 'borrow' one after dark. To hire one would be too dangerous. Later, when I am at the palace and you are pretending to rest, Hanif and Yali will go off together like lovers trying to find a nest, and they will bring the boat to the same place you met me when I returned from Bombay. Be there at midnight. Wear your darkest clothes. Slip out this very window into the kitchen courtyard and follow the servants' path away from the royal enclave. Come alone. Take nothing with you. I will meet you there."

Although I could think of many problems with the plan, I did not argue with my husband. When we returned to our rooms, we tried to act as normally as possible. We ordered an enormous meal, which I ate with gusto. My lethargy had passed, for bitter anger fueled my movements. I took a last walk around the confines of the Orchid House, which had never been more than an elegant prison. I surveyed the elaborate wardrobe for court appearances and some infant apparel the talented Travancore seamstresses had been fashioning. The thought of wearing any of the garments I had worn to the palace or dressing my baby in the handiwork of the state appalled me. I could not wait to be gone from this place forever.

\\/   \\/   \\/

The merest slip of a moon shone a pale line of light along the trail to the wharf. At first I did not see anyone. Then Yali cooed birdlike in the reeds. The craft was well-hidden in the marsh. Hanif rowed it around and Yali helped me in. We went to hide and wait for Edwin. An hour passed. With every minute my heart pounded more fiercely. Finally, out of the blackness he came wading through the low-tide muck. There was a sucking sound as he climbed into the craft. Wordlessly he took up the oar opposite Hanif and pushed us off into the stygian night.

By dawn we had almost reached Kadhinamkulam Lake. There Edwin had hoped to hire a larger boat with a team of oarsmen who would propel us faster on our way north. "In the morning Amar will learn of our disappearance."

"I can't believe he would come after us."

"He will be furious. He will think it a point of honor."

"Even if he catches us, what can he do? Kill us?"

"He does rule the state. He could have us jailed on a pretense: theft or fraud or . . ."

"Only under the watchful eye of the British resident," I said.

"Sir Mortimer offers more of a blind eye than anything else, and it would take a good long time for our plight to come to the attention of the viceroy."

"Amar is a modern prince, not some crazed medieval ruler."

"Why are you defending him?"

"I'm not! I think he's the most horrid, spoiled, disgusting man I have ever known, and I am sorry I didn't heed my better judgment and stop this before it ever happened."

"You agreed about the ship!"

"Yes, that did sound like a good idea at the time, but if you remember, I never wanted to come to this dreadful place. I knew the gift of the Orchid House had to be tainted. I knew that slimy man wanted more than the purity of 'friendship.' For your sake I always buried my fears. I thought his attentions to me were odd, but I tried to convince myself I was misinterpreting them. If only I had trusted my instincts sooner!" I buried my face in the crook of my arm as I thought about the comparisons to Nissim Sadka that I had discounted for too long.

Edwin put down one oar for a moment and stroked my back. "Let's not argue. We must find a faster boat. Hanif and I cannot row to Cochin."

After an hour of paddling around the lagoon, Edwin had made a deal with the owner of a sleek *wallam*, which had a curved dragon neck at both the bow and stern. Normally a crew of two propelled it, but Edwin had more than enough coins to entice four men aboard. With our head start, it would be difficult for anyone to beat us to Quilon.

From the floating market Hanif and Yali purchased supplies, including a small charcoal stove and teakettle, to prepare meals. The day was warm and mild, the water calm, and my baby seemed lulled by the gentle movement of the boat. We ate, we slept in each other's arms, and the nightmare of Trivandrum fell farther and farther away.

In Quilon, Hanif ran ahead to alert the Cliffords. They sent a chair to carry me to the hillside mansion. There we were bathed and cosseted like storm-tossed children. Edwin told an abbreviated version of the tale: the loss of the *Luna Sassoon*, the professor's death, and Amar's outrageous proposal.

"I have been worried about you," Jemima admitted. "When the maharajah invited us on the elephant hunt, I was concerned then— not about you, but about myself. I tried to refuse, due to my condition at the time, but he was so insistent."

"What do you mean?" Edwin asked.

Jemima flushed.

"You owe it to them to explain," the resident urged. "It might help them now."

"Shortly after our arrival at the camp, the maharajah made up some tale that it was considered good luck to touch the belly of a pregnant foreigner, and he asked if he might place his hand on mine."

"I was there at the time," Dennis added. "Jemima was so taken aback, she didn't know how to respond. Foolishly, perhaps, I joked that since she had been through this so many times, I could see no harm."

"Did you let him?" I asked, aghast.

"For a moment." Jemima bit her lip.

"She was fully clothed and there were servants everywhere," her husband replied tensely.

"I have to admit the experience was unpleasant. There was something about his touch"—she shuddered—"it felt unclean." She looked at me for confirmation.

"Yes." I nodded. "I felt the same way whenever he looked at me. Sometimes I chided myself for being silly. Now I wish—"

"Never mind! You are here now and safe with us," Dennis said firmly. "Come see our beautiful baby, Robert."

When we were calmer, Dennis confided that he was not astonished by the turn of events. "The man has been unstable from the first. Before his uncle died, he was moody and depressed. Ever since his brothers became ill he has had few periods of contentment. Once he went swimming in the backwaters at night and almost drowned. Some think it was a suicide attempt. The first time I had seen him happy in many months was when he was on his way back from Cochin after attending your wedding. We had hopes you both would be good for him, help him settle in. If I could have predicted this tragic result . . ." The resident trailed off.

"If I could not see what was happening, nobody else is at fault," Edwin replied kindly.

The men went on to discuss the serious problems in the capital. "The gross mismanagement concerned me and I was planning a trip to Madras to consult with the viceroy. Now I must not delay any further. I will leave in the morning."

"Perhaps you should wait a few more days in case they come looking for us. I would not want Mrs. Clifford to have the burden—"

"You are absolutely correct. I do not know what I was thinking. The whole situation is a perfect muddle, isn't it?"

"You don't think Amar will send his soldiers after us, do you?" I asked the resident.

"A rational man would not, but I do not trust Amar's faculties. Besides, since there is no point in second-guessing him, you are not safe in Quilon."

"I agree," Edwin added. "We must get on our way tonight. If the maharajah's launch has set out with a full crew, they could catch up to us if we delay."

"You must not go to Cochin. The Maharajah of Cochin is one of Amar's closest allies. The resident there would never trust your word above the royals'."

"My mother is waiting for our return, and Dinah is going to have her child there. Where else could we go?"

"Why don't you take Dinah to Calcutta?"

"How can she cross the country in this heat and in her condition?"

"I am sorry, young man, you do not have a choice."

"In any case, we have to go to Cochin to get to Calcutta," I offered. "We could see your mother, even take her with us."

"No, Dinah, Edwin, please listen to me." The resident's eyes narrowed. "Didn't you know the maharajah has a steam launch? I haven't seen it used for more than a year, but the old maharajah was especially proud of its shiny engine. He used to toot the whistle himself."

"How fast is it?" Edwin wondered.

"It could make the journey from Trivandrum to Quilon in less than a day, certainly outrunning any numbers of oarsmen. The waters may be too low in spots this time of year, but there is a chance it could get through."

"We must leave at once!" I gasped.

"You cannot attempt the inland sea."

Edwin shook his head. "What other choice do we have?"

"There is a small freighter that called here a few days ago. I believe it is heading up the coast to Bombay. There you could get the train for Calcutta."

While the resident located the captain of the ship, Jemima burst into action, gathering a suitable wardrobe for me and a small packet for an infant. "It's always wisest to be prepared," she said in an offhand manner.

"The baby is not due for at least six weeks."

"Well, my dear, babies have a clock of their own."

"I should not be traveling now, should I?"

"You seem to be doing splendidly. Take tea and stimulants sparingly, and if you feel any cramps, drink one brandy an hour for three hours, then sleep. If they return, you can continue the brandy as long as you take plenty of bread and fruit with it."

"I will pickle the baby."

"Do as I say, and just in case . . ." She went on to discuss how to deliver a baby in an emergency. "Your Yali will know what to do." She patted my arm. "Don't worry, I am certain you will make it to your father's house. You will be in my prayers every minute."

By nightfall we were pulling out of Quilon's harbor and chugging north along India's western coast. If the maharajah, his soldiers, or a herd of wild elephants had been clamoring after us, we were beyond their reach.

The master of the rusty steamer, a pitiful cousin of the *Luna Sassoon*, had managed to find comfortable quarters for the "esteemed owner of the Salem Steamship Service." Along the way to Bombay, Hanif and Yali tended us dutifully. There we booked a first-class compartment to Calcutta, but it was hardly a match for the private car that had taken us across country the first time.

The baby did not appreciate the motion of the train. Pains began right after we left Nagpur, diminished before Raipur, then increased on the outskirts of Calcutta. Brandies and fruit drinks were offered, wet towels cooled my limbs, while Edwin crooned, "Wait, baby, wait."

As we passed the outskirts of the city, I heard Yali muttering that I might make it to Calcutta.

"I agree," I said, then sat up and announced that the contractions had gone away.

"But, Dinah . . ." Edwin tried to restrain me as I combed my own hair, and insisted that I change into one of Jemima's prettiest gowns.

"No, really, this baby is so pleased to be getting off the train, he has gone back to sleep." Peering into the reflecting glass, I saw my sweating, disheveled face. "I look a fright. I cannot let my family see me like this. What would they think?"

"Indeed," Edwin muttered as he thought about facing his father-in-law with the news that he had squandered his generous dowry and almost lost his wife to a deranged maharajah.

The train slowed. Familiar images were framed in the moving window: the Hooghly River . . . the bathing ghats and country boats . . . the tangled web of rigging on the sailing ships . . . the pontoon bridge. And soon . . . soon . . . Theatre Road.

PART IV

❦ ❦ ❦

The Harvest

In this age of civilisation we are unwilling to
see anything that can detract from that distinguished character which in former times gained
to the Merchants the title of "Princes" and to
traffickers that of the "Honourable of the Earth."

—JAMES MATHESON, *The Canton Register,*
19 April 1828

41

❧ ❧ ❧

Calcutta, 1892–1897

The egg of our marriage survived intact. Our sojourn in Travancore may have contaminated its pristine surface, but once it was washed clean after our return to Calcutta, not even a hairline crack could be found. Edwin's concern for my health and mine for his loss, coupled with our mutual disgust for the maharajah's despicable proposal, united us further. Although we knew we could weather the storm together, we had still to face my father and the other Sassoons.

I would recommend that anyone running away from a wrathful maharajah and having to confront parents after disposing of a munificent dowry arrange to give birth within a week of returning home. Our son, Aaron David, was delivered by Dr. Hyam, who was assisted by the Jewish midwife Saleh Arakie and Yali on the first of October. In the feverish hours of my labor, everyone tried to hide the significance of this date from me, yet I eventually realized that my child had arrived on the fourteenth anniversary of my mother's murder. Rather than dwell on the bizarre coincidence, Edwin prodded me to remember that our lusty son proved there was much more goodness than sadness in life.

Aaron had been born several weeks early, and being a small baby, required feeding every two hours. Heeding Jemima's advice, I nurtured him myself, much to the dismay of the Sassoon aunts. However, Zilpah thought mine the most sensible course, especially in the anxious aftermath of the plague.

One benefit of my postpartum state was that explanations of our predicament had been left to Edwin. He must have handled them admirably, for I received sympathy in place of reprimands. Only after the baby passed the crucial three-month mark with plump cheeks and a glowing report from the doctor did my father sit down with us to address our future. The January morning was so cool, a patina of moisture fogged the windows, and he asked us to join him in the parlor, where a pungent fire burned in the hearth. Aaron, wrapped in muslin, slept in my arms.

"As much as we would like to have you at Theatre Road, you need to continue to make a life of your own," Papa began gently.

"Absolutely," Edwin responded with an agreeable smile.

"These days it is costly to set up a family in a suitable house." His expression became more somber. "Also, we have experienced tragic losses, proving once again that families must share responsibilities along with their fortunes."

There was a long pause that I felt I had to fill. "What do you have in mind, Papa?"

As Aaron stirred in his sleep, I patted his back, and my father asked, not unkindly, "Don't you think the child could be laid down now?"

"He prefers to be close to someone."

"Babies need to learn to sleep alone."

"I can't imagine why," I replied sweetly. "Now, please tell us what is on your mind."

"In one way your return is a blessing. I never cared to have you far away, and now I never want you to leave again." He shot a glance at Edwin. "I know your ties are in Cochin. If your mother would consider moving to Calcutta, I would assist in the transition."

"That is very kind, but—"

My father cut him off. "Let me explain my proposition. When my brother Jacob died, his wife, Sumra, was left without a husband and grieving for the loss of four of her children, all of whom had been living at home. As you might know, Dinah, the three eldest are married and on their own. The youngest one remaining, Yedid, is a shy boy who has not begun to recover from the trauma. However, his case is nothing compared to his mother's. Poor Sumra walks about as if she is in a trance. She rarely even speaks. Without a firm hand, the servants have allowed the house to deteriorate."

While he spoke, I recalled Uncle Jacob's gloomy house in Free School Street, which always seemed filled with too many children and not enough light or air. It was not difficult to imagine why the plague had struck there.

". . . Sumra wasn't much of a manager before the sickness, and the situation has worsened considerably since then. . . ."

Slowly an understanding of my father's intentions clarified. Flinching at the idea of living in that crowded older quarter, I exclaimed, "Are you suggesting that we move to Free School Street?"

"I am asking you to consider the possibility. Your aunt is incapable of making decisions. She would defer to you. There should be no quarrels on that score. Yedid needs a man like Edwin around. I realize the house—which Sumra inherited from her mother—is north of Park Street, but funds are available for a renovation. Many of the smaller bedrooms could be combined, new windows could be installed, the parlor refurbished to your tastes . . ."

Edwin, who had never seen the ghastly place and was probably as glad to leave his father-in-law's domain as I had been to leave his mother's, spoke up cheerfully. "Dinah does prefer to rule her own roost—doesn't any woman?—and I would do anything I could to help your family. Our Aaron might even bring some sunshine into those dark corners. Don't you agree, darling?"

"If I can be assured the house is a healthy place to live," I replied hesitantly.

"There is no rush to leave Theatre Road, Dinah," my father added to seal my cooperation. "The kitchen and pantries must be torn out so that the plumbing can be repaired. Sumra can live with her eldest son, Mir, until then." He rubbed his hands to signal the matter was concluded to his satisfaction.

Aaron began to cry. Yali rushed into the room and offered to take him from me.

"No, he is fine now," I said as I calmed him. "I'll bring him up in a short while."

I thought a shadow of disapproval crossed my father's face, but he said nothing about my reluctance to let anyone else care for my child. "Yali and Hanif will go with you, of course," he continued smoothly. "The household budget from Jacob's share should enable you to have at least four, possibly six servants, if you wish."

Edwin shook his head. "I don't think that will be—"

My father waved for him to be quiet. "There is another matter. You will be wanting to make yourself useful," he said, staring my husband in the eye. "I know you have been looking around and I realize you have not wanted to ask any more favors of me, but it makes no sense to have such a bright mind at the service of another company. Everyone makes mistakes, perhaps not of the magnitude you suffered, but let me say that I believe you thought you were making the correct decisions and those decisions might well have held you in good stead if a confluence of unfortunate events had not occurred." My father went to stand behind the chair where I sat rocking Aaron. "We learn from our errors. We become more cautious. We mature. Thus, today you are more valuable than you might have been a year ago."

"That is very kind of you, but—"

"No, let me finish. Now you are a family man. You can see what it means to want to do the best you can for your child, your wife. For better or for worse, you are also a member of the Sassoons, a clan that has been decimated by the loss of my two brothers Saul and Jacob. I am trying to fill the shoes of my eldest brother, but there is nobody groomed to fill Jacob's place. He was our link to the ryots in the Patna region."

"That is not the place for Edwin," I said, less gently than I could have.

My father's expression darkened. "I don't believe he has many options at the moment, Dinah."

"There are always complications in a family business," I added quickly, as if that, not the nature of the crop, had been my objection.

Sensing my discomfort, Edwin leapt in. "What I think she meant was that I know nothing about the cultivation of opium. Perhaps I could be more useful in Clive Street or . . ." He trailed off as he observed my father's disparaging expression. Avoiding my pleading gaze, he capitulated. "Well, I will help you in any way possible."

"Then that settles it." My father reached down and stroked Aaron's ruddy cheek, then turned on his heel and left the room abruptly.

❦ ❦ ❦

The house in Free School Street was scrubbed from the inside out. The grimy exterior was painted a lemon yellow, and the hideous green shutters—so common in Calcutta—were painted a more tolerable shade of cream. The interior required white on every wall. Marble tiles replaced wormy wood floors. Dusty panels were removed. Unfortunately, along with the increased light, noise and dust from the busy intersection filtered in as well. I added more cleaning staff and punkah-wallahs and moved our bedroom to the back side of the house, giving Aunt Sumra the noisy front room. I did not mean to be unkind. I thought the commotion might stimulate her, and if it didn't, then at least she was used to it.

I would like to say that I worked as impressive a miracle with my aunt as I did with her house. At most, I managed to have her maintained, like a piece of the furniture. All the idealistic plans I had—which included having her tend Aaron—fell flat. She could not be trusted with the baby, for she had no sense of where his body began or stopped. Once she almost dropped him, so that ended that. Aaron learned first to crawl, then to walk around her. If she noticed him, or anything else for that matter, I never knew it. Her face never lost its flat, bleak stare. Thus our domestic life proceeded without her, although we hoped she was able to absorb a portion of our contentment, if only subconsciously.

Yedid, on the other hand, bloomed under Edwin's tutelage. "Every night when he goes to sleep, he must be afraid," my husband had remarked perceptively when we first went to live in Free School Street.

"Why do you think that?"

"Because there was a period when every time he woke up, he found someone else had died in the night."

He asked Hanif to sleep in the boy's room, and each evening he was home he would read the child to sleep. In less than a year Yedid's energy returned. He ran down the halls knocking lamps, furrowing runners, but was never chastised. Aaron toddled after the boy with worshiping eyes.

Against my wishes, Edwin went to work for the Sassoons. Was there no way I could disassociate myself from opium, or was it in my blood? For his part, Edwin shrugged off my aversion to the family trade much as Silas had done. And, given our reduced circumstances, I could hardly demand my husband refuse my father's offer.

I was troubled by another matter. I had always looked down at the positions that Aunt Bellore's husband, Samuel Lanyado, and Cousin Sultana's husband, Gabriel Judah, held, because their salaried status was that of poor relations compared to the brothers, who divided the vast profits. They lived well—Aunt Bellore at the Kyd Street mansion, Sultana and Gabriel in a much smaller house in the fashionable section south of Park Street—but everybody knew they would never be partners in the firm. My brother Jonah, who was being groomed to work beside my father, would be Gabriel's superior in a year or two; and my father, who was younger than Samuel Lanyado by many years, was expected to take Uncle Saul's place as head of the family in Calcutta. If Edwin remained with the firm, he would never be more than a clerk, subservient to Uncle Samuel and even Gabriel.

Nevertheless, Edwin thought he could make his mark. "Your Uncle Jacob gave the ryots too much latitude. It won't take much to bring a finer grade to market, one that will raise prices in China without the competition at the auction being any the wiser. If I can make a difference in the balance sheet rapidly, I will have earned my position in the family. I might be able to make back fifty thousand rupees in less than two years—for the company, of course."

I thought his predictions optimistic, but did not dispute him. Nor did I let him know there was no possible way he would ever end up with a share, no matter how deserving he was. Instead I concentrated on making a happy home and participating in the seasonal rounds of events that I had missed after leaving Calcutta.

❦   ❦   ❦

Other mothers must look back on the infancy of their children and see the months and years as a blur as I do. Three years after Aaron's birth, I was again pregnant. This time I was uncomfortable almost from the first, and gained an enormous amount of weight. The worst part of my pregnancy came during the harvest in Patna, when Edwin was away for weeks at a time. I was pleased he could be spared my complaints, and yet I was so lonely, I was distraught without him. Zilpah thought I should come to Theatre Road, where it was cleaner and quieter, but I was loath to uproot Aaron and Yedid. When Edwin returned, my grossly swollen ankles, puffy face, and enormous belly shocked him. Within two hours of his arrival he had Dr. Hyam examine me.

"Twins," he announced.

Edwin was ecstatic. I was frightened. Immediately we returned to Theatre Road. Saleh Arakie, who had assisted in Aaron's birth, was hired to attend me day and night. The doctors considered surgery. They checked my babies' heartbeats several times a day. They insisted I eat special foods. My task was to remain calm and to do as I was told until the babies could be born safely.

Edwin and I spent long hours contemplating the names of the twins, trying to make selections for every combination. He did not approve of the Middle Eastern custom of adding the child's name to that of its father and grandfather, with the last name in the series being dropped when the train of names became too cumbersome. Trying to keep track of relatives named David Joseph David and Moses David Joseph David and David Moses David (who were grandfather, father, and son, respectively) convinced us to search for less common names.

By the time I went into a long, drawn-out labor, we had not come to a final decision. The pains were intermittent and not especially acute, but they went on for days and days. I became irritable as fingers and hands and instruments prodded and poked incessantly. Trying to distract me, Edwin brought out our name list.

"Pick anything you want," I said irritably at high noon in the hottest, dampest season of the year. All at once my water broke with an explosive splash, soaking the midwife. A curl of pain seemed to split my spine. The midwife banished Edwin from the room. Within minutes the first child tumbled from my loins.

"A boy," the doctor told me.

"Is he all right?" I gasped.

"Listen to him crying. What a fighter!"

Ten minutes later another slid down, leaving a tremor in his wake.

"Another boy . . . smaller than the first," the doctor said so softly I became frightened.

"He isn't crying."

"Don't worry, he's breathing."

"Yes," the midwife added. "He's nice and pink. And delicate. More like a girl, but he's a boy . . . most definitely a boy!"

I squeezed the attendant's hand and closed my eyes as the prodding and wiping continued below my waist. The doctor gave me an injection and I fell into a rolling sea of sleep. When I awoke, I thought I was in the midst of a dream. Aaron sat at the foot of the bed. Two baby boys were wrapped in muslin, with only their hands and faces exposed. Aaron held the plumper one's fingers in one hand.

"That's Jeremiah," Edwin said softly, glancing at me for confirmation, since that had been my preference for a boy's name. I nodded my approval. As Aaron bent over and touched the smaller one's cheeks, a long lock of black hair covered his right eye. In the last, complicated weeks of my confinement, I had neglected to have his thick hair trimmed.

"That's Zachariah," Edwin said as he selected the name that had been his favorite.

Aaron stumbled as he tried to pronounce the names. "Jeremeeah . . . Zachameeah . . ."

I laughed. "That's good enough."

Aaron beamed up at me, and as he lifted his head, he used his fingers to comb back the errant hair in a gesture that perfectly mimicked his father's.

❦ ❦ ❦

Other milestones marked the passage of those busy years. In 1894, when Ruby was fourteen, she married twenty-year-old Ariel Bassous, a true Talmudic scholar—in fact he was ill-suited to anything but a life of study. While my brother Jonah was trained in the opium business, Asher and Zilpah's two sons were sent away to school. Seti thrived in the Jewish Girls' School and enjoyed being the center of attention at Theatre Road.

These relatively pleasant years were marred by two deaths. Edwin went to Cochin twice to see his ailing mother. I admit I thought she was once again using her health as an excuse to bring him home, but two weeks after he came back from the second visit, she died. I refused to return to Cochin or the Malabar Coast, and after his mother's death, neither did Edwin. A short while later, Aunt Sumra passed away in her sleep. I felt as though she had been released from a living hell, and did not grieve for long, Even Yedid, who had just completed his bar mitzvah the month before, showed more relief than despair.

By the time he was sixteen, Yedid was almost ready to leave us. His eldest brother, who ran the godown inventory desk at the Sassoon company, offered to take him on as an apprentice. Yedid, who was impatient to leave a household where one child was always screaming in the night, welcomed the move to his elder brother's house.

Reminiscing on that period, I realize that I was too exhausted by the demands of the children to be aware of what was happening with the Sassoons. I had not seen a balance sheet in many years. The older sons of the brothers now formed a second tier of managers who competed for favors. There were rumors of Gabriel Judah's discontent, of Samuel Lanyado's clashes with my father, but Edwin assured me these were minor struggles. Indeed, the family seemed harmonious, at least on the occasions when I saw everyone: at synagogue, for parties, and at holidays. Edwin's responsibilities, which were limited to his supervision and reporting on the Patna fields, kept him out of the fray, or so I was led to believe. Later I would berate myself for being too absorbed by my growing family to notice the signs of dissatisfaction, but as long as my father was at the helm, nothing seemed amiss. However, his specialty was the Chinese trade, and it was during the last of his journeys—the first time Jonah accompanied him—that the equanimity in the Clive Street offices of Sassoon and Company was shattered forever.

42

♦♦ ♦♦ ♦♦

Too many Sassoon children," Edwin explained in an exasperated voice. "That's actually what Samuel said!" He strutted about our cramped sitting room clenching his fists. Rarely had I ever seen my husband so perturbed. "The words sounded as though that wife of his was putting them into his mouth."

"After living for so long with Aunt Bellore, her nasty ways were bound to wear off on him." I patted the double settee for him to sit beside me. "What was my uncle's point?"

Edwin plopped down for a second, but bounced up again. "The problem is who shall control the company. When Moses Sassoon began the trade, he held the reins. The business was rich enough to include generous shares for his five sons and to provide lucrative employment for his one son-in-law. What Moses did not anticipate was that his daughter's husband would come to resent his position."

I caught Hanif's eye as he passed by the half-closed door. "A brandy and soda for Mr. Salem," I called. "Now, Edwin, we have less than an hour before we have to go to Theatre Road for dinner, and I still don't know what you are getting at."

"Who is coming?"

"With Papa away, I expect it will be a quiet evening. Just Zilpah, Seti, Grandmother Helene, Ruby, and Ariel."

"I hope they won't bring the baby."

"Edwin, you are upset. It's not like you not to want to see Sharon."

Hanif presented Edwin's drink on a silver tray. "I can't help thinking that because she looks like her father, she must have the brains of her mother." Edwin stared morosely into the glass of the amber liquid.

"Now, exactly which children are upsetting Samuel and Bellore?" I asked to bring him back to the point.

"*All* the offspring of the Sassoon dynasty. Ever since Saul and

Jacob died, the balance has been distorted. As I understand it, when Saul was alive, he would render a final decision, and if that was unpopular, its effect could be leavened by Jacob."

"What about Uncle Reuben and Uncle Ezra?" I asked for the sake of form, although I knew that both had weaknesses: Reuben was slow and obese, Ezra fancied himself above any sort of labor.

As Edwin sipped his drink, I noticed that the skin under his eyes was dark and his chin sagged. "Reuben spends his days translating to and from Chinese," he replied glumly. "I can see why your father replaced him in China. Anyway, he seems happy enough to leave decisions to the others and take his considerable share." He finished the brandy and looked desolately at the empty glass. "And Ezra is an odd one. He almost never comes into town, except when he is invited to visit Government House or to have lunch at the Great Eastern Hotel."

"Or to see his tailor at Ranken's."

"Exactly."

"My father saw value in his social interests. 'Somebody's got to kiss the viceroy's boots and fortunately Ezra has volunteered' was how he put it."

Edwin laughed for the first time that evening. "He didn't really say that, did he?"

"Absolutely. My uncle is not the first Sassoon to be seduced by the glitter of royalty and privilege. Before his death, Great-Uncle Abdullah— excuse me, Sir Albert Sassoon, the first Baronet of Kensington Gore— was happily ensconced at his 'ancestral' home halfway around the world from steamy India."

"Nobody realizes the advantages—as well as the dangers—of having friends in high places better than I do," Edwin said with a self-deprecating laugh. "The point is: where does that leave matters at Sassoon and Company? In a muddle, there's where. When your father is here, he runs the show, but he spends half his time in China. For a few months after his departure, everyone stays in his proper channel, until slowly they begin to alter his orders, confusing the staff. You can't imagine what it is like to have three or four people giving me conflicting assignments. Then, when everything is murky, your Uncle Samuel leaps in and supposedly sorts matters out."

"At least somebody takes the helm," I said in a conciliatory voice, even though I was reluctant to commend Bellore's officious husband.

"It is not his place to do that, and everyone knows it!" Edwin's face turned dusky with rage. "Some comply; others rebel. That is how the problem of too many children comes in. Thus far, none of our genera-tion has any power. As you know, each of the sons of the brothers takes his compensation from his father's shares. The sons-in-law have salaries that cannot compare with what the other men get, even divided four or five ways. I am not complaining, but Gabriel makes his displeasure obvious. And I admit he has a point, since he does ten times the work of someone like Reuben's son, Nathaniel, who rarely shows his face except at auction time. And Samuel, who has devoted his whole life to the company, makes less than Yedid will when he starts."

While he was talking, I counted up the male Sassoons who divided the spoils. Saul had two sons, Adam and Nathan, who were in the company. Reuben had Nathaniel and Noah. Ezra had only Sayeed, who was more interested in horse racing than business, but took his share anyway. That was five. Of Jacob's ten children, only his eldest son, Mir, was a part of the company, but counting Yedid—who soon would be—that made seven. Bellore had only girls, and for some unexplained reason twenty-one-year-old Lulu had refused every suitor and was unmarried. The prettiest, Abigail, had wedded a distant cousin of the Rothschilds' and moved to France. And Sultana's Gabriel was part of the problem. My father had already added Jonah to his side of the firm, and Asher would certainly follow. Zilpah's sons were being groomed for the law, since Benu could never give them a share and Zilpah did not want them to be in an inferior position to any Sassoon. That left at least nine young Sassoon men pushing into the fray. Samuel had every reason to feel threatened.

Before I could formulate a solution, Yali appeared at the door. Aaron wore a sailor shirt and short pants. The twins, who were learning to walk, held on to her sari. Zachariah fell down. Jeremiah ran to Edwin.

"Time to go," I said. "Let's talk about this later. There must be a way to settle it."

"That I doubt," Edwin replied. He sounded grim, but his face had already puckered into a funny expression that made Jeremiah giggle with glee.

☙ ☙ ☙

Even though Edwin's days may have been unpleasant, he withstood the tensions stoically. Many evenings when he returned from Clive Street, he went to the small bedroom on the top floor that had become his study. After a quiet hour to himself, he would join the family, mellowed from the time alone. I suspected he chafed at working under Samuel Lanyado and Gabriel Judah, but his resentment was muffled because of his chagrin at having lost the fifty thousand rupees. I tried to let him know there were other options, even if he felt he had none.

"Opium is not the only business in the world," I began one evening when he seemed especially relaxed. "When you traded with your uncle, you exported gunny and rope, coriander and beeswax to Singapore. What's more, the Sassoons of Bombay deal almost exclusively in products manufactured in their own mills, and they have prospered."

Edwin squinted at me. "What is this about?"

"I can see you are miserable."

"Who says I am?"

"Edwin . . ." I sighed in frustration.

He was quiet for a time before he spoke again. "Do you know what your trouble is? You are not content unless you have something to worry about. You must not let your mind wander into dark corners that you easily could avoid."

"Now, darling," I replied smoothly, "some housekeepers may be able to ignore the corners, but a good one makes certain to dust them before the spiders and their nasty webs take over."

"What do you expect me to do?" he snapped. "Shall I say to your father, 'Thank you very much, but I have decided to seek my fortune elsewhere'?"

"Why not? With your experience you could get a position with any number of Jewish firms."

"That's true, but then we could not continue to stay in this house. In fact, we shouldn't be here now that poor Sumra is gone, since it rightfully belongs to her son, Mir. With what I could earn we could find some place on Harrison Road or Bow Bazaar, but never anything nearly as large as we have and certainly never anything south of Park Street."

"I don't care where we live, darling."

"That is not true," he said, restraining his ire.

"We are not exactly paupers living on Sassoon crumbs. I have my small legacy from Grandmother Flora, and your mother's estate has provided a cushion. Anyway, that is not what I had in mind to discuss."

"Well?" he asked wearily.

"I know you pretend to be content for my sake, but the time is coming when you will have to go on your own before my brothers and cousins push you aside."

"That won't happen. They may receive more money, but my place is secure."

"Is it? Look at the Lanyados. Aunt Bellore might not have become such a monster if she had had more prestige."

"You are being melodramatic, Dinah. Their lofty perch in Kyd Street is hardly a stinking *bustee*. If anything, Samuel has become the biggest fish of them all. With his wheedling and conniving, everyone defers to him. Besides, when your father returns, he will sort everything out."

"And if he doesn't?"

"Dinah, the company has been going strong since before you were born. A few conflicts between brothers and sisters will hardly sink the ship." He gulped at the unfortunate choice of words, giving me a chance to make my final point.

"Nothing lasts forever," I said firmly. "The Chinese used to think they had a monopoly on tea until Robert Fortune and his friends brought the plants to India. Now that the Chinese are growing their own opium, we have seen a decline in the price. One of these days that market may dwindle as well."

"The whole world buys opium."

"They do this year, but what if the laws change? Many people of high moral character want to outlaw it entirely."

"That will never occur. Too many people would revolt if denied their daily pipe. India supplies more than two million Chinese smokers, and even the most exaggerated estimates say that native opium supplies less than four percent of them. Anyway, too many people of power have a vested interest."

"People have a way of losing power." I groaned in frustration. "Edwin, couldn't you consider expanding your horizons? If the opium market changes, you would be ahead of the others in finding a new situation." I winced as Edwin closed his eyes. Perhaps I had pushed him too far after a tiring day.

"Theories are entertaining, but there is no practical way to implement them. If we had any capital left, I could open a trading company of my own. Nothing could stop us from bidding on anything from tea to opium if we had the wherewithal to cover the auction prices."

"We might be able to borrow the money."

"No! I'll be damned if I'll ever ask anyone in your family for a single anna."

"What about your friends?" I suggested hesitantly.

"It is difficult enough being in business with one's family," he said obliquely.

"What do you mean?"

"That's enough for now," he said with a firmness that silenced me. "When your father returns, things will right themselves."

I let the matter drop for a while. At least Edwin enjoyed the trips to Patna. In fact, the less he was around the Sassoons, the happier he seemed to be. When he was in Calcutta he joined friends for a game of billiards and conversation over cheroots and port. I was pleased he had renewed friendships with boys he had known during his brief stay at St. Xavier's: Howard Farrell, Abdul Moquith, and Ahmed Majid, men of different faiths whom we never entertained at home. There was also a group of Bengali friends including Shyamdas Chauduri and Krishna Mukerji. Perhaps one of these contacts might be his avenue out of the opium business, I decided, and reminded myself to keep encouraging

Edwin in that direction. In any case, since I was exhausted by my domestic routines, Edwin's absences were sometimes a relief. Time for myself was precious: to read, to keep my journal, to sleep an extra hour. I knew that a household filled with demanding babies was no place to unwind after a day with formidable in-laws. Unlike many a wife, I never worried that other women might tempt Edwin. When we were alone together, the magic embraced us like an impervious veil. No husband had ever been as ardent, as attentive, as superb a lover as Edwin. Maybe he was right. Maybe this simple life was what happiness was about.

❦   ❦   ❦

A matter more profound than the problems of leadership at Sassoon and Company occupied Edwin's mind. When we received word that my father and Jonah's return would be delayed a month, his agitation was more acute, but he did not share his concerns with me. Unaware as yet that the consequences of my uncle's dissatisfaction were soon to propel me into the center of the family arena, I did my best not to provoke Edwin.

When my father did arrive, we were relieved to learn that business had gone well: the price of opium had stabilized at a record high. Illness had kept my father in Hong Kong for several extra weeks, a malady he described as a monsoon fever. He looked tired, but that was to be expected after a sea journey. I thought his skin seemed more ashen than usual, his voice shakier, but Edwin reminded me these voyages were strenuous and the man was not getting younger. Jonah, who was flushed with success, had escaped the ailment.

"When the fever first struck, we had to postpone the journey, but once it broke, I kept after Father to start home. There was an awful stench to Hong Kong and I thought the sea air would do him good. I was right, as it turned out. Except for one relapse during the crossing, he's been looking better and better."

"That's true," my father said to console everyone, especially Zilpah. "All I need is a few bowls of *marag* to set me right."

With several nights of rest, we did see a change for the better in my father. And after a week back at his desk in Clive Street, Edwin reported the pecking order was becoming reestablished and the churning seas of discontent were subsiding to postmonsoon levels. Unfortunately, the relief we experienced at my father's revival was short-lived. His chills and fever returned. Without hesitation Dr. Hyam made the diagnosis: malaria.

"Are you certain?" Zilpah asked outside the door to the sickroom.

"Every sign is positive. His spleen is enlarged, the periodic attacks come at the expected intervals, and he has been in a malarious region lately."

"Can he be cured or . . . ?" Zilpah pursed her lips, letting the unfinished question hang in the air.

"We can treat the febrile spells, but they probably will return."

"People live for many years with malaria. If they didn't, the British Empire would have faded away long ago." I forced a weak laugh.

"What can I do?" Zilpah asked the doctor.

"During an attack he must rest in a cool, darkened room. First we'll try this prescription." He made certain we understood the correct proportions of the dosage, consisting of strychnine, arsenious acid, iron by hydrogen, quinine, and aloe. "That should be made up into twenty tablets and Benu should take one pill every three hours."

"When will he be well enough to return to work?" I wondered, thinking of the chaos at Clive Street that would ensue in his absence.

"In a week or two. He will know when he is able, but he must not travel to areas where the disease is endemic."

"You mean China?"

"Yes, I do."

Zilpah paled. "Never again?"

"At least not until he has been free of the acute state of the illness for a year, probably two."

"He won't obey," Zilpah said helplessly.

The doctor shrugged. "A reinfection could be fatal."

☙ ☙ ☙

My father did not visit his office for a week, nor two, nor even after a month had passed. Frequent malarial bouts racked his body. Between them he gathered strength for the next onslaught. Either Zilpah or I had to be in the house to medicate the various stages. Cinchona was to be administered at the first signs. If he had not rallied after twelve hours, ipecacuanha had to be offered. In the early morning, when the cold state racked his bones, arnica was taken. Veratrum was substituted when he felt icy on the outside but feverish internally. If the sweating became profuse, somebody had to force him to drink drafts laced with sambucus. During the worst periods, when he would have two or more attacks within twenty-four hours, belladonna alternated with hyoscyamus was required to prevent seizures.

In the brief periods of relief, my father tried to cheer us. "I don't know why you are making a fuss. Just a touch of malaria. Most fellows live with it quite peacefully, accepting it as a visit from an old, if not entirely congenial, friend." In a few hours, or if he was fortunate, a few days, it would start again. Each time, the fever broke as suddenly as it came, leaving him soaking wet and weaker than when it had begun.

"A terrible case. One of the worst in my career," Dr. Hyam said, as though that were consolation for my father's inability to respond to the treatments.

One evening nothing helped my father's misery. The night was hot and damp, he was surrounded by hot-water bottles, but still he shivered. "I can't take it!" he shouted. "Every bone feels as if it is being twisted by some malevolent hand."

"Dr. Hyam said this would pass, but it only gets worse," I said, feeling desperate. "Can't we do *something*?" I begged Zilpah, but she had no answers, either.

While tending to my father occupied all my time away from my children, Edwin toiled harder at the office, since matters there had deteriorated. One day when it seemed my father was on the mend at last, Edwin approached me at Theatre Road as I assisted Seti with her Hebrew. "I need to talk to you, Dinah."

"Of course, darling. Is something wrong?" His grim expression made me think he had some news about my father's condition that I had not yet been told. "Seti, copy the next three lines. I'll check your work later."

I followed Edwin out to the terrace. We stood a few feet from the spot where we had discovered how much we had in common. Nothing had changed; and yet everything had changed.

"I need your help," he began.

"What can I do? All the doctors haven't—"

"The problem concerns a matter at Clive Street." At first I thought he meant the usual discontent, but his look was far too pained for that. "For a long time now I have been suspicious. Since I don't have access to any of the books except those from the ryots, I decided to wait for your father's return and match up his figures. His first days back didn't give me enough time, and now . . ."

"What is it?"

"There are discrepancies. I confirmed the matter with Jonah. He told me some of the figures on his side, and they don't balance with mine."

"What can I do?"

"You've worked with these ledgers before. Maybe you can detect what I cannot."

"How would we get hold of them? I can't ask my father. We wouldn't want to worry him now, not when he is finally improving. Perhaps in a few weeks—"

"I've waited too long already. We could go to Clive Street together late some afternoon. The durwan would let us in. I know where everything is kept. We could say we were getting papers for your father."

"When?" I asked with a mixture of excitement and dread.

"Saturday evening, just after sundown."

This seemed like a prudent time. Family members often stopped by for a few hours' work on Sunday, especially during busy seasons, but it was rare for anyone to come in on the Sabbath, except a few of the non-Jewish employees, and they would be gone by one o'clock. To set the stage, Edwin worked right up until sundown on Friday. When he left, he complained to Ram Singh, the evening durwan, about how much work was yet undone and how he might have to return to complete it before Monday morning. "Besides," he had said, "with all this rain, the children are out of sorts and it isn't always serene at home."

The durwan readily nodded, for it had poured for two days and nights. Everyone was anxious for the monsoon to break. The following evening, the clouds had blown out to sea, and the quiet streets of the commercial section gleamed in the glow of the setting sun.

"Sahib, this is a surprise," Ram Singh said to Edwin when he opened the door to our office jaun. "When the rain stopped, I thought you would stay at home."

"The rain from above may have ceased, but the storm on my desk remains," Edwin said as he helped me out of the carriage.

"Memsahib!" the durwan said with a bright smile when he saw me alight. "A pleasure to see you again. How is your father?"

"Better every day, Ram Singh."

As the Indian put his hands together and bowed, I followed Edwin to his office on the third floor.

Edwin opened a drawer in his rolltop desk and pulled out a tall ledger book. "These are the Patna accounts for the past three seasons." He showed me the totals on the summary sheets, which I noted on a paper I had already prepared for entering the calculations. "Come, follow me." We walked down the hall to Uncle Reuben's larger office, where there were also desks for his sons, Noah and Nathaniel. The Chinese accounts kept there were based on figures supplied by my father. The room was extraordinarily tidy thanks to Noah, who had the reputation for being as meticulous about his work as he was sloppy about his person. The figures in his ledger, translated from the Chinese notes by his father, looked as if they had been engraved upon the page. Since I had seen these records in the past, I knew exactly where to look.

Immediately my sheet showed an enormous shortfall when one compared what had been earmarked for purchase at auction and what had been sold overseas. Before I could reach any conclusions, however, these figures had to be reconciled with several other sources: the auction records, the amount of opium in storage, the amount held back for poor quality, grades to determine market value, additional expenses to customs agents, shipping companies, railroads, and the "special fees" that greased the way to China.

"Did you check Uncle Saul's office while I was talking to Ram Singh?"

"Yes, it is locked."

"Do you want me to ask for the key?"

"No, I'll do it. You stay here. If you come downstairs, he will feel he has to accompany you up the stairs and unlock it for you, and then he will wait around for us. If I go down, I can give him a bit of *baksheesh* for his trouble and send him off to buy some refreshment. After all, we're here to look after the premises."

A few minutes later he returned with the ring of keys. "All's well. He bought my story about leaving a folder there on Friday. We did have a conference and I did leave it, so it wasn't a lie."

"How long do we have?"

"An hour at least. Ram Singh has many friends on the street, and enough money to buy several rounds."

"Good. But we will have to hurry."

Once inside, I walked around the corner room with the long mahogany table which had belonged to my grandfather. I still thought of the office as belonging to his eldest son, Saul, even though it had been taken over by Samuel Lanyado on a "temporary" basis until it was decided who would be Saul's successor. Neither Reuben nor Ezra had embraced the responsibility, and Saul's eldest son, Adam, showed little aptitude for heading the firm. When I reached the end of the conference table, I stood behind the green leather chair and ran my fingers over the polished curve of the back rail. If my father retired from his travels, he might take this position at the head of the table.

At the far side of the room, Edwin unlocked the chest that held the remainder of the record books. He opened each one, checked its contents, and marked which pages I should examine. "Sit down, I'll bring them to you."

"Where?"

"Right there is fine."

A thrilling sensation shot up my spine as I eased myself into the founder's seat. Leaning back, I could see all the way along Clive Street. In the distance, factories belched curls of black smoke, smudging the yolk of the setting sun. I thought about how much money was controlled from this chair, the many lives affected by the opium commerce, Uncle Saul's benevolent approach to managing the family trade compared with Samuel's bullying tactics. What right did Bellore's husband have to sit here in the first place? No more than I did. I smiled to myself. The sooner my father deposed his brother-in-law from his "temporary" perch, the better!

In the distance the bells of St. John's Church tolled, and a wave of anxiety swept over me. "Edwin, we should hurry."

"If it was simple to mark the right pages, this wouldn't have turned into such a puzzle." He flipped open the last ledger. "Here they are."

There were so many ledgers and so many pages to check, I had to walk around the table, stopping to mark various totals on my work sheet.

"What do you think?" Edwin asked when I wasn't even halfway finished.

"I can't say. I'm taking down the figures. I can do the calculations later. There are several ways to do it, and there isn't time now."

"Shall I put the books away?"

I scanned the table. "I suppose you can." He closed the first one. "Wait!" Edwin froze. "Which one is that?"

He read the heading: "Accounts Payable to Vendors."

I looked down at my sheet. "Just a minute." I walked over and reopened the book. In the waning light the figures were blurry, and I carried it over to the window to see better. Flipping through the pages, I mentally rounded off the totals and added them. For six pages the cumulative totals seemed in order, but on the seventh the total fell short by ten thousand rupees. A simple clerical error. This incorrect total was carried forward for another six pages. Then another ten thousand rupees vanished! With my heart beating wildly, I counted ahead six more pages. Again! I pulled over the next ledger. This one seemed in order on the sixth page, the seventh, the tenth, but on the twelfth—there is was! And on the twenty-fourth, the thirty-sixth, and so on. There were no discrepancies in the volume listing salaries to nonfamily employees, or none that I could immediately discern. We both began opening books at random and trying to find the system, for each was different.

"Look at this!" Edwin shouted. He pointed to the second page from the back. One figure at the top of the horizontal columns was underlined: the figure four. "In this book, the shortfall must occur every fourth page," he guessed. He opened to the next-to-last page in another ledger. There the underlined figure was seven. "In this one it occurs every seventh page. That's the clue!"

I rushed to check several other ledgers. He was absolutely right. "You are a genius!"

"No, you are the one who found this in the first place."

"There isn't time to pat ourselves on the back. It's getting dark, and I don't want to light the lamps."

"You're right. Anyhow, Ram Singh could return any minute."

"It would take the whole night to figure this out, maybe longer. Hundreds of thousands of rupees have disappeared, and we have no idea where. Who keeps these journals?"

"A group of clerks make the entries under Gabriel Judah's command, and he reports to his father-in-law."

I checked a few of the pages in different volumes. "The line items are in different hands, but the totals may be in the same one. It is difficult to tell, though, because the ink matches and the work is very standard, very tidy." As I looked up at Edwin, his gaze locked with mine. We both had realized that my Uncle Samuel was the thief.

Just then we heard footsteps outside. I tiptoed to the door, and when I peeked out, a shadow on the wall caught my eye. Was he coming . . . or going? "Ram Singh?" I whispered.

"Does he know we are in here?"

"I'm not certain. I will see to him while you put the books away." I strolled down the hallway and called nonchalantly, "Ram Singh? Hello! We are about to leave, but I want to use the toilet. Would you mind checking to see if it is safe?"

"Certainly, memsahib." We rounded the corner that put us out of sight of Uncle Saul's office. The durwan opened the door to the Sassoons' private toilet. He banged around inside, then reported, "Everything is in order. I will wait by the door."

"Thank you, Ram Singh."

Sitting on the toilet, I held my head in my hands. My knees would not stop shaking. My stomach contracted as my bowels emptied. Was my distress from the fright at almost having been caught or at the horror of the magnitude of our discovery? I heard voices in the hall.

"Dinah!" Edwin called. "Are you all right?"

My stomach lurched. I thought I might be sick, and had to face the dismal dilemma of whether to stand up or remain sitting.

"Dinah?" The voice was closer. He had opened the door.

"Yes," I answered weakly. "I'm coming." I thought I could stand. I straightened my skirts. At the basin I splashed cool water on my wrists and face. Yes, I'm calmer now, I told myself, walking to the door. Edwin offered me his hand and we started down to the street. I had taken the last step when my stomach churned so violently I thought I would lose control. I gripped Edwin. And he lunged for me. The huge chandelier rattled above us and I heard a clattering on the roof. We were a few yards from the entrance, where Ram Singh was holding open the heavy wooden door. Both Ram Singh and the door were swaying. Outside, a horse reared up. A carriage toppled. Ram Singh ran back into the building and grasped the rails of the staircase.

There were screams, and then a terrible roar like a train charging down the center of Clive Street.

"What?" I tried to ask, but my teeth were chattering.

Edwin pulled me out the door. We could barely stand upright. Bent over, we half-ran, half-crawled to the steps. Across the way an awning crashed to the pavement. Reflexively Edwin backed us inside. I stared at Ram Singh's terrified face and in his eyes read the meaning of what was happening. It was an earthquake! A flash of light captured my attention, and I looked up.

"No!" Edwin screamed at Ram Singh. He pushed me away from the door and out to the sidewalk, instinctively covering my body with his. Behind us the chandelier fell and shattered on the marble floor. Shards of crystal shot through the air. A veil of glass blanketed us. With my eyes tightly closed, I shook my head and cleared my face. I squinted one eye and looked back inside Sassoon and Company. Ram Singh lay in a twisted maze of metal and broken glass. Rivulets of blood, like roving tentacles, seeped in every direction. As I started to crawl toward him, the ground heaved. Edwin held me down until the last tremor passed, only four minutes after the first had begun.

In the momentary calm, Edwin moved us away from the building, but kept me out of the street, where frightened ponies ran loose. Too soon, another tremble began to lurch from the once-steady base of earth. The government and bank buildings swayed like ships at sea. Sheets of plaster fell in flakes several yards long.

During the next lull my thoughts went to Ram Singh. "We must help him."

"He's dead."

"How do you know?"

"He took the full weight on his head."

"We should see—"

"I saw—"

"But—"

"It cracked . . . like a melon."

43

♨ ♨ ♨

Oh, no!" I shuddered miserably. "The children!"
Our hired carriage was nowhere in sight, and in the chaos it was unlikely we could find anyone to take us home, so we made our way on foot. Because it was dark, it was difficult to assess the extent of the destruction. Here and there fires flared. Fallen debris blocked some streets; others were remarkably clear. Finally we found a rickshaw-wallah willing to take us home. Gathered in the living room, the children and servants were agitated but unharmed. Books had fallen from the shelves, ornaments were shattered, but the scene of Jeremiah yanking Zachariah's hair while Aaron tried to pull them apart was wonderfully ordinary.

The discovery of the juggled books at Sassoon and Company was dwarfed by the calamity. None of the Sassoon residences were badly damaged, although a house farther down Theatre Road lost a balcony. The steeple of the Maghen David Synagogue required extensive repairs, but a few contrary members of the congregation decided this was a sign the steeple should be removed entirely, since it had no place on a Jewish house of worship. Others disagreed, saying that if it was a sign, the sign was also meant to deter Christians as well, since they had more damage to their steeples than we had to ours. "Besides," Zilpah sniffed, "that is what makes our synagogue unique."

I thought petty arguments like these took away from the misery around us. Many had died in pitiful accidents like the one that had befallen poor Ram Singh. Even though I came to believe the durwan had been killed instantly, I never could shake the feeling we should have gone back to him. As it was, we never acknowledged being there, for it was imperative to keep our findings a secret until we could determine our course of action.

News spread along the railway lines. Telegrams brought reports that the whole of northern India had felt some degree of the shocks,

476

especially around the Himalayas. Picturing Xanadu Lodge perched on that steep slope, I searched for news from Darjeeling as the dispatches came in. At last a correspondent got a message into *The Englishman* under the headline: "DARJEELING CUT OFF FOR THREE DAYS." I read rapidly to see if there was mention of the Luddys or their friends.

> The shock, which was first felt on Saturday, electrified hills and valleys with startling suddenness. People who were standing on the viceroy's tennis court describe how they had to balance themselves and plant their feet so as not to be thrown over. Those who were out saw, after hearing a terrible rush of sound like a whirlwind, chimneys swaying and falling, trees beaten to and fro, walls falling like cards in a toy house, and people rushing frantically out of their houses to save themselves from the crashing and falling interiors. . . . Sunnyside, Hillside, Annandale, Manor Mansell's House, and Mr. Gayer, the private secretary's, house have fallen inside, and some of the outer walls of other houses have fallen and have to be deserted!

Finding no indication of loss of life, I felt a sense of profound relief, even though the next day's news included the times and dates of severe secondary shocks that continued to sway the area. Coolingridge, the Maharajah of Cooch Behar's residence, was declared uninhabitable. Many houses had been destroyed by chimneys collapsing inward. My pulse leapt with anxiety when I read that "the surrounding tea plantations have suffered greatly. Bloomfield is a ruin and Mr. Nash's estate at Soom is totally destroyed. Tukvaar reports many injuries." The Luddy houses were in that region! I wondered how Silas and Maurice had fared. In fact, I wondered if Maurice was still alive. Since my marriage to Edwin, I had had no word of the Luddys and nobody who might have known them had volunteered any information.

Zilpah had family in the area and we were anxious about them as well. A few days later the papers brought further descriptions of the events in Darjeeling as the repaired railroad brought back home hundreds of families who were fleeing the hills in the height of the season. My heart pounded as I scanned the listings for any mention of Silas. I was encouraged when one reporter wrote, "The south side of the hill seems to have been the least affected." What a relief! Xanadu was south of the town. I leaned back in my chair and closed my eyes. A defused image of Silas' pale face hovered in my mind. It had been so long since I had given him a moment's thought. . . .

"Mummy!" Aaron ran into the room. "A man has come."

"What sort of a man?"

"A *small* man with a *big* knife!"

"Aaron!" I chastised, for my eldest son sometimes told fanciful tales.

"Really, Mummy! Hanif said I should fetch you," he cried, tugging at my sleeve.

Tilting my head, I gave in reluctantly. "All right, Aaron, but this had better not be one of your games." As I stood up, the newspaper fell to the floor. No matter, I thought, I would get back to it later. I allowed Aaron to lead me into the entranceway. There, standing at attention beside the front door of Free School Street, was Gulliver, his kukri curving beneath his belt. He gave a little bow, then squared his shoulders. The moment my eyes met his, I knew something terrible had happened.

His cap was filthy and his snowy coat was torn and stained. How had he found me? My churning mind recalled that he had come to Calcutta for my wedding. He had accompanied us back to Darjeeling, serving us on the train, wrapping me in blankets, arranging the tongas . . . so very long ago. He must have gone to Theatre Road looking for me, and they had sent him here.

"Gulliver? Why have you come?"

"The sahib sent me."

"Silas!" Thank God he was all right!

He nodded.

"Is he in Calcutta?"

Gulliver shook his head.

"He sent you from Darjeeling? The earthquake was terrible there, wasn't it?"

He nodded.

"Does Silas need help?"

He shook his head.

"Oh, that is good news. I was just reading about the disasters in the region, thinking about all of you and—" Gulliver's usually impenetrable eyes flashed a signal that silenced me.

"Mr. Luddy sent me to you."

"I don't understand."

"Mr. Luddy said I was to come to you if anything happened to him."

"No!"

"Mr. Luddy has perished."

"Mummy?" Aaron was beside me. "Mummy?" Feeling him pulling my skirt, I swatted him away. He began to cry. I lifted him to me and nuzzled my face in his hair.

"How?" I managed weakly. "When?"

"They were on the balcony having a drink. The rains had stopped. The evening was warm. I had served them and gone downstairs for some more soda water. The earth moved. In the cellar we felt a shaking and then the timbers above creaked. There was a crash. The ceiling opened to face the sky. By the time we climbed upstairs, the house was gone."

I thought of Xanadu perched on the cliff, of the cantilevered balcony miraculously balanced in the treetops. What was below? Nothing— nothing for thousands of feet.

Gulliver shook his head. "All gone . . . everything above the top of the stairs."

"Did you find him?"

"Yes, the next morning. They say the fall killed them instantly."

Them? "Who else?"

"Mr. Euclid."

Together. Having a drink, watching the sunset dapple the hills, the burnished snows. Together savoring the last light of the day . . . the last light for eternity.

"Anyone else? What about his father?"

"He has been dead for more than three years."

Yes, I felt as if I had known that all along. Just as I had sensed something had happened to Silas the moment I had heard the quake had reached Darjeeling. I should have followed my instincts more. From the moment we had met, I had perceived Silas was the wrong man, as I had sensed instantly that Edwin was the right one. What else? I had never trusted Amar. I had felt Travancore would be a mistake from the moment the Orchid House was offered. What else? Since childhood I had known there was something devious about Aunt Bellore, and something amiss as soon as Uncle Samuel began to act in Uncle Saul's stead. The confirmation found in the altered totals was merely the black-and-white proof of a far deeper knowledge.

The unpleasant memories wove in and out of my grasp like a moth in the moonlight. I blinked my eyes. Gulliver was standing before me straight and proud.

"Gulliver, you must be tired and hungry. Please, come in and have a rest." I looked around for Hanif. He stood in the shadows awaiting my instructions. "Take this old friend and make him comfortable."

"Yes, memsahib."

Aaron wiggled down. "Hello." He gave Gulliver a shy smile.

"This is your son," Gulliver said softly.

"Yes."

"May I ask, where are the other two?"

The question stunned me. How could he have known about the twins? "They are upstairs. You shall meet them later, but who told you about them?"

"The sahib," he said matter-of-factly.

"But . . . ?"

"He always reported how you were doing. From time to time there were messages from the family of your father's wife."

"Oh!" Zilpah's relations must have kept Silas informed about my marriage, my travels, my children, and probably my troubles. Silas might have known about the *Luna Sassoon*, about Free School Street, and what else? I hoped he had known how content I was with Edwin, and wished I had been able to learn that his life had been as satisfactory. It was too late now. . . . Tears streamed down my face unexpectedly.

"Gulliver, I am sorry, this has been a shock. I need time alone." As I backed toward the parlor, Yali came forward and scooped Aaron into her arms. Hanif escorted Gulliver away.

The poor man, I thought as I sank into the nearest chair and covered my eyes with my hands. My tears could not blot Gulliver's tragic face. Nor the image of Silas, of Silas and Euclid, of Silas and Euclid talking together, feeling a tremor, staring with surprise and then horror as the bottom fell away . . . away . . . Over and over I replayed the scene. First they were standing, smiling; then they were two bodies pinned under piles of debris. The suspended seconds when they must have known their fate were too harrowing to contemplate. Had they died on impact? Might they not have been conscious for minutes or hours? The rescuers could not have known whether they suffered or not. They had said that to comfort the relatives. . . .

I saw scenes moving in front of me as though I were watching from a long distance off. Nepalese and Tibetan natives climbing down the ravine, lifting timbers, branches, using tree trunks like fulcrums to move boulders. I pictured Gulliver pushing through the crowd, clawing at the earth, and pulling Silas away. A jagged edge of a branch ripped Gulliver's sleeve. Mud dripped onto his cap as he lifted Silas' broken body from the soggy earth. Had he told me this? No! Yet the image was as real as a burning beacon.

What else did I know?

I found my tears had dried. I looked around the shabby room with its child-stained chintzes, ragged carpet, broken ornaments piled in boxes. This would not be my home for long. It had never been my home. Free School Street was but a stop on the journey—as were Xanadu and Jew Street and the Cochin cottage and Orchid House. Where would we live next? My mind focused on Theatre Road, but that was illogical. The knowledge would come.

I heard footsteps behind me. When I turned, I saw Hanif was waiting. "The man would like to speak to you again. He says he cannot eat or rest until he delivers his message."

Was there more? "All right, Hanif."

Gulliver appeared in the doorway. "Mr. Luddy sent me to you. He told me that if anything happened to him I was to come to you."

"And so you have, Gulliver. I am thankful you told me yourself."

"You do not understand, memsahib. I am to stay with you."

"Oh, Gulliver, that is impossible. My home is now Calcutta. You would miss your people."

"That is not important to me. It is my duty."

"But, Gulliver, as you can see, we already have a bearer. This is a small household. Don't worry, if you want to stay in Calcutta, I can find you a position."

"I will work only for you," he said resolutely. I had forgotten how fine-boned and sensitive his face was. I hadn't meant to hurt him. My heart pounded as he added simply, "I can live on my own. Mr. Luddy provided for me."

There was no use protesting. The gentle servant had no place to go. When he had overcome his own grief, we could settle the matter. "Very well, Gulliver. We'll make the necessary arrangements later. Is there anything else, or do you think you now could take that well-deserved rest? You must have been traveling for several days."

"Yes, there is another matter. I was told to come to you and ask you to attend to something without delay."

"What do you mean?"

"Many years ago Mr. Luddy sent you a bureau. Do you still have it?"

The bureau? For a moment I was puzzled. The Clive desk! "Yes, certainly."

"Will you take me to it?"

"It is not here." I had never moved it from my room at Theatre Road and now I wondered why. Cochin had been too far, Travancore too temporary. But why not Free School Street? Because it had never felt like home, I reminded myself with the new clarity of vision the shock had bestowed. "I have kept it at my father's house."

"May we go there now?"

"Is it that important?" I asked, and as I did so I knew it was. In a moment I had ordered a carriage, made arrangements for the children, and was on my way. Before leaving the house, I turned to Hanif. "Go to Mr. Salem at the office and tell him to meet me at Theatre Road at once."

"Yes, memsahib," he said with a bow.

As we rode past the ruined houses and littered lanes of Calcutta, I didn't know what was happening and yet I felt that Edwin should be at my side when I discovered the mystery of the Clive desk.

❦ ❦ ❦

My father was asleep, Zilpah was out, and Edwin had not yet arrived as I took Gulliver directly to my old room, now used for guests.

The Clive desk looked as magnificent as ever. The rosewood gleamed a burnished bronze. The intricate ivory inlay of leaves and flowers and swirls glinted in the sun. I remembered how respectfully Silas had described the Vizagapatam workmanship. Rubbing my hand across the silver encrustations, I thought about the desk surviving a hundred and fifty years, outliving its creator; Clive, its plunderer; and now Silas, its latest, but not last admirer.

Gulliver also seemed to need a few moments to contemplate the desk, which must have brought him his own flood of memories. At last he spoke. "The bottom drawer, memsahib." His voice was deep and hollow.

"I don't recall anything there," I protested, but Gulliver seemed confident in his mission, so I asked, "Which one?" The desk had thirteen drawers: one top drawer that extended across the width, four smaller ones down each side, and four in the center, which curved like crescents to allow knees to fit under the writing surface.

"The center one on the bottom."

I opened the top drawer, which I kept unlocked. The key for the other drawers was at the back tucked in an envelope with the note that had accompanied the desk to Calcutta. My heart leapt at the first sight of Silas' elegant handwriting. I again read the quotation from Wordsworth:

Every gift of noble origin
Is breathed upon by Hope's perpetual breath.

What had Silas meant? What did it mean now that he had breathed his own last mortal breath? With a surefooted expectation of impending discovery, I turned back to the desk. Nothing of value was stored in it, just some of my school papers, old letters, and a few books I had not taken to either Cochin or Free School Street. I unlocked the bottom drawer. Since it was deeper than the rest, this is where I had stacked the most items. I removed two bundles of letters, including the last ones I had received from Silas that contained his responses to my moral queries about opium as well as his encouragement to ask my father for a salary. How long ago that seemed! I turned to Gulliver for direction. "There is nothing here except my books and papers."

"Please lift them out."

I made a neat stack of the letters. Underneath were the Dickens books I had never returned, including *The Mystery of Edwin Drood*. Below that was a wrapped volume tied with faded ribbons: *The Kama Sutra*! I had not looked at it in years. Now the drawer was empty.

"Can you pull the drawer out any farther?" Gulliver asked.

It slid halfway, then resisted my tug. "It doesn't come out."

"It does."

I gave a firmer yank, but could budge it only another inch.

Gulliver fell to his knees. "May I?" Even under his muscular grasp the drawer refused to budge. Frowning, he removed his kukri from its scabbard and, using the curved sharp tip to push back the wood that had swollen in the humidity, he was able to wriggle it forward, first on one side, then on the other. With a radiant smile of triumph he lifted the drawer out and turned it upside down.

"What now?" I asked, perplexed, for the drawer was obviously empty.

With one hand he supported the bottom of the drawer frame. With the other he coaxed what had seemed to be the bottom panel forward. Once its front edge was exposed, I reached over and pulled it farther. Out fell a pristine vellum envelope with the thunderbolt crest. My name was on it.

11 December 1890

My dearest Dinah,

This is being written the day after the writing of our divorce papers, but will be seen by you someday far in the future, if ever. If you are reading this, something will have happened to me. If Gulliver outlasts me, he shall be at your side when this is found. I have given the matters that shall be addressed in this and subsequent documents deep consideration. The legal papers will more completely describe the nature of how the transactions will be undertaken. Here let me explain that the intent of my last will and testament is to leave all my worldly goods, including Xanadu, any other real estate I may own, my shares in the Luddy Tea Company, and other business interests in your hands.

I cannot know what time and place in your life this finds you. Possibly, this may be an additional burden you have no desire to undertake. In that case you have the freedom to sell any portion of these holdings to the benefit of yourself, your family, or anyone else you may assign. Most probably you have been well-provided for by your father, and if you have remarried, your spouse and his family. Perhaps my goods will be a small but pleasant addition to your wealth. Or, if luck would have it, and you might truly benefit from this bequest, use it to your advantage.

But, you are asking, why me? Why indeed! You know the reasons as well as I do, but I will state them as a reminder.

First, I married you with the full expectation that I would share my fortune with you. But I married you under false pretenses and did not bring a single benefit to you. In fact, I may have harmed your chances of finding a companion for life. You would not accept my help afterward, and I could not force you to. These documents are irrevocable and cannot be voided, thus I know that my last wishes to right a wrong will be met.

Second, I cannot leave my interests to Euclid or another man who may

have taken his place, for this would remove their considerable value from
a chain of inheritance through a Jewish family line. If you yourself do not
have children, I would hope you might (although this entails no legal ob-
ligation) leave these interests to a member of your family with heirs.

Third, you may be wondering why I have overlooked the most obvious
answer and not left my shares to other members of my own family. Be-
cause of my circumstance, I have been deeply hurt by them, and although
this may be my fault, I have never been able to change my nature, any
more than my sisters could make their eyes blue. Also, there was wisdom
in my father's structure giving control to me. The Luddy Tea Company
would not have survived without this division, and it may not survive past
my death. You have a basic understanding of the business and a strong
mind that will certainly become more astute with age. I have confidence
you either will manage the business yourself or find intelligent lieuten-
ants . . .

Tears flooded my eyes. I could not read any further for a few
minutes. When I was able to continue, I shuffled the many pages of
explanations and instructions until Gulliver's name caught my eye.

As a special favor to me, I would like you to keep Gulliver in your
employ. A fund for his maintenance is a part, though not a condition, of
this trust. You may not feel you need Gulliver, but he will be of service
if you are ever in the Darjeeling region, for he knows much about how my
business and home are run. If you should wish him to manage Xanadu
while you live elsewhere, that would be acceptable. However, my advice is
to keep him with you as your personal servant. From my experience, wealth
breeds danger as a swamp breeds mosquitoes. I realize that I may have be-
queathed you enemies as well as rupees. There will be many who will be
displeased with what I have done. Gulliver is a simple man with excellent
instincts. Trust him with anything: your money, your children, your life.
This Gurkha is as brave as a lion and would not hesitate to sacrifice his life
to protect yours. . . .

I looked over. Gulliver stood watching me with his dark, piercing
eyes. He had brought me here and given me this letter. Had he known
what it contained? He must have. What else did he know? I realized I
could not handle the Luddy matters without him, nor did I want to. I
thought about Silas' suggestion that he remain at Xanadu. Silas would
never have expected that he and his house would have perished in
unison.

"What is it? What are you doing here?" Edwin burst into the room.
"Your father?"

"No, he is sleeping."

"Then what . . . ?" Edwin caught sight of Gulliver, who was holding his kukri in front of him like a shield. "My God, who is that?"

I waved for Gulliver to stand back, and rose to greet my husband. "These papers were in the Clive bureau." I shook them in the air. "They are from Silas Luddy of Darjeeling. He was killed in the earthquake."

Edwin's eyes shifted warily as he wondered why I was in contact with my first husband. "I see," he said slowly, "but who's the mountain man?"

"His name is Gulliver, at least that is what he has been called for many years. He's the Gurkha who was Mr. Luddy's bearer."

Edwin glanced over his shoulder. The kukri dazzled in the midday sun.

"Gulliver, I must speak to my husband alone."

When Gulliver had backed into the hall, Edwin said, "Dinah, you look terrible. Are you certain you are all right?"

"The news was dreadful. Silas' house slid down the mountainside and he must have plunged thousands of feet. He was a good man, Edwin. I never loved him, but I never disliked him either."

"You don't have to explain about—"

"Yes, I do." I showed him the drawer with the false bottom. "He gave me this desk as a wedding present. After the divorce he hid some papers here and sent the desk to Calcutta. I never would have known about them if Gulliver hadn't come."

"What is this all about?"

"I do not fully understand it yet myself, but it seems as if Silas Luddy has left me all his worldly goods—including the controlling interest in the tea plantations and anything else he might have owned."

"Why you?"

"The letter clarifies it somewhat, but it's an unexpected shock."

"What does this mean?"

My knees trembled as I sat down at the desk chair. "I'm not certain." I leafed through the papers. One contained an inventory that was at least seven years old. "When the desk was sent to me, there was a capital account held personally for five hundred and seventy-five thousand rupees, another account in London worth sixty-five thousand pounds sterling—that's a total of almost one hundred thousand pounds! When we were together, Silas was taking more than five thousand rupees a month from the tea business. Xanadu, his home, is gone, but he was to inherit his father's house, and his father has died. There are the tea-processing machines—his father's inventions—a great deal of land . . ."

"And this is yours free and clear?"

"I don't know exactly. He mentions solicitors . . . everything here is outdated . . . but . . ." I looked up and saw he was as perplexed as I was.

Then he beamed. "But we don't need the Sassoons anymore!"

"No . . . we don't," I said in a quavering voice. "We are independent at last." I looked up with a frown. "A week ago we could have walked away from the company. But how can we do that now . . . with what we know?"

"We don't need them," Edwin repeated with a snort. He grinned as a fresh realization lit his face. "They need us."

\\/   \\/   \\/

The Luddy Tea Company had prospered. Silas had implemented his plan to concentrate on producing what he had called a "brisk tea" for the British working-class markets, and a very brisk business had followed. In order to popularize his Luddy brand, he had set aside far more funds for promotion than his predecessors. Considering the enormous quantities of Luddy's Finest Orange Pekoe that were shipped to England each month, the concept had been a huge success.

All this I learned in the offices of Mason, O'Malley, and Woodruff, the Luddys' Calcutta solicitors. Fifty percent of the Luddy family's combined holdings were mine free and clear. Maurice Luddy's two daughters and their husbands had inherited twenty-five percent each, but only of the tea-company shares. The land itself was mine, as was the homestead on the tea plantation. The parcels near Tiger Hill were mine, as were any effects that could be salvaged from the landslide. Silas' income and capital from other sources were mine, including the portion that had come to him on his father's death. Gala and Gracia had not shared in their father's personal estate. Although much of the value of the inheritance was tied up in real estate and company assets, the cash more than quadrupled the original inventory. In all, the bequest made me one of the richest women in the community.

My father was delighted with the news. In fact, the excitement surrounding the legal work rallied him for a week, for he insisted on examining every document.

"He's looking for the fatal flaw," Edwin said, not unkindly. "He thinks there must be some detail that has been overlooked."

"I feel the same way. I fully expect Gracia or Gala to charge in waving a new will in their favor or to contest this one."

"Mr. Woodruff assured us your original was in accordance with Silas' latest directives."

"I know, but my father pointed out that the most recent updates were at the time of Maurice's death. There could have been something—"

"We must go to Darjeeling," Edwin stated.

I agreed that we should see Silas' sisters and make arrangements for the management of the tea company. Less than a month after the earthquake, we made the journey, accompanied by Mr. Woodruff and Gulliver, our trusty Gurkha, who never left my side voluntarily, sometimes to Edwin's dismay.

"I wonder if I should be jealous."

"Edwin, he's here to protect us both."

"Nonsense. If I go to the left and you to the right, Gulliver follows you."

"I wouldn't care if he followed you."

Edwin laughed. "He's no fool. Besides, I feel better knowing you have him as a shadow."

"Why? You have never worried about my safety before."

"Silas was not stupid. Everyone knows about your inheritance. The money has placed you in danger."

"That's absurd. How is this any different from being the daughter of Benu Sassoon?"

Edwin shook his head. "I don't know, but I have a sense there is a change. Even your Uncle Samuel has never been nicer."

"That's because he expects you will be leaving the firm."

"That's what everyone thinks. What they don't know will hurt them!"

"First things first," I reminded him. "Let's settle the Luddy business and then we can make our plans."

\\/   \\/   \\/

The trip to Darjeeling brought memories both bitter and sweet. Not much had changed in seven years. Even the town, perched on the ridge, seemed unaltered from a distance. Up close the fissures in the plaster walls, the piles of chimney brick beside the houses, the incessant clanging of hammers, and the diminished holiday population were reminders of the disaster. Like Calcutta, Darjeeling had suffered a surprisingly small loss of life. The tremors had hit at a propitious time of day: after tea and before supper. If everybody had been in bed, many more would have been killed by countless collapsing roofs. The few casualties were the result of sad coincidences: an unfortunate passerby who was hit by a falling awning, two children trampled by a runaway horse, burns from overturned stoves, and the terrible plunge of the eccentrically perched Xanadu Lodge.

Gala's husband, Harold Ezekiel, and Gracia's husband, Israel Cohen, met us at the door to the Luddy offices. Their congenial greetings did nothing to allay my suspicions the meeting would be unpleasant. We were led to the conference room, where a sumptuous tea was set out. Six uniformed bearers wearing bright sashes that matched the various colored labels on the green tins manned six silver teapots, each marked with the name of a Luddy blend.

Once the tea was poured and introductions made, Harold cleared his throat. "We want you to know that it is our intention to cooperate with you in every way possible."

"Thank you," I responded, even though his words had been directed in Mr. Woodruff's direction. "Before we attend to the specific items that must be settled, I would like to know if you intend to challenge Silas Luddy's will."

Harold shot a glance at Israel. Israel, the older of the two, spoke so softly I had to strain to catch his first words. "Since you have been frank in asking the question, I will tell you the idea was discussed and we did receive advice that we might have a case. Yet how would that improve our position? Years might pass before the estate was settled, and in that time irreparable harm might be done to the business. And if we lost, the enmity that would have built up would ruin our ability to cooperate with you."

"Besides," Harold interjected more forcefully, "you have seen the figures. There is more than enough to go around. You do have fifty percent, but if we vote our shares together, we could block anything you tried to do. The best way to push forward is to work together for everyone's benefit."

With this announcement a great weight was lifted from my mind. I smiled at the two men whom I had hardly known because of the distance Silas had placed between himself and his family. Long ago my father had admired Maurice Luddy's acumen at running a family business gracefully. Considering the morass in the Sassoon Company, I thought his achievement was even more remarkable. I wondered what difference it would have made, for instance, if Bellore's husband had been given a share from the beginning.

"Where are Silas' sisters?"

"Here. They want to visit you after the business concerns are settled," Harold replied.

"Might you ask them in now? I know they have never been involved in the company, but what I have to say is as much a family matter as a financial one."

Harold excused himself and returned with Gracia and Gala. I greeted them each with a handshake and introduced Edwin and the solicitor. Stiffly we returned to our seats. "First, let me say that I am as surprised by these developments as you—that is, if Silas did not warn you of his intentions." Their furtive glances indicated they had expected a different outcome. "I do not believe I have any moral claim to the Luddy fortune. What happened between Silas and me was settled at the time our marriage was dissolved. I never felt he owed me anything, and I told him this on many occasions. However, it seems I have a valid legal claim. In his documents Silas has explained why he wanted me to have his share. Though you or I may argue with his reasoning, his messages do reflect his wishes. Even if I were to be foolish enough to relinquish this gift, Silas made it clear he did not desire to increase the shares of the members of his family. Any action I might take to remove myself from the company would bring an unknown third party into your midst. I do not think that I will be better—or worse—than someone else. My intention is to continue my life in Calcutta and to have the company run essentially as it has always been, with minimal interference from me. If, however, either or both of you would like to sell your shares, I would like a written agreement permitting me to make the first offer. If you would negotiate an option agreement to that effect, I would pay ten thousand rupees on signing." I looked around the room. Gracia's knees were shaking. Gala was pale but composed. Edwin brushed his hair back to conceal the grin that was spreading across his face.

Israel stood up. "Since you have spoken so honestly and graciously, Mrs. Salem, let me open my heart to you. Ever since I married into the Luddy family, I have been treated like a beloved son. I grieved for Maurice as much as for my own father. In his lifetime, he was generous with both his money and his affection. I knew nothing about tea cultivation when I came into this business and I have learned as the company grew. Gala and I have a pleasant life in Darjeeling. Now that our children are older, we have been wanting to travel more, but that is the extent of our ambitions. You know the figures. You know there is more than enough wealth to sustain everyone. All the money in the world cannot purchase health or happiness. I don't think I speak out of turn when I say the greatest tragedy is that Silas was never able to find contentment. His appalling end was only the final pathetic chapter in a dismal life."

His wife interrupted. "Israel, this is hardly the time—"

"When is the time if not now? For most of his life your brother was wretched. The reason we are here today is that Dinah gave him something the rest of us could not. We should be grateful to her for that. And from what has transpired thus far, I can see some of the reasons he placed so much faith in her."

Edwin coughed to get everyone's attention. "Transitions are always confusing," he began hesitantly. With my eyes I prodded him to stand. "This whole situation came as much of a shock to us as it did to you." He shifted to face the sisters. "We have come to tell you that as long as you are not going to object to your brother's wishes, we are not going to alter anything. The tea company is doing splendidly. We are more than content with its present level of income, and we have become the beneficiaries of ample bank deposits as well. We are not going to sell off any tea-company assets. Later, after we learn more about the direction the tea markets are taking in general and the goals of the company in particular, we may have suggestions to contribute. For now, the status quo is the way to go." He smiled at his silly rhyme and sat down.

After a cursory inspection of the landholdings, which Silas had extended when he came into his father's share, and a more thorough examination of the account books, Edwin and I returned to Calcutta, leaving the solicitors to transfer everything into my name. Xanadu had been declared a total loss. Nothing besides the bodies had been removed from the treacherous site. Thinking of Silas' paintings, books, and other precious collections, I financed an expensive salvage effort. "Take as much time and as many men as necessary. Move every timber and bring back anything of value," I ordered. "Do what is required, as long as no lives are risked." Eventually a portion of the treasures was recovered.

I directed that a simple platform with a sturdy railing be built over the exposed cellar, and mandated it be open to any pilgrim who wished to make darshan or tourist who wanted to view the snows. A wooden plaque noting this had been the site of Xanadu Lodge, the home of Silas Luddy, was placed where the balcony had once stood. Underneath was carved the Wordsworth quotation that had come with the Clive desk:

Every gift of noble origin
Is breathed upon by Hope's perpetual breath.

Nobody would ever live near Tiger Hill again.

44

❦ ❦ ❦

Edwin and I and, of course, Gulliver, returned to Calcutta victorious. We could not wait to tell my father everything that had evolved and to get his advice on how to proceed. When we arrived at Theatre Road, however, we heard he was in the throes of another attack.

"The next time he is stable, we must speak to him," I said to Edwin. He nodded glumly, for I had already told him that keeping Uncle Samuel's theft from my father had been a terrible strain for me.

"He is too weak. We'll have to wait."

"We can't wait forever. People never recover from malaria entirely."

"They gain strength between attacks," Edwin said optimistically. "Soon he will be much better."

"How can you be certain? The doctor says he has a very bad case. Every time he has a spell, other organs are affected. His heart is weak . . ."

"That is why we must manage this without him. The shock might be too much. Together we can work this out, if you think you can put your prejudices about opium aside and work with me on the solution."

Prejudices! Is that what they were? In any case, whether the commodity were opium or tea or dung, the family's honor—and assets—had to be protected. Edwin, who had known about the problem longer than I, had formulated an ingenious idea about how to foil Uncle Samuel. All during our trip to Darjeeling, I had not been convinced it would work.

"I have been giving our plan some thought and have decided that we don't have to tell your father everything to get his counsel," Edwin continued earnestly. "If he will help us with the auction, we can handle the rest on our own."

"I don't know . . . He will become suspicious and demand an explanation for our queries," I demurred.

491

"Haven't you seen how happy he is now that you have the Luddy estate? You are his oldest child. He wants you—he wants us both—to succeed."

"Not at the expense of his brothers, or their children, or his other children."

"Someone has to take charge before Samuel's stealing destroys everything. Without secrecy, none of this will work."

No matter what I felt, there was no contradicting this point. "I suppose you are correct, Edwin," I replied dejectedly.

"The next auction is only a few weeks away. If we are going to do it, there is no time to waste."

\\/　\\/　\\/

"A contrived conspiracy to do business" was how my father described the opium auctions to Edwin and me. Wrapped in a rug and wearing a cap on his head, even though the day was warm, my father sat on the sunny side of the rose garden and shivered. "The crown owns the Patna fields, always has, and always will, for this is how they control their share of the revenue," he rambled on, telling us what we knew perfectly well, but once he started, he might clarify several areas we needed to understand more about. "What a brilliant system! The government grants licenses to ryots who apply for them, and—here is the key—they advance money for cultivators without interest. Does the crown do that for cotton or jute or potatoes or rice? No. Not a rupee do they give for any other agricultural purpose. Their condition has always been that every drop of juice the cultivator extracts from the poppy head must be delivered to the government agent at a price set by the government. Now, why do we get involved at this stage even though we don't own any part of the fields or crop?"

"Because the government pays by the pound weight," Edwin filled in. "A pound of water or a pound of Patna's finest will bring the same three to four rupees."

"Right. We supervise the ryots and the processors to have a voice in quality. If we didn't know who grew the poppy or how it was prepared, we would have no say over which lots we would want to purchase, and so the grades would decline." His cheeks pinked, his eyes brightened. His enthusiasm for his subject had overcome his debility for the time being. "But is that the extent of the government's participation? Of course not. With a small extension of credit they not only own the crop, they have set the price. Do they bother grading, storing, shipping, or marketing the substance? Absolutely not! That is where we, the merchants, come in. Every chest of opium finds its way to the periodic auctions in Calcutta. Here the British don't exactly set the final price, they control their revenues by placing a reserve and then taking an excise tax on the final sale price to profit from any upswing in the market. Clever, eh?" As he began to cough, Edwin handed him a glass of water.

When he recovered, he continued, but with less zest than before. "Now, the reserve price means they will not sell below a figure, minimizing any loss. The excise tax guarantees they will not be cut out of the proceeds. The way we merchants win is by creating favorable trading conditions with our customers. If we buy carefully, assure a fine product that sells for the top price, and control the flow to sustain the high rate, we make money. If the market becomes flooded and the price drops below our costs—which includes that minimum price, the crown's taxes, the costs of doing business, shipping, Chinese taxes, and more—we lose. On paper it seems simple enough, but out there, whether in the fields of Patna or the warehouses of Hong Kong, only the smart ones survive."

As he finished, his voice cracked with the strain of talking, and I rolled my eyes at Edwin to warn him against going on. He avoided me, however. "Tell us more about the auctions."

"Not now," I said, since he hadn't heeded my gesture. "Maybe tomorrow we—"

"Nonsense. How tired can I get sitting about all day?" my father asked, throwing off the rug. "Another drink . . ."

Edwin poured from a pitcher of lemonade laced with quinine. Papa took a few sips, then spat in the grass. "Too bitter. Water!"

I passed the water. With the covers removed I could see how badly his body had wasted. His wrists were smaller than mine and his skin sagged on his upper arms. Once he had emptied the glass, he looked up. "Now, what do you want to know?"

"Does the reserve price change, and is it made public?" Edwin asked.

"Yes and no. Yes and no." He grinned. "Remember what I said about a conspiracy."

"They don't tell you, but you have ways of finding it out."

"Very good deduction, Edwin." My father's eyes twinkled out from his gaunt face.

Maybe I was wrong. Maybe this was the medicine Papa required.

"The reserve never varies by more than ten percent, even less if one studies the seasonal aspects of the price," he said excitedly. "There are tables for the last ten years. We research the average for the previous auctions in, say, August, and then use other figures to pinpoint the price."

"What other figures, Benu?"

"Why do you want to know?"

"Curiosity," I said, to deflect his suspicion from Edwin.

"Well, you will have to be curious a bit longer. Several clerks work diligently to estimate what it will be on each lot. The total number of chests coming to auction is one factor, as are quality and certain climactic variables. Anyway, the question is academic and has no bearing on your participation in the company." After a few seconds he gave each of us a sly smile. "Tell me, what are you two scheming to do?"

I laughed to distract him. "Now, Papa, aren't you the suspicious one?"

"What do you think we are going to do?" Edwin asked smoothly.

"I suspect you want to bid for a few lots on your own. You think that is the way you will garner a share of the opium trade for yourself. Why bother? If I were you, I would get as far away from the Sassoon enterprises as I could and concentrate on the Luddy situation. You have more than you will ever need as it is, although you could develop it into an even more substantial pile for the sake of your children." He gave Edwin a piercing look as he continued: "I know a man your age has personal scores to settle. These last years in Calcutta have not been easy, my son, but you have weathered the difficulties admirably. You can leave with your head high."

"If we make an attempt, what harm could there be?" Edwin asked.

"Samuel Lanyado tried it five years ago, but it got him nowhere."

My eyebrows lifted at this news, but Edwin seemed to know all about it and asked simply, "Why?"

"Let me explain what happens next. None of us merchants want to give the crown more than we have to, thus we have a gentleman's agreement, called 'lot division,' designed to hold the price down. This ensures that we aren't bidding against each other and thereby inflating the price. If we were, the government could try tricks of their own: keeping some lots back to make a false shortage, flooding the market with poorer grades. As it is, one company bids for a lot at the lowest, fairest price—calculated to beat the reserve—and then it is split among the others by proportions determined previously, based on investment levels."

"I see. Therefore, in order to even stay in the auction, one has to make an agreement beforehand for a portion of the lots."

"That is correct, Dinah."

"How is that done?" Edwin wondered.

"It isn't. The same dealers have controlled the business since my father's time. There is no reason to permit outsiders to change the system and enormous reason to prevent their success at all costs."

"What did Uncle Samuel try to do?" I asked in a way I hoped seemed nonchalant.

"He had saved enough to buy a substantial number of lots. He wasn't foolish enough to bid for himself, so he hired an agent through a middleman. However, the secret could not be kept, and everyone knew that when the agent bid for a lot, Samuel's money was behind a portion of it. The others cleverly bid those lots up, not enough to seem unusual, but enough to make his the highest-priced chests of the day. Then they refused to lot-split. Your uncle was left with the most expensive opium. This would not have been so bad if he could have sold directly in China, but like many others, he underestimated what went on at the other end. There was no way he could manage without another middleman. This drove his price out of the range of the marketplace. He took a loss on every chest."

"Poor Uncle Samuel." I laughed. "How did he cover the losses?"

"He must have taken loans. He didn't come crawling to the family, at least not for money. There were some—I won't say who—that did not want him to stay in the firm afterward. Your Uncle Saul insisted he stay because the Sassoons had not been harmed by his shenanigans and he had been taught a lesson. Since that time, Bellore has tightened the purse strings at Kyd Street and they undoubtedly have recovered."

"Do you think he would attempt it again?" Edwin wondered.

"There is a difference between foolishness and lunacy."

"Aren't there any conditions under which a new person could enter the opium market?" Edwin dared.

Unwilling to see my father's reaction to this confrontation, I focused my gaze on a nearby bush bursting with yellow roses.

Watchful as ever, my father straightened his back and swung his legs down from the settee. "Dinah!" As I turned toward him, he patted the cushion. "Dinah, come sit beside me." Crooking a bony finger at my husband, he commanded, "Edwin, sit here too." Once Edwin had slid into the other seat, Papa went on, "Yes is the answer to your question. If someone had considerable resources to throw into the wind, one could outbid for most of the lots at a single auction. Then, for a short time, the winner would control the price. If that company had agents in place to handle the shipping and sales in China, they might make a profit. One thing about opium is there is always an anxious group of customers on the other end who are not willing to wait until the price drops before they buy. But where would that get the newcomer in the long run? To prevent a monopoly, the auctions are held frequently. With the money they had saved, the other merchants would rush in and buy up the next stock of chests. I would guess they would be so irate at what had occurred, they might try any number of tricks to hurt the upstart." He squeezed my hand tightly and stared from me to my husband. "Listen to me, Dinah and Edwin, and listen well. I don't know what you two have been thinking, but you must never use your Luddy funds to try a run on the auction.

First, it won't work. Second, you promised the Luddy sisters you would leave their tea holdings intact. Third, you don't require more than you already have. And if that isn't enough, I shall have to remind you the last time you made an impetuous investment, it landed on the bottom of the sea—where much opium has also ended up, by the way."

As he pressed my hand to his lips and kissed it, tears welled in my eyes. "I am a very sick man, Dinah. I cannot pretend that I will be around to protect you or the others for much longer. You can't imagine how much lighter my heart has been since Silas left you his shares. Promise me that you will be judicious in the future."

"Yes, Papa," I said, and Edwin nodded also.

He closed his eyes and leaned back against Edwin. "Is that a promise?" This question was directed at me.

I stared at my pitiful father. His cheeks were sunken, his lips parched. Only the husk of the vibrant man remained. "I promise to act responsibly now and in the future."

His eyes flew open and met mine. I was able to hold them without flinching.

"Good." He sighed.

Edwin stood up. "Dinah, we should let your father rest," he said.

I didn't let go of his hand, though, for there was something else I had to say. "One more question, Papa. Do you think there will ever be an end to the opium business in India?"

"Everything ends sometime," he said sadly. "But I can't envision it happening in my lifetime or yours. Last year the net opium revenue for India was more than ten percent of the total revenues from the colony."

This sounded so similar to Edwin's apologies for the substance that I felt outnumbered. Didn't anybody share my scruples? "Wouldn't it be beneficial to some people if there was less available?"

"There will always be those who cry out in moral outrage, but the pragmatists who run the show will silence them."

"Are you a pragmatist?" I asked softly, though I meant it as a rebuke.

"We Sassoons have always been beyond reproach in our dealings," he said with a defensive retort.

Not in what they have dealt in, I thought to myself. My father sighed again. Whether he was allowing himself to meditate along the same lines as I had been or whether he was only tiring, I was not certain. Although he voiced no remorse, I had a sense there was some ambivalence—especially because of what had happened to my mother—he had never been able to express.

Zilpah was coming across the lawn. Knowing she was going to chide us for interrupting my father's rest, Edwin and I stood and said our good-byes. "One last word," Papa added, barking a hoarse cough. "Remember, they may outlaw opium someday, but they will never outlaw tea."

❦ ❦ ❦

"I don't think we should go ahead with the plan," I said when Edwin and I were alone.

"Dinah! How can we back down now?"

"Very easily. We have not done anything irrevocable."

He switched on a lamp in our parlor. Since returning from Theatre Road, we had reviewed every point, looking for flaws. In the waning light of the day, my enthusiasm had also dimmed. "What are you frightened of?"

"You heard what my father said. I am afraid of failure."

"We have agreed that the possible losses are within tolerable limits."

"You have agreed. I have assented to nothing! Don't you recall what it is like to lose fifty thousand rupees?"

Edwin blanched, and I immediately regretted the outburst.

"For years I have borne the weight of that responsibility. Even today I am not free of the burden."

I knew that was true. He never would have acquiesced to working for the Sassoons or suffered the indignities had he not been mortified by the loss.

"This time I know we are taking the right course."

"My father doesn't."

"He doesn't understand what we actually are going to attempt."

"He came close, though, and he made me promise we would not go after a share."

"No, you knew better than to do that. You promised you would act responsibly to guard your inheritance. And you shall—we shall. This time we are not betting the whole account. At most, we could lose a fraction of the cash assets. If the Luddy Tea Company does as well as it did the past five years, the income from the balance alone will support us grandly. What more do we need? Besides, if all goes as planned, we will have lost nothing and we will have rid ourselves of Samuel—and your Aunt Bellore—forever."

"Aren't there less expensive, less risky ways to do that?" I asked in a shaky voice.

"Dinah, we've gone over this a thousand times."

"We could tell my father about the embezzlement."

"The malaria has severely debilitated him. It would be too much of a shock."

"And this won't be?"

"A pleasant surprise could restore him."

"And if it does not work the way you think it will?"

"Then he will have to be told. Besides, even if we did inform him or your brothers, you know as well as I what would happen: they would recover the money as best they could and bury the matter."

"I don't agree."

"I work with them every day and I know the way they think." Edwin brushed off his jacket and stood authoritatively. "There is one other possibility."

"What is that?" I asked, fired with the hope there was a course we had overlooked.

"Take the matter to court. A criminal case would accomplish what you want and there would be some justice in seeing your uncle— possibly even your aunt—in the dock."

"Justice! There is no justice in the courts. My uncle would hire a bunch of slimy solicitors who would do anything—including bribery—to free him." My voice lowered to a husky pitch. "There is no justice in the courts of Calcutta, or anywhere else probably. My mother was murdered by two men whose guilt was proved to everyone except the judge. There was evidence, there were witnesses, and still they were released."

"What happened to them?"

"Dr. Hyam believes they went to Singapore or Macao. Once he heard that Sadka returned to Calcutta and was said to have even bragged about the crime, but that indiscretion forced him to disappear again."

"Where are they now?"

"Who knows? Somewhere in the world Sadka and Chachuk are free. My mother never had a second chance. So don't tell me I should try to seek justice in the courtroom."

"Dinah, you don't have to convince me."

My arguments were crumbling. Was there no other choice? I gulped and added, "I thought we agreed that even at the largest estimate of what Samuel may have accumulated, he couldn't afford the reserve of even the lowest-priced chests."

"Do you think it is a coincidence that he has been meeting with *Indian* moneylenders?"

As I looked up in astonishment, he smiled like a man holding the trump card. "How do you know that?"

"Gulliver has made himself useful to me in this matter. The list includes Shyamachurn Banerjee of the Agra Bank and Surroop Dutt of Tagore and Company. Why else would he be going to the Bengalis? You can imagine the terms he must be getting. Banks lend money to a credit society at six percent; the society then advances it to the money-lenders at ten percent; and if Samuel persuades the moneylenders, he'll pay in the area of twenty-five percent. His risk is enormous. Only if he corners the market and can set his price will he be able to pay them back."

"But my father said these raids won't work unless he also has the shippers and Chinese merchants in his pocket."

"By now he must have a plan of his own. He's not going to repeat old mistakes. Perhaps he has hired the resources of one of our competitors, or perhaps he is planning a merger with one of them."

"Is that possible?" I gasped.

"Yes," Edwin replied resolutely. "We don't have a monopoly on China."

"If he joined with someone else or put together strong associates, he could continue to parlay his gains this time into building another company, couldn't he?"

Edwin nodded morosely. "There is another possibility. If we lose our chance to make a profit this season, he could arrange to have almost the entire network of the Sassoons at his disposal. Don't you see? If Samuel owns the crop, he will control the market price. The gains he can make could be so enormous that he could do this again and again. In fact, he could end up commanding Sassoon and Company. We could all be working for *him*."

45

♦ ♦ ♦

Everything was in place. Or so I thought. We had studied the plan repeatedly, and though there were many eventualities we could not anticipate, we framed strategies to master any deviations. My folly was to have probed behind every door—except my own.

The evening before the auction, Calcutta was all pastels beneath the setting sun. Even the bustling throng along Free School Street seemed softer, more muted as I walked with Aaron, and Yali followed with a twin on each hand. Smiling at a pleasant breeze that ruffled the children's sun-streaked locks, I looked back toward the drab facade of Uncle Jacob's house. When this was over, my first task would be to find us a new place to live. Several possibilities near Grandmother Helene's appealed to me, or I might consider one of the large houses across from St. Xavier's, which would be convenient when the boys were older. Edwin might even want to teach there from time to time. The business had wasted his intellectual gifts. Now that there was no need for him to struggle, he should be able to manage some aspects of the Luddy holdings and devote himself to a more satisfying task.

What would I do? The tea business required my attention. After the lesson of Uncle Samuel's duplicity, I knew I had to take an active interest in the Luddys' enterprises. I wanted to make certain Silas' promotional ideas continued, and was pondering new tea blends for special markets. Did the Americans like brisk tea? I wondered. What did the Continentals prefer? We might travel and discover the various tastes, then tailor our product to suit the market instead of trying to sell what we had in stock. These thoughts danced about without choreography, for the main music in my mind was a replay of the last exciting days, when we had seen the pieces on the chessboard line up for tomorrow's checkmate.

500

First of all, Edwin had calculated how much cash my uncle had embezzled and had estimated between two and two and a half million rupees, or twenty-five lacs. Almost ten thousand chests were to be sold at the next auction. The reserve was figured at an average fourteen hundred rupees per excise chest. If the purchase price averaged close to the reserve, say fourteen-fifty per chest, the sale would gross over one crore, thirty lacs. In order to monopolize the price, Uncle Samuel would have to garner close to seventy-five percent of the crop. That was almost one hundred lacs. How could twenty-five buy my uncle a hundred? It couldn't. If he had bankers willing to lend him money until he made back his price, he would have to come up with only twenty-five percent of three-quarters of the crop. Amazingly, that figure was 2,501,250 rupees—a pinch over our estimate. With that calculation I was firmly convinced of his intentions.

In order to succeed, however, we required the support of the other merchants. After giving the matter careful thought, we decided not to meet each individually. Instead we would discuss the situation with Abner Raphael, head of the second-largest Jewish opium house. A close friend of Uncle Saul's and the Maghen David synagogue's principal benefactor, Raphael was among the most-respected men in the community. I myself had had a special fondness for the gentleman since the time my father first had been trying to find me a husband and Raphael had remarked, "If I had a son the right age, I would welcome your daughter into my house." I hoped he would receive us in the same benevolent spirit when Edwin and I called at his home ten days before the auction.

"Your father, is he recuperating?" Abner Raphael had asked with a concerned expression after we were seated in his study. The man was not ten years older than my father, but his traditional Baghdadi dress and long beard made him look like portraits of my Sassoon forefathers: Moses, David, even Sheikh Sason ben Saleh.

I tried to put my awe aside and responded with confidence. "We hope so. The fevers are less frequent, but he requires complete rest. He won't return to China this year."

"Who will go in his stead?"

"We are not certain. Possibly my brother Jonah, and Reuben's son Noah."

"Nathaniel might be better," he judged, stroking his creamy beard. "Is that what you have come about? Do you require advice on the China trade?"

"No, Mr. Raphael," Edwin replied. He had remained in the background until he was required to bolster the argument, for he had said this was a favor that had to be requested by a Sassoon.

"Then to what do I owe this pleasure?" Raphael replied slowly. "Are you soliciting for a charity? I know of your family's estimable work after the earthquake and your own interests in helping in Darjeeling. I would be pleased to—"

I held up my hand and laughed uneasily. "Only if you consider Sassoon and Company a charity."

"Indeed I do." His eyes crinkled to slits as he guffawed. "The Raphaels have lost out often enough to feel we have been giving to the Sassoons—albeit against our will—for half a century."

I observed his expression carefully. There was no hint of hostility. The Raphael mansion was even grander than Theatre Road. This palatial residence next to the residence of Calcutta's commissioner of police included a private zoo that my children often visited. Their favorite creature was a venerable tortoise that must have given rides to every Jewish child. However, I could no longer trade on our friendship. The time had come to win Raphael with facts. Without any further preliminaries I told him what we had discovered, with me outlining the broad problem, Edwin reading from his notes on the details of the theft.

Raphael leaned farther and farther forward as the magnitude of the deception mounted. "A tragedy," he clucked. "Samuel Lanyado! Who would have thought he could do such a thing?" He shook his head sadly. "Are you sure? Couldn't there be another explanation?"

"If we had found a few isolated errors, I would agree with you," I replied softly.

"How long has this been going on?"

"We aren't certain," Edwin added. "The oldest records are in storage and we have not been able to retrieve them."

"I suspect he has been taking what did not belong to him since Uncle Saul and Uncle Jacob died," I continued. "Possibly even before then."

"No!" Raphael spat. "He would not have dared."

I backed down instantly. "I suppose you are right. Even so, we place the loss between twenty and thirty lacs."

Edwin nodded somberly. "We are also fairly certain Gabriel Judah helped his father-in-law."

For about a minute Raphael was silent. "How could they conspire against their own family?"

"Greed," Edwin filled in simply. "What else could it be?"

I stared at our host imploringly. "We need your help to put an end to it."

Raphael threw up his hands. "What can I do? This is a matter for the Sassoons to settle. Why doesn't your father step in?"

"He doesn't know," Edwin replied resolutely.

"The doctor warned us that his heart was weak," I added.

Raphael's face seemed carved in ice. For a moment I didn't think we would succeed with him. "What can I do?" he repeated with a catch in his throat.

I took a deep breath. "We have reason to believe that Samuel has saved the bulk of the money to make a run on the opium auction."

"Ridiculous! Nobody has ever been successful at it. We work together to sustain our shares. Besides, as I recall, he tried once before. He learned his lesson then."

"He didn't have twenty-five lacs then," Edwin offered.

Raphael gave us an indulgent smile. "That is not nearly enough."

"It's enough if he buys on margin," I said. "He has made deals with Bengali moneylenders." Doing his part to back me with solid figures, Edwin went over the mathematics.

Raphael shook his head. "Even if the numbers worked in his favor and he bought enough chests, he would have to sell the stuff in China. How could he get rid of it—and at a higher price at that—without an organization?" Suddenly the color drained from his cheeks, and he filled in his own answer. "If he amassed seventy-five percent, he would control the Sassoons."

"We cannot allow him to get that far," I said, hoping the bold use of the "we" wouldn't put him off.

Before Raphael could interrupt, Edwin launched into our plea. "The way he will gain control of the lots is to outbid everyone else. He'll be clever, probably working through several of the independent bidders who pay more for smaller lots of the medicinal grades. We estimate that he might let some chests go close to reserve, escalating the price as slowly as possible. In the end it will be obvious that a run is on, and unless the rest of you band together to fight him, he'll garner what he needs."

"How do you children know this?" Raphael asked with a tinge of condescension in his tone.

"We spoke with my father."

"You said he was ignorant of the Lanyado matter."

"He is," I insisted. "We told him we wanted to learn more about the business. Then he became suspicious. He accused us of trying to do our own run, using the Luddy money."

"How do I know your story about your uncle isn't a falsehood to get the others and me to back down while you take over the Sassoons? I have more confidence in your holdings than the amount your uncle supposedly embezzled."

"I promised my father I would not attempt to control the auctions for my own gain. I am trying to protect the Sassoons now, and the rest of you in the future. Do you really want a man like Lanyado running the show in Calcutta?"

"You are a clever girl, Dinah, but what do you know about the opium trade? Why should a Jardine or a Davidson, a Gubbay or the Meyer brothers, an Eliahu or a Raphael, for that matter, want to give up any fraction of this year's profits to help you settle a family feud?"

"Nobody will have to give up a single anna," I said, laying most of our cards on the table. "If you will orchestrate the auction so the rest of the merchants bid up to twenty percent above your highest agreed lot price, I will cover the difference."

"That is crazy! You might lose everything."

"I can afford that out of my capital. None of the Luddy Company assets will be affected. We must be certain to give my uncle enough rope to hang himself, then recapture the balance of the chests so he has no ability to repay the Bengalis."

"But we will have forced the price up twenty percent," Raphael said before he had thought through my offer. "The Chinese won't tolerate that much of an increase." I didn't reply. At last comprehension illuminated his face. "The rest of us come on the market with a price close to the usual, while you personally absorb the loss. . . ."

"Yes," Edwin said with a lopsided, nervous grin.

I was also on the edge, wondering if I would fall off the precipice as we played our last card. I glanced at Edwin. This was his hand.

"In return, we would want a small concession."

Raphael lifted his bushy white eyebrows and waited.

"Because we accept the entire risk—and don't forget, we are protecting your interests as well as the Sassoons'—we are asking that each of the merchants return to us twenty percent of his revenue after expenses on each chest, or twenty percent of the chests themselves, whichever we choose."

I squeezed in before Raphael could reply. "In other words, if the reserve was calculated at fourteen-seventy-five, you normally might bid up to fifteen-fifty. With us covering an additional twenty percent, you could bid another three hundred and ten per chest, paying up to eighteen-sixty."

"Nobody has ever paid eighteen-sixty based on that reserve!" Raphael said in a shocked tone. "Nor would the Chinese pay over fifty-five hundred, which we would need to stay in line with last year's profits."

"I agree you might not do as well as last year, but that doesn't mean you couldn't unload it in China for around five thousand. You probably multiply the auction price times three hundred percent, the way the Sassoons do, and have something like our seventy-percent margin to work with, but even at five thousand you are making almost seventeen percent on your investment."

"But—" Raphael was about to jump in, but I didn't give him an opening.

"If everything works out, I will have a chance to make a small profit. If the Chinese merchants accept a higher price, I would make substantially more, but if you are unable to get a price that gives you that level of profit, I lose. No matter what, I will have accomplished the goal of ridding Sassoon and Company of my uncle, and I will have kept a promise to my father to act responsibly with my Luddy inheritance."

"Are you suggesting the rest of us should forfeit twenty percent of our market this season?"

"Yes," Edwin agreed affably. "Look at it another way: if Samuel takes over, you will lose a minimum of fifteen percent for the whole year. However, twenty percent of this season is only one-sixth, or three percent, for the year, plus you will have purged yourself of a rival whom you could never again trust. On the other hand, think of what Samuel might do with those profits. What might he attempt at the next auction? By working with us, you limit your losses to three percent, and even those losses are a phantom penalty on income you *hoped* to make, not losses on funds depleted."

Raphael sighed. "Do you plan to take delivery of your chests?"

"I'm not certain," I answered truthfully. "Probably not, even if the Sassoon situation is secure. I do not want to mingle my money with theirs. As you know, I have no shares in the company. If I decide against delivery, you and the other merchants would sell my twenty percent and pay me with the last of the *sycee* from the season. I can afford to wait."

"How generous," Raphael responded facetiously.

I let his sarcasm slide. "Not at all. I wanted to offer sweet coating for a bitter pill."

"You actually expect me to endorse this ridiculous scheme?" Raphael asked gruffly.

"Only your word would convince the others," I added softly.

"You haven't done so badly yourself," he complimented. He was thoughtful for a moment. "What if you hadn't found the evidence of the embezzlement?"

"Samuel would have an easy time at the auction, wouldn't he?" Edwin answered.

"Probably. What about after? How would he have explained having the capital?"

"With lies about the size of his loans, I suppose," I added. "Flushed with his success, he would have taken the reins at Clive Street, reorganizing his account books and the other evidence."

"Don't forget your uncle continues to think nobody knows what he's going to do." Edwin stood up. "Secrecy is essential."

"I wish your Grandfather Moses could be here now." Raphael pushed his bulk up with a groan. "Or your Uncle Saul." He turned to Edwin.

"Write out those figures for me and I'll see what I can do."

After that meeting, I had not returned to Raphael's house. Edwin had seen him again to organize the details. My husband came back from the last encounter with a startling suggestion.

"Raphael wants you to attend the auction."

"Why? Women never do."

"Not true. Apparently some of the English ladies have been finding it entertaining. He told me that even Bellore went once. Nobody thought too much of it because she likes to do whatever is fashionable, and if Olivia Davidson finds some place new to parade about in her latest Parisian confection, your aunt is not to be outdone."

"But why me?"

"Give the old man some credit. He's thought of some angles we neglected. Eventually the merchants will figure out that a run is on. Of course, almost everyone—except the independent agents and a few of the smallest houses who cannot be in on the plot because of secrecy—will know what is happening. Everyone except Samuel's coterie, of course."

"I don't understand. What good will it do for him to see me when he knows that he is the one, not me?"

"What if he thinks that we might be trying to play the same game? He knows you have a fortune to invest. Raphael has a few independent agents who will bid a portion of his shares at a higher price early in the day so it will *appear* as though someone besides your uncle is trying to take over. If your uncle sees you there, you will be the prime suspect. Remember, he doesn't know that we surmise him guilty of anything. Our interference should escalate the bidding more rapidly and, more important, destroy his equilibrium. The sooner Samuel backs down, the cheaper the later chests will be, minimizing our risks."

I had been thrilled by this latest addition to the scheme. Earlier qualms about the nature of what we were bidding for diminished with the larger goal of using the lots and rupees to rout Uncle Samuel. And when this was over, Edwin and I would be able to wash our hands of the opium business forever.

Yes, everything was almost perfect, like an ungilded dome with the promise of golden foil about to be pressed in place. My mind turned back to the children, who were running ahead as we left Wellington Square and made our way back to Free School Street. I liked this time of day best. After tea I was refreshed, filled with a balance of energy and patience. The children's vitality infused me. Now that the twins were able to converse, I had taken to supervising their nursery suppers while the ayahs had their own meal.

A short while later we sat at the table together. Aaron entertained with a song he had heard me sing only once. His memory showed every sign of being as exceptional as his father's. Zachariah fussed about having too much rice on his plate. Jeremiah could not eat fast enough. Aaron used his implements with the precision of a little old man. The differences amused me. I idly wondered what a daughter might be like.

"Ow!" Aaron cried as I wiped Jeremiah's mouth. I turned to see blood dribbling down his chin.

"What happened?" I asked in alarm.

Aaron was grinning, not crying. In his hand he held up a little pearl of a tooth. He stuck his tongue through the gap between his lower front teeth. "First one!" he said triumphantly.

I clapped my hands in appreciation for the threshold he had crossed.

"Papa! I want to show Papa."

I went out into the hall and called for Hanif. "Is the sahib home yet?"

"Yes, memsahib, he came in while you were out. Shall I call him for you?"

"No," I said, because Edwin might be lying down, something he often did before dinner, since he liked to stay up and work in the coolness of the late evening. "Ask Yali to watch the little ones." After I wiped Aaron's lip, he pulled the bloody napkin away and waved it around like a banner. I placed the tiny tooth in the other hand. "Hold this tightly and we'll show it to Papa." I urged him upstairs, and in so doing opened a door that led not to a happy family celebration, but to a black shaft of despair.

❦ ❦ ❦

The man I loved lay on his side, his back away from me, as Aaron and I entered the room at the end of the corridor on the top floor, which had become Edwin's study. He said he liked this corner room because it had shutters on two sides and good ventilation in the hottest months. Even on this mild evening, the moment the door opened, a breeze rippled through the room and lifted my skirt. My husband's books lined one wall. The bed was covered with a silk rug and dotted with cushions. "My reading nest," Edwin called it. The children were never permitted to disturb him there. Even I respected his privacy, for I had wanted to encourage his intellectual pursuits, which were his relief from the pressures of his work. However, the loss of his first son's first tooth justified a special exception.

The room was darkened. Shafts of twilight spilled through the wide-open slats. One shutter that was not completely fastened creaked slightly. My instinct was either to latch it firmly or to lock it open. I decided on the latter course so Edwin would see his son's toothless grin better.

"What a funny smell," Aaron said, wrinkling his nose.

"Shhh!" I hushed him. Turning to admire the husky curve of Edwin's back, I moved around to see if he was asleep.

His eyes were closed, but he was not asleep. Oblivious of our entrance, he was smoking a silver pipe.

An opium pipe.

"Edwin!"

"Di-nah . . ." His mushy reply reminded me of Amar's awful speech.

"Papa, I lost my first tooth!" Aaron crowed, starting to climb onto the bed.

Grabbing his shirt, I pushed the child back roughly. "Go to Yali!"

"I must show Papa my tooth!"

"Do as I say!"

"Mama, no!"

"Aaron!"

The child burst into tears. Supporting himself on his elbow, Edwin sat up slightly. "Truth. He must show me the truth. Never too early for the truth . . ."

Aaron's tears stopped as he giggled. "No, Papa, *tooth*."

Was this the truth? Had everything else been imagined? How could I not have known? The ungilded dome shattered like a raw egg rapped with a spoon.

Mechanically I had Aaron give his father the tooth and a kiss on the cheek. Using enormous control, I steered him out the door and turned him over to the *dhobi*, who was stacking diapers on a table. "Go finish your supper, Aaron." This time the child had the sense to do as told.

When I returned to my husband, he sat at his desk. The pipe was no longer in sight.

"How long?"

"What does it matter?"

"It matters to me. Is this something new?"

"No."

"Why didn't you tell me?"

"I knew you would never approve. Anyway, what difference does it make? A pipe of Patna's finest now and then has never affected me."

"How can you say that? I have always abhorred opium users!"

"Then you must abhor me, for I have been fond of the essence of poppy since long before I met you." There was a mocking quality in his expression I had never before heard, and it penetrated my heart.

"Tell me this is a mistake," I begged. "I can understand you needing something on a day like today, a day when we are both on the brink. I too have been worried, wishing it would be over," I continued in the hope that his response to one of my statements would ease the stabbing pain.

Edwin's voice was soft and faraway. I felt I was falling into an abyss. "I never wanted you to know . . . I have always been careful. I don't usually smoke at home, and when I do, it is up here with the windows open wide."

"Do you use it every day?" I could barely speak above a whisper.

"It depends. A few puffs in the early evening is what I prefer, but if I cannot have it, I do not suffer. What is the difference between a brandy or a pipe or a cheroot—or a four-o'clock cup of bloody tea?" he added in a burst of anger.

"Opium is evil."

"Then you are as corrupted as I am—and worse, you are a hypocrite. The profits from that flower have supported you your entire life. Tomorrow you will barter your future with the black balls of its sap."

"It killed my mother."

"No, it did not! Some jealous madman murdered your mother."

"If my father had not been in China—"

"What difference did that make? He could have been selling saddles or bricks or silver bars, and he might still have been away from home. Nothing could have saved her."

"If I had awakened earlier . . ." A sob enveloped me. Could I have saved her? Had I worried about this all these years without ever acknowledging it?

Edwin tried to put his arms around me, but I pushed him away. He returned to his desk and shuffled a few papers. "It is true that a few people use opium to their detriment. The world is filled with failures who drink too much or smoke too much, but that shouldn't ruin the substance for the rest. A modern physician cannot cope without opium." He read from the paper in his hand, his dark pupils wide and shiny in the dim light: " 'In Great Britain, the chief manufacture of these salts of opium for medicinal purposes is carried on in Edinburgh by two firms, Mssrs. T. and H. Smith, and J. F. Macfaran and Co. Opium is undoubtedly the most valuable remedy for the whole *materia medica*. For other medicines, we have one or more substitutes; but for opium none—at least in the large majority of cases in which its peculiar and beneficial influence is required.' "

"I have no objection to medicinal preparations."

"Stop deceiving yourself. In your book, it is perfectly acceptable for a Chinese coolie to support your sumptuous life, yet not your own husband."

"No! I have never felt it was right for anyone—at least not since I learned more about opium and the harm it could do. You know full well I have always resisted the family trade and often questioned my father. If you remember, I never wanted you to work for the Sassoons and have been encouraging you to find another line. I thought that with the Luddy inheritance, we would free ourselves of it—once we had settled the situation with the Lanyados. But now I see you have never agreed with me about any of this. The whole while you have lied to me!"

"No, I have kept a secret. Nobody can know everything about the next person. You have secrets from me."

"That is not true. I have no secrets from you." My voice became strident. "What else don't I know?" I shouted. Then, more menacingly: "How can I ever trust you again?" The ooze of the broken egg could not be restrained.

"When will you learn you can never control everything?" he said, as though that followed logically.

"What are you talking about? I have never tried to control you."

"Haven't you? Then how did we end up back in Calcutta, where you wanted to be from the beginning?"

A great force churned inside me. There was no release but words— awful words, horrid words, that should never have been spoken aloud. "Who insisted we go to Travancore? Who was dazzled by the princely offering? Who wanted to use that connection to make a quick fortune? Not me. I was happiest in the seaside cottage in Cochin. Why didn't you see Amar's design from the first, when you knew he had perverted tastes? Or were your own perverted by the same poison? Who selected the ship and said it was ready to sail? Who lost my dowry? Who?"

"Yes. *Your* dowry. *Your* inheritance. Yours. Everything has always been yours. When you talked to Raphael you said: '*I* do not want to mingle *my* money . . . pay *me* with the last of the *sycee* . . . *I* can afford to wait.' "

Blackness swirled around me as I sat down hard on the bed. I no longer could see Edwin. If he was still speaking, I could not hear him. An hour earlier I had thought I was on the brink of having everything. Would a moral victory over Uncle Samuel and Aunt Bellore now cost me my happiness? Me! My happiness! Edwin was right! I was thinking only of myself. What about *us*? What about *our* children, *our* marriage?

"Edwin . . . darling . . ." I managed as I swam up past the blinding pain to the light. "Edwin, you are right. I am sorry. It's not the opium, it's—"

Where was he? "Edwin?"

The door was open. "Edwin!"

He was gone.

46

❦ ❦ ❦

He would be back in time for supper.

He would be back in time for bed.

To avoid a confrontation, he would slip in beside me in the night. . . .

I was up most of the night waiting, and when I drifted off, it was for but a few moments. Each time I opened my eyes, I was startled anew to find myself alone.

At dawn I lay in bed unable to move. Any twist of my body drove the stake that impaled me deeper.

He would arrive in the morning to dress for the auction. . . .

When Yali came to wake me, I had to force myself to stand.

"You are ill?" she asked, worried.

"No." I sent her away. If I took shallow breaths, the sharp twinges could be mastered. I could not drink or eat. Swallowing was impossible. The clock was a demon ticking away. I had to dress. I had to walk downstairs. I had to call for a carriage.

He would meet me there. . . .

The auction rooms were in a hall near Dalhousie Square. Pools of limpid light poured through the arched windows two stories in height and illuminated the polished benches where the agents and merchants sat. Six times every year these modestly attired gentlemen gathered to bid a price for a commodity that controlled the empire's balance of trade in China.

From the number of office jauns and phaetons waiting in front of the building, I ascertained that most of the people had already arrived. If I hadn't been waiting for Edwin, I would have been earlier myself. At the last possible minute I had left without him. Now I had to muster the courage to enter the room alone—except for Gulliver. Dressed in a long white jacket and shiny boots, he was an imposing companion, but he would hardly deflect questions on my husband's whereabouts.

I had chosen my own garments with care. Vacillating between a utilitarian walking dress and a more frivolous creation, I had selected something in the height of fashion to counter my usual practical image. Here I was: the new heiress ready to flaunt her good fortune to everyone from the Jardines to the Lanyados. Some would speculate whether I was there just to be seen or if my new streak of daring had extended from my wardrobe to trying for a stake in the opium business. I especially hoped that my plum gown with the high officer stand-fall collar, wide satin revers, and the matching bonnet crowned with ostrich feathers would agitate Aunt Bellore.

Heads turned when I entered the room. The men's glances were brief, the women's more intrigued. Just as they must have appraised me, I was equally interested in them. Olivia Davidson was wearing a sailor-style jacket with a jaunty white linen collar. Her friend Natalie Matheson was in a pink gown with a close-fitting bodice and frilled *jabot*. I did not recognize some of the younger women, but Sultana and her sister Lulu sported jackets with wide leg-o'-mutton sleeves. In front of them—sitting with the wives of the several smaller bidders— their mother was bedecked in black cotton with white lace collar and cuffs. Feeling satisfied I had not underestimated what to wear, I went over to the short trellised barrier that separated the ladies' and visitors' gallery on the right side of the room from the trading floor.

"How nice to see you again," Olivia fussed. "Do sit next to me, Mrs. Salem, for I must hear about your recent trip."

I took the seat that was offered to me between Olivia Davidson and Sultana Judah. "To Darjeeling?" I asked in a syrupy voice. Before I had inherited the Luddy estate, Olivia had barely looked in my direction. Nor had I ever taken an interest in the society in which Bellore and her kin had longed to become accepted. The British ladies would suppose my appearance as nothing more than a desire to establish myself at the pinnacle at last. I hoped Aunt Bellore's thoughts might range beyond the obvious.

"The earthquake's ravages are not apparent, at least not on the surface, but some of the homes will have to be refurbished. Many need new roofs."

"Such a pity," Olivia clucked. "Well, it is good to have you back. We must have you both over for supper."

"Thank you." I forced myself to smile past my pain. From the corner of my eye I watched as Gulliver stationed himself behind me. A punkah-wallah on his right looked at the imposing Gurkha in awe and stopped pulling on the rope. Gulliver gave the skinny boy a discreet kick. He stirred the air twice as fast.

Reluctantly Cousin Sultana acknowledged my presence. "This is my first auction," she began sweetly.

"Mine too," I said as I eyed my mother's pearl bracelet on her wrist. "I have come to see what the fuss is about."

Olivia leaned over. "It's not often one gets to see so much money exchanging hands," she said in her charmingly husky voice. "You must watch the expressions on the men's faces. There is one other time they ever look so intense." She smiled slyly.

"I don't see Edwin," Cousin Sultana said with her face screwed in a perplexed expression. Everyone knew that we were rarely apart.

"He doesn't usually come to the auction." Aunt Bellore turned about and looked at me suspiciously. "Will he be here today?"

The words twisted the spike that continued to pierce my heart, but I refused to wince. "I don't know," I said with forced nonchalance. "I was curious to find out what people have been finding amusing. He probably has more important business to attend to in Clive Street."

Three men dressed in gray lounge suits appeared from a side door. The tallest one mounted a small platform and stood in front of a lectern under a brass chandelier. The others carried leather cases. Each went to a table on either side of the lectern and began to remove stacks of documents.

"Who are they?" I asked Olivia brightly.

"The auctioneer is Jack Chappell," she said as the man on the left handed the one in the middle a set of papers. "The other two are the government agents. The one with the black hair is Christopher Haythornthwaite. Isn't that the most adorable name? He's a cousin of the viceroy's wife. The other one, with the blond mustache, is Michael MacGregor, recently out from England and quite green."

To me the three looked like ordinary gentlemen, but in Calcutta's small European world they were intriguing morsels to the Olivias and Natalies, who were bored with their routine friends. The auctioneer pounded a silver gavel, and the ringing sound silenced the room. The women settled their skirts. The few men who still mingled about took their places. Papers shuffled, throats cleared. Six burly Indians carried in three mangowood chests and placed them on benches in front of the room. The lids were opened to reveal two levels of twenty opium balls.

"Lot one hundred and one," the auctioneer began, "comprising twenty-four chests of Malwa opium, grade double-A, processed in Nimach. Thirty thousand to open."

"Why don't they start with number one?"

"Tradition, I suppose," Olivia replied airily.

Although I did not notice a flicker in the crowd, someone must have indicated a bid, for the auctioneer had moved on rapidly. "Thirty-two, thirty-two-five, thirty-four, thirty-four-five, thirty-four-five . . . and forty . . . and fifty and sixty." The gavel fell. "Thirty-four thousand, five hundred and sixty for the lot."

"Who bought it?" I asked, perplexed that I had seen so little take place.

"Probably Jardine, Matheson," Olivia replied. "By custom, they always take the first lot. Not that it matters—they will share it later."

"Is that a good price?" I wondered aloud, even though I knew the fourteen-forty per chest I calculated was considerably better than the thirteen-fifty rupee reserve that we had estimated for the paste of Malwa flowers.

Olivia tossed her honey curls. "Who knows? Who cares? But look, do you see that divine man behind my brother Thomas? He's from our Hong Kong office. If only my husband would consider transferring him here." She giggled.

Where was Edwin? Had he spent last night with his friend Howard Farrell? And if he had, could Olivia know about that already? No, there had not been time. . . .

The auction had droned on while my mind wandered to the whereabouts of my husband. Several more lots were bought, yet they could not have disposed of even a hundred chests. With over nine thousand slated to be sold that day, I realized this could be a tedious business indeed. Thus far hardly a muscle had moved among the merchants scribbling figures on their bid sheets, and I had no idea to whom the lots had gone. If I were going to follow the auction, it would require my full attention. Better concentrate, I admonished myself as I straightened my back and turned away from Olivia's animated whispers.

Uncle Samuel sat on the far left side of the third row with a weary expression frozen on his pinched face. Throughout the room I picked out the other members from Sassoon and Company. In the second row I saw Reuben's son Nathaniel, our company's designated bidder. With a pang I realized he was not privy to our plans, and hoped when everything came to light he would not be furious. Gabriel Judah sat at the end of the third row closest to us. Uncle Reuben and Uncle Ezra were side by side in the fifth row. The next generation was also represented, by Mir, Adam, and Noah, who were scattered randomly around the chamber. None of these people knew what was planned. Representatives from Jardine, Matheson held most of the prestigious front-row seats that were theirs for seniority.

In the center of the front row was an empty chair. "Who sits there?" I asked my cousin curiously.

"That was Uncle Saul's place and our grandfather's before him. I think it is shameful to leave it empty, for everyone thinks we do not have a leader worthy to head the company."

I tested the water. "Perhaps when my father has recovered . . ."

Sultana shrugged and turned to say something to her sister. At least Uncle Samuel had not had the audacity to take it for himself—yet.

I wondered if he was eyeing it covetously at that very moment. But no, his full attention was on the sheet of paper in front of him. His pen ticked the squares as the auctioneer continued his singsong soliloquy, punctuated by gavel drops that gave me no hint of who had won the round.

The sample crates were being carried in and out rapidly. The lots varied in size from twenty-four to sixty chests each. Even so, I calculated that at this rate the auction would take five to six hours to complete. How was I ever going to follow the action? If I asked for papers, I would be suspect. Oh, but I had forgotten the scheme. I was supposed to be suspect! Ever since I had walked into the room and had not seen Edwin, I had been disoriented. It was fortunate the execution of the plan had not been left to me, because I would have muddled it already.

I turned around and signaled for Gulliver.

"Yes, memsahib."

I whispered my request for some sheets of paper like the ones the men had. Gulliver nodded and left the room. A few minutes later he handed me a sealed packet.

"Sold. Lot one hundred fifty-three!" called the auctioneer.

I shuffled the pages until I turned to where we were. Nudging Natalie, Olivia bent over and muttered, "Aren't you the serious one?"

"I will fall asleep if I don't have something to look at," I said with a laugh that sounded forced. Natalie rolled her eyes in a gesture I recalled from my school days, when a friend thought me too studious for my own good.

"Lot one hundred fifty-four." Chappell was at the top of the third of sixteen pages. "Patna, grade double-B, from Ghazipur." A prickling sensation shot up my back. The ryots in that area had always had close ties with the Sassoons. Long ago I had been in Ghazipur with my father. This was Edwin's domain. "Thirty-six chests."

What was the reserve that Abner Raphael had set for lower-grade Patna? Edwin had taken down the figures, but he was nowhere in sight. Less than thirteen hundred, I recalled. I did a quick multiplication: forty-six thousand was the minimum.

"Forty-five . . . forty-six . . . forty-six and five hundred . . . forty-eight . . . fifty . . . fifty-one . . ." Was I imagining the slight catch of excitement in the auctioneer's voice? Was that a high price for double-B? Had Uncle Samuel begun his run?

"Fifty-one and five hundred and fifty!" was finalized by a gavel thump. I scribbled some figures. That was over fourteen hundred rupees per chest—a slight elevation, but not an absurd price. Who had made the purchase? My eyes, which had adjusted to the nuances in the men's frugal movements, had caught a slight wave of the fingers of an agent sitting behind my Uncle Ezra. And Uncle Samuel had shifted slightly in his seat, not turning around but twitching enough that I sensed he had garnered that group of chests. What was Gabriel doing? Making careful notations—after he nodded respectfully to Olivia Davidson, the woman closest to him. I was right! I had to be right! Before I could calm my rushing pulse, another bid was under way.

The next lot of twenty-four higher-graded crates of Patna went for 1,468 rupees. Had the same agent got both lots? I was not certain, but the climate in the room seemed changed. The men were more alert. The choicest grade of Patna was on the block: triple-A. Abner Raphael whispered something to the man one chair to his left, an Indian with a high forehead, who I presumed was either his manager or agent. A raise of this man's dark finger indicated he was opening the next round of bidding. Again the crates were sold to someone sitting behind my Uncle Ezra.

"Seventy-four and four!" I overheard Haythornthwaite say as he filled in his documents.

"Is that a great deal?" I asked Olivia innocently, even though I had already calculated this was over fifteen hundred rupees per chest.

"I suppose so, but the lots were large. Did he say thirty-six or forty-eight chests?" Olivia bent over and asked Sultana.

"I'm not sure," Sultana replied nonchalantly.

My cousin always pretended to be dense when in fact she had a conniving streak that had presented difficulties when we were children. I had a feeling she knew almost as much as I did about what was going on.

"At least your friend from Hong Kong seems pleased," I mumbled to Olivia.

"A pity. If he is cheerful, my husband is bound to be grumpy." She babbled on about something that had happened at a previous auction, when the auctioneer had made a mistake and they had got a parcel under the reserve, while I tried to concentrate on who was bidding for the next lot.

Two more loads seemed to go to agents. The quality was high and the price more than ten percent above the reserves I recalled.

"Who buys the higher-priced opium?" I asked Olivia.

"Usually those who need it for medicinal purposes," she replied officiously. "Surely you know the more expensive grades contain a higher percentage of morphine. Anyway, the independents, who buy particular chests for special customers or the pharmaceutical interests, will be finished shortly and then the merchants will settle up the rest. Everything moves more swiftly once the smaller fish are out of the pond."

"Good," Sultana said, fanning herself, for the September day was turning out to be typically warm and moist. "I don't plan to stay here the whole afternoon."

Was that what was going on? Had the expensive parcels gone to the pharmacists? Had I misread the higher prices as the beginning of Uncle

Samuel's move? My searching glance caught Abner Rapahel's eye. He made an exaggerated nod in my direction. I remembered my presence was supposed to be obvious, and I gave him as expansive a smile as possible. Perhaps the agent who had accrued the recent lots had been working for him (and thus me) all the while. Being on the outskirts was infuriating. If I only knew where matters stood . . .

I tried to concentrate on what was happening. New chests were opened and several men had gone up to the front of the room to handle the sample balls as the bidding continued. Whether it was considered finer than usual, I was not certain, but the price was over sixteen hundred rupees. The murmurs in the room indicated that something exceptional was happening. The next time the gavel fell, most of the men busily made notes on their sheets. I calculated 1,690. Could I have been in error? I looked around. Others were scratching their heads. I hoped that Raphael's comrades were following exactly how much Uncle Samuel was now controlling, for the whole scheme would collapse if he were allowed to purchase too much of the crop, no matter the price. I went back to my sheet and made tiny ticks next to those lots I thought the same questionable agent had purchased and circles next to those about which I was unsure. Jack Chappell carried on with his fluid song of numbers. "Forty thousand, five hundred . . . five-fifty . . . six hundred . . . eight hundred . . . nine hundred, do I hear ten . . . twenty . . . nine hundred and twenty!"

Twenty-four chests divided into 40,920—was 1,705 rupees! My heart beat wildly. Merchants in the front rows near the Jardines mopped their brows. I forced myself to look at Uncle Samuel. He sat straight and unruffled. His confidence churned my stomach. I gripped the railing. The room swam in a hot mist of rage. He couldn't win! He couldn't! A black waistcoat blocked my view of the gallery.

"Now, you listen to me, Dinah . . ." came a stricken voice that I did not recognize immediately.

I gasped as the spike drove deeper into my chest. I lifted my head, fully expecting to see Edwin. A body blow could not have shocked me more. The face that loomed above me was grimacing with fright.

"I told you to stay away from here. How could you defy me like this?"

"Oh, Papa!" I said with alarm. "It is not what you think."

"Isn't it?" he boomed so everyone could hear.

I was on my feet in an instant, and Gulliver maneuvered beside me protectively. I felt as though every eye in the room followed my movements as I made my way down the aisle past Mir Sassoon, the members of the Davidson firm, even Gabriel Judah. Once outside, I blinked in the bright noon light of the courtyard. "Now, Papa, please listen to me."

"How could you do this?" His voice quavered.

"Hush," I said as I pointed to the open windows that led into the chamber, "or you will ruin everything."

"So, you *are* the one! How could you pay more than seventeen hundred rupees for a chest of inferior Patna?"

"I didn't, I promise I didn't."

"Don't lie to me!" he sputtered, his face turning a dusky red. His eyes, which were sunk deeply into his devastated face, protruded with disbelief. Noticing that his hands were trembling, I signaled for Gulliver to take one arm while I supported the other. We forced him to sit on a bench. "What else could you be doing here? Look at you!" he raved. It was almost as though I could hear his feverish brain spinning with confused thoughts. "You are dressed like a hired consort, not like a mother of three young sons. The Luddy money has ruined you! Ruined you! And I thought you were the sensible one!"

"Papa, please, let me explain. Uncle Samuel is making a run on the business."

"Stop patronizing me," he snarled.

"I'm trying to prevent it," I responded evenly.

"You! How could you prevent it?" As Gulliver quickly moved beside me, Papa demanded, "What is he? Your shadow?"

I waved for Gulliver to back off, but he remained in place. "Papa, don't mind Gulliver. He always—"

"Gulliver! Ridiculous name." He began to cough so hard that he spat up phlegm before he could continue. "I am sorry I lost control of myself." He shivered and took a deep breath. "I don't know what comes over me these days." He blotted his lips with his handkerchief. "Now, please tell me—how could Samuel be making the same blunder again?"

As hurriedly as possible, I explained about the embezzled money and our suspicions that his brother-in-law was leveraging what he had stolen to seize this season's opium crop. "What I am doing is helping Abner Raphael and the others prevent this from happening."

"How can you do that?"

"With certain . . . guarantees."

"I don't understand."

I glanced in the direction of the auction room. If I missed much more of the bidding, I would never follow what was happening. "It's complicated. I'll explain more fully when it is realized, but I am not risking the Luddy money. I am keeping my promise."

My father patted my arm. "You are a good girl, Dinah, but I don't know . . ." His voice faded as though he had forgotten what he was going to say. Then his face twisted. "But where is Edwin? I did not see him—"

"He's not here yet."

A thought burned briefly in his eyes, then seemed to drift away. "You should go back inside, you must want to see . . ." He seemed tired, beaten.

"Yes, Papa. Watch the agent who is sitting behind Uncle Ezra and next to Uncle Saul's son Adam. I think he is working for Samuel. Also, there is another behind the Davidsons. And the Indian with a shiny forehead to Abner Raphael's left is probably working for us. The other bidders in the consortium will split the lot, even if they buy at a premium. Already prices have been going over seventeen hundred."

"I know, Dinah. I heard the last two rounds." As he stood awkwardly, Gulliver took his arm.

"Papa, Uncle Samuel needs about seventy-five percent of the crop to make the numbers work. That means he will have to monopolize almost seven thousand chests. I estimate he's cornered a thousand so far, if that. We can ruin him if we stick him with two thousand and don't let him take any more."

"Who says?"

"Abner Raphael agreed with me."

"Raphael is helping you?"

"Yes, Papa."

My father blew his nose loudly as we entered the room together. He took a seat in the last row next to his nephew Mir. I slid next to Olivia.

"Good to see your father well enough to be here today," she murmured. "I heard he was ill."

"He didn't want to miss another auction."

"I am surprised Zilpah permitted it," Sultana said disapprovingly.

"He had to sneak away. And was he ever surprised to see me here!" I said to minimize the effects of his harsh words in front of the other ladies. "Why, he thinks that only men should attend these functions. I tried to explain the modern notions, but he wasn't convinced," I said with a playful shake of my head. "We are both naughty today. Like father, like daughter, I suppose." I grinned at Sultana. My cousin shot a wary glance to her mother, who had followed every word.

Jack Chappell droned on in the background. "Where are my papers?" I asked.

Aunt Bellore handed them back to me. "Here they are. I kept them in case you came back."

"Thank you," I said, furious that she might have attempted to follow my notations. At least I had used ticks and circles, not names or initials. Anyway, even if she suspected the worst, she would not have been able to communicate anything to her husband or their agents before the luncheon break. And even if she decided I was trying to buy lots for myself and told her husband later, it would help push him over the edge. I hoped that my running total of what I suspected he now owned would have been taken for unintelligible figurings. I bent toward Olivia. "Do the prices continue to run high?"

"Yes, they were up to eighteen hundred rupees for a time, but now are running closer to seventeen hundred. A most amusing morning. The men are quaking. Old man Jardine was forced to buy at over seventeen-fifty. He almost had apoplexy on the spot."

If Jardine had bought at seventeen-fifty, that meant that twenty percent of that batch was mine. "Which lot was that?"

"I don't know." She waved her hand as if it were of no consequence.

"Lot two hundred fifty-four," Sultana replied stiffly. "Why?"

"Everything is so much more fascinating if you follow the flow," I answered smartly.

"Sixty-six thousand and three hundred, and four hundred, and five . . . and six hundred . . ." the auctioneer called out with a tinge of excitement obvious in his tone. I could see Abner Raphael's white beard moving up and down as he mouthed the numbers. ". . . Eight hundred, nine hundred . . . nine-fifty . . . nine-sixty . . . sold!"

The room buzzed with the result. A new high. The Raphaels had it. Pens flew. If Raphael had the lot, that meant I did as well. Instead of calculating that I now owed more than thirteen thousand rupees, I saw the chests as they were taken away and realized that seven were now mine. Where was Uncle Samuel? In the commotion he had left the room. What a wonderful sign! With Jardine, Matheson willing to outbid him and the Raphael Company entering the fray, he had to be feeling the pressure. We had been right. He thought that everybody else would back away at the inflated prices—and well they might have if it hadn't been for my guarantees. If only I knew how many chests he had committed to already. He probably could recover from a thousand, considering that he had bought some earlier close to reserves. Now it was crucial for the others to back off long enough for him to regain his confidence and bid for the second thousand that would plunge him into ruinous debt. Then the merchants could jump in to pay whatever necessary to wrest control away from him.

Mesmerized, I watched while these esteemed men of commerce wiggled a callused finger or blinked a cloudy eye or lifted a proud chin in an elegant ballet of money and power. Jack Chappell was the maestro: strutting, bowing, nodding, gesticulating, frowning, prodding as if he were conducting a symphony. On either side, the British agents, Mr. MacGregor and Mr. Haythornthwaite, were the nervous musicians anxious that every note be modulated to perfection. The merchants—their dancers—fluttered through their paces as the crescendos at the end of each bid were reached. As an audience, we ladies might not have had a deep appreciation for the music, but we knew enough to realize we were witnessing a singular performance.

There was a lull in the action. The auctioneer mentioned the next chests were in batches of forty-eight, and after that set he would adjourn for the noon meal. Murmurs of approval met the announcement. Most of the prices hovered close to the seventeen-hundred mark, some dipped below sixteen hundred. I guessed that Uncle Samuel was drawing ever closer to the two-thousand-chest figure, and I didn't want him to get there cheaply. On the other hand, the less he had to pay, the less my twenty percent would cost me later in the day. This latest predicament consumed my consciousness until a movement directly behind Gabriel Judah caught my attention.

Someone was taking that vacant seat. Could it be . . . ? Yes! My chest swelled with excitement. Edwin had arrived. For the first time that day the stabbing sensation subsided. Edwin wore a gray single-breasted morning coat fastened in front with two pearl buttons. This was not anything I recognized from his wardrobe. His striped trousers became closer-fitting at the bottom, in the latest fashion. He must have spent the morning being outfitted at Ranken's. But why? Why the narrow stiff collar, the silk top hat, the blue-and-silver-striped tie?

"Your husband looks splendid," Olivia Davidson fawned.

"Yes, he does," I concurred boldly.

"I wish mine would dress as well, but he favors comfort over style, especially in this heat," she muttered on, but my attention was not directed at her.

Edwin's seat on the far right of the room was quite near mine. I tried to catch his eye, but he stared at the auctioneer. Was he not about to quell our dispute? Then why was he here? I wondered in a flush of fury.

"Seventy thousand . . . seventy-five . . ." The pace slackened considerably. There were longer and longer spaces between bids. Mr. Chappell had to call smaller increments in between. "Seventy-five and six hundred . . . and seven hundred . . . and eight, do I hear eight? . . ."

Olivia yawned.

Aunt Bellore squirmed.

My eyes were riveted on Edwin, who sat as stiffly as a man about to be photographed for a portrait. There was a movement. His head turned slightly, but not far enough to see me. He was making a movement in my direction. He did want a reconciliation! Just in case, I pasted a slight smile on my lips. I wanted him to know I was not holding a grudge. I was certain the opium pipe had been a momentary lapse. It could be explained. This would pass. If only we could get through the next tense hours.

Edwin raised his arm and brushed back his hair.

". . . Eighty thousand, one hundred and sixty!" The gavel came down at the same moment as Edwin's hand. Mr. Haythornthwaite gestured toward Edwin. Mr. MacGregor marked something on his pad.

Gabriel Judah swiveled around to stare at Edwin.

No, it had been a mistake! Edwin had been straightening his hair, not bidding! Edwin nodded to Gabriel. He did not think he had made a mistake. He was not trying to get out of the sale!

The world of the auction room tilted. What was going on? Had Edwin gone crazy? He was not supposed to bid! There were a few more lots, and then the room began to empty. Stunned, I could not move. Where was my father? What would he think? And Abner Raphael and the others? Not to mention Samuel. Was Edwin going to ruin everything now? How could he do this? How and why?

ᾧ   ᾧ   ᾧ

Outside, I gasped for air. From the corner of my eye I could see the comforting whiteness of Gulliver's waistcoat. The other figures swirled past in a blur. Nobody approached me. Olivia and Natalie brushed by on their way to their carriages. Aunt Bellore and Sultana had left from the opposite exit.

"Dinah!" came my father's raspy voice. "I thought you said—"

"I . . . I don't know what happened. There must have been a change in strategy . . ." I glanced around furtively for Edwin. Surely he would explain.

"Why did Edwin leave without you?"

"He did?"

"Yes, I couldn't catch up to him. I thought you were together until I saw you waiting here. Come with me. I demand a better explanation of these events."

Docilely I followed my father. Where was Edwin headed? Tears flooded my eyes as I strained to make sense of what was happening. In the silent minutes of our journey, I wondered where Uncle Samuel was going and with whom he would be conferring. What could he have thought of Edwin's brash maneuver? He had to have some suspicions that we were trying to buy lots of our own. Since nobody had yet been aggressive enough to outbid him for many chests, he could not have taken the threat seriously. If he backed off now, he could handle his losses, which would ruin our plan.

Once we were at Theatre Road, Zilpah made my father sit in the small parlor and sip his medicines. Only when the glass was drained did she chide him for not following doctor's orders. After that was accomplished, she stared at my outfit. "Dinah, where have you been, dressed like that?"

"At the auction," I replied, feeling as ashamed as a child who has done something wrong but does not know quite what.

"What happened there? You are pale, and your father looks on the verge of a relapse."

"Nonsense," he said in a domineering voice that silenced his wife. He continued with an explanation of the morning's events.

"Where is Edwin?" Zilpah asked reprovingly.

"I do not know," I said, hoping we could move on to the details of Uncle Samuel's machinations.

Zilpah would not let the matter drop. She pursed her lips and fixed me with a maternal glare. "There is something else going on here . . ."

"We had a small quarrel last night."

Zilpah sucked in her bright red lips. "How unlike you two." Suddenly she turned sympathetic. "Most couples have tiffs. Don't let it worry you."

"I know that, but this is the first time for us."

"You must have been under a considerable anxiety since your discovery of the altered records. Such a burden to accept on your own! You should have come to us—or at least to me," she admonished gently. "And then to have the Luddy matter on top of that . . ."

"Unfortunately, money brings out the worst in most people," my father added, thinking our dispute had something to do with my inheritance.

"Not money exactly," I said, then wished I had left his guess stand.

"Why the hell is he bidding?" Papa shouted.

"Benu, calm yourself," Zilpah hissed. She pressed the back of her bronzed hand to his milky-white forehead. I noticed a relieved sigh at no sign of fever. "You had both better have something to eat before returning to the auction." She led us to the table on the terrace. The day was fair, the afternoon breeze a promise of the end of the hot-and-wet season, the roses fragrant in the moist air. The silver utensils glistened, the linen was white and crisp, the bowls of curry and rice steamed their spicy promise. For a second I wished I could sit there forever and blot out the nasty arena of commerce and duty. I reached for a slice of bread and tried to ease the unrelenting stabbing with food, but my churning stomach would not permit me to accept more than a few bites. I sipped tea and managed a handful of almonds while Zilpah and Benu heatedly discussed the predicament.

When my father checked his pocket watch, Zilpah swooped up like a butterfly flying into the wind. "I am coming with you."

My seat in the ladies' section had been taken by one of Natalie's sisters who had not been there in the morning. Sultana had moved beside her mother in the front. Zilpah and I were content to take over the last row. Gulliver stood protectively behind my chair. Edwin's place remained empty until a few minutes after the auctioneer and the agents entered from the side room.

I hurriedly looked at the sheets of paper. Most of the subsequent lots were in groups of forty-eight or sixty. Matters would move more swiftly now. There were only six pages of figures remaining, each line representing considerably more than a mere printed number and description.

"We resume with lot two hundred eighty-one," Mr. Chappell said, his rested voice as bright as a brass bell. "Sixty chests, grade-A Patna, processed at Monghyr. Do I hear a hundred thousand?"

A communal gasp rumbled through the room. A hundred thousand? What audacity to open at almost seventeen hundred per chest! And he was staring at Edwin! Edwin nodded his chin. Mr. Haythornthwaite could not master his grimace of satisfaction. The competing bids flew in fast and furious.

"One hundred and seven thousand, four hundred." The gavel fell. An anonymous agent at the back of the room purchased the lot. Uncle Samuel, I suspected, had taken it for 1,790. At least Edwin hadn't managed to succeed again.

Edwin also started the next few lots, which were closed by a broker at around the eighteen-hundred level. Was Edwin merely compelling my uncle into higher and higher ranges? Had Samuel's hostility toward my husband forced his hand sooner than he had expected? If so, I suspected Edwin would tone down his efforts for a while. And indeed quite soon my husband refrained from beginning any bids and merely nodded halfheartedly in the center of the action, quieting long before the gavel fell closer and closer to the nineteen-hundred mark.

Energy flowed through the room as the lots in the three-hundred numbers came up. Some of the choicest grades from Dinapur were on the block. I watched as Jardine paid 1,925 for a double-A and the Gubbay firm bested him for a similarly ranked Benares at 1,932.

"A new record," murmured the crowd.

Uncle Samuel was perspiring openly. True, the room had become stuffier in the late afternoon, but the punkahs were flapping and few of the ladies were as perturbed. Obviously the prices at these unimaginable levels distressed him. And if he was going to wrest control of the market, it was at this high range where he would have to make his play to buy everything in sight.

Edwin bid again. Why would he go after an inferior Gorakhpur that had opened at a measly fifteen hundred? Instead of letting others pick up the pace, Edwin stayed in the fray. I was aghast when I realized my husband had purchased his second batch for seventy-seven thousand rupees—over sixteen hundred per chest! Not a huge amount, considering the numbers we had been hearing, but a great deal more than the reserve. What in the world was he doing now? My palms began to perspire. I felt dizzy, for after Edwin's purchases the prices went soaring. While Raphael, Gubbay, and the Meyer brothers bid aggressively, they ended up deferring each overpriced lot to anonymous agents. I circled a figure on my page, 2,700, and whispered to Zilpah, "That's how many I think Samuel has taken. Although he's been conservative and the average price is under fifteen hundred, he must have spent more than forty lacs by now. That is way over what he can afford—almost double our estimate of his capital."

"Probably he was waiting for the price to fall before taking everything. Now he has no choice," Zilpah added knowingly. "Won't he need most of the balance to take control?"

I looked up. The gavel had fallen. I was relieved that Jardine, Matheson had taken the lot. "Yes, he will."

Davidson had the next two. Jardine stole a few in the fifteen hundreds because of the auctioneer's seeming to ignore the agent behind Uncle Ezra. Gabriel Judah was on his feet about to register a protest when Edwin reached forward and pushed him down. Gabriel spun around and shot him a malignant glance. The whole room noticed the altercation, but the auctioneer did not miss a beat. For a while the prices soared to panicky heights near the two-thousand-rupee mark. Haythornthwaite did a merry jig as the numbers peaked. A pity the crown will profit handsomely from my uncle's evils, I thought sourly.

There was no evidence that anyone other than our tight circle of conspiring merchants had paid inflationary prices. We had scared Uncle Samuel off! Gabriel trembled openly. Sultana dabbed her eyes, pretending she had a difficulty with a lash to hide her anguish. Aunt Bellore's shoulders sagged.

"Lot four hundred twelve."

The numbers were getting higher and higher.

We were on the next-to-last page. "Lot four hundred twenty-five."

My uncle could never recover now!

"Seventy thousand . . ." There were no longer any bidders willing to open at over sixteen hundred per chest. Nonplussed, Mr. Chappell backed off to sixty thousand. Silence. Aware the room had cooled significantly, but ignorant of the forces at play, the confused auctioneer fell to forty thousand and finally sold the lot for the paltry—if more ordinary—figure of 1,345 rupees per chest.

As if propelled by something painful on his seat, Uncle Samuel stood up. His arms jerked wildly before he sank back into his chair clutching his chest. Abner Raphael turned around and directed the man next to my uncle to unbutton his jacket. The agent who had won many earlier rounds—probably for Samuel—passed up a flask. Samuel pushed his helpers away. Stumbling up the aisle, he scattered curses. Weeping openly, Aunt Bellore followed him out.

Somehow the others managed to conclude the sale. Over nine thousand chests had passed from the hands of the crown to those of the merchants. Zilpah took my hand, and together we walked onto the trading floor. In the aftermath, men gathered around in tight circles, comparing versions of what had occurred, those not in the know gleaning what they could.

Abner Raphael greeted my father with a luminous smile. "Benu! I did not expect to see you here. I thought this was to be a secret from you."

"It was, but I had a premonition."

"Now that you know, you won't be too hard on them, will you?" He lifted his furry eyebrows, which seemed crested with frost.

"I don't think I know the half of it yet, Abner, but it seems to me you made out rather well."

"Indeed I have."

Winston Davidson patted my father on the back. "Wasn't that amusing, Mr. Sassoon?" He chuckled. "I am pleased you were able to see what evolved, for no words would have done it justice, eh?"

"I suppose it is easier to enjoy oneself when the risks have been assumed by another party." My father gave a sardonic laugh.

"I doubt there will be any regrets in the house of Sassoon, my dear friend," added the plumper of the Meyer brothers. "Your daughter is a treasure. How many men, let alone sons, would have taken that chance to save the family firm?"

"She's a wonderful girl," my father agreed. "I always said she had the flowers in her blood."

"And gold in her pocket," Abner Raphael interjected. "Do you have any idea of what her position is now?"

My father scratched his head, for I had not explained the details of my twenty-percent guarantee. As Raphael filled him in, a realization began to dawn. My percentage gave me ownership of about twelve hundred chests, plus the several hundred Edwin had bought for some crazed reason of his own. After lot splitting on the usual basis, the Sassoon company would control at least another two thousand. And then there were the approximately twenty-five hundred that Samuel was stuck with at prices too high to market on his own. If I could make a deal to get Samuel's lots and combine them with mine *and* those of the Sassoons, I would monopolize the essential seventy-five percent to rule the marketplace!

My thoughts were diverted by the sound of Edwin's voice. "That is very kind of you." He was talking to Awad Meyer, beaming under the man's lavish compliments. "No, I wasn't planning on bidding. I wasn't even planning to come . . ."

Raphael tugged at Edwin's sleeve. "Then why did you bid, my boy?" he said without rancor.

I held my breath for my husband's explanation.

"I knew you wanted Dinah there as bait for her uncle, but I was afraid I could not hide my emotions, so I forced myself to stay away. Throughout the morning I thought I would go mad wondering what was happening. Then, as I humored myself at Ranken's"—he touched his showy lapel with a chagrined smirk—"I realized I did not want to miss the moment a man who stole from his own family was put in his place. That sort of creature deserves no pity. Nor even the slightest chance to wheedle out of the mess! I thought: If only the bastard could be coerced to bid beyond any limits he had set for himself, he would disintegrate that much sooner. After that I wondered what would make him bid the highest. Suddenly I realized that the reason he had always treated me abominably was that he was *afraid* of me. If he saw me openly making a move on behalf of Dinah, he could not tolerate it."

"I suppose my plan for Dinah to be there might have been too soft," Raphael interjected gracefully. "Ladies have been coming for many months now, so there was no novelty."

"Right," Edwin agreed. "Samuel could have dismissed her as another gawker, but he could not dismiss a direct bid from me." He gave Raphael an embarrassed shrug. "I know I was a bad boy. Honestly, I could not find a fault in my plan, especially if I arrived late in the morning, after the attack was under way."

Raphael smiled like a teacher recognizing a worthy pupil. "Splendid idea. I should have thought of it myself."

"And it worked!" Awad Meyer pounded Edwin on the back. "I thought I was going to see the Benares top grade go for over two thousand. Historic highs! Did you notice Haythornthwaite? He turned every color of the rainbow." He laughed heartily.

"The boy should put in for a bonus," Jardine added with a wink to me.

Did I believe Edwin's tale? I mulled over his reasoning and decided the act had been more impulsive, less calculated, than Edwin had admitted. Fortunately, the result had been successful.

The circles broke up as everyone congratulated one another. My father moved into a corner along with Uncle Reuben and Uncle Ezra, and several of the next generation, including Mir and Nathaniel, stood on the outskirts listening. In the front of the chamber, Edwin signed some documents for Mr. MacGregor. Zilpah and I waited to see where we would be going next. To avoid a public confrontation with my husband, I kept away from him, studiously watching the faces of my uncles as they absorbed the scope of the Lanyados' crimes. Then, one by one, they turned to stare at me.

My face burned as if a hot light had been focused on me. A queer sensation, like a tug from a source far removed from my volition, propelled me toward my father. I felt myself resisting this unbidden urge. If I hesitated, I would be cementing my place as a dutiful daughter. If I moved forward, I staked my claim. Rigid with indecision, I swerved my neck slightly to catch Edwin's whereabouts. From the other end of the room his eyes were on me, but he did not move in my direction.

He should be at my side! We should be approaching them together. I did not want to make another mistake. Should I go to my husband and bring him along with me? No, that would be patronizing. Shouldn't he take my arm and insist I cross the chasm, or did he think this was something I had to do on my own? Maybe he was so furious he chose not to join me in this moment of triumph. The crucial seconds ticked by with the pounding of my heart.

As I straightened my shoulders, the high officer collar on my gown pinched my neck. With an enormous effort I steadied my head so the ostrich feathers would not tremble. Then I crossed the emptying auction room. The plum satin trim on my gown shone like a puddle of wine under the gleaming lights of the chandelier.

My uncles and cousins stood in respectful silence. Even my father did not speak at first. "We should adjourn to Kyd Street," I said in the slow, clipped way in which I gave instructions when I was nervous.

"Before supper?" Uncle Reuben asked with polite surprise, but there was no challenge to his tone.

"We cannot rest until a few loose ends are tied," I replied more steadily.

"Yes, of course you are right," Uncle Ezra said, deferring to me.

After a hurried discussion of who would travel with whom, I climbed into an office jaun with my father and Gulliver, while Zilpah had commandeered Edwin, promising to meet us there.

My father lay back and unbuttoned his collar. His breathing was strident, his flesh moist. We did not speak for we both knew he needed to rest.

When we approached the house where he had been born, I broke the silence. "Are you certain you are up to this, Papa? It could wait until tomorrow . . ."

"No, you were right, we must resolve it now."

"One more question, Papa. May I assume Jonah will inherit Theatre Road?"

My father nodded sadly. "By rights the property goes to Jonah."

"Certainly it does. Don't apologize. I needed to know for certain," I said, curious as to why I was baffled by this natural course of events. For some reason I had imagined myself living there again. Perhaps many people dream of inhabiting their childhood homes as adults in charge instead of as dependents, I decided as I put the whim aside.

Gulliver assisted my father down, buttoned his shirt, and dusted his jacket. My father stumbled on the steps, but the Gurkha caught him and took his arm. I plunged ahead toward the one uninviting lamp that burned by the door. And as I crossed the threshold into the gloomy colonnaded hall, I knew I had crossed over into a new phase of my life.

47

✿ ✿ ✿

randy and soda, Bombay gin and tonic, bottles of imported
Scotch as dear as liquid gold, decanters of sherry and port,
bottles of lemonade, and crystal glasses were reflected in the
mirrored sideboard in the Lanyados' dining room. Bowls of
fruit, vases of flowers, and silver platters of pastries and savories had
been readied. But not for us. A very different set of guests for a very
different celebration had been expected.

For half an hour we had milled about in the entrance hall waiting for
everyone to reconvene. The bearer's entreaties that we take seats in the
parlor had been ignored. Nobody turned down the offer of cocktails,
though, and soon most of my relatives were fortifying themselves.
When everyone had been accounted for, I marched them into the
dining room because the long formal table—center of so many Passover seders and Sabbath suppers and family transitions—seemed the
place to congregate.

The news had gone out rapidly. Almost everyone was there: my
father and Zilpah, Jonah and Asher from my family; Uncle's Saul's son
Adam; Uncle Reuben and his sons Noah and Nathaniel; Uncle Ezra
and his son, Sayeed; Jacob's Mir and Yedid. Aunt Bellore and Uncle
Samuel, of course. Curiously absent were Gabriel Judah, his wife,
Sultana, and Lulu Lanyado. Edwin and I milled about on the fringes
while the family was seated amid coughing and sputtering and the
creaking of chairs. Suddenly the room fell silent. There were two seats
left: one in the center of the table near the festive sideboard, the other
at the head of the table.

With an expansive gesture to the far end, Edwin said, "Come sit
here, Dinah."

The expectant faces of my family clouded like those at the end of a
dream. Edwin had stepped past me to the high carved chair that had
once belonged to the patriarch of our family: Moses Sassoon. I held my

breath tightly in check, trying not to cry. The click of my heels echoed in the room. With a flourish and a bow, Edwin pulled out the chair. Did everyone realize he was playacting? I looked up. No one was smiling. There was not a single expression of scorn or displeasure. At the far end, Aunt Bellore's face was a blank page ready to be written on by my words. Her husband seemed dazed, as though he did not know what was going on. Was he ill? Had he really suffered an attack in the auction hall? No, I realized he was drunk.

My father half-stood on wobbly legs. Leaning on the table, he began, "My daughter Dinah has agreed to explain the extraordinary events of the day." He was interrupted by a spate of coughing. With some difficulty he cleared his throat. "Then, as a family, I believe we have some very serious decisions to undertake." Zilpah pushed him back in his seat.

With a nod to Edwin, who had seen that I had this place at the head of the table, I returned the favor. "My husband," I began, infusing the word "husband" with a halo of respect, "is the one you must thank. Without his alertness, the fact that someone was robbing our company might have gone undiscovered. Since the older records are in storage, we do not know the full extent of the loss, but as a preface to what we must do next, Edwin will explain the details of the altered accounts."

Everyone turned his attention to Edwin, who had come prepared with a list of our discoveries. In a businesslike manner he began to explain the trail of missing money and how the deed had been accomplished. Only Aunt Bellore, the woman whom throughout my life I had most feared, seemed distracted. She could not stop gawking at me.

For a few seconds I squirmed under her gaze like a child. Then, as a terrible monsoon sky clarifies after a downpour, my mind sharpened. And possibly for the first time I saw myself from a long way off, as a newcomer might. It was as if there had always been two of me: twin sisters—one dark and difficult, one light and intelligent. I realized that many of my negative self-images had stemmed from Bellore's disapproval. She had disdained my height because it demonstrated a superiority her daughters did not have, so throughout my life I had seen my tallness as ungainly. My position at Theatre Road—the house Bellore had always coveted—the love of my father, Grandmother Flora, Grandmother Helene, and others had also upset her. Even my horrifying discovery of my mother's body had singled me out as special. Though I was bereft, lonely, lost in the world of ideas and books, my aunt had seen me as aloof and arrogant. Though I did not comprehend how she could have envied my childhood or my sad marriage to Silas, the fact was that—despite her wishes to the contrary—neither had harmed me permanently. Then my alliance with Edwin had brought a palpable joy we had flaunted, once again inciting her ire. And certainly our three sons could spawn covetousness in a woman who had no living grand-children yet.

Relentlessly Edwin read off the figures. ". . . At least ten lacs were missing from the shipping ledgers, and then we turned to the disbursements to foreign agents," he continued steadily.

Proudly I watched his angular jaw, his somber eyes, his magnificent brow. From Bellore's perspective I had it all: the ideal family, the inherited wealth, the newfound maturity, the power earned by triumph over transgression. In her tormented eyes she was not condemning me, but admiring me—if grudgingly.

There I sat, tall and proud, from my purple satin slippers to the luxurious ostrich feathers on my hat, at the head of one of the most important families in Calcutta, if not India. Two days earlier my pride would have been overweening, but ever since I had discovered Edwin's nasty secret, I conceded that the reality of our perfect life was a gossamer curtain that could be dissolved by the pull of a silken cord. If only Aunt Bellore knew . . . But she won't, I vowed. My penetrating stare made the woman at the other end of the table cringe. So this was the moment I had waited for all these years. I wondered if retribution would taste as sweet as I hoped it would. Perhaps it was wrong, perhaps it showed a flaw in my character, but I could not wait for my time to speak, my turn to grind that husk of a human being into dust!

Edwin had finished. Everyone turned to me. They seemed a long way off, as though I had suddenly sighted them from the wrong end of the telescope. For some unexplained reason I reached up, removed my hat, and handed it to Gulliver. The tableau righted itself. My family was in perfect focus. And then I stood up.

❦ ❦ ❦

"My husband has estimated that Sassoon and Company is short by at least twenty-six lacs—this year. Would you agree with that figure, Uncle Samuel?"

My uncle purpled under the scrutiny. "Well, I—"

His brother-in-law Ezra pounded the table. "Come now, you bloody *pukka badmash*," he cursed in two languages, "you might as well make this easier on yourself—and us."

"Your figures are not out of line," he whispered hoarsely.

"And, from what we can deduce, today you spent about forty-five lacs in your futile attempt."

Samuel covered his face with his hands and wept.

"Save your tears for the Bengali moneylenders." I sat down and waited for him to look up. "How do you expect to cover the debt?" I asked sweetly. I leaned back in my chair. "At your *salary* it could take a hundred years. From this moment you are ruined. Isn't that correct, Uncle?"

His pitiful nod gave me no satisfaction.

"Then let us examine if there is any way to protect the family name despite this disgrace." I glanced down the row of my relations. Their eyes were with me! I plunged on, "You have many debts to settle— with the Bengalis, with your brothers-in-law—but first, let us begin with those to me."

I pointed to Aunt Bellore. "Please hold up your hand. No, not your left, your right. Yes. Now turn it and show everyone the ring on the middle finger. Does anyone recognize that ring? Does anyone recall that my Grandmother Flora's mother once wore it? And Flora gave it to Luna, her daughter—my mother. Does anyone remember Luna?" Several pairs of eyes looked away. "Aunt Bellore, do you think you could remove the ring and pass it along to me? Yes, I see that it is tight. It came from my mother's side of the family, not the Sassoons. It was never meant for your finger, was it?" My voice burst from the control I had been straining to maintain. "Was it?"

Aunt Bellore trembled so excitedly she could not remove the ring. I waited patiently while she dipped it into a glass of sherry to lubricate it. At last the ring was passed to me. I held it up. The large stone glowed with a tinge of pink among a circlet of smaller matched pearls. "This pearl was handed down in the Cohen family from my Great-Great-Grandfather Shalom, who was court jeweler to princes and maharajahs, including Ranjit Singh in the Punjab. One day the maharajah asked Shalom to appraise his most prized possession, the Koh-i-noor diamond. 'It is worthless,' Shalom declared. As you might imagine, this enraged the ruler. Then my ancestor explained, 'The jewel can be secured only as a gift or by the shedding of blood, not by an exchange of currency.' This reply won the maharajah's favor."

A murmur of approval went around the table, but Aunt Bellore's mouth was set in a grim line. "Did my mother give you this ring?" Bellore shook her head. "Did my mother leave you her pearls or any of her possessions by written or oral agreement?" Bellore shook her head again.

"She w-was k-keeping them for you," Samuel stuttered.

My brother Jonah laughed. "That's preposterous."

"How many other pieces are there?" Nobody answered. "I remember the necklaces with pearls as big as marbles, the double-strand bracelet that Sultana has, two or three smaller rings, a gold tiger brooch with emeralds for its eyes, and more. . . . Am I right?"

"I don't recall," Bellore replied in a surly manner. I wanted to lash out at her, to scream, but held myself in check.

"What does this have to do with the problem at hand?" Cousin

Noah asked foolishly. Must remember to use him in the business sparingly, I thought, making a mental note.

"Please allow me a personal indulgence. My family's jewels may not be the Koh-i-noor, but they are priceless to me. Since I did not receive them as a gift and since I am not violent by nature, I must demand their return. In any case, I am as entitled to recover my mother's stolen possessions as the company is to recover its losses, especially since it was my personal guarantee to cover the overbids that saved the situation." Perhaps I sounded overbearing, but I did not care. The respect that registered on the faces of those who did not yet know that fact was immensely satisfying.

"I'll be brief with the private portion of this business." I rose to my feet again. "Aunt Bellore, I want everything that belongs to me returned at once. That includes the jewels you own and the ones you gave to your daughters."

"That's impossible," Bellore moaned. "Abigail is in France—"

"France is not the far side of the moon. Tomorrow you will deliver the jewels that are in Calcutta, plus a note listing missing items and swearing to their timely return."

Bellore bowed her head in defeat, but that was not enough. "Do you agree?"

"Yes, I do," she muttered.

"Good. That makes the next part simpler. Now, Uncle Samuel, we have estimated that today you have purchased something in the area of twenty-five to twenty-seven hundred chests. Is that correct?"

"I am not certain."

"Refer to the receipt in your breast pocket if you must," Edwin said contemptuously.

With a stare of astonishment at Edwin's audacity, my uncle fumbled for the document. "There were two thousand, six hundred and forty."

My own guess had been only sixty off. My spine tingled. How right I had been from the first! Ever since my promise to go along with my intuition, everything had fallen into place. Well, almost everything, I reminded myself so I would not explode with arrogance.

Edwin, pen in hand, boldly scribbled a series of calculations on the linen cloth. "We will purchase your chests for seven hundred rupees each."

"What? You are a thief!"

"No," Edwin reminded him gently. "You are."

"But I paid more than *seventeen* hundred for many of them," Samuel sputtered.

"With stolen Sassoon money and usurious credit."

It was as if Samuel hadn't heard Edwin. "You spurred the price to record highs, you—"

Now most everyone was laughing. The man was unhinged.

I rapped the table and the room silenced. "The seven hundred rupees should almost pay off your debt to the Bengalis, since that will bring in one million, eight hundred and forty-eight thousand rupees, and I presume you owe them one million, eight hundred and eighty-eight thousand—or less, since you bought some earlier lots close to the reserve."

Uncle Samuel tried to blurt something, but choked on his words. Edwin's rising voice stifled his feeble sputters. "You will complete the payments for the lots by using your stolen capital. Then, when the Sassoons resell the opium in China, we will retrieve our losses."

I turned from my distraught uncle, and with a wave of my hand I captured everyone's attention. "Here is the situation: if we take Samuel's twenty-six hundred and forty chests, combine them with the three hundred that Edwin managed to obtain for the sake of baiting Samuel, and add them to the Sassoon percentage, we control almost five thousand, or more than half of the current crop. However, because I covered the overages in the auction, I may either take the profits from, or take possession of, twenty percent of the lots in the splitting group. If Sassoon and Company agrees to go in with me—on my terms—my twenty percent, or twelve hundred chests, brings us to six thousand, one hundred and forty, enough to establish control of the marketplace."

"Easily," Uncle Reuben said with confidence. "The auction was extremely fragmented because people were unsure of what was happening. And certainly the consortium will go along with our pricing."

"That means we can set the prices in Hong Kong and thus we will lose nothing," I said, beaming at Uncle Reuben, then at my father. "In fact, what I propose is not to raise the rates by the twenty-percent premium we had to pay, but by, say, fifteen percent across the board. Then, working with the others, we could maintain that price for a long while. With the next auction bound to be more predictable, the increased profits could average out to be substantial over a few years." I was about to suggest that some of the profits might be moved into other industries when Uncle Reuben cleared his throat. I acknowledged him.

"Hong Kong may not agree entirely," he warned.

"I could assist in that arena," my father promised.

My brothers clapped their hands and Edwin joined in. I could not help grinning as the others expressed their elation at the scheme. There would be plenty of time to discuss my other ideas.

"Where does that leave us?" Aunt Bellore asked weakly after the commotion subsided. "We will have nothing."

"I am certain you have put something away for a rainy day," my father said to his sister.

"This house costs a fortune to run. I have an unmarried daughter and . . ." She threw up her hands. "What could I do? A woman must follow her husband."

"Bellore!" Samuel bellowed. "Don't start blaming me! If it wasn't for your endless demands . . . your declaration that what we did wasn't wrong, since you had never received the same share as your brothers and—"

Bellore stood and tried to leave the room, but Zilpah was swift on her feet and blocked the way.

"Yes, I can see your expenses have been a burden," I said over the din. "I know the strain you have been under. We have had to stretch my own husband's salary to support the much smaller household in Free School Street. I will be happy to pay you a fair market price for Kyd Street. That would give you a nice account to settle your other affairs in Calcutta."

"Where would they live?" Zilpah asked facetiously.

"In France. I am certain Abigail would be honored to have her family nearby."

"You can't make us leave the country!" Uncle Samuel shouted stubbornly.

"What about my other children?" Bellore gasped.

"By the way, where are Sultana and Gabriel and Lulu?" Edwin asked. "Their absence condemns them. I expect they should follow you to hell or wherever you will be going." Bellore struggled under Zilpah's grasp. Zilpah steered her back to her seat and passed her a brandy. She gulped it like a thirsty peasant. When she finished, the silence was as welcome as the calm after a squall.

Uncle Reuben stood up. "We have had enough for one day. Also, it is fair to admit the guilt for this debacle must be shared by those who put too much trust in the wrong man and who did not have the sense to check the records more thoroughly. Each of us who works in the firm can probably recall items that did not seem quite right, but in our indolence we did not analyze the situation thoroughly. Ever since Saul passed on, we may have been too content to take our portion and too lax on many matters. I am not trying to minimize the shocking behavior of a member of our family. All I am saying is that unfortunate circumstances made a tempting situation for a weak and greedy person." Pouring from the decanter, he gave me a charming smile, then turned to my father. "My dear brother, we must thank you for giving us Dinah and bringing Edwin into the family." He raised his glass. "To Dinah and Edwin, who have earned everything they have and who deserve more than they will receive."

One by one the Sassoons joined in the toast. I tried to acknowledge each with a nod. When Edwin avoided my smile, I locked my eyes on my father's, which were swimming with tears of pride. He coughed. The glass wobbled in his hand. He managed a respectful sip before he had to set it down. He coughed again. This time his cheeks puffed and his watering eyes streaked his face. His chest contracted and his head snapped back. Zilpah and I both leapt in his direction as his mouth opened. Blood flowed out and coated his chin like a red beard.

\\/   \\/   \\/

It was long past midnight before we were able to get back to Free School Street. The doctor had not been alarmed by my father's attack. "These things happen from time to time because the parasites lodged in his lungs cause hemorrhages. However, he must have complete quiet or more unpleasantness may result," he chided Zilpah.

I felt responsible, but Zilpah reassured me. "He would not have missed today for anything in the world. Even if he has a setback, we are in your debt."

Edwin had supported me while I wept. "Take her home," Zilpah insisted, "or she will have her own collapse."

Edwin and I were too exhausted to do more than crawl into the carriage that Gulliver had standing by. There was no discussion of the previous night, which seemed eons ago, nor any review of the stunning events of the day. Concerns about my father's health had muted our victory. I doubted if he would ever recover, and I brooded that despite what the doctor and Zilpah said, the strain of the auction had been a fatal blow.

Once we were inside the house, I began to climb the stairs, using the banister to inch my weary body along. Edwin followed behind. For a moment I thought I could blot out the opium incident like a bad dream. We had triumphed. We were together. What more could we want? At the door to our bedroom I paused. Edwin was no longer behind me. He was heading up another flight of stairs.

"Where are you going?" I asked in a strangled voice.

"To my study."

"Are you going to sleep there?"

"Possibly."

"No!" I gasped. "Don't do it."

"What do you mean?" he said with a challenging edge I had never heard him use before.

"You don't need it!" I shouted.

"How dare you tell me what I need? Today has been the longest of my life. I did my part and more. Now, leave me to find peace the only way I know how."

"Once you found peace in my arms," I quavered.

"You may now be the head of Sassoon and Company, but you are not master of my soul."

"How can you say that? We did it together. I told everyone how you found the discrepancies—"

"Did you, now? You gave me credit when it was in your interests to do so. Then you made certain everyone knew who was boss."

"What do you mean?"

"Oh, Dinah, really." He sounded weary. "Let's not pretend anymore. Let me see if I can recall some of your phrases . . ." It was almost as though I could hear the latch click as those tidy compartments of complete recall opened in his mind and he spewed forth the evidence with a vengeance. " '. . . I may either take the profits from, or take possession of, twenty percent of the lots . . .' and '. . . If Sassoon and Company agrees to go in with me—on my terms—my twelve hundred chests establishes control of the marketplace.' "

I had made the same mistake in my discussions with Abner Raphael. Even after Edwin had told me how offended he had been by my arrogance, I had thoughtlessly repeated the error. "I am sorry, Edwin, I cannot help myself, it is how I think. Everybody knows we act together—"

"Do they? Do they know you were against the plan and I had to convince you? No! I'll let you take the credit, but I must be allowed to have something of my own. If I choose to go upstairs and have a quiet smoke to relax myself with the very substance you and your kin have been buying and selling today, then I shall."

"How long has this been going on?"

"What difference does it make? It has never affected you one way or the other."

"I must know."

"I told you yesterday. Since before we ever met. Since my first visit to Travancore when Amar and I were boys."

"Amar! I should have known." I recalled the last time I had been with the maharajah, and he had tried to turn Edwin against me and me against Edwin. Because Amar had lied about me, I had assumed he had lied about my husband. How ironic that he was telling the truth when he had said, "Even your husband can be corrupted, if the pipe is filled with something sweet to smoke and the woman who wants him is persistent enough." If the first part was true, could the second be as well? I shuddered, but said nothing.

"Come now, Dinah. Not every opium smoker is a criminal. Many of my friends, and yours, enjoy a pipe now and again."

"Who?"

"Abdul Moquith, Howard Farrell, and Krishna Mukerji, among others. I am not a crazed addict, nor are my friends. Sometimes I go for days, maybe a week, without a pipe. Other times I enjoy one nightly."

"Then you could stop."

"I suppose I could if I wanted to."

"You must."

"Why, because you say so?"

"No, because it is harmful."

"The only harm that has ever come has been your recent discovery and objection. You would not have complained if you had found me pickled in gin or tamping a tobacco pipe or smoking a cheroot, so why shouldn't I have the right to be amused by the poppy's blush?" He smiled at the attractive allusion he had conjured.

Who was this man? I did not know him. I opened my mouth to reply, then saw it was no use. The selfish ugly sister that had been mirrored in Aunt Bellore's eyes reappeared. There was nothing here to keep Edwin away from his pipe or anything else. I turned my contorted face from him and opened the door to our room. His footsteps moved up the stairs, irrevocably widening the fissure between us.

I leaned against the door for balance. How had it come to this? We had won our battle with the Lanyados, but at what cost? My father's bloody sputum convinced me that he was certain to die soon. How had I managed to prevail at the auction and garner the approval of my whole family—as well as obtain justice from my deceitful aunt and uncle—yet insult my husband in the process?

What was wrong with me? What was wrong with him? I might have a quick, insensitive tongue, but at least I did not smoke opium, as did my husband . . . as had my mother. Images of Luna and Sadka and the hookah blurred together with those of Edwin lying on his bed sucking from his pipe and of Amar doing the same. Was I cursed with this problem for the rest of my days? Was there no way I could extricate myself from this world of opium?

I staggered into our bedroom. Without Edwin it was hollow and drab. I let my clothes lie where they fell. The long, treacherous day was finished. But something else had begun. There was Hong Kong to think about, and the subsequent management of the company. Maybe this was a time to begin again—in more ways than one. If I could salvage the money I had committed, I might find a way to diversify later investments. . . . There had to be a way out of this morass.

I fell across my bed, limp with terror at what the future might bring without Edwin beside me. A wave of apprehension crashed over me, dissolving any sense of satisfaction over my revenge. How could I have survived a day in which so many dreams had come true, only to discover I had not enjoyed it at all?

48

※ ※ ※

Only the servants knew. Did Yali and Hanif and Gulliver discuss our separate sleeping arrangements or that we hardly ever took meals together or spoke except when it was necessary to converse about strategic matters? Many marriages had rifts established by disagreements. Others, the result of arrangements that had not proved satisfactory over time, had agreements to respect mutual privacy. Then why did I feel ashamed of my predicament? Was it because it had happened without warning? One day Edwin and I had been the passionate pair servants sometimes espied in an unhurried embrace. The next we were singular icebergs floating in a common strait.

We were careful to hide our estrangement from everyone else. The children hardly sensed anything, for we tended them as before. Even more critical, the rest of the Sassoons were to have no doubts about our abilities to lead the company out from the murky management of Samuel into a new regime headed by our "partnership." The natural course seemed for Edwin to move into Uncle Saul's corner office and to act as the senior man on a daily basis. Every few days I would arrive, hold meetings, sign documents, examine account books randomly, and finalize decisions, including the ones Edwin had made in my absence.

"You are the Sassoon," he had explained in a practical tone. "You are the person they will trust, especially after being defrauded by another in-law."

Thus I was the one who sat in Uncle Saul's chair and I was the one to whom everyone deferred. My dream of seeing my father return to Clive Street was not to be realized.

Abner Raphael was jolted when I asked to take delivery of my twenty percent of the shares, but he agreed it was within my rights to do so. I softened the blow by sending a ten-thousand-rupee check for the restoration of the synagogue steeple and another in the same amount for classroom space for the Hebrew school in memory of Luna Sassoon. Neither payment was refused.

The major issue in the business was how to convince the Chinese merchants to accept higher prices. My father insisted he would have to go to China to handle the negotiations.

"Impossible," replied the usually jolly Dr. Hyam. "Even if Benu defied us and booked passage, he would never return."

This was the first statement of the hopelessness of my father's condition, although we had suspected he was dying after the hemorrhage. Initially we discussed Reuben's going in his stead, since he spoke Chinese and had handled the trade before Benu had taken over. Eight years older than my father and "sickly" by his own standards, Reuben vetoed the idea. "I have lost my contacts. The business is a personal one. Benu has the touch with the Chinese, knows what makes them tick. They always confounded me. Besides, the trade wants someone younger. Jonah can do it."

But Jonah demurred. "I have been only once. I cannot speak the language yet. And while we were there, Father did everything. I merely looked on."

Though disappointed by his lack of faith in himself, I realized that he did not want the fate of these difficult negotiations falling upon his shoulders.

"This is our doing," I told Edwin, "and we must resolve it."

"We could commission someone from Jardine, Matheson or the Raphael office to take it on," my husband suggested.

"No! This is a point of pride for the Sassoons."

"We won't feel very proud if we can't unload our crates at the higher rates and the season is an enormous loss."

"That is why we must go to China, to cement old ties and forge new ones. Jonah also could go along, since he knows a few of the ropes."

Edwin sighed with exhaustion. "Dinah, we cannot do everything ourselves. Already I am spending fourteen hours a day in Clive Street."

"Your choice," I reminded him pointedly.

"Hardly," he sniffed. "When this family trade flourished, there were a father and five sons working together."

"And one son-in-law," I said with a rueful laugh.

"Exactly. Now four of the seven are out of the picture. Despite everything"—he was alluding to our rift—"together we have managed to keep matters afloat in Calcutta. If we both went to China, whom would we leave behind to run Clive Street?"

"You have provided the answer."

"Have I?" He raised an eyebrow in the rakish way I once found so appealing. Now it irritated me. I did not want to play his games, not if he would not take the first step and throw away the toxic opium pipe that had come between us. How he could continue to justify—no, to flaunt!—his vice was as irksome a question as ever.

"Oh, stop being coy, Edwin. You know as well as I do that one of us must go to China. And if you won't do it, I suppose I must."

His mouth dropped open. "You? Don't be ridiculous."

"What is ridiculous about it?"

"The Chinese won't deal with a woman. Anyway, I did not refuse to go."

"You said you were engaged at the office."

"I was going to suggest you take over there for the time being."

"I don't suppose they will deal with a woman any better in Calcutta. In any case, you're the one who knows the day-to-day operations, not me. You should remain here."

"But you are the Sassoon."

"Exactly. And as such I suppose I must go in my father's stead. Jonah can travel with me—and Gulliver, of course. What could be wrong with that plan?"

"A thousand reasons come to mind, but what do I know?" he said, not masking his scorn.

"Name two."

"How about three: Aaron, Jeremiah, and Zachariah?"

A clutch at my heart told me he was right, yet I felt compelled to disagree. "I would not choose to leave the children, but they would be well cared for."

"Why don't you ask your father? If he can't dissuade you, nobody can."

❦ ❦ ❦

My father was appalled. "You cannot leave your husband, let alone your children. Besides, you have no idea of the conditions. No woman should be asked to tolerate them. I forbid it!" he sputtered, and began to cough.

Zilpah, who had been sitting with us in the small parlor, warned me with her eyes. Even though the day was warm, a fire had been set to help combat his shivering paroxysms, which had begun shortly before my arrival. Fearing he again might spit up blood, I sat quietly until he was in control.

Mopping my face in the overheated room, I continued softly, "All right, Papa, I only wanted your opinion. Do you think Edwin might be a better choice?"

"What does he know about China?"

"Nothing, but you could teach him."

"I expected it would take five years at my side before Jonah could handle any negotiations on his own, so why should Edwin be able to take over after a few hours of discussion?" He halted until he could stop his teeth from chattering. "There are no formulae that can be employed. Everything is based on the situation of the moment. We drink tea, we talk about our families, we size each other up, we trade points. One year I give in; the next year the other fellow does. This is where the tally is kept." He pointed to his forehead.

"Then Edwin is right. We must hire someone from Jardine, Matheson or Raphael's company to sell our chests," I said sadly. "A middleman's commission might be the difference between making or breaking this season. And what do we do next time?"

"I . . ." he started to say, then looked down at his wasted arms and bony hands. "I suppose I won't ever return."

"No, Papa." I looked to Zilpah for support.

Tears welled in her eyes, but she managed to speak crisply. "The time has come for the children to take over, Benu. Of course they will make mistakes, but look how wonderfully they have done already."

Lost in some private torment, he hadn't heard her. "My God, it is hot in here!" he moaned.

Zilpah and I took his arms and led my father out to the shade of the terrace. He drank two glasses of lemonade laced with quinine before leaning back and closing his heavy eyelids.

"Very well," he began slowly, "I will tell you everything. The truth is that I am too tired to worry about who goes where or does what." His eyes shot open. They were bright with feverish excitement. "Zilpah is right. At least I have confidence that somehow, in some way, you and the others will get by, and yet . . ." Involuntarily he closed them again. ". . . I cannot fathom how. . . ."

❦   ❦   ❦

For the next two weeks I spent every available moment at my father's side, taking notes on his ramblings. When I attempted to question him about specific names, locations, or previous dealings, he might answer one question lucidly, then drift off onto a tangent that seemed useless. Later, though, I would find that a seemingly disconnected thought was a vital link in the commercial chain. In the evenings I would rewrite my notes, cross-referencing them into folders. Soon a pattern began to emerge, though it was a pattern with pieces missing. If I attempted to question my father in an attempt to fill a hole, "Don't know . . . what are you talking about? . . . I never said that!" were common responses to my inquiries.

Even more frustrating were his lapses into Chinese. For a few days I tried to transliterate his husky digressions in the hope of later sorting them out. When time seemed to be running short, I brought in an interpreter, who took notes in Chinese.

Zilpah objected. "He's not up to these interrogations."

"But, Zilpah, we may not have much more time," I protested.

"That may be the case, but I can't have you robbing what few good hours he has left."

I wanted to argue with her, but I constrained myself. "He wants to tell us everything."

"Does he?" she inquired pointedly. "He could care less."

"May I still come every day to see him?" I asked when I resigned myself to her wishes.

Zilpah nodded her head sadly. "Of course, Dinah."

The next morning I arrived at the usual time—without the interpreter or my notebooks—and found Dr. Hyam and two nurses flanking my father's bed. His breathing was raspy and shallow. Zilpah stood next to the bed, as cold and inanimate as a statue.

"Send for the brothers and his other children," Dr. Hyam said to me.

But before anyone else could get to his bedside, he died.

❦ ❦ ❦

A loss expected is not necessarily a loss accepted. Zilpah went through the paces with a wooden stiffness. I shed enough tears for the two of us. Although Edwin treated me kindly, I could find no solace in his arms, and turned to Zilpah. My stepmother and I clung together, supporting each other. Asher was desolate. Ruby avoided the family because her husband did not want her to be upset. Seti, who was eleven, acted mature beyond her years. She dealt with servants and guests and pampered her mother. Fortunately, Jonah handled the necessities with admirable efficiency.

If we were going to manage the Chinese trade, Jonah said we must depart directly after the month of mourning for our father. At first I objected, but his logical arguments won me over. The two of us spent many hours with Uncle Reuben, trying to decipher my notes and planning our journey.

"We actually won't know how much we can command until we deliver the merchandise and see what the market will bear," Jonah summarized after a long meeting.

"Very sensible," Reuben complimented, then turned to Edwin. "Jonah could do quite well on his own," he told Edwin pointedly, "if you can't see your way to convince Dinah you would be more suited to the trip than she would."

Edwin laughed genially, saying, "Haven't we learned by now that my wife has a mind of her own?" The subject was not discussed again.

My father's will left Theatre Road and the bulk of his estate to Jonah, who graciously told Zilpah she might stay on as long as she wanted. Edwin and I had continued to live in Free School Street even though we had taken possession of Kyd Street when the Lanyados left for France. With the complications of reorganizing Sassoon and Company, the plans for traveling to China, my father's illness—not to mention the impossibility of our reaching any agreement on a domestic issue— moving had been an absurd consideration. Besides, I could not envision myself walking in Aunt Bellore's garden or eating from her dishes, let alone sleeping in her bedroom.

Jonah chided me for my bias. "Why not have the place redecorated to suit your fancy? Look what you did to brighten Free School Street. With half the attention, Kyd Street would be a palace."

I was not about to admit anything about my personal confusion to my brother. Besides the obvious reason, I also did not want him to question the wisdom of matrimony. He should have been wedded already, but had resisted every match suggested to date.

"With Father's illness and the commotion, I can't take any steps in that direction," he protested. "I'll consider the next round when we return from China, if you will pledge not to prod me until then."

One afternoon when he was delivering some documents for our journey, Jonah looked around the crowded, shabby Free School Street parlor and clucked his tongue. "Why don't you have Edwin move while we are away? Wouldn't it be wonderful to come home to a new house without having to undertake the packing yourself?"

"I've told you before, I can't see myself as the mistress of Kyd Street," I replied peevishly.

"Would you sell it?" he asked, shocked.

"Possibly," I replied, although I had never before considered the idea.

"You can't do that," my brother protested good-naturedly, "any more than I could sell Theatre Road."

"Don't you want Theatre Road?"

"What would I do with such a large house?"

"Fill it with children!"

He wagged his finger at me. "You promised . . ."

"Jonah . . ." I began as an idea formed. "Wouldn't you rather have Kyd Street? It should have been handed down to a male Sassoon heir from the beginning."

"Kyd Street is even larger. How many children do you suppose I will have?"

"Don't forget, there is a separate wing, which would be convenient if you had to take in any members of your wife's family."

"What are you getting at, Dinah?"

My eyes twinkled impishly. "We could trade. I would much rather live in Theatre Road than anywhere else in the world. And if you were in Kyd Street, your position in the family would be solidified."

"As second to you," he replied flatly.

I shrugged. "You are a man. That will always make you superior in everyone's eyes. I have to fight for every ounce of respect, and frankly, I am finding it wearisome. After this trip I plan to sit back and let the others manage matters."

"What about Edwin?" he asked uneasily.

Avoiding the issue of Edwin's position in the company, I replied, "Edwin will be as content at Theatre Road as anywhere else."

Jonah backed off. "Do you really want to swap houses?"

"I believe it would be fair, as long as you agreed. Theatre Road is newer but smaller. Kyd Street is larger but requires more renovation. If you want, I will pay you a premium."

"Does it mean that much to you?"

"Why are you surprised?"

Jonah swallowed hard and spoke warily. "I thought you had some unpleasant memories . . ." He trailed off.

"And you don't?"

"I was much younger than you. I have no recollections of our mother."

"There are happy memories also," I mumbled softly.

Jonah shook his head. "Father always said women were more perplexing than the Chinese."

I forced myself to smile. "Soon you will have substantial experience with both."

My brother was quiet for several seconds, then brightened. "I believe I would prefer Kyd Street," he replied slowly. "Just as you and Edwin don't want to appear like the next Bellore and Samuel, I do not want to live in the shadow of Benjamin Sassoon."

To seal the matter, my brother and I shook hands formally. And without consulting Edwin or anyone else, Theatre Road was mine.

❦ ❦ ❦

Everything was arranged. Zilpah agreed to stay on at Theatre Road until she determined where else she might go. She had ties in Darjeeling she wanted to renew, but she did not want to be apart from her children, who were settled in Calcutta.

"Why not consider living part of the year in each place?" I suggested. "You could follow the seasons." It was too soon for her to decide, thus the temporary solution of assisting us while I was in Hong Kong seemed logical.

Before our departure I left a list of renovations for Theatre Road. None would inconvenience the family drastically, but were necessities if I were to claim the house as my own.

Edwin, however, was more difficult to rearrange. "I will stay on in Free School Street," he announced shortly before the children were to make the transition with their ayahs.

"But, Edwin, the boys should have their father with them," I said amid the boxes and bundles stacked in the corridor.

"I shall see them daily and be available whenever they require me. I expect they will also visit me here. In fact, having me in a familiar environment should ease their confusion."

"No, it will confound them further. They must know they will be making their home at the new house and are not just visiting Grandmama."

"As far as I am concerned, they can remain with me here or go with Zilpah, but you cannot transport me along with the furnishings and the servants." He sat down on a crate and leaned back against the wall with studied nonchalance.

"This argument is not about houses—it is about opium!" I challenged forthrightly. "You want your privacy so you may indulge to your heart's content." I clenched my fist at him. He did not flinch.

"Exactly," he replied in the bitter tone that I had come to know well in the past few weeks. "The moment you leave, I will convert the house into a den of iniquity. I shall stop going to Clive Street and spend my days, as well as my nights, lost in a miasma of woeful Oriental dreams. As De Quincey said, 'Thou only givest these gifts to man; and thou hast the keys of Paradise, oh, just, subtle, and mighty opium!' "

"Don't forget that De Quincey not only wrote *The Pleasures of Opium*, but *The Pains of Opium* as well."

"Pity I did not marry an ignorant woman. Or did I? Education does not necessarily breed common sense. Why can't you understand that I am not affected adversely by a few puffs from a pipe? Until you discovered me, you did not suspect that I had ever inhaled a whiff." He stood and stretched languidly. "Besides, what difference should it make to you? If I were dissolute, if I had left your bed, if I had failed at my work, you might have some cause for complaint."

"That is not the point. Who knows how your body is being poisoned? Who knows when the pleasure will turn to pain? What if you begin to see 'crocodiles with leering eyes' and other 'unutterable monsters' like De Quincey?" I began to sob with anxiety. "What I want is to have the man I dearly love back in my arms again!"

"Nonsense." He moved farther away from me. "The man you love smoked before he met you, and at times throughout your marriage. In truth, you have never loved a man who did not smoke opium. If I stopped, you might find me a hateful creature. Perhaps it is the opium itself that made me so desirable to you."

"No!" I gasped.

"Why won't you look at the facts instead of some imagined horror?" he concluded before shutting himself off in his study.

There was no middle ground where we could meet to discuss his habit rationally. Edwin believed we could be reconciled if I accepted him as he was. This I could never do. If he truly loved the children and me, he would see that giving up this minor yet dangerous pleasure was the way to give us peace. I began to hope that while I was away, he might miss me so dreadfully he would be willing to undertake the sacrifice. Yet I also worried that he might find the solitary life satisfactory, and I would return to find he had left us forever.

What choices did I have? Someone had to go to China. And anyway, arguing was not bringing our estrangement to an end. There was one more option. Even though it involved a risk to our reputation, I had to take it.

✿ ✿ ✿

Before I set sail, I went to see Dr. Hyam to acquire antimalaria tablets and to be inoculated against the plague. As I lay down on my stomach on the examining table, the doctor's assistant lifted my skirt and pulled down my undergarments. The doctor approached me from the front and prepared the treatment while I watched.

"To think of the lives this vial of serum has saved." Dr. Hyam held up the syrupy substance reverently. "I suppose you know the connection between it and your esteemed family."

"No . . ." A more serious matter on my mind distracted me.

"Come now, you must recall that Waldemar Haffkine, a Russian Jew who studied with Pasteur, discovered the serum. First he worked on a cure for cholera, and then the British ambasssador in Paris encouraged him to extend his studies in India to find a serum for plague. After the last terrible outbreak, your family was one of the first to accept his newest vaccine. I am surprised you did not get one then."

"I was in Travancore when the plague struck."

"How fortunate that you were protected by distance. Now you will have a more secure shield." He injected the stinging dose into my buttock.

I winced, then said, "So our family inspired others to be protected."

"They did more than that. When Haffkine was working in Bombay, the government gave him a bungalow on Malabar Hill for his use as a laboratory. That's how the doctor came to know his neighbor and your distant relation, Flora Sassoon." With a clink the doctor dropped the syringe in a dish and told me to press the spot where he had stabbed me.

"Really?" Suddenly I was intrigued. Ever since I had taken charge at Clive Street, there had been mumblings that I was going to turn into Calcutta's Flora Sassoon, the grande dame of the Bombay clan who managed their cotton mills and other aspects of the family's business after the death of her husband.

"Such a devout man, and so humble," Dr. Hyam prattled on. "Without her encouragement, some say Haffkine might never have made the breakthrough."

"Dr. Hyam, I . . ." Long ago I had trusted this old friend with the embarrassing problems Edwin and I had confronted on our honeymoon. Desperate again, I had to confide in him.

"Yes?" he asked as he washed his hands. When he turned around, he went on as though I hadn't spoken. "To think Haffkine caused himself to be inoculated with his own preparation to prove its harmlessness. What courage! What vision!"

"Vision." I embraced the word. "That's another matter I wanted to speak with you about." I sat up and straightened my skirts.

The doctor took my wrist in his hand. "Are you feeling light-headed?"

"No."

"Excellent. Now you must sit awhile to make certain there are no ill effects." He turned to make a note on his chart. With his back to me, he added, "Is there anything else?"

I took a deep breath and blurted, "Is it possible for someone to smoke opium in moderation with no ill effects?"

"What brought this about?"

Echoing in my mind were my father's words of explanation in that Patna field long ago: "This is *Papaver somniferum*, the most prized flower in the world . . ."

"Yes?" the doctor prompted.

I wiped my brow with the handkerchief crumpled in my hand. "My father used to say the poppy eliminated pain and cured diseases."

"And so it does. You see the black balls that are shipped to China, but I see a compendium of morphine, narcotine, codeine, narcine, thebaine, opianine, meconine, pseudomorphine, porphyoxine, papavarine, and meconic acid—a total of eleven useful organic compounds available in every ounce of opium. From them we compound morphine tablets, ointments, solutions, tinctures, suspensions, and clysters. Asthmatics clear their lungs with it, racking coughs are quelled, stomach cramps are ended, and people with pain—pain so hideous you would prefer to put them out of their misery rather than see them suffer another second—can function between doses."

I had not expected the doctor would make me almost as defensive as Edwin had. "I realize opium for medicinal purposes might be essential, but he also told me it made men happy. What do you think about people who use opium purely for pleasure?" I asked as I fought to control my voice's timbre.

"The quantity consumed by the masses is immense, as you well know, and yet in the end, we doctors find it does not do irreparable harm to the majority who use it. There is no disease directly caused by moderate use, and although some physicians say the course of one's life is shortened, how can this be proved?"

I wondered whether my perspiring forehead was a symptom of my emotional anguish at the thought of Edwin's perpetual dependence or from the new drug inside my body. "So you would argue that opium is a harmless substance."

"My own conviction is that if someone chooses to take a stimulant, the juice of the poppy is as benign as any other artificial source of excitement. At least it never makes a man foolish, it never casts him into a ditch or under the table, it never deprives him of his wits or his limbs. Frankly, opium permits a man to be a gentleman."

I tried again. "The visions . . ."

"Yes, it may give him visions, but these visions create no noise, no riots. They deal no blows to himself or to his fellows. To a man who is despondent, if offers an unoffending relief to his miseries."

"What if a man is not miserable and takes it only out of habit?"

Dr. Hyam wheeled around. "Why this sudden interest? Anything to do with your voyage abroad?"

"Not exactly."

I accepted his outstretched hand and stepped down from the table. "Would you prefer to continue this discussion in my office?"

"Yes, I would." My bottom was aching, but I did not care as I took the hard seat in the Lower Chitpur Road clinic office. This is where so much of what I am today began, I thought as I looked around the familiar room where I had first tried my hand at keeping account books.

"Now, what is this about?" the doctor asked in a genial yet probing manner.

Anger overcame my reticence. "This is about my husband," I replied. "Edwin has been smoking for years and years and refuses to give it up."

Dr. Hyam shook his head with disbelief. "How long have you known this?"

"I discovered it quite recently."

"How many years?"

"Since before we married. Somehow he hid it from me the whole time. How could I have been so blind?"

"Don't berate yourself. Didn't I mention earlier the opium user does not display the disgusting habits of the imbiber? He smokes a pipe, is that right?"

"Yes, I saw him myself."

"Perhaps it will alleviate some of your distress to know that opium smokers, unlike opium eaters, have the mildest form of dependence."

"Why are you defending Edwin?" I jumped up and started for the door.

"Dinah, please . . ." The rotund man came around to my side of the desk and took my hands in his plump ones. "You must not leave for an hour, in case you have a reaction to the vaccine. In any case, we have not arranged your medicines for the journey." He took the seat next to mine and waited until I seemed calmer. "I gather you have asked your husband to abandon this habit and he has refused."

"Yes, he thinks the only obstacle is my objection."

"Edwin does not even think he has a problem. He wonders why you have bothered to excite yourself over the matter."

The doctor's accuracy alarmed me. "Have you spoken to Edwin about this already?"

"No, this is experience speaking. For your part, you cannot understand why, if he loves you and the children, he will not refrain from what is, after all, a useless vice."

Deflated, I sighed. "I want him to be healthy."

"In my opinion, there seem to be other reasons you object. You do not want him to be a slave to another mistress. You do not want him pursuing an activity that you perceive is out of your sphere of control."

Was I so monstrous? My shoulders sagged and my chin dropped as though a weight were pressing me from all around. I stared at my feet.

"Even before you came into the Luddy fortune or had to confront the Lanyados, you were a determined young lady. That is not meant as criticism, rather as a compliment." He leaned away from me, his bald head tilting backward. "I remember you after the death of your poor mother, and I recall myself thinking: This is the strongest child I have ever known. I wonder, though, if that strength has not made it impossible for you to bend."

"I cannot see how I could be at fault—" I choked. "Edwin began smoking when he was a boy. Also, if this habit is innocuous, why did he hide it from me?"

"He was ashamed. He did not want to appear weak, which he would have, at least in comparison with you. 'Admiration' is the word I would use as regards your husband, my dear. The loss of the ship might have shattered a lesser man. He swallowed his pride and got on with it. And now look where he is, where you both are, today. You two are the most esteemed couple in Calcutta."

"That is not true," I objected.

"Rarely do we see ourselves as others see us."

"Then you don't think he should discontinue the vice."

"To my mind, there is but one difficulty with smoking opium: the loss of free will. Alas, my dear, your husband cannot throw his pipe out the window any more than you can agree to go without food."

"That is an unfair comparison. Food is a requirement for life."

"Is it?" The doctor tilted his head. "What if I were to offer you a tablet that contained everything you needed to sustain yourself each day. Wouldn't you continue to crave food? Wouldn't delicious odors tempt you? Could you resist your favorite sweets, which are certainly unnecessary? You see, my dear, there are two reasons that people take opium: either to restore themselves to the condition they regard as normal, such as to take away pains or symptoms or disease, or to liberate themselves from normality—to change their mood, to make them feel more excited or more relaxed, actually to alter their perceptions of normalcy. If, as you say, Edwin has been taking the pipe for many years, normalcy to him includes the opiate in his bloodstream."

"He doesn't think about it like that."

"Not in his conscious mind perhaps, yet his body sends powerful signals to his brain warning him not to tamper with the status quo."

"Could he stop if he really wanted to?"

"I would guess he may have tried on his own—most sensible people do at one time or another—and knows the unpleasant sequelae that follow."

"Would he get very sick?"

"Yes, for a short time. At least that is the case with most smokers. He would have respiratory problems. His eyes would discharge tears and mucus. He would have ringing in his ears and severe intestinal colic. There would be vomiting, purging, chills followed by flashes of heat—much like the terrors of malaria—tearing pains in the legs, the loins, between the shoulders. He would find no relief in sleep for months. Frankly, most people who try to break themselves seldom carry the struggle to a successful conclusion."

"Couldn't you assist him?"

"If he wished it. There are ways to manage the distress. One treatment consists of the use of capsicum, digitalis, and cannabis Indica tincture in large doses. If there is much reflex nervous trouble, potassium and sodium may be given. There are also several methods that diminish the effect of the drug slowly."

"If only he would try it!"

"I could offer him the treatment, but it is more complicated than I have made it sound. Dozens of medicines must be employed to counteract the various symptoms: catechu in large doses for the diarrhea, chloride of gold and soda for the pains in the limbs, oxide of zinc for the profuse perspiration, and more. He would have to submit to my regimen religiously and be watched and restrained for at least two weeks. From what you have said, I doubt he would be willing."

My moment of exhilaration was crushed. "You are right. There is no hope."

"Don't say that. There are further possibilities. Unless you have been a brilliant actress, I believe you have been a very happy wife. Why not go on as you were?"

"That is impossible."

Dr. Hyam shook his gleaming head. "I fear you are also suffering from an addiction—the addiction of having your own way." There was no rancor in his voice, but the spike that continued to lodge in my heart was driven deeper.

"Perhaps if I am away, I will appreciate what I have," I said as tears blurred my view of the doctor's concerned face. "The discovery of the pipe was a shock. Everything since the earthquake has been a shock." I sobbed openly. "How has everything gone so wrong?"

"I agree that you both might benefit from perspective. How long have you been together?"

"Almost seven years."

"Often a time when men and women tire of each other."

"I haven't tired of Edwin! Not for a second! If it weren't for the opium, everything would be perfect."

"If it weren't for the opium, you might be paupers."

"I know," I replied soberly, "and that is a matter I will confront after the journey," I said, standing.

"No ill effects from the vaccine. Good."

"If Edwin would make the attempt . . ." My mind cleared. "Yes, if Edwin tried to shake the habit—even if he failed—I would agree to turn the other way. It's the attempt that matters to me. If his constitution does not allow him to relinquish the drug, then I will bow to the inevitable. Does that sound reasonable?" My voice was as childish as my desire for the doctor's acceptance.

"Very. Why don't you tell him how you feel?"

"I can't. He won't listen. Not any longer. I surrendered my chance when I reacted violently. Besides, he has lost his common sense."

"You both are armored by anger. Do you know the prime disadvantage of armor?" He smiled benevolently. "When you fall down, you cannot stand again without assistance."

"Would you . . . ?"

"I'll see what I can do. After you have gone, I will make it a point to speak with him. I will say you left the matter in my hands."

"That will infuriate him."

"I think not. My prodding will hardly persuade him, but his love for you might."

"If any love remains."

"While I am not a physician of the heart, I can assure you this rift could not shake the foundations of a marriage as rooted in compatibility as yours."

Heading back to Theatre Road, I tried fervently to believe the doctor was right, but my own doubts crowded out his parting words. Whatever Edwin decided, whatever happened with his cure, the shell of perfection had shattered. Mended, we might continue, but the flawlessness we had shared in the past was gone forever.

PART V

✸ ✸ ✸

Flowers in the Blood

The greatest pleasure in life is doing what people say you cannot do.

— Chinese Proverb

49

❧ ❧ ❧

Hong Kong, 1898

Dare I admit it was a relief to depart for China? I kissed the tender necks of my sons—but not the lips of my husband—and walked up the gangplank of the China and Manila Steamship Company's most luxurious steamship, the *Zafiro*, without looking back.

As I stood at the rail of the ship, staring at the fading coastline of India, I believed every mile passed was a marker on a much longer journey, one that would not end with my arrival in China. I had no idea whether I would be successful selling our chests in Hong Kong or with my long-range plan to wean our family's dependence from the opium trade. Nevertheless, I reminded myself that small steps, one after the other, could cover a distance as well as leaps. Besides, leaps would be foolhardy when I knew nothing of what waited on the opposite shore.

My bitterness toward Edwin's obstinacy solidified my determination to obliterate opium from my life. The knowledge that my mother had been corrupted by that flower intermingled sourly with an acceptance that the same substance had sustained me in luxury. This dichotomy had never been reconciled despite conversations with Silas and my own lofty ideals. Edwin knew this. No wonder he had accused me of duplicity. How quickly I had condemned him! How easily I had absolved myself! Why should I have expected him to relinquish his physical dependence on the substance when I had been unwilling to extricate myself from the spoils of the trade?

Much in the manner of a cork being dislodged from an ancient bottle of wine, the tossing of the ship loosened something in my mind. I saw clearly what must be done. I would liberate the Sassoons from the opium trade, yet not at once. Just as the body could not take the assault of sudden withdrawal, neither could the enterprise. The Chinese were producing more and more of their own supply. Soon it would be unprofitable to compete with them. Also, there were moralists in England who were trying to persuade the government to curtail Indian production. One of these days the Sassoons might awaken to find that our one and only commodity had been taken from us. If we planned ahead, we could pick and choose from investments in products that would increase in value. Tea was one area where the Sassoons might thrive alongside the Luddys, and there were other alternatives: cotton, jute, even ships. Wouldn't it be wonderful if Edwin could put the *Luna Sassoon* behind him and control the fleet of his dreams? I suspected there would be discord at first, but eventually the family would see the merit of my proposition.

If I remained sensible, I would be able to find solutions as each problem presented itself. With or without Edwin, I would settle each question. The realization that I might not have dared attempt to control the auction without his prompting, and might flinch from other bold yet essential decisions, was banished with resolutions to pursue my aims with single-minded diligence. With a sure and steady pace I would reach my goal, I concluded confidently as I turned eastward, the direction of the rising sun.

Thanks to the dependability of the mild northeasterly winds, we made the passage past Siam, through the South China Sea, and into the immense bowl of Hong Kong's harbor in less than two weeks. The ship slowed as the vessel approached the myriad islands that punctuated the approach to the harbor. Alongside came a native ship, and a pilot was hoisted on board. "Jardine's Lookout," a sailor on the flag mast called out when he sighted a purple peak that struggled out of the mist like a finger pointing to the sky.

Jonah turned his back to the wind. "Father explained it was named the lookout because in the days before the Opium War, the clipper ships would circle until the smugglers received a signal that the moment was right to proceed across to Chuanpei Bay and into the Pearl River."

"Why? Would they be attacked or impounded?"

Jonah threw back his head and laughed. "No, the 'danger' was the opium price on Lintin Island was too low. Only when the supplies were so diminished that the Chinese would pay a premium would they tell the ships that it was 'safe' to head into port. In that, they were hardly any different from us."

The bustling harbor, filled with every size ship from ocean steamers to large sailing clippers, reminded me of Calcutta, except for the junks and sampans moored so closely to each other that they seemed an extension of the land itself.

"Today Hong Kong thrives on the spoils of entrepôt trade, but when Lord Palmerston first saw it, he was disappointed because the barren island had hardly a house upon it. Just look at it fifty years later." Jonah went on to point out the government buildings, commercial structures, and warehouses, including the most impressive: Jardine, Matheson's.

"So this is the prize won in the Opium War," I said, astonished at the prosperous port.

I remained on board until Jonah and Gulliver had seen to our luggage and had found us transportation.

"What took so long?" I said after they were done, cross because of the chilly wind and raw smells of the wharf.

"I had to find something suitable." Jonah pointed out the closed black-and-silver sedan chair that shone in the sun. Beside it, six liveried Chinese laborers stood at alert.

"Lavishness was not necessary," I chided.

"That is where you have made your first mistake, my dear sister. If you want the Chinese to respect you, your arrival must herald your status as the head—or as they would say, the *taipan*—of the Sassoon clan. Anyhow, the better class of Chinese women rarely are seen in public."

"What do they do with them?"

"They are hidden behind their garden walls and the curtains of their palanquins."

"Is that what I am expected to do?"

"Not exactly. From time to time they may catch a glimpse of you, but never so much as to make too many assumptions. Already tongues will wag from Kowloon to Aberdeen.They must think of you of as powerful and elusive—the Chinese love secrets."

"I will not be locked away," I said with good-natured peevishness in my tone, since my father had made a similar suggestion.

"That will hardly be the case. Tomorrow night you will be a guest at the governor's home. On Friday you will meet the cream of Hong Kong's Chinese society. By Monday your position should be well-established."

"That will not make me elusive."

"If a woman keeps her eyes open and her mouth shut, the technique can be mastered," Jonah said, ducking playfully as I pretended to swat him.

"What do you know about women?"

"More than you think, less than I would like."

I ruffled my brother's hair, thinking how much I liked him. A half-head taller than I and even more slender, he had a wiry yet not extremely masculine appearance. His face was pale, his bone structure delicate. Although nobody dared mention it, he most resembled our mother. He had inherited her oval face and chiseled chin, long eyelashes, and pink bow mouth. At twenty-two, many young men had a mature demeanor, but my brother had not lost his youthful softness. As much as I was charmed by his boyishness, I worried that this, added to the irrevocable fact of my sex, would handicap our negotiations. Fortunately, my brother did have a pragmatic streak.

How much better an appearance Edwin would have made, and how much I would miss his nimbleness and ability to recall precisely what he had heard or read! However, Edwin was not here, I thought with an immense longing I had not felt since I had left India. At least Jonah had been to Hong Kong previously. And, I reminded myself, we were controlling more than six thousand chests of opium—three-quarters of the current crop—opium the Chinese wanted dearly. Opium that accounted for one-sixth of the colony's revenues. My resolve stiffened. Together we could do this.

Together we had to do this.

☸ ☸ ☸

As we made our way along the quay, Gulliver, in full Gurkha regalia, caused quite a stir. Proudly he walked next to the sedan chair through the narrow streets along the wharf. Unsettled by the crowds of Orientals, he kept one hand on the scabbard of his kukri. In a short while we came to a tramway station. After a ten-minute uphill ride through a primeval forest, improbable mansions loomed along the high ridges seventeen hundred feet above the harbor. Jonah directed the sedan-chair bearers to Mount Gough, the Peak. The chair seemed to tip as we wound our way up a steep hillside path in so convoluted a manner I preferred to look at the verdant mountainside rather than the precipitous drop. At last we halted at a high gate.

"Best to walk from here," my brother suggested as he helped me down. "The Sassoon company's pied-à-terre in Hong Kong," he said with a sweeping gesture toward a small stone house that from the outside looked like a charming home for a fairy-tale character. A glimpse of the vertiginous drop on either side, though, made my heart lurch.

"Should be pied-à-ciel, if I recall my French," I noted as I walked down the lane to the house perched high above Hong Kong harbor. A quick comparision to Xanadu extended the sinking feeling. Once inside, however, all similarities ended.

The Sassoons had purchased the house from a British banker whose wife's tastes ran to floral chintzes and lace curtains. Since our father spent little time in the house, he had not bothered to redecorate. Because nobody had known when to expect us, the house was tidy, but much too cold for that dank January day. No logs burned in the fireplaces. No flowers adorned the tables. Gulliver seemed determined to have matters put right, but his Nepalese-tinged English could not be understood by the Chinese servants: a skinny, solemn houseboy called Chen Ah Bun and a rotund, smiling lady who said she was Su Sum. Jonah found himself in the middle, interpreting clumsily between the bewildered retainers. Within an hour we were served a passable English-style tea and plans were under way for some sort of supper, although whether Chinese or Indian or English, I could not determine.

\v/   \v/   \v/

The next morning Mr. Ming Hien Chang, the *compradore* for Sassoon and Company's Hong Kong offices, called on us. Jonah explained the term came from the Portuguese *comprar*, or buyer, and referred to the Chinese agent used by the merchant houses to buy, sell, and negotiate with his own people.

"My sympathy on the death of your esteemed, honorable father," Mr. Ming said, bowing to Jonah and ignoring me.

My brother introduced me. The compradore gave me a perfunctory bow and turned back to Jonah.

My brother cleared his throat. "Compradore, I do not think you understand. My elder sister, Dinah Sassoon Salem, is at present the taipan of Sassoon and Company." His bemused smile perplexed Mr. Ming. His eyes darted back and forth. Was this boy joking with him? He watched my expression for a clue.

What should I do? If I permitted Jonah to explain further, my power could be compromised. If I spoke, I might sound defensive. Yet if I could not convince this man who was in our employ, there was little likelihood I would be respected anywhere else on the island. Slowly, and in the deeper register that made me sound more serious, I began. "Mr. Ming, I must ask for your agreement to hold much of what will be discussed here in the strictest confidence."

I waited for Mr. Ming to face me before I went on.

"Our family has suffered from the actions of a greedy and dishonest relation. With the assistance of my father, my husband and I found the discrepancies and worked to make the situation right. Because I was successful in Calcutta, my family has selected me to represent them here in Hong Kong. I cannot be successful here, however, without your advice and assistance."

Mr. Ming's eyes flicked back to Jonah. He noted my brother's youth, and once again focused on me. I had remained sitting. Now I stood. The man's head did not reach my shoulders. He looked up. I kept my face immobile, my hands at my side. This time he bowed to me. "I am at your service, taipan."

I offered him a seat. In a few minutes a Chinese-style tea was served in little round cups with no accompaniments of milk or sugar. Gulliver waited at attention behind my chair. Rain poured from the sky, obliterating the view. My bones began to ache with the dampness while I listened to the compradore's report on business enacted on behalf of the company. At first the man's accent was hard to follow, but soon I had caught the rhythm and was able to understand the words. The meanings behind them, though, were far more obtuse.

My father had tried to educate me in the confused state of opium trade in China: "Every time we work out an arrangement with our merchants, the governments of India, Hong Kong, and China vacillate on their positions and everything must be recalculated. I have nightmares whenever the crown sends a new governor out to Hong Kong or his celestial majesty appoints a new commissioner in Canton."

Here was a place to begin. "Tell me, compradore, have you recent estimates on how much opium the merchants of Hong Kong require this season?"

"We keep those at the office, madam. Were you planning to come to the Prince's Buildings this week?"

I shot a glance at Jonah. Reminding me of our decision to keep me behind the scenes, he shook his head slightly. "No, most of the time I will remain here and let you gentlemen act for me." In the compradore's eyes I thought I saw respect dimming, so I added, "That is what my father wished."

This was true. On his deathbed my father had said repeatedly that if I were going to go to Hong Kong with Jonah and Edwin, I should leave the talking to the men. "Stay in the background, even remain in your lodgings, and have the men report back to you." When he saw the distress his advice had given, my father had calmed me by saying how much faith he had in my ability "to put intellectual fires to work to solve a problem. It is always wisest to have someone thinking matters through while someone else acts as the mouthpiece." Then he added, "Never try to think and speak simultaneously, or you will inevitably make mistakes. Anyway, the Chinese have enough trouble putting trust in any 'foreign devil,' and it is unwise to stretch their fragile faith to extend to negotiating with a female."

After only a half-hour with Mr. Ming, I saw my first hurdle would be convincing our own man to follow my directives. Evasiveness had been his calling card. How could I assure him that I was really in charge? Best to press on and learn from my blunders, I decided.

I asked the question a different way. "Don't you recall any figures from the Royal Commission on opium? I understand they do a yearly report."

There was a slight motion in the compradore's chin that might have counted as a quiver. Then he spoke. "One recent paper compiled by Governor Robinson himself estimates the consumption in Hong Kong at three chests per day."

"That is over a thousand a year in the colony alone. Do you think that is a fair estimate?"

My question took the compradore aback. "No, I do not, taipan."

I waited for a further explanation, but none was forthcoming. This is like pulling teeth, I seethed silently, yet I replied firmly. "Do you think the colony requires more or less?"

"More."

"How much more?"

"Another private report circulated among the merchants showed 67,429 chests paid import excises, while 61,808 paid export taxes in 1896."

A man clever enough to remember those figures was surely a font of essential information. If only I knew how to extract it! "That means 5,621 chests remained on the island."

Mr. Ming Hien Chang's eyes gleamed with respect for the first time. To think simple arithmetic was all it took. "Yes, that indicates that more than five times the official amount is required. However, there is a small opium-growing industry on the island that cuts into that figure significantly."

"How far?"

No response.

"By half?"

"No, possibly by a third."

"Even so, most of the chests merely pass through Hong Kong on their way to the mainland. Is that correct?"

"Yes, taipan."

Good, I thought silently. As we had hoped, everything pointed to an exceedingly healthy marketplace. If we remained firm with our Chinese merchants, we could drive the prices to the levels we desired. Matters had gone so well that I almost broached the matter with the compradore then and there. Some streak of caution, however, warned me not to rush. I turned the topic to the inclement weather for the duration of the tea.

❀   ❀   ❀

The next morning an invitation to the governor's dinner party was delivered with the breakfast tray. Along with the handwritten card came a letter from the governor's secretary apologizing for the last-minute nature of the invitation, which had been necessary since we had arrived just the day before. "We will understand if you are too exhausted from your journey to visit tonight. Unfortunately, the weekend is complicated by the festivities that accompany the Chinese New Year." He went on to explain that we were also welcome the week after that, either for the first time or as a second visit.

"How did they know we were in Hong Kong, and how did you know we would be invited?" I asked my brother in amazement.

"There are few secrets on a small island." He winked, then explained, "When we wired ahead to the office, they took care of everything, from opening the house to planning our social calendar. Anyway, do you want to go?"

"Certainly. I do hope the British will be more forthcoming than the compradore."

"Now, sister, I hope you won't interrogate the governor."

"Why ever not?" I teased, and went off to enlist Su Sum's help with my clothes.

I decided on the plum gown, sans ostrich plumes, that I had worn to the auction. It had brought luck, and besides, it was the most astonishing item in my wardrobe. Though Jonah looked handsome in his evening clothes, he was no match for Gulliver, resplendent in his white uniform.

"Where will Gulliver remain while we are in the dining room?" Jonah asked.

"At my side, as always."

"He can't stay with you during dinner."

"I will ask him to wait outside."

"He doesn't always do as you say."

"He will if I promise to leave the room through the doorway he is guarding."

"Dinah, he isn't your jailer. He's your servant."

"I feel safer when he is around."

"What do you have to worry about?"

Jonah would never know how much Gulliver's presence allayed the myriad fears that floated in my mind. Memories from my mother's murder, to my experience with the thugs in Patna, to running from Amar mingled with being a woman, a rich woman, in a foreign land. Gulliver's devotion might have been excessive to some, but to me it was most welcome.

Shrugging, Jonah led me to the waiting sedan chair.

When we arrived at Government House, we had to wait our turn to be announced. Outside the entryway I looked back toward the Peak, the highest point of the mountain range that formed the backbone of the island, wondering if I could pick out our cottage, but it was lost in a veil of bluish mist. At last they called our names. Light and warmth replaced the bone-chilling gloom of the night air. Fires blazed in every room.

I was introduced to a selection of public servants, British subjects, and distinguished visitors as Dinah Salem, the daughter of Benjamin Sassoon. Many present had known my father. A few of the older gentlemen recalled my Uncle Reuben, and some knew Sassoon relations who had settled in Shanghai and even England. Accustomed as I was to having the family name open doors, I had never before witnessed the magic among strangers in another country. Even though everyone was too polite to mention it directly, I could tell there was curiosity about why I was escorted by my brother instead of my husband.

After seeing that all his guests had arrived, the governor himself became attentive to me. The last time I had talked privately with a governor had been in Darjeeling shortly after my marriage to Silas, I thought with a pang at his memory. Steering me to the front gallery, which offered a splendid view of the town and harbor, Governor Robinson spoke in an accent that was a wistful reminder of Dennis Clifford. "I like it best before the moon has risen. In this haze the small-magnitude stars are not visible, yet you can see some of the larger ones plainly. Below, the air is usually clear, and though the vessels are invisible, their lights remind me of another hemisphere of stars even more numerous than the others. I have no control over the comings and goings of celestial bodies: nevertheless those in that lower firmament are mine to keep in order."

I looked at the man to see if he was serious. His rigid demeanor gave no hint of a joke. I managed to hide my disbelief at his pomposity behind a smile he could have taken for feminine deference.

During dinner, I took my seat between a Lord Hargreaves, who was traveling around the world with his wife, and a Commodore Treadwell. Jonah was seated next to Lady Hargreaves and the wife of the surveyor-general. Gulliver took his station outside with the Chinese servants, who wore long blue gowns, white gaiters, thick shoes with white soles, and had pigtails hanging past their waists.

"Have you had an opportunity to taste much of the Chinese cuisine?" Lord Hargreaves asked as the lightly seasoned consommé was served.

"No, only a few tidbits prepared by our houseboy at the Peak."

"I must warn you that while some is delicious, there are many items you might find disagreeable. For instance, their delicacies include bird's-nest soup, sharks' fins, and eggs said to be fifty years old."

I grimaced. "How do they taste?"

"The soup is not bad, rather bland actually, and although I cannot say that anything else is nasty, the brown sauces that cover the mysterious ingredients worry me. At least I like rice."

"I do too."

"Then you shall get on just fine. A lady can be more particular than a man without offending the host, so you mustn't feel compelled to try anything you find repulsive."

I went back to my soup and decided nothing could be blander. Because I liked every sort of Indian dish, even the spicy platters served in Travancore, I wouldn't turn against Chinese food on one man's critique.

When the buttered fish fillets were set before us, Commodore Treadwell, a man with a mustache that looked more like a bristle brush, focused on me with typical questions about our crossing and how I was finding Hong Kong.

"I have barely had time to unpack. If the rain stops tomorrow, I hope to take a proper look around."

"May I suggest you first visit the Victoria Peak via the Upper Level Tramway. From there you will gain perspective on the whole island."

"That sounds perfect, since I know nothing of the area."

"I would be happy to answer any questions you might have."

I was about to give an expected response when something perverse in my nature—or merely the desire to get on with what I had come for—caused me to startle the gentleman. "Frankly, Commodore, I had not considered the effects devaluation of the Spanish dollar would have. Presently it is at a five-year low. Don't you find that disturbing?"

"What I find disturbing is that a woman as lovely as you has any concern about such matters," he said without condescension in his tone.

"I have come to Hong Kong as a woman of commerce, not as a lady of leisure. Some other time I hope to bring my husband and have a purely social visit. This trip, I represent the Sassoon interests."

"As I said, Mrs. Sassoon—I mean, Mrs. Salem—I would be honored to answer any questions you might have."

I waited while a lemon ice decorated with a sliver of peel carved like a leaping fish was placed in front of me. When the governor's wife lifted her spoon, I tasted mine and said, "How delicious!" After the next bite I continued, "I wonder if you could tell me anything about the Chinese opium merchants."

"I am a naval man, inexperienced in commercial matters. The person you should speak with is Godfrey Troyte, who likes to say he's been here longer than anyone else. I suppose he's right. His father captained one of the original opium clippers and settled here after an accident at sea crippled him."

"He sounds most interesting. How could I meet him?"

"He's at the far end of the table, next to the lady in the royal-blue dress."

I caught a glimpse of a man with snowy white hair floating about his youthful, clean-shaven face. Just then he looked in our direction. The commodore caught his eye, which twinkled back in acknowledgment.

"If you like, I'll introduce you after dinner."

"Thank you, I would like that," I said.

There was a whoosh of satin as the ladies, following a signal from the governor's wife, stood. The men leapt up, pulled out chairs, and made gracious bows. Across the way my brother gave a broad smile that I understood to mean: Sorry the taipan must take tea with the ladies instead of port with the men.

What would he think if he knew how much more comfortable I felt in the drawing room than among the booming camaraderie and the cigar smoke? The governor's wife was easy to talk to, and we had a cordial chat about one of her favorite places, Darjeeling.

Deciding I had little time to waste before the men joined us, I ventured, "What can you tell me about Mr. Troyte?"

"Now, what would you want with him?" Lady Robinson asked archly.

"The commodore thought he might answer some of my questions about Hong Kong."

"Well, if it is historical information you are requiring, you could not do better. Actually, if you want present-day gossip, you need look no farther either." She placed her curly head next to mine and whispered, "Just watch out, he's a bit of a scoundrel."

"In what way?"

"With other people's money."

"That's a relief, because if he had another sort of reputation, I could not risk mine with his company."

"How wise you are, my dear. Pity your husband could not accompany you this time. Ah, and here are the gentlemen now."

As promised, the commodore ushered Mr. Troyte my way. "Mrs. Salem, what a pleasure. I believe I have known every Sassoon to pass through this port. Even your Grandfather David once kissed me when I was a boy."

"He was my great-grandfather."

"Certainly."

"Then you knew my father."

"We were acquainted." His bright blue eyes shifted from side to side. "May I say how much you remind me of him?"

I gave a little shiver.

"Are you cold?"

"A bit. Calcutta gets chilly, but it doesn't seem to penetrate the bones quite as thoroughly."

"That's the dampness." He steered me toward one of the three fires that blazed in the massive drawing room. "Winter on the island is always like this. Two months earlier would have been ideal." Perceptively, the man noticed impatience in my expression and quickly ceased the small talk. "The commodore said I might be of assistance to you."

"Possibly." I gave a nervous laugh, since Lady Robinson's warning had put me on guard. "I feel abysmally ignorant about Hong Kong, almost as if I'm adrift without flotation."

Godfrey Troyte threw back his head and laughed heartily. "What an original allusion!" His wispy long hair settled long after his head stilled. "Because my father was an old sailor, I have many safety lines around. Shall I toss you one?"

"Please."

"Where should I begin?" He leaned against one of the stone lions carved into the face of the hearth and cocked his head.

"I suppose you know that I, along with my brother, am here in my father's stead. What it took him a lifetime to know must be assimilated by us more quickly if we are to represent the Sassoon interests to the Chinese opium dealers this season."

The sharp blue eyes darted from side to side, almost like mechanical attachments to the man's thinking gears. When they steadied, I knew he had made a decision. Had he realized we were in some difficulty? Did he already know about our need to raise the prices sharply? Even if he did, all he replied was: "Opium is not my field."

"Lady Robinson thought you had historical perspective," I said, pronouncing "historical" in the same exaggerated manner as our hostess.

Godfrey Troyte's amused expression let me know he caught the mimicry. "I imagine your father told you that most of the Chinese merchants descend from the original Cantonese Co-Hong traders. They form ten guilds licensed by the emperor in Peking to trade with foreigners, a situation forced upon him against his better judgment by the results of the opium wars. Just as yours is a family trade, so is theirs." He paused and looked around. Nobody was paying any attention to us. In fact, the room was emptying.

"Go on," I urged.

"Caught in the middle of a trade they find difficult to control, these merchants have banded together to resist those who do not share their interests."

"Who would that be? The Indian opium dealers?"

"Yes, but there are others, including the Mandarin import-export officials, who impose the traditional Cantonese bribery ritual—not affectionately known as the 'squeeze.' Also, Peking regularly punishes the merchants whether they go along with the squeeze or fight it. Thus the trade is in perpetual disorder, for one never knows if one's associates are currently in or out of favor."

"Now I understand why my father had nightmares over the business."

"Telling family secrets?" Jonah asked pleasantly, having come to collect me. We were almost the last guests in the room.

"I believe Mr. Troyte already knows them." I introduced the two men.

"A pity it is time to leave," Godfrey replied to Jonah. "Monday-night suppers always end early, for most of the guests have to work tomorrow. This week will be especially busy because the new year begins on Saturday."

"Is it an important holiday?"

The two men exchanged bemused smiles. "Your sister is in for a proper welcome to Hong Kong, isn't she?"

"There I go floating out to sea," I said as we three walked over to the governor and his wife to say our farewells.

Gulliver handed me my cape, which Godfrey helped settle around my shoulders. "My offer of a line extends past the evening."

"Would it be presumptuous of me to invite you to call?"

"I was hoping you would ask."

"Would tomorrow be convenient, or do you also have a great deal to accomplish before the holiday?"

"Hardly," he chuckled. "Tomorrow around four?"

"Perfect. Do you know . . . ?"

"Mount Gough, the White Chalet," he filled in.

"I didn't realize that's what the house was called." I climbed into the waiting sedan chair and gave my new friend a wave.

"My, you move quickly," Jonah commented. I looked to see if he was upset with me. If anything, he seemed delighted.

"Someone needs to explain what is going on. Ever since we arrived, I have felt in a fog."

"That is because the fog has barely lifted."

I cuffed my brother's shoulder. "You know what I mean." He shrank back playfully. "And you, did you have a pleasant evening?"

"Not especially."

"A pity your dinner companions were both married."

"That sort of woman is of no interest to me."

"I could see that," I said lightly, even though I felt a sudden twinge and thought of Silas. No, not Jonah! He had never met anyone he cared for, that was it. When we returned to Calcutta, I would attempt to find him a few good candidates for a wife, I mused.

"What sort of girl would you like?" I asked in the foyer. Jonah's tense expression caused me to back off. "Or haven't you given the matter much thought?"

"On the contrary," he replied, but did not clarify further.

If I had not been so tired or if his face had registered an invitation to press forward, I might have continued. All I said was, "That's a start."

50

❀ ❀ ❀

I already scheduled a meeting with the compradore," Jonah said, "so I shall not be able to greet your latest conquest."

"Mr. Troyte is hardly that." I grimaced. "I wonder why the gentleman does not cut his hair properly. He looks quite extraordinary."

Jonah idly fingered an ivory letter opener on the desk where I was working on some preliminary figures. "That is probably why."

"Here is our version of the reports you may give to the compradore." I handed him a packet of papers. "Remember, though, do not discuss firm prices yet. We need to gather more information before we present our case to Mr. Ming."

"Why don't you want to confide in him? He works for us, not the Co-Hong merchants."

"I have a feeling these Chinese stick together as tightly as the Baghdadi Jews."

"Father trusted him implicitly."

"Father trusted no one implicitly."

"I do not care to argue with you, Dinah."

"Good, then do as I say and be discreet with him. Only offer these figures for now."

"As you wish, taipan," he said with an exaggerated bow. He backed out of the room.

Promptly at four, Godfrey Troyte arrived, soaked from the late-afternoon downpour.

"It is you who need the lifeline this afternoon," I said, shaking my head. "Come, sit by the fire and I will pour some tea." The man's lips were blue. "Would you like some brandy added?"

"Please" was his grateful reply.

By the time he was warmed in body, Godfrey had also come up to steam as far as his tales went. "What many newcomers find hard to

568

comprehend is that while European nations have thrived because they settled near the sea and ventured out, the Chinese believe they prospered because they discouraged sea trade. They take pride in being the Inner Land. Only the Cantonese, perhaps because they are so far from the center of imperial power in Peking, have ever relished trading. Why, then, did the emperor allow them to indulge in this dangerous intermingling? Because we barbarians had developed a passion for tea. Once our tongues had been tempted with the noble leaf's brew, the Chinese found we would pay ludicrous prices to satisfy our craving. This is why they licensed the original ten Co-Hong families to control the trade and agreed to keep the Pearl River open so tea could flow out—not realizing that traffic would soon flow the other way when the barbarians tired of dumping vast amounts of bullion and not finding the Chinese willing to take anything in exchange."

"Why opium?" I asked.

"Opium was the single product that did not exist in China and for which there was not only a demand but also an increasing urgency." Godfrey went on disgorging a prodigious amount of knowledge on the conflicts between the Cantonese dockworkers and the tea merchants, the Co-Hong guilds and their handling of foreign currency exchanges, and the blow-by-blow details of the two opium wars. ". . . Curiously, nobody knew what happened once the opium chests were brought into Canton's port. The keepers of the Heavenly Empire jealously guarded the secrets of the Inner Land. Nevertheless, what the Jardines, Sassoons, and their compatriots realized was that a considerable number of the three hundred million Chinese harbored a bottomless appetite for opium."

"The situation is different nowadays, isn't it?"

"Not really. To them, we are but a new breed of *Huang-Maou*, redheaded barbarians." He gestured to my hair, which from the days at sea had streaks of ruddy gold around my face. "Literally, in your case."

"And the Chinese appetite for opium has not dimmed, has it?"

"The business will never be curtailed unless the young reject it and the old addicts die out. Nevertheless, customers are not your problem." Godfrey's strange blue eyes roamed the room while waiting for me to comment.

"I see . . ." I said, not wanting to rise to the bait.

He stood and stretched. "I must be going. If I stay any longer, your fine brandy and mesmerizing fire will conspire—against my will in such splendid company—to put me to sleep."

I leaned back in my chair. "What *is* my problem, Mr. Troyte?"

A nuance of triumph registered on his face. "The districts of Yunnan and Szechuan are being blanketed in poppies. Word has it the Szechuan is turning up a higher morphine content than premium Patna." He reached into his vest pocket. "I brought you this article by the Shanghai correspondent for the *Times* of London saying the Chinese plant is 'all but universal' in the central regions."

"I had not realized that." My concern must have shown on my face, for he came over to me, took my hand in his, and patted it. "Your saving grace is that Indian opium is considered the finest by the wealthiest users. There will always be those who prefer to pay a steep price because it makes them think they are getting a superior product. The common people might be swayed to accept the cheapest version."

Gulliver, seeing the strange man holding my hand, edged forward. Godfrey acknowledged his concern with a nod of his head, but did not let go. Because I did not feel in the least bit attracted to or threatened by the man, I did not withdraw. "You have been most helpful. I do hope we shall meet again."

"Tomorrow, then," he said without any query in his manner. He bent forward and kissed my hand, then left before Gulliver could open the door for him.

That evening, after I had told Jonah about my encounter, he seemed uninterested. I suppose I had expected him to be disapproving, and when he was not, I decided it was more satisfactory having a brother as a companion than a father, a mother, or even a husband. Not that Godfrey was the slightest rival for Edwin. The man's pallor, darting eyes, and exotic mannerisms were intriguing, but held no romantic charms.

"What did the compradore have to say today?" I asked next.

"I approached the matter of prices—without mentioning specifics, as you desired—and he was resistant to anything but last season's figures."

"I expected he would be. After all, when we are gone, he will have to live with the wrath of the merchants."

"That brings another matter to mind," Jonah slipped in silkily. "I have been thinking that a Sassoon should remain in Hong Kong year-round. Perhaps our father might have found the Chinese less confounding if he had become a resident."

I stared at him with a fresh regard. His point was well taken, but who would want to live on this rugged ridge of lofty granite? "Are you volunteering?" I teased.

"Perhaps I am." His expression was unflinching.

"You cannot possibly decide that now. What if your wife would not want to leave Calcutta? It is harder for a woman to adjust to a new society. I know, I was miserable in Cochin."

He opened his mouth, then closed it. Every time marriage or women were mentioned, he shut himself off from me. Since he had not provoked me about Godfrey, I extended him the same courtesy and changed the subject.

❦ ❦ ❦

The next afternoon Godfrey began our conversation with a discussion about the upcoming festivities. "This week the Chinese will begin the Year of the Dog and the twenty-fourth year of the reign of the Emperor Kwang Hsu."

"Why is it called the Year of the Dog?"

"Chinese astrologers base their calculations on a cycle of twelve lunar years. The signs follow each other in the same order. Each year is represented by an animal, which influences the lives, destiny, and character of the people born that year. For instance, the rooster has to scratch about to find food, the rat is destined to be trapped, the cat always lands on his feet." He went on to explain that the actual choice had been made by Buddha, who had summoned the beasts in creation to visit him, and only twelve turned up. "To each he offered a year to bear its name. The animals accepted and now the years run in the order of their arrival at the party."

"Will the Year of the Dog be a productive one?"

"Actually, it's an unsettled period in which we'll be pessimistic, anxious, and worrying about our future. How this affects the individual depends on the year of the person. When were you born?"

"In 1872."

"A monkey. I might have guessed! This year the monkeys will wait patiently for the end of their difficulties, particularly in the arena of finance and romance. May I ask when your husband was born?"

"The same year."

"How splendid for you both! Monkeys produce extraordinary people. They are intellectuals with a thirst for knowledge. Also, they are great readers, cultured, with fantastic memories. Some can recall the tiniest details of everything they have seen, read, or heard."

"My husband can do that."

"Monkeys are also excellent problem solvers."

"Are there any negatives?"

"Well . . ."—Godfrey grinned mischievously—"since you asked. They can be independent and selfish, determined that nobody will put anything over on them. A monkey must be in charge, even if it means bending his scruples to get his way. Despite this, people always seek out monkeys for their intelligence and wit."

"How do we fare in romantic matters?"

"Monkeys fall in love too rapidly, but later may become critical of their partners."

My heart began to hammer in my chest. I did not want to hear any more about myself—or Edwin. "You seem to know a great deal about this."

"One of my specialties. The wisdom of the signs continues to confound me."

"What animal are you?"

"I am a cat. Refined, reserved, ambitious. Nobody ignores cats because we are good company."

"How true."

"Now, even though you were too polite to ask, here are the unpleasant aspects. Cats are social yet superficial. The indiscreet cat is sometimes a gossip to the point of scandalmongering. He is conservative, abhorring anything that disturbs his quiet life. In speculations, he is fortunate and he has the gift for nosing out bargains. To others, the placid cat is a formidable entrepreneur, which is to his advantage. Fortunately, the cat is an astute businessman and anybody who signs a contract with one need not worry."

Lady Robinson's warning came to mind. "Is that something you would agree with?"

"Certainly."

"Where would you speculate these days?"

"In Hong Kong real estate. The crown is about to sign a ninety-nine-year lease with the Chinese for the rest of the peninsula of Kowloon together with seventy-five islands. Once the documents are sealed, real-estate prices will soar."

I was intrigued by this, especially in light of Jonah's interest in remaining in Hong Kong. "What if the lease is not enough to attract buyers who don't want to lose their investment in a hundred years?"

"In my experience, most people think more about what they will eat tomorrow than their grandchildren's future."

"I suppose that may be true, however some may not trust a cat," I dared.

His sharp eyes steadied on me. "I agree. Some believe witches and wizards change themselves into cats. Our mysterious nature puzzles others. What you must remember is the cat's weaknesses can be mutated into its strengths."

Suddenly uncomfortable with the man's defensive posture, I turned to Jonah. "My brother is four years younger. What does that make him?"

"A rat."

"Poor Jonah."

"No, it is a rather good sign, except this year he should pay more attention to his business affairs rather than his love affairs. The rat seems to be calm and well-balanced, but beware! Beneath that placid exterior there is a restlessness that can get him into trouble. Interestingly, the monkey casts a spell over the rat, although the rat will never admit it."

"What are you saying?"

"The rat will come into his own once the monkey leaves his side. If possible, he should couple with a dragon or a buffalo."

"Neither sounds very romantic. Tell me, should two monkeys be married to each other?" I asked gently, even though the spike twisted anew in my heart.

"Total complicity links monkeys. Together they should go far, unless they compete, playing 'I'm-smarter-than-you.' "

I gulped at the last, but managed to reply steadily, "How intriguing this is. How could I learn more about it?"

"Tomorrow I will bring you a chart I have translated into English," he said, standing and stretching.

"Are you leaving already?"

"Not if you would like me to stay."

"I did have a few more questions."

"I expected you would. A monkey is not satisfied until she is versed in what is happening in the world."

"My interests here extend only to the small yet hidden world of the opium trade."

"There is some problem you are trying to solve and you think I can help you. Why not get to the point directly?"

"Do I hear the cat speaking to the monkey?"

"Exactly." He grinned, revealing stained yellow teeth and gray gums.

What did I have to lose? I told him—without mentioning that my own uncle was the culprit—of the problem at the Calcutta auction and the need to raise prices by almost twenty percent. "The compradore is balking at presenting new prices."

Godfrey paced in front of the windows, which dripped with moisture, blanking out the view. "Mr. Ming did not gain his position by trampling on his customers."

"He works for us."

"Now, Madam Monkey, you must be shrewd enough to see the Co-Hong merchants are the ones who really work for you. Without them you would have no sales. Or, looking at it from a cat's perspective, *you* work for the merchants."

Squirming, I replied, "I hadn't thought of it that way." There was something about the man that made me feel as though I was tied in knots. Then, after a few moments' quiet, my brain began to unravel the twisted skein, until I found the end. "There is another point that shifts the balance back in our favor. According to everything we have been able to learn, there is more demand than supply. Therefore we should be able to set the prices."

"Yes, you have a point. However, while opium eaters may not be able to stop, they can cut back on consumption, dilute their pipes, buy more locally grown flowers, make deals on the side with some of the other Indian merchants . . ."

"I see." This was something I had to work out for myself. What was the worst that might happen? Prices could not be moved more than, say, five percent, and I would have lost a considerable portion of the currency from the Luddy inheritance. Even so, I would not have to touch the land and other assets I had promised to keep intact; and no matter what, the Lanyados still would have been routed.

Godfrey interrupted my contemplations. "Cats and monkeys can go around and around forever. I will not string you along when I have an answer to your problem."

I sat up straighter. "Yes?"

"There is a man who works outside the system of Indian trading companies and Co-Hong merchants." He drew Chinese characters on the window while he spoke. "Sometimes he buys whole shipments and keeps them back until he senses a shortage, then brings his on the market at a higher price. As you might imagine, he is not well-liked, since he squeezes his share from each side of the deal. But he is influential." My mentor turned to face me. "If anyone can help you, he can"—he gave a lopsided grin—"as long as he would profit in the end."

"Who is he?"

"Song Kung Ni is the name he goes by. He's not Chinese, or at least not full-blooded. His past is somewhat mysterious. Some say he was born in Macao from parents of mixed backgrounds—some combination of Portuguese, Chinese, Indian . . . who knows? Others suggest he came from India, since he knows Hindustani." He gestured for Chen Ah Bun to bring his coat. "If you are willing, I could arrange an introduction."

"Does the monkey need to tell the cat what she would like to do?"

"No," he replied as he dressed to leave. "Consider it done."

$$ \text{\Large ❦ ❦ ❦} $$

On Friday we were expected at the compradore's dinner party. Mr. Ming had not visited Mount Gough since our arrival because I preferred for Jonah to deal with him at a distance until, armed with a deeper knowledge, I was ready to discuss our pricing structure. In preparation, I was using the time to pump Godfrey further and study the data Jonah supplied. After the New Year was over, I would commence discussions in earnest. For the present, I thought it best to keep our evening at the Ming home purely social.

"I wonder what year Mr. Ming was born?" I asked my brother as we made our way down the mountain.

"Why?"

"Remember what I told you about Chinese astrology?"

"That nonsense!"

"I thought the same at first, but the coincidences I found in Godfrey's chart were uncanny."

"In what way?"

"It said you are a rat and so was our father, which means you should be able to follow in his footsteps with ease."

"I'm flattered, I suppose."

"And Amar is a charming goat with a weak will who makes noises like a leader but fools nobody."

"That sounds like the man you described."

"Also, poor Silas was a typical dragon: idealistic, a perfectionist, demanding, but generous. The chart suggested that dragon men should choose artistic professions instead of business, said they usually marry late or not at all. Even odder, dragons are often the cause of some drama of despair. How can the system be so uncannily accurate?"

"Perhaps because you interpret generalities too closely."

"What do you mean?"

"What did it say about Uncle Samuel?"

"I believe he is a dog. They're always on the defensive, alert, watching for an opportunity. That fits."

"Aren't dogs supposed to be loyal?"

"Yes, but—"

"You can read anything into those descriptions you want, picking and choosing what applies, discarding what does not."

"I suppose you are right, Mr. Rat, but I find it amusing nevertheless." Piqued that he had found holes in my new interest, I changed the subject. "Have you ever been to the compradore's house before?"

"Once with Father, but not for dinner. This is quite an honor, especially for a woman." He gave me an apologetic smile. "I am certain you will like his family. He has four sons."

"Any daughters?"

"No, but he has a niece who was sent to live with him as a child." Jonah's placid face became animated. "Her name is Wu Bing. 'Bing' means 'ice,' which doesn't suit her, for she has a round, gentle face . . . and the prettiest hands you ever saw, even if she does act as the Mings' unpaid servant."

"What do you mean?"

"She's their *mui tsai*, literally a younger sister, who was given to the family because they were better able to feed and clothe her. To the Chinese, a daughter is a financial drain. Only sons carry on the family name and inherit its wealth."

"Do they treat her well?"

"Yes, by their standards. She waits on the wife and does other household chores."

"What does she get in return?"

"Her parents received a packet of 'lucky money' to help pay off their debts, and the Mings have assumed responsibility for her future."

"Does she ever get to leave?"

"If she contracts a suitable marriage."

"When did you meet this girl?" I asked slowly.

"I told you, when we visited the Mings last year."

"You said you were there only once. She must have made quite an impression."

He looked away. "She did."

I would have pursued the matter if the carriage had not stopped in front of a moon gate. The house, built up on several terraces, had many layers of tiled roofs curved like prows at the corners. It was as opulent as many on the Peak.

"Why has the compradore chosen to live close to the harbor, when the government officials and wealthier families prefer the Peak?"

"Only the members of the British and European community are permitted to live on the Peak."

"That seems unfair, when it was Chinese originally."

Jonah seemed distracted as he took my arm. "Come, there is someone I want you to meet."

Mr. Ming Hien Chang, who was wearing his Victoria Jubilee medal, greeted us cordially. He introduced us to the compradores of Melchers and Co., Siemssen and Co., the Chartered Bank, the Davidson Company, and of course Jardine, Matheson. Each had three names, with the last name first, generational name second, and first name last. In a few moments I was hopelessly confused. As soon as possible, Jonah bowed to the men and whisked me away to a humid conservatory.

"This is Wu Bing," he said, his voice echoing off the glass panels.

I looked around. From the leafy shadows came a trembling movement. A hesitant girl kowtowed to me. "An honor to meet the venerable sister of Mr. Jonah."

Startled by her lilting accent and sweet upturned face, I looked at my brother for an explanation. He was watching me intently. Turning back to the child, I found her not as young as I had first thought. Her wide, luminous eyes studied my reaction. Something in her hopeful expression touched me.

"Who is this?"

"The youngest daughter of Mr. Ming's second brother."

"That is not what I meant." I saw his gaze lock with hers. As though she bathed in the light of a dozen candles, Wu Bing glowed in my brother's presence. Phrasing my words carefully so as not to hurt the girl's feelings, I continued, "Who is she to you?"

"I care for her," he said simply.

"No wonder the compradore has been suspicious of us," I said too harshly, then lowered my voice. "Has he seen you with her?"

"I have never spent more than a few minutes with her."

"Then how could you ever consider his niece if you hardly know her?"

"Who are you to criticize me?" he asked, grinning mischievously. "I seem to remember you fell in love with Edwin after one glimpse from a balcony—and he with you."

"That's not what happened."

"Oh, no? That first evening when you thought he might accept Ruby, you became hysterical. We wondered whether you had lost your mind. Have you forgotten?"

"I suppose I did become entranced rather quickly with him," I said, feeling a bit dizzy in the fragrant closeness of the hothouse, "but our friendship deepened when we became better acquainted."

"Anyway, it worked out in the end for you both. There has never been a happier marriage in our family, at least that is what everyone says." Jonah waited for me to contradict him.

Unwilling to confess anything about our current estrangement, I did not argue. Thankfully, a gong clanged. We were being called to dinner.

At the doorway, the compradore introduced me to his wife, a bony woman with snow-white hair, and then with the inverse modesty of the Chinese, to his sons. "My eldest son, a lazy boy who needs to study harder; my second son, who eats too much to play a proper game of tennis; my third son, who prefers girls to hard work; and my fourth, who is probably the most backward of the lot."

Jonah knew the ritual. "Oh, but isn't your eldest son the top boy in his class and your second the captain of his team . . . ?" Pleased that he had learned so much on his earlier trip, I nodded and smiled and let my brother smooth our way.

Instead of one long table, the dining room contained many round ones with eight to twelve places at each. In a side room a small army of cooks tended woks over charcoal fires. Jonah and I were given seats at the table with the eldest son and some of the other compradores we had met earlier, including a plump man who was with Russell and Company, the leading American opium firm. Immediately I noticed that no other women were seated in the room. Even Mrs. Ming had disappeared.

During the week Jonah had coached me in the use of chopsticks, so I did not feel overly awkward as I attempted the first platter: stewed pigeon eggs and vegetables. Lord Hargreaves' warning made me wary at first, but it was tasty. I went on to enjoy fried quail with bamboo shoots, a soup which did include the controversial sharks' fins, a dish with slippery noodles and prawns (I avoided the shellfish not entirely successfully), and chicken flavored with a curious spice. Only a mushroom-and-fish concoction did not please my palate, and Jonah warned me when pork was served. Since the Chinese did not seem to include milk products in their cuisine, I finished most of the courses feeling relatively secure that I had not violated the dietary laws too blatantly, although I had far exceeded the usual limits of my stomach's capacity.

Just when I was certain the meal was ending, platters of carp were passed. Mr. Ming, who was circulating through the room, stopped at our table and asked, "May I offer you some fish?"

I thanked him politely.

The head of the fish was placed before me. Its huge glassy eye stared at me accusingly.

"The guest of honor is given the head," Jonah explained.

"I am flattered," I said, trying to hide my queasiness.

"To eat the eye is to bring good luck," Mr. Ming said in a manner that did not indicate this was a joke.

Carefully I lifted the eye from its socket and deftly offered it to Jonah. "Fortune has smiled upon me. I have a wonderful husband and three fine sons. My brother should be the one to have this honor." I gave Jonah a sly grin. As far back as childhood, he had had a reputation for eating anything. He did not disappoint me.

With one gulp he swallowed the eye. "What could be better to see in the new year?" he quipped, pleasing Mr. Ming and astonishing me.

The compradore gave him a bow of respect, then asked me, "Would you like to see my garden?"

Grateful for the excuse to avoid more food, I nodded and went outside. Gulliver followed at a safe but respectful distance without rankling the compradore, who accepted that a woman required protection, even from him.

The house, which looked impressive from the road, climbed several levels on the hill behind to reveal a substantial mansion. The compradore walked me out into his terraced garden, linked by flights of steps and winding pathways. There was a concrete tennis court, currently used as a nursery for plants, and a large vegetable patch at the highest level, where Mr. Ming said he preferred to do much of the work himself, "to clear my head after a day in the office." From there we had a fine view of the harbor below. He pointed out the mat-sheds, temporary structures of bamboo and palm leaves which were being set up for the next day's celebrations, then led me into a rose arboretum.

Gardening had never been a particular interest of mine, so I could not uphold my end of the conversation. After dutifully admiring the blossoms, I impulsively abandoned my decision to avoid business that night and asked the main question running around in my head. "Compradore, are you acquainted with a Mr. Song Kung Ni?"

Even in the dimness of the garden lanterns, the man could not hide his consternation. "Why do you ask?"

"I have been told he could be of some use to us."

"Impossible!"

"But why? Isn't he an important man in the trade?"

"Not to us." He made a raw, hawking noise deep in his throat and spat into the night. "No. Never."

This finality, without explanation, was most exasperating. Since the subject was obviously sensitive, I decided to tread lightly. "I have heard it said that he might be of assistance with our particular difficulty."

"What difficulty is that, may I ask?"

"I must apologize for not being more forthcoming earlier, compradore, but I am new to this business as well as to Hong Kong." I took a deep breath. "Due to some singular circumstances, the auction prices in Calcutta ran more than twenty percent higher than usual."

The man's cheeks sucked in with surprise. "The merchants will never buy from us at that price!"

"What if we raised it by . . ." I was going to suggest fifteen percent, but an inner voice told me to minimize it further. ". . . say, ten to twelve percent? Then, if we held it there for three seasons to come, we would make up the difference eventually."

"There has never been an increase of more than a few points. Don't forget, we have competition from other traders and the Chinese themselves."

"You yourself estimated the demand was there."

"Not at ridiculous prices. You will have to accept a loss if you are to stay in business."

"If *we* are to stay in business, compradore, I suggest we look beyond the narrow horizons of the past. Why not open your mind and think about Song Kung Ni? What could it hurt to talk with him?"

The man's eyes bulged. "You do not know what you are asking."

"Explain it to me."

"Companies of the caliber of the Sassoons or Jardine, Matheson do not do business with men of his sort." He wrinkled his nose, as if the very idea gave off a bad odor. "If you force my hand, I will resign."

I backed off. "My apologies, compradore." There was a mystery here. Perhaps Godfrey could help me unravel it. This might be a personal feud between our compradore and Mr. Song. If Godfrey thought it worthwhile to meet Song Kung Ni, I would do so. My father had warned me about the complexities of dealing with the Chinese, for they had to save "face." By acting on my own, we might secure the help we needed, while not compromising the compradore's pride.

When we returned to the others, tea was being served in the drawing room. I looked around for Jonah, but he was nowhere in sight. Putting my concerns about the opium business aside, I decided to concentrate my worries on his potentially disastrous flirtation.

❦ ❦ ❦

The morning of Chinese New Year's Eve dawned clear, with mauve and purple and pink slashes across the harbor sky. Sampans and junks dotted the horizon, their sails like the wings of distant insects. I sipped a cup of green tea and tried to organize my thoughts. The novel sights, sounds, questions, languages, and personalities had exhausted me. My new acquaintances—Godfrey Troyte, the compradore, Wu Bing—were utterly perplexing, each in his or her own way. Why did Godfrey want to bother himself with me? How could I win Mr. Ming's trust? And where would Jonah's concern for his niece lead? Thoughts of my children crowded in. What were they doing at the moment? Did they miss me? Had it been a mistake to leave them for so long? And what of Edwin?

Jonah sauntered into the room wearing his flannel dressing gown. *"Kong Hey Fat Choi,"* he greeted. "Happy New Year."

Chen Ah Bun served him tea. "Kong Hey Fat Choi," they said to each other.

"We will have to give the servants time off after midday. This is the most momentous holiday of their year."

"We can manage with Gulliver."

"Right. Now, how shall we celebrate?"

"Must we?"

"When in Rome . . ."

I sighed deeply. "I would give anything for a quiet evening at home."

"We have several invitations," he reminded me. "The compradore would like us to join his family, and the Davidsons are giving a party for foreigners."

The Davidsons reminded me of Olivia and the tense auction. "I would rather not attend that one."

"There is a gathering at Government House to see the fireworks. Your friend Godfrey Troyte will be there."

"Couldn't I have a headache and spend the evening home?"

My brother looked crestfallen. "I suppose . . ."

"That doesn't mean you shouldn't go where you like. I'll be fine here with Gulliver."

Brightening, he asked slowly, "Are you certain?"

"Absolutely. Which gala will you attend?"

"I thought I might return to the compradore's."

"Do you think that would be wise?"

"I need to talk to Wu Bing. Tonight, with the confusion, we might have some time alone."

"I suppose you need to settle this infatuation. When the girl learns how hopeless her quest is, she will be more realistic about her future."

"This is not an infatuation!"

"Jonah, don't be absurd. If you want to have a fling with a servant girl, that is one thing. Anything more is absurd."

"Wu Bing is doomed to a life of servitude because of circumstances. She comes from a good family—the same family as the compradore—and is far from ignorant. She reads and writes in Chinese and has taught herself English."

"What are you doing, Jonah, trying to rescue her?"

"On the contrary, she will rescue me."

"It would never work. What would Father . . . ?" I caught myself. Tears billowed behind my eyes. We were alone in the world, alone to make our own decisions for better or worse. Zilpah would be shocked, but with her own unusual background she could hardly complain. Why, even Silas' Nepalese mother had been a convert to Judaism, and Zilpah had approved of him.

"Would Wu Bing consider converting?"

"Yes, I mentioned it. Truthfully, she has no idea what being a Jew means and she would be doing it only to please me. Nevertheless, I would want our children to be Jewish; therefore it would be necessary."

"You *are* serious about this."

Jonah blinked anxiously. "Actually, I am unsure. As I said, I need to be with her in private. Do you remember when Edwin came to Calcutta? Didn't the time you had together help settle your minds on whether to marry?"

"Yes, it did."

"Time for us will never be given freely. I must steal what I can and see what happens."

"Maybe you will discover you are not suited. These matters are more obvious than one would believe. For instance, I knew from the first that Silas was the wrong match for me, but I was so young, so inexperienced, I did not know how to interpret the signals. Then, when Edwin came along, the message of rightness was indisputable. Even so"—I searched for the words to convince him—"people who are deeply compatible continue to have difficulties as they traverse the mountains and valleys of a life together. Edwin and I shared the same faith, had agreeable parents, were of the same age and similar background. In my experience, the differences become magnified over the years, but the similarities are what pull you through."

Jonah was quiet for a long while. The sky turned bluer and bluer. White clouds, like sails without hulls, hovered over the islands in the harbor. "You may be right," he said, startling me, for I had expected an argument. "I must discover this truth for myself."

51

❧ ❧ ❧

The house was quiet. Two clocks, a porcelain one on the mantelpiece and a grandfather in the hall, ticked in opposition to each other. I drank a glass of claret as I watched the sunset dapple the harbor with an oddly greenish hue. Gulliver cooked me a supper of eggs and toast. For a moment I was so lonely, I almost asked the stocky Gurkha to take his meal with me. Fortunately, I quickly discarded the notion. Gulliver would have felt awkward, but would not have known how to agree or refuse. How inexperienced I was with being on my own. Not since Edwin had left me in Travancore had I been without a busy family life. If I was this lonely, how must my babies be feeling? Where did they think I was? Did they worry I might never return? Could the twins possibly forget me? When this business was concluded, I would rush back to Calcutta and smother my children with love.

Outside, firecrackers splintered the air. The long evening stretched before me. It had been foolhardy to presume the night would be peaceful. Perhaps something to read might be diverting. Perusing bookshelves, I pulled out Kipling's *Plain Tales from the Hills*, then closed it after the first few sentences reminded me of Darjeeling. Ignoring the row of Stevenson and Henry James in favor of Sir Arthur Conan Doyle's *A Study in Scarlet*, I settled into the lumpy armchair by the window and tucked a woolen coverlet over my legs.

I opened the book.

In the year of 1878 I took my degree of Doctor of Medicine of the University of London, and proceeded to Netley to go through the course prescribed for surgeons in the Army. Having completed my studies there, I was duly attached to the Fifth Northumberland Fusiliers as assistant surgeon . . .

582

Gulliver brewed a perfect cup of Luddy's finest Darjeeling tea and placed lemon biscuits on a tray. He laid an extra log on the fire. In the distance, flares of vermilion and jade green were inverse comets in the void. Intermittent showers of gold and silver rained down. The constant bangs, pops, and crackles that punctuated the night were becoming a familiar but not annoying distraction, like someone else's boisterous children. I became absorbed in the tale.

"You have been in Afghanistan, I perceive."

"How on earth did you know that?" I asked in astonishment.

"Never mind," said he, chuckling to himself . . .

Engrossed in the story and no longer sensitive to the din, I missed the knock on the door of the White Chalet. Gulliver's announcement of a visitor came as a heart-thumping jolt.

"No, please don't get up," Godfrey Troyte insisted. "You look wonderfully settled."

I pushed aside the comforter and straightened my gown. "Kong Hey Fat Choi," I said.

"Well done. Kong Hey Fat Choi to you as well. I was concerned when you did not arrive at Government House."

"We sent our regrets."

"I heard. I hope you are not ill. Some visitors experience distress because of the new food or the water."

"Not in the least. Only tired."

"And your brother?"

"He had another engagement, and frankly, I was looking forward to a quiet evening at home."

A nearby rocket boom caused the windows to tremble. "You have chosen the wrong night in Hong Kong."

"Obviously."

"There will be plenty of time to rest over the next few days. Why not come out and enjoy the merriment in the streets?"

"I am quite content." I realized that Godfrey was still standing and had not even taken off his coat. "That doesn't mean I am not delighted to see you. Why not stay for a few minutes? I opened a bottle of claret for my dinner, or there is sherry or port . . ."

"The claret, please."

As Gulliver took Godfrey's coat, did I notice a flicker of displeasure in his eyes? No matter, I couldn't be impolite to the man who had come all this way on my behalf. I placed the book aside and smoothed my hair.

Sitting down, Godfrey tasted the wine and licked his pink lips. "I told Song Kung Ni about you," he began without preface.

I decided not to react, and waited for him to continue.

"He is most anxious to meet you."

"How kind of you to make the arrangements so swiftly. I am looking forward to hearing what assistance he might offer."

"Excellent. I have a feeling he will clarify matters for you."

"If so, I shall be grateful," I said, and noticing his slight smirk, wondered if I would owe Godfrey money or favors or both. "When can the meeting be organized?"

"Whenever you wish."

"I am available anytime."

"How about right now?"

"Tonight?"

"Why not?"

"In the midst of the celebrations?"

"It won't make any difference to Song Kung Ni."

"Where does he live?"

"On the other side of the city in an area called Happy Valley."

That sounded pleasant enough, but I could not imagine going there so impulsively.

Godfrey realized I was hesitating. "The drive will take us past the most impressive illuminations. If we time it right, we can arrive at a propitious moment for you to negotiate: the Hour of the Monkey."

"Even the hours have animal names."

"Right. The Chinese divide the day into twelve two-hour portions, beginning at four A.M. with the Hour of the Rooster, then moving to the Hour of the Dog at six A.M. and ending at two A.M. with the Hour of the Sheep."

"What time is the Hour of the Monkey?"

"Ten in the evening."

A burst of white light glowed in the southern sky. "I suppose it would be foolish to ignore the festivities," I said, slowly giving in. The sooner I finished up in Hong Kong, the sooner I would be on my way home to the children . . . and Edwin. "I'll need half an hour to prepare myself." I stood and clapped for Gulliver. "Have another glass of wine, won't you?"

❦ ❦ ❦

Gulliver was jittery, and every fusillade of firecrackers unnerved him further. Seeing the tension etched in his normally placid face, I realized that I had been selfish to drag him out so late. Both of us had required a respite. I should have insisted he remain behind to guard the house. Not that he would have obeyed. All I could do was hope Godfrey would not keep us out the whole night.

Huge bonfires glowed on the hilltops as we made our way down from the Peak. Houses on the terraces glowed with Chinese lanterns that looked like molten oranges. A large open carriage awaited us at the bottom of the tramway, but our passage to the road closest to the harbor was tedious because of a procession blocking the road. Dragons with frightful heads and burnished scales pranced through the streets on hundreds of legs. Drums, gongs, and bells jangled and boomed raucously as musicians weaved in and out of the lanes.

Bracelets of lights outlined many of the vessels in the harbor. At the water's edge we passed bamboo structures over three hundred feet high. "What are those for?" I wondered.

"When illuminated later, they will make pictures in fire."

"It must look wonderful from the bay."

"Actually, the worst place to be tonight is on a ship," Godfrey explained. "Last year I joined a party on a large Canton riverboat, the *Hankow*. The night navigation, what with all the launches rushing about, was even riskier than getting around on land."

That hardly seemed possible, since the crowds formed one long sinuous river. The horses weren't able to pick up speed until we were away from the densest population around the waterfront. Even along the lonely rim road, fires blazed, rockets splintered the sky, and children's faces glowed in the glare of their hand-held sticks of dazzling light.

As we arrived in Happy Valley, Godfrey pointed out the cemetery situated on the sides of the mountain that sloped gently into the valley. "A most picturesque place to spend eternity," he assured me, although not much could be appreciated at night. "Over there is the race course. Song Kung Ni owns some of the fastest ponies on the track."

"Is that why he chooses to live out here?"

"I suppose," Godfrey said, launching into a description of local racing customs.

When I could slip in a word, I tried to focus on the reason for the journey. "What does Mr. Song know about me?"

"More than I told him."

"What do you mean?"

"He knew you were the taipan of the Sassoons, that your father was Benjamin of Calcutta, even your age."

"How did he learn that?"

In the twinkling light of the lamps that lined the road, Godfrey's cat eyes gleamed with a golden tinge. "None of it is a secret."

"Does he know about my need to raise the price of opium?"

"I hinted at your predicament."

"What did he say?"

"He said he would like to meet you, no more, no less." Godfrey pointed at the high wall that loomed in front of us. Beyond it I could make out the roofs of a house situated on a rise. "And here we are." A guard with a rifle slung across his back opened the creaky iron gate. "Do you know why the Chinese like to wall their houses?" He did not wait for a reply. "To keep evil spirits out. That's the same reason their roofs curl at the corners."

At the entrance, two eight-foot porcelain statues of fierce tigers bracketed the doorway. In the torchlight their saber teeth gleamed menacingly, and for a moment I thought I saw blood dripping from their mouths, but dismissed the image as a shadow.

Once inside, we walked along a dim hallway. The floors, walls, and ceiling were constructed from an aromatic wood that made our foot-steps reverberate with the muffled beat of a faraway drum. Two servants wearing white silk caftans and black pantaloons bowed and opened double doors to a chamber lit by candles in stone lanterns. Elongated shadows curving from the floor up a red-silk-covered wall preceded our entrance into the room.

A heavyset man wearing a black Chinese cap was lying on a divan on the distant side of the room. His back was turned to us. After a long moment he rolled partially on his other side, but not enough to look directly at us. "Kong Hey Fat Choi, Godfrey," he said with a rumbling voice.

"Happy New Year to you too. May I present Mrs. Salem, the taipan of Sassoon and Company."

The man cocked his head to the side too quickly for me to see much of his face, then turned away as if the light bothered him. "The world of the new year appears better and better if the taipans of the future are going to look like you, madam." Just as Godfrey had hinted, the man's lilting accent seemed slightly Indian.

A faint rustling caught my eye, and I turned to find two guards dressed in black from head to foot leaning against columns. Only their shuffling feet and the whites of their eyes betrayed them. Gulliver glided closer to me.

Slowly Mr. Song Kung Ni backed his bulky frame into a chair behind a table and sat down. His arm extended to point out cushioned stools. "Make yourselves comfortable in my lair."

"Mr. Song, are you by any chance a tiger?" I asked to break the tension.

Without turning around, the man tilted his head deferentially. "God-frey, you did not warn me the taipan was well-schooled in our ways."

"Mr. Troyte taught my classes."

"How splendid for you." The man's jowls vibrated. "What did he tell you about us tigers?"

"Tigers are rebels," I began, editing my remarks rapidly, since I could recall only negative images: the fault-finder, the hothead, the ringleader, the reckless and irresponsible one. "And leaders. People respect them, even those working against them, which is just as well, for the tiger prefers being obeyed to obeying."

Song clapped his hands, although they were too padded to make much sound. "Well done. But that is what I would expect from a monkey."

"How did you know?" I asked, shooting a glance at Godfrey. He threw up his hands as if to say he was innocent. He must have mentioned it and then forgotten, or else he did not want me to realize how thoroughly he had briefed our host.

"My friends, I see you are well-matched," Godfrey began in a syrupy voice. "Only the snake, who is too wise for him, and the monkey, who is too clever, can outwit the tiger." He leaned back and waited to see who would pick up that lead.

Song did not snap at the lure. I thought he was waiting to see how I would react. Feeling that I had to reestablish myself as someone besides a monkey, I backed off the subject entirely and asked, "Did you build this magnificent house?"

"I did," Song said, sounding bored.

"And you picked Happy Valley to be near the race course."

"That is true."

"Do you own many horses?"

"Many."

A long silence ensued. No servants moved forward to offer refreshment. The room reeked with a fruity smell of incense and something I could not identify. My stomach churned. Faraway fireworks sounded like rifle shots. There was a loud blast from the settlement outside the walled enclosure, then stillness. Across the room a brass clock chimed. I counted along. Ten! The Hour of the Monkey. Now what? I tried to catch Godfrey's eye. Purposely he looked the other way.

Our host stood on wobbling legs. Without turning toward us, he walked to a table, lifted a long silver implement, and stroked it. "Don't allow Godfrey to fill your head with too much peasant nonsense," he said with his back still to us, causing me to wonder if he was disfigured or had some other reason he didn't want us to see his face. "Primitive people are easier to manipulate if you understand their crude logic. The more external rules and regulations, the simpler it is to get them to do what you want." The man spoke in a whining, grating voice that sounded like a nail upon glass. "A wise man uses superstitions when they are useful to him, and discards the rest."

"I see."

"Do you?" he challenged, but before I could respond, he asked, "Has our mutual friend told you about *fung shui*?"

The term was unfamiliar. "No."

"Fung shui," he repeated disgustedly. "Literally it means 'wind and water.' It is a divination system the Chinese use to determine where the site for anything—from a grave to a house to an office building—should be placed to have the most propitious influence on the people concerned. All it does is create a high-paying job for the local charlatan who claims to have special powers to arrange these matters."

"Fung shui created Happy Valley," Godfrey rebutted in a conciliatory manner. "A grave in the southern cleft between two hills helps the dead appreciate the warm winds of winter, the cool winds of summer—as you do."

"Ah, but that is where you are wrong, my friend. The experts rejected this site for a house," he went on in an irritating whine. "They said the 'expression of its dragon was wrong.' Apparently even on this hill it is too low for a tiger, thus placing me at risk." He gave a hollow laugh.

"You seem well enough guarded to me," Godfrey said.

"That doesn't have anything to do with fung shui," Song said with annoyance. "Enough of this nonsense." Seeing him turn at last, I tried to take in his features, but they were hard to discern in the gloom. At least there was nothing abhorrent about them, although the long nose, which had a sharp twist, and the ripples of fat on his jowls and chin were hardly handsome. Godfrey had been right: the man definitely was not Chinese. He looked more like an Arab with golden skin.

There was something else, though. I swallowed hard, fighting nausea. Must be the incense, I told myself. No, it was Song. My baffled expression alerted Gulliver, and he sidled even closer behind me.

Our host looked out from the squinting eyes that had seemed Oriental at first. "A Gurkha—how clever. More devoted than dogs, or so I have been told." The candlelight seemed to disturb him, so he shielded his face.

I felt insulted for Gulliver, who never would have registered his feelings.

"My first husband left him to me. I am afraid he takes his responsibilities seriously."

"Have him wait outside."

"He would not do that. He has sworn to protect me. Besides, you yourself have guards."

"Fung shui," Godfrey reminded.

"Phooey on fung shui!" Song said, laughing uproariously at his joke. "Guards! Those cowards? Ha! They are here to light my pipe and fetch my slippers."

Pipe! That was what he twisted in his hand. What I smelled was opium mixed with a sandalwood incense. The man was under its effect right now. I would have to be more circumspect. I could settle nothing with someone who was impaired, for he might come back with a different version of a deal or claim I had taken advantage of him unfairly.

"Then why not send them away?" Godfrey wondered testily.

"Shall I tell them to leave us?" Song asked me.

"As you wish," I said in a deliberately offhand manner.

Song shot a terse Chinese command and the men in black fled the room. I waited for him to return to the subject of Gulliver, but a huge explosion, followed by myriad poppings and sparks, diverted him. He blinked his eyes and waved the air in front of him, as though shooing invisible flies. Was this the opium or some other distortion in his mind? "Now, where were we?" he said, scratching his genitals through his silk trousers.

"Why don't we discuss the reason we are here?" Godfrey interjected mercifully.

"You know how I hate to be rushed, God." He chortled. "Our mutual friend quite likes my pet name for him." His next laugh was more like a cackle.

There was something I had to know. "When did you leave India?" I forced myself to ask in a steady voice.

Song picked at his coat. "How did you know?"

"Your accent."

"It must be twenty years . . . a long time ago."

"Have you been back?"

"Once."

There were shouts of children running inside the walls; then a long string of firecrackers trembled the floor beneath our feet. Godfrey stood and went to look out. He waved the youngsters away, but remained at the window to make sure they did not return. I was forced to fend for myself with the revolting man. The sooner I brought up the matter of the opium prices, the sooner we could get away.

"I suppose you know both sides of the trade."

Song's face relaxed slightly and a tinge of a smile raised his many chins. "Yes, I do."

"Then you understand the needs of a Calcutta as well as a Co-Hong merchant."

"You might say that."

"Mr. Troyte seems to think you could assist us this season."

"Perhaps." His voice oozed like rancid oil. "What do you require?"

"Customers willing to purchase Benares and Patna at prices significantly higher than last year's."

Song waved his hands as though he was dismissing me. "I know about that. Who cares about the price? You tell me the figure you want and I will find someone who will pay it."

"Up to twenty percent higher?"

"Why not? The demand is always larger than the supply, the demand does not diminish, and the customer cannot ignore his desire."

"Will they take seven thousand chests?"

"Eventually. It might take a year to sell them into depleted markets. My name, 'Song,' is from the same Chinese character as 'deliver.' Ask around. See if I do not deliver what I say I will." An odd obsequiousness had crept into his voice, one that put me on guard. "I would welcome this opportunity to represent the Sassoon interests in Hong Kong."

I was about to ask how we would work together, since I was certain the matter could not be as simple as he made it seem, when he placed the mouthpiece of his pipe to his lips and closed his eyes. Long eyelashes fluttered as the smoke satisfied his urgency. The pipe drooped in his hand. He gave a mild shudder and his lower lip protruded, moist and florid. A flash—either of fireworks or my memory—brought a picture to mind: a man on a veranda, with his lip puckered in the same unflattering position, mimicking the sweet song of a bulbul for a little girl.

A wave of dizziness washed over me. Sensing I would need my wits about me, I summoned strength from every cell. "You know Calcutta, don't you?"

"How perceptive you are, Madam Sassoon," he said as his eyes flickered open.

"Salem," Godfrey interrupted. "She is Mrs. Salem now."

Ignoring my escort, I plunged on, while trying desperately to recall who had imitated the songbird. "Obviously, Song Kung Ni is not your birth name," I said, and as I did, comprehension washed over me. Ni . . . was for 'Nissim.' Song Kung was for . . .

"Sadka?" The word bubbled from my mouth like rising vomit. "My God!" I jumped up and stumbled backward, but one of the posts that supported the high peaks of the ceiling blocked my escape.

Taking my violent reaction for the thrill of coincidence, Godfrey asked, "You know him?" with bemused amazement.

Our host nervously licked his lips. Then his face became more composed and he spoke genially. " 'Uncle Nissim' is what she once called me."

"He killed my mother!"

"Now, Dinah, I did not," he crooned, advancing on me. Reacting to his fetid breath, I recoiled. Gulliver was just to one side of me. "I may call you Dinah, may I not? After all, that is what I knew you as many years ago in Theatre Road." He saw the distress in my eyes at the familiarity, but pressed on. "Yes, Theatre Road. Is it still the same? Such a splendid house." He spoke very slowly. Each word seemed an enormous effort. "That is why I wanted so much to meet you again. Perhaps my own inquisitiveness got the better of me. Perhaps I should have restrained myself, since an old cat like Godfrey would lecture on the adverse effects of curiosity. Nevertheless, I hoped you would not recognize me after so much time had passed. You were a young child. I thought you would have forgotten. Besides, I am thrice the size of my old self." A guttural laugh shook his belly.

Sparks burst in front of me. Whether they were from without or within, I could not tell. "I was at the trial! I know what happened. There were witnesses. Everybody agreed you did it."

"The judge did not concur," Sadka replied with infuriating confidence as he waddled back behind the wide lacquered table where his pipe had been.

"Who killed her then?" My voice was high and thin, like a child's.

"Why dredge up that sad case? Wouldn't it be better to move forward? Let us resume the business at hand. Perhaps I can make it up to you now by extricating you from the terrible mess the Sassoons are in."

"We are not in a mess," I spat. "We had a business deal to propose, but now that I know your identity, we could never work with you." I stood boldly in front of the table, supporting myself by gripping the edge slightly.

"Come now, let us not become sentimental, taipan."

His condescension cut through me like a knife, but after the first painful slice, something changed inside me. It was as if my blood had frozen. The wild churning diminished. My heartbeat slowed from erratic pips to long, steady beats. Even my hands did not tremble. I released the table and took one step backward. My eyes focused on his double chin and drooping cheeks. Behind that flesh was a glimmer of the man in that Calcutta courtroom long ago. "If you did not murder Luna Sassoon, who did?" I asked without a quaver.

"I cared for your mother. If you must blame someone," he groaned, "I suppose you must look to Moosa Chachuk."

"And you had nothing to do with it?"

Sadka shrugged. "These affairs cannot be reduced to simple explanations. Your mother was a confused woman. She was dangerous to herself, to others." His mouth turned down ominously at the corners.

"And dangerous to you?" I thought of placid, dreamy Luna lying on her chaise longue reading *Lorna Doone*. Nobody was less deserving of the savage, hideous end. . . . "What could she have done to you?" I watched Sadka for any sign that he would rise up and strike me, but he seemed deflated. Something I had said had touched him. What? What had she done to him to cause him to want her dead? I had never thought this through before. Always I had seen my mother as the innocent victim of a senseless crime. Now she was something else. She had become a target because she had frightened him.

"But why? If you really cared for her, you would have protected her, unless what they said was true."

"And what is that?"

"You were jealous."

"I might have been, but crimes of passion are not planned."

He was right. Ladders weren't purchased, or knives, or chloroform. Yet if you loved someone and had decided you had to kill her, chloroform would have been a kindness. The doctor had thought Luna had not cried out because she had not felt the pain. The memories of her wounds rose up like tentacles and clutched me, pulling me down.

"Then you were angry with my mother for something she did to you," I guessed in a subdued voice.

"Not really."

I pursued him. "You arranged for Chachuk to kill her for a reason. She refused to see you anymore. There was another man"— I was groping blindly—"my father was returning . . ." Sadka allowed me to struggle on. "You were worried she would tell someone else, tell my father . . ." There! A shadow passed in front of Sadka's heavy-lidded eyes. The irises opened wide and wondering. I pointed a finger at him. "You were frightened she would . . ." Glassy buttons of sweat beaded on his brow as he removed his silk cap and revealed a shiny bald head. He was twitching. The vulnerable spot had been pressed. Sadka reached over the table and opened a tiny box. He popped something in his mouth and closed his eyes momentarily.

The sight sickened me. As I backed farther away, a piece of furniture— the divan—tripped me. Gulliver reached to catch me, but I sat right down. For a few seconds I held my head in my hands. I could not force the truth. My only hope was to coax it, but how? There is a soothing tone mothers revert to when mollifying angry children. I harnessed it like a lifeline and looked up. "How terrible for you. You must have been concerned that somehow she could hurt you. Is that what it was?"

"In a manner of speaking," he rasped.

"She knew about . . ." I prompted.

"About my business dealings. We had shared many pipes of opium, many glasses of wine, many nights of love. She was easy to be with, undemanding, amusing, but silly. She lacked common sense. One day she tired of me. I am not certain why. I had not tired of her. On the contrary, the rejection excited me. She became more of a challenge. I determined to win her back, and for a while I did. Then she told me not to return. I was impulsive. I pressed her too hard. She became unhinged—women do at times like those—and told me . . . no, threatened me . . . to stay away. And if I did not . . ." With sinister speed he came around the table and loomed over me.

"Yes," I said, forcing myself not to shrink from his bulk.

"She warned that she would tell what she knew. I became deranged. In those days I was afraid of the police. I had smuggled, had dealt in stolen goods. In retrospect, I doubt she would have said anything to anyone, because she would have had to tell how she knew. Why would she want to compromise herself? But I was young, scared. And my friend Chachuk was alarmed. He stood to lose even more."

How ordinary he made it sound. A woman knew too much about his illegal dealings. She did not want to see him anymore. He pressed her. She frightened him. He had her killed. I fought my mounting fury. "You admit this freely now. Why didn't the judge—?"

"By then I had learned about sprinkling rupees."

"You couldn't bribe a High Court justice!"

"Everyone has a price. His was less than you might imagine." Sadka's tone was tinged with pride.

My head pounded. There was something else I had to know. "Where is Moosa Chachuk?"

Sadka shook his head. "Such an idiotic man. He could never learn to stay out of trouble. About five years ago he was killed in a brawl in Singapore in some dispute over a woman. Doesn't that come as a relief to you? As far as you are concerned, the sad business is over. We were found not guilty by a court of law and the perpetrator is dead. Now, let me make this up to you in a deal that will be advantageous to us both." His lips curled with a smile of satisfaction.

My forbearance exploded. Sadka was near enough for me to grab, and this I did by leaping up and throwing myself at him. I pummeled his shoulders, his chest. Noticing Gulliver's hand hovering near mine, I defiantly pushed him away with one hand. "No! This is for me to do!" With the other hand I continued to pelt Sadka. The heavyset man was more muscular than flabby. He accepted a few blows, then pushed me aside roughly, making it impossible for me to encircle his thick, corded neck. I fell against his table, gasped for a breath, and started back to claw him.

"Dinah . . ." Sadka warned harshly. He raised a knee to ward me off while his arms slapped at invisible insects. I was too hysterical to remember I was dealing with a man in an opium stupor. Some moments he had been lucid, others crazed. My fingernails grazed his cheek before he raised his leg. His swift kick to my abdomen stunned me for a second.

Gulliver moved forward to block me as I heard Godfrey's hiss from the far corner of the room. "My God, Dinah! Stop!"

Wheeling around, I caught a glimpse of him cowering and then shot a look back to Sadka. His face was bleeding from the one long scratch I had managed to inflict. He was pointing a pistol at me. Where had it come from? He might have armed himself behind the table or he might have had it in his pocket the entire time.

My mind calculated the threat with a peculiar precision: Sadka had no idea who else knew I was there. My brother, my servants, even Governor Robinson could know my whereabouts. "You wouldn't be foolish enough to kill me . . ." I took a long, shuddering breath as I tried to tell myself the weapon was his way of settling me down, warning me off. ". . . or Mr. Troyte."

"I can control Godfrey without a pistol. Bad boys can't afford to tell tales out of school, can they?" Sadka gave a wicked laugh.

The man was impaired. Best not to incite him further, I told myself. I backed away from the barrel in the direction where I sensed Gulliver had been standing.

"That is better. Don't want you to lose control of yourself," he said soothingly. "Godfrey said you were a sensible lass. Must be to have been given so much authority." He grinned patronizingly. "Another child might have been ruined by what happened." The barrel of the pistol drooped in his lazy fist. For a second my hate melted like the ebb of a strong tide before it yawned up in an immense wave and crashed down, crushing me. "Yes," I whispered as I continued to move away. My arm brushed Gulliver's rough coat. Now he stood in front of me, kukri in hand.

Sadka laughed. "Down, boy, down." He brandished the pistol as a malevolent reminder. "A bullet will beat a Gurkha. Tell him to put it away." He pointed his weapon in the direction of Gulliver's scabbard.

My belief in my own safety did not extend to Gulliver, who was frozen in position. Sadka could claim self-defense against an overzealous guard. "Gulliver," I began gently. "Please. Everything will be all right now." Unthinking, I moved in front of Gulliver to shield him.

Sadka's mouth distorted viciously. "Tell him!" His order had the sting of a whiplash. Just then firecrackers rumbled among the hills. The lights in the sky were like flashes from faraway storms. Nobody flinched.

"What a foolish girl. Like mother . . ." Sadka released the safety on the pistol. The tiny metallic click reverberated in the silence.

"Gulliver!" I cried in desperation, and moved aside.

Gulliver had been coiled like a spring: every muscle wound, concentration honed on his target. My cry released him. Bending his knees, he rose from the floor in an impossible arc. The dazzling kukri echoed the movement in the air and it was this metallic gleam that my eyes followed as it sliced through the air, met a brief resistance, then came full circle in front of his white waistcoat.

I looked down. Blood pooled from the pointed sword's tip like tears. "Aiii!" swelled Sadka's gruesome cry.

Something skidded across the floor "What . . .?" I sputtered. It was the pistol—attached to what had been Sadka's right hand.

"Aiii!" Sadka held up his bloody stump and gawked in disbelief.

At the sound of their master screaming, three servants burst into the room. The sight of the spurting arm stunned them. Gulliver spun around and flashed his kukri, ending their advance.

At that moment Sadka rallied. He lunged forward, bellowing curses at me from a face contorted by pain and fear, rage and revenge. Again he lifted his leg—he's trained in martial arts, I realized—and delivered a sharp blow to the side of my head. I recoiled from the wave of pain, only to realize he was on top of me. His remaining hand pressed into my throat. Gagging, I tried to push him away with hands slippery with his blood. Fighting to protect myself, I did not notice that Gulliver's knees were bent again. Or that his elbows were drawn in. Or that his chin was close to his chest. There was a swishing sound before the shining steel caught my eye. The kukri had begun its second spin.

Seeing it coming at him for the second time, Sadka flung himself against a pillar and held his one whole arm across his face to fend it off. But Gulliver had picked out his mark long before. The tapered edge of the elegantly angled blade completed its destined trajectory and cupped Nissim Sadka's neck.

I closed my eyes and heard voices from the past: *"Papa, what will they do to them?"* And my father's face, solemnly promising, *"In the Bible it says, 'Eye for eye, tooth for tooth . . .' "* And me wondering, *"How?"* And the images of amputations and his response: *"They shall hang by the neck until they are dead. . . ."*

There was a bump. I looked down. Sadka slumped toward the floor. At first it appeared he had gone to sleep. When his buttocks landed, however, his head, attached by a slender rope of sinew, flopped over to one side like a child's broken toy. Sadka's servants thundered out, screeching. I turned away. Behind a screen Godfrey retched. I pivoted back. Gulliver stood erect, kukri raised, waiting to take on anyone who dared approach us.

Again I glanced down at Sadka.

I stared at the face that in death held the twisted paroxysm of his final seconds. The mouth gaped, the tongue lolled. His glazed eyes bulged like those of the giant carp. I felt nothing—not loathing, not disgust, not regret, not dread. It was as if I were floating above him: remote, detached, as though I had come from a long, long way to see this, and would journey on.

Someone was speaking. I heard the voice, but I did not understand it. At last it broke through the shimmering barrier. It was Godfrey and he was saying we had to leave. He tugged my sleeve and we followed Gulliver out. The grisly kukri led the procession. Nobody detained us.

Once outside, I ran past the tiger statues. Shadows had not cast an illusion. Their mouths did drip painted blood. I made it to the carriage. The wind carried an acrid smell of gunpowder. Godfrey jumped beside the terrified driver, who whipped the horses. We burst through the gate. Away we rushed, away from the walled enclosure, which I hoped would confine the evil spirits in, rather than out.

Happy Valley was plunged in darkness. Most of the lanterns had been extinguished. The children had run out of fuses to light. The solitary sound was the hooves of the horses blasting against the hardness of the rim road.

The Year of the Dog had begun.

52

✿ ✿ ✿

"Now what do we do?" I asked when I had caught my breath.

"We go directly to Government House," Godfrey replied thickly.

"How can we?" I noticed a metallic odor permeating the carriage. My skirt was encrusted in blood. "I must change my clothes first."

"No, you mustn't."

My mind swirled with other thoughts. I was haunted by my own childish cries after the trial of "Not fair . . . not fair . . ." and my farfetched vow to settle the score with Nissim Sadka. And as I considered the biblical injunctions about vengeance belonging to the Lord, I marveled at the events which had spiraled out of my control, even though justice had been served at last.

Thinking that my silence meant I might not agree with him, Godfrey continued, "If your man is to be vindicated, the governor must see the horror you faced."

Too exhausted to argue and too stunned to know what would ensue, I allowed him to orchestrate the events of the next hours.

We roused Governor Robinson from his bed. By the time the first morning of the new year dawned, many more authorities were sobered from their revels by the crime. Over and over Godfrey explained what he had witnessed: Nissim Sadka, formerly of Calcutta and known in Hong Kong as Song Kung Ni, had asked to meet with me to discuss purchasing a quantity of opium. Godfrey had taken me to his home in Happy Valley, ignorant that Sadka had had prior dealings with the Sassoons. Upon my realization that Sadka had been an accomplice to the murder of my mother—and Sadka's confession of the same—a struggle between the two of us had ensued. Sadka had pulled a gun, pointed it at me, and undone the safety catch. My bodyguard had acted swiftly to protect me, by cutting off the man's offending arm. When

597

this did not halt his attack, Gulliver had swung his kukri a second time to scare him off, accidentally decapitating him.

"No point in suggesting that Gulliver wanted to kill the man. Since Song was disarmed, a case could be made against Gulliver," Godfrey had explained before we saw the governor. Even though I was dazed, I had seen the sense in this. Besides, I was not certain what had happened. Part of the time my eyes had been closed.

Pity at my plight was the universal reaction. Lady Robinson bathed me herself and put me to bed. My stained clothes were turned over to the police.

Jonah and the compradore arrived to manage the details. The case absorbed several days, although it seemed the officials were merely going through the motions. Nobody doubted that I had been in mortal danger. Gulliver had to appear before a judge, and statements were sworn. Known to be exceptional members of the British military, Gurkhas' loyalty was unquestioned. Sadka's servants, who all had conveniently disappeared, were never questioned. Publicly, the chief magistrate ruled that Sadka had been killed accidentally in the defense of my life, commenting that Gulliver, in acting on my behalf, was "a fine example of his people." Privately, he commented that Gulliver had served the colony as well, for Song Kung Ni, whose dealings skirted the fringes of the law, had been a thorn in his side. In police circles Gulliver was a hero. He would have received a medal if there had been any to give.

ॐ   ॐ   ॐ

Anxious to leave for India as soon as possible, I spent my days sequestered at Mount Gough, while my brother and the compradore attended to the legal and company affairs.

"A representative of the Co-Hong merchants has accepted our rise in rates without a quarrel," Jonah reported to me. I was sitting in the green leather armchair, staring out at the low black clouds that swirled above the harbor in an eerie counterclockwise motion that looked as if a giant was stirring a steaming caldron.

I should have been elated, but I was merely relieved. Now we could go home! I listened patiently while Jonah described the favorable terms of the deal. "For the finest triple-A Patna they have agreed to a twenty-three-percent increase," my brother said, preening. "The average was eighteen percent. For the least expensive chests we've conceded to a twelve-percent rise. Even so, there will be no reason to lower those rates next season. That means we'll make up the difference by the end of the year, with a tidy profit." My expression did not reflect the excitement he exuded. "We've done it, Dinah! Mr. Ming was astonished. He said he had never seen the merchants agree to anything that quickly."

"Why do you think they assented?"

"Perhaps in gratitude. Sadka's tactics had squeezed profits from them as well." He touched my shoulder. "Aren't you pleased?"

"They settled because they were afraid of us. I do not think fear should be the basis of negotiations. Goodwill and a handshake should be our calling cards, not murder and blood—" I choked on my words.

"It is over, Dinah. Can't you forget it?"

"You weren't there! You don't know!" Tears flooded my eyes. For days they had welled up at the slightest provocation. Jonah had no recollection of our mother, let alone the vivid memories of her bludgeoned body. He had not been to Happy Valley and had no images of Sadka's menacing face taunting me in life—and death.

Perching on the chair arm, he took my hand in his. "What can I do for you?"

"Nothing. Nobody can help me now."

"Edwin should be here with you."

"What difference would that make? I am floundering in a nightmare of my own creation. Most of the time I feel as if I am stumbling in a thick fog. Now and then, when it lifts, I catch sight of something unspeakably horrible."

Fortunately, my brother did not press the point. He gave a hopeless sigh, moved away from my chair, and paced in front of the windows. I was too engrossed in my own misery to realize that another matter racked him.

At last he spoke. His voice rang out clear, bold, and compelling. "Believe me, I am sympathetic to you, Dinah. I don't want to diminish your troubles, but the fact of the matter is that everything is settled. It has come full circle. By some quirk of fate, you have avenged our mother's murder. With your diligence and cleverness you have succeeded in clobbering Uncle Samuel and salvaging the company. In a few days we will be on our way back to Calcutta and you will be crowned for your latest triumph." He whirled around and gave me an opaque stare. His dark eyes reflected the sky like mirrors. "Yes, *your* triumph. I feel privileged to have been your assistant, your brother, and I hope your friend." Swallowing hard, he pursued his objective. "All I ask is that you widen your circle to include me and my predicament. I would not make this request, not after everything you have endured, if it were not essential to my happiness."

"What is this about?" I asked foolishly. The color drained from his face. His lips looked as if they had been outlined in chalk. "Wu Bing?"

"Yes," he murmured, "Wu Bing." The words fell from his mouth like the peal of a bell.

"You will be sad to leave her."

"I cannot leave her."

My heart pounded in empathy with his dilemma. "Jonah, how terrible for you!"

"Not terrible, wonderful. While you were in Happy Valley, I spent the evening with her. We managed to be alone for hours, and she is everything I have ever wanted—and more, far more!"

Alternating between feeling appalled at the consequences and thrilled for him, I had no words of advice. "What will you do?" I asked slowly, while reminding myself that I must not interfere in the matter. I had enough difficulty leading my own life to presume to order his.

"Yesterday I asked the compradore if I might marry her."

I swallowed hard, but remained silent.

"And he said he would release her. If you don't object, I will bring her back with us. There will be a period when she will study our ways, and if she continues to want to convert, the arrangements will be made, and we shall be married."

"And if she does not convert?" I trembled as I took the poor girl's side over my brother's. "What then? She would not be able to return to her people with honor, and she would be a pariah in India."

"We have arrived at an agreement on that," he replied simply and firmly. "If in her heart she does not wish to become a Jew, then we will come back to Hong Kong together and be wedded in her traditions. Here it will be easier for each of us to remain true to our beliefs. In any case, I hope to return eventually and work for the family here. A Sassoon is needed permanently. At least you'll agree with me about that." He gave a charming, lopsided grin.

"Tell me, Jonah, what is Wu Bing?" He gave me a questioning glance. "Under what animal sign was she born?"

"That nonsense again?" He laughed with relief. "She's a buffalo. Is anything wrong with that?"

"On the contrary." I jumped up and went to the shelf where Godfrey's compatibility table had been placed. "If she's a buffalo and he's a rat, the woman will be the perfect housewife and an exceptional hostess." I chuckled as I scanned the box matching buffaloes and rats.

"What's wrong with that?"

" 'In this union, *she* wears the trousers,' " I read. " 'Besotted by the buffalo, the rat will remain faithful, and she will make the rat very happy.' " I looked up. My brother's eyes had filled with tears.

"Oh, Jonah! In this world where there is so much pain and misery, so much bloodletting, brutality, and death, should anything matter except the time spent caring for one another?" My brother reached his hands out to me and I clasped them. "Wu Bing is as worthy of love as anyone." I choked on my tears. "Take your happiness, Jonah, take it and run to the end of the earth if necessary."

＊＊＊＊＊＊

On the voyage home the weather was mild and the steamship *Morning Star* made good time because of the advantage of a following sea. For propriety's sake, I shared my stateroom with Wu Bing, but she took every opportunity to visit with Jonah. During the day they roamed the decks. When night fell, they settled into one of the public rooms and talked until midnight. I preferred to be alone. As the shock of the last weeks in Hong Kong wore off, a legion of disparate emotions flooded my mind: remorse, anxiety, fear, anger, punctuated by odd moments of ecstasy. A constant headache was my companion. Sleep was my solace.

As we rounded Singapore and headed into the Strait of Malacca, we were greeted by a punishing sea. Rains, brought by gale-force winds, lashed the decks for two days and nights. Once the cataclysmic downpour began, the ship shuddered under the impact. The lurching motion was unpredictable. A simple walk to the toilet required forethought as to where to place one's hands, one's feet. In a more positive frame of mind I might have coped better with the temporary adversity, but since it mirrored my inner turmoil, I gave myself over to the sea and suffered immensely.

Wu Bing, whose love apparently had vanquished any natural frailty, did not succumb to sickness. Within a few hours she had mastered the rolls and pitches and moved around with impunity. Seeing my distress, she was reluctant to leave me. She fed me tea and broth and rice gruel and had the steward concoct a soothing juice of coconut milk. When I could not contain my nausea, she held the bowl and sponged my brow. Her ministrations were offered with a knowing gentleness that reminded me of my grandmother's touch.

Jonah visited me several times a day. "Tonight the rains should end," he reported when, with every forward thrust of the engines, ferocious waves crashed over the deck.

"How do you know that?"

"I've been talking with the crew. By this time tomorrow we will have put the Malay Peninsula behind us. After that, it should be clear sailing."

I smiled gratefully, but Wu Bing and my brother hardly noticed. Hand in hand, they were oblivious of the thundering sea that rushed beyond the thin steel skin of the hull. "Why don't you two go upstairs for a while? I am going to try to sleep through this. It's the only way I can cope."

Seemingly torn between her duty and her desire, Wu Bing looked to Jonah for direction. Concerned, he checked back with me. "Are you certain?"

"Absolutely." I pulled up my covers and turned away from them to prove my point. I heard the door click closed. It was a relief to be alone. Alone to absorb the shudders and shakes, the pummelings and poundings that were the outer manifestations of the churnings that racked my mind. My life was like the sea: one moment the placid, cosseted stream of Theatre Road; the next agitated by the tumultuous storms of maharajahs, murders, and opium. In the delirium of my anguish, images of my mother mingled with those of Sadka. From a long way off I heard my children calling, but they vanished behind a wall of water. I lost track of the days and nights. This roiling hell was my whole world. The awful odors of oil, of sickness, of fried foods and spoiled fruit and urine combined with the noise and the humidity to debilitate me further.

I recall fragments: a doctor attending me, Wu Bing helping me to take medicines, Jonah assisting. "Nobody ever died of seasickness," he quipped during a moment when I had rallied enough to sit up in a chair and sip a cup of jasmine tea. "They only wish they had."

The winds had diminished and the rains had ceased by the time we entered the Bay of Bengal. Nevertheless, we were buffeted by waves rolling perpendicular to the movement of our hull. The ship, our aberrant cradle, rocked from side to side. Sometimes we rode deep in troughs with waves the size of mountains looming alongside. Later we were at the mercy of the ocean's sadistic power to sway us to and fro like beans in a jar.

"This time of year the crossing is supposed to be fairly tranquil," Jonah explained apologetically. "Unfortunately, the southwest wind has come early."

The hardiest sailors began to flounder. Jonah took to his bed. Even Gulliver, who had fetched and carried through the worst of the gale, succumbed. Wu Bing was not spared either. She developed dark blotches above her translucent cheeks and her lips lost the natural rosiness that gave her a doll-like prettiness. Valiantly she tried to hide her retching, and putting aside her own tribulation, she continued to tend me. I was immensely grateful, but also shamed by her unselfish ministrations. If we ever saw Calcutta again, I promised myself that I would defend my brother and Wu Bing with my last breath.

❁ ❁ ❁

Thinking of the trials the two would soon endure, I momentarily diverted my thoughts of past terrors and whatever was in store for me. An hour later, I was on the same treadmill of unanswered questions. The future of the company was secure for the present, thanks to the transactions the compradore had concluded. How long would this last? How soon would the negotiations begin anew? The greater issues of the Sassoons of my generation struggling to establish themselves would bring more dissension over time. For the present I was the designated leader, yet was that what I wanted? Although flattered by the position, I wondered how I could manage it effectively and not upset my uncles, cousins—or my husband. Had my Grandfather Moses or Uncle Saul been disturbed by the disadvantages of leadership? Was it different because they were the heirs—the male heirs—whose authority was never questioned? And when all was said and done, did I wish to spend my days in Clive Street? No. Theatre Road was where I imagined myself being happiest.

Who could take over for me? The person I preferred was Edwin, but they would not accept an in-law after Samuel's disastrous rule. Nor did I believe that Edwin could be content if I was given the final say over him, a situation which would be implied even if it wasn't true. Who else? There was Jonah, but he was inexperienced and had done little to win respect. What if I played up his part in the negotiations with the Co-Hong merchants? Even so, I had forgotten about Wu Bing and his choice to make China his permanent home. No, Jonah was out. Then who?

The more immediate problem of making my way to the lavatory halted that train of thought. Catching the motion of the rolls, I swaggered across the cabin and managed to tend to myself. Triumphant with that minor accomplishment, I eased myself to the porthole and studied the watery world below. The sea was the vivid green of emeralds. Foam fluttered from the whitecaps like blossoms in the wind, reminding me of poppies blooming in Patna's fields. How thrilling my first sight of them had been before I understood that the ephemeral loveliness of those delicate petals was transformed into globs of tarry exudate that men—fine men like my father, odious men like Nissim Sadka—lusted over.

For the first time in days, my head cleared. I took a deep breath and was accosted by the staleness of the stateroom. I yearned for fresh air. In rhythm with the bobbing of the floorboards, I managed to dress myself. Holding tightly to the rails fastened along the corridors, I made my way on deck.

My eyes squinted in the harsh light. The fresh salt spray stung my pallid flesh. Filling my lungs was painful at first, but subsequent breaths were easier. Somewhere to the west was the coast of India. There was no land in sight, yet the demarcation of sky greeting the sea on the horizon shone with promise. Much as the thick moisture of a summer's day congeals into puffy white clouds, my future began to evolve from an amorphous cluster into organized segments.

First, I would forgive Edwin and help him to accomplish whatever he wanted. If the man required the comfort of the poppy, why should he be denied it? Now I understood there were far worse vices than a pipe of Patna now and again. After admitting that I might lose the battle to rid my husband of the blight of opium, I determined to lead Sassoon and Company into other lucrative industries. Even though I might not have wanted to stay at the helm, I had to—at least until I had shepherded them into different pastures. Yes, the moment to broach the subject was at hand. I gathered my arguments: the Chinese were growing more and more of their own poppies, the crown was leaning away from supporting the trade, and India was booming.

Visions formed on the horizon. If the various cousins were responsible for different industries, but were supported by a financially sound structure, Sassoon and Company could be like a great tree rooted in prosperity, with each branch bearing fruit. I remembered Edwin once saying that trading was like a tree. The root of the profession was buying and selling, and everything branched from there. As long as an idea could be traced to the root, it was an acceptable investment. Following the same concept, a small jute mill on the Hooghly might be an excellent place for Asher to begin. Reuben's sons could investigate cotton in Bombay. I would oversee the tea, Edwin the ships. Jonah and Wu Bing might consider handling the Sassoon interests—or even diversifying into real estate—in Hong Kong. And there would always be a need for people like Sayeed and Yedid and their children to administer matters in Clive Street.

The motion of the ship was no longer my enemy, for every heave and recoil brought me closer to Calcutta, closer to my latest revelation, and most of all to Edwin. If only he would forgive my stubbornness!

For several leagues across the trackless ocean, I feared the outcome of our reunion. How mysterious the world was. We always knew what had just passed, but we never knew what even the next second would bring. My life was an ever-evolving story. I helped write the chapters, but an unseen hand manipulated my fate. *The Mystery of Edwin Salem . . . The Mystery of Mr. and Mrs. Edwin Salem. . . .* Mustering the same determination I had felt when I swore to make Edwin mine the first time, I would win him back. Unlike the unfinished *Mystery of Edwin Drood*, this story's ending would be written, and written by an author determined to make it a happy one. After all, didn't the Chinese horoscope say it was auspicious if a monkey married a monkey?

The wind drew my mouth back into a smile. Every moment, I was sailing nearer to Edwin and my children. The yawning gap of the vast Bay of Bengal was narrowing. Soon I would be with the man I loved more than anyone else in the world, and with my adorable Aaron, the good and true, like the quick-witted horse in the Chinese zodiac. And in my arms I would clasp Jeremiah and Zachariah, my two mischievous twin monkeys.

53

♦ ♦ ♦

Theatre Road shimmered in the midday sun, a brilliant jewel of a palace in the City of Palaces. A fresh layer of stones covered the drive. The first summer rains had revived the lawns into verdant carpets. Huge hibiscus blossoms yawned in the breeze. As Jonah, Wu Bing, Gulliver, and I arrived at the portico, there was something else that caught my eye. For a few long moments I could not define what dazzled me. Every surface gleamed under recent paint and polish. Varnished trim winked from the casements. A fresh coat of chunam had been applied to whitewash the facade. What were those winking eyes staring back at me? My breath caught in my throat. Windows! Every shutter had been removed. Fresh panes of polished glass reflected earth and sky.

Hanif opened the huge double doors with a flourish. Yali hugged me. My children clustered at my feet. And there, coming from the shadows into the pool of light streaming from the garden, strolled Edwin with an easy smile.

After the clamor of the welcome had settled, we sat in the hall and chattered on. Asher, Pinhas and Simon Tassie, and Seti bubbled with questions for Jonah. I held Edwin's hand and tried to attend the tugs and hugs from the three boys with equal doses of affection.

"The Chinese have accepted our pricing structure," Jonah announced in a lull.

Edwin was delighted, but his raised eyebrows registered his surprise. "How did you accomplish it?"

"A long story" was all I would contribute, and went back to questioning Zilpah about how the children had fared. Aaron had given the twins chickenpox. The boys lifted their shirts and pulled down their pants to point out the few remaining scabs. We chatted on about family matters: Ruby was expecting again, the Lanyados and Gabriel Judah had vanished well before our arrival, a match had been found for

605

Yedid. This went on for some time, until I noticed that Wu Bing was standing on the far side of the room, in the manner of a servant. Gulliver hovered at her side protectively.

I extricated myself from the embrace of the children and went to her. "This is Wu Bing, the niece of Ming Hien Chang, compradore of our company in Hong Kong." Perplexed, Zilpah looked from her to Jonah and then back to me. During the difficult voyage, Wu Bing has been like a sister to me." I kowtowed to Wu Bing and then to my brother. "Happily, she will always be my sister, for she has agreed to marry Jonah."

Asher blanched visibly. Pinhas gave a low whistle. "When?" Seti asked in a high, excited voice.

My stepmother's eyes flickered across Wu Bing's flat abdomen and up to her hopeful eyes. She sucked in her lips and waited for Jonah to respond.

"After she has received instruction in our faith, she will convert. Until then we will not set a wedding date."

Asher shook his brother's hand. Edwin came around and patted Jonah on the back. With my arms around Wu Bing's fragile shoulders, I steered her into the circle of Sassoons and kissed her cheek.

❦ ❦ ❦

Later, when we were alone, I told Edwin about Sadka. We lay in the room where my mother had died, a room transformed by the hush of ivory satin draperies that brushed the floor. A light breeze stirred the silk panels that blocked out the starry night. A thick coverlet with squares of silver and ivory brocade covered the bed. A canopy of pleated fabrics further enshrouded us in a private world.

Edwin held me tightly while I gave a truncated version of Sadka's death and the aftermath. "Thank you for being here," I concluded, drying my eyes.

"Where else would I be?"

"You said you were going to remain at Free School Street."

"I did, for as long as it was necessary."

"I don't understand . . ."

"Don't you?" He brushed back his hair with an exaggerated gesture that forced me to smile.

"No."

"I can see why the governor of Hong Kong immediately absolved you of any guilt. Your guise of innocence would fool anyone, except a husband."

"What . . . ?"

"Have you forgotten your conversation with Mordecai?"

"Dr. Hyam!" I pulled away from Edwin. "You spoke with him."

"Indeed."

My heart pounded. Don't criticize him, I warned myself, not when we are together at last. Not when I need him so desperately. "I am sorry. You were right about everything, even about how being apart would bring me around. How foolish I was to think you were somehow different because of what I discovered. You had not changed, I had! If we can begin anew, I promise I will never mention it again."

He pressed his finger to my lips. "It's over, Dinah."

"No!" I cried. "Please, I know I can make it up to you. I cannot live without you."

"And I cannot live without you, my darling girl. The opium is finished. I have thrown away my pipe."

Somehow I survived the gyrations of my heart, from the plummeting rush of blood to the momentary stoppage, to the wild beating that ballooned in my chest. "How did . . . ?"

"I always wanted to stop, but I never knew how. You cannot imagine how afraid I was. Fear is what made me reject your concerns. An even greater fear, though, that of losing you and everything we had together, made me want to change. When the doctor told me there were medical ways to assist me, I leapt at the chance."

"Was it difficult?"

"Yes. Terribly. Suspecting it would be, I remained alone at Free School Street. The doctor sent a medical student to live with me to see me through. Without him I could never have managed."

"Did you stop all at once?"

"No. I tried the Chinese method."

"What did that entail?" I asked slowly, guessing it had been torturous.

"The doctor dissolved opium ash, or *yen tshi*, in sherry wine, and I took a tablespoonful three times a day, each time adding wine to the bottle. Soon I was taking only clear wine."

"And you didn't become ill . . ."

"On the contrary. I underwent a horrible spectrum of incapacitating symptoms. There were stomach pains, diarrhea. My eyes ran perpetually and my nose would tickle, causing attacks of sneezing by the hour. The whole time I felt itchy, restless. I could not sit still. When I tried to rest, my body would twitch, almost convulse. I prayed for sleep and yet could not. Exhausted, I lay prostrate in my bed. If I dozed, there were the nightmares of monsters and murder—straight out of De Quincey. Even more frightening was the lack of control over my sex. Sometimes I would feel myself spurting for no reason, although even that was devoid of pleasure."

"Oh, my poor darling . . ." I clutched at him and stroked his face. "How do you feel now?"

"As if I have plunged out of the darkness and burst into the light."

"Is it over?"

"Yes, but I must be vigilant. There may be times when my body will ache for solace. I must resist every temptation."

"Can I help?"

"Yes."

"I will do anything . . ."

"My requirements are simple."

"Tell me."

"Love me."

There was an awkward moment of mutual hesitation. Where to begin? A tentative touch. A kiss. A button undone. A petticoat drawn over the head. A gathering confidence narrowed the channel and we melted together, like well-trained dancers. The merging was so natural I could not imagine life without it ever again. He exhausted me with his insistence on my pleasure, which was propelled by the imposition of his own.

In the stillness that followed, we were silent for a long while. My mind brimmed with the infinite possibilities. I did not yet realize that ten months after the night of my return, our fourth child—and only daughter—would be born there in the brocaded bed. We would name her Clara Luna Salem. When I look at her now, I think I must have, in some small measure, known about her on that glorious night when almost simultaneously some mysterious stirring had us again reaching for each other and we began anew.

I lifted myself atop Edwin and he drew me onto him. We kissed fervently. I arched my back and opened my eyes. Tiny lights, like diwali lamps floating in a misty current, sprinkled the room. Blinking at the fantastic vision, I moaned, "Never, never have I felt like this before."

"What do you mean?" he mumbled as he kissed my breasts.

"Every time you touch me, I see bright lights," I murmured in awe.

He glanced around. "I cannot take the credit for that." His chest and pelvis heaved with laughter. "Fireflies have arrived to welcome you home." He plunged even deeper into me.

Closing my eyes to the luminescence, I gave myself up to the concentric circles of pleasure that crested over me. In the pause between the mild and violent bursts, my thoughts wandered back in time to the days after our wedding on the country boat, and I realized that we had known nothing compared with this. It was miraculous that something this precious could be renewed. Memories, splendid memories, could be revived. Pains, hideous pains, could be buried. My fingers burrowed into his back. His face nestled in the curve of my neck. I marveled in the forgetfulness of love. This is what endures, nothing else. Only this. Banishing Luna and Sadka and Amar and Edwin's addiction and my intransigence, I released a flood of adoration from every pore. Hungrily we grappled with each other, dispelling ghosts and renewing pledges.

Edwin shuddered. "I love you!"

"Yes, me too," I gasped as, expertly, with measured bursts of force and release, we satisfied each other again. And again. And again.

\\/ \\/ \\/

The story continued, but my record ends today, the last day of May 1953, because there is no more time. Outside the window I can see the last of the furniture from the hall being carried out in the crates destined for London. Following in the footsteps of my children, my family, my friends, and so many members of the Jewish community in Calcutta, I am leaving Theatre Road and Calcutta. In less than an hour they will be coming for the bed in which Clara Luna was conceived and born. Soon they will be carrying the Clive desk halfway around the world. What will happen in the future seems of little consequence compared with what we accomplished in the past.

On the day Edwin and I were reunited, I did not know that the stand I would take to diversify the Sassoon investments would be in line with the most progressive thinking of the era. A few years later, an International Opium Commission would meet in Shanghai. To forestall criticism at home, the British government would decide to reduce the export of opium from India by one-tenth each year after 1907, if China would reduce her home-produced opium by the same amount. In 1908 the government of Hong Kong would be ordered to close the opium divans in the colony. By then the Sassoons were out of the flower business entirely and were prospering with a galaxy of other investments that have sustained the family until now and, with prudent management, should suffice for generations to come.

How pleased I would have been to know that Jonah and Wu Bing would marry and return to Hong Kong to raise a family of eight. Eventually they would control enormous parcels of prime real estate. The leader who emerged in the next generation of Sassoons turned out to be Yedid, convincing me that people who have experienced pain and loss in childhood learn they can rise above other difficulties to accomplish great deeds. Although no parent wishes to subject his child to the agonies that Yedid or I suffered, he might consider the advantages in not sheltering his offspring from absolutely all the world's woes.

Together Edwin and I would watch our children strike off in directions we might not have selected for them, but which led them to adventures, sorrows, and fulfillments of their own. And while our family expanded and progressed, we also endured the upheavals that accompanied two wars, the finale of the British raj, and India's struggle for independence and its bloody aftermath. As was true for Jews around the world, the formation of the state of Israel united us in a different direction. Thousands of us—Baghdadis and Bene Israels and Cochinis—from across the subcontinent chose to make *aliya* and return to our restored homeland. Others sought to protect our prosperity in London and New York. Unlike many other places in the world, India had always welcomed Jews. Edwin used to say the various religious and political factions of Indians had no time to hate us, for they were too busy hating one another.

I never wanted to leave Calcutta, but there is no one left for me. The house echoes with emptiness. The choice has been made. The hour is here. With this task completed, I can rest knowing my story has been chronicled by me and not merely conjectured by someone else. Now that the tale has filled these notebooks, it seems not very different from the secrets that other families keep. My beloved Edwin has been gone for over five years now. During the period of his illness, I blamed his pulmonary problems on the years he had been addicted to opium, although no physician suggested this was the cause. When he required pain relief, Edwin rejected morphine. I dared not encourage him lest he think his case was hopeless. The longer one lives, the more paradoxical our positions become, for in the end I secretly laced Edwin's tea with tears of the poppy and he died peacefully in my arms.

Almost everyone else has died, but what happened to them and what they did about it will live on in this memoir. What now to do with my inept scratchings? This record of that time in my life is everything I intend to say. I leave this as my explanation for who I was and what I did. Others may have a different version of the same events. I cannot relate anyone else's perspective. This is how I lived it, how I saw it, and yes, how I choose to remember it. And once my pen is put away, this is all I will tell. I do not want to answer questions. Before I close the lid of Clive's bureau, I shall lock this memoir inside for safekeeping. What happens when it is found will be someone else's concern.

Clara Luna Weiss
605 Park Avenue
New York, New York
20 July 1960

Aaron S. Salem
11 Alwyne Place
London N1

Dear Aaron,

You all guessed wrong! The mysterious bundle contained an extraordinary memoir Mother must have written—or at least completed—during the last months she lived in Calcutta. Since it ends before I was born, there is a frustrating gap. Although it covers some familiar ground, there are myriad questions satisfied. For instance, haven't you always wondered why Mother would never visit Cochin or Travancore or what the truth was behind our grandmother's murder? Also explained is how Uncle Jonah got his start in Hong Kong and the true origins of the enigmatic Wu Bing, who has left us that legacy of lawsuits. Best of all, here is our parents' story and it is the tale of true love we always suspected. There are a few disconcerting revelations about Papa. However, knowing them helped me to understand so much more.

Please ask Mr. Jhirad in exactly which drawer in the Clive desk he found the manuscript. This is of significance, as you will learn when you read the copy I am enclosing for you. I have also forwarded one to Zachariah, who should be back in Israel by now, and I will save one for when Jeremiah returns from his circumnavigation on Luna Two.

I think you will agree this is a record of the singular life of a woman and her times. After the family has read it, we might consider having the book published (perhaps deleting the intimacies that might embarrass some), either by my publishing firm or another, depending on the offers we receive. Besides, with so few of us left in India, it does chronicle a society that—at the rate it is going—will soon disappear and will never be again.

Somehow I think that must have been what Mother had in mind when she directed that it be sent to me.

Love to you, Nancy, and the children,

Clara

P.S. As to the "bureau," please have a firm accustomed to crating and shipping valuable furniture prepare the desk for transport to New York.

Author's Note

❦ ❦ ❦

The fictional murder of Luna Sassoon on the first of October 1878 is based on the real murder of Leah Judah on the first of October 1858. Like Luna, Leah was a member of Calcutta's Baghdadi Jewish community, her husband was an opium trader who traveled to China much of the time, and she was killed by a jealous suitor who had been rejected. Two men were arrested for the murder: Ezekiel Shurbanee on a charge of willful murder and Nissim Gubbay as his accomplice. The trial that ensued was much like the one described in the novel, and the verdict, despite much evidence and the sworn testimony of servants, identical. Afterward, both freed men fled Calcutta. In the Jewish cemetery in Calcutta, the murdered woman's tombstone describes her as Leah, daughter of Abigedor Ezriel, not as her husband's wife, for he had disowned her in death. Years later it was rumored that Nissim Gubbay met a violent end in a Hong Kong opium den. This tale is covered in *Turning Back the Pages, A Chronicle of Calcutta Jewry*, by Esmond David Ezra, and *Remarkable Criminal Trials in Bengal*, by the pseudonymous "Lex," who is thought to be Robert Reid.

The Arabic-speaking Jewish community of India did have as two of its progenitors Shalom Cohen of Aleppo (1762–1836), who is regarded as the founder of the community in Calcutta; and Sheikh Sason Ben Sason of Baghdad (1750–1830). The latter never went to India, but his son David Sassoon did settle in Bombay and built up the family fortune. These men, and a few of their descendants, including David Sassoon (1792–1864), Abdullah Sassoon (1818–1896), who moved to England, and Flora Sassoon (1859–1936), have been mentioned for historical purposes. The real names of the Baghdadi Jews of Calcutta add to the confusing line between fact and fiction. Often the Jews who came from the Middle East did not have surnames. Elias Ezra Aaron would be Elias, the son of Ezra, the son of Aaron. As the names became longer through the generations, those at the end would be dropped. Eventually, any common connection was lost, and because many biblical names were used repeatedly, genealogies in different families have almost identical names. To assist the reader, I have given families surnames and have tried not to duplicate names, but since I have attempted to use mostly typical names of the period, I may have inadvertently named a fictional character after a real one. Nevertheless, all other descendants of those clans described in the novel are entirely fictional.

This was a unique culture, which can hardly be reproduced in a novel with any accuracy. For the most part the Calcutta Jews were rather unsophisticated in their language. Among themselves, the older characters would have spoken Arabic, interspersed with Hindustani and English. And while the opium trade was practiced by a few members of the community, a majority of the Jews plied a variety of professions. Also, opium, which was perfectly legal in India at the time, was traded by Indians themselves as well as British and other merchant groups.

While few had the financial resources of my fictional family, many real Sassoons went on to become leaders of the Jewish community in Bombay. One extraordinary woman, Flora Sassoon, was a scholar, philanthropist, and famed hostess, and for many years was managing partner of the firm's Bombay office. The fictional Dinah's life was not based on any of Flora's experiences, only inspired by her successful example.

The princely state of Travancore (in the area now called Kerala) did exist. It was matrilineal and headed by a maharajah. However, Amar and his family are entirely imaginary and are not based on any real persons in Travancore or elsewhere. Except for a few other people mentioned in their historical context, every other character is fictional and any resemblance to those living or dead is coincidental.

An outbreak of the plague occurred at approximately the date mentioned and was more severe in Bombay than in Calcutta. Flora Sassoon did assist Dr. Haffkine in his work to develop the first plague vaccine. The earthquake of 1897 is based on actual accounts of this disaster, which, though severe in Calcutta, was even more so in Darjeeling.

While I have attempted to place people and events in the approximate times they did occur, certain railways, schools, and less important events may not have been in operation or actually occurred exactly as recorded here. Usually there is less than a three-year discrepancy, if any. Please see scholarly works for any accurate information on the people and places described.

Today the fields of Patna continue to flower with opium poppies. India remains the world's largest—and only legitimate—poppy producer. A United Nations treaty, signed by 116 nations, acknowledges the medicinal value of opium, while denouncing illegal poppy cultivation, which possibly doubles India's output and is usually converted to heroin. Even with the latest in modern pharmacology, the derivatives of the poppy—morphine and codeine—are unrivaled in their ability to alleviate pain. If there is codeine in your medicine cabinet, it was probably processed by an authorized Indian company and grown in the fields that once supplied the Sassoons, the Jardines, and their compatriots.

In 1947, India's Jewish population reached a peak of about thirty thousand. The combined political influence of Indian and Israeli independence, which happened almost simultaneously, led to widespread emigration. The Baghdadi Jews, in particular, always thought of themselves as members of the European community and thus did not expect to thrive under the new regime. Also, they were influenced by the economic restrictions that were introduced in the country and by regulations that affected dealings in foreign exchange. Many of the Calcutta Jews migrated to England, Canada, the United States, and Australia. Israel called to many other Jews. At first, those Cochin Jews who tried to emigrate were delayed due to Israel's concern for their endemic disease—elephantiasis. Once the disease was proved to be noncontagious, the Cochin Jews left en masse. Of the twenty-five hundred who once lived there, less than fifty Jews remain. Today, in the whole of India, fewer than five thousand Jews (mostly Bene Israel) are left. The once-thriving Jewish community of Calcutta has dwindled to just about one hundred.

For readers curious to learn more about this culture and period, the following sources are recommended:

Elias, Flower, and Judith Ellis Cooper. *The Jews of Calcutta.* New York: Sephardic House, 1974.

Ezra, Esmond David. *Turning Back the Pages, A Chronicle of Calcutta Jewry.* London: Brookside Press, 1986. (Includes a separate genealogy and tape recording.)

Jackson, Stanley. *The Sassoons.* New York: E. P. Dutton, 1968.

Musleah, Rabbi Ezekiel N. *On the Banks of the Ganga—The Sojourn of Jews in Calcutta.* North Quincey, Mass.: Christopher Publishing House, 1975.

Roland, Joan G. *Jews in British India: Identity in a Colonial Era.* Hanover, N.H.: University Press of New England, 1989.

Ross, Cecil. *The Sassoon Dynasty.* London: Robert Hale, 1941.

I am indebted to experts in many fields who assisted with the research for this book. Members of the scattered Jewish community of

India who were very generous to me include Ellis Jhirad, Daniel and Hannah Jhirad, Sam and Erna Daniel, Benjamin Hayeem, Vilma Hayeem-Ladani, Rabbi Ezekiel N. Musleah, Joseph Sargon, Zeke Barber, Sylvia Wisenfeld, Lionel Alroy, and the members of Congregation BINA, the organization of Indian Jewry settled in the United States, as well as several others who preferred to remain anonymous. Specialists who shared their expertise include food writer Copeland Marks; chemist Jim Cossey; Latin scholars Warren J. Myers, Marguerita Avellaneda, and Candace Hoflund; doctors Josh Madden, Mario Mendizabel, Dick Stewart, and Robin Weisman Madden; sailors Gerard Pesty and Don Corman; chess expert Leonard Weisman; Chinese queries were fielded by Adrienne, Kendall, and Jennifer Su. Of course all errors, omissions, and fictional digressions remain the responsibility of this author.

Robert Singerman of the Price Judaica Library at the University of Florida was a font of information, and the university's interlibrary loan department worked overtime for me. Mr. Robert Hayday and the India Office Library in London provided access to a wealth of material on the period of the British raj. I appreciate the continuing assistance of Vanda Carnes and the Coastal Region Public Library and the Ocala Public Library.

Researchers Kathleen Cossey in Florida and Alexander Clifford in London worked on my behalf. Information was also gathered by Jem Cohen, Ruth Mandel Chevat, and Nancy Porter. Thanks to Caroline Caughey, Jenny and David Clifford, Pru Trew, and Angela Sanford for helping me in London.

Insightful editorial work by Maureen Baron, Hilary Ross, and John Paine is gratefully acknowledged.

My personal assistants and readers who offer valuable support daily include my mother, Elsie Weisman; Mary Ann Boline; Beverly Crane; Mary Wanke; Barbara Miller; and Rebecca Stanley Bunch.

I rely on the continuing counsel of my wise agent and friend, Don Cutler.

Essential to this project were the love, cooperation, and encouragement of my husband, Philip, who reads everything first, and my sons, Blake and Joshua, who tolerated a mother whose heart is always theirs, but whose mind was often continents away in India.

0-595-24249-9

Printed in the United States
64028LVS00003B/4-6